*Criti*

'McBain

*s Weekly*



'A virtuoso *Guardian*

'Ed McBain police procedural . . . McBain delive story with panache and real zest . . . *Money Mo y Money* may be the fifty-first of the series but it's as fresh and vivid as the first. Great' *Observer*

'Sick, taut, inventive, modern and (as always) funny'
*Glasgow Herald*

'This much-loved and seminal writer is a national treasure. If you're a mystery reader, you've undoubtedly read Ed McBain. If you haven't read one for a while, try this one. It's so good it will immediately send you scurrying back for the ones you missed' Otto Penzler

'A master . . . as always in his novels, sharp, clear sentences trot briskly one after another . . . As always, the funny stuff is funny and the scary parts scary. McBain gets it right, of course . . . as he has done for dozens of books and years'
*Time*

'One of the masters of crime fiction' *Sunday Telegraph*

'McBain steadily unrolls a tapestry of adultery, jealousy, and revenge. Amazingly, all the mind-boggling complexities are kept perfectly clear, thanks to McBain's unsurpassed mastery of exposition, the story's still gaining in force when the curtain finally thunders down' *Kirkus Reviews*

'McBain has a great approach, great attitude, terrific style, strong plots, excellent dialogue, sense of place, and sense of reality' Elmore Leonard

'A master storyteller' *Washington Times*

The name Ed McBain is one of the most illustrious in crime fiction. In 1998, he was the first non-British author to be awarded the Crime Writers' Association/Cartier Diamond Dagger Award and he was also holder of the Mystery Writers of America coveted Grand Master Award. He passed away in 2005. Visit his website at www.edmcbain.com.

*By Ed McBain*

THE 87TH PRECINCT NOVELS

Cop Hater • The Mugger • The Pusher • The Con Man
Killer's Choice • Killer's Payoff • Killer's Wedge • Lady Killer
'Til Death • King's Ransom • Give the Boys a Great Big Hand
The Heckler • See Them Die • Lady, Lady, I Did It!
The Empty Hours • Like Love • Ten Plus One • Ax
He Who Hesitates • Doll • Eighty Million Eyes • Fuzz • Shotgun
Jigsaw • Hail, Hail, the Gang's All Here • Sadie When She Died
Let's Hear It for the Deaf Man • Hail to the Chief • Bread
Blood Relatives • So Long As You Both Shall Live
Long Time, No See • Calypso • Ghosts • Heat • Ice • Lightning
Eight Black Horses • Poison • Tricks • Lullaby • Vespers • Widows
Kiss • Mischief • And All Through the House • Romance
Nocturne • The Big Bad City • The Last Dance
Money Money Money • Fat Ollie's Book • The Frumious
Bandersnatch • Hark! • Fiddlers

THE MATTHEW HOPE NOVELS

Goldilocks • Rumpelstiltskin • Beauty & the Beast
Jack & the Beanstalk • Snow White and Rose Red
Cinderella • Puss in Boots • The House That Jack Built
Three Blind Mice • Mary, Mary • There Was a Little Girl
Gladly the Cross-Eyed Bear • The Last Best Hope

OTHER NOVELS

The Sentries • Where There's Smoke • Doors • Guns
Another Part of the City • Downtown • Driving Lessons
Candyland • The Moment She Was Gone • Alice in Jeopardy

# Ed McBAIN

## THE PUSHER

## KING'S RANSOM

## MONEY MONEY MONEY

*The Pusher*
First published in Great Britain by T.V. Boardman in 1959

*King's Ransom*
First published in Great Britain by T.V. Boardman in 1962

*Money Money Money*
First published in Great Britain by Orion in 2001

This omnibus edition published in 2009
by Orion Books Ltd
Orion House, 5 Upper St Martin's Lane
London WC2H 9EA

An Hachette UK company



The city in these pages is imaginary. The people, the places are all fictitious. Only the police routine is based on established investigatory technique.

A CIP catalogue record for this book is available
from the British Library.

ISBN 9781407221038

Printed in Great Britain by Clays Ltd, St Ives plc

www.orionbooks.co.uk

# THE PUSHER

The city in these pages is imaginary. The people, the places are all fictitious. Only the police routine is based on established investigatory technique.

# CHAPTER ONE

Winter came in like an anarchist with a bomb.

Wild-eyed, shrieking, puffing hard, it caught the city in cold, froze the marrow and froze the heart.

The wind roared under eaves and tore around corners, lifting hats and lifting skirts, caressing warm thighs with icy-cold fingers. The citizens blew on their hands and lifted their coat collars and tightened their mufflers. They had been enmeshed in the slow-dying lethargy of autumn, and now winter was upon them, rapping their teeth with knuckles of ice. The citizens grinned into the wind, but the wind was not in a smiling mood. The wind roared and bellowed, and snow spilled from the skies, covered the city with white and then, muddied and dirtied, yielded to the wind and the cold and turned to treacherous ice.

The citizens deserted the streets. They sought pot-bellied stoves and hissing radiators. They drank cheap rye or expensive Scotch. They crawled under the covers alone, or they found the warmth of another body in the primitive ritual of love while the wind howled outside.

Winter was going to be a bitch this year.

The patrolman's name was Dick Genero, and he was cold. He didn't like winter, and that was that. You could sell him ice skating and skiing and bobsledding and hot rum toddies and all the other fictions of a happy, happy snowy season and he would still tell you to go drop dead someplace. Summer was Genero's season. He was one of those people, that's all. He liked warm sand and a hot sun and blue skies with hardly any clouds in them, and he also liked summer storms with lots of lightning, and he liked flowers blooming and gin-tonics and you could take all the winters that ever were and stuff thern into a beat-up old tin can and dump them in the River Dix and Genero would have been a very happy man.

His ears were cold.

'When your ears are cold, you're cold all over,' Genero's mother used to say, and Genero's mother was a well of wisdom on weather conditions. Genero walked his beat with his cold ears, and he thought of his mother, and then unrelatedly and belatedly thought of his wife and wished he were home with her in bed. It was two o'clock in the morning, and any man in his right mind would not be walking the streets of the city at two in the morning with the temperature in the low twenties and a pretty woman at home in bed.

The wind ripped at his winter overcoat, pierced the heavy blue material, and licked at his winter blouse. The cold soaked into his undershirt, and Genero shivered and thought of his ears, remembering not to touch them because if you touched them when they were cold, they would fall off. His mother had told him that, too. He had been tempted on several occasions in his life to touch his ears when they were cold, just to see if they *would* fall off. He was, in truth, afraid they would not – and there would go a son's faith in his mom. So he dutifully kept his gloved hands away from his head, and he ducked his head against the wind and thought of Rosalie home in bed, and thought of Florida and Puerto Rico and the Virgin Isles and Africa, working his way south until he realized abruptly he had reached the South Pole, where the cold still persisted.

*It's warm,* he told himself. *Come on, now – it's warm.*

Look at all the bathing beauties in their scanty suits. Jesus, but this sand is hot today. Listen to that ocean, ah, thank God for the cool breeze, we can certainly use a cool breeze on a scorcher like today, that's for sure. And . . .

*And I'll bet maybe they will fall off if I touch them.*

The streets were empty. Well sure, that figured. Only idiots and cops were out tonight. He walked to the candy store and automatically tried the doorknob, cursing the proprietor for not having the store open so that a cop with his ears ready to fall off could go in and have a cup of coffee. Ingrates, he thought, all ingrates. Home and asleep while I'm trying the stupid doorknob. Who'd pull a burglary on a night like this, anyway? A man's fingers would freeze solid to the burglar's tools, the way fingers freeze solid to metal in the Arctic. There's a cheerful thought. Jesus, *I am cold*!

He started up the street. Lanny's Bar was probably still open. He would stop there to see that no fights were in progress and perhaps sneak an against-regulations nip to take the edge off this cold. He could see nothing wrong with a little nip. A man could pretend he was chilly, true, but when a man's underwear showed the ability to stand unaided and independently in the middle of the street, it was time to dispense with the 'chilly' fantasy and realize that freezing was but a stone's throw away. Genero clapped his gloved hands together and lifted his head.

He saw the light.

It came from somewhere up the street. The street was black except for the light. Genero stopped and squinted his eyes against the wind. *The tailor shop*, he thought instantly. That stupid ass Cohen is pressing clothes in the wee hours of the morn again. He would have to warn him. 'Max,' he would have to say, 'you're a hell of a nice guy, but when you're going to be pressing late at night, give the house a ring and wise up us poor bastards, will you?'

Then Max would nod and smile and give him a glass of that sweet wine he kept behind the counter. All at once, Max didn't seem so stupid.

Max was the kind benefactor of all cops walking beats everywhere. Max's light was a shining beacon, the shop a sanctuary for ice-bound freighters. *Get the bottle out, Max*, Genero thought. *I'm on my way.*

He headed for the tailor shop and the light, and he would

have really enjoyed that glass of wine with Max, were it not for one thing:

The light was not coming from the tailor shop.

The light came from farther up the street, spilling from the open mouth of the basement steps under one of the tenements. For a moment, Genero was puzzled. If not Max . . .

Genero quickened his step. Quite unconsciously, he drew off his right glove and yanked his service revolver from its holster. The faces of the buildings were closed with sleep. Only the light pierced the darkness, and he approached the light warily, stopping before the steps where they descended beyond the hanging chain to enter the bowels of the tenement.

A door was hooded in shadow beneath the brick stoop of the building, and a window was set high up in the brick alongside the door. The window was caked with grime, but it glowed like a single wakeful eye. Cautiously, Genero climbed over the chain and started down the steps.

A narrow alley ran straight as an arrow to the back yard of the tenement. The garbage cans were in for the night, stacked haphazardly in the alleyway, dispelling their stench on the crisp December air. Genero glanced quickly up the alleyway, and then walked quietly to the door.

He stood listening. There was no sound from beyond the door. He held the revolver ready in his right hand, and with his left hand, he twisted the doorknob.

Surprisingly, the door swung open.

Genero backed away suddenly. He was sweating. His ears were still cold, but he was sweating. He listened to the sound of his own breathing, listened for other sounds in the cold sleeping city, listened for the silent scrape of a foot, something, anything. He listened for a long time, and then he entered the basement room.

The light came from a naked bulb suspended from a thick wire cord. It hung absolutely motionless. It did not swing, it did not make the slightest movement, so that the wire cord seemed almost to have been frozen into a slender steel rod. An orange crate rested on the floor beneath the light bulb. There were four bottle caps on the crate. Genero pulled out his pocket flash and swung the arc around the room. There were pin-up pictures on one of the walls, pasted close together, breasts to buttocks, cramped for space. The opposite wall was bare. There was a cot at the far end of the room, and there was a barred window over it.

Genero swung the light a little to the left and then, startled, pulled back, the .38 jerking upward spasmodically.

A boy was sitting on the cot.

His face was blue. He was leaning forward. He was leaning forward at a most precarious angle, and when the first cold shock of discovery left Genero, he wondered why the boy didn't fall forward on to his face. That was when he saw the rope.

One end of the rope was fastened to the barred window. The other end was knotted around the boy's neck. The boy kept leaning forward expectantly as if he wanted to get up off the cot and break into a sprint. His eyes were wide, and his mouth was open, and there seemed to be life coiled deep within his body, ready to unspring and catapult him into the room. Only the colour of his face and the position of his arms betrayed the fact that he was dead. The blue of the face was a sickly hue; his arms lay like heavy sleepers at his sides, the hands turned palms upward. Several inches from one hand was an empty hypodermic syringe.

Tentatively, somewhat frightened, somewhat ashamed of his superstitious dread of a dead body, Genero took a step closer and studied the blue face in the beam of the flash. To prove he wasn't frightened at all, he stood looking into the blank eyes for a moment or two longer than he felt he had to.

Then he hurried from the room, trembling, and headed for the nearest call box.

# CHAPTER TWO

The word had gone out long before Kling and Carella arrived.

Death had silently invaded the night, and death – like Macbeth – had murdered sleep, and there were lights in the windows now, and people leaned out into the bitter cold of winter, staring down at the five patrolmen who clustered in an uneasy and somehow guilty-looking knot on the pavement. There were people in the streets, too, talking in hushed whispers, wearing overcoats thrown over pyjamas. The Mercury sedan swung into the block, looking like any pleasure car except for the short radio aerial protruding from the centre of the roof. The car carried MD licence plates, but the two men who stepped from it were not doctors; they were detectives.

Carella walked briskly to the patrolmen. He was a tall man, dressed now in a brown sharkskin suit and charcoal-brown overcoat. He was hatless, and his hair was clipped close to his head, and he walked with the athletic nonchalance of a baseball player. He gave an impression of tightness, tight skin drawn taut over hard muscle, tight skin over high cheekbones that gave his face a somewhat Oriental appearance.

'Who called in?' he asked the closest patrolman.

'Dick,' the cop answered.

'Where is he?'

'Downstairs with the stiff.'

'Come on, Bert,' Carella said over his shoulder, and Kling followed obediently and silently. The patrolmen studied Kling with pretended aloofness, not quite able to hide their envy. Kling was a new detective, a twenty-four-year-old kid who'd come up from the ranks. 'Come up,' hell. 'Shot up' was a better way to put it. 'Streaked up' was, in fact, the best way to put it. Kling had cracked a homicide, and the other patrolmen called it dumb luck, but the Commissioner called it 'unusual perceptiveness and tenacity', and since the Commissioner's opinion was somewhat more highly respected than the opinions of beat-walkers, a rookie patrolman had been promoted to 3rd Grade Detective in less time than it took to pronounce the rank.

So the patrolmen smiled bleakly at Kling as he climbed over the chain after Carella, and the greenish tint to their faces was not caused by the cold.

'What's the matter with *him*?' one of the patrolmen whispered. 'Don't he say hello no more?'

If Kling heard him, he gave no sign. He followed Carella into the basement room. Dick Genero was standing under the light bulb, biting his lip.

'Hi, Dick,' Carella said.

'Hello, Steve. Bert.' Genero seemed very nervous.

'Dick,' Kling acknowledged.

'When'd you find him?' Carella asked.

'Few minutes before I called in. He's over there.' Genero did not turn to look at the body.

'You touch anything?'

'Jesus, no!'

'Good. Was he alone when you got here?'

'Yeah. Yeah, he was alone. Listen, Steve, you mind if I go upstairs for some air? It's a little . . . a little stuffy in here.'

'In a minute,' Carella said. 'Was the light burning?'

'What? Oh, yeah. Yeah, it was.' Genero paused. 'That's how I happened to come down. I figured maybe a burglar. When I come down, there he was.' Genero flicked his eyes toward the body on the cot.

Carella walked to where the boy sat suspended by the rope. 'How old can he be?' he asked of no one. 'Fifteen, sixteen?' No one answered.

'It looks . . . it looks like he hung himself, don't it?' Genero asked. Studiously, he avoided looking at the boy.

‘It looks that way,’ Carella said. He did not realize that he was unconsciously shaking his head, or that there was a pained expression on his face. He sighed and turned to Kling. ‘We’d better wait until the Homicide boys get here. They raise a stink if we leave them seconds. What time is it, Bert?’

Kling looked at his watch. ‘Two eleven,’ he said.

‘Want to start keeping a timetable, Dick?’

‘Sure,’ Genero said. He took a black pad from his hip pocket and began writing into it. Carella watched him.

‘Let’s go up and get that air,’ he said.

Most suicides don’t realize the headaches they cause.

They slash their wrists, or turn on the gas jets, or shoot themselves, or bang a slew of parallel wounds into their skulls with a hatchet, or leap from the nearest window, or sometimes chew a little cyanide, or – as seemed to be the case with the boy on the cot – they hang themselves. But they don’t give a thought to the headaches of the law enforcers.

A suicide, you see, is initially treated exactly like a homicide. And in a homicide, there are a few people concerned with law enforcement who must be notified. These few people are:

1. The police commissioner.
2. The chief of detectives.
3. The district commander of the detective division.
4. Homicide North or Homicide South, depending upon where the body was found.
5. The squad and precinct commanding officers of the precinct in which the body was found.
6. The medical examiner.
7. The district attorney.
8. The telegraph, telephone, and teletype bureau at headquarters.
9. The police laboratory.
10. The police photographers.
11. The police stenographers.

Not all of these people, of course, descend simultaneously upon the scene of a suicide. Some of them have no earthly reason for climbing out of bed at an ungodly hour, and some of them simply leave the job to lesser paid and highly trained subordinates. You can always count on a diehard contingent of night owls, however, and this group will include a few Homicide dicks, a photographer, an assistant medical examiner, a handful of patrolmen, a pair or more of dicks from the local precinct, and a few lab technicians. A stenographer may or may not come along for the show.

At 2.11 or thereabouts in the morning, nobody feels much like working.

Oh sure, a corpse breaks up the dull monotony of the midnight tour; and it's nice to renew acquaintances with old friends from Homicide South; and maybe the photographer has a few choice samples of French postcard art to pass around; but all in all, nobody has much heartfelt enthusiasm for a suicide at 2.11. Especially when it's cold.

There was no questioning the fact that it was cold.

The dicks from Homicide South looked as if someone had pulled them from the freezer compartment a few moments before. They walked stiff-legged to the sidewalk, their hands thrust into their coat pockets, their heads bent, their fedoras pulled low over their faces. One lifted his head long enough to say hello to Carella, and then they both followed him and Kling into the basement room.

'Little better down here,' the first cop said. He rubbed his hands together, glanced over at the body, and then said, 'I don't suppose anybody has a flask with him?' He looked at the faces of the other cops. 'No, I didn't suppose so,' he said sourly.

'Patrolman named Dick Genero discovered the body at about 2.04,' Carella said. 'The light was burning, and nothing's been touched.'

The first Homicide cop grunted, and then sighed. 'Well, better get to work, huh?' he asked with eager enthusiasm.

The second Homicide cop looked at the body. 'Stupid,' he mumbled. 'Why didn't he wait until morning?' He glanced at Kling. 'Who are you?' he asked.

'Bert Kling,' Kling said, and then – as if the question had been burning his throat since he'd first seen the body – he asked, 'I thought the body had to be swinging free in a hanging suicide.'

The Homicide cop stared at Kling, and then turned to Carella. 'Is this guy a cop?' he asked.

'Sure,' Carella said.

'I thought maybe you brought one of your relatives along for a thrill.' He turned back to Kling. 'No, son,' he said, 'the body don't have to be swinging free. You want proof?' He pointed to the cot. 'There's a hanging suicide, and the body ain't swinging free, now, is it?'

'Well, no, it isn't.'

'You're quite a whiz,' Carella said. He was not smiling. He caught the Homicide cop's eyes and held them.

'I get by,' the Homicide cop said. 'I ain't from the crackerjack 87th Precinct, but I been on the force twenty-two years now, and I've broken up a few ticktacktoe games in my time.'

There was no irony or sarcasm in Carella's voice when he answered. He played it deadpan, apparently serious. 'Men like you are a credit to the force,' he said.

The Homicide cop eyed Carella warily. 'I was only trying to explain . . .'

'Sure,' Carella said. 'Stupid kid here doesn't realize the body doesn't have to be swinging free. Why, Bert, we've found them standing, sitting, and lying.' He turned to the Homicide cop. 'Isn't that right?'

'Sure, all positions.'

'Sure,' Carella agreed. 'A suicide doesn't have to look like one.' A barely concealed hardness had crept into his voice, and Kling frowned and then glanced somewhat apprehensively toward the Homicide dicks. 'What do you think of the colour?' Carella asked.

The dick who'd blown his top at Carella approached him cautiously. 'What?' he asked.

'The blue. Interesting, isn't it?'

'Cut off the air, you get a blue body,' the Homicide cop answered. 'Simple as all that.'

'Sure,' Carella said, the hardness more apparent in his voice now. 'Very simple. Tell the kid about side knots.'

'What?'

'The knot on the rope. It's on the side of the boy's neck.'

The Homicide cop walked over and looked at the body. 'So what?' he asked.

'I just thought a hanging-suicide expert like yourself might have noticed it,' Carella said, the hardness of his voice completely unmasked now.

'Yeah, I noticed it. So what?'

'I thought you might want to explain to a new detective like the kid here the coloration we sometimes get in hangings.'

'Look, Carella,' the other Homicide cop started.

'Let your pal talk, Fred,' Carella interrupted. 'We don't want to miss the testimony of an expert.'

'What the hell are you talking about?'

'He's needling you, Joe,' Fred said.

Joe turned to Carella. 'You needling me?'

'I wouldn't know how,' Carella said. 'Explain the knot, expert.'

Joe blinked. 'Knot, knot, what the hell are you talking about?'

'Why, surely you know,' Carella said sweetly, 'that a side knot will completely compress the arteries and veins on one side of the neck only.'

'Sure, I know that,' Joe said.

'And you know, of course, that the face will usually be red

when the knot's been tied at the side of the neck – as opposed to the face being pale when the knot's tied at the nape. You know that, don't you?'

'Sure, I know that,' Joe said arrogantly. 'And we've had them turn blue in both side-knot and nape-knot cases, so what the hell are you telling me? I've had a dozen blue strangle cases.'

'How many dozen blue cyanide-poisoning cases have you had?'

'Huh?'

'How do you know the cause of death was asphyxiation?'

'Huh?'

'Did you see those burnt bottle caps on the orange crate? Did you see the syringe next to the boy's hand?'

'Sure I did.'

'Do you think he's a junkie?'

'I guess he is. It would be my guess that he is,' Joe said. He paused and made a concerted effort at sarcasm. 'What do the masterminds of the 87th think?'

'I would guess he's an addict,' Carella said, 'judging from the 'hit' marks on his arms.'

'I saw his arms, too,' Joe said. He searched within the labyrinthine confines of his intelligence for something further to say, but the something eluded him.

'Do you suppose the kid shot up before he hanged himself?' Carella asked sweetly.

'He might have,' Joe said judiciously.

'Be a little confusing if he did, wouldn't it?' Carella asked.

'How so?' Joe said, rushing in where angels might have exercised a bit of caution.

'If he'd just had a fix, he'd be pretty happy. I wonder why he'd take his own life.'

'Some junkies get morose,' Fred said. 'Listen, Carella, lay off. What the hell are you trying to prove, anyway?'

'Only that the masterminds of the 87th don't go yelling suicide until we've seen an autopsy report – and maybe not even then. How about that, Joe? Or do *all* blue bodies automatically mean strangulation?'

'You got to weigh the facts,' Joe said. 'You got to put them all together.'

'There's a shrewd observation on the art of detection, Bert,' Carella said. 'Mark it well.'

'Where the hell are the photographers?' Fred said, tired of the banter. 'I want to get started on the body, find out who the hell the kid is, at least.'

'He's in no hurry,' Carella said.

# CHAPTER THREE

The boy's name was Aníbal Hernandez. The kids who weren't Puerto Rican called him Annabelle. His mother called him Aníbal, and she pronounced the name with Spanish grandeur, but the grandeur was limp with grief.

Carella and Kling had trekked the five flights to the top floor of the tenement and knocked on the door of apartment fifty-five. She had opened the door quickly, as if knowing that visitors would soon be calling. She was a big woman with ample breasts and straight black hair. She wore a simple dress, and there was no make-up on her face, and her cheeks were streaked with tears.

'Police?' she asked.

'Yes,' Carella said.

'Come in, *por favor.* Please.'

The apartment was very still. Nothing broke the silence, not even the sullen sounds of sleep. A small light burned in the kitchen.

'Come,' Mrs Hernandez said. 'In the parlour.'

They followed her, and she turned on a floor lamp in the small living-room. The apartment was very clean, but the ceiling plaster was cracked and ready to fall, and the radiator had leaked a big puddle on to the scrubbed linoleum of the floor. The detectives sat facing Mrs Hernandez.

'About your son . . .' Carella said at last.

'*Sí,*' Mrs Hernandez said. 'Aníbal would not kill himself.'

'Mrs Hernandez . . .'

'No matter what they say, he would not kill himself. This I am sure . . . of this. Not Aníbal. My son would not take his own life.'

'Why do you say that, Mrs Hernandez?'

'I know. I know.'

'But why?'

'Because I know my son. He is too happy a boy. Always. Even in Puerto Rico. Always happy. Happy people do not kill themselves.'

'How long have you been in the city, Mrs Hernandez?'

'Me, I have been here four years. My husband came first, and then he send for me and my daughter – when it was all right, you know? When he has a job. I leave Aníbal with my mother in Cataño. Do you know Cataño?'

'No,' Carella said.

'It is outside San Juan, across the water. You can see all the city from Cataño. Even La Perla. We live in La Perla before we go to Cataño.'

'What's La Perla?'

'A *fanguito.* How do you say – a slom.'

'A slum?'

'*Sí, sí,* a slum.' Mrs Hernandez paused. 'Even there, even playing in the mud, even hungry sometimes, my son was happy. You can tell a happy person, *señor.* You can tell. When we go to Cataño, it is better, but not so good as here. My husband send for me and Maria. My daughter. She is twenty-one. We come four years ago. Then we send for Aníbal.'

'When?'

'Six months ago.' Mrs Hernandez closed her eyes. 'We pick him up at Idlewild. He was carry his guitar with him. He plays very good the guitar.'

'Did you know your son was a drug addict?' Carella asked.

Mrs Hernandez did not answer for a long time. Then she said, 'Yes,' and she clenched her hands in her lap.

'How long has he been using narcotics?' Kling asked, looking hesitantly at Carella first.

'A long time.'

'How long?'

'I think four months.'

'And he's only been here six months?' Carella asked. 'Did he start in Puerto Rico?'

'No, no, no,' Mrs Hernandez said, shaking her head. '*Señor*, there is very little of this on the island. The narcotics people, they need money, is that not right? Puerto Rico is poor. No, my son learned his habit here, in this city.'

'Do you have any idea how he started?'

'*Sí*,' Mrs Hernandez said. She sighed, and the sigh was a forlorn surrender to a problem too complex for her. She had been born and raised on a sunny island, and her father had cut sugar cane and fished in the off seasons, and there were times when she had gone barefoot and hungry, but there was always the sun and the lush tropical growth. When she got married, her husband had taken her to San Juan, away from the inland town of Comerío. San Juan had been her first city of any size, and she had been caught up in the accelerated pace. The sun still shone, but she was no longer the barefoot adolescent who walked into the village general store and exchanged banter with Miguel, the proprietor. Her first child, Maria, was born when Mrs Hernandez was eighteen. Unfortunately, her husband had lost his job at about the same time, and they moved into La Perla, a historic slum squatting at the foot of Morro Castle. La Perla – The Pearl. Named in high good humour by the poverty-stricken dwellers, for you could strip these people of their belongings, strip them of their clothes, toss them naked into wooden shacks that crouched shoulder to haunches in the mud below the proud walls of the old Spanish fort – but you could not steal their sense of humour.

La Perla, and a girl-child named Maria and two miscarriages that followed in as many years, and then another girl-child who was named Juanita, and then the move to Cataño when Mrs Hernandez's husband found a job there in a small dress factory.

When she was pregnant with Aníbal, the family had gone one Sunday to *El Yunque*, and the *Bosque Nacional del Caribe*

– the Rain Forest. And there Juanita, barely two, had crawled to the edge of a fifty-foot precipice while her father was snapping a picture of Mrs Hernandez and his older daughter. The child had made no sound, had screamed not at all, but the plunge had killed her instantly and they came home from the national forest that day with a corpse.

She feared she would lose the baby within her, too. She did not. Aníbal was born, and a christening followed on the heels of a funeral, and then the factory in Cataño closed down and Mr Hernandez lost his job and took his family back to La Perla again, where Aníbal spent the early years of his boyhood. His mother was twenty-three years old. The sun still shone but something other than the sun had deepened what used to be laugh wrinkles at the corners of her eyes. Mrs Hernandez was coming to grips with Life. Life and Fortune combined to find more work for Mr Hernandez. Back to Cataño went the family, moving their scant belongings, convinced that this time the move was for good.

It seemed a permanent job. It lasted for many years. Times were good, and Mrs Hernandez laughed a lot, and her husband told her she was still the prettiest woman he knew, and she accepted his lovemaking with hot-blooded passion, and the children – Aníbal and Maria – grew.

When he lost the job that had seemed permanent, Mrs Hernandez suggested leaving the island and heading for the mainland – heading for the city. They had enough for a plane ticket. She packed him a chicken lunch to eat on the plane, and he wore an old Army coat because he had heard the city was very cold, not like Puerto Rico at all, not with the sun shining all the time.

In time, he found a job working on the docks. He sent for Mrs Hernandez and one child, and she took the girl Maria because a girl should not be left without her mother. Aníbal she left with his grandmother. Three and a half years later, he was to be reunited with his family.

Four years later, he was to be an apparent suicide in the basement of a city tenement.

And thinking over the years, the tears started silently on Mrs Hernandez's face, and she sighed again, a sigh as barren and hollow as an empty tomb, and the detectives sat and watched her, and Kling wanted nothing more than to get out of this apartment and its echoes of death.

'Maria,' she said, sobbing. 'Maria started him.'

'Your daughter?' Kling asked incredulously.

'My daughter, yes, my daughter. Both my children. Drug addicts. They . . .' She stopped, the tears flowing freely, unable to speak. The detectives waited.

'I don't know how,' she said at last. 'My husband is good. He has worked all his life. This minute, this very minute, he is working. And have I not been good? Have I done wrong with my children? I taught them the church, and I taught them God, and I taught them respect for their parents.' Proudly, she said, 'My children spoke English better than anybody in the *barrio*. Americans I wanted them to be. Americans.' She shook her head. 'The city has given us much. Work for my husband, and a home away from the mud. But the city gives with one hand and takes back with the other. And for all, *señores*, for the clean white bathtub in the bathroom, and for the television set in the parlour, I would not trade the sight of my happy children playing in the shadow of the fort. Happy. Happy.'

She bit her lip. She bit it hard. Carella waited for it to bleed, amazed when it did not.

When she released her lip, she sat up straighter in her chair.

'The city,' she said slowly, 'has taken us in. As equals? No, not quite as equals – but this too I can understand. We are new, we are strange. It is always so with the new people, is it not? It does not matter if they are good; they are evil because they are new. But this you can forgive. You can forgive this because there are friends here and relatives, and on Saturday nights it is like being back on the island, with the guitar playing and the laughter. And on Sunday, you go to church, and you say hello in the streets to your neighbours, and you feel good, *señores*, you feel very good, and you can forgive almost everything. You are grateful. You are grateful for almost all of it.

'You can never be grateful for what the city has done to your children. You can never be grateful for the narcotics. You can remember, remember, remember your daughter with young breasts and clean legs and happy eyes until those . . . those *bastardos*, those *chulos* . . . took her from me. And now my son. Dead. Dead, dead, dead.'

'Mrs Hernandez,' Carella said, wanting to reach out and touch her hand, 'we . . .'

'Will it matter that we are Puerto Rican?' she asked suddenly. 'Will you find who killed him anyway?'

'If someone killed him, we'll find him,' Carella promised.

'*Muchas gracias*,' Mrs Hernandez said. 'Thank you. I . . . I know what you must think. My children using drugs, my daughter a prostitute. But, believe me, we . . .'

'Your daughter . . . ?'

'*Sí, sí*, to feed her habit.' Her face suddenly crumpled. It had been fine a moment before, and then it suddenly crumpled, and she sucked in a deep breath, holding back the racking sob, and then she let it out, a sob ripped from her soul. The sob stabbed at Carella, and he could feel himself flinching, could feel his own face tightening in impotency. Mrs Hernandez seemed to be clinging to the edge of a steep cliff. She hung on desperately, and then sighed and looked again to the detectives.

'*Perdóneme*,' she whispered. 'Pardon me.'

'Could we talk to your daughter?' Carella asked.

'*Por favor*. Please. She may help you. You will find her at El Centro. Do you know the place?'

'Yes,' Carella said.

'You will find her there. She . . . she may help you. If she will talk to you.'

'We'll try,' Carella said. He rose. Kling rose simultaneously.

'Thank you very much, Mrs Hernandez,' Kling said.

'*De nada,*' she answered. She turned her head toward the windows. 'Look,' she said. 'It is almost morning. The sun is coming.'

They left the apartment. Both men were silent on the way down to the street.

Carella had the feeling that the sun would never again shine on the mother of Aníbal Hernandez.

# CHAPTER FOUR

The 87th Precinct was bounded on the north by the River Harb and the highway that followed its winding course. Striking south from there, and working block by block across the face of Isola, you first hit Silvermine Road and the fancy apartment buildings facing on the river and Silvermine Park. If you continued walking south, you crossed The Stem, and then Ainsley Avenue, and then Culver Avenue, and the short stretch of Mason known to the Puerto Ricans as 'La Vía de Putas'.

El Centro, despite the occupation of Maria Hernandez, was not located on Whore Street. It crouched in a side-street, one of the thirty-five running blocks that formed the east-to-west territory of the 87th. And though there were Italians and Jews and a large population of Irish people in the 87th, El Centro was in a street that was entirely Puerto Rican.

There were places in the city where you could get anything from a hunk of cocaine to a hunk of woman – anything in the alphabet, from C to S. El Centro was one of them.

The man who owned El Centro lived across the river in the next state. He very rarely visited his establishment. He left it in the capable managerial hands of Terry Donohue, a big Irishman with big fists. Donohue was, for a precinct Irishman, most unusual: he liked Puerto Ricans. This is not to say that he liked only Puerto Rican women. That was certainly true. But there were many 'Americans' in the 87th Precinct who detested the influx of the 'foreigners' while secretly admiring the tight wiggle of a foreign female's backside. Terry liked them both, male and female. He also liked running El Centro. He had worked in dives all over the world, and he was fond of saying El Centro was the worst, but he still liked it.

In fact, Terry Donohue liked just about everything. And, considering the joint he ran, it was surprising that he could find anything to like in a cop – but he liked Steve Carella, and he greeted him warmly when the detective showed up later that day.

'You lop-eared wop!' he shouted. 'I hear you got married!'

'I did,' Carella said, grinning foolishly.

'The poor girl must be nuts,' Terry said, shaking his massive head. 'I'll send her a basket of condolences.'

'The poor girl is in her right mind,' Carella replied. 'She picked the best available man in the city.'

'Hoo! Listen to him!' Terry shouted. 'What's her name, lad?'

'Teddy.'

'Terry?' Terry asked unbelievingly. 'Terry, is it?'

'Teddy. For Theodora.'

'And Theodora *what*, may it be?'

'Franklin, it used to be.'

Terry cocked his head to one side. 'An Irish lass, perhaps?'

'Catch me marrying an Irish girl,' Carella said, grinning.

'A mountain guinea like you could do worse than a sweet Irish lass,' Terry said.

'She's Scotch,' Carella told him.

'Good, good!' Terry bellowed. 'I'm four-fifths Irish myself, with a fifth of Scotch thrown in.'

'Ouch!' Carella said.

Terry scratched his head. 'I usually get a laugh from the cops on that one. What're you drinking, Steve?'

'Nothing. I'm here on business.'

'And business was never harmed, by God, by a tiny bit of alcohol.'

'Have you seen Maria Hernandez around?'

'Now, Stevie,' Terry said, 'with a sweet little Scotch lass at home, why would you . . .'

'Business,' Carella said.

'Good,' Terry said. 'A constant man in a city of inconsistencies.'

'Inconstancies,' Carella corrected.

'Whatever, she hasn't been in yet today. Is this about her brother?'

'Yes.'

'A junkie, too, huh?'

'Yes.'

'One thing gets me sore,' Terry said, 'is narcotics. Have you ever seen a pusher in here, Steve?'

'No,' Carella said. 'But I've seen plenty outside on the sidewalk.'

'Sure, because the customer's always right, and he gets what he wants. But you never saw one of those scurvy bastards in my shop, and you never will, that's the truth.'

'When do you expect her?'

'She doesn't roll around until about two. That's if she gets here at all. You know junkies, Steve. Figuring, figuring, always figuring. I swear to God, the president of General Motors doesn't have to do as much conniving as a junkie does.'

Carella glanced at his watch. It was 12.27.

'I'll be back later,' he said. 'I want to grab lunch.'

'You're offending me,' Terry said.

'Huh?'

'Can't you read the sign outside? Bar and *Grill.* Do you see that hot table back there? The best damn lunch in the city.'

'Yeah?'

'*Arroz con pollo* today. Speciality of the house. Got this beautiful little girl who cooks it up.' Terry grinned. 'She cooks by day and hooks by night – but the *arroz con pollo* is out of this world, lad.'

'How's the girl?'

Terry grinned more widely. 'I couldn't say, having only sampled the dear thing's cooking.'

'I've been poisoned in worse places,' Carella said. 'Let's have it.'

Maria Hernandez did not walk into El Centro until three that afternoon. A john from downtown on a romance-seeking excursion would probably have passed her by as a sweet, innocent high-school senior. For whereas the common stereotype puts all prostitutes in tight silk dresses slit to the navel, such is not the case. As a general rule, most of the prostitutes in the 87th were better and more stylishly dressed than the honest women in the streets. They were well-groomed and very often polite and courteous, so much so that many of the littte girls in the neighbourhood looked up to the hookers as the cream of society. In much the same way as the pamphlets that go through the mails in a plain brown wrapper, you couldn't tell what these girls had under their covers unless you knew them.

Carella did not know Maria Hernandez. He looked up from his drink when she walked into the bar, and he saw a somewhat slight girl who looked no more than eighteen. Her hair was black, and her eyes were very brown, and she wore a green coat open over a white sweater and a straight black skirt. Like a suburban housewife, she wore nylons and loafers.

'There she is,' Terry said, and Carella nodded.

Maria sat on a stool at the far end of the bar. She nodded hello to Terry, glanced at Carella quickly to ascertain whether or not he was a prospective client, and then fell to staring through the plate glass window at the street. Carella walked over to her.

'Miss Hernandez?' he said.

She swung the stool around. 'Yes?' she said coyly. 'I'm Maria.'

'I'm a cop,' Carella said, figuring he'd set her straight from go, before she wasted any effort.

'I don't know anything about why my brother killed

himself,' Maria said, all coyness gone now. 'Any other questions?'

'A few. Shall we sit in a booth?'

'I like it here,' Maria said.

'I don't. A booth or the station house. Take your choice.'

'You get down to business, don't you?'

'I try.'

Maria climbed off the stool. They walked together to a booth opposite the steam table. Maria took off her coat and then slid into the booth opposite Carella.

'I'm listening,' she said.

'How long have you been on the junk?'

'What's that got to do with my brother?'

'How long?'

'About three years.'

'Why'd you start him on it?'

'He asked to start.'

'I don't believe you.'

'Why should I lie to you? He came in the bathroom one night while I was shooting up. The little snot didn't even knock. He wanted to know what I was doing. I gave him a snort.'

'And then?'

'He liked it. He wanted more. You know.'

'I don't know. Tell me about it.'

'He got on mainline a couple of weeks later. End of story.'

'When did you start hustling?'

'Aw, listen . . .' Maria said.

'I can find out.'

'A little while after I got a habit. I had to make money some way, didn't I?'

'I suppose so. Who supplies you?'

'Oh, come on, cop, you know better than that.'

'Who supplied your brother?'

Maria was silent.

'Your brother is dead, do you know that?' Carella said harshly.

'I know it,' Maria answered. 'What do you want me to do? He always was a stupid little snotnose. If he wants to kill himself . . .'

'Maybe he didn't kill himself.'

Maria blinked, seemingly surprised. 'No?' she said cautiously.

'No. Now who supplied him?'

'What difference does it make?'

'Maybe a lot.'

'I don't know anyway.' She paused. 'Listen,' she said, 'why don't you leave me alone? I know cops.'

'Do you?'

'Yeah. You looking for something free, is that it? You figure on scaring me so I'll . . .'

'I'm not looking for anything but information about your brother,' Carella said.

'Yeah, I'll bet.'

'You'd win,' Carella said.

Maria kept staring at him, frowning. 'I know cops who . . .' she started.

'I know hookers with syphilis,' Carella said flatly.

'Listen you got no right to . . .'

'Then let's drop this whole goddamn routine,' he snapped. 'I want information, period.'

'Okay,' Maria said.

'Okay,' Carella repeated.

'And I still don't know anything,' Maria added.

'You said you started him.'

'Sure.'

'All right, then you probably made a contact for him after he was hooked. Now, who?'

'I didn't make any contact for him. He always went his own way.'

'Maria . . .'

'What do you want from me?' she said, suddenly flaring. 'I don't know anything about my brother. I even found out he was dead from a stranger. I haven't been inside my own house for a year, so how would I know who supplied him or who didn't supply him, or even if he was supplying himself and others besides?'

'Was he pushing?'

'I don't know nothing. I didn't know him any more, can you understand that? If I saw him on the street, I wouldn't recognize him. That's how much I knew about my own brother.'

'You're lying,' Carella said.

'Why should I lie? Who's there to protect? He hung himself, so . . .'

'I told you once,' Carella said. 'Maybe he didn't hang himself.'

'You're making a federal case out of a lousy junkie,' Maria said. 'Why knock yourself out?' Her eyes clouded momentarily. 'He's better off dead, believe me.'

'Is he?' Carella asked. The table was very silent. 'You're holding something back, Maria. What is it?'

'Nothing.'

'What do you know? What is it?'

'Nothing.'

Their eyes met. Carella studied her eyes, and he knew what was in them, and he knew she would tell him nothing more. He had just stared into a pair of opaque hoods. Her eyes had closed her mouth.

'All right,' he said.

The coroner didn't like to deal with new people. That was the way he'd been raised. He hated new faces, and he didn't like to confide secrets to strangers. The coroner's secret was a big one, and Bert Kling was a stranger, and so the coroner studied his face and reluctantly dredged through the facts in his mind, wondering how much he should reveal.

'How come they sent you?' he asked. 'Couldn't they wait for our official report? What's the big rush?'

'Carella asked me to check with you, Dr Soames,' Kling said. 'I don't know why, but I suppose he wants to get moving on this thing, and he figured he didn't want to wait for the report.'

'Well, I don't know why he couldn't wait for the report,' Soames said. 'Everybody else waits for the report. In all my years here, everybody's waited for the report. So why can't Carella wait?'

'I'd appreciate it if . . .'

'You people think you can just barge in and expect immediate results. You think we have nothing else to do? You know how many corpses we have in there waiting for examination?'

'How many?' Kling asked.

'Don't get factual with me,' Soames advised. 'I'm trying to tell you this is an imposition. If I weren't a gentleman and a doctor, I'd tell you this is a big pain in the ass.'

'Well, I'm sorry to trouble you, really. But . . .'

'If you were really sorry, you wouldn't trouble me. Listen, don't you think I'd love to forget typing up the report? I type with two fingers, and no one on my staff can do any better. Do you know how understaffed I am here? Do you think I can afford to give each case the special attention you're asking for? We've got to process these things like an assembly line. Any break in the routine, and the whole shop goes to pieces. So why don't you wait for the report?'

'Because . . .'

'All right, all right, all right,' Soames said testily. 'All this fuss over a drug addict.' He shook his head. 'Does Carella think this was a suicide?'

'He's . . . I think he's waiting to hear from you people on it. That's why he . . .'

'Do you mean to tell me there's a doubt in his mind?'

'Well, from . . . from outward appearances . . . that is, he's not sure the boy was . . . was asphyxiated.'

'And what do you think, Mr Kling?'

'Me?'

'Yes.' Soames smiled tightly. 'You.'

'I . . . I don't know what to think. This is the first time I . . . I ever saw anybody hanging.'

'Are you familiar with strangulation?'

'No, sir,' Kling said.

'Am I supposed to give you a course in medicine? Am I supposed to run a seminar for every uninvited, uninformed detective on the force?'

'No, sir,' Kling said. 'I didn't want . . .'

'We're not talking about a technical hanging now,' Soames said. 'We're not talking about hanging with a hangman's noose where the bulky knot and the sudden drop break the neck. We're talking about death by strangulation, death by asphyxia. Do you know anything at all about asphyxia, Mr Kling?'

'No, sir. Choking is something I . . .'

'We are not talking about choking, Mr Kling,' Soames said, gaining momentum, annoyed by strangers, equally annoyed by ignorance. 'Choking, in police work, presupposes hands. It is impossible to choke yourself to death. We are now discussing asphyxia induced by pressure on the neck arteries and veins through the use of ropes, wires, towels, handkerchiefs, suspenders, belts, garters, bandages, stockings, or what have you. In the case of Aníbal Hernandez, I understand the alleged means of strangulation was a rope.'

'Yes,' Kling said. 'Yes, a rope.'

'If this were a case of strangulation, pressure from the rope on the neck arteries . . .' Soames paused. 'The neck arteries, Mr Kling, carry blood to the brain. When they are pressed upon, the blood supply is terminated, resulting in anaemia of the brain and loss of consciousness.'

'I see,' Kling said.

'Do you indeed? The pressure on the brain is increased and further aggravated because the veins in the neck are also under pressure from the rope, and there is interference of the return flow of blood through those veins. Eventually, strangulation proper – or asphyxia – will set in and cause the death of the unconscious person.'

'Yes,' Kling said, swallowing.

'Asphyxia, Mr Kling, is defined as the extreme condition caused by lack of oxygen and excess of carbon dioxide in the blood.'

'This is . . . is very interesting,' Kling said weakly.

'Yes, I'm sure it is. The knowledge cost my parents something like twenty thousand dollars. Your own medical education is coming at a much cheaper rate. It's only costing you time, and *my* time at that.'

'Well, I'm sorry if I . . .'

'Cyanosis in asphyxia is not uncommon. However . . .'

'Cyanosis?'

'The blue coloration. However, as I was about to say, there are other examinations to be made in determining whether or not death was due to asphyxiation. The mucous membranes, for example, and the throat. . . . Let it suffice to say, there are many tests. And, of course, cyanosis is present in many types of poisoning.'

'Oh?'

'Yes. We have, considering this poisoning possibility, conducted tests on the urine, the stomach contents, the intestinal contents, the blood, the brain, the liver, the kidneys, the bones, the lungs, the hair and nails, and the muscle tissue.' Soames paused. Dryly, he added, 'We *do* occasionally work here, you know.'

'Yes, I . . .'

'Our concern, despite popular misconception, is not chiefly with necrophilism.'

'No, I didn't think it was,' Kling said, not at all sure what the word meant.

'So?' Soames demanded. 'Add it all up, and what do you get? Do you get asphyxia?'

'Do you?' Kling asked.

'You should wait for the report,' Soames said. 'You should really wait for the report. I like to discourage these special requests.'

'Is it asphyxia?'

'No. It is not asphyxia.'

'What then?'

'Alkaloidal poisoning.'

'What's alka –?'

'An overdose of heroin, to be exact. A large overdose. A dose far in excess of the fatal 0·2 gramme.' Soames paused. 'In fact, our young friend Hernandez took enough heroin to kill, if you'll pardon the expression, Mr Kling, a bull.'

# CHAPTER FIVE

There were about eight million things to do.

There always seemed to be more things wanting doing than a man could possibly get to, and sometimes Peter Byrnes wished for two heads and twice that many arms. With coldly rational illogic, he knew the situation was undoubtedly the same in any kind of business, while simultaneously telling himself that no business could be the rat race police work was.

Peter Byrnes was a detective and a lieutenant, and he headed the squad of bulls who called the 87th Precinct their home. It was, in a somewhat wry way, their home – the way a rusty L.C.I. in the Philippines eventually becomes home to a sailor from Detroit.

The precinct house, in all honesty, was not a very homey place. It did not boast chintz curtains or pop-up toasters or garbage-disposal units or comfortable easy chairs or a dog named Rover who eagerly bounced into the living-room with pipe and slippers. It presented a cold stone façade to Grover Park, which hemmed in the precinct territory on the south. Beyond the façade, just inside the entranceway arch, was a square room with a bare wooden floor and a desk that looked like the judge's bench in a courtroom. A sign on the desk sternly announced: ALL VISITORS MUST STOP AT DESK. When a visitor so stopped, he met either the desk lieutenant or the desk sergeant, both of whom were polite, enthusiastic, and pained in the neck to please the public.

There were detention cells on the ground floor of the building, and upstairs behind mesh-covered windows – mesh-covered because the neighbourhood kids had a delightful penchant for hurling stones at anything faintly smacking of the Law – were the Locker Room, the Clerical office, the

Detective Squad Room, and other sundry and comfortable little cubicles, among which were the Men's Room and Lieutenant Byrnes's office.

In defence of the lieutenant's office, it is fair to say there were no urinals lining the walls.

It is also fair to say that the lieutenant liked this office. He had occupied it for a good many years now, and had come to respect it the way a man comes to respect a somewhat threadbare glove he uses for gardening. At times, of course, and especially in a precinct like the 87th, the weeds in the garden grew a little thick. It was at such times that Byrnes devoutly wished for the extra head and arms.

Thanksgiving had not helped at all, and the approaching holidays were making things even worse. It seemed that whenever the holidays rolled around, the people in Byrnes's precinct declared a field day for crime. Knifings in Grover Park, for example, were a year-round occurrence and certainly nothing to get excited about. But with the approach of the holidays, the precinct people burst with Christmas spirit and happily set about the task of decorating the park's scant green patches with rivers of red in honour of the festive season. There had been sixteen knifings in the park during the past week.

The fencing of stolen goods along Culver Avenue was a well-known pastime of the precinct people, too. You could buy anything from a used African witch doctor's mask to a new eggbeater if you happened to come along at the right time with the right amount of cash. This despite the law that made receiving stolen goods a misdemeanour (if the value of such goods was less than $100) and a felony (if the value was more than a C-note). The law didn't disturb the professional shoplifters who toiled by day and sold by night. Nor did it bother the drug addicts who stole to sell to buy to feed their habits. It didn't bother the people who bought the stolen goods, either. Culver Avenue was, in their eyes, the biggest discount house in the city.

It bothered only the cops.

And it bothered them especially during the holiday season. The department stores were very crowded during that joyous season and shoplifters enjoyed the freedom and protective colouring of the sardine pack. And, too, customers for the hot stuff were abundant since there were Christmas lists to worry about, and there was nothing like a fast turnover to spur on a thief to bigger and better endeavours. Everyone, it seemed, was anxious to get his Christmas shopping done early this year, and so Byrnes and his bulls had their hands full.

The prostitutes on Whore Street also had their hands full. Whatever there was about the Yule season that led a man uptown to seek a slice of exotica, Byrnes would never know. But uptown they sought, and Whore Street was the happy hunting ground – and the climactic culmination of a night's sporting was very often a mugging and rolling in an alleyway.

The drinking, too, was beginning to get a little wilder. *What the hell, man has to wet his whistle for the holidays, don't he?* Sure he does, no law against that. But drinking often led to flaring tempers, and flaring tempers often led to the naked revelation of somewhat primitive emotions.

*What the hell, man has to slit another man's whistle for the holidays, don't he?*

Sure he does.

But when the wetting of a whistle led to the slitting of a whistle, it very often led to the blowing of a whistle by a cop.

All those whistles blowing gave Byrnes a headache. It wasn't that he didn't appreciate music; he simply found the whistle a particularly uninventive instrument.

So Byrnes, though devoutly religious, was devoutly thankful that Christmas came but once a year. It only brought an influx of punks into the Squad Room, and God knew there were enough punks pouring in all year round. Byrnes did not like punks.

He considered dishonesty a personal insult. He had

worked for a living since the time he was twelve, and anyone who decided that working was a stupid way to earn money was in effect calling Byrnes a jackass. Byrnes liked to work. Even when it piled up, even when it gave him a headache, even when it included a suicide or homicide or whatever by a drug addict in his precinct, Byrnes liked it.

When the telephone on his desk rang, he resented the intrusion. He lifted the receiver and said, 'Byrnes here.'

The sergeant manning the switchboard behind the desk downstairs said, 'Your wife, Lieutenant.'

'Put her on,' Byrnes said gruffly.

He waited. In a moment, Harriet's voice came on to the line.

'Peter?'

'Yes, Harriet,' he said, and he wondered why women invariably called him Peter, while men called him Pete.

'Are you very busy?'

'I'm kind of jammed, honey,' he said, 'but I've got a moment. What is it?'

'The roast,' she said.

'What about the roast?'

'Didn't I order an eight-pound roast?'

'I guess so. Why?'

'Did I or didn't I, Peter? You remember when we were talking about it and figuring how much we would need? We decided on eight pounds, didn't we?'

'Yes, I think so. What's the matter?'

'The butcher sent five.'

'So send it back.'

'I can't. I called him already and he said he's too busy.'

'Too busy?' Byrnes asked incredulously. 'The butcher?'

'Yes.'

'Well, what the hell else does he have to do but cut meat? I don't under –'

'He'd probably exchange it if I took it down personally.

What he meant was that he couldn't spare a delivery boy right now.'

'So take it down personally, Harriet. What's the problem?'

'I can't leave the house, Peter. I'm expecting the groceries.'

'Send Larry down,' Byrnes said patiently.

'He's not home from school yet.'

'I'll be damned if that boy isn't the biggest scholar we ever . . .'

'Peter, you know he's re . . .'

'. . . had in the Byrnes family. He's always at school, always . . .'

'. . . hearsing for a school play,' Harriet concluded.

'I've got half a mind to call the principal and tell him . . .'

'Nonsense,' Harriet said.

'Well, I happen to like my kid home for supper!' Byrnes said angrily.

'Peter,' Harriet said, 'I don't want to get into a long discussion about Larry or his adolescent pleasures, really I don't. I simply want to know what I should do about the roast.'

'Hell, I don't know. Do you want me to send a squad car to the butcher shop?'

'Don't be silly, Peter.'

'Well, what then? The butcher, so far as I can tell, has committed no crime.'

'He's committed a crime of omission,' Harriet said calmly.

Byrnes chuckled in spite of himself. 'You're too damn smart, women,' he said.

'Yes,' Harriet admitted freely. 'What about the roast?'

'Won't five pounds suffice? It seems to me we could feed the Russian Army with five pounds.'

'Your brother Louis is coming,' Harriet reminded him.

'Oh.' Byrnes conjured up a vision of his mountainous sibling. 'Yes, we'll need the eight pounds.' He paused, thinking. 'Why don't you call the grocer and ask him to hold off on delivery for a few hours? Then you can go down to the butcher and raise all sorts of Irish hell. How does that sound?'

'It sounds fine,' Harriet said. 'You're smarter than you look.'

'I won a bronze scholarship medal in high school,' Byrnes said.

'Yes, I know. I still wear it.'

'Are we set on this roast thing, then?'

'Yes, thank you.'

'Not at all,' Byrnes said. 'About Larry . . .'

'I have to rush to the butcher. Will you be home very late?'

'Probably. I'm really swamped, honey.'

'All right. I won't keep you. Good-bye, dear.'

'Good-bye,' Byrnes said, and he hung up. He sometimes wondered about Harriet, who was, by all civilized standards, a most intelligent woman. She could with the skill of an accountant balance a budget or wade through pages and pages of household figures. She had coped with a policeman-husband who was very rarely home, and had managed to raise a son almost singlehanded. And Larry, despite his damned un-Byrnesian leaning toward dramatics, was certainly a lad to be proud of. Yes, Harriet was capable, level-headed, and good in bed most of the time.

And yet, on the other hand, something like this roast beef thing could throw her into a confused frenzy.

Women. Byrnes would never understand them.

Sighing heavily, he turned back to his work. He was reading through Carella's D.D. report on the dead boy when the knock sounded on his door.

'Come,' Byrnes said.

The door opened. Hal Willis came into the room.

'What is it, Hal?' Byrnes asked.

'Well, this is a weird one,' Willis said. He was a small man, a man who – by comparison with the other precinct bulls – looked like a jockey. He had smiling brown eyes, and a face that always looked interested, and he also had a knowledge of judo that had knocked many a cheap thief on his back.

'Weird how?' Byrnes asked.

'Desk sergeant put this call through. I took it. But the guy won't speak to anyone but you.'

'Who is he?'

'Well, that's it. He wouldn't give his name.'

'Tell him to go to hell,' Byrnes said.

'Lieutenant, he said it's got something to do with the Hernandez case.'

'Oh?'

'Yeah.'

Byrnes thought for a moment. 'All right,' he said at last. 'Have the call switched to my wire.'

# CHAPTER SIX

It was not that Steve Carella had any theories.

It was simply that the situation stank to high heaven.

Aníbal Hernandez had been found dead at two o'clock on the morning of 18 December. That had been a Monday morning, and now it was Wednesday afternoon, two days later – and the situation still stank to high heaven.

The coroner had reported that Hernandez died of an overdose of heroin, which was not an unseemly way for a hophead to meet his end. The syringe lying next to Hernandez's hand had been scrutinized for latent prints, and those prints were now being compared with the prints lifted from Hernandez's dead fingers.

Carella, with dead certainty, was sure the prints would not match. Someone had tied that rope around Hernandez's neck *after* he was dead, and Carella was willing to bet that the same person had used that syringe to administer the fatal dose of heroin.

Which situation brought up a few problems. Which problems combined to lend the entire situation its air of putrefaction.

For assuming that someone wanted Hernandez dead, an assumption that seemed to be well-founded, and further assuming that someone had used an overloaded syringe of heroin as his murder weapon, why then was the murder weapon not removed from the scene of the crime?

Or why then, for that matter, was the body then hoisted by its own petard, more or less, in an attempt to simulate a hanging suicide?

These were the knotty trivialities that disturbed the normal thinking of Detective Steve Carella. He knew, of course, that there could be a thousand and one motives for murder in the tangled world of drug addiction. He knew, too, that someone unfamiliar with the ways of the coroner's office might innocently hope to palm off a poisoning as a hanging. But he further knew that every man and boy in the United States had been raised on the Fingerprint Legend. *Commit a crime? Wipe off the prints, boy.* The prints had not been wiped from the syringe. The prints were there, as big as life, waiting to be lifted and studied. The syringe was there, too, and if someone were trying to palm off a *hanging*, would he leave a syringe around? Could he be so stupid as to believe the cops wouldn't automatically connect the syringe to a possible death by overdose?

Something stank.

Everything stank.

Carella had a sensitive nose and perhaps a sensitive mind. He walked the streets of the precinct, and he thought, and he wondered where he should begin because the right beginning was very often the most important time-saving device in detective work. And whereas he was, at the moment, primarily concerned with the Hernandez case, he couldn't very well forget the fact that he was a cop being paid to enforce law twenty-four hours a day, three hundred and sixty-five days a year.

When he saw the automobile parked at the kerb near Grover Park, he gave it but a cursory glance. Were he an ordinary citizen out for a mid-afternoon promenade, the cursory glance would have sufficed. Because he was a law-enforcing cop, he took a second glance.

The second glance told him that the car was a 1939 Plymouth sedan, grey, licence number 42L-1731. It told him that the right rear bumper had been smashed in, and it told him that there were two occupants on the back seat, both male, both young. Two young men sitting in the back seat of a car presupposed the absence of a driver. Why were these kids waiting in a car alongside Grover Park, and for whom?

In that instant, Aníbal Hernandez left Carella's mind

completely. Casually, he sauntered past the car. The occupants were no more than twenty-one years old. They watched Carella as he passed. They watched him very closely. Carella did not turn to look at the parked car again. He continued walking up the street, and then stepped into the tailor shop of Max Cohen.

Max was a round-faced man with a fringe of white hair that clung to his balding pate like a halo. He looked up when Carella came in, and said, 'Hallo, Stevie, what's new?'

'What could be new?' Carella asked. He had already begun taking off his brown overcoat. Max eyed him curiously.

'Some tellor work, maybe? You want someting sewed?' he asked.

'No. I want to borrow a coat. How about that tan one on the rack? Will it fit me?'

'You vant to borrow . . . ?'

'I'm in a hurry, Max. I'll bring it right back. I'm watching some people.'

There was urgency in Carella's voice. Max dropped his needle and went to the rack of clothing. 'Dun't get it doity, please,' he said. 'It's already been pressed.'

'I won't,' Carella promised. He took the coat from Max, shrugged into it, and then went outside again. The car was still up the street, standing at the kerb alongside the park. The boys were still on the back seat. Carella took a position across the street from the car, standing so that the blind spot in the rear of the car hid him from view. Patiently, he watched.

The third boy appeared some five minutes later. He walked out of the park at a brisk clip, heading directly for the car. Carella shoved himself off the lamp-post instantly and began crossing the street. The third boy did not see him; he walked directly to the car, opened the door on the driver's side, and climbed in. An instant later, Carella threw open the door opposite him.

'Hey, what . . . ?' the driver said.

Carella leaned into the car. His coat was open, and his gun butt lay a few inches from his right hand. 'Sit tight,' he said.

The boys in the back seat exchanged quick, frightened glances.

'Listen, you got no right to . . .' the driver started.

'Shut up,' Carella said. 'What were you doing in the park?'

'Huh?'

'The park. Who'd you meet there?'

'Me? Nobody. I was walking.'

'Where'd you walk?'

'Around.'

'Why?'

'I felt like walking.'

'How come your pals here didn't go with you?'

'They didn't feel like walking.'

'Why are you answering my questions?' Carella hurled.

'What?'

'Why are you answering me, goddamnit? How do you know I'm a cop?'

'. . . I figured . . .'

'Were you expecting cop trouble?'

'Me? No, I was just going for a wa –'

'Empty your pockets!'

'What for?'

'Because I say so!' Carella shouted.

'He's got us cold,' one of the boys in the back seat said.

'Shut up!' the driver snapped without turning his head.

'I'm waiting,' Carella said.

The driver fished into his pocket slowly and cautiously. He placed a package of cigarettes on the seat of the car, and then quickly covered it with a comb, a wallet, and a key ring.

'Hold it,' Carella said. Gingerly, he shoved the package of cigarettes to one side with his forefinger. The cigarettes had been resting on, and covering, a small envelope. Carella picked up the envelope, opened it, spilled some white powder on to the palm of his hand, and then tasted it. The boys watched him silently.

'Heroin,' Carella said. 'Where'd you get it?'

The driver didn't answer.

'You make the buy in the park?'

'I found it,' the driver said.

'Come on! Where'd you buy it?'

'I found it, I told you.'

'Mister, you're getting a possessions charge whether you found it or inherited it. You might be helping yourself if you told me who pushed the junk to you.'

'Leave us out of this,' the boys in the back said. 'We ain't got none of the junk on us. Search us, go ahead. Search us.'

'I'm booking the three of you for acting in concert. Now, who pushed it?'

'I found it,' the driver said.

'Okay, smart guy,' Carella agreed, 'you found it. Have you got a licence to drive this car?'

'Sure I do.'

'Then start driving it.'

'Where to?'

'Take a long guess,' Carella answered. He slid on to the seat and slammed the door behind him.

There was nothing Roger Havilland liked better than questioning suspects, especially when he could question them alone. Roger Havilland was probably the biggest bull in the 87th Precinct, and undoubtedly the meanest son of a bitch in the world. You couldn't really blame Havilland for his attitude about punks in general. Havilland had once tried to break up a street fight and had in turn had his arm broken in four places. Havilland had been a gentle cop up to that time, but a compound fracture that had to be rebroken and reset because it would not heal properly had not helped his disposition at all. He had come out of the hospital with a healed arm, and a somewhat curious philosophy. Never again would Havilland be caught unawares. Havilland would strike first and ask questions later.

So there was nothing he enjoyed more than questioning suspects, especially when he could question them alone and unassisted. Unfortunately, Carella was with him in the interrogation room on that Wednesday afternoon, 20 December.

The boy who'd been caught with the deck of heroin sat in a chair with his head high and his eyes defiant. The two boys who'd been in the back seat of the car were being questioned separately and respectively by Detectives Meyer and Willis outside. The objective of these related questioning sessions was to discover from whom these kids had made their buy. There was no fun in picking up a hophead. He took a fall, and then the city bore the expense of a thirty-day cold turkey ride. The important man was the pusher. Had the detectives of the 87th wanted to pull in a hundred addicts a day, all of whom would be holding one form or another of narcotics, they had only to walk the streets of their precinct. Unauthorized possession of any quantity of narcotics was a violation of the Public Health Law Section and a misdemeanour. The offender would undoubtedly pull a term on Bailey's Island – thirty days or more – and then come out ready to seek the drug again.

On the other hand, the pusher was in a more vulnerable position. State law made the possession of certain quantities of narcotics a felony, and those quantities were:

1. One-quarter ounce or more of one-per-cent compounds of heroin, morphine, or cocaine.
2. Two ounces or more of other narcotics.

And this possession was punishable by imprisonment of from one to ten years. Then, too, the possession of two or more ounces aggregate weight of compounds containing three per cent or more of heroin, morphine, or cocaine – or sixteen ounces or more of other narcotics – created, according to the law, an unrebuttable presumption of intent to sell.

It was not a crime to be a drug addict, but things could be made tough for you if you possessed either drugs or instruments for using drugs, which possession *was* a crime.

The boy who'd made his buy in Grover Park had been caught holding a sixteenth of H, which had probably cost him something like five bucks. He was small fry. The bulls of the 87th were interested in the man who'd sold the stuff to him.

'What's your name?' Havilland asked the boy.

'Ernest,' the boy answered. He was tall and thin, with a shock of blond hair that hung on to his forehead dejectedly now.

'Ernest what?'

'Ernest Hemingway.'

Havilland looked at Carella and then fumed back to the boy. 'All right, champ,' he said, 'we'll try again. What's your name?'

'Ernest Hemingway.'

'*I got no time to waste with a wise punk!*' Havilland shouted.

'What's the matter with you? the boy said. 'You asked me what my name was, and I –'

'If you don't want to be picking up your teeth in a minute, you'd better give me a straight answer. What's your name?'

'Ernest Hemingway. Listen, what's with –'

Havilland slapped the boy quickly and almost effortlessly. The boy's head rocked to one side, and Havilland drew his hand back for another blow.

'Lay off, Rog,' Carella said. 'That's his name. It's on his draft card.'

'Emest *Hem*ingway?' Havilland asked incredulously.

'What's the matter with that?' Hemingway asked. 'Listen, what's bugging you guys, anyway?'

'There's a fellow,' Carella said. 'A writer. His name is Ernest Hemingway, too.'

'Yeah?' Hemingway said. He paused, then thoughtfully said, 'I never heard of him. Can I sue him?'

'I doubt it,' Carella said dryly. 'Who sold you that sixteenth?'

'Your writer friend,' Hemingway answered, smirking.

'This is going to be cute,' Havilland said. 'I like them when they're cute. Kid, you are going to wish you were never born.'

'Listen, kid,' Carella said, 'you're only making things tough for yourself. You can get thirty out of this or ninety, depending on how cooperative you are. You might even get a suspended sentence, who can tell?'

'You promising?'

'I can't make promises. It's up to the judge. But if he knows you helped us nail a pusher, he might be inclined toward leniency.'

'Do I look like a stoolie?'

'No,' Havilland answered. 'Most stoolies are better looking than you.'

'What was this lug before he turned cop?' Hemingway asked. 'A television comic?'

Havilland smiled and then slapped Hemingway across the mouth.

'Put your hands away,' Carella said.

'I don't have to take crap from a snotnose junkie. I don't have to –'

'Put your goddamn hands away!' Carella said, more loudly this time. 'You feel like a workout, go down to the Headquarters gym.'

'Listen, I –'

'How about it, kid?' Carella asked.

'Who the hell do you think you are, Carella?' Havilland wanted to know.

'Who the hell do you think *you* are, Havilland?' Carella

said. 'If you don't want to question this kid properly, then get the hell out. He's my prisoner.'

'You'd think I broke his head or something,' Havilland said petulantly.

'I don't want to give you the opportunity,' Carella said. He turned back to Hemingway. 'How about it, son?'

'Don't give me the 'son' routine, cop. I blab who pushed the junk, and I'll still go the limit.'

'Maybe you'd like us to say we found you with a quarter instead of a sixteenth,' Havilland suggested.

'You can't do that, big mouth,' Hemingway said.

'We pulled in enough narcotics today to fill a steamboat,' Havilland lied. 'Who's to know what *you* were carrying?'

'You know it was a sixteenth,' Hemingway said, weakening.

'Sure, but who else besides us knows it? You can get ten years for holding a quarter-ounce, pal. Slap on to that the intent to sell the junk to your pals outside.'

'Who was trying to sell it? Jesus, I only bought it! And it was a sixteenth, not a quarter!'

'Yeah,' Havilland said. 'But it's a pity we're the only ones who know that, ain't it? Now, what's the pusher's name?'

Hemingway was silent, thinking

'Possession of a quarter-ounce with intent to sell,' Havilland said to Carella. 'Let's wrap this up, Steve.'

'Hey, wait a minute,' Hemingway said. 'You're not gonna railroad me like that, are you?'

'Why not?' Havilland said. 'You're no relative of mine.'

'Well, can't we . . .' Hemingway stopped. 'Can't we . . .'

'The pusher,' Carella said.

'A guy named Gonzo.'

'Is that his first name or his last?'

'I don't know.'

'How'd you contact him?'

'This was the first I heard of him,' Hemingway said. 'Today, I mean. The first time I ever copped from him.'

'Yeah, sure,' Havilland said.

'I snow you not,' Hemingway answered. 'I used to buy from another kid. The meet was in the park, near the lion house. I used to get from this other kid there. So today, I go to the meet, and there's this new character. He tells me his name is Gonzo, and he's got good junk. So, okay, I gambled on getting beat stuff. Then the law showed.'

'What about the two kids in the back seat?'

'Skin poppers. You want to be smart, you'll throw them out. This whole business has scared them blue.'

'This is your first fall?' Carella asked.

'Yeah.'

'How long have you been on the junk?'

'About eight years.'

'Mainline?'

Hemingway looked up. 'There's another way?' he asked.

'Gonzo, huh?' Havilland said.

'Yeah. Listen, you think I'll be able to get a fix soon? I mean, I'm beginning to feel a little sick, you dig me?'

'Mister,' Havilland said, 'consider yourself cured.'

'Huh?'

'They don't meet near the lion house where you're going.'

'I thought you said I might get a suspended sentence.'

'You might. Do you expect us to keep you hopped up until then?'

'No, but I thought . . . Jesus, ain't there a doctor or something around?'

'Who'd you used to buy from?' Carella asked.

'What do you mean?'

'At the lion house. You said this Gonzo was new. Who pushed to you before?'

'Oh. Yeah, yeah. Listen, can't we talk a doctor into fixing me? You know, I mean, like I'll puke all over the floor or something.'

'We'll give you a mop,' Havilland said.

'Who was the other pusher?' Carella asked again.

Hemingway sighed wearily. 'A kid named Annabelle.'

'A broad?' Havilland asked.

'No, some spic kid. Annabelle. That's a spic name.'

'Aníbal?' Carella asked, his scalp prickling.

'Yeah.'

'Aníbal what?'

'Fernandez, Hernandez, Gomez? Who can tell with these spics? They all sound alike to me.'

'Was it Aníbal Hernandez?'

'Yeah, I think so. Yeah, that sounds as good as any. Listen, can't I get a fix? I mean, I'll puke.'

'Go ahead,' Havilland said. 'Puke.'

Hemingway sighed heavily again, and then he frowned, and then he lifted his head and asked, 'Is there *really* a writer named Ernest Hemingway?'

# CHAPTER SEVEN

The lab report on the rope and the I.B. report on the fingerprints came in later that afternoon. There was only one piece of information in either of them that surprised Carella.

He was not surprised to learn that an analysis of the rope found around Hernandez's neck completely discounted the possibility of the boy having hanged himself. A rope, you see, has peculiar properties of its own, among which are the fibres of which it is constructed. Had Hernandez hanged himself, he undoubtedly would have first tied one end of the rope on the barred window, then tied the other end around his neck, and then leaned into the rope, cutting off his oxygen supply.

The fibres on the rope, however, were flattened in such a way as to indicate that the body had been pulled *upwards.* In short, the rope had first been affixed to Hernandez's neck and then the loose end had been threaded through the bars and pulled upon until the body assumed its leaning position. The contact of the rope's fibres with the steel of the bar had given the fibres a telltale direction. Hernandez may have administered his own fatal dose of heroin, but he had certainly not strung himself to the barred window.

The fingerprints found on the syringe seemed to discount the possibility of suicide completely, and this hardly surprised Carella either. None of the fingerprints – and there were a good many, all from the same person, all clear sharp prints – matched up with the fingerprints of Aníbal Hernandez. If he had used the syringe at all, then he had wiped it clean before handing it to a second unknown party.

The *unknown* party bit was the part that surprised Carella. The Identification Bureau had done a runthrough on the prints, and come up with a blank. Whoever had handled the syringe, whoever had allegedly pumped that heroin into

Hernandez, did not have a criminal record. Of course, the F.B.I. had not yet been heard from, but Carella was none the less disappointed. In his secret heart, he was halfway hoping that someone who had access to a syringe and the staggering amount of heroin it had taken to kill Hernandez would also be someone with a record.

He was mulling over his disappointment when Lieutenant Byrnes poked his head out of the office.

'Steve,' he called. 'See you a moment?'

'Yes, sir,' Carella said. He rose and walked to Byrnes's door. The lieutenant was silent until Carella closed the door.

'Bad break, huh?' he asked then.

'Sir?'

'Couldn't get a make on those fingerprints.'

'Oh, no. I was kind of hoping we would.'

'I was, too,' Byrnes said.

The two men stared at each other thoughtfully.

'Is there a copy around?'

'Of the prints?'

'Yes.'

'May I have it?'

'Well, it's already been checked. I mean, we couldn't . . .'

'I know, Steve. It's just that I have an idea I want to . . . to work on.'

'About the Hernandez case?'

'More or less.'

'Feel like airing it?'

'No, Steve.' He paused. 'Not yet.'

'Sure,' Carella said. 'Whenever you feel like.'

'Get me those prints before you check out, will you, Steve?' Byrnes asked, smiling weakly.

'Sure,' Carella said. 'Will that be all?'

'Yes, go ahead. You're probably anxious to get home.' He paused. 'How's the wife?'

'Oh, fine,' Carella said.

'Good, good. It's important to have . . .' Byrnes shook his

head and let the sentence trail. 'Well, go ahead, Steve, don't let me keep you.'

He was bushed when he got home that night. Teddy greeted him at the door, and he kissed her in a perfunctory, most un-newlywedlike way. She looked at him curiously, led him to a drink waiting in the living-room and then, attuned to his uncommunicative mood, went out to the kitchen to finish dinner. When she served the meal, Carella remained silent.

And because Teddy had been born with neither the capacity for speech nor the capacity for hearing, the silence in the small kitchen was complete. She looked at him often, wondering if she had offended him in some way, longing to see words on his lips, words she could read and understand. And finally, she reached across the table and touched his hand, and her eyes opened wide in entreaty, brown eyes against an oval face.

'No, it's notbing,'Carella said gently.

But still her eyes asked their questions. She cocked her head to one side, the short raven hair sharply detailed against the white wall behind her.

'This case,' he admitted.

She nodded, waiting, relieved that he was troubled with his work and not with his wife.

'Well, why the hell would anyone leave a perfect set of fingerprints on a goddamn murder weapon, and then leave the weapon where every rookie cop in the world could find it?'

Teddy shrugged sympathetically, and then nodded.

'And why try to simulate a hanging afterwards? Does the killer think he's dealing with a pack of nitwits, for Christ's sake?' He shook his head angrily. Teddy shoved back her chair and then came around the table and plunked herself down in his lap. She took his hand and wrapped it around her waist, and then she snuggled up close to him and kissed his neck.

'Stop that,' he told her, and then – realizing she could not see his lips because her face was buried in his throat – he caught her hair and gently yanked back her head, and repeated, 'Stop it. How can I think about the case with you doing that?'

Teddy gave an emphatic nod of her head, telling her husband that he had exactly understood her motivations.

'You're a flesh pot,' Carella said, smiling. 'You'll destroy me. Do you think . . .'

Teddy kissed his mouth.

Carella moved back gently. 'Do you think you'd leave a . . .'

She kissed him again, and this time he lingered a while before moving away.

'. . . syringe with fingerprints all over it on a mmmmmmmm . . .'

Her face was very close to his, and he could see the brightness in her eyes, and the fullness of her mouth when she drew back.

'Oh God, woman,' he said.

She rose and took his hand and as she was leading him from the room he turned her around and said, 'The dishes. We have to . . .' and she tossed up her back skirts in reply, the way cancan dancers do. In the living-room, she handed him a sheet of paper, neatly folded in half.

'I didn't know you wanted to answer the mail,' Carella said. 'I somehow suspected I was being seduced.'

Impatiently, Teddy gestured to the paper in his hand. Carella unfolded it. The white sheet was covered with four typewritten stanzas. The stanzas were titled: ODE FOR STEVE.

'For me?'he asked.

*Yes*, she nodded.

'Is this what you do all day, instead of slaving around the house?'

She wiggled her forefinger, urging him to read the poem.

ODE FOR STEVE

I love you, Steve,
I love you so.
I want to go
Where e'er you go.

In counterpoint,
And conversely,
When you return
'Twill be with me.

So darling boy,
My message now
Will follow with
A courtly bow:

You go, I go;
Return, retum I;
Stay, go, come –
Together.

'The last stanza doesn't rhyme,' Carella said.

Teddy pulled a mock mask of stunned disgust.

'Also, methinks I read sexual connotations into this thing,' Carella added.

Teddy waved one hand airily, shrugged innocently, and then – like a burlesque queen imitating a high-priced fashion model – walked gracefully and suggestively into the bedroom, her buttocks wiggling exaggeratedly.

Carella grinned and folded the sheet of paper. He put it into his wallet, walked to the bedroom door, and leaned against the jamb.

'You know,' he said, 'you don't have to write poems.'

Teddy stared at him across the length of the room. He watched her, and he wondered briefly why Byrnes wanted a copy of the fingerprints, and then he said huskily, 'All you have to do is ask.'

*

All Byrnes wanted to do was ask.

The lie, as he saw it, was a two-part lie, and once he asked about it, it would be cleared up. Which was why he sat in a parked automobile, waiting. In order to ask, you have to find the askee. You find that person, you corner that person, and you say, 'Now listen to me, is it true you . . . ?'

Or was that the way?

What was the way, damnit, what was the way, and how had a man who'd lived honestly all his life suddenly become enmeshed in something like this? No! No, damnit, it was a lie. A stupid lie because there was a body and someone was trying to . . . but suppose it were not a lie?

Suppose the first part of the lie was true, just the first part alone, what then? Then, then, then something would have to be done. What? What do I say if the first part of the lie is true? How do I handle it? This first part of the lie, this first thing was enough. It was enough to cause a man to doubt his sanity, if it was true, if this first thing was true, no, no, it cannot be true!

But maybe it is. Face that possibility. Face the possibility that at least the first thing may be true, and plan on handling it from there.

And if this other thing was true, and if it broke, what untold harm would be done then? Not only to Byrnes himself, but to Harriet, God, why should Harriet have to suffer, Harriet so innocent, and the police department, how would it look for the police department, oh Jesus let it not be true, let it be a lousy punk lie.

He sat in the parked car and he waited, certain he would recognize him when he came out of the building. The building was in Calm's Point, where Byrnes lived, and it was surrounded by lawn, and there were trees placed all around it, trees bare now with winter, their roots clutching frozen earth, the bases of their trunks caked with snow. There were lights burning in the building, and the lights were a warm amber against the cold winter sky, and Byrnes watched the lights and wondered.

He was a compact man, Byrnes, with a head like a rivet. His eyes were blue and tiny, but they didn't miss very much, and they were set in a browned and weathered face that was seamed with wrinkles. His nose was craggy like the rest of his face, and his mouth was firm with a weak upper lip and a splendid lower lip. He had a chin like a cleft boulder, and his head sat low on his shoulders, as if it were hunched in defence. He sat in the car, and he watched his own breath plume whitely from his lips, and he reached over to wipe the fogged windshield with a gloved hand, and then he saw the people coming from the building.

Young people, laughing and joking. A boy stopped to roll a snowball and hurl it at a young girl who shrieked in gleeful terror. The boy chased her into the shadows then, and Byrnes watched, searching for a face and figure he could recognize. There were more people now. Too many to watch without being close. Hastily, Byrnes stepped out of the car. The cold attacked his face instantly. He hunched his shoulders and walked toward the building.

'Hello, Mr Byrnes,' a boy said, and Byrnes nodded and studied the faces of the other boys who were swarming past. And then suddenly, as if a dam hole had been plugged, the tide stopped. He turned and watched the kids as they sauntered away, and then he sucked in a deep breath and started up the steps, passing beneath an arch upon which were chiselled the words CALM'S POINT HIGH SCHOOL.

He had not been inside this building once since his visit during Open School Week back in . . . how many years had it been? Byrnes shook his head. *A man should take more care*, he thought. A man should watch these things. But how could anyone have even suspected, and how could anyone have prevented, Harriet, Harriet, she should have watched more carefully, if this thing is true, *if* it is true.

The auditorium, he supposed. That was where they'd be. If

there were any more of them, they would be in the auditorium. The school was very quiet, closed for the night, and he could hear the hollow tattoo of his own shoes against the marbled main floor of the building. He found the auditorium by instinct, and he smiled wryly, reflecting that he wasn't such a bad detective after all, Christ, what would this thing do to the police department?

He opened the door. A woman stood at the far end of the auditorium, near the piano. Byrnes pulled back his shoulders and started down the long aisle. The woman was the only other person in the large, high-ceilinged room. She looked up expectantly as he approached her. She was in her mid forties, a stoutish woman who wore her hair in a bun at the back of her neck. She had a mild, pleasant face with cowlike brown eyes.

'Yes?' she asked, her head lifted, her eyebrows lifted, her voice lifted. 'May I help you?'

'Perhaps so,' Byrnes said, mustering up a genial smile. 'Is this where you're rehearsing the senior play?'

'Why, yes,' the woman said. 'I'm Miss Kerry. I'm directing the show.'

'How do you do,' Byrnes said. 'I'm very happy to know you.'

He felt suddenly awkward. His mission, he felt, was a basically secretive one, and he did not feel like exchanging pleasant cordialities with a high-school teacher.

'I saw the boys and girls leaving,' he said.

'Yes,' Miss Kerry replied, smiling.

'I thought since I was in the neighbourhood, I'd stop by and give my son a lift home. He's in the show, you know.' Byrnes forced another smile. 'Talks about it at home all the time.'

'Oh, is that right?' Miss Kerry said, pleased.

'Yes. But I didn't see him outside with the other kids. I was wondering if you . . .' He glanced up at the darkened empty stage. '. . . had him in here working with the . . .' His sentence lost momentum. '. . . sets or . . . or something.'

'You probably missed him,' Miss Kerry said. 'The cast and crew all left just a few minutes ago.'

'All of them?' Byrnes asked. 'Larry, too?'

'Larry?' Miss Kerry frowned momentarily. 'Oh, yes, Larry. Of course. Yes, I'm sorry, but he left with the others.'

Byrnes felt an enormous sense of relief. If nothing else, the show accounted for his son's evenings. He had not lied on that score. The smile mushroomed on to his face. 'Well,' he said, 'I'm sorry to have troubled you.'

'Not at all. It's I who should apologize, not remembering Larry's name instantly. He's the only Larry working on the show, and he's really doing a fine job.'

'Well, I'm glad to hear that,' Byrnes said.

'Yes, Mr Schwartz,' Miss Kerry replied, 'you should be very proud of your son.'

'Well, I am. I'm happy to hear . . .' Byrnes stopped. He stared at Miss Kerry for a long, terrible moment.

'My son is Larry *Byrnes*,' he said.

Miss Kerry frowned. 'Larry Byrnes. Oh, I'm sorry. I mean . . . your son isn't in the show at all. Did he say he was? That is . . . well, he didn't even try out for it.'

'I see,' Byrnes said tightly.

'I do hope I haven't . . . that is, well, perhaps the boy had reasons of his own for wanting you to believe he was . . . well . . . you can't always take these things on face value, Mr Byrnes. The boy undoubtedly had reasons.'

'Yes,' Byrnes said sadly. 'I'm afraid he had.'

He thanked Miss Kerry again, and then left her in the big, empty auditorium.

# CHAPTER EIGHT

Byrnes sat in the living-room and listened to the methodically monotonous tocking of the grandfather clock. The clock had always been a comfort to him, a possession he'd desired ever since he'd been a boy. He could not have told why he'd wanted a grandfather clock for his own, but he had wanted one, and one day he and Harriet had driven out to the country and stopped at an old barn repainted red and white, displaying the sign ANTIQUES.

The proprietor of the shop had been a thin, wispish man with an effeminate walk, dressed like a country squire, complete with waistcoat and leather-elbow-patched sports jacket. He had floated around among his rare pieces of china and cut glass, fluttering anxiously whenever Harriet lifted a piece of crockery. Eventually, they had got around to the grandfather clock. There were several clocks, and one was going for $573, and had been made in England, and was signed and dated by the craftsman who had fashioned it. It was still in fine working order, a stately, proud time-telling machine. Another clock had been made in America, and it was unsigned and undated, and it would probably need repairs – but it cost only $200.

When the proprietor saw that Byrnes's interest was in the cheaper clock, he immediately disqualified them as true *aficionados.* Caustically, he said, 'Well, of course, if you want the *garden* variety of grandfather clock,' and then concluded the deal with barely disguised distaste. Byrnes had taken his garden variety of grandfather clock home. The local jeweller had charged $14 to set it in fine running condition. It had never given Byrnes a bit of trouble since. It stood now in the hallway, and it tocked off the minutes in a deep monotonous voice, and its delicately wrought hands held the white moon face in a wide-angled grin, and the grin read ten minutes to two.

There was no comfort in the clock now, no comfort in the ordered, well-regulated spacing of its breathing. There was neither – and curiously – a sense of time attached to the clock. There was instead a desperate feeling of urgency, the hands advancing, the mechanism whirring, as if time-disconnected, separate and apart from the living universe, the clock would suddenly clasp its own hands and then explode into the hallway leaving Byrnes alone, waiting for his son.

The house creaked.

He had never before noticed how the house creaked. There was sound everywhere around him, the sound of an old man with rheumatic joints. From the bedroom upstairs, he could hear Harriet deep in slumber, the sound of her even breathing superimposed on the dread tocking of the clock and the uneasy groaning of the house.

And then Byrnes heard a small sound that was like an earsplitting thundercrack, the sound he had been waiting for and listening for all night long, the sound of a key being turned in the front-door latch. All other sounds vanished in that moment. He sat tensed and alert in his chair while the key twisted, and then the door swung wide, creaking a little, and he could hear the malicious gossip of the wind outside, and then the door quietly easing shut and snuggling into the jamb, and then the boards in the hallway creaking as feet fell upon them.

'Larry?' he called.

His voice reached out of the darkened living-room, and fled into the hollows of the house. For a moment, there was complete silence, and then Byrnes was aware of the tocking of the grandfather clock again, his garden-variety clock complacently standing against the wall and watching life rush by, like an idler leaning against the plate-glass window of a corner drug store.

'Dad?' The voice was surprised, and the voice was young,

and the voice was a little breathless, the way a voice will sound when its owner has come into a warm room after facing a sullen cold outside.

'In here, Larry,' he said, and again the silence greeted him, a calculating silence this time, broken only by the steady punctuality of the clock.

'Sure,' Larry said, and Byrnes listened to his footfalls as he came through the house and then paused outside the living-room door.

'Okay to put on a light?' Larry asked.

'Yes, go ahead,' Byrnes said.

Larry came into the room, walking with the familiar skill of a person who has occupied a house for a long time, walking in the darkness directly to an end table and then turning on a lamp there.

He was a tall boy, much taller than his father. His hair was red, and his face was long and thin, with his father's craggy nose, and his mother's guileless grey eyes. His chin was weak, Byrnes noticed, nor would it ever be any stronger because adolescence had forged the boy's face, and it was set now for eternity. He wore a sports shirt and slacks, over which had been thrown a sports jacket. Byrnes wondered if he'd left his overcoat in the hallway.

'Doing some reading?' Larry asked. His voice was no longer the voice of a child. It sprang full-chested and deep from the long, reedy body, and somehow it sounded ludicrous in a boy so young, a boy hardly eighteen.

'No,' Byrnes said. 'I was waiting for you.'

'Oh?' Byrnes watched his son, listening to him, amazed at how the single word 'Oh?' could have conveyed so much sudden wariness and caution.

'Where were you, Larry?' Byrnes asked. He watched his son's face, hoping his son would not lie, telling himself a lie would shatter him now, a lie would destroy him.

'At school,' Larry said, and Byrnes took the lie, and it did not hurt as much as he expected it would, and suddenly something inside the man took over, something alien to a father-son relationship, something he reserved for the squad room at the 87th. It came into his head and on to his tongue with the ready rapidity of years of familiarity. In the space of three seconds, Peter Byrnes became a cop questioning a suspect.

'The high school?'

'Yes, Dad.'

'Calm's Point High, isn't it? Isn't that where you go?'

'Don't you know, Dad?'

'I'm asking you.'

'Yes. Calm's Point.'

'Late to be getting home, isn't it?'

'Is that what this is all about?' Larry asked.

'What kept you so late?'

'We're rehearsing, you know that.'

'For what?'

'The senior play. Holy cow, Dad, we've only gone over this about a hundred times.'

'Who else is in the play?'

'Lots of kids.'

'Who's directing it?'

'Miss Kerry.'

'What time did you start rehearsals?'

'Hey, what is this?'

'What time did you break up?'

'About one o'clock, I guess. Some of the kids stopped for a soda afterwards.'

'The rehearsal broke up at ten-thirty,' Byrnes said clearly. 'You weren't there. You're not in the play, Larry. You never were. Where did you spend the time between three-thirty yesterday afternoon and two o'clock this morning?'

'Jesus!' Larry said.

'Don't swear in my house,' Byrnes said.

'Well, for Christ's sake, you sound like a district attorney.'

'Where were you, Larry?'

'Okay, I'm not in the play,' Larry said. 'Okay? I didn't want to tell Mom. I got kicked out after the first few rehearsals. I guess I'm not a good actor. I guess . . .'

'You're a terrible actor, and a bad listener. You were *never* in the play, Larry. I said that just a few seconds ago.'

'Well . . .'

'Why'd you lie? What have you been doing?'

'Now what would I be doing?' Larry said. 'Listen, Dad, I'm sleepy. If you don't mind, I'd like to get to bed.'

He was starting from the room when Byrnes shouted, 'I DO MIND! COME BACK HERE!'

Larry turned slowly to face his father. 'This isn't your grubby squad room, Pop,' he said. 'Don't yell at me like one of your lackeys.'

'This has been my squad room longer than the 87th has,' Byrnes said tightly. 'Wipe the sneer out of your voice, or I'll kick your ass all over the street.'

Larry's mouth fell open. He stared at Byrnes for a moment, and then said, 'Listen, Dad, I'm really . . .'

Byrnes came up out of the chair suddenly. He walked to his son and said, 'Empty your pockets.'

'What?'

'I said . . .'

'Oh now, let's just hold this a minute,' Larry said heatedly. 'Now, let's just slow down. What the hell is this, anyway? Don't you play cop enough hours a day, you have to come home . . .'

'Shut up, Larry, I'm warning you!'

'Shut up yourself! For Christ's sake, I don't have to take this kind of . . .'

Byrnes slapped his son suddenly and viciously. He slapped him with an opened, calloused hand that had been working since its owner was twelve years old, and that hand slapped Larry hard enough to knock him off his feet.

'Get up!' Byrnes said.

'You better not hit me again,' Larry muttered.

*'Get up!'* Byrnes reached down, catching his son's collar with his hand. He yanked him to his feet, and then pulled him close and then said through clenched teeth, 'Are you a drug addict?'

Silence crowded into the room, filling every corner.

'Wh . . . what?' Larry asked.

'Are you a drug addict?' Byrnes repeated. He was whispering now, and the whisper was loud in the silent room. The clock in the hallway added its voice, commenting in a monotone.

'Who . . . who told you?' Larry said at last.

'Are you?'

'I . . . I fool around a little.'

'Sit down,' Byrnes said wearily.

'Dad, I . . .'

'Sit down,' Byrnes said. 'Please.'

Larry sat in the chair his father had vacated. Byrnes paced the room for several moments, and then stopped before Larry and asked, 'How bad is it?'

'Not too bad.'

'Heroin?'

'Yes.'

'How long?'

'I've been on for about four months now.'

'Snorting?'

'No. No.'

'Skin pops?'

'Dad, I . . .'

'Larry, Larry, are you mainlining?'

'Yes.'

'How'd you start?'

'At the school. Some kid was shoving muggles. Marijuana, Dad. We call it . . .'

'I know the names,' Byrnes said.

'So that's how I started. Then I forget, I think I had a snort of C, and then somebody gave me a snort of H, and that . . . Well, I tried a skin pop.'

'How long before you went on mainline?'

'About two weeks.'

'Then you're hooked solid,' Byrnes said.

'I can take it or leave it alone,' Larry answered defiantly.

'Sure. Where do you get your stuff?'

'Listen, Dad . . .'

'I'm asking as a father, not a cop!' Byrnes said quickly.

'Up . . . up in Grover Park.'

'From whom?'

'What difference does it make? Look, Pop, I . . . I'll ditch the habit, okay? I mean, really, I will. But let's knock this off. It's kind of embarrassing, you know?'

'It's more embarrassing than you think. Did you know a boy named Aníbal Hernandez?'

Larry was silent.

'Look, son, you went all the way to Isola to buy. You bought in my precinct, in Grover Park. Did you know Aníbal Hernandez?'

'Yes,' Larry admitted.

'How well?'

'I bought from him a couple times. He was a mule, Dad. That means he pushed to other kids. Mostly because he had a habit himself.'

'I know what a mule is,' Byrnes said patiently. 'How many times, exactly, did you buy from him?'

'A couple times, I told you.'

'Twice, you mean?'

'Well, more than that.'

'Three times?'

'No.'

'Four? For God's sake, Larry, *how many times*?'

'Well, like . . . well, to tell you the truth, I bought from him mostly. I mean, you know, you fall in with a pusher and if he gives you good stuff you stick with him. Anyway, he . . .

he was a nice guy. Few times we . . . we shot up together, you know? Free. I mean, he didn't charge me anything for the junk. He laid it on me free. He was all right.'

'You keep saying *was.* Do you know he's dead?'

'Yes. He hanged himself, I heard.'

'Now listen to me carefully, Larry. I received a phone call the other day. The caller . . .'

'From who?'

'An anonymous call. I took it because it was related to the Hernandez death. This was before we got the coroner's report.'

'Yeah?'

'The caller told me a few things about you.'

'Like what? Like I'm a junkie, you mean?'

'Not only that.'

'What then?'

'He told me where you were and what you were doing on the night of December 17th, and the early morning of December 18th.'

'Yeah?'

'Yes.'

'So where was I supposed to have been?'

'In a basement room with Aníbal Hernandez.'

'Yeah?'

That's what the caller told me.'

'So?'

'Is it true?'

'Maybe.'

'Larry, don't get smart again! So help me God, I'll . . .'

'Okay, okay, I was with Annabelle.'

'From what time to what time?'

'From about . . . let me see . . . it must have been nine o'clock. Yeah, from about nine to midnight, I guess. That's right. I left him about twelve or so.'

'Were you with him at all that afternoon?'

'No. I met him in the street about nine. Then we went down to the basement.'

'When you left him, did you come straight home?'

'No. I was high. Annabelle was already nodding on the cot, and I didn't want to fall asleep there. So I cut out, and I walked around a little.'

'How high were you?'

'High,' Larry said.

'What time did you get home?'

'I don't know. Very late.'

'What's very late?'

'Three, four.'

'Were you alone with Hernandez until midnight?'

'Yes.'

'And he shot up, too, is that right?'

'Yes.'

'And you left him asleep?'

'Well, nodding. You know – not here, not there.'

'How much did Hernandez shoot?'

'We split a sixteenth.'

'Are you sure?'

'Sure, Annabelle said so when he took out the deck. He said it was a sixteenth. I'll tell you the truth, I'm glad we shot up together. I hate to shoot up alone. It scares me. I'm afraid of an overdose.'

'You say you shot up together? Did you both use the same syringe?'

'No. Annabelle had his spike, and I had mine.'

'And where's your outfit now?'

'I got it. Why?'

'You still have your syringe?'

'Certainly.'

'Tell me exactly what happened.'

'I don't follow you.'

'After Annabelle showed you the deck.'

'I got out my spike, and he got out his. Then we cooked the stuff in some bottle caps, and . . .'

'The caps found on that orange crate under the light?'

'Yeah, I guess so. Yeah, there was an orange crate across the room.'

'Did you take the syringes with you when you went to that orange crate?'

'No, I don't think so. We left them on the cot, I think.'

'Then what?'

'We cooked the junk and went back to the cot, and Annabelle picked up his spike, and I picked up mine, and we loaded them and fixed ourselves.'

'Annabelle picked up his syringe first?'

'Yes, I think so.'

'Is it possible he picked up the wrong syringe?'

'Huh?'

'Is it possible he used your syringe?'

'No. I know the feel of mine. No, it's impossible. I shot up with my own syringe.'

'What about when you left?'

'I don't know what you're saying, Dad.'

'Could you have left your syringe there and taken Annabelle's by accident?'

'I don't see how. Right after we shot up, Annabelle . . . now wait a minute, you're getting me mixed up.'

'What happened exactly?'

'Well, we fixed ourselves, and I guess we put the syringes down. Yes, yes. Then Annabelle saw he was about to nod, so he got up and took his syringe and put it in his jacket pocket.'

'Were you watching him closely?'

'No. I only remember he was blowing his nose – addicts always got colds, you know – and then he remembered the spike, and he went over to get it and put it in his pocket. So that was when I went over for mine, too.'

'And you were high at the time?'

'Yeah.'

'Then you could have taken the wrong spike? The one Annabelle had been handling? Leaving your own spike behind?'

'I guess so, but . . .'

'Where's your syringe now?'

'On me.'

'Look at it.'

Larry reached into his pocket. He turned the syringe over in his hands studying it. 'It looks like mine,' he said.

'Is it?'

'It's hard to tell. Why? I don't get it.'

'There are some things you should know, Larry. First, Hernandez did not hang himself. He died of an overdose of heroin.'

'What? What?'

'Second, there was one and only one syringe found in the room with him.'

'Well, that figures. He . . .'

'The man who called me is after something. I don't know what yet. He said he'd call me again after I talked with you. He said you and Hernandez argued that afternoon. He says he has a witness who will swear to it. He says you were alone with Hernandez all that night. He says . . .'

'Me? Hell, I didn't argue with Annabelle. He laid a fix on me free, didn't he? Does that sound like we argued? How does this guy know all about this, anyway? Jesus, Dad . . .'

'Larry . . .'

'Who is this guy?'

'I don't know. He didn't give his name.'

'Well . . . well, let me get his witness! I didn't argue with Annabelle. We were friendly as hell. What's he trying to say, anyway? Is he trying to say I gave Annabelle that overdose? Is that what? Let him get his goddamn witness, go ahead, let him.'

'He doesn't need a witness, son.'

'No? I suppose a judge is just going to . . .'

'The man who called me said we'd find *your* fingerprints on the syringe in that basement room.'

# CHAPTER NINE

At three o'clock that morning, Maria Hernandez was ready to call it a day. She had thirty-five dollars in her purse, and she was tired, and it was cold, and if she fixed herself now and then went straight to sleep, she'd be set for the night. There was nothing like a nice warm fix before hitting the sack. For Maria, a shot of heroin was something that attacked her entire body. It made her tingle everywhere, even in what the Vice Squad and she herself referred to as her 'privates'.

The euphemistic use of the word by members of the Vice Squad was prescribed by law, since that law demanded that no arrest for prostitution could be made by a detective posing as a prospective client until the alleged prostitute's 'privates' had been exposed. Whether or not Maria had picked up the term from her Vice Squad associates, or whether it was a modestly maiden expression she herself had invented was a question for debate. She did have a good many Vice Squad associates – with some of whom she had going business arrangements, and with others of whom she had got into trouble. The trouble had been either of a legal-sexual nature or a socio-sexual nature. The Vice Squad because of its unique pincerlike position was thought of by many prostitutes as the Vise Squad. Again, this was a euphemism.

There were many euphemisms in Maria's business. She could discuss sex the way most other women discuss the latest fashion trends, except that Maria's discussion would have been far more coldly dispassionate. But she *could* discuss sex and generally did in no uncertain terms with other women in her trade. She discussed sex differently with men.

A man seeking her body was, when she discussed him with

the other prostitutes, a 'john'. But in the polite society of a brew shared between male and female in a polite neighbourhood bistro, Maria invariably referred to a client as a 'friend'.

When Maria said, 'I have some very important friends,' she did not mean she could have a speeding ticket fixed. She simply meant that many of the men who, euphemistically, slept with her were perhaps both wealthy and respected.

Nor would Maria ever stoop to describing in a vulgar manner the services she performed. Maria never 'slept' with a man. Maria, euphemistically, 'stayed with a friend'.

Whatever she did, and for whomever, she did it with a strangely detached attitude. There were, she realized, a good many more respectable ways of earning money. But Maria needed about forty dollars a day to feed her habit, and girls of Maria's age – unless they were movie stars – simply didn't earn that kind of money. It seemed provident to her that she had come fully equipped with a readily marketable commodity. And, following the age-old hand-in-glove practicality of supply and demand, she dutifully set about supplying whenever there was a demand.

There was a demand for Maria.

The suburban housewives, knitting and sewing, secure in the golden circle of their own wedding bands, would have been surprised to learn just how much of a demand there was for Maria. They might, in all truth, have been shocked.

For Maria had a good many friends who enjoyed the innocent, high-school-girl look about her. Being with Maria was like being a boy again, and even suburban housewives know that every man is just a little boy grown up. Maria's friends ranged from wealthy executives to file clerks, and her places of assignation ran the gamut from plush-lined private offices to blankets thrown on a factory floor. When she operated within the confines of the 87th Precinct, she generally enjoyed the rental of a room supplied at the rate of $3 per friend. The rooms were rented by various and sundry people, but usually by old women who derived their sole sources of income from such rentals. Maria did not enjoy working uptown. Her prices, because of the clientele, had to be lower there, and that meant entertaining more friends in order to accrue the boodle necessary for her daily drug requirement.

To say that Maria despised the sex act would be untrue. To say that she enjoyed it would be equally untrue. She neither enjoyed it nor despised it. She tolerated it. It was part of her job, and since there were many white-collar workers in the city who neither despised nor enjoyed but simply tolerated their jobs, her attitude was understandable. Her tolerance was helped by the peculiar ability of narcotics to quell the normal sex appetite. So, armed with the double-barrelled shotgun of understimulation through narcotics and indifference through prostitution, Maria stalked her game and quite miraculously led the game to consider her a hot-blooded huntress.

Her stalking, by three o'clock in the morning, left her a little weary. She had thirty-five dollars in her purse, and an eighth of heroin in her hotel room, and hell, it was time to call it a day. But thirty-five dollars was not forty dollars, and forty dollars was what Maria needed for her next day's supply, and so her relief at the day's work being over was partially clouded by a reluctance to quit when that additional five dollars was still lacking.

It was perhaps this reluctance that led to a chain of events that put her in the hospital.

She was walking with her head ducked against the wind, wearing high-heeled shoes and an unlined raincoat. She wore a smart blue silk skirt and white blouse under the raincoat. She had dressed in her best because she'd had a call downtown that afternoon, one of her important friends, and she'd hoped to cop the entire forty from him. But he'd been short on cash, and he'd asked her if it couldn't wait until next time, and knowing he had done this before, and knowing that payment had always followed the next time with perhaps a little bonus thrown in for her patience, Maria had smiled and said *certainly next time*, and then gone uptown to see what could be hustled. Dressed in her finery, she had managed very well. Still dressed in her finery, she headed now for the subway kiosk, anxious to get home for her fix, yet reluctant, but still anxious.

When she heard the footsteps behind her, she became a little frightened. Muggings were not uncommon uptown, and she didn't want to lose the thirty-five dollars she'd worked hard for all day. Her fright ebbed when a voice behind her whispered, 'Maria.'

She stopped, and then turned and waited, squinting into the wind. The man walked directly to her, grinning.

'Hello, Maria,' he said.

'Oh, you,' she said. 'Hello.'

'Where are you going?'

'Home,' she told him.

'So early?'

There was a lilt to his voice, and Maria had been in the business a long time, and whereas she had never been very fond of this particular man, and whereas she really did want to get home to that waiting fix, she nonetheless considered the five dollars or perhaps more which could just possibly be earned in a very short time, and she accepted the lilt in his voice and answered it with a mechanical smile.

'Well, it's not really as early as all that,' she said, still smiling, her voice somehow changed.

'Oh, sure,' he said, 'it's very early.'

'Well,' Maria answered, 'it depends on what you do with your time, I suppose.'

'I can think of a few things to do with the time,' he said.

'Can you?' She lifted one brow coquettishly and then moistened her lips.

'Yes, I can.'

'Well, I'm curious,' Maria said, stalking her game carefully now, knowing there was no joy to the hunt unless the hunted felt he was being chased. 'If it was early enough, and I'm not saying it is, but if it was, what would you like to do with the time?'

'I'd like to lay you, Maria,' he said.

'Oh now, that's vulgar,' Maria said.

'Is twenty dollars vulgar?' he asked, and suddenly Maria had no desire to play the game any more. Maria wanted that twenty dollars, the game be damned.

'All right,' she said quickly. 'Let me arrange for a room.'

'Do that,' he told her. She started away from him, and then she turned suddenly.

'I'm a one-way girl,' she warned him.

'Okay,' he said.

'I'll get the room.'

It was very late, she knew that, and perhaps she could not get a room for the usual three. But with twenty dollars promised, she could afford to risk five on a room, oh, this was wonderful, this was more than she could have hoped for. She climbed to the second flight of the tenement and knocked on one of the doors. At first, there was no answer, and so she knocked again, and then knocked repeatedly until a voice from within called, '*Basta! Basta!*' She recognized the 'Enoughs' as having erupted from the mouth of Dolores, and she grinned in the hallway, picturing the old woman getting out of bed. In a few moments, she heard the slap of bare feet approaching the doorway.

'*Quién es?*' a voice asked.

'Me,' she answered. 'Maria Hernandez.'

The door swung open. '*Puta!*' Dolores shouted. 'Why you break down the door at . . . *qué hora es?*'

Maria looked at her watch. '*Son las tres.* Look, Dolores, I need . . .'

Dolores stood in the doorway, a small thin woman in a faded nightgown, her grey hair straggly and hanging at the sides of her face, her collarbones showing sharply where the gown ended. The rage began building inside her, finally spread into her face, and then exploded from her mouth in a string of epithets. '*Puta!*' she screamed. '*Hija de la gran puta! Pendega! Cahapera!* Three o'clock in the morning, you come here and . . .'

'I need a room,' Maria said hastily. 'The one downstairs, is it . . . ?'

'*Bete para el carago!*' Dolores hurled, and she started to close the door.

'I can pay five dollars,' Maria said.

'*Me cago en los santos!*' Dolores went on, still cursing, and then the door stopped. '*Cinco?* You said five?'

'*Sí.*'

'The room downstairs is empty. I get the key. You stupid whore, why didn't you say five dollars? Come out of the hallway, you'll get pneumonia.'

Maria stepped into the apartment. In the kitchen, she could hear Dolores opening drawers, cursing mildly as she searched for the key. In a few moments, Dolores came back.

'The five,' she said.

Maria opened her purse and gave her five dollars. Dolores gave her the key. 'Good night,' Dolores said, and she closed the door.

He was still waiting in the street when Maria went to him. 'I got a room from Dolores,' she said.

'Who?'

'Dolores Faured. An old woman who . . .' She stopped and grinned. 'Come,' she said, and she led him to a room at the rear of the ground floor. She opened the door, flicked on the wall light, and then locked the door behind him.

He reached for her almost instantly, and she danced away from him and said, 'I heard a proposal of twenty dollars.'

He took out his wallet, grinning. He was a big man with big hands, and she watched his hands, and she watched the methodical way in which he counted out the bills. He handed her the bills and because she didn't want to seem cheap – even though she'd already laid out five for the room – she didn't count them. She put them in her purse, and then took off her coat.

'Last time I saw you,' she said, 'you didn't seem interested in me personally. You were more interested in cards.'

'That was last time,' he said.

'Well, I'm not complaining,' she said.

'I've been looking for you all night,' he said.

'Really?' She walked toward him, wiggling suggestively. Now that the twenty dollars was in her purse, the game could proceed again. 'Well, you found me, baby.'

'I wanted to talk to you, Maria.'

'Come, baby, we'll talk horizontally,' she said.

'About Gonzo,' he told her.

'Gonzo?' She seemed puzzled. 'Oh, are you still saying that silly name?'

'I like it,' he said. 'Now, about your arrangement with Gonzo.'

'I have no arrangement with Gonzo,' she said. Slowly, she began unbuttoning her blouse.

'Ah, but you do.'

'Listen, is this all you want to do? Talk, I mean? You didn't have to pay me twenty dollars to talk.'

She took off the blouse and draped it over the back of a chair. The chair, a bed, and a dresser were the only pieces of furniture in the room. He studied her and then said, 'You're small.'

'I'm not Jane Russell,' she answered, 'but I'm in proportion to the rest of me. For twenty dollars, you don't get movie queens.'

'I'm not complaining.'

'Then what's the holdup?'

'There's more to say first.'

Maria sighed. 'You want me to undress, or no?'

'In a minute.'

'This room ain't exactly warm, you know. Whatever I got,

I don't want to freeze 'em.' She grinned, hoping he would grin back. He did not.

'About Gonzo,' he repeated.

'Gonzo, Gonzo, what's with you and Gonzo, anyway?'

'A lot,' he said. 'I asked Gonzo to make that arrangement with you.'

'Wha . . .' She stared at him, surprised. 'You? You asked him to . . . ?'

'Me,' he said, and now he was grinning again.

Warily, she asked, 'What arrangement are you talking about?'

'The arrangement with Gonzo and your brother.'

'Go ahead,' she said, 'tell me more.'

'Where you promised Gonzo you'd swear you saw your brother and this Byrnes kid arguing.'

'Yeah?' she asked suspiciously.

'Yeah,' he answered. 'Gonzo was working on my orders. He gave you twenty-five dollars, didn't he?'

'Yes,' Maria said.

'And he said there'd be more, didn't he, if you swore you heard them arguing.'

'Yes,' Maria said. She shivered and said, 'I'm cold. I'm getting under the covers.' Unselfconsciously, she slipped out of her skirt, and then ran to the bed in her brassiere and panties and pulled the covers to her throat. 'Brrrrrrr,' she said.

'Did Gonzo tell you what it was all about?'

'Only that this would be a good deal, and that my brother was in on it.'

'What about since your brother died? Has Gonzo said anything about that?'

'He said my brother fouled up the works. Listen, I'm cold, Come on over here.'

'Do you feel any differently about the deal since your brother died?' he asked, walking toward the bed. He took off his overcoat and draped it at the foot of the bed.

'No,' she said, 'why should I? He committed suicide. So why should . . .'

The man was grinning. 'Good,' he said. 'You keep thinking that way.'

'Sure,' she answered, puzzled by his grin. 'Why shouldn't I? The deal had nothing to do with Aníbal's death.'

'No,' he said. 'But just forget there ever was a deal, do you hear me? All you know is that your brother and this Byrnes kid argued, that's all. Do you understand? If anyone asks you – cops, reporters, anybody – that's your story.'

'Who is this Byrnes kid, anyway?' He was sitting on the bed now. 'Aren't you going to take off your clothes?' she asked.

'No, I'll leave them on.'

'Well, Jesus, I . . .'

'I'll leave them on.'

'All right,' she said quietly. She took his hand and guided it to her breast. 'Who is this Byrnes kid?'

'That doesn't matter. He argued with your brother.'

'Yes, yes, all right.' She was silent for a moment. 'Now, that's not so small, is it?'

'No,' he said.

'No,' she repeated. 'That's not so small at all, is it?' They were silent for several moments. He lay back on the bed, holding her.

'Remember,' he said again. '*Anyone* who asks you; cops, anyone.'

'I already spoke to one cop,' she said.

'Who?'

'I don't know his name. A good-looking one.'

'What did you tell him?'

'Nothing.'

'About the argument?'

'No. Gonzo said I should wait until I got the word on that. He said I should keep quiet until then. This cop . . .' She frowned.

'What?'

'He said . . . he said maybe Aníbal didn't commit suicide.'

'What did you say?'

Maria shrugged. 'He must have committed suicide.' She paused. 'Didn't he?'

'Sure, he did,' the man said. He held her tighter now. 'Maria . . .'

'No. No, wait. My brother. He . . . he didn't die because of this deal, did he? This deal had nothing to do with . . . I said *wait*!'

'I don't want to wait,' he told her.

'Did he commit suicide?' she asked, trying to hold him away from her.

'Yes. Yes, dammit, he committed suicide!'

'Then why are you so interested in making me lie to the cops? Was my brother killed? Was my . . . oh? Stop, you're hurting me!'

'Goddamn you, can't you shut your mouth!'

'Stop!' she said. 'Stop, please, you're hurting . . .'

'Then shut up about whether he was killed or he wasn't killed, who the hell gives a damn about that? What kind of a whore are you anyway?'

'He *was* killed, wasn't he?' she asked, bearing his weight now, the pain disappearing. 'Who killed him? Did you kill him?'

'No.'

'Did you?'

'Shut up! For Christ's sake, shut up!'

'Did you kill my brother? If you killed him, I'll never lie. If you killed him for one of your deals . . .' She felt something warm on the side of her face quite suddenly, but she didn't know what it was and so she kept talking. '. . . I'll go straight to the cops. He may have been a crumb, but he was my brother, and I'm not going to lie to . . .'

There was more warmth on her face, and then her throat. She reached up suddenly and then, over his body, she studied her hand, and her eyes went wide with terror when she saw the blood. *He's cut me*, she thought. *Oh God Jesus, he's cut me!*

He backed away from her, arching his body, and she saw the knife in his right hand, the blade open, and then he slashed at her breasts and she rolled with all her strength, flinging him off her. He caught her arm and flung her back into the room, coming at her with the knife again. She held out her hands to ward off his blows, but he slashed, and then slashed back, and she began screaming as he continued swinging the knife, cutting the palms and fingers of her hands. She rushed to the door, groping with the lock, her fingers slashed, fumbling with the lock and unable to open it because her fingers would not do what she wanted them to do.

He swung her around, and she saw him pull back the knife, and then thrust forward with it, and she felt the blade when it tore skin just below her rib cage and then ripped across her body and slashed upwards. She fell back against the door, and he slashed at her neck and her face, and then he shouted, 'You don't have to lie for me, you bitch! You don't have to say another word, any more!' He threw her away from the door, and he unsnapped the lock, and then he scooped his coat from the bed, and went to her and stood staring at her for a moment, staring at the blood-smeared caricature that had once been Maria Hernandez, and then maliciously he thrust the knife deep into her breast and brought it across her body, sure he had struck her heart. He watched as she fell to the floor, and then he ran through the door and out of the building.

She lay in a pool of her own blood, thinking *He killed my brother and now he has killed me. He killed my brother because of his deal, I was to lie, I was to say Byrnes and Aníbal argued, Gonzo told me that, a good deal he said, he gave me twenty-five dollars, more to come, he killed my brother.*

And miraculously, she crawled to the open doorway,

naked, running blood every inch of the way, and she crawled into the hallway, not screaming because there was no strength in her to scream with, crawling the long, long length of the hallway while her life drained out of her, running red into the bare brown wooden floor of the building, and then into the entry-way with its mailboxes, and she reached up and managed to hold the doorknob in her tattered fingers, and managed to twist the doorknob, and then fell face forward on to the sidewalk, still bleeding.

A patrolman named Alf Levine found her a half-hour later as he was making his round. He called an ambulance immediately.

# CHAPTER TEN

There were four bulls in the Squad Room of the 87th on the night Maria Hernandez was stabbed.

Detectives Meyer and Willis were sitting at one of the desks, drinking coffee. Detective Bongiorno was typing up a D.D. report to be turned over to the Safe and Loft Squad. Detective Temple was sitting at the telephone, catching.

'I don't like coffee in containers,' Meyer said to Willis. Meyer was a Jew whose father had a hilarious sense of humour. And since Meyer had been a change-of-life baby, which, in a sense, had been a big practical joke on the old man, the old man had decided to play his own little joke on his son. And since his son's surname was Meyer, he could think of nothing more side-splitting than to make his son's given name Meyer, too. In those days, babies were born at home, delivered by midwives. There was none of the hospital pressure to name a child. Meyer's father withheld his choice of a name until the *briss.* He announced it just as the *moile* was performing the circumcision, and the resultant shock almost caused him to have a castrated son.

Fortunately, Meyer Meyer emerged intact, if not altogether triumphant. A name like Meyer Meyer is a difficult burden to bear, especially if you live in a neighbourhood where kids were wont to slit your throat if you happened to have blue eyes. Remarkably, considering the Meyer Meyer handle, and considering the unfortunate coincidence that had provided Meyer with blue eyes, he had managed to survive. He attributed his survival to an almost supernaturally patient attitude. Meyer Meyer was the most patient man in the world. But when a man bears the burden of a double-barrelled name, and when a man is raised as an Orthodox

Jew in a predominantly Gentile neighbourhood, and when a man has made patience his credo, something's got to give. Meyer Meyer, though he was only thirty-seven years old, was as bald as a cue ball.

'It simply doesn't taste like coffee,' he expanded.

'No? Then what does it taste like?' Willis asked, sipping.

'It tastes like cardboard, if you want to know. Now, don't misunderstand me I like cardboard. My wife often serves cardboard for dinner. She has some wonderful recipes for cardboard.'

'She must have got them from my wife,' Temple called over.

'Well,' Meyer said, 'you know how wives are. Always exchanging recipes. But my point is that I wouldn't want you to believe I'm prejudiced against cardboard. Not at all. In fact, I might honestly say that the taste of cardboard is a taste cultivated among gourmets and civilized humans all over the world.'

'Then what's your beef?' Willie asked, smiling.

'Expectancy,' Meyer said patiently.

'I don't get it,' Willis said.

'Hal, when my wife serves dinner, I *expect* the taste of cardboard. We have been married, God bless her, for twelve years now and she has never disappointed me on the matter of dinner. I expect the taste of cardboard, and it is the cardboard taste I get. But when I order coffee from the local luncheonette, my taste buds are geared to enjoy the tongue-tingling tang of coffee. As you might say, my face is fixed for coffee.'

'So?'

'So the disappointment, after the great expectations, is almost too great to bear. I order coffee, and I'm forced to drink cardboard.'

'Who's forcing you?' Willie asked.

'To tell you the truth,' Meyer said, 'I'm beginning to forget what coffee in a cup tastes like. Everything in my life tastes like cardboard now. It's a sad thing.'

'I'm weeping,' Temple said.

'There are compensations, I suppose,' Meyer said wearily.

'And what are they?' Willis asked, still smiling.

'A friend of mine has a wife who has cultivated the knack of making everything taste like sawdust.' Willis laughed aloud and Meyer chuckled and then shrugged. 'I suppose cardboard is better than sawdust, already.'

'You should switch wives every now and then,' Temple advised. 'Break the monotony.'

'Of the meals, you mean?' Meyer asked.

'What else?' Temple said, shrugging grandly.

'Knowing your filthy mind,' Meyer began, and the telephone on Temple's desk rang. Temple lifted the receiver.

'87th Squad,' he said, 'Detective Temple.' He listened. The Squad Room was silent. 'Uh-huh,' he said. 'Okay, I'll send some men. Right.' He hung up. 'Knifing on South 14th,' he said. 'Levine's already called an ambulance. Meyer, Hal, you want to take this?'

Meyer went to the clothes rack and began shrugging into his coat. 'How come,' he wanted to know, 'you're always catching when it's cold outside?'

'What hospital?' Willis asked.

'General,' Temple said. 'Call in later, will you? This looks pretty serious.'

'How so?' Meyer asked.

'It may turn into a homicide.'

Meyer had never liked the smell of hospitals. His mother had died of cancer in a hospital, and he would always remember her pain-wracked face, and he would always remember the smells of sickness and death, the hospital smells that had invaded his nostrils and entrenched themselves there for ever.

He did not like doctors, either. His dislike of doctors

probably had its origin in the fact that a doctor had originally diagnosed his mother's malignant cancer as a sebaceous cyst. But aside and apart from this indisputably prejudiced viewpoint, he also found doctors unbearably conceited and possessed of, to Meyer, a completely unwarranted sense of self-importance. Meyer was not a man to scoff at education. He himself was a college graduate who happened to be a cop. A medical man was a college graduate who happened to have a doctorate. The doctorate, in Meyer's mind, simply meant four years of additional schooling. These years of schooling, necessary before a physician could begin practice, were akin to the years of apprenticeship any man had to serve in any given field before he became a success in that field. Why then did most doctors feel superior to, for example, advertising men? Meyer would never understand it.

He supposed it broke down to the basic drive for survival. A doctor allegedly held survival in his hands. Meyer's impression, however, was that the physicians had inadvertently and quite unconsciously correctly labelled the pursuit of their chosen profession: practice. As far as Meyer was concerned, all doctors were doing just that: practising. And until they got perfect, he would stay away from them.

Unfortunately, the intern in whose hands the life of Maria Hernandez lay did not help to raise Meyer's opinion of medical men in general.

He was a young boy with bright blond hair clipped close to his scalp. His eyes were brown, and his features were regular, and he looked very handsome and very clean in his hospital tunic. He also looked very frightened. He had perhaps seen cut-up cadavers in medical school, but Maria Hernandez was the first live person he'd seen so mutilated. He stood in the hospital corridor, puffing nervously on a cigarette, talking to Meyer and Willis.

'What's her condition now?' Willis asked.

'Critical,' the young doctor said.

'How critical? How much longer has she got?'

'That's . . . that's hard to say. She's . . . she's very badly cut. We've . . . we've managed to stop the blood, but there was so much loss before she got to us . . .' The doctor swallowed. 'It's hard to say.'

'May we talk to her, Doctor Fredericks?' Meyer asked.

'I . . . I don't think so.'

'*Can* she talk?'

'I . . . I don't know.'

'For Christ's sake, pull yourself together!' Meyer said irritably.

'I beg your pardon?' Fredericks said.

'If you have to vomit, go ahead,' Meyer said. 'Then come back and talk sensibly.'

'What?' Fredericks said. 'What?'

'All right, listen to me,' Meyer said very patiently. 'I know you're in charge of this great big shining hospital, and you're probably the world's foremost brain surgeon, and a little Puerto Rican girl bleeding her guts out over your floors is an inconvenience. But –'

'I didn't say –'

'*But*,' Meyer continued, 'it so happens that someone stabbed that little girl, and our job is to find whoever did it so that it won't happen again and cause you further inconvenience. A dying declaration is competent evidence. If the person has no hope of recovery, and if we get a declaration, the courts will admit it. Now – is that little girl going to live, or isn't she?'

Fredericks seemed stunned.

'Is she?'

'I don't think so.'

'Then may we talk to her?'

'I would have to check that.'

'Well then, would you please, for the love of God, go check it?'

'Yes. Yes, I'll do that. You understand, the responsibility is not mine. I couldn't grant permission for questioning the girl without check –'

'Go, go, already,' Meyer said. 'Check. Hurry.'

'Yes,' Fredericks said, and he hurried off down the corridor in a fury of sudden starched energy.

'You know the questions we're supposed to ask?' Willis said. 'To make this admissible?'

'I think so. You want to run over them?'

'Yeah, we'd better. I think we should get a stenographer up here, too.'

'Depends on how much time there is. Maybe there's a loose secretary hanging around the hospital. A police stenographer would take –'

'No, not enough time for that. We'll ask Fredericks if someone can take shorthand. Think she'll be able to sign?'

'I don't know. What about the questions?'

'The name and the address first,' Willie said.

'Yes. Then, *Do you now believe that you are about to die?*'

'Yeah,' Willis said. 'What comes next?'

'Jesus, I hate this, you know?' Meyer said.

'Something about *Do you hope to recover . . . ?*'

'No, no, it's *Have you no hope of recovery from the effects of the injury you have received?*' Meyer shook his head. 'Jesus, I hate this.'

'And then the business about *Are you willing to make a true statement of how you received the injury from which you are now suffering?* That's all of it, isn't it?'

'Yes,' Meyer said. 'Jesus, that little girl in there . . .'

'Yeah,' Willis said. Both men fell silent. They could hear the quiet *thrum* of the hospital all around them, like a giant white heart pumping blood. In a little while, they heard footsteps echoing down the corridor.

'Here's Fredericks now,' Willis said.

Dr Fredericks approached them. He was sweating, and his tunic looked rumpled and soiled.

'How about it?' Meyer said. 'Did you get us permission?'

'It doesn't matter,' Fredericks said.
'Huh?'
'The girl is dead.'

# CHAPTER ELEVEN

Because the room in which Maria Hernandez kept her fatal assignation with a person or persons unknown was the last known place to have enclosed her murderer, it was open to particular scrutiny by the police.

This scrutiny was of a non-theoretical nature. The laboratory technicians who descended upon the premises were not interested in exercising their imaginations. They were interested solely in clues that might lead to the identity of the person or persons who had wantonly slashed and murdered the Hernandez girl. They were looking for facts. And so, after the room had been sketched and photographed, they got down to business, and their business was a slow and laborious one.

Chance impressions are, of course, fingerprints.

The three kinds of chance impressions are:

1. Latent prints – these are invisible. Sometimes they can be picked up with the naked eye unaided, provided they are on a smooth surface and provided indirect lighting is used.
2. Visible prints – which happen to be visible only because the person who left them behind was a slob. And, being a slob, he'd allowed his fingers to become smeared with something containing colour. The colour was usually provided by dirt or blood.
3. Plastic prints – which, as the definition implies, are left in some sort of a plastic material like putty, wax, tar, clay, or the inside of a banana peel.

Naturally, plastic prints and visible prints are the nicest kinds of chance impressions to find. At least, they entail the least amount of location work. But chance impressions being what they are – that is, fingerprints inadvertently and unconsciously left behind – the person leaving them is not always so considerate as to leave the easiest kind to find. Most chance impressions are latent prints, and latent prints must be made visible through the use of fine-grained, lumpless powders before they can be photographed or transferred on foils. This takes time. The lab boys had a lot of time, and they also had a lot of latents to play around with. The room in which Maria Hernandez had been slashed, you see, was a room used to the steady going and coming of men. Patiently, slowly, the lab boys dusted and dusted, and photographed and transferred, coming up with a total of ten different men who had left good clear latents around the room.

They did not know that none of these men was the one who'd killed Maria. They could not have known that Maria's murderer had worn gloves until he'd climbed into bed with her that night. They did not know, and so they passed the prints on to the detectives, who checked them through I.B. and then indulged in a time-consuming roundup of available possible killers, all of whom had readily accessible (and generally true) albis. Some of the prints had been left by persons who had never had a brush with the police. The I.B. could not identify those prints. Those men were never pulled in for questioning.

Considering the nature of the murder room, the lab boys were not surprised to find a good many naked footprints here and there, especially in the dust-covered corners near the bed. Unfortunately, the I.B. did not keep an active footprint file. These footprints then were simply put away for possible comparison with suspects later on. One of the footprints, unsurprisingly, had been left by Maria Hernandez.

The lab boys could find no usable shoe impressions in the room.

They found many head hairs and several pubic hairs on the bloodstained sheets of the bed. They also found semen stains. The blanket that had been on the bed was vacuumed, and the dust collected on filter paper. The dust was then examined and analysed carefully. The technicians found nothing in the dust that proved helpful to them.

They found one thing in the room that was of possible real value.

A feather.

Now, the work they performed in that room may sound very simple and very unstrenuous, especially when all they could turn up was a lousy little feather, a handful of unimportant latents, and a few soleprints, and some hairs, and some blood, and some semen.

Really now! How much work could all that have involved?

Well, a semen stain looks like a geographical map and has the feel of a starched area. Unfortunately, looks alone are not enough for the purposes of identification. The suspected stain had to be packed. It had to be packed so that no friction ensued, because semen stains are brittle and can fracture into tiny, easily lost pieces. Friction could also break the spermatozoa. In other words, the stain could not be rolled, and it could not be folded, and it could not be haphazardly tossed into a bag of old clothes. It had to be packed so that its sides were absolutely free of friction of any sort, and this took time and trouble.

When the suspect stain reached the laboratory, its real examination began.

The first microchemical test it underwent was called the Florence reaction test, wherein a small part of the stain was dissolved in a solution of 1.56 grammes of iodide of potassium, 2.54 grammes of pure crystalline iodine, and 30 c.c. of distilled water. The test showed only that there was a probability of semen in the stain. It showed this because brown and rhombic-shaped Florence semen crystals appeared under the microscope. Unfortunately, however, similar crystals could have been obtained with either mucus or saliva, and so the test was not conclusive. But it did admit to a probability, and so the second test was performed, and the second test was the Puranen reaction test.

The Puranen reagent, into which a part of the stain extracted with several drops of saline was placed, consisted of a five-per-cent solution of 2, 4-dinitro-1-naphthol-7-sulphonic acid, flavianic acid. The stain portion, the saline, and the solution were put into a micro tube, and the tube in turn put into a refrigerator for several hours. At the end of that time a yellowish precipitate of spermine flavianate was visible at the bottom of the tube. This precipitate was put under the microscope, and the all-powerful eye revealed crosslike crystals characteristic of seminal fluid.

And then, of course, the further microscopic examination included a search for at least several spermheads – defined by shape and staining – with necks attached. Luckily, the stain had not been changed by either friction or putrefaction. Had it been so altered, the search for the presence of spermatozoa might have been even more time-consuming and less fruitful.

So that's what they did with one stain. It consumed the major part of the day. Nor was it very exciting work. They were not searching for elusive cold germs. They were not seeking the cure for cancer. They were simply trying to compile a list of facts that might lead to the killer of Maria Hernandez or that, at a later date, might help to identify a suspect positively.

And if these men devoted long hours to the death of one junkie, another man was devoting long hours to the life of another junkie.

The junkie happened to be his son.

Peter Byrnes would never know how close he had come to washing his hands of the whole matter. He had fought first with the idea that the entire concept was a hoax. *My son a drug addict?* he had asked, *my son? My son's fingerprints on an alleged murder weapon?* No, he had told himself, it is a lie, a complete lie from start to finish. He would seek out this lie, pull it from beneath its rock, force it to crawl into the sunshine where he could step upon it. He would confront his son with the lie, and together they would destroy it.

But he had confronted his son, and he had known even before he asked 'Are you a drug addict?' that his son was indeed a drug addict, and that a portion of the lie was not a lie. The knowledge had at once shocked and disgusted him, even though he had somehow expected it. For a lesser man than Byrnes, for a lesser cop than Byrnes, the knowledge might have beeen less devastating. But Byrnes despised crime, and Byrnes despised punks, and he had learned that his son was a punk engaged in criminal activities. And they had faced each other in their silent living-room, and Byrnes had talked logically and sensibly, Byrnes had outlined the entire predicament to his son, never once allowing his disgust to rise into his throat, never once crying out against this punk criminal who was his son, never once saying the words of banishment.

His instinct told him to throw this person out into the street. This was an instinct nurtured over the years, an instinct that was an ingrained part of Byrnes's character.

But there was a deeper instinct, an instinct shared at fires in paleolithic times, when men clasped sons against the night, and the instinct had been passed down through the blood of man, and it coursed through the veins of Peter Byrnes, and Byrnes could think only *He is my son.*

And so he had talked levelly and calmly, exploding only once or twice, but even then exploding only with impatience and not allowing the disgust to overrule his mind.

His son was an addict.

Irrevocably, irreconcilably, his son was an addict. The caller had not lied on that score.

The second half of the lie turned out to be true, too. Byrnes checked his son's fingerprints against those that had been found on the syringe, and the fingerprints matched. He revealed this information to no one in the department, and the concealment left him feeling guilty and somehow contaminated.

The lie, then, had not been a lie at all.

It had started out as a two-part falsehood, and had turned into a shining, shimmering truth.

But what about the rest? Had Larry argued with Hernandez on the afternoon of the boy's death? And if he had, were not the implications clear? Were not the implications that Larry Byrnes had killed Aníbal Hernandez perfectly clear?

Byrnes could not believe the implications.

His son had turned into something he could not easily understand, something he had perhaps never understood and might never understand – but he knew his son was not a murderer.

And so, on that Thursday, 21 December, he waited for the man to call again, as he had promised; and he bore the additional burden now of a new homicide, the death of Aníbal's sister. He waited all that day, and no call came, and when he went home in the afternoon, it was to a task he dreaded.

He liked a happy home, but there was no joy in his house now. Harriet met him in the hallway, and she took his hat, and then she went into his arms, and she sobbed against his shoulder, and he tried to remember the last time she had cried like this, and it seemed very long ago, and he could not remember except that it was somehow attached to a senior prom and a corsage, and the insurmountable problems of an eighteen-year-old girl. Harriet wasn't eighteen any more. She had a son who was almost eighteen now, and that son's problem had nothing to do with senior proms or corsages.

'How is he?' Byrnes asked.

'Bad,' Harriet said.

'What did Johnny say?'

'He's given him something as a substitute,' Harriet answered. 'But he's only a doctor, Peter, he said that, he said he's only a doctor and the boy has to *want* to break the habit.

Peter, how did this happen? For God's sake, how did it happen?'

'I don't know,' Byrnes said.

'I thought this was for slum kids. I thought it was for kids who came from broken homes, kids who didn't have love. How did it happen to Larry?'

And again, Byrnes said, 'I don't know,' and within himself he condemned the job that had not left him more time to devote to his only son. But he was too honest to level the entire blame on the job, and he reminded himself that other men had jobs with long hours, irregular hours, and their sons did not become drug addicts. And so he started up the steps to his son's room, walking heavily, suddenly grown old, and beneath his own feelings of guilt ran the pressing undercurrent of his disgust. His son was a junkie. The word blinked like a neon sign in his head: JUNKIE. Junkie. JUNKIE. Junkie.

He knocked on his son's door.

'Larry?'

'Dad? Open this, will you? For Christ's sake, open it.'

Byrnes reached into his pocket and took out his key ring. He had locked Larry into his room only once that he could remember. The boy had broken a plate-glass window with a baseball and then flatly refused to pay for the damage out of his allowance. Byrnes had informed his son that he would then deduct the money from the meals Larry ate, and that all meals would stop as of that moment. He had put the boy in the room and locked the door from the outside, and Larry had capitulated shortly after dinner that night. The incident, at the time, had not seemed terribly important. A form of punishment and really, really now, if Larry had still refused, Byrnes would certainly have fed him. Byrnes had felt, at the time, that he was teaching his son a respect for other people's property as well as a respect for money. But now, looking back, he wondered if he had not behaved wrongly. Had he isolated his son's affection by punishing him in that way? Had his son automatically assumed there was no love for him in this house? Had his son assumed Byrnes was taking the side of the shopkeeper and not that of his own flesh and blood?

But what is a man supposed to do? Consult a psychology textbook before he says anything or does anything? And how many other small incidents were there, how many incidents over the years, how many incidents piling up, inconsequential in themselves, gathering force and power as they accumulated until, together, they conspired to force a boy into drug addiction? How many incidents, and for how many of them could a father be blamed? Was he a bad father? Didn't he truly and honestly love his son, and hadn't he always tried to do what was best for him, hadn't he always tried to raise his son as a decent human being? What is a man supposed to do, what is a man supposed to do?

He unlocked the door, and then stepped into the room.

Larry stood just before the bed, his fists clenched.

'Why am I a prisoner?' he shouted.

'You're not a prisoner,' Byrnes said calmly.

'No? Then what is it when the door's locked? What the hell, am I a criminal or something?'

'To be technical, yes, you are.'

'Dad, listen, don't play games with me today. I'm not in any goddamn mood to be playing games.'

'You were found by a law-enforcement officer to be carrying a hypodermic syringe. That's against the law. That law-enforcement officer also found an eighth of an ounce of heroin in your dresser drawer, and that's against the law. So you are, in effect, a criminal, and I am aiding and abetting you – so shut up, Larry.'

'Don't tell me to shut up, Dad. What was that crap your friend gave me?'

'What?'

'Your big friend. Your big-shot doctor friend. He's probably never seen an addict in his whole life. What'd you drag him in for? What makes you think I need him? I told you I could drop the stuff any time I wanted to, didn't I? So what'd you have to call him in for? I hate that son of a bitch.'

'He happened to bring you into the world, Larry.'

'So what am I supposed to do? Give him a medal or something? He got paid for the delivery, didn't he?'

'He's a friend, Larry.'

'Then why'd he tell you to lock me in my room?'

'Because he doesn't want you to leave this house. You're sick.'

'Oh, Jesus, I'm sick. I'm sick, all right. I'm sick of everybody's attitude around here. I told you I'm not hooked! Now what do I have to do to prove it?'

'You're hooked, Larry,' Byrnes said quietly.

'I'm hooked, I'm hooked, I'm hooked, is that the only goddamn song you know? Is that the only one you and your bigshot doctor friend rehearsed? Jesus Christ, how'd I ever get such a goddamn square for a father?'

'I'm sorry I disappoint you,' Byrnes said.

'Oh boy, here we go. Here comes the martyred-fatherhood routine! I saw this in the movies ever since I was eight. Turn it off, Pop, it doesn't reach me.'

'I'm not trying to reach you,' Byrnes said. 'I'm trying to cure you.'

'How? With that crap your friend gave me? What was that crap, anyway?'

'A substitute drug of some sort.'

'Yeah? Well, it's no damn good. I feel exactly the same. You could have saved your money. Listen, you want to do me a real favour? You really want to cure me?'

'You know I do.'

'All right, go out and scare me up some junk. There must be plenty of it down at the station house. Listen, I got a better idea. Give me back that eighth you took from my dresser.'

'No.'

'Why not? Dammit, you just said you wanted to help me!

Okay, so why won't you help me? Don't you want to help me?'

'I want to help you.'

'Then get me the stuff.'

'No.'

'You big son of a bitch,' Larry said, and the tears suddenly started on his face. 'Why don't you help me? Get out of here! Get out of here! Get out of here, you lousy . . .' and the sentence dissolved into a series of animal sobs.

'Larry . . .'

'Get out!' Larry shrieked.

'Son . . .'

'Don't call me your son! Don't call me that! What the hell do you care about me? You're just afraid you'll lose your cushy job because I'm a junkie, that's all.'

'That's not true, Larry.'

'It *is* true! You're scared crap because you think somebody'll find out about my habit and about those fingerprints on the syringe! Okay, you bastard, okay, you just wait 'til I get to a telephone.'

'You're not getting to a phone until you're cured, Larry.'

'That's what you think! When I get to a phone, I'm gonna call the newspapers, and I'm gonna tell them all about it. Now, how about that? How about it, Dad? HOW ABOUT IT? Do I get that eighth?'

'You're not getting the heroin, and you're not getting near a phone, either. Now relax, son.'

'*I don't want to relax!*' Larry shouted. 'I *can't* relax! Listen, you! Now listen to me, you! Now you just listen to me!' He stood facing his father, his face streaked with tears, his eyes red, pointing his finger up at his father's face, shaking the finger as if it were a dagger. 'Now listen to me! I want that stuff, do you hear me? Now you get that stuff for me, do you hear?'

'I hear you. You're not getting any heroin. If you want me to, I'll call John again.'

'I don't want your snotnose doctor here again!'

'He's going to keep treating you until you're cured, Larry.'

'Cured of *what*? Can't you get it through your head that I'm not sick? What's he going to cure?'

'If you're not sick, why do you want a shot?'

'To tide me over, you damn jerk!'

'Over what?'

'Until I'm okay again. Dammit, do I have to spell everything out? What's the matter, are you stupid? I thought you were a cop, I thought cops were supposed to be smart!'

'I'll call Johnny,' Byrnes said. He turned and started for the door.

*'No!'* Larry screamed. 'I don't want him here again! That's it! That's final! Now that's it!'

'He might be able to lessen your pain.'

'What pain? Don't talk to me about pain. What do you know about pain? You've been living all your stupid life, and you don't know half the pain I know. I'm eighteen, and I know more pain than you'll ever know. So don't tell me about pain. *You don't know pain, you bastard!'*

'Larry, do you want me to knock you down?' Byrnes asked quietly.

'What? What? You going to hit me? Okay, go ahead. Be a big muscle man, what the hell will that get you? You going to beat me out of this?'

'Out of what?'

'Out of what, out of what, I don't know what! Oh, you're a tricky bastard. You're trying to get me to say I'm sick, ain't you? You're trying to get me to say I'm hooked, I know. I know. Well, *I'm not*!'

'I'm not trying to get you to say anything.'

'No, huh? Well then, go ahead, why don't you beat me? Why don't you make believe this is your squad room, go ahead, start using your fists, start beating me up. You can take me easy. You can . . .' He stopped suddenly and clutched at his stomach. He stood doubled over, his arm crossing his middle. Byrnes watched him helplessly.

'Larry . . .'

'Shhh,' Larry said softly.

'Son, what . . . ?'

'Shhhh, shhhh.' He stood rocking on his heels, back and forth, clutching his stomach, and then finally he lifted his head, and his eyes were wet, and this time the tears coursed down his face, and he said, 'Dad, I'm sick, I'm very sick.'

Byrnes went to him and put his arm around his shoulder. He tried to think of something comforting to say, but nothing would come to his tongue.

'Dad, I'm asking you, please. Please, Dad, would you please get me something? Dad, please, I'm very sick, and need a fix. So please, Dad, please, I'm begging you, get me something. Please get me something, just a little bit to tide me over, please, Dad, please. I'll never, never ask you for anything else as long as I live. I'll leave home, I'll do whatever you say, but please get me something, Dad. If you love me, please get me something.'

'I'll call Johnny,' Byrnes said.

'No, Dad, please, please, that stuff he gave me is no good, it doesn't help.'

'He'll try something else.'

'No, please, please, please, please . . .'

'Larry, Larry, son . . .'

'Dad, if you love me . . .'

'I love you, Larry,' Byrnes said, and he held his son's shoulder tightly, and there were tears on his own face now, and his son shuddered and then said, 'I have to go to the bathroom. I have to . . . Dad, help me, help me.'

And Byrnes took his son to the bathroom across the hall, and Larry was very sick. At the foot of the stairs, Harriet stood with her hands wrung together, and after a while her husband and her son crossed the hall again, and then Byrnes came out of Larry's bedroom and locked the door on the outside and went down the steps to his wife.

'Call Johnny again,' he said. 'Tell him to get right over.'

Harriet hesitated, and her eyes were on Byrnes's face, and Byrnes said, 'He's very sick, Harriet. He's really very sick.'

Harriet, with the wisdom of a wife and mother, knew that this was not what Byrnes wanted to say at all. She nodded and went to the telephone.

The lions were really kicking it up.

Maybe they're hungry, Carella thought. Maybe they'd like a nice fat detective for dinner. It's a pity I'm not a fat detective, but maybe they're not very choosy lions, maybe they'll settle for a lean detective.

I am certainly a lean detective.

I have been leaning against this stupid cage since 2 p.m., and waiting for a man named Gonzo whom I have never seen in my life. I have been leaning and leaning, and the lions are roaring inside the building, and it is now 4.37, and my good friend Gonzo or anything resembling my good friend Gonzo has still not appeared.

And even when he does appear, he may not be very important at all. Except for the fact that he's a pusher, and it's always nice to grab another pusher. But he may not be important in the Hernandez case, even though he seems to have inherited at least some of the boy's customers, God, the girl! God, the job somebody did on that poor girl! Was it because of her brother?

What, what?

What is it? What's behind such a fishy goddamn suicide? It looks like a suicide set-up, but it's obviously not a suicide setup, and whoever killed that boy knew that, whoever killed that boy wanted us to know it was *not* a suicide! He wanted us to dig deeper, and he wanted us to come up with a homicide, but why? And whose fingerprints are on that syringe? Do they belong to this Gonzo character I'm now waiting for, a nice grubby pusher who hasn't got a record? Are they his prints and will we find out what this whole goddamn mess is about the minute we get him? And is he the one who slashed the girl to ribbons or was that something separate and apart, something that just happened to a prostitute, an occupational hazard, something not at all connected with the earlier death of her brother?

Will Gonzo know the answers?

And if you know the answers, Mr Gonzo, or Gonzo Mr, because I don't know whether Gonzo is your first name or your last name, you certainly have kept yourself well hidden in this precinct, you certainly have operated on a small quiet scale, but if you know the answers where the hell are you now?

Have you been operating before this, Gonzo?

Or did you suddenly inherit a nice business the night you knocked off Aníbal Hernandez? Was that why you killed him?

But what kind of a business did the kid have, when you really examined it closely? Kling beat that whole neighbourhood with his feet, and he scared up a handful of Hernandez's erstwhile customers. A mule, pure and simple, shoving only enough stuff to keep him in the junk himself. So is a business of such minuscule size a reason for murder? Do people kill for a handful of pennies?

Well, yes, people *do* kill for a handful of pennies sometimes.

But usually the pennies are in plain sight, and the pennies are the temptation. Hernandez's business was a non-tangible thing, and if he were killed for that business then why, why in Christ's holy name, had the killer gone out of his way to indicate homicide?

Because surely the killer must have known that death by overdose could have been suicide. Had he left the body where it lay, syringe on the cot next to it, chances are a suicide verdict would have been delivered. The coroner would have examined the boy and said *yes, death by overdose*, as he had in fact said. Aníbal Hernandez would have been chalked off as a careless junkie. But the killer had affixed that rope to the kid's neck, and the rope had been placed there after the boy was dead, and surely the killer *knew* this would draw suspicion, surely the killer knew that. He had wanted suspicion of homicide.

Why?

And where is Gonzo?

Carella took a bag of peanuts out of his pocket. He was wearing grey corduroy slacks, and a grey suede jacket. He wore, too, black loafers and bright red socks. The socks were a mistake. He realized that after he'd left the house. The socks stood out like lights on a Christmas tree, God, what was he going to get Teddy for Christmas? He had seen some nice lounging pyjamas, but she'd murder him if he spent $25.00 for lounging pyjamas. Still, they would look beautiful on her, everything looked beautiful on her, why shouldn't a man be allowed to spend $25.00 on the woman he loved? She had told him with her lips that his love was enough, that he himself was the biggest and best Christmas present she had ever received, and that anything in excess of $15.00 worth of merchandise would be the silliest sort of extravagance for a girl who already had the nicest gift in the world. She had told him this, and he had held her close, but dammit, those lounging pyjamas were still very pretty, and he could visualize her wearing them, so what the devil was an additional $10.00 when you got right down to it? How many people threw away $10.00 every day of the week without giving it a second thought.

Carella popped a peanut into his mouth.

Where was Gonzo?

Probably doing Christmas shopping, Carella thought. Do pushers have wives and mothers, too? Of course they do. And of course they exchange Christmas gifts and they go to baptisms and bar-mitzvahs and weddings and funerals just like everybody else. So maybe Gonzo *is* doing his Christmas shopping, the idea isn't such a far-fetched one at that. I wish *I* were doing *my* Christmas shopping right now instead of munching on stale peanuts in this bitter cold outside the lion house. Besides, I don't like working outside my own precinct. All right, that's an idiosyncrasy, and I'm a crazy cop, but there's no place like home, and this park belongs to two other precincts, none of which is the 87th, and I like the 87th, and that makes me a crazier cop, have another peanut, idiot.

Come on, Gonzo.

I'm dying to make your acquaintance, Gonzo. I've heard so much about you that I feel I actually know you, and really, hasn't our meeting been postponed for just an unbearably long time? Come on, Gonzo. I am beginning to resemble the brass monkeys, Gonzo. I'd like very much to go inside and look at the lions – how come they're so quiet now? Feeding time already? – and toast myself by their cages rather than stand out here where even my red socks are turning blue from the cold. So how about it, Gonzo? Give a flatfoot a break, will you? Give a poor honest cop a dime for a cup of coffee, willya? Oh brother, would I love a hot cup of coffee right this minute, mmmmm.

I'll bet you're having a cup of coffee in some department-store restaurant right now, Gonzo. I'll bet you don't even know I'm here waiting for you.

Hell, I sure hope you *don't* know I'm waiting for you.

Carella cracked open another peanut and then glanced casually at a young boy who turned the corner of the lion house. The boy looked at Carella and then walked past. Carella seemingly ignored him, munching happily and idiotically on his peanuts. When the boy was gone, Carella moved to one of the benches and sat, waiting. He glanced at his watch. He cracked open another peanut. He glanced at his watch again.

In three minutes, the boy was back. He was no older than nineteen. He walked with a quick, birdlike tempo. He wore a sports jacket, the collar turned up against the cold, and a pair of shabby grey flannel slacks. His head was bare, and his blond hair danced in the wind. He looked at Carella again, and then went to stand near the outdoor cages of the lion house. Carella seemed interested only in cracking open and eating his peanuts. He barely gave the boy a glance, but the boy was never out of his sight.

The boy was pacing now. He looked at his wrist, and then seemingly remembered he didn't have a watch. He pulled a grimace, glanced up the path, and then began pacing in front of the cages again. Carella went on eating his peanuts.

The boy suddenly stopped pacing, stood undecided for a moment, and then walked over to where Carella was sitting.

'Hey, mister,' he said, 'you know what time it is?'

'Just a second,' Carella answered. He finished cracking a peanut, popped it into his mouth, put the shell on to the little pile he'd formed on the bench, dusted his hands, and then looked at his watch.

'About a quarter to five,' he said.

'Thanks,' the boy answered. He looked off up the path again. He turned back to Carella and studied him for a minute. 'Pretty cold, ain't it?' he said.

'Yeah,' Carella answered. 'Want a peanut?'

'Huh? Oh, no. Thanks.'

'Good,' Carella said. 'Give you some energy, build body warmth.'

'No,' the boy answered. 'Thanks.' He studied Carella again. 'Mind if I sit?'

'Public Park,' Carella said, shrugging.

The boy sat, his hands in his pockets. He watched Carella eating the peanuts. 'You come here to feed the pigeons or something?' he asked.

'Me?' Carella said.

'Yeah you.'

Carella turned to face the boy fully. 'Who wants to know?' he asked.

'I'm just curious,' the boy said, shrugging.

'Listen,' Carella said, 'if you haven't got any business here near the lion house, go take a walk. You ask too many questions.'

The boy considered this for a long time. 'Why?' he said at last. 'You got business here?' 'My business is my business,' Carella said. 'Don't get snotty kid, or you'll be picking up your teeth.'

'What're you getting sore about? I was only trying to find out . . .' He stopped abruptly.

'Don't try to find out anything, kid,' Carella said. 'You'll do better to keep your mouth shut. If you've got business here, just keep it to yourself, that's all. You never know who's listening.'

'Oh,' the kid said thoughtfully. 'Yeah, I hadn't thought of that.' He glanced over both shoulders, first peering to the left, then to the right. 'There's nobody around, though,' he said.

'That's true,' Carella answered.

'So, you know . . .' The boy hesitated again. Carella pretended to be interested in his peanuts. 'Listen, we're here for the same thing, ain't we?'

'Depends on what you're here for,' Carella said.

'Come on, mister, you know.'

'I'm here to get some air and eat some peanuts,' Carella said.

'Yeah, sure.'

'What are *you* here for?'

'You tell me first,' the boy said.

'You're new at this, ain't you?' Carella asked suddenly.

'Huh?'

'Look, kid, my advice to you is don't talk about the junk to anybody, not even me. How do you know I'm not a bull?'

'I never thought of that,' the boy said.

'Sure, you never thought of it. So if I was a bull, I could take you right in. Listen, when you've been on it as long as I have, you don't trust nobody.'

The boy grinned. 'So why you trusting me?' he asked.

' 'Cause I can see you're not a bull, and 'cause I can see you're new at the game.'

'I could be a bull,' the boy countered.

'You're too young. How old are you, eighteen?'

'I'm almost twenty.'

'So how could you be a bull?' Carella glanced at his watch. 'Dammit, what time was this meet supposed to be, anyway?'

'I was told four-thirty,' the boy said. 'You think anything happened to him?'

'Jesus, I sure hope not,' Carella said honestly. He was aware of a tense anticipation that began spreading through him. He had established now that there was to be a meet today, and that the meet was to have taken place at four-thirty. It was now almost five, which – barring any unforeseen accidents – meant that Gonzo should be showing any minute now.

'You know this Gonzo character?' the boy asked.

'Shhh, Jesus, don't use names,' Carella said, making a big show of looking around. 'Boy, you're real green.'

'Argh, nobody's here to listen,' the boy said cockily. 'Only a nut would be sitting out here in the cold. Unless he wanted to make a buy.'

'Or a pinch,' Carella said knowingly. 'Them damn cops can lay as still as a rock if they want to. You'd never know they was there until the cuffs are on your wrists.'

'There ain't no cops around. Listen, why don't you take a look for him?'

'This is my first time with him,' Carella said. 'I don't know what he looks like.'

'Neither do I,' the boy answered. 'Was you getting from Annabelle?'

'Yeah,' Carella said.

'Yeah, me too. He was a nice kid. For a spic.'

'Well, spics are okay,' Carella said, shrugging. He paused. 'You got no idea what this Gonzo looks like?'

'He's supposed to be a little bald. That's all I know.'

'He's an old man?'

'No, I don't think so. He's just a little bald. Lots of guys get a little bald, you know that, don't you?'

'Sure,' Carella said. He looked at his watch again. 'He should've showed by now, don't you think?'

'What time is it?'

'A little after five.'

'He'll be here.' The boy paused. 'How come this is your first time? I mean, with this Gonzo. Annabelle hung himself couple days back, didn't he?'

'Yeah, but I copped big from him before he pulled the plug. I had enough to tide me.'

'Oh,' the boy said. 'What I done, I've been shopping around, you know? I got some good stuff, but I also got a couple bum decks. I figure you got to do business with somebody you trust, don't you?'

'Sure, but how do you know you can trust this Gonzo?'

'I don't. What've I got to lose?'

'Well, hell, he may stick us with beat stuff.'

'I'm willing to chance it. Annabelle's stuff was always good.'

'Sure, it was. The best.'

'He was a good kid, Annabelle. For a spic.'

'Yeah,' Carella said.

'Don't get me wrong,' the boy said. 'I got nothing against spics.'

'Well, that's a good attitude,' Carella said. 'There are two things I can't stand, and that's bigots and spics.'

'Huh?' the boy said.

'Why don't you go take a walk and look for Gonzo? Maybe he's coming down the path.'

'I don't know him.'

'Neither do I. You check now, and if he ain't here in five minutes, I'll check next time.'

'Okay,' the boy said. He rose and walked away from the

bench, toward where the path angled down sharply alongside one wall of the lion house.

The things that happened next happened with remarkable rapidity and in almost comic succession. Later, when Carella had a chance to think about the events clearly, unhampered by the subjective viewpoint of having been caught in them while they were happening, he was able to put them in their right sequence. As they happened, they only succeeded in annoying him and in stunning him somewhat. But later, he was able to see them clearly as a pattern of unfortunate coincidence.

He first watched the boy walk up to the path, stand there for a moment, and then shake his head at Carella, indicating that Gonzo was nowhere in sight. Then the boy turned and looked up the other end of the path and, perhaps so that he could get a better view, climbed to a small knoll and walked several paces until he was hidden by one corner of the lion house where the path swung around it. The instant the boy stepped out of sight, Carella was aware of someone approaching him from the opposite side of the lion house.

The someone approaching was a patrolman.

He walked briskly, and he wore ear muffs, and his face was very red, and he carried his night stick like a caveman's club. His direction was unmistakable. He was walking in a quick straight line that would take him directly to the bench upon which Carella was sitting. From the corner of his eye, Carella watched the turn in the path around which the boy had disappeared. The patrolman was closer now, walking purposefully and rapidly. He came up to the bench, stopped before Carella, and stared down at him. Carella glanced toward the path again. The boy had not yet returned into view.

'What're you doing?' the patrolman asked Carella.

Carella looked up. 'Me?' he said. He cursed the fact that the park was not part of his own precinct territory, cursed the fact that he did not know this patrolman, cursed the stupidity of the man, and at the same realized he could not show his credentials because the boy might return at any moment, and all he needed was for the boy to see him. And suppose Gonzo should arrive at this moment? Good God, suppose Gonzo should arrive?

'Yeah, you,' the patrolman said. 'There's only two of us here, ain't there?'

'I'm sitting,' Carella said.

'You been sitting for a long time now.'

'I like to sit in the fresh air,' Carella said, and he weighed the possibility of quickly flashing his shield, and the possibility of the patrolman quickly grasping the situation and taking off without another word. But as if to squash that possibility, the boy suddenly reappeared around the corner of the lion house, then stopped dead in his tracks, seeing the cop, and then reversed his field. But he did not disappear completely this time. This time he took up a post at the corner of the lion house, peering around the brick of the building like an advancing street soldier looking for possible snipers.

'Kind of cold to be sitting out here in the open, ain't it?' the patrolman asked. Carella looked up at him, and he could still see the boy watching behind the patrolman's back. There was nothing he could do but try to talk himself out of this without revealing himself. That and pray that Gonzo would not arrive and be scared off by the sight of a uniform.

'Listen, is there any law against sitting on a bench and eating peanuts?' Carella asked.

'There might be.'

'Like what? I'm not bothering anybody, am I?'

'You might. You might try to molest the first young schoolgirl who walks by.'

'I'm not going to try to molest anybody,' Carella said. 'All I want to do is sit here and mind my own business and get some fresh air, that's all.'

'You could be a vagrant,' the patrolman said.

'Do I look like a vagrant?'
'Not exactly.'
'Look, officer . . .'
'You'd better stand up,' the patrolman said.
'Why?'
'Because I'll have to search you.'
'What the hell for?' Carella said angrily, constantly aware of the boy's prying eyes at the corner of the building, aware too that a search would uncover the .38 Detective's Special tucked in its holster into his waistband, and the gun would require an explanation, and the explanation would necessitate the flashing of tin, and there would go the set-up. The kid would know he was a cop, and the kid would take off, and if Gonzo showed at the same time . . .
'I got to search you,' the patrolman said. 'You may be a dope peddler or something.'
'Oh, for Christ's sake!' Carella exploded. 'Then go get a search warrant.'
'I don't need one,' the patrolman said calmly. 'You're either going to get searched or I'm going to clout you on the head and drag you into the station house as a vagrant. Now, how about it?'
The patrolman didn't wait for Carella's answer. He began running his night stick over Carella's body, and the first thing he hit was the .38. He yanked up Carella's jacket.
'Hey!' he shouted. 'What's this?'
His voice could easily have carried to the reptile house at the other end of the zoo. It certainly carried to the corner of the lion house not fifteen feet away, and Carella saw the boy's eyes open wide, and then the patrolman brandished the gun like a Carrie Nation hatchet, and the kid saw it, and his eyes narrowed suspiciously, and then his face vanished from the corner of the building.
'What is this?' the patrolman shouted again, holding Carella's arm now. Carella listened, and he heard footsteps beating a rapid retreat on the asphalt path. The boy was

gone, and Gonzo hadn't shown either. In any case, the day was shot clear up the ass.

'I'm talking to you!' the patrolman shouted. 'You got a permit for this gun?'

'My name,' Carella said slowly and precisely, 'is Stephen Carella. I'm a 2nd Grade Detective, and I work out of the 87th Precinct, and you just prevented me from making a possible narcotics pinch.' The patrolman's red face turned a little pale. Carella looked at him sourly and said, 'Go ahead, panic. It'll serve you right.'

# CHAPTER TWELVE

A feather.

It was only a feather, but it was perhaps the most meaningful bit of evidence turned up in the room where Maria Hernandez had been stabbed.

There are all kinds of feathers.

There are chicken feathers, and duck feathers, and quail feathers, and goose feathers, and flamingo feathers, and horse feathers, and even Leonard Feathers.

Feathers are divided into two groups, down feathers and contour feathers.

The feather found in the room was a down feather.

Now, when a kid in the 87th Precinct held another kid in high regard, considered this kid an all-right guy, a courageous fighter, a lover, a hero, he might very well refer to the boy as a 'down cat'. The *cat* signifying *boy*, and the *down* signifying *all right*.

A down feather, on the other hand, was not an all-right feather. That is to say, there was nothing really wrong with it, but it was in no way courageous, amorous, brave, or trustworthy. It simply happened to come from a certain part of a bird's body, as opposed to other parts of the body, and so it was called down rather than contour.

The down feather found in the room was allowed to soak in soapy water for a while, then rinsed under running water, and then rinsed again in alcohol, and then put under the microscope.

The feather had long knots consisting of several protruding tips.

In the order of sparrows, the knots are close together and conical.

In the order of wading birds, the knots are pointed and conical, the barbules hairy and hard.

Climbing birds have feathers with strongly protruding knots with four tips.

Aquatic birds have strong knots with dull points.

Chickens and other birds in the Gallinae order have feathers with the same characteristics as wading birds.

Pigeons . . . ah, pigeons.

Pigeon feathers have long knots consisting of several protruding tips.

The feather in the room was a pigeon feather.

The feathers in the one pillow on the bed were duck down. The feather found, therefore, had not come from the pillow. It was found stuck to a smear of blood, so chances were it was left by the killer and not left by someone who'd been in the room previous to the killer.

If the killer, therefore, had a pigeon feather stuck to his clothes, chances were he was a pigeon fancier.

All the cops had to do was track down every pigeon fancier in the city.

That job was for the birds.

The department stores on Friday, 22 December, were a little crowded. Bert Kling could not honestly say he disliked the crowds because the crowds forced him into close proximity with Claire Townsend, and there was no girl he'd rather have been proximately close to. On the other hand, however, the alleged purpose of this excursion was to pick up presents for people like Uncle Ed and Aunt Sarah – whom Kling had never met – and the sooner that task was accomplished, the sooner he and Claire could begin spending an uncluttered afternoon together. This was, after all, a day off and he did not enjoy trudging all over department stores on his day off, even if that trudging were being done with Claire.

He had to admit that of all the trudgers around, he and Claire made the nicest-looking pair of trudgers. There was a tireless sort of energy about her, an energy he usually associated with Phys Ed majors. Phys Ed majors were easily identified by short, squat bodies with muscular legs and bulging biceps. Claire Townsend had none of the attributes of the Phys Ed major, except the tireless energy.

Claire, in Kling's estimation, was perhaps the most beautiful woman alive. She was certainly the most beautiful woman he had ever met. Her hair was black. There are blacks, you know, and then there are blacks. But Claire's hair was a total black, a complete absence of light, a pure black. Her eyes were a warm brown arched with black brows. She had the pale complexion of a high-bred Spanish girl coupled with the high cheek bones of an Indian. Her nose was straight and her mouth was full, and she was obviously the loveliest woman in the world. Whether she was or not doesn't matter. Kling thought she was.

He also thought she was a dynamo.

He wondered when the dynamo would run down, but the dynamo kept right on discharging electrical bolts and buying gifts for Cousin Percy and Grandmother Eloise, and Kling trailed along like a dinghy tied to a schooner in full sail, mixing his metaphors with reckless abandon.

'You should see what I got you,' she told him.

'What?' he asked.

'A gold-plated holster for your ridiculous weapon.'

'My gun, you mean?' he asked.

'And a carton of soap for your dirty mind.'

'I'll bet I could make 2nd Grade in ten minutes just picking up shoplifters here,' he said.

'Don't pick up any who are young or blonde.'

'Claire . . .'

'Look at those gloves! Only $2.98 and perfect for . . .'

'Cousin Antoinette in Kalamazoo. Claire . . .'

'As soon as I get these gloves, darling.'

'How do you know what I was going to say?'

'You want to stop all this nonsense and get some drinks, don't you?'

'Yes.'

'Just what I had in mind,' Claire said. And then, being in a gay and expansive mood, she added, 'You should be delighted. When we're married, *you'll* have to pay for all this junk.'

It was the first time the subject of marriage had come up between them and, being towed as he was, Kling almost missed it. Before he became fully aware of the miracle of what she had said, Claire had purchased the $2.98 gloves and was whisking him along to the roof garden of the store. The roof garden was packed with matronly women who were bulging with bundles.

'They only serve those triangular little sandwiches here,' Kling announced. 'Come on, I'll take you to a shady bar.'

The shady bar he took her to was really not quite so shady as all that. It was dim, true, but dimness and shadiness are not necessarily synonymous.

When the waiter tiptoed over, Kling ordered a Scotch on the rocks and then glanced inquisitively toward Claire.

'Cognac,' she said, and the waiter crept away.

'Are you really going to marry me some day?' Kling asked.

'Please,' Claire told him, 'I'll burst. I'm full of Christmas cheer, and a proposal now will just destroy me.'

'But you *do* love me?'

'Did I ever say so?'

'No.'

'Then what makes you so impetuous?'

'I'm sure you love me.'

'Well, confidence is a fine quality, to be sure, but . . .'

'Don't you?'

Claire sobered quite suddenly. 'Yes, Bert,' she said. 'Yes, Bert darling, I do love you. Very much.'

'Well then . . .' He was speechless. He grinned foolishly and covered her hand with his and blinked.

'Now I've spoiled you,' she said, smiling. 'Now that you know I'm in your power, you'll be unbearable.'

'No, no, I won't.'

'I know you policemen,' she insisted. 'You're brutal and cruel and . . .'

'No, Claire, no really, I . . .'

'Yes, yes. You'll take me in for questioning and . . .'

'Oh Jesus, Claire, I love you,' he said plaintively.

'Yes,' she said, smiling contentedly. 'Isn't it wonderful? Aren't we so lucky, Bert?'

'You were lucky,' the man said.

Gonzo looked at him sourly. 'Yeah? You think so?'

'You could have taken a fall. How much were you holding?'

'About an ounce. That's not the point. What I'm trying to tell you is that this is getting hot, you see?'

'We want it to get hot.'

'Listen, friend, hot is hot, but getting my own ass in a sling is another thing.'

'You weren't nabbed, were you?'

'No, but only because I happened to be on my toes.' Gonzo lighted a cigarette, and then exhaled a cloud of smoke. 'Listen, don't you understand what I'm saying?'

'I understand perfectly.'

'Okay, okay. This guy was a dick. And he was sure as hell looking for *me*! That means they're on to me some way, and that means they may know what happened in that room with Annabelle.'

'It doesn't matter what they know.'

'You keep saying that. Okay, play it cool. I'm saying we're in this pretty deep now, and I say let's get it over with. Make your goddamn call, do what has to be done. Get it over with.'

'I'll make the call when I'm ready,' the man said. 'I want to go up and look at the pigeons first. This cold weather . . .'

'You and your goddamn pigeons,' Gonzo said.

'Pigeons are good,' the man said simply.

'All right, look at them. Tuck them in. Do whatever you want. But call Byrnes, will you? Let's square this thing away. Remember, I got nothing to do with this but . . .'

'You've got a lot to do with it!'

'Nothing! That's what I'm trying to tell you. You made me a lot of promises, okay, I don't see nothing happening. All I see is bulls looking for me. Okay, what happened to the promises? What happened to your big idea? Goddammit, who was it told you Byrnes's kid was a junkie in the first place?'

'You, Gonzo.'

'Okay. So how about it? When do the promises pay off?'

'You've got Annabelle's trade, haven't you?'

'Peanuts!' Gonzo said vehemently. 'You laid this out like big time. Okay, where's the big time? Didn't I do everything you said? Didn't I risk my neck setting up the Hernandez girl? You think it was easy getting her to agree to lie?'

'Yes, I think it was easy. I think all you had to do was flash the twenty-five dollars.'

'Yeah, well, it wasn't all that easy. The guy was her brother, you know. And she sure as hell didn't figure he was getting measured for a coffin. Anyway, he was a nice kid. That part of the idea stunk.'

'It was the only way to do it.'

'You coulda done it plenty ways,' Gonzo said, 'but I don't even want to talk about it. I don't know nothing about murder, nothing. Annabelle and his sister are your headaches. That's another thing, you know? Why'd you hafta cut . . . ?'

'Shut up!'

'Okay, okay. All I'm saying is this. That goddamn 87th is wise to something, and I got to protect myself. I ain't taking a fall for you or nobody else. If that dick starts giving me trouble – well, don't think I'm going along with him, friend.

Nobody's going to work me over in no goddamn squad room.'

'What'll you do, Gonzo? If a cop tries to take you in?'

'I'll kill the son of a bitch,' Gonzo said.

'I thought you didn't know anything about murder.'

'I'm talking about these fancy wash jobs you figure out. I'm clear out of that mess, friend. All I want is what I was promised. For giving you the lead in the first place, and for setting up the Hernandez girl. Without me, you never woulda . . .'

'You'll get everything you were promised. Do you know what's wrong with you, Gonzo?'

'No, tell me. I'm dying to hear what's wrong with me.'

'You still think small time. You're playing with something that's big time, and your mind is still laying on the garbage heap.'

'Well, your mind is up in the clouds. Congratulations. Excuse me for being in the garbage.'

'Start thinking big, you fool! Once I explain to Byrnes . . .'

'When? Call him, will you? Let's get this thing rolling.'

'As soon as I check my pigeons.'

'Check on the pigeons!' Byrnes shouted into the intercom. 'If you've got stoolies, why the hell aren't you using them, Steve?'

At the other end of the instrument, Carella sighed patiently, unable to understand Byrnes's curious irritation these past few days.

'Pete, I *have* been checking with our stoolies. None of them seem to know anybody named Gonzo. I've got a call in right now to Danny Gimp. As soon as I . . .'

'I find it impossible to believe that nobody in this goddamn precinct has ever head of Gonzo!' Byrnes shouted. 'I find it impossible to believe that with a squad of sixteen detectives, I can't locate a two-bit pusher when I want him!

I'm sorry, Steve, but I find that pretty damn impossible to believe.'

'Well . . .'

'Have you checked the other precincts? A man doesn't simply materialize out of thin air. That doesn't happen, Steve. If he's a pusher, he may have a record.'

'He may be a new pusher.'

'Then he may have a J.D. card.'

'No, I've checked that. Pete, maybe the Gonzo is a nickname. Maybe . . .'

'What the hell do we have aliases files for?' Byrnes shouted.

'Pete, be reasonable. He may not be an old-timer. He may be one of these young punks who's just cut himself into the business. So he has no record and he . . .'

'A young punk suddenly becomes a pusher, and you're telling me he has no J.D. record?'

'Pete, he doesn't necessarily have to be listed as a juvenile delinquent. It's just possible, you know, that he's never been in trouble. There are hundreds of kids in the streets who don't have cards on . . .'

'What are you telling me?' Byrnes said. 'Are you telling me you can't find a snotnosed punk for me, is that what? This Gonzo took over Hernandez's trade, and that's a possible motive for murder, don't you think?'

'Well, if it were a big enough trade, yes. But, Pete . . .'

'Have you got a better motive, Steve?'

'No, not yet.'

*'Then find me Gonzo!'*

'Ah, Jesus, Pete, you're talking to me as if . . .'

'I'm still running this squad, Carella,' Byrnes said angrily.

'All right, look. Look, I met a kid yesterday who was ready to make a buy from Gonzo. I know what the kid looks like, and I'll try to scout him up today, okay? But first let me see what Danny Gimp has.'

'You think this kid knows Gonzo?'

'He said he didn't yesterday, and he panicked when a

patrolman showed. But maybe he's made contact since, and maybe he can lead me to Gonzo. I'll look around. Danny should be calling back in a half-hour or so.'

'All right,' Byrnes said.

'I don't know why you're getting so hot about this case Carella ventured. 'We're getting hardly any pressure at . . .'

'I get hot about *every* case,' Byrnes said tersely, and he snapped off the connection.

He sat at his desk and stared through the corner window of the room, looking out over the park. He was very weary and very sad, and he hated himself for snapping at his men, and he hated himself for concealing important evidence, evidence that might possibly help a good cop like Carella. But again he asked himself the question, and again the question had the same hollow ring to it: *What's a man supposed to do?*

Would Carella understand? Or would Carella, being a good cop and a smart cop, beat those fingerprints to death, track them down, get to work in earnest and come up with a murderer named Larry Byrnes?

*What am I afraid of?* Byrnes asked himself.

And, faced with the answer, a new despondency claimed him. He knew what he was afraid of. He had met a new Larry Byrnes in the past few days. The new person masquerading as his son was not a very nice person. He did not know that person at all.

That person could have done murder.

*My son, Larry, may have killed that Hernandez boy*, Byrnes thought.

The phone on his desk rang. He listened to it ring for several moments, and then he swung his swivel chair around and picked up the receiver.

'87th Squad,' he said. 'Lieutenant Byrnes here.'

'Lieutenant, this is Cassidy at the desk.'

'What is it, Mike?'

'I've got a call for you.'

'Who is it?'

'Well, that's just it. The guy won't say.'

Byrnes felt a sudden sharp pain at the base of his spine. The pain spread, suffused slowly, became a warm dissipating glow. 'He . . . he wants to talk to me?' Byrnes asked.

'Yes, sir,' Cassidy said.

'All right, put him on.'

Byrnes waited. His hands were sweating. The receiver was slippery in his right hand, and he wiped the palm of his left hand on his trouser leg.

'Hello?' the voice said. It was the same voice as before. Byrnes recognized it instantly.

'This is Lieutenant Byrnes,' he said.

'Ah, good afternoon, Lieutenant,' the voice said. 'How are you?'

'I'm fine,' Byrnes said. 'Who is this?'

'Well now, that's not exactly a very bright question, is it, Lieutenant?'

'What do you want?'

'Ah, are we alone on this wire, Lieutenant? I'd hate to think that any of your colleagues were about to hear the personal things we'll discuss.'

'No one listens in on my calls,' Byrnes assured him.

'You're quite certain of that, are you, Lieutenant?'

'Don't take me for a fool,' Byrnes snapped. 'Say what you've got to say.'

'Have you had a chance to chat with your son, Lieutenant?'

'Yes,' Byrnes said. He shifted the phone to his left hand wiped his right hand, and then switched again.

'And has he confirmed the accusations I made the last time I spoke to you?'

'He's a drug addict,' Byrnes said. 'That's true . . .'

'A pity, isn't it, Lieutenant. Nice kid like that.' The voice grew suddenly businesslike. 'Did you check those fingerprints?'

'Yes.'

'Are they his?'

'Yes.'

'It looks bad, doesn't it, Lieutenant?'

'My son didn't argue with Hernandez.'

'I've got a witness, Lieutenant.'

'Who's your witness?'

'You'll be surprised.'

'Go ahead.'

'Maria Hernandez.'

'What!'

'Yes. That makes it look even worse, doesn't it? The one witness to the argument suddenly winds up dead. That makes it look pretty bad, Lieutenant.'

'My son was with me on the night Maria Hernandez was killed,' Byrnes said flatly.

'That'll sit pretty nicely with a jury, won't it?' the voice said. 'Especially when the jury learns Pop had been concealing evidence.' There was a pause. 'Or have you told your colleagues about your son's prints on that syringe?'

'No,' Byrnes said hesitantly. 'I . . . I haven't. Look, what is it you want?'

'I'll tell you what I want. You're supposed to be a pretty tough customer, aren't you, Lieutenant?'

'Goddammit, what do you want?' Byrnes paused. 'Are you looking for money? Is that it?'

'Lieutenant, you underestimate me. I . . .'

'Hello?' a new voice said.

'What?' Byrnes asked. 'Who . . . ?'

'Oh, gee, I'm sorry, Lieutenant,' Cassidy said. 'I must've plugged into the wrong hole. I'm trying to get Carella. I've got Danny Gimp for him.'

'All right, Cassidy, get off the line,' Byrnes said.

'Yes, sir.'

He waited until the clicking told him Cassidy was gone.

'All right,' he said. 'He's gone.'

There was no answer.

'Hello?' Byrnes said. 'Hello?'

His party was gone. Byrnes slammed down the receiver, and then sat morosely at his desk, thinking. He thought very carefully, and he thought very clearly, and when the knock sounded on his door five minutes later, he had reached a conclusion and a certain peace.

'Come,' he said.

The door opened. Carella came into the office.

'I just spoke to Danny Gimp,' Carella said. He shook his head. 'No luck. He doesn't know any Gonzo, either.'

'Well,' Byrnes said wearily.

'So I'm going to take another run over to the park. Maybe I'll see this kid again. If he's not there, I'll try around.'

'Fine,' Byrnes said. 'Do your best.'

'Right.' Carella turned to leave.

'Steve,' Byrnes said, 'before you go . . .'

'Yes?'

'There's something you ought to know. There's a lot you ought to know.'

'What is it, Pete?'

'The fingerprints on that syringe –' Byrnes said, and then he girded himself for what would be a long and painful story. 'They're my son's.'

# CHAPTER THIRTEEN

'Mom!'

Harriet stood at the foot of the steps and heard the voice of her son again, a plaintive voice that penetrated the wood of his door and then fled wildly down the steps.

'Mom, come up here! Open this door! Mom!'

She stood quite still, her eyes troubled, her hands clenched one over the other at her waist.

*'Mom!'*

'What is it, Larry?' she said.

'Come up here! Goddammit, can't you come up here?'

She nodded gently, knowing he could not see her reply, and she started up the steps to the upper level. She was a full-breasted women who had been considered something of a beauty in her Calm's Point youth. Her eyes, even now, were a clear bright green, but the red of her hair was threaded with grey strands and she had put on more weight in the behind than she'd wanted. Her legs were still good, not as strong as they used to be, but good, clean legs. They carried her upstairs, and she stopped outside the door to Larry's bedroom and very quietly asked, 'What is it, son?'

'Open the door,' Larry said.

'Why?'

'I want to come out.'

'Your father said you are not to leave your room, Larry. The doctor . . .'

'Oh, sure, Mom,' Larry said, his voice becoming suddenly oily, 'that was before. But I'm all right now, really I am. Come on, Mom, open the door.'

'No,' she said firmly.

'Mom,' Larry continued persuasively, 'can't you tell I'm all right now? Really, Mom, I wouldn't try to fool you. I'm fine.

But I feel sort of cooped up here, really. I'd like to walk around the house a little, stretch my legs.'

'No.'

'Mom . . .'

'No, Larry!'

'For Christ's sake, what the hell do I have to do around here, anyway? Are you trying to torture me? Is that what you're trying to do? Listen to me. Now listen to me, Mom. You go call that lousy doctor and tell him to get me something fast, do you hear?'

'Larry . . .'

'Shut up! I'm sick of this damn mollycoddle attitude around here! All right, I'm a junkie! I'm a goddamn junkie, *and I want a fix!* Now, get it for me!'

'I'll call Johnny if you like. But he will not bring any heroin.'

'You're a pair, aren't you? You and the old man. Ike and Mike. They think alike. Open this door! *Open this goddamn door!* I'll jump out the window if you don't open it! You hear me? If you don't open this door, I'm gonna jump out the window.'

'All right, Larry,' Harriet said calmly. 'I'll open the door.'

'Oh,' he said. 'Well. It's about time. So open it.'

'Just a moment,' she said. She walked quite calmly and quite deliberately to her own bedroom at the end of the hall. She heard Larry call 'Mom!' but she didn't answer. She went directly to her dresser, opened the top drawer and took out a leather case. She snapped open the case, dust-covered because it had not been used since Peter gave it to her as a gift, and lifted the pearl-handled .22 from where it lay on its velvet bed. She checked the gun to make sure it was loaded, and then she walked down the corridor to Larry's door, the gun dangling loosely at her side.

'Mom?' Larry asked.

'Yes, just a moment.' She reached into the pocket of her apron for the key, inserting it into the lock with her left hand. She twisted the key, shoved open the door, levelled the .22, and stepped back.

Larry rushed for the door almost immediately. He saw the gun in his mother's hand, and then pulled up short, staring at her unbelievingly.

'Wh . . . what's that?'

'Back away,' Harriet said, holding the gun quite steadily.

'Wh . . .'

She entered the room, and he moved away from her and the gun. She closed the door behind her, moved a straight-back chair to a position in front of the knob, and then sat in it.

'Wh . . . what's the gun for?' Larry asked. There was something in his mother's eyes that he could remember from his childhood days. It was something stern and reprimanding, something with which he could not argue. He knew. He had tried arguing with it when he was a little boy.

'You said you were going to jump out the window,' Harriet said. 'It's at least a forty-foot drop to the pavement, if not more. If you jump, Larry, you're liable to kill yourself. That's what the gun's for.'

'I . . . I don't understand.'

'This, son,' Harriet said. 'You're not leaving this room, either by the door *or* the window. And if you make a move toward either of them, I'll have to shoot you.'

'What!' Larry said incredulously.

'Yes, Larry,' Harriet said. 'I'm a good shot, too. Your father taught me, and he was the best damn shot at the academy. Now sit down and let's talk, shall we?'

'You're . . .' Larry swallowed. 'You're k . . . kidding me, of course.'

'It would,' Harriet answered, 'be a little foolish to gamble on that premise, son, considering the fact that it's me who's holding the gun.'

Larry looked at the .22 and then blinked.

'Now sit,' Harriet said, smiling pleasantly, 'and we'll talk about all sorts of things. Have you thought of what you're giving Dad for Christmas?'

There's a trouble with murder.

There are, to be truthful, a lot of troubles with murder – but there's one in particular.

It gets to be a habit.

No one's claiming, you understand, that murder is the only habit-forming activity around. That would be untrue and somewhat foolish. Brushing the teeth is habit forming. So is taking a bath. So is infidelity. So is going to the movies. Living, if one wanted to be a little morbid, is also a little habit forming.

But murder is, and in a non-exclusive way, definitely habit forming.

That's the main trouble with murder.

The man who killed Aníbal Hernandez had a very good reason, according to his own somewhat curious way of thinking, for wanting Aníbal dead. Now, if you're going to justify murder at all, you'd have to admit that so far as good reasons went, this fellow had a pretty good one. All within the framework of murder, of course. There are good reasons and bad reasons for everything, and there are doubtless many people who might feel that there simply is no such thing as a good reason for murder. Well, there's no arguing with some diehards.

But this fellow's reason was a good one, and once the somewhat gory task of murder had been done, the reason seemed even better because a *fait accompli* seeks and generally finds its own justification.

The reason for killing Aníbal's sister also seemed to be a pretty good one at the time. Hadn't the fool girl exhibited all the symptoms of a tongue about to start wagging? Besides, a girl shouldn't start arguing with a man when he . . . well, it served her right. Of course, she really hadn't known anything, except about Gonzo, well, that was reason enough.

Tell the police that Gonzo had asked her to lie, and then the police would pick up Gonzo, and Gonzo would empty his stomach of everything. That was dangerous.

Standing now in his pigeon coop on the roof, he could see how dangerous it would be if Gonzo got picked up. He was still a little rattled by the fact that Byrnes had put a tap on their call, even though he'd been assured no one was listening. That would seem to indicate a foolhardiness on the part of Byrnes, and one doesn't get very foolhardy when his son might be involved, unless one has an ace up his sleeve. And what could that ace be?

God, it was windy up here on the roof. He was glad he had put tar paper over the wire mesh of the coop. Sure, pigeons are hardy, don't they go gallivanting around Grover Park all winter long, but still he wouldn't want any of his birds to die. There was one in particular, that little female fantail, who didn't look good at all. She had not eaten for several days now and her eyes, if you could tell anything at all from a pigeon's eyes, didn't look right. He would have to watch her, maybe get something into her with an eye-dropper. The other birds were looking fine, though. He had several Jacobins, and he would never tire of watching them, never tire of admiring the hoodlike ruff of feathers they wore around their heads. And his tumbler, God, the way that bird somersaulted when it flew, or how about the pouters, they were magnificent birds, too, what the hell could Byrnes have up his sleeve?

How had a dick got on to Gonzo's tail?

Was it possible the girl had talked? Before she'd died? No, that was not possible. If she had talked, the police would have come to him directly and damn fast. They wouldn't be fooling around trying to pick up Gonzo. Then how? Had someone seen Gonzo talking to her on the afternoon of Annabelle's death? That was possible, yes.

How had this thing got so complicated?

It had started as a simple plan, and now the plan didn't

seem to be working, should he call Byrnes again, tell Byrnes there had better not be anyone listening this time, tell him the whole damned story, lay the cards right on the table? But who could have seen the girl with Gonzo? Had they talked together in the same room she'd taken him to? The room Maria got from that woman, what was her name? Dolores? Wasn't that what she'd said? Yes, Dolores. Had Dolores known about Gonzo's talk with Maria? Had she recognized Gonzo from seeing him before, not knowing his name perhaps but . . . no. No, the police were probably keeping all known pushers under surveillance. But Gonzo is *not* a known pusher.

Gonzo is a punk who happened to stumble across some valuable information and who fortunately placed that information in the hands of someone who realized its potential: me.

Gonzo has no record, Gonzo is not a known pusher, Gonzo is in this only for the promise of quick unhindered riches, and he is not even known in the neighbourhood, not as Gonzo, anyway. So if he has no record, and if he is not known as Gonzo, and if he is not a known pusher, how did the police find out about him?

The woman.

Dolores.

No, not her, but someone perhaps saw them talking together that afternoon, saw him extract from her the promise of a lie, saw the twenty-five dollars exchange hands. Someone perhaps . . .

How much did Maria tell the woman Dolores?

Good Christ, why am I worrying about Gonzo? How much did Maria tell that old woman? Did she mention my name to her? Did she say, 'I have this friend who wants to sleep with me, and I need a room?' Did she then say who the friend was, God, could she have been so stupid?

What does Dolores know?

He took a last look at the female fantail, stepped out of the coop, locked the door, and then went downstairs to the street. He walked with a brisk spring in his step. He walked with a purpose and a goal, and that goal was the tenement building in which he and Maria had shared a room. When he reached the building, he looked both ways up the street, thankful the streets were not crowded, thankful for winter because if this were summer, the front stoop would be crowded with old women yacketing.

He checked the mailboxes, finding one marked DOLORES FAURED. Yes, that was the name Maria had mentioned. Dolores Faured. The apartment was on the second floor. He walked through the hallway quickly. There was no pain of remembrance in his mind. What had happened with Maria Hernandez had happened, and murder is habit forming.

He found the apartment and knocked.

'*Quién es?*' a voice called.

'*Un amigo*,' he answered, and he waited.

He heard footsteps, and then the door opened. The woman standing there was thin and frail, a frail old witch, he could pick her up and break her in half if he wanted to. With sudden insight, he realized that he was now committed. He had come here, and if the old woman knew nothing, if Maria had indeed told her nothing, what then? How did he question her and still leave her with no knowledge?

'Who are you?' the woman asked.

'May I come in?'

'What do you want?'

She would not let him into the house until she knew who he was, that was certain. But if he mentioned the name of Maria Hernandez, would he not then be tied to this frail old hag? Would she not then have a glimmer of knowledge? And was not even a glimmer of knowledge dangerous, how had this thing got so complicated?

'I'm from the police,' he lied. 'I want to ask some questions.'

'Come in, come in,' Dolores said. 'More questions, always questions.'

He followed her into the apartment. It was a dirty, smelly apartment, this woman was nothing but a female pimp, a frail witch of a pimp.

'What now?' she asked.

'On the night Miss Hernandez was killed? Did she mention to you who she was seeing? Who the man was?'

Dolores was staring at him. 'Don't I know you?' she asked.

'Not unless you've been inside the 87th Precinct,' he answered quickly.

'Haven't I seen you in the neighbourhood?'

'Well, I work in the neighbourhood. Naturally . . .'

'I thought I knew all the bulls from the 87th,' Dolores said speculatively. 'Well.' She shrugged.

'About this man.'

'*Sí.* Don't you cops work together?'

'What?'

'I already told them this. The others who came. Detectives Meyer and . . . who was the other?'

'I don't remember.'

'Hengel,' Dolores said. 'Yes, Detective Hengel.'

'Of course,' he said. 'Yes. Hengel. You already told them this?'

'Certainly. The next day. That room downstairs was flooded with police. Meyer and . . .' She stopped suddenly. 'It was Temple,' she said, her eyes narrowing. 'Temple was the other cop's name.'

'Yes,' he said. 'What did you tell them?'

'You said Hengel.'

'What?'

'Hengel. You said it was Hengel.'

'No,' he said, 'you're mistaken. I said Temple.'

'I said Hengel, and you said yes, it was Hengel,' Dolores insisted.

‘Well, we have a Hengel at the station house, too,’ he said irritably. ‘In any case, what did you tell them?’

Dolores looked at him long and hard. Then she said, ‘Let me see your badge.’

*Well, here we are doing the lion house bit again,* Carella thought.

This is Steve Carella, folks, coming to you again from atop lovely Hotel Grover in the charming Lion House room. Ah, I hear the orchestra tuning up, ladies and gentlemen, so perhaps we’ll have some delightful cocktail music. We broadcast from this spot every day at the same time, you know, through the auspices of the National Foundation for Contracting Double Pneumonia. We get a lovely little breeze here atop the Hotel Grover, and the breeze is never quite so charming as when it whips around the corners of the Lion House room. So stay tuned, folks, for a lot of laughs and a few surprises.

The surprises today include an announcement from Detective-Lieutenant Peter Byrnes, my immediate superior, who wishes you to know that his son Larry Byrnes was today voted Drug Addict of the Year cum Murder Suspect. Now, how’s that for a little surprise, folks? Knock the wind out of you? Damn near knocked me flat on my ass, so the least it should do is knock a little wind out of you. What’s that? Excuse me, folks, I’m being signalled from Hy Auerglass in the control booth. What is it, Hy? Oh, we’ve been cut off the air? That last ‘ass’ did it, huh? Well, those are the breaks. I can always go back to being a cop.

Oh, that poor son of a bitch. I like that guy. There are cops who don’t like him, but I do, and I wouldn’t have another skipper if he came gold-plated. But what’s he going through right now? What’s he going through, with some bastard sitting out there and dangling a carrot in front of his nose, what’s he . . .

He spotted the boy.

The same boy he’d talked to yesterday afternoon, only the

boy wasn't heading for the lion house this time. Was it possible that run-in with the patrolman yesterday had scared Gonzo into calling the meet for elsewhere in the park?

The boy had not seen him, and chances were he would not recognize him even if he did see him. Carella was wearing a battered felt hat with the rim rolled down front, sides, and back. He wore a wide box raincoat which gave him an appearance of girth. And, even though it made him feel a little silly, he was wearing a false moustache. The raincoat was buttoned from top to bottom; Carella's .38 was in the right-hand pocket.

Quickly, he took off after the boy.

The boy seemed to be in a hurry. He walked straight past the lion house, up the knoll in the path, and then hesitated at a sign which read – pointing in several directions – Seals, Reptiles, Children's Zoo. The boy nodded, and then began walking in the direction of the reptiles.

Carella thought of overtaking the boy and asking him some pointed questions. But if the boy were rushing to meet Gonzo, wouldn't it be a little ridiculous to stop him? The object all sublime was to net a pusher who may have had something to do with the demise of Aníbal Hernandez. Junkies making buys could be had by the basketful. Gonzo was the important character in this business transaction, and so Carella bided his time, following the blond boy and waiting for the big deal the way a stockbroker waits for a merger between Ford and Chrysler.

The boy seemed in no particular hurry. He seemed intent, instead, on making a thorough inspection of what the zoo offered. Wherever there was an animal, the boy stopped to look at it. Occasionally, he glanced over his shoulder. Once he stopped to consult a big clock set in the face of the monkeys', apes', and gorillas' house. He nodded and then moved on.

Apparently, there was still time. Apparently, the meet had been called for – what time was it now? Carella looked at his watch. It was three-fifteen. Was three-thirty a safe estimate? Was that why his young friend was dawdling all over the park?

The dawdling eventually took the blond boy to the men's room. He walked up the flag-covered path, and Carella watched him. As soon as the boy entered the building, Carella circled it, checking for a second exit door. There was none. Satisfied that the boy could not leave the building in any way but through the door by which he had entered, Carella sat on a bench and prepared to wait out the vagaries of nature.

He waited for five minutes. At the end of that time, the boy reappeared and began travelling at a fast trot in the direction of the reptile house. Whatever other faults there may have been in the boy's judgement, Carella could not venture to guess. But he had certainly been astute in choosing the snake pit as an appropriate spot to meet a pusher. Carella grinned and followed toward the snakes, a sudden gay mood overtaking him. He was looking forward to the pinch, the way a good coon dog looks forward to the moment of the kill, just before the wounded coon drops out of the tree.

As if to add to his sudden happy outlook, a crowd magically appeared. It was as if a movie director cued his musicians for a crescendo, and then signalled for throngs to swarm out of the hills, building to a climactic scene.

The people who suddenly appeared were not exactly what Carella would have called throngs. They were, instead, the students of a junior high school class, led by a slightly embarrassed-looking male teacher whose principal had undoubtedly decided his charges were not getting enough 'real' experience. The principal had decided to introduce them to 'life', and so the science teacher had probably been asked to take his class to the zoo, where they could smell the animals. The teacher's face bore the expression of a man sitting next to two drunks in a subway; his mouth yearned to shout, 'They're not with me!'

But, unfortunately, the kids were with him, and they were the noisiest damn kids Carella had ever seen or heard. He did not mind the noise because there was a noise within him now, an excitement that mounted as he followed his prey past the school kids and hurried down the path toward the reptile house.

Behind him, one of the kids was saying, 'They got a snake in there can eat a pig whole, how about that?'

Another kid answered, 'There ain't no snakes can eat pigs whole.'

'No? That's how much you know. My father saw a Frank Buck pitcher where the snake eats a pig whole. And they got that snake here.'

'The *same* snake?'

'Not the one in the pitcher, stupid. But a snake like him.'

'Then how do you know this one can eat pigs?'

Fascinated as Carella was, he concentrated on his quarry. His quarry was entering the house with the snakes, and Carella did not want to lose him. For a ridiculous moment, he had the sneaking suspicion his moustache was falling off. He stopped, touched the area beneath his nose, and then, satisfied, entered the building. The boy seemed to know exactly where he was going. He didn't look at any of the snakes he passed, even though the zoo officials had gone to considerable expense in capturing, transporting, and suitably enclosing the reptiles. He walked directly to a cage behind whose thick plate-glass window lay two cobras. He stood watching the cobras, fascinated – or at least seemingly fascinated. Once or twice he rapped on the glass.

Carella took up a station alongside a small glass-fronted cage that contained a Rocky Mountain rattler. The snake was asleep, or dead, or some damn thing. It lay in a despondent coil, looking for all the world as if an earthquake would not have disturbed it. But Carella was not interested in the snake.

Carella was interested in the colour of the glass cage that held the snake. For the back wall of that cage was painted a deep green, and from where Carella was standing, the plate-glass front combined with the green back wall to provide an excellent mirror effect. He could, while ostensibly marvelling over the rattle on the surely dead snake in the cage, study the boy across the room with considerable ease.

The boy was undoubtedly a snake lover. He was making sounds at the cobra cage, and he was rapping on the plate-glass front again, and he looked something like a new father in a hospital nursery, making an ass of himself through the nursery window.

The boy did not make an ass of himself for long, nor was he alone for very much longer. Carella couldn't hear any of the sounds emanating from the vicinity of the cobra cage because the junior high school class suddenly burst into the reptile house *en masse*, and the resultant chaos was a tribute to the city's school system. But Carella's quarry was no longer rapping on the glass. A second boy had come up to the cobra cage, a boy with a mane of wild black hair, wearing a black leather jacket, wearing black pegged trousers and black shoes.

Carella took one look at the newcomer and instantly thought: Gonzo.

Gonzo or not, the newcomer was the person Carella's young friend had been waiting for. Still unable to hear anything because of the science class, Carella was nonetheless able to witness a quick shaking of hands. Then both boys reached into their pockets simultaneously, and then there was another shaking of hands, and Carella knew the junk and the money for the junk had been exchanged.

Carella was no longer interested in his young friend. He was now interested in the boy with the black leather jacket. The blond boy he'd been following grinned, turned, and headed off in one direction. Carella let him go. The other boy lifted the collar of his black jacket, hesitated just a moment, and then headed off in the opposite direction. It was Carella's devout wish to collar him with a pile of narcotics on his person. It was also his desire to get him in the Squad Room and question him about the late Aníbal Hernandez.

Unfortunately, the school system was working against Carella that day.

He had shoved himself away from the front of the rattler cage and was taking off after the black leather jacket when a blood-curdling shriek split the air.

'There he is!' an adolescent voice screeched.

The screech, had it come from behind a tree in the heart of the jungle, would have been enough to send the brave hunter scurrying for the nearest trading depot. As it was, it almost lifted the false moustache from Carella's upper lip.

In a moment, he realized what all the commotion was about. The kid had spotted the python cage, and was rushing over to it to see if any pigs were being devoured whole that afternoon. In another moment, Carella realized that he was in the direct path of a headlong stampede, and – unless he sidestepped damned fast – he might very well be devoured whole himself. He sidestepped damned fast, and the thundering herd rushed past him, and trailing in its wake came the weary and abashed shepherd, still wearing his 'They're not with me!' look.

The shouts and cries from the python cage were almost inhuman. Carella turned The black leather jacket was gone.

He rushed to the door, cursing principals and science classes and Frank Buck, coming out into the cold air, feeling the bite of it on his cheeks, feeling it attack his teeth. The black leather jacket was nowhere in sight.

He began running, running aimless actually, not knowing which side of the path the boy had chosen. He kept running until it became obvious he had lost the boy. He was ready to start cursing all over again when he spotted the blond boy he'd been following earlier.

The blond boy was certainly not the one he wanted, but any port in a storm. The kid had just made a buy from

Gonzo, hadn't he? All right, he'd found out about the meet someplace, and maybe he knew where Gonzo could be located. In any case, there was no time to lose. What with the city system rampaging all over the town, one never knew when one might run into a kindergarten class out hunting snipes. Carella moved fast.

He came up behind the boy almost soundlessly, and then he moved alongside him, and reached for his sleeve.

'All right . . .' he started, and the boy turned.

For a moment, the boy's face was blank. And then his eyes penetrated the false moustache, widened in recognition, and then turned alert with the knowledge of imminent danger. He shoved out at Carella instantly, surprising him, knocking him backward several paces.

'Hey!' Carella shouted, and the boy was off.

The boy may not have been a track star, but he certainly could run like a bastard.

Before Carella caught his breath, the kid was turning the bend of the path and heading into the trees. Carella started after him. He couldn't understand why the kid was risking more trouble than a small narcotics buy was worth, but he didn't stop to question motive too long. There was a time for thinking and theorizing, and a time for doing; and this was definitely a time for using legs and not brains. It was also a time for using firearms, but Carella wasn't aware of this as yet, and so the .38 stayed where it was in his right-hand coat pocket. There certainly didn't seem to be any danger attached to the simple task of overtaking and putting a collar on a junkie. Sublimely unaware of what was in store for him, Carella began climbing off the side of the path and into the trees.

He saw the blond head duck behind a boulder. He quickened his pace, panting hard, reflecting that he was not as young as he used to be. He was deep in the trees now, climbing over big boulders and smaller rocks, far from the path that wound through the park. He could see the blond head bobbing along in the distance, and then he didn't see it again, and he was afraid he'd lost *this* boy, too. He swung around a huge outcropping of rock, and then pulled up short.

He was looking into the open end of a .32.

'Don't open your mouth, cop,' the boy said.

Carella blinked. He had not expected a gun, and he cursed his own stupidity, and at the same time he sought for a way out of this. He looked at the kid's eyes, and the kid didn't seem to be high, so perhaps he could be talked to, perhaps reason could penetrate. But the .32 was held in a steady fist, and the eyes above the gun were unreasonable eyes.

'Listen . . .' he started.

'I said keep the mouth closed. I'll shoot you, cop.' The boy delivered the speech so simply that all of its lethalness seemed innocuous. But there was nothing innocuous about the boy's eyes, and Carella watched those eyes carefully. He had been on the business end of a gun before, and it was his contention that a man always telegraphed the tightening of his trigger finger by a previous tightening of his eyes.

'Keep your hands away from your sides,' the boy said. 'Where is it?'

'Where's what?'

'The gun that patrolman turned up yesterday. Still got it in your waistband?'

'How do you know I'm a cop?' Carella asked.

'The holster. Don't ask me about intuition. None of the guys I know who carry pieces carry them in holsters. Fish it out for me, cop.'

Carella's hand moved.

'No!' the boy said. 'Tell me where it is. I'll get it myself.'

'Why are you buying yourself trouble, kid? You could have got out of this with a simple misdemeanour.'

'Yeah?'

'Sure. Put the gun up. I'II forget you ever had it.'

'What's the matter, cop? You scared?'

'Why should I be scared?' Carella asked, watching the boy's eyes. 'I don't think you'd be silly enough to shoot me here in the park.'

'No, huh? You got any idea how many people are shot in this park every day?'

'How many, son?' Carella asked, stalling for time, wondering how he could get the .38 out of his pocket, divert the kid for an instant while he drew and fired.

'Plenty. Why are you following me, cop?'

'You won't believe this . . .' Carella started.

'Then don't waste it. Give me the real story the first time around.'

'I was after your pal.'

'Yeah? Which pal? I got lots of pals.'

'The one you met by the cobra cage.'

'Why him?'

'I've got some questions to ask him.'

'About what?'

'That's my business.'

'Where's your piece, cop? Tell me that first.'

Carella hesitated. He saw the boy's eyes tighten almost imperceptibly. 'My right-hand coat pocket,' he said quickly.

'Turn around,' the boy said.

Carella turned.

'Put the hands up. Don't try any tricks, cop, I'm warning you. You feel this? It's the muzzle of this piece. It'll be right up against your spine all the while I'm reaching into your pocket. You start to turn, you start to run, you even start to breathe crooked, and you've got a broken spinal cord. I ain't afraid to pull this trigger, so don't test me. You got that?'

'I've got it,' Carella said.

He felt the boy's hand move quickly into his pocket. In an instant, the reassuring weight of the .38 was gone.

'All right,' the boy said, 'turn around again.'

Carella turned to face him. He had not, up to that moment, really believed the situation to be a serious one. He had talked himself out of similar situations before, and he had been fairly certain – up to now – that he could either talk his way out of this one, or somehow get to the gun in his coat pocket. But the gun was no longer in his coat pocket, and the boy's eyes were hard and bright, and he had the peculiar feeling that he was staring sudden death in the face.

'You'd be stupid,' he heard himself say, but the words sounded hollow and insincere. 'You'd be shooting me for no reason. I told you I'm not after you.'

'Then why were you asking me all those questions yesterday? You thought you were playing it real cool, didn't you, cop? Sounding me out about the meet. I was sounding you at the same time. It ain't easy, you know, not when you don't know what faces are gonna be at a meet. It ain't easy at all. I let you think I was stepping right into your pitches, but I saw your curves coming a mile off. That patrolman clinched it for me. When he dug that piece out of your pants, I knew for sure you were a bull. Up to then, I could only smell it on you.'

'I'm still not after you,' Carella said patiently. They were standing on loose rock in the shadow of the big boulder. Carella weighed the possibility of lunging at the boy suddenly, throwing him off balance on the loose rock, getting the gun away from him. The possibility seemed extremely remote.

'No, huh? Look, cop, don't snow me. I've been snowed by the best. You think you're going to tie me in to something big, don't you? You think you're gonna get me in your cosy little precinct house and beat the crap out of me until I'll confess to having raped my own mother. Well, you're wrong, cop.'

'Goddammit, what do I want with a two-bit junkie?' Carella said.

'Me? A junkie? Come off it, will you? This time I'm not taking the pitches, cop. Don't try to sell me a new line of spitballs.'

'What's with you, anyway?' Carella asked. 'I've seen junkies panic before, but you're the uneasiest. Are you so scared of taking a fall? Dammit, I was only going to ask some questions about the guy you met. Can't you get that through your head? I don't want you. I want him.'

'I thought you weren't interested in two-bit junkies,' the boy said.

'I'm not.'

'Then why bother with him? He's eighteen years old, and he's been hooked since he was fourteen. He goes to bed with H. You're inconsistent, cop.'

'He's a pusher, isn't he?' Carella asked, puzzled.

'Him?' The boy began laughing. 'Cop, you're a riot.'

'What's . . .'

'All right, listen to me,' the boy said. 'You were tailing me yesterday, and you were tailing me today. I'm carrying enough junk on me right now to make a pinch pretty much worth your while. I'm also violating the Sullivan Act because I ain't got a licence for this piece. You've got me on resisting an officer, and there's probably some kind of law against taking a cop's gun from him, too. You got me, cop. You can throw the book at me. And if I cut out now, you'll grab me tomorrow, and then it's your word against mine.'

'Listen, take off. Put up the gun and take off,' Carella said. 'I'm not looking for a slug, and I'm not looking for trouble with you. I told you once. I want your pal.' Carella paused. 'I want Gonzo.'

'I know,' the boy said, his eyes tightening. '*I'm Gonzo.*'

The only warning was the tightening of Gonzo's eyes. Carella saw them squinch up, and he tried to move sideways, but the gun was already speaking. He did not see it buck in the boy's fist. He felt searing pain lash at his chest, and he heard the shocking declaration of three explosions and then he was falling, and he felt very warm, and he also felt very ridiculous because his legs simply would not hold him up, how silly, how very silly, and his chest was on fire, and the sky was tilting to meet the earth, and then his face struck the ground. He did not put out his arms to stop his fall because his arms were somehow powerless. His face struck the loose stones, and his body crumpled behind it, and he shuddered and felt a warm stickiness beneath him, and only then did he try to move and then he realized he was lying in a spreading pool of his own blood. He wanted to laugh and he wanted to cry at the same time. He opened his mouth, but no sound came from it. And then the waves of blackness came at him, and he fought to keep them away, unaware that Gonzo was running off through the trees, aware only of the engulfing blackness, and suddenly sure that he was about to die.

It is to the credit of the 87th that it worked faster than either of the two precincts that reigned over Grover Park. Carella was not found by a patrolman until almost a half-hour later, at which time the blood around him resembled a small swimming pool.

But another act of violence had been done in the 87th at about the same time Carella was being shot outside his precinct, and the results of that violence were discovered not ten minutes later

The patrolman who called it in said, 'She's an old woman. Her neighbours tell me her name is Dolores Faured.'

'What's the story?' the desk sergeant asked.

The patrolman said, 'Her neck is broken. She either fell or was pushed down an airshaft from the second floor.'

# CHAPTER FOURTEEN

In the heart of the city, the shoppers went about their business. The store fronts glowed like hot pot-belly stoves, inviting the cold citizens to come in and toast awhile, come in and browse awhile, come in and buy a little. The swank shops lining plush Hall Avenue were decked not in holly but in an austerely shrieking display of Christmas white and red and green electrical wizardry. The front of one department store was covered with a two-storey-high display of blue angels, and the outdoor gardens across the street picked up the theme, multiplied it by a hundred, splashed the concrete with ethereal winged messengers of the Lord, escorting the passers-by to the giant Christmas tree near the skating rink. The tree climbed to the sky, ablaze with red and blue and yellow globes as big as a man's head, competing with the stiff formality of the giant office buildings around it.

The other shops dripped with incandescence, molten Christmas trees fashioned of light, giant white wreaths, windows aglow with the pristine brilliance of a new snowfall. The shoppers hurried in the streets, their arms loaded with packages. The office parties were in full swing behind the stiff formal fronts of the buildings. File clerks kissed file clerks behind banks of file cabinets. Bosses lifted the skirts of secretaries, and promotions were promised, and raises were bandied about like memo slips, and boys from the shipping departments tilted glasses with executives from wood-panelled offices. There were lipstick stains, and Scotch stains, and hurried phone calls to waiting wives, and hurried phone calls to husbands who were enjoying their own Christmas parties behind the equally stiff fronts of other buildings. There was happiness of a sort because this was late Friday afternoon, 22 December, and this was the culmination of a long year's waiting. And the accountant who'd had his discreet marital eye on the pretty, young, blonde receptionist could now greet her with more than a polite 'Good morning'. Sharing a highball by the water cooler, his arm could encircle her waist in Christmas friendliness. Her head could rest upon his shoulder in yuletide camaraderie. He could take her lips beneath the mistletoe, and he could do all this without the slightest feeling of guilt because the Christmas Party was an established tradition of the American culture. Husbands went to Christmas parties, and wives were never invited. Wives did not expect to be invited. For one day a year, the marital contract was temporarily revoked. Christmas parties were joked about later, the way a person will joke about a bloody dagger on his living-room coffee table, unwilling to acknowledge how it got there.

And in the streets, the shoppers walked. Time was short, and time was running out. The advertising executives who had goaded the public since before Thanksgiving were now busy getting drunk in their offices. But the public, caught in the commercial machinations of a holiday that had somehow grown out of all proportion to the simple birth in Bethlehem it represented, hurried and scurried and wondered and worried. Had Josephine's gift been expensive enough? Were all the Christmas cards mailed? What about the tree, shouldn't the tree have been bought by now?

Beneath it all, despite the gaudy plot of the advertising master minds, despite the frantic commercial rat race it had become, there was something else. There was, for some of the people, a feeling they could not have described if they'd wanted to. This was Christmas. This was the holiday season. Some of the people saw through the sham and the electrical glitter and the skinny Santa Clauses with straggly beards lining Hall Avenue. Some of the people felt something other than what the advertising men wanted them to feel. Some of the people felt good, and kind, and happy to be alive. Christmas did that to some people.

And so the city was drunken, and the city was goaded into near panic, and the streets were jammed with shoppers, and maybe the concrete looked cold and stiff and aloof – but it was the most wonderful city in the world, and it was never more wonderful than at Christmastime.

'This is Danny Gimp,' the man told the desk sergeant. 'I want to speak to Detective Carella.'

The desk sergeant didn't enjoy talking to stool pigeons. He knew that Danny Gimp often came up with good information, but he considered all stool pigeons unclean, and it was an offence just talking to them.

'Detective Carella isn't here,' the desk sergeant said.

'Do you know where I can reach him?' Danny asked. Danny was a man who'd been stooling for the police for as long as he could remember. He knew he was not respected for his talkative traits among members of the underworld, but the ensuing ostracism did not disturb him. Danny made his living as an informer and, quite curiously, he enjoyed helping the police. He had had polio as a child, with the result that one leg still carried a slight limp. His real surname was Nelson but very few people knew that, and even his mail came addressed to Danny Gimp. He was fifty-four years old, and very small all over, looking more like an undernourished adolescent than a full-grown man. His voice was high and reedy, and his face bore hardly any of the wrinkles or other telltale signs of age. He could not honestly say he liked cops, even though he liked helping them. There was one cop he did like. That cop was Steve Carella.

'Why do you want to reach him?' the desk sergeant asked.

'I think I may have some dope for him.'

'What kind of dope?'

'When did you get promoted to the detective division?' Danny asked.

'If you want to get smart, stoolie, you can get off the line.'

'I want Carella,' Danny said. 'Will you tell him I called?'

'Carella ain't taking any messages,' the desk sergeant said.

'What do you mean?'

'He got shot this afternoon. He's dying.'

'What!'

'You heard me.'

'What!' Danny said again, stunned. 'Steve got . . . Are you kidding me?'

'I'm not kidding you.'

'Who shot him?'

'That's what we'd like to know.'

'Where is he?'

'General Hospital. Don't bother going down. He's on the critical list, and I doubt if they're letting him talk to stoolies.'

'He's not really dying,' Danny said, almost as if to reassure himself. 'Listen, he's not really dying, is he?'

'They found him half-froze and almost bloodless. They've been pumping plasma into him, but he took three slugs in the chest, and it don't look good.'

'Ah, listen,' Danny said. 'Ah, Jesus.' He was silent for a while.

'You finished, stoolie?'

'No, I . . . General Hospital, did you say?'

'Yeah. I told you, stoolie, don't bother going down. It'd make you uncomfortable. Half the bulls on the squad are there.'

'Yeah,' Danny said thoughtfuly. 'Jesus, that's a tough break, ain't it?'

'He's a good cop,' the desk sergeant said simply.

'Yeah,' Danny said. He was silent again, and then he said, 'Well, so long.'

'So long,' the desk sergeant said.

Because of the sergeant's warning, Danny Gimp did not get to the hospital until the next morning. He wrestled with the problem all that Friday night, wondering if his presence would be welcome, wondering if Carella would even recognize him. And even if Carella was in condition to say hello,

Danny doubted if he'd want to. They had a going business arrangement, but Danny was keenly aware of the fact that an informer is not the most respected of men. Carella might very well spit at him.

He wrestled with his problem, and he didn't sleep that night. He awoke on Saturday morning with the problem still fresh in his mind. He did not know why, but he wanted to see Steve Carella before he died. He wanted to see him and say hello, and maybe shake hands with him. Perhaps it was the Christmas season. Whatever it was, Danny took some coffee and a doughnut and then he dressed carefully, putting on his good suit and a clean white shirt and choosing his tie carefully as well. He wanted to look respectable. He was going to the hospital on a respectable visit, and the entire unrespectability of his life seemed suddenly in very sharp focus. It seemed very important to him that he show his concern for Steve Carella, and it seemed equally important that Carella should respect him for it.

On the way to the hospital, he bought a box of candy. The candy gave him a good many moments of doubt. There would undoubtedly be cops at the hospital. Hadn't the desk sergeant said so? And wouldn't it look stupid for a stool pigeon to come carrying a box of candy? He almost threw the candy away, but he did not. When a man went to visit someone in the hospital, he brought something, something to say 'You're still with us and you'll get well.' Danny Gimp was entering the polite, respectable world of civilized society, and so he would obey the rules of that society.

The sky beyond the hospital was very grey on that Saturday 23 December. It looked like snow, and Danny thought fleetingly of the hundreds of people who were wishing for a white Christmas, and he felt a total sadness as he pushed through the hospital's revolving doors and entered the wide white entrance lobby. There was a big Christmas wreath on the wall opposite the reception desk, but there was nothing festive about the hospital itself. The girl behind the desk was polishing her nails. On a bench opposite the desk, an old man sat with his hat in his hands, glancing anxiously every few moments toward the Emergency Room down the corridor.

Danny took off his hat and walked to the desk. The girl did not look up. She painted her nails with the precision and skill of a Japanese dollmaker.

Danny cleared his throat. 'Miss?' he said.

'Yes,' the girl said, working the brush over her extended forefinger, covering the moon, splashing the oval with carmine brilliance.

'I'd like to see Steve Carella,' Danny said. 'Stephen Carella.'

'What is your name, sir?' the girl asked.

'Daniel Nelson,' he replied.

The girl put down the brush, held the fingers of the painted hand widespread, and reached for a typewritten sheet with the other hand. She reached for it automatically, without even looking for it. She put it down in front of her, studied it, and said, 'Your name's not on this list, sir.'

'What list?' Danny asked.

'Mr Carella is in a critical condition,' the girl said. 'We are admitting only members of his family and, because of the nature of the case, certain people from the police department. I'm sorry, sir.'

'Is he all right?' Danny asked.

The girl looked at him dispassionately. 'It's not usual to put a man on the critical list unless we feel his condition is critical,' she said.

'When . . . when will you know?' Danny asked.

'I have no way of telling, sir. He may rally, or he may not. I'm afraid it's out of our hands.'

'Is it all right if I wait?'

'Certainly, sir,' she said. 'You may sit on the bench there, if you like. It may be some time, you realize.'

'I realize,' Danny said. 'Thank you.'

He wondered why one of the few honest emotions he'd

ever felt should be frustrated this way by a young chippie who was more interested in painting her nails than in life and death. He shrugged, blaming bureaucracy, and then went to sit on the bench alongside the old man. The old man turned to him almost instantly.

'My daughter cut her hand,' he said.

'Um?' Danny said.

'She was opening a can, and she cut her hand. Is that dangerous? A cut from a tin can, I mean?'

'I don't know,' Danny said.

'I heard it was. They're dressing the cut in there now. She was bleeding like a pig. I hope it isn't dangerous.'

'She'll be all right,' Danny said. 'Don't worry.'

'Well, I sure hope so. Did you come here to see somebody?'

'Yes,' Danny said.

'A friend?'

'Well,' Danny said. He half shrugged, and then began reading the list of ingredients on the candy box, wondering what lecithin was.

In a little while, the girl came out of the Emergency Room, her hand bandaged.

'Are you all right?' her father asked.

'Yes,' the girl said. 'They gave me a lollipop.'

Together, they went out of the hospital.

Alone, Danny Gimp sat on the bench, waiting.

Teddy Carella sat in the room with her husband, watching him. The blinds were drawn, but she could see his face clearly in the dimness, the mouth open, the eyes closed. Beside the bed, the plasma ran from an upturned bottle, slid through a tube, and entered Carella's arm. He lay without stirring, the blankets pulled up over the jagged wounds in his chest. The wounds were dressed now, but they had leaked their blood, they had done their damage, and he lay pale and unmoving, as if death were already inside him.

*No*, she thought, *he won't die.*

Please God, please dear God, don't let this man die, please.

Her thoughts ran freely, and she didn't realize she was praying because her thoughts sounded only like thoughts to her, simple thoughts, the thoughts a girl thinks. But she was praying.

She was remembering how she'd met Carella, the day he'd come to the small office she'd worked for after they'd reported a burglary. She could remember exactly how he had come into the room, he and another man, a detective who was later transferred to another precinct, a detective whose face she could no longer remember. She had been concerned only with the face of Steve Carella that day. He had entered the office, and he was tall, and he walked erect, and he wore his clothes as if he were a high-priced men's fashion model rather than a cop. He had showed her his shield and introduced himself, and she had scribbled on a sheet of paper, explaining that she could neither hear nor speak, explaining that the receptionist was out, that she was hired as a typist, but that her employer would see him in a moment, as soon as she went to tell him the police were there. His face had registered mild surprise. When she rose from her desk and went to the boss's office, she could feel his eyes on her all the way.

She was not surprised when he asked her out.

She had seen interest in his eyes, and so the surprise was not in his asking, the surprise was that he could find her interesting at all. She supposed, of course, that there were men who would try anything once, just for kicks. Why not a girl who couldn't hear or talk? Might be interesting. She supposed, at first, that this was what had motivated Steve Carella, but after their first date, she knew this wasn't the case at all. He was not interested in her ears or her tongue. He was interested in the girl Teddy Franklin. He told her so, repeatedly. It took her a long while to believe it, even though she intuitively suspected its truth.

She had gone to bed with Carella because going to bed

with him seemed the natural thing to do. He asked her to marry him often, but she never quite believed he really wanted her for his wife. And then one day, belief came, the way belief suddenly comes, and she realized he really and truly did want her for his wife. They were married on 19 August, and this was 23 December, and now he lay in a hospital bed, and it seemed he might die, it seemed possible he might die, the doctors had told her that her husband might die.

She did not concern herself with the unfairness of the situation. The situation was shockingly unfair, her husband should not have been shot, her husband should not now be fighting for his life on a hospital bed. The unfairness shrieked within her, but she did not concern herself with it, because what was done was done.

But he was good, and he was gentle, and he was her man, the only man in the world for her. There were those who held that any two people can make a go of it. If not one, then another. Throw them in bed together and things will work out all right. There's always another streetcar. Teddy did not believe this. Teddy did not believe that there was another man anywhere in the world who was as right for her as Steve Carella. Somehow, quite miraculously, he had been delivered to her doorstep, a gift, a wonderful gift.

She could not now believe he would be torn rudely from her. She could not believe it, she would not believe it. She had told him what she wanted for Christmas. She wanted him. She had said it earnestly, knowing he took it as jest, but she had meant every word of it. And now, her words were being hurled back into her face by a cruel wind. Because now she really wanted him for Christmas, now he was the only thing she really wanted for Christmas. Earlier, she had been secure when she asked for him, knowing she would certainly have him. But now, the security was gone, now there was left only a burning desire for her man to live. She would never again want anything more than Steve Carella.

And so, in the dimness of the room, she prayed, not knowing she was praying, and the words ran through her mind over and over and over again:

*Let my husband live. Please let my husband live.*

Detective-Lieutenant Peter Byrnes went down to the lobby at six fifteen that evening. He had been waiting in the corridor outside Carella's room all day long, hoping he could get to see him again. He had seen Carella only for a brief moment before Carella went unconscious again.

Carella had whispered a word, and the word was 'Gonzo'.

But Carella could say nothing more about the pusher, and so Byrnes still had only a flimsy description, a description he'd got from the three kids Carella had pinched in the car that day. No one else had heard of Gonzo, so how could Byrnes possibly pick him up? If Carella died . . .

He had put the thought out of his mind, sitting in the corridor. He called the precinct every half hour. And every half hour, he called home. The precinct had nothing to report. There were no leads to the new death of Dolores Faured. There were no leads to the old deaths of Aníbal and Maria Hernandez. There were no leads to Gonzo.

Things weren't much better at home. Larry was still in the process of shaking his sickness. The doctor had come again, but nothing seemed to displease Byrnes's son more. Byrnes wondered if he would ever be cured, and he wondered if they would ever find the man or men who were committing murder in his precinct. It was two days before Christmas, but Christmas would be a bleak time this year.

At six fifteen, he left the corridor and went down to the lobby. He stopped at the reception desk and asked the girl there if there was a decent eating place in the neighbourhood. She suggested a greasy spoon on Lafayette.

He was heading for the revolving doors when a voice called, 'Lieutenant?'

Byrnes turned. He didn't recognize the man at first. The man was small and thin, and he carried a box of candy under his arm, and he looked seedy, the way a normally seedy-looking person appears when he's trying to look dressed up. And then the face fell into place, and Byrnes said gruffly, 'Hello, Danny. What're you doing here?'

'I came to see Carella,' Danny said. He blinked and looked up at Byrnes.

'Yes?' said Byrnes, untouched.

'Yeah,' Danny said. 'How is he?'

'Bad,' Byrnes said. 'Look, Danny, you don't mind but I was on my way out to dinner. I'm kind of in a hurry.'

'Sure, sure,' Danny said.

Byrnes looked at him, and perhaps because it was almost Christmas, he added, 'You know how it is. This Gonzo character shooting Carella hasn't . . .'

'Who? Did you say Gonzo? Is he the one shot St – Detective Carella?'

'That's the way it rooks,' Byrnes said.

'What are you telling me?' Danny asked. 'A punk kid like that? He took Steve Carella?'

'Why?' Byrnes said. He was interested now, but only because Danny had referred to Gonzo as if he knew him. 'What do you mean, a punk kid?'

'He can't be more than twenty, not the way I got it.'

'What do you know, Danny?'

'Well, like Ste – Well, Carella asked me to scout around on Gonzo, and I didn't come up with nothing. I mean, I scouted around because Ste . . .'

'For Christ's sake, call him Steve,' Byrnes said.

'Well, some cops are touchy about . . .'

'What have you got to say, Danny, goddamnit!'

'Even Steve don't like me calling him Steve,' Danny admitted, and then – seeing the look on Byrnes's face – rapidly went on. 'Nobody knew this Gonzo, you dig? So with me, it becomes a mathematical problem. How come these three kids coming to make a buy from this guy know him by

Gonzo, and how come nobody on the scene knows him? It figures he ain't from the neighbourhood, am I right?'

'Go ahead,' Byrnes said, interested.

'Then I ask myself, if he ain't from the neighbourhood, how come he inherits the dead Hernandez's junk route? This don't figure. I mean, it looks like he at least knew Hernandez, don't it? And if he knew Hernandez, maybe he knew the sister, too. This is the way I was thinking, Lieutenant, putting together all the things Steve told me.'

'So what'd you get?'

'I got a guy who's a stranger in the neighbourhood, but who maybe knew the Hernandezes. So I went to see the old lady Mrs Hernandez. I talked to her, you know, fishing around, figuring this Gonzo was maybe a cousin or something, you know these Puerto Ricans – strong family ties.'

'*Is* he a cousin?'

'She don't make a cousin named Gonzo. She was talking true, too, because she knows me from the neighbourhood. Gonzo don't ring a bell.'

'I could have told you that, Danny. My men questioned Mrs Hernandez also.'

'But she tells me her son had a friend. He used to belong to the Sea Scouts, she says, and he used to go to these meetings up in Riverhead at a high school there. I check around, and I find out this is called the Junior Navals, a thing where some ex-Navy jerk got a bunch of kids together and slapped them in monkey suits so they could march around once a week. Only Hernandez don't go there to march. He goes there to push his junk. Anyway, the kid he knows there is called Dickie Collins.'

'How does this tie with Gonzo?'

'Well, listen,' Danny said. 'I start snooping around about this Dickie Collins kid. He used to live around here, moved a while ago, his old man got a job selling storm doors up in Riverhead, so the little extra dough enabled him to get the hell out of the neighbourhood. But Dickie's still got ties here, like that, you know? Comes back every now and then, and visits with the boys – including Aníbal Hernandez, the late. Met the sister a coupla times, too. Okay, so one night there's a card game. Small time, penny-ante stuff. This was only about two weeks ago, so it explains why there's nobody knows this Gonzo bit except four people, one of which is now dead. Luckily, I latched on to an alive one.'

'Spill it,' Byrnes said.

'There was four people in the game. A kid named Sam Di Luca, this kid Dickie Collins, Maria Hernandez, and an older guy from the neighbourhood.'

'Who was the older guy?'

'The Di Luca kid don't remember – and Maria Hernandez can't say any more. From what I could gather, they were shooting up that night, and this Di Luca's only sixteen, so he was probably blind. I got to explain this Di Luca kid, he calls himself Batman. That's his nickname. They all got nicknames which is maybe why this Gonzo thing appealed.'

'Get to the point, Danny.'

'Okay. Sometime during the night, the four of them having a ball and playing cards, the older guy mentioned something about a cheap gunsel in the neighbourhood. Well, it turns out this kid Dickie Collins, he's never heard the word "gunsel". It's kind of a dead expression, you know, Lieutenant? I mean, hardly anybody but old-timers use it nowadays. Like "torpedo", you know? Out of fashion. So it's understandable, him being a snothouse kid, that he never heard it. But dig this. He says, "A gonzo? What the hell's a gonzo?" Now this broke up the joint. Maria fell off her chair, and the older guy was practically rolling on the floor, and Batman damn near wet his pants, it was so funny.'

'I see,' Byrnes said thoughtfully.

'So for the rest of the night, they kept calling him Gonzo. That's what this Batman tells me, anyway. But like there's only the four of them who know about it – just Batman,

Maria, Dickie, and the older guy. And like Maria's pretty dead now, you know?'

'Dickie Collins is Gonzo,' Byrnes repeated blankly.

'Yeah. Batman, he forgot about the whole thing after that night. He was stinking drunk, anyway. But when I start asking about Gonzo, he remembers. The older guy, Christ alone knows who he is.'

'Dickie Collins,' Byrnes repeated.

'Sure. Lives in Riverhead now. One of the cheaper neighbourhoods there. You going to pick him up?'

'He shot Carella, didn't he?' Byrnes asked. He reached into his wallet and took out a ten-dollar bill. 'Here, Danny,' he said, offering the money.

Danny shook his head. 'No, Lieutenant, thanks.'

Byrnes stared at him unbelievingly.

'One thing you can do for me, though,' Danny said, somewhat embarrassed.

'What's that?'

'I'd like to go upstairs. I'd like to see Steve.'

Byrnes hesitated a moment. Then he walked to the desk and said, 'I'm Detective-Lieutenant Byrnes. This man is working on the case with us. I'd like him to go upstairs.'

'Yes, sir,' the girl said, and then she looked over toward Danny Gimp, who was smiling from ear to ear.

# CHAPTER FIFTEEN

They caught Dickie Collins on Christmas Eve.

They caught him as he was coming out of church, where he had just lighted a candle for his dead grandmother.

They took him to the Squad Room of the 87th Precinct, and four detectives surrounded him there. One of the detectives was Peter Byrnes. The others were Havilland, Meyer, and Willis.

'What's your name?' Willie asked.

'Dickie Collins. Richard.'

'What aliases do you go by?' Havilland asked.

'None.'

'Ever own a gun?' Meyer asked.

'No. Never.'

'Know Aníbal Hernandez?' Byrnes asked.

'The name sounds familiar.'

'Did you know him, or didn't you?'

'Yeah, I knew him, I guess. I knew lots of kids in the neighbourhood.'

'When did you move?'

'Coupla months ago.'

'Why?'

'My old man got a new job. I go where he goes.'

'Did you want to move?'

'Makes no difference. I'm a free agent. I travel where I want to, no matter where I live. What's all the questions for? What did I do?'

'What were you doing on the night of 17 December?'

'How do I know? When the hell was that, anyway?'

'A week ago today.'

'I don't remember.'

'Were you with Hernandez?'

'I don't remember.'

'Start trying to remember.'

'No, I wasn't with Hernandez. What was that, a Saturday night?'

'It was a Sunday night.'

'No, I wasn't with him.'

'Where were you?'

'In church.'

'What?'

'I go to church every Sunday night. I light candles for my grandmother.'

'How long did you stay in church?'

'About an hour. I say a coupla prayers, too.'

'From what time to what time?'

'From about . . . from about ten to eleven.'

'And then what'd you do?'

'I drifted around.'

'Who saw you drifting?'

'Nobody. What do I need witnesses for? You trying to hang the Hernandez kill on me?'

'What makes you think he was killed?'

'He hung himself,' Collins said.

'Okay, but what made you call it a kill?'

'A suicide's a kill, ain't it?'

'Why should we try to hang a suicide on you?'

'How do I know? What else you got me in here for, if not that? You're asking questions about that night, ain't you? You're asking me if I knew Annabelle, ain't you?'

'You did know him.'

'Sure, I knew him.'

'From the neighbourhood or from the Sea Scouts?'

'What Sea Scouts?'

'In Riverhead.'

'Oh, you mean the Junior Navals. That ain't Sea Scouts. Yeah, yeah.'

'Where'd you know him from?'

'I used to say hello when I lived in the neighbourhood. Then, when I met him at the Navals, we got a little friendly.'

'Why'd you say you guessed you knew him? If you got friendly, then you knew him.'

'Okay, I knew him. Is that a crime?'

'Why'd you go to the Navals?'

'I didn't belong. I only went to watch the marching. I like to watch guys march.'

'You'll do a lot of marching where you're going,' Havilland said.

'Yeah, you got to send me there first, cop. I still ain't heard no charge. Are you booking or just looking?'

'You're a pusher, aren't you, Collins?'

'You're dreaming.'

'We've got three kids who made a buy from you. One is ready to identify you.'

'Yeah? What's his name?'

'Hemingway.'

'What're the other two called? Sinclair Lewis and William Faulkner?'

'You read a lot, Collins?'

'Enough.'

'This kid Hemingway doesn't read. He's a junkie. He bought a sixteenth of heroin from you on the afternoon of 20 December. One of our detectives nabbed him right after he made the buy.'

'So that's why I was being fol . . .' Collins cut himself short.

'What?'

'I didn't say nothing. If your Hemingway made a buy, he didn't get it from me.'

'He said he did. He said it came from you.'

'I don't know what a sixteenth of H looks like.'

'Did you know Hernandez was a junkie?'

'Yeah.'

'He ever shoot up with you?'

'No.'

'You never saw him shoot up?'

'No.'

'How do you know he was a junkie?'

'Word gets around.'

'Ever see him with any other junkies?'

'Sure.'

'Who?'

'I don't know their names.'

'Ever see him with a junkie named Larry Byrnes?' Byrnes asked.

Collins blinked.

'I said Larry Byrnes,' Byrnes repeated.

'Never heard of him,' Collins said.

'Think hard. He's my son.'

'No kidding? I didn't think cops had junkie sons.'

'Did you happen to see my son on the night of 17 December?'

'I wouldn't know your son from a hole in the wall.'

'How about the morning of 18 December?'

'I still don't know him, night or morning. How would I know him?'

'He knew Hernandez.'

'Lots of guys knew Hernandez. Hernandez was a pusher, didn't you know that?' Collins paused. 'Hell, he even pushed at the Navals.'

'We knew it. How'd you know it?'

'I seen him sell a couple of times.'

'To whom?'

'I don't remember. Listen, you think I know the names of every junkie in the neighbourhood? I never fooled with that crap myself.'

'You fooled with it on the twentieth, Collins. Two days after we found Hernandez dead, you were fooling with it. This Hemingway kid used to be one of Hernandez's customers.'

'Yeah? Maybe he bought that sixteenth from Hernandez's ghost, then.'

'He bought it from you.'

'You're gonna have a hell of a time proving that, cop.'

'Maybe not. We've had a man following you for the past few days.'

'Yeah?'

'Yeah.'

'So why didn't he pinch me? Listen, you find any stuff on me when you pulled me in? What am I here for, huh? I want a lawyer.'

'You're here on suspicion of murder,' Byrnes said.

'You mean . . .' again, Collins stopped short.

'What, Collins?'

'Nothing. Hernandez hung himself. Just try pinning that one on me.'

'Hernandez died of an overdose.'

'Yeah? So he was careless.'

'Who put that rope around his neck, Collins?'

'Maybe your son did, Lieutenant. How about that?'

'How do you know my rank?'

'What?'

'If you don't know my son, and if you don't know anything about my son, how the hell do you know my rank?'

'One of your bulls called you Lieutenant. What do you think?'

'Nobody's called me anything since you got here, Collins. Now how about it?'

'I guessed. You look like you got leadership qualities, so I figured you were the boss. Okay?'

'Larry says he knows you,' Byrnes lied.

'Who's Larry?'

'My son.'

'Yeah? Lots of guys know me who I don't know. I'm popular.'

'Why? Because you're pushing junk?'

'Only thing I ever pushed was my sister's baby carriage. Get off that kick, cop. It leads nowhere.'

'Let's try another kick, Collins. Let's try cards.'

'What about them? Want to play some?'

'You ever play cards?'

'Sure, I do.'

'You ever play with a kid named Batman Di Luca?'

'Sure.'

'Who else was in that game?'

'Which game?'

'The night you played.'

'I played cards with Batman a lot. He can't play to save his ass. I always win.'

'What's a gunsel, Collins?'

'Huh?'

'A gunsel.'

'Oh.' Again, Collins blinked. 'A guy who's hired to wash somebody.'

'Pronounce it.'

'Gunsel. Say, what is this, an English class?'

'When did you find out what a gunsel was?'

'I always knew.'

'You found out that night of the card game, didn't you?'

'No, I didn't. I always knew.'

'Which night, Collins?'

'Huh?'

'You said you knew what a gunsel was before that night of the card game. Which night are we talking about?'

'The . . . the last time we played, I guess.'

'And when was that?'

'About . . . about two weeks ago.'

'And who played?'

'Me, Batman, and another guy.'

'Who was the third guy?'

'I don't remember.'

'Batman says you brought him down.'

'Me? No, it was Batman. I think he was a friend of Batman's.'

'He wasn't, and he isn't. Why are you protecting him, Collins?'

'I ain't protecting nobody. I don't even know who the guy was. Listen, I'd still like to know what you're driving at. You guys think –'

'Shut up!'

'Well, I got a right –'

'What happened on that night of the card game?'

'Nothing.'

'Who first mentioned the word "gunsel"?'

'I never heard it mentioned.'

'Then why'd you mispronounce it?'

'I didn't mispronounce it.'

'You pronounced it correctly?'

'Sure, I did.'

'How'd you pronounce it?'

'Gunsel.'

'When was this?'

'The night we . . .' Collins stopped. '*Anytime* I pronounced it.'

'You said it wasn't mentioned on the night of the game.'

'I said I never heard it. Maybe it was mentioned, how should I know?'

'If it wasn't mentioned, where'd you get the nickname "Gonzo"?'

'Gonzo? Who's got a nickname Gonzo? Everybody calls me Dickie.'

'Except those three kids who came to make the buy from you.'

'Oh? Well, that explains it. You've got the wrong guy. You're looking for a Gonzo. My name is Dickie. Collins. Hey, maybe that's where you slipped up. Collins and Gonzo sound a little –'

'All right, let's cut the crap,' Havilland said sharply.

'Well, I . . .'

'We know what happened at the card game. We know all about the gunsel routine and the way you goofed and called it "gonzo" and the way it brought down the house, and the way you were called Gonzo the rest of the night. Batman told us all about it, and Batman'll swear to it. We figure the rest like this, pal. We figure you used the Gonzo tag when you took over Hernandez's trade because you didn't figure it was wise to identify your own name with your identity as a pusher. Okay, so these kids were looking for Gonzo, and they found him, and one of them bought a sixteenth from you, and he'll swear to that, too. Now how about the rest?'

'What rest?'

'How about the cop you shot?'

'What?'

'How about that rope you put around Hernandez's neck?'

'What?'

'How about the slash job you did on Maria?'

'Listen, listen, I didn't –'

'How about shoving that old lady down the airshaft?'

'Me? Holy Jesus, I didn't do –'

'Which one did you do?'

'None of them! Holy Jesus, what do you take me for?'

'You shot that cop, Gonzo!'

'No, I didn't.'

'We know you did. He told us.'

'He told you nothing.'

'Who?'

'This cop, whoever you're talking about. He couldn't have said it was me because I had nothing to do with it.'

'You've got a lot to do with all of this, Gonzo.'

'Stop calling me Gonzo. My name's Dickie.'

'Okay, *Dickie*. Why'd you kill Hernandez? To get his two-bit business?'

'Don't be stupid!'

'Then why?' Byrnes shouted. 'To drag my son in on it?

How'd Larry's fingerprints get on that syringe?'

'How do I know? What syringe?'

'The syringe found with Hernandez.'

'I didn't know there was one.'

'There was. How'd you swing it?'

'I didn't.'

'Were you trying to frame my son for this?'

'Stop harping on your son. Your son can go drop dead, for all I care.'

'Who's the man that calls me, Gonzo?'

'I didn't know anybody called you Gonzo.'

'Look, you rotten punk . . .'

'I don't know what you're talking about.'

'Somebody called to tell me about my son and that syringe. Somebody's got something on his mind. Was he the guy at that card game?'

'I don't know who that guy was.'

The same guy who called me, isn't he?'

'I don't know who calls you.'

'The guy who helped you kill Hernandez, isn't it?'

'I didn't kill Hernandez.'

'And Maria, and the old lady . . .'

'I didn't kill anybody.'

'You killed a cop,' Willis snapped.

'Is he dead?' Collins asked.

The room was suddenly very quiet.

'What's wrong with that?' Collins said.

'You tell us, pal.'

'You told me a cop got shot. You didn't say he was dead.'

'No, we didn't.'

'Okay, so how was I supposed to know about the goddamn bull? You didn't say he was dead, only that he got shot.'

'We didn't say he was a bull, either,' Byrnes said.

'What?'

'We said a cop. What makes you think he's a detective?'

'I don't know, I just thought so. From the way you were talking.'

'His name is Steve Carella,' Willis said. 'You shot him on Friday, Collins, and he's still fighting for his life. He *told* us you shot him. Why don't you tell us the rest of it, and make it easy for yourself?'

'There's nothing to tell. I'm clean. If your cop dies, you ain't got a thing on me. I ain't got a gun, and I wasn't carrying no junk. So do me something.'

'We're gonna do you a lot, pal,' Havilland said. 'In about three seconds flat, I'm gonna beat the crap out of you.'

'Go ahead. See what that gets you. I ain't involved in none of this. Your cop is crazy. I didn't shoot him, and I got nothing to do with Hernandez, either. You going to build a friendship at the Junior Navals into a federal case?'

'No,' Willis said, 'but we're going to build your footprint into a murder case, that's for sure.'

'My *what*?'

'The footprint we found near Carella's body,' Willis lied. 'We're going to check it against every pair of shoes you own. If it matches up, you're –'

'We were standing on stone!' Collins shouted.

And that was it.

He blinked, realizing it was too late to turn back now, realizing they had him cold. 'Okay,' he said, 'I shot him. But only because he was going to take me in. I didn't want to get tied in with this other stuff. I had nothing to do with killing Hernandez or his sister. Nothing. And I never saw that old lady in my life.'

'Who killed them?' Byrnes asked.

Collins was silent for a moment.

'Douglas Patt,' he said at last.

Willis was already starting for his coat. 'No,' Byrnes called, 'I want him. What's his address, Collins?'

# CHAPTER SIXTEEN

It was very cold up on the roof, colder perhaps than any place in the city. The wind swept around the chimney pots and ate into a man's bones. You could see the entire city almost from up there on the roof, the lights winking, a city of secrets, little secrets.

He stood for a moment and looked out past the rooftops, and he wondered how everything could have gone so wrong. The plan seemed like such a good one, and yet it had gone wrong. *Too many people*, he thought. Whenever there are too many people, things go wrong.

He sighed and turned his back to the cutting wind that whipped the clothes lines and the fragile panes of glass in the walls of the buildings. He felt very tired, and somehow very lonely. It shouldn't have worked out this way. A plan so good should have worked out better. Despondently, he walked to the pigeon coop. He took a key from his pocket and unlocked the door, hanging the lock back on the latch. He stepped into the coop, and the pigeons – alarmed for a moment – beat their wings and then resolved their private fears and settled down again.

He saw the female fantail almost instantly.

She lay on the floor of the coop, and he knew at once that she was dead.

Gently, he bent down and picked her up, and he held her on his widespread hands, staring at her, as if staring would bring her back to life.

Everything seemed suddenly too much to bear. Everything seemed to have been leading to this ultimate, crushing defeat: the death of his fantail. He kept watching the bird, aware that his hands were trembling, but unable to stop them. He went out of the coop then, still holding the bird in his hands. He walked across the roof, and he sat with his back to one of the chimney pots. He put the bird down gently at his feet, and then – as if his hands were too idle now that they were empty – he picked up a loose brick and turned it over and over in his hands, like a potter working with wet clay. He was turning the brick, slowly, slowly, when the man came up on to the roof.

The man looked around for a moment and then walked directly to where he was sitting.

'Douglas Patt?' the man asked.

'Yes?' he answered. He looked up into the man's eyes. The eyes were very hard. The man stood with his shoulders hunched against the wind, his hands in his pockets.

'I'm Lieutenant Byrnes,' the man said.

'Oh,' Patt answered.

They looked at each other silently for a long time. Patt made no motion to rise. Slowly, he kept turning the brick over in his hands, the dead bird at his feet.

'How did you get to me?' he asked at last.

'Dickie Collins,' Byrnes said.

'Mmm,' Patt said. He didn't seem to care very much. He didn't seem at all interested in how the police had found him. 'I figured he would be a weak link if you got on to him.' Patt shook his head. 'Too many people,' he said. He looked down at the bird. He gripped the brick more tightly in one hand.

'What'd you hope to get out of this, Patt?' Byrne asked.

'Me?' Patt said. He made a motion to rise, and Byrnes moved quickly and effortlessly, so that by the time Patt was squatting on his haunches he was looking into the level muzzle of Byrnes's pistol. But Patt seemed not to notice the gun. He seemed intent only on studying the dead bird at his feet. He moved the bird with one hand, holding the brick in the other hand. 'Me? What did I want out of this? A chance, Lieutenant. Big time, Lieutenant.'

'How?'

'This kid, Gonzo – you know about the Gonzo, don't you? Silly damn thing, isn't it? But sort of weird – this kid, Gonzo, he came to me and said, "How do you like that? Annabelle tells me he's got a junkie friend whose old man runs the dicks at the 87th." That's what Gonzo said to me, Lieutenant.'

Byrnes watched him. Patt had lifted the brick slowly, and now he brought it down almost gently, but with a gentle force, smashing it against the body of the dead pigeon. He brought back the brick again, and again he hit the bird with it. There was blood on the brick now, and feathers. He brought it back unconsciously, and then down again, almost as if he were unaware of what he was doing to the bird.

'I figured this was it, Lieutenant. I figured I'd get your son into a set-up that looked pretty bad, and then I'd come to you, Lieutenant, and lay my cards on the table and say, "This is how it stands, Lieutenant. Your son's story gets blabbed all over the newspapers unless I get your cooperation." I had your son rigged for a murder rap, Lieutenant. I was sure you'd cooperate.'

He kept pounding with the brick. Byrnes pulled his eyes away from the disintegrating bird.

'What kind of cooperation did you expect?'

'I push,' Patt said. 'But I'm afraid. I could really expand if I didn't have to be afraid all the time. I didn't want to take a fall. I wanted you to help. I wanted hands off from you or any of your dicks. I wanted to be free to roam the precinct and push wherever I wanted to, without being afraid of getting pinched. That's what I wanted, Lieutenant.'

'You'd never have got it,' Byrnes said. 'Not from me, and not from any cop.'

'Maybe not from you. But, oh, it was sweet, Lieutenant. I sold this little Annabelle jerk a bill of goods. I told him all I wanted was a syringe with your son's prints on it. He dragged your son in and gave him a free fix, and then he switched syringes before your son left that night. I was waiting. When your son took off, I went in to see Annabelle. He was nodding, half blind. I loaded a syringe with enough H to knock the top of his head off. He didn't even know I was injecting it. Then I took your son's syringe out of Annabelle's pocket, and I laid it on the cot beside him.

'Why the rope?' Byrnes asked.

Patt kept hitting the bird, pulverizing it with the brick, spewing feathers and blood on to the tar of the roof. 'That was an afterthought. It occurred to me – Jesus, suppose they think it is a suicide? Or suppose they think it was just an accidental overdose? Where does that leave my murder frame? So I put the rope around Annabelle's neck. I figured the police would be smart enough to know it was tied there after he was killed. I wanted them to know it was homicide, because I was measuring your son for the rap. Your son was my bargaining tool, Lieutenant. My bargaining tool for a free precinct.'

'A free precinct,' Byrnes repeated.

'Mmm, yes,' Patt said. 'But it didn't work out, did it? And then Maria, and the old woman – how do these things get so complicated?'

He stopped pounding and looked down at the tar suddenly. The bird was a crushed mass of bloody pulp and feathers. Tho brick was stained with blood, as were Patt's hands. He looked at the pigeon, and then he looked at the brick and his hands as if he were seeing them for the first time. And then, quite suddenly, he began sobbing.

'You'd better come with me,' Byrnes said gently.

They booked him at the 87th. They charged him with the murder of three people. And after he'd been booked, Byrnes went up to his office, and he stood looking out over the park, and then he saw the clock in the park tower, and the clock told him it was five minutes to midnight.

Five minutes to Christmas.

He went to his telephone.

'Yes?' the desk sergeant said.

'This is the Lieutenant,' Byrnes said. 'Can I have a line, please?'

'Yes, sir.'

He waited for his dial tone, and then he dialled his Calm's Point number, and Harriet answered the phone.

'Hello, Harriet,' he said.

'Hello, Peter.'

'How is he?'

'I think he's going to be all right,' she said.

'He's better?'

'Better than he was, Peter. He doesn't seem . . . he hasn't been vomiting or fidgeting or behaving like a wild man. I think he's licked it physically, Peter. The rest is up to him.'

'Yes,' Byrnes said. 'Is he awake?'

'Yes, he is.'

'May I talk to him?'

'Certainly, darling.'

'Harriet?'

'Yes?'

'I know I've been chasing around, but I wanted you to know . . . 'I mean, all this running around these past few days . . .'

'Peter,' she said gently, 'I married a cop.'

'I know you did. I'm grateful for it. Merry Christmas, Harriet.'

'Come home as soon as you can, darling. I'll get Larry.'

Byrnes waited. In a little while, his son came to the phone.

'Dad?'

'Hello, Larry. How are you feeling?'

'Much better, Dad.'

'Good, good.'

There was a long silence.

'Dad?'

'Yes?'

'I'm sorry for the way . . . for, you know, what I've done. It's going to be different.'

'A lot of things are going to be different, Larry,' Byrnes promised.

'Will you be coming home soon?'

'Well, I wanted to wind up . . .' Byrnes stopped. 'Yes, I'll be home very soon. I want to stop off at the hospital, and then I'll be right home.'

'We'll wait up, Dad.'

'Fine, I'd like that.' Byrnes paused. 'You really feel all right, Larry?'

'Well, I'm getting there,' Larry said, and Byrnes thought he detected a smile in his son's voice.

'Good. Merry Christmas, son.'

'We'll be waiting.'

Byrnes hung up and then put on his overcoat. He was suddenly feeling quite good about everything. They had caught Patt, and they had caught Collins, and his son would be all right, he was sure his son would be all right, and now there remained only Carella, and he was sure Carella would pull through, too. Damnit, you can't shoot a good cop and expect him to die! Not a cop like Carella!

He walked all the way to the hospital. The temperature was dipping close to zero, but he walked all the way, and he shouted, 'Merry Christmas!' to a pair of drunks who passed him. When he reached the hospital, his face was tingling, and he was out of breath, but he was more sure than ever before that everything would work out all right.

He took the elevator up to the eighth floor, and the doors slid open and he stepped into the corridor. It took a moment to orient himself and then he started off toward Carella's room, and it took another moment for the new feeling to attack him. For here in the cool antiseptic sterility of the hospital, he was no longer certain about Steve Carella. Here he had his first doubts, and his step slowed as he approached the room.

He saw Teddy then.

At first she was only a small figure at the end of the

corridor, and then she walked closer and he watched her. Her hands were wrung together at her waist, and her head was bent, and Byrnes watched her and felt a new dread, a dread that attacked his stomach and his mind. There was defeat in the curve of her body, defeat in the droop of her head.

*Carella*, he thought. *Oh God, Steve, no . . .*

He rushed to her, and she looked up at him, and her face was streaked with tears, and when he saw the tears on the face of Steve Carella's wife, he was suddenly barren inside, barren and cold, and he wanted to break from her and run down the corridor, break from her and escape the pain in her eyes.

And then he saw her mouth.

And it was curious, because she was smiling. She was smiling and the shock of seeing that smile opened his eyes wide. The tears coursed down her face, but they ran past a beaming smile, and he took her shoulders and he spoke very clearly and very distinctly and he said, 'Steve? Is he all right?'

She read the words on his mouth, and then she nodded, a small nod at first, and then an exaggerated delirious nod, and she threw herself into Byrnes's arms, and Byrnes held her close to him, feeling for all the word as if she were his daughter, surprised to find tears on his own face.

Outside the hospital, the church bells tolled.

It was Christmas Day, and all was right with the world.

# AFTERWORD

For reasons that will soon become clear, this is an afterword rather than an introduction. For those of you with lengthy memories (my own grows shorter every day), I do not need to reiterate the basic premise behind the 87th Precinct novels – but I will, anyway because it's so short and easily memorized: conglomerate hero in a mythical city.

Meaning that one cop can step into the spotlight in one novel, another in the next novel, cops can get killed and disappear from the series, other cops can come in, all of them visible to varying extents in each of the books, all of the books set against the backdrop of a city with an invented historical past and place names that do not exist, all of which I've said two thousand times before.

Long before any genius producer began singing the blues on an imaginary hill in an unnamed city where a mix of a dozen or so cops came and went in what was known to script writers as 'the usual squadroom boil,' *Cop Hater* set the tone and the pattern for a police series in which – so far as I was concerned – there were no restrictions on content or style. Detective Steve Carella was the hero in that first novel. In the second one, he was on his honeymoon and the murder was solved by a uniformed cop (Bert Kling) who got promoted ino the squadroom in time for the third book, the one you've just finished reading.

I had a contract for only three books, but that wasn't why I decided to kill Steve Carella in the third book. In fact, by the time I began writing it, Pocket Books, Inc. had already renewed for another three books, and the lifetime of the series was assured for at least that long. But I kept remembering what I'd said when I first described the series, all that stuff about cops going and coming, cops getting *killed* and replaced by other cops, and it seemed to me that a very classy thing to do would be to kill off a guy that we'd all come to like and admire – so long, Steve-a-rino!

Toward that end some two-thirds of the way through *The Pusher*, Carella found himself looking into the open end of a .32 calibre pistol and only several pages later he was shot by someone he thought was named Gonzo – as you now know, having already finished the book, unless you read backwards.

Confusion about names, by the way, is something I've used frequently in book after book, a sort of recurring theme, perhaps because I myself legally changed my name to Evan Hunter back in 1952, and then to further complicate matters – started using the McBain name in 1956. In *Lady Killer*, the essential clue hinges on a name. Ditto in *Killer's Choice.* In the book I've just finished writing, *Widows*, there's also some confusion about a name. I like confusion about names. But I digress.

Steve Carella was supposed to die in this book.

The way the book originally ended, in fact, the way I delivered it to my agent, and the way he delivered it to my editor was that Lieutenant Byrnes came into the hospital, just as he does now, and saw Teddy Carella coming down the corridor toward him, just as she does now, and she was crying, and he wanted to break away from her to escape the pain in her eyes and all that, everything just as it is now.

Except that Teddy wasn't smiling.

The way the book read in the version I delivered, Teddy kept crying as the lieutenant took her in his arms and the church bells tolled outside the hospital. The last two lines of the book were:

*It was Christmas day, and all was right with the world.*

*But Steve Carella was dead.*

I thought that was hot stuff, I mean, I thought nobody in the history of crime fiction had ever done that, kill off a guy we'd been rooting for all through the book? I mean talk about *innovation*! Gleefully, I wrapped the book, hand-delivered it to my agent, and walked out into Fifth Avenue again, grinning as if I'd just discovered penicillin.

He called me the next morning.

He said, 'What did you do?'

I said, 'What do you mean?'

He said, 'You killed the hero.'

I said, 'No, no.'

He said, 'What do you mean, no, no? What's this if it isn't a dead hero? It's Christmas day, Carella is dead, you have killed the hero, yes, yes.'

I said, 'No, no, Carella isn't the hero.'

He said, 'What do you mean he isn't the hero? This is the second whole book he's been in.'

I said, 'Yes, and the last one.'

He sighed heavily.

The next day, I got a call from my editor.

He said, 'What did you do?'

I said, 'I didn't kill the hero, if that's what you're suggesting.'

'Yes, that's what I'm suggesting,' he said. 'Because unless I'm reading this wrong, it's Christmas day, Carella is dead, and you've killed the hero.'

I said, 'No, no.'

He said, 'Then please explain who this dead person at the hospital is.'

'It's Carella,' I said. 'But he isn't the hero. Remember what we talked about when I first came up with the series idea? About cops coming and going . . .'

'That didn't mean . . .'

'. . . cops getting killed, other cops replacing them, remember all that?'

'Yes, but nobody said you could kill the hero.'

'But he isn't the hero,' I said. 'He was only in one book before this one.'

'He's the hero. Period.'

I sighed heavily and went back to the typewriter.

I gave Teddy a big smile and at first a small nod and then a delirious nod in answer to Byrne's question, 'Is he all right?' And I cut the last line of the book, and all at once it was Christmas day, and all was right with the world, and Steve Carella was alive again. Magic!

He's still alive.

Maybe somebody knew something I didn't know.

Ed McBain

# KING'S RANSOM

This is for my dear wife, Dragica

# 1.

**THE LONG CURVE** of the bay window faced the River Harb and the late-afternoon traffic of tugboats and barges plying their way between the two states. The scene beyond the window was clear with the pristine snappishness of October growing into November, each orange-and-gold leaf boldly shrieking its colour against a sky too blue, too cold.

The room itself was clouded with cigar smoke and cigarette smoke, lacking the sharply defined clarity of the outdoors, hazing over the people who had come to the room to transact business. The smoke hovered on the air like the breath of banished ghosts, clinging like early-morning cemetery mist to the wide hand-pegged planks of the flooring, rising to the exposed hand-hewn timbers in the ceiling. The room was immense, but it was cluttered now with the trivia of an extended skull-cracking session, ash trays over-brimming with butts, used and half-used glasses strewn about the room like the debris of a drunken army in retreat, empty bottles cluttering the tables, the men themselves exhausted and drawn as if they too, like the clinging shifting smoke, were ready to dissipate into the air.

With dogged weariness, the two men sitting opposite Douglas King rapped out their staccato argument with the precision of vaudeville tap dancers. King listened to them silently.

'All we're asking, Doug, is that you think in terms of net profit, that's all,' George Benjamin said.

'Is that a lot to ask?' Rudy Stone said.

'Think of shoes, yes. Don't forget shoes. But only as they apply to net profit.'

'Granger Shoe is a business, Doug, a *business*. Profit and loss. The black and the red.'

'And our job,' Benjamin said, 'is to keep Granger in the black, okay? So keep that in mind, and think of net profit, and then take another look at these shoes.'

He rose from his position in the easy chair. He was a thin waspish man wearing black-rimmed spectacles which overpowered the narrowness of his face. He moved with the swiftness of a bird of prey, walking rapidly, almost gliding to the brass-stemmed, glass-topped teacart which stood some few feet from the sofa. The top of the cart was covered with women's shoes. Benjamin picked up one of these shoes now and, with the same swift gliding movement, a peculiar grace which gave the impression that he was walking several inches above the actual surface of the expensive flooring, walked to where King sat in noncommittal silence. He extended the shoe to him.

'Is that a shoe to stimulate sales?' he asked.

'Don't misunderstand George,' Stone put in hastily. Standing alongside the bookcases which lined one wall of the living room, he looked like nothing less than a Nordic god, muscularly blond, a man of forty-five with all the litheness of an adolescent. He dressed, too, with an arty flair, the checked waistcoat, the off-blue of his sports coat, which seemed too young for his years. 'It's a good shoe, a fine shoe, but we're thinking in terms of net profit now.'

'The red and the black,' Benjamin repeated. 'That's what we're interested in. Am I right, Frank?'

'A hunnerd per cent,' Frank Blake said. He sucked in on his cigar and blew a smoke wreath at the high ceiling.

'This shoe simply doesn't stimulate the masses, Doug,' Stone said, moving away from the bookcases. 'It has no flair.'

'It has no guts,' Benjamin said, 'that's what it hasn't got. Not only can't the average American housewife afford it, she wouldn't buy it even if she *could* afford it. Mrs America, that's who we're after. The little woman who sweats over a hot stove and wipes snotty noses. Mrs America, our customer. Mrs America, the stupidest damn customer in the universe.'

'We've got to excite her, Doug. That's elementary.'

'We've got to bring women to a fever pitch.'

'What excites a woman, Doug?'

'You're a married man. What excites Mrs King?'

King studied Benjamin blandly. Standing some six feet beyond him, mixing a drink at the bar, Pete Cameron looked up suddenly and caught King's eye. He smiled secretly, but King did not return the grin.

'Clothes excite a woman!' Stone said.

'Dresses, hats, gloves, bags, *shoes*!' Benjamin said, his voice rising. 'And shoes are our business, and nobody's in business for his health.'

'But nobody!' Stone said. 'Net profit depends on stimulation, excitement. You can't excite a woman with these shoes. These shoes wouldn't excite a mare in heat!'

The room was silent for a moment.

Then Douglas King said, 'What are we selling? Shoes or aphrodisiacs?'

Frank Blake rose instantly, his thick Southern accent dripping from his thick Southern lips. At fifty-six, he gave the impression of a man who'd been weaned on molasses. 'Doug is makin' a joke,' he said. 'You'll fo'give me, but I din't come all the way from Alabama to hear jokes. I've got money invested in Granger, and from what George Benjamin tells me about how the firm's bein' run, well, I can see why it's almost in the red.'

'Frank is right, Doug,' Benjamin said. 'This is nothing to joke about. Unless we do something fast, Granger Shoe is going to be right up the proverbial creek.'

'Without the proverbial paddle,' Stone added.

'What do you want from me?' King asked softly.

'Now you're asking the right questions,' Benjamin said. 'Pete, let me have another drink, will you?'

From the bar, Cameron nodded. Quickly he began mixing the drink. There was an economy to his motions, as if they too had been pared down to fit the requirements of his well-tailored, grey-flannelled frame. A tall and handsome man of thirty-five, he continued mixing the drink, his brown eyes flicking alternately to each person in the room.

'What do we want from you, Doug?' Benjamin said. 'Okay, here's what we want.'

'Spell it out for him,' Stone said.

Cameron carried the drink over. 'Anybody else?' he asked.

'None fo' me,' Blake said, and he covered the top of his glass.

'You might freshen this one, Pete,' Stone said, handing him his near-empty glass.

'All right, Doug,' Benjamin said. 'In this room, at this moment, we've got the top brains of Granger Shoe, am I right? I represent sales, you represent factory, and Rudy here is fashion co-ordinator. We're all on the board of directors, and we all know damn well what's wrong with the firm.'

'What's that?' King asked.

'The Old Man.'

'His policy is dictating the kind of shoe we produce,' Stone said. 'His policy is driving this company into a hole.'

'He doesn't know a shoe from a corn plaster,' Benjamin said.

'What does he know about women's tastes? What does he know about *women*, for God's sake?' Stone said.

'He's seventy-four years old, and I think he's still a virgin,' Benjamin said.

'But he's president of Granger, and so Granger goes as the Old Man goes,' Stone said.

'But why is he president, Doug? Have you ever stopped to ask yourself that question?'

'Doug isn't a moron, George. He knows why the Old Man's president.'

'Because he has enough votin' stock to swing any election his way,' Blake put in, interrupting the two other men.

'So year in and year out, he's president,' Stone said, nodding.

'And year in and year out, we stand by while he puts out these . . . these *maternity* shoes!' Benjamin said.

'And year in and year out, we watch the company sink into the slime.'

'An' my stock *dee*-preciates in value. Now, tha's no good, Doug.'

Benjamin moved quickly to the teacart. King had been silent while the men spoke. Still silent, he watched Benjamin pick up a red pump from the clutter of shoes on the cart's top.

'Now look at this shoe,' Benjamin said. 'Take a peek at this! Style! Flair! Excitement!'

'I supervised the design of that bitch myself,' Stone said proudly.

'We had samples made up when you were on vacation, Doug.'

'I know what happened at the factory while I was on vacation, George,' King said softly.

'Oh? Oh?'

'Yes.'

'Give him the shoe,' Stone said. 'Let him take a close look.'

Benjamin handed the pump to King and then turned to glance at Blake, who was puffing on his cigar. King turned the shoe over in his big hands, studying it carefully, saying nothing.

'Now how about that, boy?' Benjamin asked. 'The women'll go nuts for that shoe. What do women know, anyway? Do they care about quality, so long as a shoe flatters the foot?'

'I can read his mind,' Stone said. 'He's thinking the Old Man would never let a shoe like that go through.'

'Ah, but the Old Man won't have a thing to say about it, Doug. That's why we're here today.'

'Oh, is that why we're here today?' King asked mildly, but the irony in his voice was lost on everyone but Pete Cameron, who caught it and smiled.

'The Old Man's got a solid chunk of voting stock,' Benjamin said, his eyes narrowing. 'Twenty-five per cent of it.'

'I was wondering when we'd start discussing voting stock,' King said.

Benjamin laughed feebly. 'Oh, this is a shrewd one, Frank,' he said. 'You can't slip anything over on Doug here.'

King did not react to the compliment. In a flat voice he said, 'The Old Man's got twenty-five per cent, and between you, Rudy, and Frank, you've got twenty-one per cent – not enough to take an election from the Old Man.' He paused significantly. 'What's on your mind?'

'Control,' Stone said.

'Control,' Benjamin repeated. 'We want your voting stock. We want you to throw in your voting stock with us.'

'Mmmm?'

'You've got thirteen per cent, Doug. The remainder is scattered around among people who don't give a damn which way an election goes.'

'With your stock, we'll have a neat thirty-four per cent,' Stone said, 'more than enough to override the Old Man. How about it, Doug?'

'Throw in with us, boy,' Benjamin said enthusiastically. 'We'll vote in a new president. We'll put out shoes like the one you're holding in your hand there. We can sell that shoe for seven dollars. We can splash the Granger name all over the low-priced field. The hell with this quality stuff! The big money is with the masses. Invade the low-priced field with a trade name that's always stood for high fashion, and we'll kill the competition.'

'I think George's idea is sound,' Blake drawled. 'I wouldn't've come all the way up here if I dint. I'm interested in protectin' my investment, Doug. Frankly, I don't care *what* kind of shoes we sell, so long as we make money at it. That's *my* business. Makin' money.'

'Vote out the Old Man, huh?' King said. 'Vote in a new president.'

That's right, Doug,' Stone said.

'Who?'

'Who what?'

'Who goes in as president?'

There was a moment of hesitation. The men glanced at each other.

'Naturally,' Stone said, 'you've got thirteen per cent of the stock, and that's considerable, considerable. But at the same time, you can't do anything without our collective chunk, and so . . .'

'I see no reason for pussyfootin' around, Rudy,' Blake said firmly. 'Conversion to the low-priced field was all George's idea, as was this meetin' today. I'm sure Doug will recognize the fairness of our suggestion.'

'We figured,' Stone said cautiously, as if anticipating an explosion, 'that George Benjamin should go in as president.'

'Well now,' King said dryly, 'that's a surprise.'

'With you as executive vice-president, of course,' Stone said hastily, 'at a tremendous salary jump.'

Douglas King studied the men silently for a moment and then slowly rose. Sprawled on the sofa, he had given an impression of stockiness, but as he rose now, the impression was instantly shattered. He was at least six feet two inches tall, with the wide shoulders and narrow waist of an exhibition diver. At forty-two years old, it was doubtful whether or not the greying hair at his temples could be called 'premature.' It nonetheless added a feeling of dignity to the strong hard lines of his cheeks and jaw, the brittle lustre of his blue eyes.

'You'll put out a line like this, is that right, George?' he asked, holding out the red pump. 'You'll use the Granger name on a low-priced shoe?'

'Yes, that's right.'

'Figuring, of course, that we can eliminate perhaps half our normal factory operation.' He hesitated for a fraction of a second, calculating, and then said, 'Stamps and dies would knock out virtually the entire present cutting-room operation. And the machines on the fifth floor would go, and all the—'

'It's a good idea, isn't it, Doug?' Benjamin asked hopefully.

'And this would be the end result. This shoe.' King stared at the pump.

The end result would be a higher net profit,' Blake said.

'Nothing wrong with that shoe, Doug,' Stone said defensively.

'The Old Man may be running us into the ground,' King answered, 'but at least he's always put out an honest shoe. You want to put out garbage.'

'Now just a second, Doug, you wait just a—'

'No, *you* wait just a second! I like Granger Shoe. I've been working in that factory for the past twenty-six years, started in the stockroom when I was sixteen. Aside from the time I spent in the Army, I've been with this firm practically all my adult life. I know every sound and every smell and every operation in that place, and I know shoes. Good shoes. *Quality!* And I won't stick the Granger name on a piece of junk!'

'Well, all right,' Stone said, 'all right, that's just a sample you've got there. We can put out a slightly better shoe. Maybe something to . . .'

'Something to *what*? This shoe'll fall apart in a month! Where's the steel shank in this? Where the hell are the counters? Where's the box toe? What kind of a cheap sock lining is this?' King ripped out the sock lining and then tore off the strap and buckle. With one quick movement of his hands, he snapped off the heel. He held the assembled debris on his hands. 'Is *this* what you're going to sell? To *women*?'

Outraged by the demolition, Stone said, 'That sample cost us—'

'I know exactly what it cost us, Rudy.'

'Romantic notions don't boost profits!' Blake said angrily. 'If we can't make profit with quality, we've got to—'

'*Who* can't make profit with quality?' King asked. 'That'll come as a shock to the other high-fashion houses, all right. Maybe the Old Man can't, and maybe you can't, but—'

'Doug, this is business, business.'

'I know it's business! It's *my* business, the business I love! Shoes are a part of my life, and if I began making garbage my life would begin to smell!'

'I can't continue to hold stock in a firm that's constantly back-sliding,' Blake said. 'That's not sound. That's not . . .'

'Then sell out! What the hell do you want from me?'

'I'd watch the way I was talking, Doug,' Benjamin said suddenly. 'We still control twenty-one per cent, and I've known bigger men than you to be voted out of their jobs.'

'Go ahead, vote me out,' King said.

'If you find yourself out in the street . . .'

'Don't worry about me, George. I'm not going out into any damn street.' He dumped the remains of the red pump onto the teacart and then turned toward the steps which terminated just outside the entrance hall.

'If you helped me become president,' Benjamin said, 'it would mean an enormous salary increase for you. You could—' He stopped abruptly. 'Where do you think you're going? I'm *talking* to you.'

'This is still my house, George,' King said. 'I'm fed up with your meeting, and I'm fed up with your proposition, and I'm fed up with *you*! So I'm leaving. Why don't you follow suit?'

Benjamin walked after him to the steps. His narrow face was flushed with colour now. 'You don't want me to be president of Granger, is that it?' he shouted.

'That's it exactly,' King said.

'Who the hell do you think *should* be president?'

'You just figure it out,' King said, and he went up the steps and out of sight. A deadly silence followed his departure. Benjamin stared up the steps after him, contained anger rising in his face and his eyes. Blake angrily squashed his cigar in an ash tray and then stomped to the hall closet for his coat. Stone began packing the shoes into a sample case, picking up the red shoe scraps gingerly, almost lovingly, shaking his head over the destruction. Finally, Benjamin turned from the stairwell and walked to where Pete Cameron was standing near the bar.

'What's he got up his sleeve, Pete?' he asked.

'His arm, I suppose.'

'Goddammit, don't make jokes! You're his assistant. If anybody knows what he's up to, you do. Now, what is it? I want to know.'

'You're asking the wrong person,' Cameron said. 'I haven't the faintest idea.'

'Then find out.'

'I'm not sure I know what you mean.'

'Don't play it wide-eyed, Pete,' Benjamin said. 'We just offered a plan to Doug. He turned it down cold, in effect told us to go to hell. You don't tell twenty-one per cent of the voting stock to go to hell unless you're feeling mighty strong. Okay, what's he feeling strong about?'

'Why don't you ask *him*?' Cameron said.

'Don't get glib, boy, it's not becoming. What are you making now? Twenty, twenty-five grand? You can make more, Pete.'

'Can I?'

Stone took his coat from the hall closet and walked over to the two men. Pointing back at the staircase, he said, 'If that bastard thinks he's going to get away with this . . .'

'I doan like bein' kicked outa somebody's home,' Blake said angrily. 'I doan like it one damn bit! When's the next Board meetin', George, we're gonna vote Mr High-an'-mighty King right back into the stockroom!'

'He knows that,' Benjamin said softly. 'He knows that, and he doesn't care – and that means he's hooked onto something big. What is it, Pete? A deal with the Old Man?'

Cameron shrugged.

'Whatever it is,' Benjamin said, 'I want it smashed. And whoever helps to smash it may find himself in Douglas King's vacant chair. You know what that chair is worth, Pete?'

'I have some idea.'

'And I've got an idea you know just where you want to go in this company. Think it over, Pete.' Stone handed him his coat and hat. Benjamin put on the coat quickly and then, holding the Homburg in his hands, said, 'Do you know my home number?'

'No.'

'Westley Hills,' Benjamin said. 'That's WE 4–7981. Will you remember it?'

'I've been Doug's assistant for a long time now,' Cameron answered.

'Then it's time you branched out. Give me a call.'

'You're tempting me,' Cameron said, a slight smile on his lips. 'It's a good thing I'm an honourable man.'

The men locked eyes.

'Yes it's a good thing,' Benjamin said dryly. 'That's Westley Hills 4-7981.'

Stone reached down for his sample case, put on his hat and said, 'If that bastard King thinks he can—' and then stopped talking abruptly.

Diane King had come down the steps silently and she stood looking into the room now. The men stared at her speechlessly. Stone was the first to move. He tipped his hat, politely said, 'Mrs King,' and opened the front door.

Benjamin put on his hat. 'Mrs King,' he said politely, and followed Stone out.

Blake dropped his hat, fumbled for it, picked it up, placed it on his balding head, politely said, 'Mrs King,' and hastily left the house, slamming the door behind him.

Immediately Diane said, 'What did they do to Doug?'

# 2.

**THE KING ESTATE** – for such it was – lay within the confines of the 87th Precinct. It was, as a matter of fact, at the farthermost reaches of the precinct territory, since nothing lay beyond it but the River Harb. The fallow land of the estate was one section of a parcel which stretched from the river's bend to the arbitrary dividing line of the Hamilton Bridge. Within this parcel, there were perhaps two or three dozen homes which seemed to have been dropped there from another era. Incongruously, they provided the ultra-urban face of the city with an atmosphere at once countrified and otherworldly.

This section of the city was called The Club by everyone in the city except the people who lived there. The residents, of whom there were less than a hundred or so, called it Smoke Rise. They used the title casually, but they knew it represented wealth and exclusiveness; they knew that Smoke Rise was almost a city within a city. Even its geographical location seemed to verify the concept. It was bounded on the north by the River Harb. On its south, the poplars lining the River Highway created a barrier which made Smoke Rise impenetrable from invasion by the rest of the city, the rest of the world.

South of the highway was fancy Silvermine Road, a distantly wealthy (but not *that* wealthy) relative of

Smoke Rise. Continuing Southward from Silvermine Park and the apartment buildings facing it, the peripatetic stroller encountered first the gaudy commercialism, the blinking neons, the all-night restaurants, the candy stores, the shrieking traffic signals of The Stem, crossing the precinct territory like a dagger dripping blood. South of that was Ainsley Avenue, and the change from riches to rags was subtle here, the buildings still maintaining some of their old dignity, the dignity of a once stylish, now shabby Homburg; and then came Culver Avenue and the change was apparent now, striking one in the face with the sudden ferocity of naked poverty, nakedly dirty buildings stretching grime-covered façades to a cold wintry sky, bars crouched between the unemotional masks of tenements, churches huddled on street corners – Come pray to God – the wind sweeping through the grey canyon as bleakly as an icy tundra blast.

Southward, southward, through the short stretch of Mason Avenue known to the Puerto Ricans as La Via de Putas, a flash of exotic colour, a splash of eroticism on the ice floe, and then Grover Avenue and beyond that the happy hunting grounds for muggers, knifers, and rapists, Grover Park.

The 87th Precinct building was on Grover Avenue, facing the park. The detective squadroom was on the second floor of the building.

Detective 2nd/Grade Meyer Meyer sat at a desk before one of the windows overlooking Grover Avenue and the park beyond. The feeble October sunshine reflected from his bald pate, danced in his blue eyes. A pad of lined yellow paper rested on the desk before him.

Meyer scribbled notes onto the pad as the man opposite him spoke.

The man said his name was David Peck. He owned a radio supply store, he told Meyer.

'You sell radio parts, is that right?' Meyer asked.

'Well, not for commercial stuff. I mean, we sell a little of that, but mostly we sell stuff for hams, you know what I mean?' Peck tweaked his nose with his thumb and forefinger. It seemed to Meyer that Peck wanted to blow his nose, or perhaps pick it. He wondered if Peck had a handkerchief. He was going to offer him a Kleenex, but he decided the man might be offended by the gesture.

'Hams?' Meyer said.

'Yeah, hams. I don't mean like you eat. Not them hams.' Peck smiled and tweaked his nose again. 'Like, I mean, we don't run a delicatessen or nothing. By hams, I mean amateur radio operators. Like that. We sell equipment to them mostly. You'd be surprised how many hams there are in this neighbourhood. You wouldn't think so, huh, would you?'

'No, I guess I wouldn't,' Meyer said.

'Sure, lots of hams. My partner and me, we got a pretty good business here. We also sell some commercial stuff, like portables and hi-fi units and like that, but that's only a service we run, you understand, what we are primarily interested in is selling stuff to hams.'

'I understand, Mr Peck,' Meyer said, wishing the man would blow his nose, 'but what is the nature of your complaint?'

'Well,' Peck said, and he tweaked his nose, 'like somebody busted into our store.'

'When was this?'

'Last week.'

'Why'd you wait until now to report it?'

'We wasn't going to report it because the guy who busted in, he didn't steal very much, you know. This equipment is pretty heavy stuff, you know, so I guess you have to be strong to cart away a whole store. Anyway, he didn't take very much, so my partner and me we figured we'd just forget about it.'

'What makes you report it now?'

'Well, he came back. The crook, I mean. The thief.'

'He returned?'

'Yeah.'

'When?'

'Last night.'

'And this time he stole a lot of equipment, is that right?'

'No, no. This time he took even less than last time.'

'Now, just a minute, Mr Peck, let's start from the beginning. Would you like a Kleenex, Mr Peck?'

'A Kleenex?' Peck said. 'What do I need a Kleenex for?' And he tweaked his nose again.

Meyer sighed patiently.

Of all the detectives on the 87th Squad, Meyer Meyer was perhaps the most patient. The patience was not an inherited trait. If anything, Meyer's parents had been capable of behaving somewhat impulsively on occasion. Their first impetuous act involved the conception and birth of Meyer Meyer himself. He was, you see, a change-of-life baby. Now whereas news of an impending birth will generally fill the prospective parents with unrestrained glee, such was not the case when old Max Meyer discovered he was to be presented with an offspring. Max did not take kindly to the news. Not at all. He mulled it over, he stewed about it, he sulked, and finally he decided impulsively upon a means of revenge against the new baby. He named the boy Meyer Meyer, a splendid practical joke, to be sure, a gasser. It almost killed the kid.

Well, perhaps that's exaggeration. After all, Meyer *had* grown to manhood, and he *was* a sound physical and mental specimen. But Meyer had done all his growing in a predominantly Gentile neighbourhood, and the fact that he was an Orthodox Jew with a double-barrelled name like Meyer Meyer did not help him in the winning of friends or the influencing of people. In a neighbourhood where the mere fact of Jewishness was enough to provoke spontaneous hatred, Meyer Meyer had had his troubles. 'Meyer Meyer, Jew on fire,' the kids would chant, and whereas they never translated the chant into an actual conflagration, they committed everything short of arson against the Jewboy with the crazy monicker.

Meyer Meyer learned to be patient. You couldn't win a fight against a dozen other boys by using your fists. You learned to use your head instead. Patiently, intelligently, Meyer Meyer handled his problem without the aid of a psychiatrist. Patience became an ingrown trait. Patience became a way of life. So perhaps old Max Meyer's joke was harmless enough. Unless one cared to make note of the fact that Meyer Meyer was as bald as a cue ball. And even this fact assumed no real importance until it was connected with a second purely chronological fact:

Meyer Meyer was only thirty-seven years old.

Patiently now, he poised his pencil over the yellow

pad and said, 'Tell me, Mr Peck, what did this thief steal the first time he broke into your store?'

'An oscillator,' Peck said.

Meyer made a note on his pad. 'How much does the oscillator sell for?' he asked.

'Well, this is a six-hundred-volt oscillator, number 2L-2314. We sell it for fifty-two dollars and thirty-nine cents. That's including tax.'

'And that's all he took the first time?'

'Yes, that's all he took. We get a forty per cent markup on the item, so our loss wasn't really that big. So we decided like to forget about it, you know?'

'I see. But the thief broke into your store again last night, is that correct?'

'That is correct,' Peck said, tweaking his nose.

'And what did he steal this time?'

'Little items. Like a relay which we sell for ten dollars and twenty-two cents, including tax. And some batteries. And a knife switch. Things like that. He couldn't have swiped more than twenty-five bucks' worth of equipment.'

'But this time you're reporting it?'

'Yes.'

'Why? I mean, if the loss this time was smaller than the loss . . .'

'Because we're afraid he might come back a third time. Suppose he comes back with a goddamn truck and cleans out the store? It's possible, you know.'

'I know it is. And we appreciate your reporting the crimes to us, Mr Peck. We'll keep a special watch on your store from now on. Would you give me the name of it, please?'

'Pecker Parts,' Peck said.

Meyer blinked. 'Uh . . . where'd you get that name?' he asked.

'Well, my last name is Peck, as you know.'

'Yes.'

'And my partner's first name is Erwin. So we put the two names together and we got Pecker Parts.'

'Wouldn't you have done better by using some other portion of your partner's name? His last name perhaps?'

'His last name?' Peck said. 'I really don't see how we could have used that.'

'What *is* his last name?'

'Lipschitz.'

'Well,' Meyer said, and he sighed. 'And what is the address of the store, Mr Peck?'

'Eighteen twenty-seven Culver Avenue.'

'Thank you,' Meyer said. 'We'll keep an eye on it.'

'Thank *you*,' Peck said. He rose, tweaked his nose, and left the squadroom.

The theft of equipment amounting to a loss of some seventy-five dollars was certainly not important in itself. Or, at least, not important as thefts go, unless you're a stickler for the letter of the law, one of those people who insist that *any* silly little theft is really crime. In the 87th Precinct, however, seventy-five-dollar losses were commonplace, and if you knocked yourself out tracking down every bit of petty larceny, you'd have no time left for the really serious crimes being committed. No, on the face of it Mr Peck's paltry pilfering complaint was nothing to get all excited about – unless you happened to be a man named Meyer Meyer who kept abreast of what was happening around him in the squadroom and in the precinct and who was blessed with a fairly retentive memory.

Meyer studied the notes on the pad before him and then walked over to a desk on the other side of the room. Steve Carella was sitting at that desk, busily typing up a report, the forefingers of both hands beating the typewriter into reluctant submission.

'Steve,' Meyer said. 'I just had a guy in here who—'

'Shhh, shhh,' Carella said, and he continued banging away at the machine until he finished his paragraph. Then he looked up.

'Okay?' Meyer said.

'Shoot.'

'I just had a guy in here who—'

'Why don't you sit down? You want some coffee? Let's get Miscolo to make some coffee.'

'No, I don't want any coffee,' Meyer said patiently.

'This isn't a social visit?'

'No. I just had a guy in here who owns a radio parts store on Culver Avenue.'

'Yeah?'

'Yeah. So the store was broken into twice in a row. The first time the thief stole an oscillator, whatever the hell that is, and the second time just a bunch of loose junk hanging around. Now it seems to me I remember . . . '

'Yeah, how about that?' Carella said. He shoved the typing cart away from the desk and opened his bottom drawer. Dumping a sheaf of papers on the desk top, he began rifling through them hurriedly.

'A whole bunch of radio store burglaries, weren't they?' Meyer said.

'Yeah, yeah,' Carella answered. 'Where the hell's that list?' He continued scattering papers over the desk top. 'Look at this. More junk in this damn drawer. This guy was caught and is already serving his time at Castleview. Now where's that . . . ? Jewellery stores . . . bicycles . . . Why doesn't somebody add these to the stolen-bikes file? . . . Here it is. This the thing you were referring to?'

Meyer looked at the typewritten sheet.

'That's it,' he said. 'Pretty strange, don't you think?'

There was, in truth, nothing strange about the list. It simply enumerated the amount of equipment that had been stolen from several different radio parts stores over the past several months. Both men bent over the list (*overleaf*) and studied it more closely.

'What do you make of it?' Meyer said.

'I don't know.'

'Well, you must have thought there was something fishy, or you wouldn't have scribbled that note to the lieutenant.'

'Yeah,' Carella said.

'What did Pete have to say about it?'

'Not a hell of a lot. Figured it was some kids, I think.'

'What was the m.o., Steve? Do you remember?'

'A window at the back of the shop was forced in each case. And in each case, only one large item or a few small items were stolen.'

'Why do you suppose the thief did that?'

'Maybe he figured a small theft wouldn't be reported. Or perhaps not even missed. Assuming this was the same thief on each job.'

'Well, it sure as hell looks that way to me,' Meyer said.

'Mmm. In any case, it's not very serious.'

'I suppose not. Here. You'd better add these new ones

RADIO EQUIPMENT THEFTS

| DATE REPORTED | SHOP AND ADDRESS | EQUIPMENT | SERIAL NUMBER |
|---|---|---|---|
| June 11th | David Radio, 312 N. 10 | Oscillator 1600 volt | 216-81-R 17 |
| | | Dial | |
| | | Battery | |
| July 22nd | R&L Parts, 4511 Mason Avenue | Transmitter 35.66 mg. | TX 11-4812 |
| August 5th | Sparks, Inc. 7614 Grover Avenue | Receiver 43.66 mg. | RV 327-89L |
| September 8th | ~~Osigies~~ OSIKRIAS Radio Parts, Repair & Service, South 14th and Culver | four relays (one inch by three inch) | |
| | | six Batteries | |
| | | thirty-five-ft. rubberized wire | |

PETE:
M.O. SAME ON THESE.
MAKE ANY CONNECTION?
Steve

to your list.' Meyer paused and scratched his bald head. 'You suppose we're dealing with a Russian spy or something here?'

'Either that or a member of the I.R.A.'

'I mean, why else would anybody want all these parts?'

'We may be dealing with a ham who can't afford his hobby,' Carella said.

'Yeah, so why doesn't he switch his hobby?'

'One thing I stopped worrying about the minute I became a detective,' Carella said, 'is motive. If you try to figure out what motivates a crook, you go nuts.'

'You're destroying a boy's faith in detective fiction,' Meyer said. 'The Means, the Motive, and the Opportunity. Everybody knows that.'

'Except me. I just do my job,' Carella said.

'Yeah,' Meyer said.

'It always comes out in the wash, anyway. One day, all the mysterious pieces click together. And they're never what you thought they were going to be. To figure out motivation, you have to be a psychiatrist.'

'Still,' Meyer said, 'all that equipment. And the thief hit seven times to get it. That's a big chance to take for a hobby. What does it add up to, Steve?'

'Beats the hell out of me,' Carella said, and he began typing again.

# 3.

DIANE KING WAS not a beautiful woman.

She was, however, an attractive woman.

Her attractiveness was directly attributable to the bone structure of her face, which, while not adding up to the Hollywood or Madison Avenue concept of beauty, nonetheless provided an excellent foundation upon which to build. Her attractiveness, too, was indirectly attributable to a number of things like: (a) the various concoctions offered by the myriad beauty-preparation firms, (b) a life of comparative ease and luxury, (c) ready access to the hairdresser's, and (d) an innate good taste in the selection of clothes to complement a figure unendowed with a movie star's mammillary overabundance.

Diane King was attractive. Diane King, in fact, was damned attractive.

She stood just inside the entrance foyer of her luxurious home, a woman of thirty-two wearing black tapered lounging slacks and a long-sleeved white blouse open at the throat. A towel was draped over the neck and shoulders of the blouse. Her hair echoed the ebony black of the slacks, except for a fresh silver streak which rose from a widow's peak and spread like mercury to a point somewhere on the top of her head. A silver-studded belt circled her narrow waist. Her green eyes fled from the entrance doorway to Pete Cameron's face, and again she asked, 'What did they do to Doug?'

'Nothing,' Cameron said. He looked at her hair. 'What'd *you* do to your hair?'

Distractedly, Diane's hand went up to the silver streak. 'Oh, it was Liz's idea,' she said. 'What was all the shouting about, Pete?'

'Is Liz still here?' Cameron asked, and there was an undeniable note of interest in his voice.

'Yes, she's still here. Why'd Doug come steaming upstairs like the Twentieth Century? I hate these damn high-power meetings. He didn't even *see* me up there, Pete, do you know that?'

'He saw *me*,' a voice said, and Liz Bellew came down the steps and into the living room. Whatever Diane King lacked in the way of beauty, Liz Bellew possessed. She was born with blonde hair that needed no hairdresser's magic, blue eyes fringed with thick lashes, an exquisitely moulded nose and a pouting sultry mouth. She had acquired over the years a figure which oozed S-E-X in capital letters in neon, and had overlaid – if you'll pardon the expression – her undeniable beauty with a polish as smooth and as hard as baked enamel. Even dressed for casual life in Smoke Rise, as she was now, wearing simple sweater and skirt, suede flats, and carrying a suede pouch-like bag, sex dripped from her curvaceous frame in bucketfuls, tubfuls, vatfuls. She wore only one piece of jewellery, a huge diamond on her left hand, a diamond the size of a malignant cancer.

'I'll be damned if I'll let *any* man rush past Liz Bellew without saying hello,' she said, obviously referring to her encounter with King upstairs.

'So hello,' Cameron said.

'I was wondering when you'd notice me.'

'I understand you've turned beautician in your spare time,' Cameron said.

'Diane's hair! Isn't it stunning?'

'I don't like it,' Cameron said. 'Forgive my honesty. I think she's quite beautiful without any gilding of the lily—'

'Oh, hush, monster,' Liz said. 'The streak gives her glamour. It emancipates her.' She paused. Underplaying the next line, she said. 'Besides, she can wash it out if she doesn't like it.'

'Well, I'll see what Doug thinks first,' Diane said.

'Darling, never ask a man what he thinks about any part of your body. Am I right, Pete?'

Cameron grinned. 'Absolutely.'

Diane glanced toward the steps nervously. 'What's he *doing* up there?'

'Your beloved?' Liz said. 'He's only making a phone call. I stopped him, and he apologized for ignoring me, and said he had an important call to make.'

'Pete, are you sure he's not in trouble? That look on his face . . .'

'Don't you know that look?' Liz said. 'My God, Harold wears it all the time. It simply means he's about to murder someone.'

'Murder?'

'Certainly.'

Diane turned sharply to Cameron. 'Pete, what happened down here?'

Cameron shrugged. 'Nothing. They offered Doug a deal, and he spit in their collective eye.'

'My Harold would have kicked them out of the house,' Liz said.

'That's just what Doug did.'

'Then everything's under control. Prepare for a homicide, Diane.'

'I'm always prepared for one,' Diane said. A troubled look had come into her green eyes. She turned away from Liz and Cameron and walked to the bar. 'But they seem to be getting more and more frequent.'

'Well, Diane,' Cameron said, 'that's business. Dog eat dog.'

'Anyway, murder can be fun,' Liz put in. 'Lay back and enjoy it, that's my motto.' She smiled archly at Cameron, who immediately returned the smile.

If there seemed to be slightly more than ultrasophisticated social palaver between Cameron and Liz, if indeed they seemed to have shared more than a passing acquaintanceship, the impression was probably nurtured by the fact that they had, over the years, and discreetly, to be sure, enjoyed that boat ride up extramarital waters. For whereas Liz Bellew was devoted to her husband Harold, and whereas Pete Cameron was a junior executive whose every waking moment was occupied with thoughts of the company, they had each managed to find the time to be mutually attracted, to arrange a first tentative meeting, and then to fall into a pattern of assignations which bordered on bacchanals.

Liz Bellew was suffering from a disease known to many thirty-five-year-old women and labelled by medical science 'itchiness.' It was all well and good to be married to a successful tycoon, and it was marvellous to live in Smoke Rise with an upstairs maid, a downstairs maid and a chauffeur, and it was delightful to be able to wear mink interchangeably with ermine – but when something like Pete Cameron strolled by, the temptation to add another acquisition to the Bellew holdings was not easily put aside. Nor was Liz a person who really struggled too valiantly against the siren calls of everyday living. Lay back and enjoy it, that was her motto. And she'd been doing just that for as long as she could remember. Happily, Pete Cameron satisfied her about as well as any mere thing of flesh and blood could satisfy her, and – thanks to him – she was saved the ugliness of becoming a real wanton. In any case, their public face, a mask they had both agreed to wear, consisted of a light sex play designed to evoke in the viewer and listener the feeling that there could not possibly be any fire where there was so much obvious smoke.

Diane poured herself a drink and turned to face Cameron. '*Is* Doug planning to slit another throat?' she asked.

'Yes, I think so.'

'I thought after what he did to Robinson, he might just possibly . . .'

'Robinson?' Liz said. 'Oh, yes, that quaint little man. He played lousy bridge. Doug's better off without him.'

'I'm better off without *whom*?' King asked from the staircase, and then he came down the steps exuberantly and walked directly to Diane where she stood near the bar.

'Did you make your call, tycoon?' Liz asked.

'The lines are tied up,' King answered. He kissed his wife lightly, backed away from her with a small take, and studied the silver streak in her hair. 'Honey,' he said, 'you've got egg in your hair.'

'Sometimes I wonder why we bother,' Liz said sourly.

'Don't you like it, Doug?' Diane asked.

King weighed his answer carefully. Then he said, 'It looks kind of cute.'

'Holy God, it looks kind of cute!' Liz mimicked. 'The last time I heard that was at a senior tea. From a football player named Leo Raskin. Do you remember him, Diane?'

'No. I didn't know many football players.'

'I wore a blouse cut down to—' Liz paused and then indicated a spot somewhere close to her abdomen – 'well, at least *here*! I was practically naked, believe me, it's a wonder I wasn't expelled from college. I asked Leo for his opinion, and he said, "It looks kind of cute." '

'What's wrong with that?' King asked.

'*It* looks kind of cute?' Liz said. 'Hell, even a football player should be able to *count*!' She glanced quickly at her watch. 'I'm getting out of here. I promised *my* tycoon I'd be back by four.'

'You're late already,' Cameron said. 'Have one for the road.'

'I really shouldn't,' Liz said, and she smiled at him archly.

'*Two* lemon peels?'

'The memory on that boy. He knows I can't resist his cocktails.'

Her eyes locked with Cameron's. Neither Diane nor King paid the slightest bit of attention to all this obvious smoke. Happily, the telephone rang, and Diane picked it up.

'Hello?' she said.

'Ready on your call to Boston now,' the operator said.

'Oh, thank you. Just a moment, please.' She handed the phone to King. 'Were you calling Boston, Doug?'

'Yes,' he said, taking the receiver.

Cameron looked up from the Martinis he was mixing. 'Boston?'

'Hello?' King said into the phone.

'We're ready with your Boston call now, sir. One moment, please.' There was a long pause, and then the operator said, 'Here's your party, sir.'

'Hello?' a voice asked. 'Hello?'

'Is that you, Hanley?' King asked.

'Yes, Doug, how are you?'

'Fine. How's it going up there?'

'Just about the way we expected, Doug.'

'Well, look, we've got to sew this thing up fast.'

'How fast?'

'Today,' King said.

'Why? Something wrong?'

'I just had the undertakers in here for a showdown,' King said, 'and they're not going to sit still for very long. What's with our man anyway?'

'He wants to hang on to five per cent, Doug.'

'What? What the hell for?'

'Well, he feels—' Hanley started.

'Never mind, I'm not interested. That five per cent is as important to me as the rest of it, so get it. Just get it, Hanley!'

'Well, I'm trying my best, Doug, but how can I . . . ?'

'I don't give a damn how you do it, just do it! Go back to him, cry on his shoulder, hold his hand, go to bed with him, get what we want!'

'Well, it may take a little time,' Hanley said.

'How *much* time?'

'Well . . . actually, I don't know. I suppose I can go over to see him right now.'

'Then go ahead. And call me back as soon as you've seen him. I'll be waiting. And listen, Hanley, I'll assume you're going to deliver and I'll act accordingly. So don't foul me up. Do you understand?'

'Well, I'll try.'

'Don't just try, Hanley. Succeed. I'll be waiting for your call.' He hung up and turned to Cameron. 'Pete, you're going to Boston.'

'I am?' Cameron said. He handed the Martini to Liz.

'How lucky you are!' she said. 'I just adore Scollay Square.'

'You're going to Boston with a big fat cheque,' King said, 'and you're going to deliver that cheque to Hanley, and we're going to close the biggest damn deal I've ever made in my life!'

'If your lawyer's in on it, it must be big,' Cameron said. 'What's it all about, Doug?'

'Now don't jinx it,' King said smiling. 'I don't like to talk about anything until it's all set. I'll tell you all about it in due time, but not until I'm sure, okay? Meanwhile, you get on the phone and find out how the flights are running to Boston. Use the upstairs phone. I want to leave this line clear for Hanley.'

'Sure, Doug,' Cameron said, and he started for the steps. He stopped, turned toward Liz and said, 'You won't leave without saying goodbye, will you?'

Liz looked up from her Martini. 'Darling, I *always* linger over my farewells,' she said.

Cameron smiled and went up the steps. King clapped

his hands together once, sharply, and began pacing the room.

'Oh, are those vultures going to be surprised! They think they're circling a dead body, but watch their faces when the body stands up and smacks them in the teeth! Asking *me* to go in with *them*, can you beat that, Diane?'

'Excuse me, Mr King,' a voice said.

The man who had come in at the other end of the living room could not have been more than thirty-five years old, but at first glance he appeared much older. It was, perhaps, the way he stood hesitantly in the doorway to the living room, his shoulders hunched, the chauffeur's uniform adding somehow to his posture of demeanour. His name was Charles Reynolds, but he was called simply Reynolds by everyone in the King household, and perhaps a man reduced to his last name is a man driven to his last retreat. Whatever the case, there was an almost tangible weakness about the man. Watching him, you felt you could reach out and touch a substance at once sticky and gelatinous. And watching him, too, you felt an extreme sympathy, a sadness. Even if you did not know his wife had died not a year ago, even if you did not know he shared the rooms over the King garage with his young son, raising the boy with the awkwardness of bereavement – even unaware of this, you felt sympathy for the man, you felt he was one of the world's strays.

'What is it, Reynolds?' King asked.

'Excuse me, sir, I didn't mean to intrude.'

'You're not intruding,' King said. There was a gruffness to his voice. Fond of the man as he was, King could not abide weakness, and weakness was this man's strength.

'I only wanted to know, sir . . . is my son . . . is Jeff here, sir?'

'That's *Mrs* King's department,' King said.

'He's upstairs with Bobby, Reynolds.'

'Oh, fine. I hope I'm not bothering you, ma'am, but it's turned a little chilly, and I figured he might need a coat if he goes outside to play.'

Diane studied the overcoat in Reynolds' hands with a practised mother's eye. 'I think that might be a little heavy, Reynolds. I've already given him one of Bobby's sweaters.'

Reynolds looked at the coat as if seeing it for the first time. 'Oh . . .' He smiled sheepishly. 'Well, thank you, ma'am. I never can seem able to decide what . . .'

'You'll probably be driving Mr Cameron to the airport, later,' King cut in. 'Plan on that, will you?'

'Yes, sir. When will we be leaving, sir?'

That's not definite yet. I'll buzz you when we know.'

A bloodcurdling scream erupted from someplace upstairs, followed by a second more chilling one, and followed immediately by the thunder of elephant hoofs on the stairs. Bobby King, wearing a blue sweater, his blond hair hanging over his forehead, charged down the steps with Jeff Reynolds in hot pursuit. At first glance, the boys seemed to be brothers. They were both blond, both of the same height and build, both carrying toy rifles, and both screaming in the same high voices. They were, however, both eight years old and did not really resemble each other in the slightest except for their build and colouration, ergo the brother concept was instantly shattered unless one admitted the possibility of their being fraternal twins. Whooping and yelling, they headed for the front door, ignoring everyone in the living room.

'Hey!' King shouted, and his son pulled up an imaginary horse.

'Whoa, boy, whoa!' Bobby said. 'What is it, Dad?'

'Where're you going?'

'Outside to play,' Bobby said.

'How about a good-bye?'

'*Good-bye*,' Liz Bellew said, rising and rolling her eyes. 'This is beginning to resemble *my* menagerie.'

'We're in an awful hurry, Dad,' Bobby said.

'Why? Where's the fire?'

'There's no fire, Mr King,' Jeff said, 'but we've got a game to play.'

'Oh? What kind of a game?'

'Creeks,' Jeff said.

'What's that?'

'It's what I'll be up unless I get home soon,' Liz said.

'It's Injuns,' Jeff explained. 'Creeks are Injuns, don't you know?'

'Oh, I see.'

'We take turns bein' Creek,' Bobby said. 'We got to find each other in the woods. When I'm the cavalry . . .'

'Oh, God, this is really all too familiar,' Liz said. 'I *must* go.'

'. . . and Jeff's a Creek, I got to find him. When I capture him . . .'

'Is that what all the artillery's for?' King asked, indicating the toy rifles each of the boys carried.

'Sure,' Bobby said solemnly. 'You can't go in the woods unarmed, can you?'

'I should say not.'

'Don't go too far from the house, Bobby,' Diane said.

'I won't, Mom.'

'Who's the Creek now?' King asked.

'I am!' Jeff said, and he let out a war whoop and began dancing around the room.

'Jeff!' Reynolds cried sharply, embarrassed.

'I'm doin' the ceremonial,' his son explained.

'Don't shout so. And take good care of the sweater Mrs King loaned you.'

'Oh, sure,' Jeff said, glancing at the bright-red sweater cursorily. 'He won't catch me, Dad, don't worry.'

'I don't care whether he catches you or not, just so—'

'Oh, won't he now?' King interrupted. 'You'd *better* catch him, son. The family name's at stake.'

'I'll get him,' Bobby said, grinning.

'What's your strategy?' King asked.

'Huh?'

'Your plan.'

'Just chase him and catch him, that's all.' Bobby shrugged.

'Never chase the other fellow, son,' King advised. 'That's no way to do it. I can see you need help.'

'Oh, Doug, let them go play before it gets dark,' Diane said.

'I will,' King said, smiling, 'but the boy needs assistance from a professional scalp hunter, can't you see that? Come here, Bobby.' He took his son aside so that Jeff could not hear the conversation. Whispering, he said, 'Climb up a tree, see? Watch him from up there. Watch everything he does. You're holding all the cards that way because he doesn't know just where you are. Then, when you're certain of what he's about to do, beat him to the punch. Pounce!'

'Doug!' Diane said sharply.

'You weren't supposed to be listening, hon,' King said.

'But climbing trees is against the rules of the game, Dad,' Bobby said.

'Make your own rules!' King said. 'So long as you win.'

'Doug, what in the world are you telling him?' Diane said.

'Only the facts of life, I'd suspect,' Liz answered.

'All they want to do, you know, is get outside and start their game.'

'How come I don't get any help?' Jeff said, turning to his father. 'What should I do, Dad?'

Reynolds, caught by surprise, obviously embarrassed in the presence of his employer, said, 'Well . . . uh . . . you can lie flat behind a rock. He'd never find you that way.'

'Unless you move, Jeff,' King said. 'Then, brother, watch out!'

'But if you don't move, son, you're safe,' Reynolds said with seeming logic.

'If nobody moves, there's no game,' King said. 'What's the sense in playing?'

'I think you'd do best, boys, to play the game just the way you want to,' Diane said, somewhat coldly. 'Go on now, have fun.'

The war whoops erupted again, the rifles were once more brandished in the air. The red sweater and the blue sweater moved in a purplish blur toward the front door, and the ensuing slam shook the house.

'Wow!' Liz said.

'I'll have the car ready whenever Mr Cameron needs it, sir,' Reynolds said.

'Fine,' King said, mentally dismissing Reynolds even before he had left the room.

'Thank you, sir,' Reynolds said, and he backed into the dining room and then turned and walked into the shadows toward the kitchen.

Diane waited until she was sure he was gone. Then she said, 'You shouldn't have told him that, Doug.'

'Huh? Told who what?'

'To . . . to climb a tree and watch and then pounce. Make your own rules! Win at any cost! What are you trying to raise? A jungle tiger?'

'Mmmm, yes,' King said, 'like his mother. Flashing eyes and sharp teeth and—'

'Doug, I'm serious!'

'Darling, so is he,' Liz said shrewdly. 'He's making love to you, can't you tell? I'd better go.'

'What kind of nonsense is that to tell a boy?' Diane said angrily. 'Pounce! For the love of— Do you want . . . do you want him to grow up to be a . . . a . . . ?'

'A rapist?' Liz supplied.

'Yes, thank you, Liz.'

'Why not?' King said. 'Like father, like . . .'

'I'm terribly sorry you think this is a joke. I don't happen to see anything so funny about it.'

Liz Bellew sighed. 'Methinks I see a storm warning for Hurricane Diane,' she said.

'Don't be silly,' Diane said with utter composure. 'You've known me long enough to tell when I'm angry or not.' She allowed her fury to smoulder silently for a moment longer and then exploded. 'Pounce, pounce,

*pounce*! The way you're doing with this Boston thing, the way you did with poor Robinson!'

'*Poor* Robinson?' King said.

'Yes, you know very well what I mean.'

'I fired a man. What's so criminal about that?'

'Harold fires men every day,' Liz said brightly.

'Of course,' King said. 'Honey, when you're in business, you can't worry about . . .'

'Yes, but *why* did you fire him? And *how*? The Robinsons were our friends.'

'Friends? Because we had them in for bridge a few times?'

'It wasn't a few times, and they were our friends!'

'All right, they *were* our friends. They're not any more.' King paused. 'He was making me look bad.'

'And is that a reason for . . .'

'Look, I told you he was charging sales trips to the cost of a shoe. Some idiot goes to Italy to buy silk, and Robinson charges that up to Cost. He was making me and the factory end look sick. He was being unfair, and I asked him repeatedly to re-evaluate his system. You know he refused.'

'So you fired him. You didn't even give him the chance to resign.'

Liz Bellew, apparently bored by the kind of talk she heard endlessly in her own house, stretched out on the couch and glanced at the staircase.

'Resign?' King said. 'The hell with resignation! When a man isn't doing his job right . . .'

'What happens when he looks for another job, when he has to tell a prospective employer he was *fired*?'

'Only a damn fool would say he was fired. If Robinson has any sense at—'

'You know they'll check with Granger, no matter what he says.'

'Well, he should have thought of that before he began holding hands with the Sales Division. Diane, he was knocking Cost 'way the hell out of line!'

'You didn't have to be so *ruthless*!'

'Ruthless? Me?' He laughed. 'Liz, am I ruthless?'

'You're a darling,' Liz said.

'What makes you think I'm ruthless? Because I get things done while other people sit around on their fannies? Honey, there are sitters and there are doers. Just because a man takes action doesn't necessarily mean . . .'

'No, but if you make a habit of stepping on people, of not caring . . .'

'Honey, if I'd sat on my duff all these years, you wouldn't be living in this house right now, you wouldn't be wearing that bracelet, you . . .'

'He's right, darling,' Liz said, and she extended the hand with the diamond on it.

'Of course I am. You either *do* or you *sit*, right, Liz?'

'Absolutely,' Liz said. She swung upright. 'I've always enjoyed a little action myself.' She looked at her watch. 'Well, back to the little shack on the hill for me. You two coming to the club tonight?'

'Maybe,' Diane said angrily.

'Mmmm.' Liz stared at Diane. 'I know what *she* needs,' she said to King.

'So do I.'

'I figured you did. By the way, if Pete asks—' She cut herself off. 'Never mind, he's a big boy now.' She waved her hand, called, 'Have fun,' and walked out of the house.

There was a dead silence after her departure. Diane stood stockstill in the centre of the room. King studied her for a moment and then began circling her slowly.

'Diane?' he said gently.

'What is it?'

'Diane, I'm sitting in a tree, and I'm looking down at you . . .'

'What?' she said, puzzled.

Circling closer, King said, 'And I'm warning you now . . . in all fairness . . . that I am getting ready to . . . *pounce*!'

He seized her suddenly, holding her close to him, his mouth an inch from hers.

'Let me go!' she said. 'If you think you can—' and King kissed her. She struggled for a moment longer, and then submitted to his kiss, and then returned it, clinging to him, and then pulled her mouth from his.

'You . . . you oaf,' she said gently.

'Yes,' he said, and he kissed her again.

'You are,' she said weakly. 'You should be ashamed of yourself.'

'I am. Deeply.' He kissed her again. 'You're beautiful. Especially with that new sexy streak in your hair.'

'I'm too good for you, that's for sure, you ape.'

'I know, I know. Listen, what time's dinner?'

'Why?' she asked suspiciously.

'I thought we might . . .' He shrugged.

'And I didn't appreciate your discussing me with Liz as if I were a head of cattle or something.'

'Mmmm, you're a gorgeous head of cattle,' he said, and again he kissed her. 'You didn't answer me.'

'What did you ask?' Diane said dizzily.

King kissed her neck. 'Dinner,' he whispered. 'The time before dinner.'

'Pete's wandering around the house, you know.'

'I'll get rid of him. I'll fire him.'

'How can you . . . ?'

'I'll send him out to the airport early.'

'Well . . .' Diane said hesitantly.

'Well?'

'Well . . .' An embarrassed smile formed on her mouth.

'Good!' King said. 'Let me check with Hanley first.'

'Check with Hanley!'

'I mean, I don't want him calling back in the . . .'

'Maybe I should arrange this through your secretary,' Diane said.

King grinned and slapped her on the rump as he went to the phone. He picked up the receiver, turned toward her, and said, 'This'll only take a minute. All I want to do is—' He stopped suddenly, aware that someone else was on the line, and then recognizing the voice as Cameron's.

'. . . yes, George,' Cameron was saying, 'that's what I'm trying to tell you. Well, I thought you'd like to know . . .'

Hastily, King pushed a button in the base of the phone, switching to another line. 'Funny,' he said.

'What's the matter?' Diane asked.

'Pete's on the other line,' King said. There was a puzzled look on his face. 'I could've sworn he was talking to . . .' He shrugged, dialled the operator and waited. 'Think you can get me Oscar Hanley at the Hotel Stanhope in Boston?' he said. He listened for a moment. 'All right, call me back, will you?' He hung up and turned toward his wife. 'In the meantime, my dear, how about a little drink to—'

The front door burst open. The Creeks were returning. Or at least one of the Creeks.

'Bobby, don't come barging into the house like that!' Diane shouted at her son as he charged up the steps to the bedroom area.

'Sorry, Mom! I forgot my powder horn! Where is it, Mom?'

'Upstairs in your toy chest, where it usually is.'

'Help me find it, will you?'

'You know where it is.'

'Yeah, but I'm in a hurry,' Bobby said. 'Jeff's already got a head start, and I-hey! There it is! Hanging on my doorknob!' He let out a wild whoop and stomped down the corridor, to return a moment later with the powder horn slung over his shoulder. 'So long!' he yelled. 'I got to find myself a tree, Dad!' and he stormed out of the house again.

'Wait,' Diane said reproachfully, 'and then pounce.'

The man in the bushes was waiting to pounce.

He was dying for a cigarette, but he knew he dared not light one. From his hidden vantage point, he could see the windowless side of the King house and the entrance to the garage. The long black Cadillac was parked in the driveway, and a chauffeur was running a chamois cloth over the sleek hood of the automobile. The man in the bushes glanced at the chauffeur, and then at his watch, and then at the sky. It would be dark soon. Good. Darkness was what they needed.

He wished for a cigarette.

He wondered if Eddie was still with the car. He

wondered if everything was okay at the house. He wondered if the whole thing would work, and, wondering about it, he began to worry about it, and his palms got damp and he wanted a cigarette more than ever.

He heard a noise in the bushes, and he felt fear crackle up his spine to explode inside his skull like a yellow sky-rocket.

*Cool*, he told himself. *Cool*.

He forced his hands to stop trembling by clenching them tightly. He squeezed his eyes shut, and then opened them again, and then saw the figure coming through the woods, and his heart gave a sudden lurch. It was the boy.

He wet his lips.

When his voice came from his mouth, it came as a hoarse cracked sound. He swallowed hard and tried again.

'Hi, sonny,' he said. 'What you doing? Playing cops and robbers?'

Dusk was beginning to shoulder its way into the city.

In October there is a special feel to dusk, the softness of a cat's muzzle, and it is accompanied by the smell of wood smoke even in the heart of the city where people do not burn wood or leaves. The smell is something ingrained on the race memory of man, and it lends a quality of serenity to October which no other month can claim. The street lamps go on a little before darkness really falls. The sun stains the sky with a brilliant red, interlaced with the solemn purple of a vault of clouds wheeling heavenward. The bridges span the city in bold silhouette, suspended cables backdropped by the stain of purple dusk, green lights winking in the coming darkness like strung emeralds.

The pace quickens a little, the step becomes a little lighter. There is a briskness on the air, and it bites the cheeks and stings the teeth, and the store fronts are coming alive with light now, like beckoning potbellied stoves, cherry-hot. There is a calm to the night because autumn is a time of stillness, and even the callous city respects the death of summer. Coat collars are lifted higher, hands are blown upon, hats are tilted lower. The wind is the only sound in the streets, and the citizens walk hastily because they are anxious to get indoors, anxious for the smell of cooking food, and the attacking force of steam heat hissing in radiators, anxious for the arms of loved ones.

Dusk is upon the city.

It will be dark soon.

It will be good to get home before it grows dark.

# 4.

**IN THE DOUGLAS** King living room, the telephone rang. King crossed the room quickly, picked up the receiver, and said, 'Hanley?'

A voice on the other end said, 'Who?'

'Oh. Oh, excuse me, I was expecting another call,' King said. 'Who is this, please?'

'All right, Mac,' the voice said. 'I'm going to make this short and—'

There's no one named Mac here,' King said. 'You must have the wrong number.' He replaced the phone and turned toward the steps. Cameron was standing there, watching him.

'Not Hanley?' Cameron said.

'No. Somebody got the wrong number.' King snapped his fingers. 'About wrong numbers, Pete.'

'Yeah?'

'Were you talking to George Benjamin a little while ago?'

'On the phone do you mean?' Cameron asked.

'Yes.'

'As a matter of fact, I was.'

'Why'd you call him?'

'To tell him I wouldn't be around tomorrow. He wanted to discuss that sales letter on the new Far Eastern Brocade line.'

'You didn't tell him you were going to Boston, did you?'

'Why, no. Should I have?'

'Hell, no. What *did* you tell him?'

'Just that I'd have to skip the meeting because I was going out of town.'

'But you didn't mention Boston?'

'Is Boston that important?' Diane asked. 'Can Benjamin smash your deal if he knows where it is?'

'I doubt it. But he'd give his eye teeth to know *who* I'm dealing with – or even that there is a deal cooking. You know, once this thing goes through, I'll be in a position to . . .'

The telephone rang again.

'There it is now,' King said, and he walked quickly to the phone.

'I'd better call for Bobby,' Diane said. 'It's beginning to get dark.'

'Honey, wait until I take this call, will you? I don't want you yelling in the background.' He lifted the receiver. 'Hello?'

'Ready on your call to Boston,' the operator said.

'Okay,' King said.

'Go ahead, sir. Your party is on the line.'

'Hello, Doug?'

'How'd you make out, Hanley?'

'It's all set,' Hanley said wearily. 'I got that five per cent for you.'

'Great! On margin? You got it on margin?'

'Just the way you wanted it, Doug. How soon can you get that cheque up here?'

'I'll send Pete up immediately. Reserve a room for him. Pete, what'd you find out about those planes?'

'Flights leaving Perry Field every hour on the hour.'

'Good.' King looked at his watch. 'Can you make a nine o'clock plane?'

'If you say so,' Cameron said.

'Hanley,' King said into the phone, 'he'll be on the nine o'clock plane. I don't know what time it arrives. You check with the terminal there.'

'Right.'

'And Hanley?'

'Yes, Doug?'

'Good work, boy.' He hung up. 'Now we move!' he said excitedly. 'Pete, call the airline and get that reservation right away!' He snapped his fingers, pushed a button in the face of the phone, lifted the receiver, paused a moment, and then said, 'Reynolds, get over here, will you? On the double.'

'Is everything all set now?' Cameron asked. 'Can you tell me about it now?'

'Now that it's in the bag, I'd even tell Benj – No, no, I guess I wouldn't.' He began chuckling. Quickly he walked to the bar and poured himself a drink.

'I'd better get Bobby,' Diane said. 'Look at how dark it's getting.'

'Let it wait a minute, Diane. Don't you want to hear this?'

'Yes, but—'

'Honey, the boy is in his own back yard, for God's sake.'

'Well . . . all right. But I really . . .'

'You heard Benjamin spouting off, didn't you, Pete? Said that I had thirteen per cent of the voting stock, am I right?'

'Right.'

'Wrong!' King said. He paused, anticipating the dropping of his bombshell. 'I've been buying stock quietly for the past six years. Right now, right this minute, I've got *twenty-eight* per cent of it.'

'Doug, that's wonderful!' Diane said.

'But where does Boston come in?' Cameron asked.

'When did we go up there, Diane? Two weeks ago? Hanley's been there since, lining this up, working on a guy who owns what I call a "disinterested" chunk of voting stock.'

Quickly he crossed to a dropleaf desk in the corner, opened it, and pulled a chequebook toward him. Sitting at the desk, he began filling out the cheque.

'How much of a chunk?' Cameron asked.

'Nineteen per cent.'

'Whaaat!'

'Add it up. Nineteen and twenty-eight make forty-seven. That's enough to swing any election my way, even if those idiots should try to work out something with the Old Man. Enough to make me president of Granger! That means I'll run the company my way, and I'll make whatever damn shoes I want to make!' He ripped the cheque from the book triumphantly and handed it to Cameron. 'Here,' he said, 'take a look at this.'

Cameron took the cheque and emitted a long, low whistle.

'Seven hundred and fifty thousand dollars,' he said, awed.

'And that's on a fifty per cent margin. That stock is costing me a million and a half bucks before this is over and done with. But it's worth it, believe me!'

'Doug, where'd you ever . . . ?'

'I've converted damn near everything we own into cash, Diane. I've even taken a mortgage on this house.'

'A mor—' Diane stared at King speechlessly and then sat, suddenly overwhelmed.

'That's . . . that's a mighty big pile of money,' Cameron said.

'Everything I own! And a tight scrape at that, believe me. I couldn't have got it for a penny less. Diane, this deal is going to make me.'

'I . . . I hope so, Doug.'

'It can't miss, honey. Nobody can stop me now.'

'Who are you buying the stock from, Doug?' Cameron asked.

'A guy who cornered it on the q.t., and who doesn't give a damn how we run the company. He'd just as soon have the cash as—'

'Who?' Cameron said. 'What's his name, Doug?'

'The beautiful part is that he's got the stock spread over about two dozen proxies. Besides us, there isn't a soul who knows he controls such a big chunk.'

'Who? Who is he?' Cameron said.

There was a slight cough at the end of the room. King turned toward the dining room. 'Ah, Reynolds, there you are,' he said. 'I want you to drive Mr Cameron to the airport.'

'What's the rush, Doug?' Cameron said. 'I haven't even got my reservation yet.'

'Well, then get on it right away, will you?'

'And *I'd* better get on Bobby right away,' Diane said. She went to the front door and opened it. 'Bobby!' she called. 'Bobby!'

'We'll have to wait until Mr Cameron makes his

reservation, Reynolds,' King said. 'That shouldn't take too long.'

'Bobby!' Diane called. 'Bob-by!'

The telephone rang. King picked it up.

'Hello?' he said.

'King?'

'Yes, this is Mr King.' He covered the mouthpiece and turned to Pete. 'Come on, Pete, get moving. There isn't much time to lose.'

At the same instant, the voice on the other end said, 'Don't hang up on me this time, King. We're not fooling around here.'

'What? I'm sorry,' King said. 'What did you say?'

'We've got your son, King.'

'My *son*? What are you . . . ?' He turned quickly toward the door.

'Bob-by!' Diane called. 'Bobby, will you *please* answer me?'

'Your son, we've kidnapped your son,' the voice said.

'You . . . you have my son?'

Diane whirled from the open doorway. 'What? What did you say?'

'My . . . my son?' King repeated blankly.

'For the last time, we got your son Bobby. Is that clear?'

'But that's . . . that's impossible.'

'*What is it, Doug?*' Diane shrieked.

'Your son was in the woods, wasn't he?'

'Yes, but— This isn't a joke, is it? If this is a joke . . .'

'This ain't a joke, King.'

'Doug, will you please, please tell me what . . .'

He motioned for her to be silent as the voice on the

phone droned on flatly. 'Now listen and listen hard because I'm only going to say this once. The kid's safe. He'll stay that way as long as you do what we say. We want five hundred thousand dollars in unmarked—'

'Just a minute, I want to take this down.' He reached over for a pencil and pad, snaring them from the desk top, the phone's wire extended to its outermost limits. 'Five hundred thou—'

'In unmarked bills,' the voice said, 'small denominations. You got that?'

'Yes, yes. I've . . . Are you sure you haven't harmed him?'

'He's okay. No consecutive serial numbers on those bills, King. Get the money by tomorrow morning, understand. We'll call you then with further instructions. Don't call the police, King.'

'No. No, I won't.'

'You understand?'

'Yes, dammit. I understand you completely.' Desperately, King's mind searched for a means of trapping the caller. When the idea finally came to him, he executed it swiftly and suddenly, as if he were consummating a long-awaited business deal.

'Okay then,' the voice said, 'five hundred thousand dollars in . . .' and King brought his finger down on the receiver bar, cutting off the connection. He whirled from the phone and shouted, 'Pete, get on the kitchen phone. Call the police first. Tell them Bobby's been kidnapped and we've had a five-hundred-thousand-dollar ransom demand.'

'No!' Diane screamed. '*No!*'

'Then call the phone company. Tell them I hung up on the bastard—'

'Why did you do that? You hung up on the man who has Bobby? You hung up on . . . ?' She could not complete the sentence. She rushed to the front door again and screamed into the gathering darkness, 'Bobby! Bobby! *Bobby!*'

'I hung up on the off chance that he'll call back,' King said. 'The phone company may be able to trace it – and in the meantime, I can think. I can . . .' He paused. 'Reynolds, get my address book upstairs. There's a private detective we used once, when Diane's pearls were missing. Di Bari, something like that, his name is in the book. Call him and get him out here right away.'

'Yes, sir.' Reynolds raced for the steps.

Diane slammed the door and ran to where King stood in the centre of the room. 'Five hundred thousand, you said. All right, call the bank. Right away! Call them this minute, Doug. We've got to get the money to them. We've got to get Bobby back!'

'We will get him back. I'll give them whatever they want, a million if they want it. I'll raise it.' He took Diane into his arms. 'Don't worry, darling. Please, please, try to stop trembling. Try to . . .'

'I'll . . . be all right. It's . . . it's . . .'

Cameron rushed in from the kitchen. 'Police are on their way over, Doug,' he said. 'Phone company standing by. Says to contact them on another line as soon as he calls again.'

'Okay, get in the kitchen. When this phone rings, get the operator to work right away.'

'Right!' Cameron said, and he rushed out of the room again.

Reynolds came down the steps, a defeated expression

on his face. 'I can't find that address book anywhere, sir,' he said. 'I'm sorry. I looked through the telephone table, but . . .'

'I'll get it,' Diane said. With a visible effort, she pulled back her shoulders, moved away from King, and started for the steps. As she passed the front door, it burst open suddenly, startling her.

'Were you calling me, Mom?' Bobby King said.

She blinked her eyes in disbelief. 'Bobby?' she said. And then the name bubbled into her throat with certainty – 'Bobby, Bobby, Bobby!' – and she ran to him and dropped to her knees and pulled him close.

'Hey, what's the matter?' Bobby said.

King looked at his son in puzzlement. 'How . . .' he started, and then he turned toward the phone and pointed a menacing finger at it and shouted, 'Why, that rotten lying . . .'

'I don't want to play with Jeff any more, Mom,' Bobby said. 'I went up a tree like Daddy told me, but it didn't work. I couldn't see him anywhere.'

'What do you mean?' King said and there was sudden fresh alarm in his voice. He glanced at the phone sharply. 'What do you mean, you couldn't see him? Where is he?'

'I'll bet he left the woods,' Bobby said. 'I looked all over, behind every rock. I don't want to play with him any more. He's not anywhere around. I don't know *where* he is!'

There was a moment of stunned silence. The name was on everyone's lips, the truth was in everyone's mind, but it was the boy's father who finally spoke the word, the single word, the name that summed up simply and explicitly everything that had taken place in the woods outside, the name that explained the phone call from a stranger.

'Jeff,' Reynolds said, and the name emerged from his lips as a thin whisper.

In the distance, they could hear a siren coming closer and closer to the cloistered sanctuary that was Smoke Rise.

# 5.

**IF THERE WERE** two things that gave Steve Carella the willies, those two things were cases involving extreme wealth and cases involving children. He was not a product of the city's slums and so he couldn't attribute his money willies to a childhood of deprivation. His baker father, Antonio, had always earned a decent living, and Carella had never known the bite of a cold wind on the seat of a pair of threadbare pants. And yet, in the presence of luxury that screamed of wealth, in the drawing rooms and sitting rooms and studies to which his work sometimes took him, Carella felt uneasy. He felt poor. He was not poor, and he'd never been poor, and even if he'd had no money at all he still wouldn't have been poor, but sitting in the Douglas King living room, facing the man who could afford a layout like this one, Steve Carella felt penniless and destitute and somewhat intimidated.

And to top it all off, this looked like a bona fide kidnapping. Even if Carella were not the father of a pair of twins which his wife Teddy had delivered to him this past summer, even if he were not experiencing the first joys of fatherhood, a kidnapping was a damn frightening thing and he wanted no part of it.

Unfortunately, he had no choice.

He sat in the King living room, intimidated, troubled, and he asked his questions while Meyer Meyer looked through the window facing the River Harb, his back to the room.

'Let me get this straight, Mr King,' he said. 'The boy who was kidnapped is *not* your son, is that right?'

'That's right.'

'But the ransom demand was made to you, is that also right?'

'Yes.'

'Then, when the demand was made, the kidnapper thought he was in possession of your son.'

'It would seem so, yes.'

'Were there any further calls?'

'No.'

'Then he may still believe he has your son?'

'I don't know what he believes,' King said angrily. 'Is there really any necessity for all these questions? I am not the boy's father, and I—'

'No, but you're the one who spoke to the kidnapper.'

'That's true.'

'And he asked for five hundred thousand dollars, is that right, Mr King?'

'Yes, yes, yes, Mr Caretta, that's right.'

'Carella.'

'I'm sorry. Carella.'

'This was a man? The person who called.'

'It was a man.'

'When he spoke to you, did he say "*I* have your son" or "*We* have your son"? Would you remember?'

'I don't remember. And I don't see why it's important. *Somebody* has Reynolds' boy, and all this damn semantic—'

'That's exactly it, Mr King,' Carella said. 'Somebody has the boy, and we'd like to find out who that somebody is. You see, we *have* to find out if we're to get that boy back safely. Now that's pretty important to us. Getting the boy back safely, I mean. I'm sure it's just as important to you.'

'Of course it is,' King snapped. 'Why don't you call in the F.B.I., for God's sake? You people aren't equipped to deal with something like this! A boy is kidnapped and . . .'

'Seven days have to elapse before the F.B.I. can enter the case,' Carella said. 'We'll notify them at once, of course, but they can't step in before then. In the meantime, we'll do our best to—'

'Why can't they come in sooner? I thought kidnapping was a Federal offence. Instead of a bunch of local Keystone cops, we could—'

'It's a Federal offence because after seven days have elapsed they can automatically assume a state line has been crossed. Up until that time, it remains in the jurisdiction of the state in which the crime was committed. And in this state, in this city, the local precinct handles the crime. That goes for kidnapping, assault, murder, or what have you.'

'Am I to understand then,' King said, 'that we're going to treat a kidnapping, where a boy's life is in danger, the same way we'd treat a . . . a . . . a fifty-cent item stolen from Woolworth's?'

'Not exactly, Mr King. We've already phoned back to the squad. Lieutenant Byrnes himself is on the way over. As soon as we know a little bit more about—'

'Excuse me, Steve,' Meyer said. 'If we're gonna get a teletype out, I'd better get a description from the boy's father.'

'Yeah,' Carella said. 'Where *is* Mr Reynolds, Mr King?'

'In his apartment. Over the garage. He's taking this pretty badly.'

'Want me to handle it, Meyer?'

'No, no, that's all right.' Meyer glanced significantly at King. 'You seem to have your hands full right here. Where's the garage, Mr King?'

'On the side of the house. You can't miss it.'

'I'll be there if you need me, Steve.'

'Okay,' Carella answered. He turned his attention back to King as Meyer went out of the house. 'Did you notice anything peculiar about this man's voice, Mr King? A lisp, a noticeable accent, a dialect, or . . .'

'I'm sorry, Mr Caretta,' King said, 'but I refuse to play this little game any longer. I honestly don't see what—'

'It's Carella, and what little game were you referring to, Mr King?'

'This cops-and-robbers nonsense. Now what the hell difference could it possibly make whether or not the man lisped or spoke in beautifully cultured English or babbled like a moron? How is that going to get Jeff Reynolds back to his father?'

Carella did not raise his eyes from his notebook. He kept staring at the page upon which he'd been writing, and he kept telling himself it would not seem fitting for a police officer to get up and punch Mr Douglas King in the mouth. Softly, evenly, he said, 'What do you do for a living, Mr King?'

'I run a shoe factory,' King said. 'Is this another one of your very pertinent questions?'

'Yes, Mr King. It is one of my very pertinent

questions. I don't know a thing about shoes, Mr King, except I have to wear them so I won't get tacks in my feet. I wouldn't dream of going into your factory and telling your employees how to nail a sole or glue a heel or sew whatever it is they sew.'

'I get your message,' King said dryly.

'You only get *part* of it, Mr King. You only get the part that's warning you . . .'

'*Warning* me!'

'. . . warning you to cut out what might be misinterpreted as resisting an officer or impeding the progress of an investigation. That's the part you get, and now I'm going to tell you the other part, and I hope both parts penetrate, Mr King, because I'm here to do a job and intend to do it with or without your help. I'm assuming you know how to run a shoe factory or you wouldn't be living here in Smoke Rise with a chauffeur whose son can be mistaken for yours in a kidnapping. Okay. You have no reason to assume I'm a good cop or a bad cop or even an indifferent cop. Most of all, you have no reason to assume I'm a silly cop.'

'I never—'

'To clear up any doubts which may be lingering in your mind, Mr King, I'll tell you now flatly and immodestly that I *am* a good cop, I am a *damn* good cop. I know my job, and I do it well, and any questions I ask you are not asked because I'm auditioning for *Dragnet*. They're all asked with a reason and a purpose, and you'll make things a hell of a lot easier if you answer them without offering any of your opinions on how the investigation should be conducted. Do you think we understand each other, Mr King?'

'I think we understand each other, Mr Caretta.'

'My name is Carella,' Carella said flatly. 'Did the man who called you have any accent?'

Reynolds sat on the edge of the bed, weeping unashamedly, shaking his head over and over again. Meyer watched him, and he bit his lower lip, and he wanted to put his arm around the man's shoulders, comfort him, tell him that everything would be all right. He could not do this because he knew how unpredictable *all* kidnappings were, the boy could be killed before the kidnappers had carried him five miles from the house. And this particular kidnapping had the added danger of error attached to it. How would the louses react when they discovered they had the wrong boy? And so he could not reassure Reynolds, he could only ask the questions he knew by rote, and he could only hope they did not sound absurd to a man who was torn by grief.

'What is the boy's full name, Mr Reynolds?'

'Jeffry. Jeffry.'

'Is that G-e-o-f or J-e-f-f . . . ?'

'What? Oh. J-e-f-f-r-y. Jeffry.'

'Any middle name?'

'No. None.'

'How old is he, Mr Reynolds?'

'Eight.'

'Birth date?'

'September ninth.'

'Then he was just eight, is that right?'

'Yes. Just eight.'

'How tall is he, Mr Reynolds?'

'I . . .' Reynolds paused. 'I don't know. I never . . . I

don't know. Who ever measures children? Who ever expects something like this to . . .'

'Well, approximately, Mr Reynolds? Three feet? Four feet?'

'I don't know. I don't know.'

'Well, average height for that age is somewhere between four and four and a half feet. He's about average height, isn't he, Mr Reynolds?'

'Yes. Or maybe a little tall. He's a handsome boy. Tall for his age.'

'How much does he weigh, Mr Reynolds?'

'I don't know.'

Meyer sighed. 'What about his build? Stout? Medium? Slim?'

'Slender. Not too stout, and not too thin. Just . . . well built for a boy his age.'

'His complexion, Mr Reynolds? Florid, sallow, pale?'

'I don't know.'

'Well, is he a dark kid?'

'No, no. He has blond hair. Very fair skin. Is that what you mean?'

'Yes, thank you. Fair,' Meyer said, and he made a note. 'Hair, blond.' He paused. 'Colour of his eyes, Mr Reynolds?'

'Will you get him back?' Reynolds asked suddenly.

Meyer stopped writing. 'We're going to try,' he said. 'We're going to try our damnedest, Mr Reynolds.'

The description of the boy was phoned in to the 87th and then transmitted to Headquarters, and the teletype alarm went out to fourteen states. The teletype read:

KIDNAP VICTIM JEFFRY REYNOLDS AGE EIGHT HEIGHT APPROX FIFTY-TWO INCHES WEIGHT APPROX

SIXTY POUNDS XXXXXXXX HAIR BLOND EYES BLUE STRAWBERRY BIRTHMARK RIGHT BUTTOCK XXXXXXXX SCAR LEFT ARM CHILDHOOD INJURY FRACTURE XXXXX FATHER'S NAME CHARLES REYNOLDS XXXX MOTHER DECEASED XXXXXX ANSWERS TO NAME JEFF XXXXXX WEARING BRIGHT RED SWEATER BLUE DUNGAREE TROUSERS WHITE SOX SNEAKERS XXXXX NO HAT XXXXX NO GLOVES XXXXX NO JEWELRY XXXXX MAY BE CARRYING TOY RIFLE XXXXX MAY BE IN COMPANY OF MALE XXXXX LAST SEEN VICINITY SMOKE RISE ISOLA SEVENTEEN HUNDRED THIRTY HOURS STD TIME XXXXX STAND BY FOR FURTHER INSTRUCTION ROAD BLOCK COOPERATION XXXXXX CONTACT HQ COMMAND ISOLA ALL INFO ETC XXXXXXXXXX

The message rolled out of teletype machines in police precincts, state trooper command posts, dinky shacks housing local one-horse police forces, anywhere in the surrounding fourteen states where the law enforcement agencies owned and used a teletype machine. It rolled out on a long white sheet with all the monotony of a foreign newspaper. The message immediately following it on the tape read:

REPORTED STOLEN XXX 1949 FORD SEDAN XXXXX EIGHT CYLS XXXX GREY XXXXX ID NUMBER 59 8L 02303 LICENCE PLATE RN 6120 XXXXXX PARKED SUPERMKT PETER SCHWED DRIVE AND LANSING LANE EIGHT HUNDRED HOURS THIS MORNING XXXX CONTACT ONE-OH-TWO PCT RIVERHEAD XXXXX

The grey Ford pulled into the rutted driveway and bounced along the road which had once belonged to a

Sands Spit potato farmer. The road, the land, the farmhouse itself had been sold a long time ago to a man who had purchased the property in the hope that the development boom would reach this isolated neck of the city's suburb. The development boom had come nowhere near reaching the erstwhile potato farm. The speculator, in fact, dropped dead before his dream was realized, and the farm and its adjacent lands, cropless now, run-down, slowly succumbing to the overwhelming encroachment of nature, was handled by a real-estate agent who managed the property for the speculator's daughter, a drunken hag of forty-seven who lived in the city and slept with sailors of all ages. The agent considered it quite a coup when he managed to rent the old farmhouse for a month in the middle of October. Suckers weren't that plentiful in the fall of the year. In the summertime, he could tell prospective tenants that the farm was near the beaches – which it wasn't, being in the centre of Sands Spit and nowhere near either of the peninsula's two shores – and possibly inveigle a city dweller or two into occupying the decrepit wreck for a while. But as soon as Labour Day rolled around, the agent's hopes vanished. The drunken daughter of the speculator would have to find other means of buying her whisky and her sailors. There would be no income from the sagging farmhouse until summer once more returned to Sands Spit. His delight at renting the hulk in the middle of October knew no bounds. Nor did he ever once realize the careful planning that had preceded the rental. He was not a man to look a gift horse in the mouth. Cash was paid on the line. He asked no questions, and expected no answers. Besides, the tenants seemed like a nice young couple. If they wanted to freeze their behinds off in the middle of nowhere, that was their business. His business, like that of the landholders of old, was simply to collect the tithes, man, simply to collect the tithes.

The Ford's headlights probed the blackness of the road, swept the grey farmhouse, the beam swinging around as the car took the curve and then came to a full-braked halt. The engine died. The lights went out. The door on the driver's side opened and a young man in his late twenties stepped into the darkness and ran toward the front door. He knocked gently, three times, and then waited.

'Eddie?' a woman's voice asked.

'It's me, Kathy. Open up.'

The door opened wide. Light splashed onto the frozen earth. The girl looked out into the yard.

'Sy?' she said.

'In the car. He'll be here. Ain't you gonna kiss me?'

'Oh, Eddie, Eddie,' she said, and she threw herself into his arms. She was a woman no older than twenty-four, nor was she a woman who could conceivably be called a 'girl' of twenty-four. For whereas there was a delicate loveliness to her face, the beauty had been overlaid with a veneer of hardness, the look of shellac worn thin, marred by years of use and misuse. Kathy Folsom was a *woman* of twenty-four and perhaps, perhaps she had even been a woman of twelve at one time. She wore a straight black skirt and a blue sweater, the sleeves shoved up to her elbows. Her hair was obviously bleached, showing dark at the roots and at the part, but on Kathy it somehow did not appear cheap, it only seemed untended, uncared for. She held her husband to her with a desperation that had been mounting ever since he had left the farmhouse that afternoon. She kissed him longingly, her arms wrapped around his waist, and then she drew away from him and stared up into his face, and she smiled with a tenderness that was embarrassing even to herself, and then, to cover her embarrassment, she touched his cheek quickly and said again, 'Eddie, Eddie,' and then, sharply, 'Are you all right? Did everything go all right?'

'Everything went fine,' Eddie said. 'How about here? Any troubles?'

'No, none. I was sitting on pins and needles. I kept thinking, This is the last one; please, God, don't let anything go wrong.'

'Well everything went just the way we figured it.' He paused. 'You got a cigarette, honey?'

'In my bag. On the chair there.'

He crossed to the chair quickly and rummaged in her purse. She watched him as he lighted the cigarette, a tall good-looking man wearing dark slacks and sports jacket, a white shirt open at the throat, a maroon sweater over the shirt.

'I was listening to the radio,' Kathy said. 'I thought they might mention something. I mean, after all, a bank and all.' She paused. 'It went all right, didn't it? There was no trouble?'

'No trouble.' He blew out a stream of smoke. 'Only, Kathy, you see . . . well . . . we didn't exactly . . .'

She kissed him again, swiftly, as if unable to keep her lips from his a moment longer. 'You're back,' she whispered. 'That's all that matters.'

'In here, kid,' the voice said, and there was a push in the voice, and a physical push in the hands of the man owning the voice. Jeff Reynolds stumbled into the room, and the man behind him chuckled and then slammed the door behind him, and then said, 'Ah, home again! How do you like it, kid? It ain't much, but it reeks, don't it?' He chuckled again. His laugh seemed to match his appearance. He was forty-two years old, nattily dressed in a dark suit, though badly in need of a shave. There was a curious air about him, the air of a man who is enjoying himself at the firm's annual picnic.

'Where's my gun?' Jeff said, and Kathy turned at the sound of his voice and then looked at him in bewilderment. He did not seem at all frightened, a little wide-eyed perhaps, slightly upset by the strange surroundings, but otherwise content.

'The boy wants his gun,' Sy said, smiling. 'Where's the gun we promised him?'

Kathy kept staring at Jeff. 'Who . . . who the hell . . . ?' she started, and Sy's grin expanded into a chuckle and then a gust of exuberant laughter.

'Ahhhh, look, Eddie, look at that beautiful piece of surprise on her face. Oh, man, this tickles me!'

'Let me handle this, Sy,' Eddie said.

'Where's the gun?' Jeff said. 'Come on, I have to be getting back.' He turned to Kathy. 'Have *you* got the gun?'

'Wh-what gun?' she answered automatically, and then she shouted, 'Who is this kid? Where . . . ?'

'Who is he?' Sy said, grinning. 'What a question to ask. Where's your manners, doll? We bring a guest home, and right away you get personal.'

She whirled on her husband instantly. 'Eddie, who . . . ?'

'Permit me, please,' Sy said, bowing from the waist. 'Son, this is Kathy Folsom, née Kathy Neal, pride of the

South Side. Beautiful, ain't she? Feast your eyes. Kathy, this is King—' he paused, reaching, and then said '—of the wild frontier!' exploding into a fresh gale of laughter, convulsed by his own humour.

'What's he talking about, Eddie? Where'd you get this boy? What's he doing here? Why . . . ?'

'I'll bet you haven't got a gun at all,' Jeff said.

'We ain't, huh?' Sy answered, 'Kid, we got enough artillery here to start a second Civil War. If General Lee had himself so many guns, we'd be asking your old man for *Confederate* bills right now.' He laughed again, a laugh of defiance which he tossed at Kathy as if challenging her intelligence. The challenge was unnecessary. The reference to bills had not escaped her. The meaning was instantly and shockingly clear. She turned to her husband and said, 'Eddie, you haven't . . .'

'Come on, kid,' Sy said. 'Let's get that gun.' He shoved Jeff to the door leading from the large parlour-kitchen of the farmhouse to one of the bedrooms. 'The gun and trophy room is right this way,' he said. 'All the comforts of home, huh?'

She waited until the door closed behind them. Then she said to Eddie, 'All right, tell me about it.'

'It's what it looks like,' Eddie said. His voice was low. He would not raise his eyes to meet hers.

'Have you lost your mind?' she asked. 'Have you gone completely out of your mind?'

'Relax now, will you? Just try to relax a little.'

Trembling to maintain control, Kathy walked stiffly to her purse, opened it, shook free a cigarette, which fell instantly from her fingers, managed to keep one in her hand while she lighted it, and then said, 'All right. I'm listening.'

'It's a snatch,' Eddie said simply.

'Why?'

'Whatya mean, why? There's five hundred grand involved here.'

'You said . . .'

'Do you need more reason than that? For Christ's sake, this is—'

'You said a bank. That was bad enough, but at least . . .'

'I was lying. It never was a bank. I only said that. We didn't go anywhere near a bank.'

'No, I see you didn't. Don't you know how serious this is, Eddie? Kidnapping is a Federal offence! You can get the electric chair for this!'

'Only if the kid ain't returned before the case goes to trial.'

'You're already in the courtroom and this is the first I'm even *hearing* of it! How long have you been planning this thing?'

'About . . . about six months now.'

'Whaaat?'

'Now look, calm down. There's no sense getting excited.'

'Who is he?'

'Bobby King.'

'And who's Bobby King?'

'His old man is a big wheel in Granger Shoe. You know the company, hon. They put out these expensive shoes for dames.'

'Yes, I know the company.' She was silent for a moment. Then, very softly, she said, 'Why didn't you tell me what you were planning?'

'Well, I didn't think you'd go along with it. I figured . . .'

'Damn right I won't go along with it!' Kathy shouted. 'Get that boy out of here this minute! Take him back where you got him!'

'How can we do that?' Eddie said. 'Come on, be sensible, will you?'

'If you don't take him back, *I* will.'

'Yeah, sure.'

'His parents must be going crazy by now. How could you do a thing—'

'Now shut up a minute, will you?' Eddie said harshly. 'He's staying right here until we get the loot, so that's that, so just shut up.'

Kathy walked to an ash tray and stubbed out her cigarette. She went to the window then and stared out at the front yard.

Eddie watched her. Gently, he said, 'Kathy?'

'You told me to shut up, didn't you?'

'Honey, there's five hundred grand in this,' he said plaintively. 'Can't you . . .'

'I don't want it.'

'Half for us, half for Sy.'

'Not any part of it! I wouldn't touch it!'

'It'll take us to Mexico.'

The hell with you and Mexico!'

'I don't understand you,' Eddie said, shaking his head. 'You said you *wanted* to go to Mexico.'

'And you said this was the last time,' she shouted, whirling from the window. The last one, you said, that's what *you* said. A bank. A simple bank. Just to set us up in—'

'All right!' Eddie said triumphantly. 'All right, it *is*

the last one. Now how about that? Five hundred thousand dollars! An express train right to Acapulco!'

'On a kidnapping! Couldn't you think of a filthier, more rotten . . .'

'A kidnapping, so what? Did we hurt the kid? Did we touch him? He's fine, ain't he?'

Remembering the boy, Kathy turned toward the bedroom door. 'What's Sy doing to him in there?' she said, and she began walking toward the door instantly.

Eddie caught her arm. 'He's all right. Sy promised him a real gun. That's how we got him here. Look honey, try to understand this, will you?'

'I don't want to understand anything about it. Dammit, don't you draw the line anyplace? What *gave* you this crazy idea to begin with? What the hell possibly gave you . . . ?'

'I just got it, that's all. We worked it out.'

'*Who* worked it out? You?' She paused. 'Or Sy?'

'We worked it out together.' He studied her face for a moment and then said, 'Well, look, what's the sense risking our necks on a stickup, huh? This is safer, ain't it? We borrow a kid, and when we return him we get five hundred grand. Now ain't that safer?'

'Borrow? Who said that? Sy?'

'No, no, for Pete's sake, I told you we worked this out together.'

'Did you, Eddie?'

'Yes. Yes.'

'You're lying, Eddie. It was Sy's idea, wasn't it?'

Well . . .'

Wasn't it?'

'Well, it was.' Then hastily, he said, 'But it's a good idea, Kathy, can't you see that? We can really quit after this one, I mean it, honey. Now look, honey, I mean it – this is the last one. Look, I can . . . I can maybe really get to be something in Mexico. Hey now, wouldn't that be great, huh? Eddie Folsom, huh? Me. Something, you know?'

'Eddie, Eddie,' she said, 'don't you even realize what you've done?'

'Honey, look, believe me, this is gonna be all right. I promise you, Kathy. Now, have I ever let you down, huh? Just stick with me, honey, willya? Please?'

She did not answer.

'Honey?'

She still did not answer.

'Aw, honey, please try to . . .'

'Bang!' Jeff shouted, and he ran into the room carrying a shotgun, Sy grinning behind him. 'Wow, what a gun!'

'The kid likes guns,' Sy said, laughing. 'Play with the gun, kid. Get to know it.'

'Sy, is that loaded?' Kathy said, alarmed.

'Now would I give a loaded gun to a mere child?' Sy asked. He clucked his tongue in imitation of an old lady.

'It sure *is* loaded, lady,' Jeff said. He aimed the gun and yelled, 'Bang! Right between the eyes!'

'Okay, kid, knock it off,' Sy said. 'Slow down a little.' He frowned momentarily and then said, 'How about tuning in the monster, Eddie?'

Eddie looked at Kathy helplessly, as if begging her with his eyes to understand. But she would not understand, and he read that on her face, and despondently he said, 'Sure, Sy,' and walked to the far wall of the parlour and immediately pulled a tarpaulin covering from a mass of radio equipment which was stacked against the wall.

'Kid,' Sy said to Jeff, 'this is Dr Frankenstein. Watch him bring that monster to life.'

The equipment did not, in truth, resemble a monster. There was however, some validity to Sy's allusion, in that the dials and switches, the needles and knobs would not have seemed inappropriate in a scientist's laboratory. Eddie walked to the setup and threw a switch.

'Go ahead, show off for the kid,' Sy said. 'Tell him what frequency the police calls are on.'

Absorbed with tuning the receiver, Eddie replied, 'Thirty-seven point fourteen megacycles.'

'Oh, the brain on that doctor,' Sy said. 'Kathy, you hooked yourself a prize, a real prize.'

'Why'd you drag my husband into this?' Kathy said tightly. 'Why didn't you leave him alone?'

'Drag? Who, me? He come in willingly, sweetheart.' A high piercing shriek erupted from the receiver. 'There she goes, kid,' Sy said. 'The monster's beginnin' to speak.'

'Hey, that's really something,' Jeff said. 'Where'd you get it?'

'I built it,' Eddie answered.

'No kidding? Boy, that musta been hard.'

'Well, it . . .' Struggling with his pleasure, reluctant to sound too proud, Eddie said, 'It wasn't *too* hard.'

'Nothing's hard for a mastermind, huh, Kathy?' Sy said. 'You're a real electronic wizard, ain't you, Eddie? That's why the little woman loves you. Learned it all in reform school, too, didn't you?'

'Cut it out,' Kathy said.

'What's the matter? I'm complimenting your husband. Someday, kid, Eddie's gonna go to a real school, be a regular schoolboy and learn radio inside out and backwards. Ain't that right, Eddie. Tell the kid here.'

Embarrassed, Eddie said, 'Yeah, that's right.'

'Thomas Alva Frankenstein, that's who he is, sonny. You want to learn how to build a set like that and have all the dames fall for you, kid?'

'I'll say I do!' Jeff said.

'Okay, then here's how. When you're fifteen years old, hold up a grocery store.'

'Sy, what are you telling him?' Kathy snapped.

'What's the matter?' Sy asked innocently. 'You don't even need a gun, kid. Just stick your hand in your pocket like Eddie did. When they catch you, they'll send you over to Youth House, and then to Children's Court, and then to reform school. Am I right, Eddie?'

More embarrassed now, twisting the radio dial intently, Eddie said, 'Yeah, that's right. Sure.'

'In reform school,' Sy concluded, 'they'll teach you how to make radios. Am I right, Eddie?'

'Only how to fix them.'

'I don't see anything funny about this, Sy,' Kathy said.

'Who's being funny? I'm teaching the kid a trade. Shall I tell him all the other things you learned in reform school, Eddie? The other *trades*?'

'Aw, tell him whatever the hell you want to.'

'Now, now, watch your language in front of the boy,' Sy said. He grinned and tousled Jeff's hair. 'Me, kid, all I ever learned was how to work in the jute mill. You ever work with jute? Don't. It makes you sneeze. It crawls into your lungs. It even crawls up your asshole.' Sy began laughing. 'How's it coming, Doctor?'

'I'm getting it,' Eddie said, and the radio suddenly erupted into intelligible sound.

'*. . . thirteen. Accident at Morrison and North Ninety-eight. Car 303, signal thirteen. Accident at Morrison and North Ninety-eight.*'

'*This is 303. Okay.*'

'A snatch right under their noses,' Sy said, 'and they're worried about a traffic jam.'

'Hey, you going to take me back now?' Jeff asked.

'I'm busy, kid.'

Jeff turned to Kathy. 'How about you?' He studied her for a moment, frankly, candidly. Then, having formed his opinion, he said, 'Aw, you're a girl. What can girls do?'

Sy burst out laughing. 'Kid,' he said, 'you'd be surprised.'

'*Car 207, Car 207*,' the police dispatcher said. '*Signal thirteen, join and assist Car 204 at Douglas King estate, Smoke Rise, adjacent River Highway on Smoke Rise Road. Signal thirteen, join and assist . . .*'

'Hey, did you hear that?' Jeff said, excited by his discovery. 'He said Douglas King!'

'*. . . Smoke Rise, adjacent River Highway on Smoke Rise Road.*'

'*This is 207. Right.*'

'The long arm of the law is beginning to reach,' Sy said. 'What'd I tell you? Ask those crumbs not to call the cops, and it's the first thing they do.' He shook his head sadly. 'You can't trust nobody nowadays.'

'Do you really expect to get away with this, Sy?' Kathy asked.

'Why, certainly. And all because Dr Frankenstein has ideas. Me, I got a worthless hobby. Swing music. Can swing music help us on a thing like this? Can Harry James blow his way out of this one? Ahhh, but Eddie's hobby, a dream, a dream. Radios.' He closed his thumb against his fingers and then kissed the collective bunch. 'I love them. I love radios. I love Eddie.' He paused. 'I even love you, Kathy. Outline it for her, Doctor.'

'She doesn't want to hear it,' Eddie said.

'She don't?' Sy said, surprised. 'What's the matter, baby, you coldhearted or something? This gig's gonna go down in history, believe me. And all because Eddie knows radio. Right now, we're listening to the bulls on his monster there. But later . . . Man, when I think of this scheme, it gives me goose bumps.'

'Sy, she's not interested,' Eddie said.

'I'm interested in anything you do,' Kathy said softly.

'Why, sure she is. The little woman. Okay,' Sy said, 'we called King on the way here. Told him we wanted five hundred grand, told him to get it ready by—'

Jeff blinked. 'Did you say you called . . . ?'

'Shut up, kid. Told him to get it ready by tomorrow morning, and we'd call him then to let him know where and when the drop's gonna be. Now here's the beauty part, honey. You listening?'

'I'm listening.'

'Okay. Tomorrow morning, we buzz King again. We tell him—'

'Are you talking about—' Jeff started, and Sy shouted, 'I said shut up, kid, now take a goddamn hint!' He glared at Jeff heatedly.

Jeff put his hands on his hips, swaggered over to Sy and, entering into the game, using his best tough-guy voice, said, 'Who do you think you are, Mac?'

'Blow kid, before you get hurt.'

Still playing, Jeff said, 'You want to get tough with me, mister?'

'I said blow!' Sy shoved the boy aside angrily. Jeff, startled, stared at him and then frowned. The room was silent. And then piercing the silence, the radio came to life again.

'*Attention all cars, attention all cars. Here's the story on that Smoke Rise kidnapping.*'

'Hey, listen,' Eddie said.

'*Be on the lookout for a blond, eight-year-old boy wearing bright-red sweater, blue dungaree trousers, white socks and sneakers, no hat, no gloves, may be carrying a toy rifle.*'

'You're famous, kid,' Sy said, grinning.

'*The boy's name is Jeffry Reynolds, answers to the name Jeff . . .*'

'What?' Eddie said.

'That man said my name,' Jeff said, startled.

'Shut up!' Sy snapped.

'*. . . is the son of Charles Reynolds, chauffeur on the King estate. There's been some kind of a foul-up here, boys, and your guess is as good as mine. There's been a five-hundred-thousand-dollar ransom demand, so chances are the kidnappers don't know who they've got yet. Beats me. Anyway, that's the story, and that's all.*'

'What's he talking about, Sy?' Eddie said. Panic had covered his face like a coat of white paint. He stared at Sy, his eyes demanding an answer, his entire body demanding an answer.

'That man said my name,' Jeff said, astonished.

'They're lying,' Sy said quickly. 'They're trying to put one over on us.'

'On police radio, Sy? They don't even know we're listening!'

'No, all they know is they want to get us, so they're pulling a cheap trick. And don't think King ain't in on this. That crooked bastard!'

'How could we have grabbed the wrong kid?' Eddie wailed.

'He *ain't* the wrong kid!'

'But suppose he is?' Kathy said calmly. 'It means you've done all this for nothing. We're in trouble for nothing.'

Eddie looked at his wife, and then at Sy. 'You . . . you gonna believe what the cops tell you?' he said. 'Kathy, you can't believe *them*!'

'Who can you believe? Sy?'

'Why not?' Sy said. 'I say this kid is Bobby King. Now how about that?'

'Me?' Jeff said, puzzled. 'I'm not Bobby.'

'One more peep out of you—'

'Let him talk,' Kathy said. 'What's your name, sonny?'

'Jeff.'

'He's lying!' Sy shouted.

'I am not!' Jeff shouted back. He glared at Sy and then said, 'I don't like you, you know that? I'm going home.'

He started for the door. Sy caught his arm and yanked him back, almost pulling him off his feet. He stood very close to the boy, and there was no humour on his face now, no laughter in his eyes. In a flat, emotionless voice he said, 'What's your name? Your *real* name.'

# 6.

**THE DRIVEWAY TO** the King estate was flanked by two stone pillars, each of which carried an ornate glass-and-wrought-iron lantern. The pillars were set back some three feet from the private Smoke Rise Road which ran past the estate, the communications link between Smoke Rise and the outside world. Between the pillars and the gravel road was a shelf of grass. Grass, in fact, lined both sides of the road, framing the grey ribbon with an October-bitten off-green.

The road was generally barren, especially on nights like this one when October was trying its best to serve as a harbinger of dead winter. A cold wind had come up, blowing off the River Harb, sending everyone but mad dogs, Englishmen, and policemen indoors. There was, perhaps, a slight difference in the motivation of the triumvirate. For whereas mad dogs stayed outside because of the vagaries of insanity, and Englishmen because of their internationally renowned *sang-froid*, the policemen were there under duress. There was not a policeman on that road that night who would not have preferred being at home with a good book, or a good woman, or a good bottle of brandy. There was not a policeman present that night who would not have preferred even a bad book or a bad bottle of brandy or, to be frankly unpatriotic, a bad woman.

There were no women, good or bad, on that road that night.

There were only men, and men engrossed in their work can be dull company to each other even when the weather is mild.

'I never seen it so cold in October in my whole life,' Detective Andy Parker said. 'I been living in this city my whole life, and I never seen it so cold like this. Tonight, they better bring in the brass monkeys, I am telling you. Tonight, everything freezes.'

Detective Cotton Hawes nodded. His fingers around the flashlight, even through the leather, fur-lined gloves he wore, felt frozen to the bone. He kept the circle of light on the patch of grass across the road from the driveway pillars. The lab technician at his feet, a man named Peter Kronig, was a person with whom Hawes had had a slight brush not too long ago. Hawes could not say now whether or not he disliked holding the light for Kronig while Kronig searched the grass on his hands and knees. He knew that he'd ridden Kronig's tail pretty shamefully on their one previous encounter, and he was rather embarrassed by their proximity now. Of course, Hawes had been working at the 87th Precinct for only a short time when he had first run across Kronig. Like any new kid on the block, he was anxious to prove himself to the other kids. In the presence of Steve Carella, whom he immediately considered the best cop on the squad, Hawes had begun riding Kronig at the police lab. Carella had chewed him out later, in a kindly fashion to be sure, and Hawes had learned a valuable lesson: Don't make enemies of the lab technicians. He had learned his lesson well. Its meaning assumed renewed importance now that he was once more working with Kronig.

'Move the light,' Kronig said. 'Over to the left.'

Hawes moved the light.

'It's only sixteen degrees,' Parker said. 'Can you feature that? It feels like twenty below, don't it? But it's only sixteen. I heard it over the radio. Man, it's cold. Ain't it cold, Hawes?'

'Yes,' Hawes answered.

'You don't talk much, do you?'

'I talk,' Hawes said. He did not particularly feel like justifying himself to Andy Parker. He didn't know the man too well, this being the first time they'd been on a squeal together, but from what he'd seen of him around the squadroom, Parker was a man it paid to stay away from. At the same time, Hawes did not want to make the same mistake he'd made with Kronig. He did not want to make an enemy where he could make a friend. 'It's just that my teeth are frozen together,' he added, hoping this would mollify Parker.

Parker nodded. He was a big man, almost as tall as Hawes, who stood six feet two inches high in his bare soles. But whereas Hawes's eyes were blue and his hair was red (except for a white streak over the left temple), Parker gave an impression of darkness, black hair, brown eyes, five o'clock shadow. And, in all honesty, the two men could not have been more dissimilar than their appearances indicated. Hawes was a cop who was still learning. Parker was a cop who knew it all.

'Hey, Kronig,' he said, 'what the hell are you searching for? Buried treasure? We got nothing better to do than crawl around on our hands and knees?'

'Shut up, Parker,' Kronig answered. 'I'm the one

who's doing the crawling. All you're doing is bitching about the weather.'

'What, you ain't cold?' Parker said. 'You got Eskimo blood?' He paused. 'Eskimos lend out their wives, you know that?'

'I know,' Kronig said. 'Let's try over here, Hawes. Come on.'

They moved several feet up the road, the flashlight playing on the grassy shoulder lining the gravel.

'It's the truth,' Parker said, 'whether you know it or not. An Eskimo goes to visit another Eskimo, he lets you borrow his wife for the night. So you shouldn't get cold.' Parker shook his head. 'And they call *us* civilized. Would you lend me your wife for the night, Kronig?'

'I wouldn't lend you a nickel for a cup of coffee,' Kronig answered. 'Over here, Hawes. This looks like something.' He stooped suddenly.

'I didn't ask for a nickel, I asked for your wife,' Parker said, and he grinned in the darkness. 'You should see this guy's wife, Hawes. Like a movie star. Am I right, Kronig?'

'Go blow it out,' Kronig answered. 'It's nothing, Hawes. Let's move up a little.'

'What are you looking for?' Hawes asked, as gently as he knew how.

Kronig stared at him for a moment, his breath pluming from his mouth. 'Footprints, tyre tracks, traces of clothing, matches, any damn thing that might give us a lead.'

'Well,' Hawes said gently, 'I don't want to stick my two cents in. You know your job, and I have no right to offer any suggestions.'

'Yeah?' Kronig said. He looked at him suspiciously.

'Seems to me the last time we met, you had a lot of suggestions, and a lot of answers. You knew all about ballistics, didn't you? The Annie Boone case, wasn't it?'

'That's right,' Hawes said.

'Yeah, so now you're shy, huh? The shy flower of the Eighty-seventh Squad.'

'I've got no quarrel with you,' Hawes said. 'I behaved like a jerk that time.'

'Yeah?' Kronig said, surprised. He kept staring at Hawes. Then he said, 'What's your suggestion? I'm not God.'

'Neither am I. But would the kidnapper be likely to park the car here, or to stand here, or to do anything here where he could be seen? I mean, right on the road?'

'Possibly not. Where do you think he parked?'

'There's a turnabout up there. About five hundred yards from the pillars. Just a little dirt cutoff. It's pretty well screened with bushes. It's worth a chance.'

'Then let's try it,' Kronig said.

'Like a movie star,' Parker said. 'This guy's wife. She's got knockers out to here. You never seen knockers like on this guy's wife except on the silver screen. Man, I'm telling you!'

'Shut up, Parker,' Kronig said.

'I'm complimenting your wife. It ain't everybody got breastworks like this woman got. Man, you could lose yourself up there. You could bury your nose, and your mouth, and your whole goddamn head if you—'

'Shut up, Parker!' Kronig said. 'I don't feel like discussing my wife's attributes with you, if you don't mind.'

'What are you?' Parker asked. 'The nervous type?'

'Yeah, I'm the nervous type.'

'And they call the Eskimos primitive,' Parker said. 'Man!'

The men trudged up the gravel road silently. The night was a piece of crystal, sharp, clear, brittle. Like work horses stamping under a heavy load, they walked to the turnabout, the vaporized moisture of their breath trailing behind them.

'This it?' Kronig asked.

'Yes,' Hawes said. 'I noticed it when we drove up.'

'Not a very big turnabout, if that's what it is.' He shook his head. 'I don't think it's a turnabout at all. Or at least I don't think it was planned as one. I think it just *became* one through use. There. See where some of those shrubs were knocked over?'

'Yeah,' Hawes said. 'But a car could have waited here, don't you think?'

'Sure, it could have. Let's have some light on the subject.'

Hawes turned on the flash. The beam covered the ground.

'Frozen mud,' Parker said disgustedly. 'Like Italy during the war. More than fifteen years go by, and I'm still up to my ass in frozen mud.'

'Any tracks?' Hawes asked.

'Anything I hated,' Parker said, 'it was trudging through the mud. You walk around in that slime all day long, and then you sleep in it all night long and next day you get up and walk around in it some more. And cold? You touched the barrel of your BAR and your hand stuck to it, that's how cold it was.'

'You should have joined the Navy,' Kronig said drily. 'I think we've got something here, Hawes.'

'What is it?'

'A skid mark. Somebody pulled out of here in a hell of a hurry.'

'That figures.' Hawes knelt beside Kronig. 'Does it look any good?'

'It's covered with a thin sheet of ice.' Kronig nodded reflectively, as if he were suddenly alone. 'Well, let's see what we can do with it, huh?'

He opened his black bag and Hawes brought the flash up so that he could see into it.

'Shellac,' Kronig said, 'sprayer, talcum, plaster, water, rubber cap, spoon and spatula. I'm in business. There's only one thing I'd like to know.'

'What's that?' Hawes said.

'Do I spray my shellac over the ice, or do I try to get rid of the ice with the possibility of damaging the tyre pattern?'

'That's a good question,' Hawes said.

'One thing you sure as hell can't do,' Parker said, 'and that's wait for the ice to melt. Winter's here to stay.'

'Andy Parker, boy optimist,' Kronig said. 'Why don't you take a walk or something?'

That's just what I'm going to do,' Parker said. 'Back to the house where I can get a cup of coffee from the cook. She's got knockers almost as big as your wife's.'

The man from the telephone company drilled another hole in the woodwork, handed the drill to Reynolds, and then blew the sawdust out of the hole. Squatting close to the floor, he eyed the hole like a cat waiting for a mouse, and then stood up.

'Okay,' he said. 'Now for the wire.' He started across

the room, passing Carella, who was busy on the telephone.

'You got nothin' to worry about, mister,' the telephone company man said to Reynolds. 'Figure it out for yourself. When they find out they got your kid by mistake, they'll just turn him loose, it figures, don't it?'

'It just seems we should have heard something by now,' Reynolds said.

'Look, don't get nervous,' the man said. 'You start gettin' nervous, you lost half the battle, it figures, don't it?'

On the phone, Carella said, 'Well, what the hell's the holdup there? Are you getting me a line to the Auto Squad, or aren't you?' He paused. 'Then would you please get the lead out of your behind? A kid's been kidnapped here!'

'Do you have any children, Mr Cassidy?' Reynolds asked the telephone company man.

'I got four,' Cassidy said. 'Two of each. That's a nice family, ain't it?'

'Very nice.'

'I'm thinking of maybe another one, round it off, that figures, don't it? Five's a good round number, I told the wife.' He paused. 'She said four is a round-enough number.' He picked up a spool of wire and began paying it out across the living-room floor. 'That's the trouble with women nowadays. You want to know something?'

'What?'

'In China, the women have their babies in the rice fields, it figures, don't it? They drop their ploughs, and they deliver the kids themselves, and then they get right up off the ground and go back to ploughing or whatever it is they do with rice. It figures, don't it?'

'Well, I don't know,' Reynolds said. 'What's the mortality rate?'

'Gee, I don't know what the mortality rate is,' Cassidy said. He paused thoughtfully. Then he said, 'But I *do* know very few of them die.' He paused again. 'It figures, don't it?'

'If they'd turned him loose,' Reynolds said, 'wouldn't someone have seen him already?'

'Mister, I told you not to start worryin', didn't I? Okay, so stop. Now that kid's all right, you hear me? For God's sake, he's the wrong kid. What can they do to him – *kill* him?'

'Well, it's about time,' Carella said into the phone. 'What's going on down there, a hot pinochle game?' He listened for a moment, and then said, 'This is Steve Carella of the Eighty-seventh. I'm up in Smoke Rise on this kidnapping. We thought – What do you mean, *what* kidnapping? Are you in the Police Department or the Department of Sanitation? It's only on every radio in the city.'

'If they turn him loose in the street,' Reynolds said, 'he won't know where to go. He isn't the kind of child who can find his way around easily.'

'Mister, *any* kid can find his way around, it figures, don't it?'

'Anyway,' Carella said into the phone, 'we thought we'd run a check on stolen cars just in case the car used in the snatch was—' He paused. 'What? Listen, mister, what's your name? . . . Okay, Detective Planier, I've already heard all the jokes about snatches, and I don't think they're very funny right now. What do you do when a guy turns up dead in a pine coffin, crack jokes about boxes? There's an eight-year-old kid missing here, and we want a rundown on stolen cars, so get a list up here right away . . . . What? . . . No, just covering the last week or ten days. Thank you, Detective Planier. . . . What? Up your mother's too,' Carella said. 'The address is just Douglas King, Smoke Rise. Off Smoke Rise Road. Goodbye, Detective Planier.' He hung up and turned to Cassidy. 'Wise guy,' he said. 'I broke up a pinochle game.'

'Did they have any news, Detective Carella?' Reynolds asked.

'I was only talking to Auto Squad,' Carella answered.

'Oh.'

'He's all worried,' Cassidy said. 'I keep tellin' him there's nothing to worry about. In fact, even puttin' in this extra phone is a waste of time. The kid'll be back before you can say Jack Robinson, it figures, don't it?'

'Do *you* think so?' Reynolds asked Carella.

'Well . . .' Carella answered, and the doorbell rang. He rose from the phone table and went to answer it. Parker came into the room, slapping his arms against his sides.

'Whoooo!' he said. 'The North Pole!'

'Cold out there?'

'Whoooo!' Parker said again. 'How's it going in here? Nice and warm in here, Stevie? You should be outside with the mad scientist.'

'What's Kronig doing?'

'Trying to make a cast from a tyre track. After that, he'll probably dust the whole damn driveway for fingerprints. These lab boys give me a fat pain in the keester. Goddamn mad scientists. The kid's probably dead already, anyway.' Carella gave him a sharp poke in the ribs. 'What's the matter?' Parker asked.

Carella glanced hastily toward Reynolds, who had apparently not heard Parker's remark. 'Any sign of the lieutenant yet?' he asked.

'No, I ain't seen him. He's probably curled up home with his wife.' He studied Cassidy, who was trailing his length of coloured wires across the room. 'What the hell is *he* doing?'

'Putting in a trunk line to the phone company's main office.'

'And what's that?' Parker asked, pointing to the instrument set up near the telephone.

'You know damn well what that is. It's a wiretap.'

'All baloney,' Parker said. 'Wiretap, trunk line, all baloney! I never seen such a commotion in my life. I won't be surprised we get the Chief of Detectives in here.'

'I imagine the lieutenant will call him,' Carella said.

'Sure, and for what? The lab's outside crawling around on their hands and knees sniffing tyre tracks, and the whole damn force is out checking rooming houses and hotels and motels and every fleabag in the city and the suburbs. We got dicks at both airports and covering every train station, bus terminal and trolley car stop. And I ask you, for what? Those cheap thieves got only two choices open to them.'

'Have they, Andy?'

'Damn right. They either turn the kid loose or they kill him out of spite.'

'They ought to take all kidnappers and burn them at the stake,' Cassidy said. 'Man sweats his head off raising a nice family, and some guy steps in and swipes a kid. There ought to be a law.'

'You . . . you don't think they'll . . . harm Jeff, do you, Detective Carella?' Reynolds asked. 'When they find out he isn't the one they wanted?'

'There ain't nobody safe nowadays, nobody,' Cassidy said. 'That's because the cops are all a bunch of—' He stopped suddenly, seemingly realizing that he was in the presence of policemen. Casually, he cleared his throat. 'Maybe I better test this phone, huh?' he said. He picked up the receiver of the new phone. Impatiently, he jiggled the bar. 'Hello? Hello?'

'I'm going to the kitchen for a cup of coffee,' Parker said. 'You want some, Stevie?'

'No. Thanks.'

'Wiretaps, trunk lines,' Parker said disgustedly, and he walked out of the room.

'Hello,' Cassidy said into the telephone, 'this is Cassidy . . . . What? . . . Never mind the Hopalong wisecracks. I'm testing this Smoke Rise installation.' He listened. 'Yeah . . . . Okay. Fine. I'm finished, then. What else you got for me?' He listened, jotting an address on to a pad. 'Right. So long.' He hung up. 'Well, that does it.'

'All finished?'

'Just pick it up, and you've got our main office. You going to try tracing a call, huh?'

'If we get another call to trace.'

'I'll let you in on something, Officer. But don't spread it around. If your man uses a dial phone, you ain't got a chance in hell of tracing the call. You know?'

'I know,' Carella said.

'Oh. You know. Well, you better pray he uses a

manual instrument. That sounds like a dirty joke, hey, don't it?' He chuckled to himself, took some papers from his pocket and then glanced at his watch. 'Are them three gonna be eating dinner all night? I gotta get somebody to sign for this installation.'

'They should be finished soon,' Carella said.

'You never seen an outfit like this one for getting things signed,' Cassidy said. 'You want to go to the toilet, you got to get somebody to sign for it, it figures, don't it?' He shook his head. 'I swear to God, one of these days, the telephone company is gonna declare war on the United States.'

'Have you heard anything yet, Detective Carella?' King said, and he came through the dining-room arch and into the living room, carrying a coffee cup in his right hand. Diane and Cameron were directly behind him.

'Not yet, Mr King,' Carella said.

'Mr King, I wonder if you would si—' Cassidy started.

'Well, what's the holdup?' King said. 'Are you sure your men are really looking? Do they have a description of the boy?'

'Yes, sir, they have a description.'

'Would you sign this—'

'Do they know he'll be wandering the streets? They can't expect the kidnappers to deliver him to our front—'

'Yes, sir, they know that.'

'Could you sign this form we—'

'Well, then, why hasn't someone seen him? Have you got men at Headquarters to take care of calls from the public? It seems likely that some citizen might—'

'That's all taken care of, sir.'

'Mr King, would you please sign for this installation?'

King turned to Cassidy as if just discovering a Martian in his living room. '*What* installation?' he asked.

'The trunk line,' Cassidy said. 'To the main office.'

'What trunk line?'

'I told you about it before we had it installed, Mr King,' Carella said.

'Oh. Oh, yes. That.'

'I have to get a few things from you first, Mr King,' Cassidy said.

'What is it?'

'Is that the only phone in the house there? I mean, the one you had before I put in the trunk line?'

'No. We've got two numbers. That one, and my private line upstairs.'

'Could I have those numbers, please?'

'Smoke Rise 8–7214 and 7215,' King said.

'And that's it, right?'

'I've got a phone in the car, too,' King said. 'Do you want that number?'

'No, just the ones in the house. Car phone's a separate thing. We just need a record of the lines going in, so we don't get all fouled up with . . . Well, it don't make no difference. Would you sign this slip, please?' He handed it to King.

'This seems like a waste of time to me,' King said, writing. 'Once they turn the boy loose . . .'

'We're taking every precaution, Mr King,' Carella said.

'Is that why there's a policeman outside my son's bedroom?'

'That's right. We have no idea what the kidnappers will do next, you see.'

'It doesn't seem to me they have much choice.' King handed the signed slip back to Cassidy.

'Thank you,' Cassidy said. 'Don't worry about this, Mr Reynolds. You'll have him back in a couple of hours. So long, now.' He went to the door and waved, opened it, stepped into the cold, and closed it quickly behind him.

'Reynolds, you'd better eat something now,' King said. 'Inge's ready for you in the kitchen.'

'I'm not very hungry, Mr King.'

'Dammit, man, you've got to eat! Now go ahead. Jeffry will be back before you know it.'

'All right, sir, thank you.' Reynolds started out of the room.

'Would you send Detective Parker in, Mr Reynolds?' Carella said. 'He should be in the kitchen.'

'Yes, I will,' Reynolds said.

Diane King waited until he was gone. Then she said, 'Mr Carella, the kidnappers *have* heard by now, haven't they?'

'They should have, Mrs King. It's been on all the radio and TV stations, and the afternoon papers have all put out extras on it.'

'Then it's just a waste of time, isn't it?'

'Well . . .'

'Isn't it?'

'I don't like to second-guess kidnappers,' Carella said. 'That's like second-guessing murderers.'

'But . . . you don't think they'll harm him, do you?'

'Of course they won't!' King put in. 'As far as they're concerned, this is a business deal that went sour, that's all.'

'They *might* harm him, Mrs King,' Carella said calmly. 'The same way a mugger will beat up a man when he finds out that the man isn't carrying any money.'

'But that would be senseless,' King said. 'I'm sure they'll simply turn him loose the moment they hear the news.'

'Well, that's a possibility, of course,' Carella said.

'But the other is a possibility too, isn't it?' Diane said. 'That they might first hurt him? Before they release him?'

'It's a possibility,' Carella said.

'A stupid possibility. I can't believe these men are stupid.'

'Kidnappers don't have to be smart, Mr King. Only ruthless.'

'We hadn't thought of that, Doug. That they might hurt him before they turn him loose,' Cameron said. 'It's a definite possibility.'

'Yes,' Carella said. 'And there's also a *third* possibility.'

'My name is Jeffry Reynolds,' the boy said.

Sy grabbed the front of his sweater and said, 'You're lying.'

'I'm not lying. My name is Jeff Reynolds. Hey, let go that sweater, will you? It doesn't belong to me. I'm supposed to—'

'You're a lying little bastard!' Sy said, and he shoved out at Jeff, sending him sprawling across the room.

'Sy!' Kathy screamed, and she took a step toward the boy.

'Get away from him,' Sy said, moving between them.

'I'm . . . I'm not lying,' Jeff said. 'Why should I lie?' He was beginning to get a little frightened now. He kept staring at Sy, not wanting to be shoved again, yet not knowing how to prevent it. Telling the truth seemed to be the wrong course of action. And yet he did not know which lie the man wanted.

'What's your father's name?' Sy asked.

'Ch-Charles.'

'What's your mother's name?'

'My mother is dead.'

'Where do you live?'

'On Mr King's estate.'

'Don't call him Mr King!' Sy shouted. 'You know he's your father.'

'My father? No. No, he's *Bobby's* father.'

Sy seized the front of the sweater again. 'You little son of a bitch,' he said, 'don't get smart with me.'

'But I'm telling you the—'

'Shut up! I know you're Bobby King, and I don't have to— What's that?'

'What?' Jeff said, truly frightened now. 'What? What?'

'In the sweater. There. Take off that sweater.' He pulled it over Jeff's head roughly, and then turned it in his hands. A slow smile crossed his face. 'So you're Jeff Whatever-the-hell, huh?'

'Yes.'

'Sure. And the name tape in your sweater says Robert King! You lying little . . .'

'That's Bobby's sweater!' Jeff said. 'Mrs King lent it to me.'

'Tell the truth!'

'I *am* telling the truth.'

'What does your father do?'

'He's a chauffeur.'

'What were you doing in the woods?'

'I was playing with Bobby.'

'And your name is Jeff, huh?'

'Yes. Yes.'

'Why didn't you mention all this before? How come you waited for the police call?'

'I didn't know. I thought – You said you had a gun for me.'

Sy nodded. He stood with his hands on his hips, a small dapper man badly in need of a shave, watching Jeff calmly, nodding, nodding. And then, suddenly, viciously, his hand lashed out, the palm catching Jeff across the cheek.

'You're full of crap!' he yelled.

'Eddie, stop him!' Kathy shouted.

Sy advanced on the boy. 'No snotnose is gonna try pulling the wool over my eyes!'

Jeff rushed into Kathy's arms, and at last the tears came, tears of fear and frustration. 'I *am* Jeff Reynolds,' he sobbed. 'I am, I am . . .'

'Shut up!' Sy said. 'Another word out of you, and you won't be *nobody*!'

'Lay off, Sy,' Eddie said. 'The kid's scared.'

'What the hell do I care if he's scared? You think he's gonna make a fool outta—'

'I said lay off.' Sy glared at him but stopped his advance. 'Let me see the sweater, Sy.' Sy tossed the sweater to Eddie. Eddie looked at the name tape. 'It *does* say Robert King, Kathy.'

'And the boy says he borrowed it. Is that so hard to accept?'

'Yeah,' Sy said. 'With five hundred grand at stake, yeah, it's goddamn hard to accept.'

'Let's take the boy back,' Kathy said softly.

'Now hold it a minute. Let's just hold it one goddamn minute. We're not—'

'He's the wrong boy, Eddie,' Kathy said plaintively. 'Why stick your neck out? What can you gain?'

'Now, look,' Sy said, 'we're in this together, right, Eddie boy? Fifty-fifty, right? So let's calm down, okay. We can't turn this kid loose.' He paused, looking first at Kathy and then to her husband. 'He *knows* us, for Pete's sake. He can lead the bulls right to us!'

'Who said we were turning him loose?' Eddie asked.

'Nobody said so,' Sy said quickly, 'but don't even let the idea get in your head. This is a sweet setup. Let's not ruin it because a dame gets hysterical.'

'I'm just trying to figure, that's all,' Eddie said.

'Okay, nothing wrong with that,' Sy said. 'But figure *right*! Our plan calls for two guys.'

'I know. I know.'

'Okay. And we've got five hundred grand invested in this kid, remember that!'

'You've got nothing invested but a little time,' Kathy said. 'What have his parents got invested in him? What have—'

'Time is right, baby. You know how *much* time we'd do on a kidnapping rap? Provided we don't get the chair? This ain't busting into a goddamn cash register!'

'Yeah,' Eddie said. 'Kathy, he's right. We *got* to hold the kid. At least until . . .'

'We don't have to! We could turn him loose right this minute!'

'Sure, and go straight to jail!' Sy said. He turned to Eddie. Seductively, he said, 'Your share of this is two hundred and fifty thousand bucks, Eddie. You know how much money that is?'

'Who wants it?' Kathy shouted. 'We don't need it!'

'Sure, she don't need it. Lady Rockefeller. Wearing a sweater with torn elbows. She don't need it!'

'I don't!'

'Well, I do,' Eddie said softly. 'That's all the money in the world. Why shouldn't I have it?' His voice rose. 'Am I supposed to be a two-bit punk for the rest of my life? What's wrong with making a grab for that kind of loot? I want it! I want that money.'

'Then don't get talked out of it,' Sy said quickly.

'What the hell, was I born with a Smoke Rise estate like this kid? What did I get, Kathy? South Nineteenth Street and David Avenue. An old man who played the numbers, and an old lady who was a rummy!'

'You can't blame this boy for—'

'I'm not blaming nobody. I'm saying I *had* nothing, and I *still* got nothing – even after all the lousy cheap stickups. Don't I ever get nothing? Ever? When the hell do I get my chance?'

'This *is* your chance, Eddie. Turn the boy loose. Then we'll . . .'

'Then we'll what? Get to Mexico? On what? Hope? Love? And do what when we get there? The same thing I'm doing here?'

'A quarter of a million bucks, boy,' Sy said. 'It'll buy

all the radio equipment you need, all the schooling. Man, you can own a whole damn radio *station*!'

'No, just . . . just a place on the beach, maybe – for me and Kathy – where . . . where I can set up . . . you know . . . with the ocean, and maybe a little boat, I don't know.' Eddie turned to Kathy, and she saw something in his eyes she had never seen there before, a look bordering on tears. 'But *mine*, Kathy. *Mine*. A place I could *own*.'

'And a Caddy, man,' Sy said, 'with them fins sticking up in the air like sharks! And fancy clothes, and a mink for the bride, how's that? Blond mink! And a string of pearls a mile long!'

'If only . . .'

'Anything, Eddie! Anything you want, boy! The world on a string! A quarter of a million bucks!'

'We got to go ahead with this, Kathy. We got to!'

'Now you're talking,' Sy said.

'But . . . but he's the *wrong boy*!' Kathy said.

'No. No,' Eddie answered. 'He . . . he ain't the wrong boy.'

'Eddie, you *know* he is. Why . . .'

'When you stop to figure it,' Sy said softly, 'what difference does it make?'

The room went suddenly still.

'What?' Eddie said.

'Whether we got the wrong kid or not.'

'I don't follow.'

'Simple. We tried for the King kid, didn't we? Okay, E for effort. Maybe we goofed. What difference does it make? We want five hundred grand. Does a lousy chauffeur have that kind of dough?'

'No, of course he—'

'All right, who's *got* the dough?' Sy waited for an answer and then gave it himself. 'King, that's who. Okay. We call King again. We tell him we don't care whether this is his kid or his chauffeur's kid or even his goddamn gardener's kid. We want the money!'

'We'll ask *King* for it?'

'Who we gonna ask? The chauffeur?'

Eddie shook his head. 'He won't pay, Sy.'

'He'll pay, all right.'

'No.' Eddie kept shaking his head. 'He won't. Maybe Kathy's right. Maybe we ought to . . .'

'Because if he don't pay,' Sy said, 'this little boy here is going to be in a goddamn big heap of trouble.' He paused and grinned at Jeff. 'And I don't think Mr King would want blood on his hands.'

# 7.

**WHEN LIEUTENANT PETER** Byrnes left the squadroom of the 87th Precinct, the telephones were jangling as if the place were an illegal racing room taking bets before the Kentucky Derby. He walked down the corridor to the end of the hall and then down the steps leading to the muster room. He nodded at Sergeant Dave Murchison, who sat behind the high desk, and then went out into the street, where a squad car and a driver were waiting for him. It was damn cold outside. Byrnes wrapped his muffler about his throat and pulled his fedora down more tightly on his head, as if this would serve as a buffer against the cold blasts which drove across Grover Park to lash the grimy stone front of the precinct building.

The patrolman got out of the car, ran to the sidewalk and opened the door for Byrnes. Byrnes nodded, slid on to the seat and thrust his hands into his coat pockets. He was a man built with all the compactness of a travelling iron, hard as steel, capable of giving off tremendous heat in the press of any situation, adaptable to the myriad currents that moved in the precinct under his command.

'Where to, sir?' the patrolman asked, getting in behind the wheel.

'Smoke Rise,' Byrnes said. 'The kidnapping.'

The kidnapping. Even the word rankled Byrnes. He

had a grown son of his own, and he knew the torments and thrills of raising a child, and he did not hold with that part of the penal law which specified 'Provided, however, that the jury upon returning a verdict of guilty against a person upon whom the death penalty would otherwise be imposed, may recommend imprisonment of the convicted person, in lieu of death.' Nor did he hold with the further wording of Section 1250, to wit: 'Provided, further, that notwithstanding the foregoing provisions of this section with respect to punishment by death, if the kidnapped person be released and returned alive prior to the opening of the trial, the death penalty shall not apply nor be imposed . . .'

Dammit, either there *was* a death penalty or there *wasn't*. A kidnapper was the lowest form of animal life, even lower than a narcotics peddler – and Byrnes had particular reason to despise any and all pushers. And if anything was going to stop the crime of stealing another man's child, the death penalty was that deterrent. Kidnapping, by its very nature, was usually a premeditated crime. Careful planning went into the actual snatch, careful psychological manipulation went into the demands made of the parents, the slow torture of uncertainty. Byrnes would rather have seen all murderers get off with prison sentences. For whereas the thin line of premeditation separated many second-degree homicides from first-degree homicides, there was very rarely a kidnapping case in which the entire filthy crime was not thoroughly and fastidiously premeditated.

'Anywhere along here, sir?' the patrolman asked.

'What's that up ahead?' Byrnes asked.

'Looks like a light, sir.'

'Pull up over there.'

'Yes, sir.'

The patrolman eased the car to a stop. Byrnes got out and walked to where Hawes and Kronig were squatted close to the ground.

'Cotton,' Byrnes said. 'Kronig. How are you?'

'Fine, Lieutenant,' Hawes said.

'Making a cast,' Kronig said. 'Looks like it's gonna be a good one.'

'Good. Those bastards call again?'

'Not that I know of, Pete,' Hawes said. 'I've been outside quite a while.'

'Where are the rest of the men?'

'Carella and Parker are up at the house. I think Meyer broke for dinner.'

'Okay,' Byrnes said. 'I put in a call to the Chief of Detectives, and he may be out.'

'May?' Kronig said, surprised.

'He's up to his ears in this income tax thing that broke yesterday. He's been waiting for a long time to clap that hoodlum behind bars.'

'Still, a kidnapping . . .' Kronig began.

'The trouble with most crimes,' Byrnes said, 'is that they don't respect any other crimes. Nothing gets priority. In any case, if the Chief shows up, I'll be—' and he stopped talking.

A figure was coming up the road. In the darkness, the men saw only a hulking shape against the sky. Byrnes's hand slipped inside the flap of his coat. Nearly all of the detectives on the 87th – with the exception of a few who were left-handed and a few who were stubborn – wore their holsters clipped to the left side of their belts during the winter months. This eliminated the necessity of delay in unbuttoning a coat, and whereas a cross-body draw was slower than a straight one, there were very rarely any wild-West theatrics which necessitated a split-second edge. On the other hand, a cop could be dead in the time it took him to unbutton his coat far enough to reach his gun. The figure came closer as Byrnes's hand tightened on the butt of the .38.

'That you, Loot?' a voice called into the darkness.

Byrnes recognized the voice as Parker's. His hand relaxed. 'Yeah, what is it?'

'Nothing. Carella was just asking a while ago whether you got here or not. How's the squad? I'll bet things are jumping.'

'They're jumping, all right.' Byrnes turned his attention back to Kronig, and then his eyes scanned the ground, coming to rest on two large boulders near the edge of the cut-off. He walked to the rocks, knelt by them and then said, 'Can you bring that light here a minute, Cotton?'

'What is it, Lieutenant?'

'Unless I'm mistaken . . .'

The light swung over to illuminate the boulders.

In the living room, the telephone rang.

'I'll get it,' King said, moving toward the phone.

'Wait a minute!' Carella shouted. He picked up the headphones attached to the wiretap equipment and then turned to Cameron. 'Mr Cameron, get on the trunk line. If this is the kidnapper, tell them to start tracing immediately. Okay, Mr King, answer it.'

King picked up the phone. 'Hello?'

'King?'

Carella nodded at Cameron. Instantly, Cameron picked up the receiver of the trunk line telephone.

'This is Mr King,' King said.

Into his phone, Cameron said, 'Hello? We've got him on the phone now. Get started.'

'All right, King, listen. We don't care whose kid this is, you got that? We heard the radio, and we don't care. He's still alive and well, and we still want that money. You get it by tomorrow morning or the kid won't see the sun go down.'

'You want . . . ?' King started, and there was a sharp click on the line.

Carella ripped off the earphones. 'Forget it, he's gone. Dammit, I was afraid this would happen.' He went to the phone and began dialling.

'What happened?' Cameron asked, hanging up his phone.

Diane, puzzled, looked at her husband. 'Is . . . is Jeff all right?'

'Yes. Yes, he's fine,' King said.

'Hello, Dave,' Carella said, 'this is Steve. Can you get me the lieutenant right away?'

'You're sure he's all right?' Diane asked, staring at King.

'Yes, dammit, he's fine!'

'I'll tell Reynolds,' she said, and she started for the kitchen.

'Diane!'

'Yes?'

'They . . . they want me to pay the ransom. They know they've got Jeff, but they still want me to pay. They want *me* to . . .'

'We'll do whatever they say,' Diane said. 'Thank God

Jeff's all right.' And she left the room. King stared after her, a frown on his forehead.

'What?' Carella said into the phone. 'Well, how long ago did he leave, Dave? I see. Then he should be here by now. I'll check outside. How's it going back there? Murder, huh? Okay, thanks, Dave.' He hung up. 'I'm going outside, see if I can scare up the lieutenant. If that phone rings, don't answer it,' Carella said. He took his coat from the hall closet. 'Detective Meyer should be back soon. Do whatever he says.'

'About this new demand,' King said. 'I think—'

'I want to talk to the lieutenant first,' Carella said, and he rushed out of the house.

'That guy knew we'd try to trace the call,' Cameron said. 'That's why he got off the line so fast.'

'Yes,' King said. The frown on his face had given way to a slightly dazed expression now. 'Yes.'

'That means we're dealing with professionals. But why would pros pull a thing like this, asking *you* to pay?'

'I . . . I don't know.'

'Hell, if you pay them – why, your Boston deal'll go right out the window, won't it?'

'Yes. Yes, it will.'

The doorbell chimed. King started for the door, but it opened before he reached it.

'Hi, Mr King,' Meyer said. 'Boy, it's turned cold out there.' He took off his hat and coat and hung them in the closet.

'Detective Carella went outside to find the lieutenant,' King said. 'He said—'

'I know. I ran into him on the way in. What was all the excitement about?'

'The kidnappers just called again,' King said.

'Yeah?'

'They want me to pay the ransom.'

'What do you mean? Do they know they got the wrong kid?'

'Yes.'

'And they still . . . ?'

'Yes.'

'First time I ever heard of a dodge like that,' Meyer said, shaking his head. 'This just about beats it all. This means that any crook can go out and steal any kid in the world, and then send a ransom demand to the richest guy he can think of.' He shook his head again. 'Screwy, all right. But nobody says kidnappers have to be normal, huh?' He shook his head again. '*Meshugah*. Plain *meshugah*.'

'What are our chances of getting him back, Detective Meyer?'

'That's hard to say, Mr King. We don't get kidnappings every day of the week, you know. What I mean is, it's a little hard to come up with actual statistics. I can tell you that the Department is working like crazy on it. Even the Sands Spit cops and the cops in the adjoining states are going on a round-the-clock schedule.'

'What about the F.B.I.?' Cameron asked.

'They don't come in till a week's gone by,' Meyer said. 'I think Carella explained that to you, Mr King.'

'Yes.'

'But we've got them on standby.'

'Would you say the boy's chances are good?'

'I don't know,' Meyer said. 'He may be dead already, for all we know.'

'We can't assume that,' Cameron said quickly. 'There'd be no sense paying the ransom if we assumed the boy was dead.'

'Mr Cameron, they may have killed him five minutes after they picked him up,' Meyer said. 'It's been done before. Figure it out for yourself. The safest kidnap victim, from the standpoint of the criminals, is a dead one. We may deliver the ransom and then find the boy in a ditch someplace.'

'In your opinion,' King said slowly, 'would paying the ransom help the boy at all?'

'If he's alive, it certainly would. If he's dead, nothing's going to help him. But the ransom bills might help in eventually catching the kidnapper.'

'I see.'

Diane came in from the kitchen. 'Doug . . .' she started, and the doorbell chimed. 'I'll get it,' she said, changing her course.

Urgently, Cameron said, 'Doug, the boy's still alive. And your money will keep him that way, remember that!'

Diane closed the door and then came into the living room. 'A telegram, Doug,' she said. 'Addressed to us.'

'You'd better let me take that,' Meyer said, 'before anyone else handles it.' He spread a handkerchief over his hand and took the telegram. 'Got a letter opener, Mr King?'

'Yes. On the dropleaf desk there.'

Meyer went to the desk. Pinning the telegram with his handkerchief, he slit the envelope, extricated the handkerchief, draped it over his hand again and, with all the dexterity of a puppeteer, reached into the envelope for the message. Still using the handkerchief, he unfolded it, read it, and then put the handkerchief back into his pocket. 'It's okay, Mr King. You can have it.'

He handed the message to King. Diane walked over to him, and together they read the wire:

PLEASE ACCEPT DEEPEST SYMPATHY YOUR MISFORTUNE. WE WILL ADD $1000 CASH TO RANSOM IF KIDNAPPERS WILL AGREE TO RETURN BOY AT ONCE. WIRE US 27–145 HALSEY AVENUE, CALM'S POINT.

MR AND MRS THEODORE SCHAEFFER

'What is it, Doug?' Cameron asked, and King handed him the wire.

'Mr and Mrs Theodore Schaeffer,' King said. 'Nobody I know.' He paused. 'But why send it to us? Our son wasn't kidnapped.'

'Half the people out there probably *still* think it was Bobby,' Cameron said, putting the wire down on the desk.

'Let me have that,' Diane said. 'I think Reynolds would like to see it. He . . . he expected them to turn Jeff loose and now . . . he's . . . he's just sitting at the kitchen table in a kind of shock. Let me show it to him. It's such a wonderful, human offer.'

King picked up the wire and handed it to his wife.

'And then I'll send a return wire,' Diane said, 'thanking them for their concern.' She started out of the room, the telegram in her hand. She stopped and turned to face King. 'Doug, have you called the bank yet?' she asked.

'No, not yet.'

'Don't you think . . . ?'

'Mommy?'

Diane turned toward the steps. Bobby King, wearing pyjamas and robe, stood on the landing.

'What is it, darling?'

'Why is there a policeman outside my room?' Bobby asked.

'Just to make sure that everything is all right,' Diane said.

'Because of what happened to Jeff?'

'Yes, Bobby.'

'Daddy, are you getting Jeff back?'

'What? I'm sorry, son, I didn't hear . . .'

'He's my best friend. You are getting him back, aren't you?'

'Your daddy's taking care of everything,' Diane said. 'Now come, I'll put you back to bed.'

'I want Daddy to tuck me in,' Bobby said.

'Doug? Will you?'

'Sure,' Preoccupied, King walked to the steps and took his son's hand. 'Come on, Bobby.'

'Poor Bobby,' Diane said, when they were out of sight. 'He still isn't quite sure about what happened. He only knows that his friend is gone, and I think he feels responsible somehow. The way I do.'

'You've no reason to feel guilty, Diane,' Cameron said. 'Once Doug pays the ransom . . .'

'Yes, I know, but I *do* feel guilty. I almost feel as if my own son is out there with those men.' She paused. 'I'd better show Reynolds this wire.' She paused again. 'Detective Meyer, I wonder if you'd come talk to him, fill him in a little on what's being done. He's so terribly shaken by all this.'

'Sure,' Meyer said. 'Be happy to.' As they walked out

of the room, he called over his shoulder, 'If that phone rings, yell for me. Don't answer it.'

'Okay,' Cameron said.

Alone in the living room, Cameron lighted a cigarette and then walked quickly to the steps, looking upstairs. He crossed the room rapidly then, looking over his shoulder toward the kitchen, walking directly to the telephone. He dialled with quick flicks of his forefinger, his eyes never leaving the steps leading to the upstairs wing of the house. Impatiently, he tapped on the telephone table.

'Hello?' he said at last. 'May I speak to Mr Benjamin, please.' He paused. 'This is Peter Cameron. Yes, I'll wait, but please hurry.' He glanced nervously toward the steps. The hand with the cigarette stopped its tapping, moved to his mouth. He sucked in on the cigarette, blew out a steady stream of smoke, looked toward the kitchen again, and was ready to hang up when the voice came onto the line.

'Hello?'

'George?'

'This is George Benjamin.'

'Pete Cameron. I've got to make this fast. Do I still get Doug's job?'

'I offered it, didn't I? I'll put it in writing, if you like.'

'I'd like. The Boston thing I called you about earlier – it is a stock deal. Doug's cornering nineteen per cent of the voting stock.'

'What!'

'And he already owns twenty-eight per cent himself. You underestimated him, George.'

'Twenty-eight . . .' There was a long silence on the

line. 'Then how can we vote him out? How the hell can we?'

'You can't,' Cameron said. 'Unless you tell the Old Man that Doug is finagling a deal behind his back. Get the Old Man on your side temporarily. It's the only way.'

'What good will that do? If Doug's stock deal goes through, he'll be sitting with forty-seven per cent of the stuff! Even *with* the Old Man's stock, we couldn't outvote him. Hell, he could get rid of *us*.'

'*If* the deal goes through. Have you been listening to the radio?'

'This kidnapping nonsense?' Benjamin said. 'What's that got to do with—'

'It has a lot to do with it.'

'It isn't even Doug's son!'

'No, but they've asked him for the ransom, anyway. If he pays, his Boston deal goes out the window.'

'Will he pay?'

'No question about it. But in the meantime, I'm trying to find out whom he's dealing with in Boston. Maybe we can beat him to the punch.'

'You're all right, Pete,' Benjamin said admiringly.

'I know I am,' Cameron answered. 'Do what I advised, George. Get to the Old Man and clasp hands with him. If Doug's deal folds and you still want him out, you're going to need a bigger club than you've got now.'

'I'll do that. And I won't forget this.'

'I'm banking on that. I've got to hang up now, George.'

'All right.'

There was a click on the line. Smiling, Cameron

replaced the receiver and lighted a fresh cigarette. He was still smiling when the doorbell chimed. He looked up at the steps, shrugged, and went to the door, opening it. A small man wearing a black overcoat and derby stood there. A black umbrella was slung over the man's arm. There was an air of secrecy about the man, the look of a Scotland Yard operative who had worked on the Jack the Ripper case. The man was easily sixty years old, perhaps older.

'Yes?' Cameron said.

'Mr King?'

'No. I'm Mr King's assistant.'

'I would like to see Mr King, please. On business.'

'What sort of business?'

'Personal business. You may tell him that Score is here. Adrian Score.'

'Just a moment, Mr Score. I'll see if he's free. Have a seat, won't you?'

'Thank you,' Score said. He walked into the living room, holding his umbrella clutched in both hands like a timid batter facing a no-hit pitcher. He studied one of the chairs as if he suspected some wild animal had befouled it, and then sat daintily on its edge. Cameron went to the steps and called, 'Doug!'

'What is it?'

'A Mr Score to see you. On business.'

'I don't know any Mr Score,' King answered.

'Tell him it's personal,' Score said over his shoulder.

'Says it's personal, Doug.'

'Okay, I'll be right down,' King said.

'Make yourself comfortable, Mr Score,' Cameron said, walking into the living room.

'Thank you, I will. This is a lovely home.'

'Thank you.'

'Thank you,' Score repeated.

King came down the steps. 'Now what is it, Pete?' Cameron shrugged. In a whisper, he said, 'Says it's personal. I'd better go get a cup of coffee.' He started toward the kitchen.

'That phone hasn't rung again, has it?'

'No. Bobby asleep?'

'Yes.'

'I'll be in the kitchen,' Cameron said, and he went out.

'Mr Score?'

'Mr King?'

'Yes.' King extended his hand.

Score rose, shook hands briefly, and nodded curtly. 'Adrian Score, sir,' he said. 'The man who always knows the score, eh?'

'Sit down, Mr Score,' King said. Score sat. 'Now then, what's on your mind?'

'Business, Mr King.'

'It's a little late for a business call, isn't it?'

'It's never too late for business, is it, Mr King?'

'Well, that depends. What sort of business did you have in mind, Mr Score?'

'Kidnapping, Mr King.'

The room went dead silent.

'What . . . what about kidnapping?'

'Do you want your son back, Mr King?'

'My son wasn't kidnapped,' King said.

'Ah-ah, Mr King,' Score said, wagging the umbrella, 'let's be honest with each other, eh? We are both businessmen, are we not? Very well then. You can tell the newspapers what you wish, but you are now dealing with Adrian Score. Honesty, eh? I asked you a question.'

'And I gave you an answer.'

'That's what I like, Mr King. Hardheaded business. Who is this Adrian Score, you are undoubtedly asking yourself. Who is this man who comes into my house in the middle of the night and asks me if I want my son back? And you've every right to ask that, Mr King, every right in the world. Sound business tactics.' He paused, nodded, put the umbrella between his legs and said, 'Well, I will tell you who Adrian Score is. Adrian Score is the man who's going to get your son back.'

'You know where the Reynolds boy is?' King asked.

Score chuckled and put a finger alongside his nose. 'All right, sir, never argue with a client, that's Score's motto. If you prefer, he's your chauffeur's son, and a very clever ruse indeed, if I may be permitted to say so. But we both know the truth, don't we, eh? In any case, you *do* want the boy back?'

'What do you know about this?'

'Ah-ah, Mr King, I asked you a question. Do you want the boy back?'

'Of course we do!'

'Now, now, don't get excited, Mr King. Don't raise your voice. If you want the boy back, Adrian Score is your man.' He paused. 'I know who kidnapped the boy, Mr King.'

Again, the room went silent.

'Who?' King asked.

'That's the big question, eh? Who? Well, Score's got the answers, and Score can get the boy back, now what do you think of that, sir? Back home safe and sound, eh? Now how would you like that?'

'I'd like that fine. Who . . . ?'

'My services are available for the asking, Mr King. Simply ask, and Score will oblige. Score will put his talents to the task of getting your boy back for you . . .'

'Well, who . . . ?'

'. . . at a nominal fee.'

'I see.'

'Yes, Mr King. I imagined you would.'

'How much?'

'Can we measure the safety and well-being of a toddler in terms of cold cash, Mr King?'

'The boy's father is a chauffeur. The five-hundred-thousand-dollar demand is far beyond his—'

'Mr King, please, please,' Score said, as if he could not tolerate the lie a moment longer. 'Please.' He leaned forward, his hands clasped over the handle of the umbrella. His voice dropped to a whisper. Intently, he said, 'I am ready to establish contact with the kidnappers, *whose* identity is already known to me, sir, and I will ascertain that the boy is alive and well, serving as a liaison between the principals, negotiating for the ransom payment, seeing that every term of the contract is strictly adhered—'

'Goddammit, how much?'

'Five thousand dollars, Mr King.'

'In addition to the exorbitant ransom demand?'

'I was thinking I might – But no, that would be far too risky.'

'What?' King asked eagerly.

'Perhaps, were you to deliver the five thousand dollars to me at once, I could get the boy back now. Tonight. Without necessity for further payment.'

'How would you manage that?'

'We are both businessmen, Mr King,' Score said, smiling. 'But does Macy's tell Gimbels?'

'Who has the boy?'

'Business, business, Mr King. Cash on the barrelhead in Score's Store.'

'How do I know you can get him back?'

'You shall have to accept my word for that, Mr King.'

'In business, Mr Score, I accept *no one's* word.'

'An admirable trait, to be sure. But a good businessman knows when his back is to the wall, Mr King. And surely you can see I'm a man to trust. You realize the danger of my position, do you not, sir?'

King's attention was momentarily diverted by Meyer Meyer, who had entered behind Score and stopped in the archway leading from dining room to living room. Score, apparently, had not seen the change of expression on King's face. Blithely unaware of Meyer's presence, he continued with his monologue

'Surely you appreciate the danger of my position, surely you do. If these ruthless men were to suspect that I was planning to get the boy away from them, my life would be placed in instant jeopardy. These men are hardened criminals, sir, cut-throats who would stop at nothing short of—

'*Which* men, Score?' Meyer called from the archway.

'Eh?' Score said, and he whirled in his seat to face the archway.

'Which men were you talking about, Score?' Meyer said.

Score studied Meyer painstakingly. 'I do not believe I've had the pleasure, sir,' he said.

'How'd you sneak past our men at the gate, Score?'

'Perhaps, Mr King, you would do me the honour of introducing this gentleman. He seems to have made an error in—'

'I'll introduce myself, Score, even though we've already met. Detective Second Grade Meyer Meyer of the Eighty-seventh Squad. Ring a bell?'

'Charmed, I'm sure,' Score said.

'I see you're still disguised as a leech.'

'Eh?'

'This is one of the biggest con men in the business, Mr King, and he specializes in human grief. If someone's kid is missing for as long as an hour, you can bet Adrian Score will be on the scene with some scheme for getting the kid back. At a nominal fee, of course.'

'This is absurd, Mr King. Surely two businessmen should be able to discuss—'

'Get the hell out of here, you rotten louse! Get out before I arrest you as an accessory to a kidnapping!'

'Accessory to a . . . ?'

'Yes, accessory!' Meyer yelled. 'A person who wilfully gives false information concerning a kidnapping while knowing that information to be false!'

'False . . . false . . . information?' Score squeaked.

'Get out, Score! I'm warning you!'

'Really, Mr King. I am a guest in your home, a respected businessma—'

'*Move!*' Meyer shouted.

Score rose rapidly and handed King a small white rectangle. 'My card, sir.' Backing off toward the door, he said, 'Call me anytime, sir, anytime at all. The name is Score. Adrian Score.' He opened the front door, shot a hasty glance at Meyer and then shouted, '*I can get your boy back!*' and slammed the door behind him.

'That rotten parasite!' Meyer said.

'He called us both businessmen,' King said. 'Why, he was nothing but a crook!'

'One of the worst. Human feelings mean nothing to him. But hang around a while, Mr King. Score is only the beginning. We'll be getting a wide range of ransom demands soon. Every filthy crook who's looking for a soft touch will hop on the bandwagon as soon as he figures a gimmick. The woods'll be full of kidnappers. We won't know the real bastards from the fake ones.'

'How do we know we have the real one now?' King asked.

'We don't. We can only assume we do.' Meyer paused and shook his head. 'One thing's for sure.'

'What's that?'

'I sure as hell wouldn't like to be back at the squad answering telephones right now.'

'Eighty-seventh Squad, Detective Willis?'

''Allo, you know the kidnap, please?'

'Who is this?' Willis said.

'Who you?' the woman said.

'Detective Willis. Can I help you, lady?'

'My name issa Miz Abruzzi,' the woman said. 'I'ma see the li'la boy.'

'The kidnap victim?'

'Yas, yas. He wass inna diner with two men. Both needa shaves, you unnerstan'? He's a li'la blond boy, no?'

'Yes, that's right.' Willis paused. 'When did you see him, lady?'

'When you tink?'

'Well, I don't know. You tell me.'

'This morn'.'

'Yeah, well the boy wasn't missing until this afternoon.'

'I see,' Mrs Abruzzi said, and then, unperturbed, she said, 'I wassa sit in the boot', an' these two men they come in wit' the boy. So right away, I'ma tink this is the li'la boy he wassa kidnap. So I watch what they—'

'Yes, Mrs Abruzzi, thank you very much,' Willis said, and he hung up. 'Holy God,' he shouted to Arthur Brown, 'I never saw anything like this in my life. You'd think we were giving away gold dollars to anybody who called Frederick 7–8024.'

'Everybody wants to help,' Brown said. 'The trouble is—' The phone on his desk rang. He picked it up quickly. 'Eighty-seventh, Detective Brown speaking.'

'I'd like the lieutenant, Detective Brown.'

'He's not here. Who's this, please?'

'Where is he?'

'Who'm I talking to?' Brown asked.

'This is Cliff Savage. I'm a reporter. The lieutenant knows me.'

'Well, he's still not here, Mr Savage. What can I do for you?'

'On this kidnapping.'

'Yes?'

'Is it true that the kidnappers have asked King for the ransom? Even though they know they've got the wrong boy?'

'I don't know what's going on out there, Mr Savage. I'm sorry.'

'Well, look, how can I find out?'

'Call me back later.'

'Where's the lieutenant? At the King house?'

'I wouldn't call there, Mr Savage. They probably want to keep those lines free for any possible contact from the—'

'The public has a right to know what's going on!' Savage said.

'Listen, you want to argue with me?'

'No, but . . .'

'Then don't. I feel like I've been working in the telephone room of the Automobile Club on the night a truck spilled a full load of tacks all over the highway. I'm getting a cauliflower ear from this goddamn phone, Mr Savage, and you sure as hell aren't helping it any.'

'Do you have the number out at the King house?'

'No.'

'I can find it, you know.'

'You may find trouble, too, Mr Savage. I'd keep off that phone if I were you. You may find yourself impeding the progress of an investigation.'

'Thanks, Brown. I'll do you a favour someday.'

'I can hardly wait,' Brown said, and he hung up. 'The son of a bitch,' Brown said. 'Wasn't he involved that time Reardon and Foster were killed? And Bush? Didn't he almost get Steve's wife in hot water?'

'Almost ain't the word,' Willis said. 'If he ever sets foot in this squadroom, the lieutenant'll drown him in the water cooler. Where's Miscolo? I want some coffee. Miscolo? Hey, Miscolo!'

'Yo?' a voice from the clerical office shouted.

'Make some joe.'

'What the hell you think this is?' Miscolo called. 'Howard Johnson's?'

'The coffee here is better,' Willis said flatteringly.

'Yeah, yeah,' Miscolo mumbled, but they could hear

him opening the file drawer to take out the can of coffee.

The telephone on Willis's desk rang.

'Come on,' he said to the phone, 'cut it out, willya?'

The phone kept ringing.

'Stop, stop, stop ringing.'

The phone shrieked into the room.

'All right, all right, all right,' he said, lifting the receiver. 'Eighty-seventh Squad, Willis. What? You saw the boy? . . . Yes, he's a blond boy . . . Yes, he's about eight . . . Yes, he was wearing a red sweater . . . Yes, sir. Yes, that certainly does sound like him . . . Yes, sir, where did you see him, sir? . . . Where, sir? . . . In a movie, sir? Which movie, sir? . . . I see. And he was sitting in the audience, is that right? . . . He wasn't? Well, then . . .' Willis paused, and an amazed look crossed his face. 'He was *in* the picture?' he said. 'You mean he was *acting* in the picture. On the screen? Mister, you mean this kid you saw – *In* the picture? Oh, mister, please, I got enough headaches.' He hung up abruptly. 'He calls me about a movie star. Says it's a remarkable coincidence. For the love of—'

The phone rang again.

'I'm gonna get a record made,' Willis said. 'It's gonna say, "Eighty-seventh Squad, Detective Willis. You saw the kid, right? Where? When? Thank you." Save my voice for the opera.' He picked up the receiver. 'Eighty-seventh Squad, Willis . . . Yes, ma'am, this is the Detective Division . . . Yes, ma'am, we are handling the Jeff Reynolds kidnapping . . . Yes, ma'am, we . . .'

The phone on Brown's desk rang.

'Eighty-seventh Squad, Detective Brown speaking . . .'

'Eighty-seventh Squad, Di Maeo . . .'
'Eighty-seventh Squad, Detective Willis . . .'
'Eighty-seventh Squad, Hernandez . . .'
'Eighty-seventh Precinct, Sergeant Murchison . . .'
'Eighty-seventh Precinct, Captain Frick . . .'
'Headquarters, Lieutenant Vinnick . . .'
'Arson Squad, Detective Hopkins . . .'
'You saw the boy, sir?'
'The boy was with three men, ma'am?'
'You saw the boy . . .'
'When, sir?'
'What street was that, sir?'
'Where, sir?'
'Where, ma'am?'
Where?
Where?
*Where?*

Lieutenant Byrnes walked into the Douglas King living room and blew on his hands.

'Hello, Steve,' he said. 'How's it going?'

'All right, sir,' Carella answered. 'Mr King, this is Lieutenant Byrnes.'

'How do you do, sir?' Byrnes said, and he took King's hand.

'How does it look, Lieutenant?' King asked.

'So-so. Has the Auto Squad delivered that list yet, Steve?'

'No.'

'Dammit. I understand "they're asking" you for the money, Mr King. That's a tough break.' He sighed. 'But maybe we've got something good outside.'

'What happened, Pete?'

'We're getting a good cast of a tyre track, and . . .'

'Will that help at all?' King said.

'It usually does. Tyre patterns are pretty easy to run down. Headquarters has an up-to-date file on tyre patterns, and once we get a good casting, half the battle is won. It's been our experience that a car will usually carry the same make of tyre on all four wheels – especially a new car. And, as funny as this may sound at first, when a tyre wears out, the owner will usually replace it with a tyre of the same make. So we can generally figure the make of car from the tyre pattern. In this case, we think we've got something else to go on, too.'

'What's that?' King asked.

'There are two boulders on the ground near where we found the tyre track. The guy driving that car was probably in a big hurry. He sideswiped one of the boulders. We got ourselves a pretty decent paint scraping from the rock. Kronig's already on the way to the lab with it. With a little luck, we may be able to come up with both the year and the make of the car. With a little luck. That's why I'm anxious to get that stolen-car list.'

'I see,' King said.

'I don't suppose Mr Reynolds is around, is he? I'd like to keep him abreast of what we're doing. The worst part of any kidnapping case is that the parents never feel we're doing enough.'

'He's in the kitchen, Pete,' Carella said. 'Want me to get him for you?'

'No, I'll go out to him in a few minutes.'

The doorbell chimed. Carella went to the door and

threw it open. A uniformed policeman stood there. 'I want Detective Carella,' he said.

'That's me.'

'You called the Auto Squad a little while ago?'

'Yes.'

'They sent me up with this.' He extended a manila envelope. 'A stolen-car list.'

'Thanks,' Carella said.

'What's the latest on the kid?' the patrolman asked.

'Nothing new, so far,' Carella said.

'Yeah.' The patrolman shook his head. 'Well, there's the list.'

'Thanks.'

'Okay.'

Carella closed the door behind him.

'Let me see that, Steve,' Byrnes said. He opened the manila envelope and studied the typewritten sheet. 'Not too bad. Couple of dozen cars, all told. Let's hope the lab boys turn up something that matches something on this list.'

'And where will that put you, Lieutenant?' King asked.

'Huh?'

'Suppose you know the car they used was a stolen one? How will that help you in finding the boy?'

'It'll give us something to look for. We've got roadblocks hemming in this whole city, Mr King. It would help if we knew the shape and size and colour of the needle, don't you think?'

'If they were smart enough to use a stolen car, they were probably smart enough to get rid of it immediately.'

'Unless they have further use for it,' Byrnes said.

'In which case they probably repainted it.'

'Unless there wasn't time. A homemade paint job is a pretty conspicuous thing, Mr King. The last thing these kidnappers want is to be conspicuous.'

'I see,' King said.

'I know it sounds slim, Mr King, but we haven't got a hell of a lot to work with here, and every little bit counts. Once the money is delivered, we'll have ransom bills to look for. And when we get the boy back, perhaps he'll be able to tell us something about his abductors. Unless we reach them before that.'

'Or unless the boy is dead already,' King said flatly.

'Yes. Unless he's dead. There wouldn't be any sense continuing then, would there?'

'None at all,' King answered.

'I want to talk to you about the ransom, Mr King. We can't mark the money, and there probably won't even be time to record all the serial numbers. They particularly specified no consecutive serial numbers, didn't they?'

'Yes. But . . .'

'Only to make the recording job more difficult. But we *will* be able to record some of those numbers, and even a partial list is a good thing to have. Those men will have to spend that money someday.' He paused. 'You haven't called the bank yet, have you?'

'No, I haven't.'

'Good. If you don't mind, I'd like to talk to them when you do. To tell them just what would be most helpful to us. If the F.B.I. comes in on this, they'll need—'

'I'm afraid I won't be able to help you, Lieutenant Byrnes,' King said.

Byrnes looked at him in puzzlement. 'I don't understand,' he said. 'You don't want me to talk to your bank?'

'No, Lieutenant, that's not it. I won't be talking to the bank, either.'

'Wh—?'

'I'm not going to pay the ransom, Lieutenant.'

'You're . . .' The room went silent. Byrnes looked at Carella. 'Well, of course . . . Well, that's entirely up to you. No one can force you to.'

'What are you saying, Mr King?' Carella said, frowning. 'You – you have to pay that ransom! That boy—'

'Knock it off, Steve,' Byrnes said.

'But he has to! That kid hasn't got a chance unless he—'

'I don't *have* to do anything!' King said tightly. 'Let's get this straight, gentlemen. I'm telling it to you, and I'll tell it to the kidnappers if they call again, and I'll tell it to anyone who cares to listen. I am not paying the ransom.' He paused. 'I am *not* paying the ransom.'

# 8.

**THERE WAS ONLY** one light burning in the parlour of the Sands Spit farmhouse, a standing floor lamp that stood close to the open sofa bed, casting a circle of light on the exposed wooden flooring. Jeff Reynolds was asleep in the centre of the bed. He turned and mumbled, and the blanket fell free of his shoulder. Kathy Folsom went to the bed and covered him again. Eddie Folsom lighted a cigarette and shook out the match.

'He asleep?'

'Yes.'

In the bathroom, Sy Barnard was singing at the top of his lungs. His shirt, tie, and gun holster were draped over the back of one of the parlour chairs. The police radio, part of the complicated equipment which stood against the wall, monotonously bleated its calls.

*'. . . proceed to intersection of Cambria and Newbridge. We want a block there to cover the whole intersection. You'll have 311 to assist. You got that, 307?'*

*'We got it.'*

*'Car 311, Car 311, proceed to intersection of Cambria and Newbridge to assist 307 in road block.'*

*'This is 311, okay. Any make on the car yet?'*

*'Nothing, 311.'*

*'Right.'*

'Sy!' Eddie called. 'Hey, Sy, you hear this?'

Sy, his face half covered with lather, came out of the bathroom. He was wearing only his undershirt. His arms and shoulders were covered with thick matted hair. 'What's the matter?' he said.

'They got road blocks springing up like mushrooms. How we gonna use the car?'

'What're you getting excited about? So they got roadblocks. So who cares?'

'You don't understand, Sy. They're stopping every car on the road. We have to use that car in the morning. How're we gonna . . . ?'

'How many times do I have to tell you? I'll be driving, right? Alone, right? In a lousy old Ford that don't attract any attention. So let's say they stop me. So I'm a guy on his way to work. I've got a driver's licence, and I'll show it to them if they ask for it. So? Do they know I'm driving a stolen car? How can they know that? We changed the plates, didn't we? So nobody's got nothing on me. So why the hell are you worried about their stupid roadblocks?'

'What about after we get the money?' Eddie said. 'How we gonna leave here? They'll still be watching.'

'And we'll still have nothing to worry about, because we won't have the kid with us. It'll be a guy, his wife and their brother-in-law. There's nothing to worry about. Let me finish shaving, will you? I feel like a Grade-A bum.' He went into the bathroom. Kathy waited until the door closed behind him.

'Eddie . . . after he gets the money, what'll happen to the boy?' 'We'll leave him right here. We'll call King to let him know where the kid is.'

Kathy nodded. 'That would be taking a . . . a big chance, wouldn't it?'

I don't think so.'

'Eddie, let's get out of here. Let's get out now, before it's too late!'

'Aw, honey, please, will you cut it out?'

*'Car 234, Car 234, are you still at the tunnel entrance?'*

*'This is 234. That's where we are, Handsome.'*

*'Okay, okay.'*

'Listen to them,' Kathy said.

'Sy says we got nothing to worry about. We've got to trust him in this, Kathy. He knows what he's doing.' Eddie walked to the ash tray and squashed out his cigarette. 'Sy never gave me a bum steer all the time I knew him. He's all right, Kathy.'

'Yes, he's fine,' she answered sarcastically.

'Well, he is. He taught me a lot.'

'Yes, he certainly taught you a lot.'

'Well, dammit, he *did*!' Eddie paused. 'He didn't have to hook up with somebody like me. Sy is big-time.'

'Big-time!' Kathy said. 'He's a hoodlum!'

'Aw, don't say that about him. He got a few bad breaks, that's all. But he's okay. Listen, you think it was easy to plan something like this? You know how many things that poor guy has on his mind?'

'He's got only one thing on his mind, Eddie.'

'Yeah? What's that?'

'He wants to kill that boy.'

'Aw, come on, willya? Wants to kill the boy! Sy's got a cool business head. He ain't yearning to get involved in a murder rap. All he wants out of this is his share of the loot.'

'And you?'

'What about me?'

'What do you want?'

'The same thing. Two hundred and fifty thousand bucks.'

'And how far will you go to get it?'

'What the hell are you talking about?' Eddie said. He went to the dresser, picked up the cigarette pack, dug into it, and crumpled it when he realized it was empty.

'How bad do you want that money, Eddie?'

'Very bad. You got a cigarette?'

Kathy opened her purse and looked into it. 'No, I haven't,' she said. She snapped the bag shut. 'Eddie, when we were kids, we used to play a game. It was called "Suppose?" and we used to say, "Suppose somebody offered you a million dollars, what would you do for it? Would you cut off a toe for it? Would you give one of your eyes? Would you spit on the cross?" Things like that. It was funny to hear the answers. All the kids had a different price for that million dollars.'

'What are you driving at?' Eddie said. 'Sy! Hey, Sy!'

'Yeah?'

'You got any cigarettes?'

Sy poked his head around the door. 'What?'

'You got any cigarettes?'

'In my jacket. You mind if I finish shaving?' He went back into the bathroom.

Eddie crossed to the jacket and went through the pockets. 'None here!' he said disgustedly. 'Sy, you ain't got any.'

'There's a carton in the car!' Sy yelled. 'Stop bothering me.'

'Where?'

'In the glove compartment. Man, will you let me shave in peace?'

Eddie started for the front door.

'What's *your* price, Eddie?'

'I don't know what you mean, Kathy.'

'Do you give an arm – but not an eye? Do you take part in a kidnapping – but stop at murder?'

The room was silent.

'What do your kid games have to do with real life?' Eddie asked at last.

'Sy is planning to kill that boy,' Kathy said.

'You're nuts.'

'It's part of his scheme, Eddie. He can't chance leaving the boy alive to identify him.' She paused. 'And I have to know where you stand.'

Eddie sighed. 'Where I stand, huh? Can't you just leave me alone?'

'No, Eddie. I have to know.'

'All right. All right, look. You were a kid, and you played your kid games and . . . and I was a kid, too, all right? Okay, and when I was a kid, I didn't have nothing. You know, Kathy? Nothing. Nothing. I . . . I . . . you say Mexico . . . you want to go to Mexico. Well, I want to go there, too. I really want to go there and . . . and I want to have a lot of money and I want waiters to treat me nice . . . and I want to have *something*. Not always nothing, all the time. I . . . I don't want to be dirt anymore, okay?'

'Okay. But—'

'So, honey, don't ask me where I stand. Don't harp on me. I don't want to start wondering about what I'm doing or why I'm doing it. This is the only way, believe me.' He paused, and when he went on there was a peculiar distress in his voice. 'This is the only way I know.'

'But it's not,' Kathy said firmly. 'Eddie, we could leave now. Sy's in the other room. If we hurried . . . Eddie, we could get out of here, and drop the boy someplace, and be free. Do you think the cops would care? If the boy is returned safely before any money changes hands, do you really think they'll try too hard to find us? We *could* get to Mexico. And we'd be together, without having to run all the time.'

'I . . . I don't know. I need a cigarette.'

'Eddie, tell me.'

'Kathy, leave me alone!' he shouted. He paused. 'I'm getting out of here.'

'Where are you going?'

'Down to the car for those cigarettes and . . , and then I'm going to take a walk.'

'I'll go with you.'

'I don't want any company. Leave me alone!' he said, and he opened the door.

'You still haven't told me where you stand, Eddie. I have to know . . .'

The door slammed on her words. She stood despondently in the centre of the room, listening to his footsteps retreating on the gravel outside. She walked to the door and locked it, and she leaned against it and sighed heavily, and suddenly Sy began singing in the bathroom again. She walked to the window and peered around the edge of the shade, stood there thoughtfully for a moment, turned to lean against the wall, facing the bathroom, studying the closed bathroom door, and then the boy asleep on the bed. When she made her decision, it showed in her face, and it showed in the sudden stiffening of her body. She took one last look at the closed bathroom door and then moved swiftly and purposefully to the sofa bed.

Seizing Jeff's shoulder, she whispered, 'Jeff! Wake up, Jeff!'

Jeff popped upright in the bed almost instantly. 'What is it?' he said. 'What? What?'

'Shhh,' she warned. She waited, watching the bathroom. 'Be quiet and do what I tell you to do.' She paused again. 'I'm taking you out of here.'

'You're taking me home?' Jeff asked exuberantly.

'Shhhh! For God's sake, keep your voice down.' She looked at the bathroom door and then the front door. Sy's voice was raised in song. There was no sound coming from the front yard. 'I can't take you home,' Kathy said, 'but I can take you out of here. I'll drop you off somewhere. Someone will find you. You'll get home. But you have to help me, and we have to move quickly and quietly. Do you understand?'

Whispering now, Jeff said, 'Yes. Are they . . . are they going to kill me?'

'I don't know. But we're not going to give them the chance.'

'Is Eddie your husband?'

'Yes.'

'He's not so hot,' Jeff said.

'He's my—'

'But he doesn't seem as if he would hurt me,' Jeff added hastily.

The singing in the bathroom stopped abruptly. Kathy glanced at the closed door sharply. The sound of running water seeped into the silent room.

'You're pretty,' Jeff said.

'Thank you. Where's your coat?'

'I don't have a coat. Only Bobby's sweater.'

'You'll need it. It's very cold out there. Where is it?'

'On the chair there.'

Kathy walked swiftly and silently to the chair. She took the sweater and began pulling it over his head.

'We'll go straight to the road,' she said. 'When we reach the road, we're going to start running, do you understand?'

'I'm a good runner,' Jeff said.

'All right then, come on.' Quickly she put on her coat and took his hand. Together, they tiptoed to the front door. Kathy unlocked it, turning the lock with all the caution of a safecracker. The tumblers clicked, and she hesitated. Then, slowly, cautiously, she opened the door a crack. The squeak sounded like a gunshot in the silent room. She peeked into the yard and then held out her hand to Jeff again. 'Come.'

'Wait!' he said, and he pulled away from her suddenly and darted back into the room.

'What . . . ?'

'My gun!' he said, rushing to the table where the empty shotgun rested. 'He gave it to me, didn't he?'

'Yes – hurry,' she whispered impatiently.

Jeff seized the shotgun by the barrel, swinging it around as it slid off the table, starting to run for the front door simultaneously. The stock of the gun clung to the table, hit an ash tray as Jeff pulled on the barrel. And then the ash tray moved to the edge, caught by the gun's stock, rushing, tilting, sliding over the edge of the table and dropping leadenly to the floor. The crash filled the room. Scattered pieces of glass ricocheted like fragments of a hand grenade. At the door, Kathy almost screamed. She brought her hand to her mouth and bit the knuckles. Jeff froze.

'Do you think . . . ?'

'Shhh!' Kathy said.

Silently, they waited. The door to the bathroom remained closed. Quickly, Kathy opened the front door again and peeked out.

'All right, let's go,' she said, and the bathroom door opened. She did not see the door opening. Looking into the yard, her hand extended behind her, waiting for Jeff, she did not know that Sy had entered the room, stopping in the bathroom doorway, his hands on his hips, instant recognition on his face.

'Hurry, hurry,' she said to Jeff, and she beckoned with her hand and then, when she realized he was not coming to her, turned from the door, starting to say, 'Jeff, will you please—' and then spotting Sy, and going pale all at once.

'Well, well,' Sy said. 'Where do you think you're going?'

'I was taking the boy out,' Kathy said.

'Oh, was you now?' His eyes flicked the room. 'Where's Eddie?'

'He went for a walk.'

Sy went quickly to the front door, locking it. 'Is that two-bit punk planning a doublecross?'

'No. He didn't know anything about this. He went to the car for cigarettes.'

'So you figured this was as good a time as any to blow the coop, huh? Boy, leave it to a dame. Lots of curves, and they're always ready to throw one of them at you. Take off your coat!'

Kathy hesitated.

'Take it off before I rip it off!' Sy shouted.

She took off the coat and tossed it onto the bed.

'The kid, too. He won't need that sweater. He ain't going anyplace.' Kathy went to Jeff and helped him to take off the sweater. 'Real buddy-buddy, ain't you? A real nice team, you and the kid.' Sy reached into his pocket and when his hand came into view again a closed switch knife was on the palm. He pressed a stud in the knife's handle, and the blade flashed into view. Slowly, he walked to where Kathy and the boy stood near the open bed.

'Listen to me, you little bitch,' he said. 'You try anything like this again, and you're gonna need plastic surgery, you understand? No matter what your darling Eddie says. And I'll personally rip this little bastard's heart out! Now you just remember that! You just remember!'

'I'm not afraid of you, Sy,' she said.

'No, huh?' He lifted the knife so that the blade was close to her throat now. 'You better even watch the way you talk to me from now on, honey. You better be real sweet to me, and maybe I'll forget what you just tried to pull. Real sweet to me from now on.'

With the blade at her throat, Sy moved his free hand down the length of Kathy's arm, caressing her. She pulled away from him quickly. The doorknob rattled, and Kathy moved toward it.

'Hey, open up,' Eddie called from outside.

Sy gestured at the door with his head. He pressed the blade of the knife shut and returned the knife to his pocket. Kathy unlocked the door. Eddie came into the room.

'You got your cigarettes, I see,' Sy said, smiling.

'Yeah.' Eddie dragged deeply on the butt. 'Gee, it's nice out. Cold, but real clear. Full of stars.'

'That means a good day tomorrow,' Sy said. 'Even the weather's with us. There ain't nothing going to foul up this job.' His eye caught Kathy's. 'Nothing,' he repeated.

'How come the kid's up?' Eddie asked.

'The little bastard can't sleep. He's worried about what's gonna happen to him tomorrow.'

'You think it'll go all right, Sy?'

'It can't miss,' Sy said. He turned to Kathy again. 'You hear that, Kathy? It can't miss. It's gonna work, and nothing's gonna stop it. We're all gonna be rich. I'll never ride another goddamn subway as long as I live. I'll wear silk underwear. You know there are guys who wear silk underwear? Me! I'm gonna be one of them.' He nodded vigorously. 'Tell her about it, Eddie. Tell her how we worked it out. Your wife here thinks we're playing games.'

'Look, let's just do it,' Eddie said. 'What do we have to talk about it for?'

'I want her to know because it's beautiful, that's why. What the hell's the matter with you? Are you ashamed of it? It's a goddamn good plan.'

'Yeah, I know, but . . .

'We're gonna call King in the morning, and give him instructions about the drop, and there won't be a cop in this city who can stop us, or who can even *find* us!' Sy paused. 'How does that sound to you, Kathy?'

'It sounds very smart,' Kathy said tonelessly.

'Yeah, very smart. *Damn smart!* Not even King is gonna know where the hell to drop that loot, so he couldn't tell the cops even if he wanted to. All he's gonna know is that we're waiting for it. But he won't know where.' He saw the puzzlement on Kathy's face. 'Yeah,' he said. 'Yeah. And it'll work. All because of Eddie's monster there.' He pointed to the radio equipment against the wall. 'Why do you think we knocked ourselves out on these radio store jobs? To give Eddie something to play with?'

'I thought you needed a radio for listening to police calls,' Kathy said, more puzzled now.

'A setup like this? For police calls? You know what those two tin cans are over there? Oscillators. And the big thing behind them? A transmitter. Am I right, Eddie?'

'Yeah, that's right. You see, Kathy, what we're gonna do—'

'What we're gonna do,' Sy said, 'is surprise the pants off King and the cops both. Once King gets started, there ain't gonna be a soul in the world but him who knows what to do. Not the cops, not nobody. Nobody but King and us. Once he leaves the house with that money in his hands—'

'*If* he leaves the house,' Kathy said. '*If* he pays the ransom.'

'I'll let you in on a secret, sweetheart,' Sy said. 'He better leave the house, and he better pay the ransom.' His hand darted into his pocket, and the switch knife appeared again. The stud made no sound when he pressed it. The blade snicked open with a slight whisper. Sy looked at Jeff, who stood by the bed, terror wide in his eyes now.

'He just *better* pay the ransom,' Sy said softly.

# 9.

THE MAN IN charge of the police laboratory was Lieutenant Sam Grossman.

The lab to the casual observer was a sterile place of long white counters and tall green cabinets. The counters were washed with fluorescent light and ultraviolet light, and the cabinets were full of laundry marks and pistols and cartridges and tyre patterns and analytical charts and pieces of glass and grass and morass and anything and everything which could be used for comparison purposes against a suspect item. There were a good many suspect items which came into the lab every hour of every day. The items ranged from the headlight glass found on a highway after a hit-and-run to a bloody hand wrapped in last Sunday's real-estate section of *The New York Times*. It was not always pleasant to deal with the packages that were dropped at the lab's doorstep like orphans on a snowy Christmas Eve. There were times when the work assumed ghoulish proportions, and many a man with a weak stomach had instantly applied for transfer to the city's Bureau of Criminal Identification, or perhaps the morgue at one of the local hospitals. It was one thing, you see, to deal with violent and sudden deaths in an active, participating way. It was another to reduce death to a scientific formula, to deal with severed limbs and errant sperm cells, hair-encrusted blunt weapons, cartridges flattened by impact with bone. The imagination soared when confronted with the grisly inarticulate by-products of murder or manslaughter. A long blond hair tangled into the sharp cutting edge of an axe shrieked more loudly than the corpse of the woman lying on a slab at the morgue. Understatement, a subtle weapon of novelists since the beginning of literature, became a daily working grindstone against which the lab technicians blunted their emotions. Sam Grossman, an emotional man by nature, an unemotional man by trade, ran the lab with the uncompromising discipline of an African missionary. The lab, Grossman knew, could very often shorten the work of the men out there in the field. The lab could bring criminals to justice. And if he could help to do this, Grossman felt his life was not being wasted. Sometimes his job was extremely difficult. Sometimes, as was the case with the casting Kronig brought back, Grossman's job was exceptionally easy. He simply went to his files and came up with the right tyre pattern in less than five minutes. The record card looked like the picture overleaf.

The name of the tyre, then, was Tirubam, and it was manufactured by the Rubber Tire Corporation of America, whose offices in this city were located at 1719 Carter Avenue in Isola. The tyre had been standard equipment in 1948 on products of the General Motors Corporation. In 1949 and 1950, the Ford Motor Company had used it on its entire line. In 1954, Chrysler Motors had equipped its automobiles with this tyre. The field seemed a rather large one from which to choose.

The size of the tyre, however, was determined from the cast to be 670×15. This was a break which

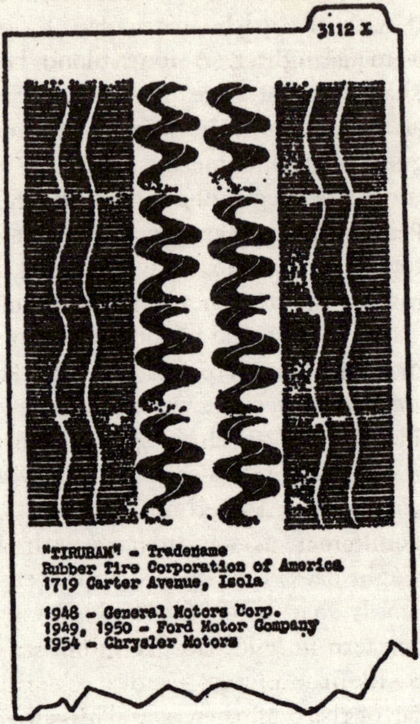


automatically eliminated any automobile manufactured before 1949, since the wheel rim had been sixteen inches in diameter up to that time and the changeover for the entire industry had come in 1949. The size of the tyre, too, eliminated any of the larger cars which both Ford and Chrysler produced in the respective years they'd used the tyres. The 1949 Mercury, for example, carried a 710×15 tyre. The 1949 Lincoln carried an 820×15. The field had been narrowed to the smallest cars produced by either of the companies in the suspect years.

The paint scraping cleared up any doubt. By the time Grossman's boys had put the sample through a spectographic examination and had made a microscopic diagnosis and a microchemical examination, they knew exactly the nature of the beast with which they were dealing. They simply took the results of their tests and compared these with facts already compiled, listed, and waiting in their files. Their record cards told them:

1. That the paint was a product of the Ford Motor Company.
2. That it was called Birch Gray by the firm.
3. That it was used on the company's 1949 models.
4. That it had been dropped in 1950 in favour of a slightly different shade which the company called Dover Grey.

Sam Grossman studied the facts. He studied them with the coldly unemotional eye of a scientist. Looking over the figures, his blue eyes guileless behind their spectacles, his face bearing the craggy, homespun look of a New England farmer, he nodded his head gently. The suspect car was a grey 1949 Ford. There was nothing more to do but call the King house and present the facts. The other policemen would take it from there. Sam Grossman took off his glasses, closed his eyes, and rubbed at them with thumb and forefinger. Then he put the glasses on again and dialled the King estate.

Meyer Meyer took the call in the living room. Douglas King, sitting in an easy chair near the fireplace, sat staring at the shifting flames while Meyer copied down the information the lab gave him. King showed no indication of listening to the call. The fire lighted the rugged planes of his face, glistened redly in the greying hair over his temples.

'I got it, Sam,' Meyer said. 'That's nice work. What? . . . Well, it doesn't look so hot on this end, but now we've got something to look for . . . . Yes, we'll get it out right away. Thanks a lot, Sam.' He hung up and turned to King. 'A grey 1949 Ford. That's what they were driving. I'd better find the lieutenant. He'll want to check this against his list.' He studied King silently for a moment. Then he said, 'Penny for your thoughts, Mr King.'

'I'm not thinking anything worthwhile at the moment, Detective Meyer,' King said.

'Mmmm. Well, I'm going outside, see if I can rustle up the lieutenant. Yell if that phone rings.'

'I will,' King promised. Meyer put on his coat and left the room. King did not look up when the door eased shut. He kept staring into the flames as if his soul were there, as if he could read himself in the leaping reds and yellows. When Diane King came into the room, he still did not look up. She walked directly to him and stood before him, blocking his view of the flames.

'All right,' she said in a voice that was barely audible. 'Pete told me.' She paused. 'You can't be serious.'

'I am serious, Diane.'

'I don't believe you.'

'I'm not paying. Start believing it, Diane. I'm not paying.'

'You have to pay.'

'I don't have to do anything.'

'They asked *you* for the money.'

'Yes, a bunch of crooks asked. Why should they make the rules? Why should I play the game according to their rules?'

'Rules? Game? There's a little boy involved here.'

'There's a whole lot more than a little boy involved,' King said.

'There's nothing more than a little boy involved,' Diane answered. 'If you don't pay them, they'll kill him.'

'He may be dead already.'

'You can't even consider that possibility.'

'Why can't I? I can consider every damn aspect of this thing. I've been asked to pay five hundred thousand dollars for a boy who means absolutely nothing to me. I've got every right to weigh the possibilities. And one possibility is that he's already dead.'

'They told you he was still alive. You know they did. You can't excuse yourself by . . .'

'And another possibility is that they'll kill him even if I do pay. Ask the police. Go ahead. See what they—'

'And if you don't pay, they'll most *certainly* kill him.'

'Not necessarily.'

King rose from his chair. He left the fire reluctantly, walking to the bar unit at the other end of the room. 'Would you like a brandy?' he asked.

'No, I would not like a brandy,' She watched him as he poured. His hand was steady on the neck of the bottle. The amber fluid filled the brandy snifter. He recapped the bottle, walked back to the easy chair and gently rolled the glass in his big hands. She continued watching him, and finally she said, 'Doug, you have no right to gamble with Jeff's life.'

'No? Who has a better right? Who'd they ask for the money? What is Reynolds doing to get his son back? He's sitting on his behind, the way he's sat all his life. Why should I have to pay for *his* son?'

'Doug, I'm trying very hard to keep from screaming. I'm trying with all my might to keep from screaming.'

'Go ahead and scream if it'll make you feel any better. Actually, there's nothing to scream about. I shouldn't have been asked to pay, and I'm not paying, and that's that. It's a closed issue as far as I'm concerned.'

'But he's a child! A *child*!'

'I don't care what he is. He's nothing of mine.' He paused as if searching for a clincher to his argument and then said, 'I don't even *like* him, do you know that?'

'He's a child, damn you!'

'All right, he's a child. What's that got to do with it? Am I responsible for him? How is he my responsibility, child or adult, or creature from the depths? How the hell is he my responsibility?'

'They meant to take Bobby,' Diane said. 'That's what makes Jeff your respon—'

'Yes, but they *didn't* take him, did they? They goofed. They took Jeff.' King paused. 'Honey, when I was in the service and the guy standing next to me got killed, I didn't feel responsible for his death. I was simply tickled to death the bullet hadn't clipped me. I felt no guilt and no responsibility. I hadn't fired the rifle that discharged the bullet that killed him. My hands were clean. And they're clean now, too.'

'This is different,' Diane said. 'You're not so stupid that you can't see this is different.'

'I'm not stupid at all. How in the hell can I give them all that money? Don't you think I'd give it if I had it?'

'You *have* got it! Don't lie to me, Doug. For God's sake, don't pretend.'

'I need every cent I have for this deal. Seven hundred and fifty thousand dollars. How can I give away two thirds of that? Don't you understand?'

'Yes, I understand completely. A boy's life against a business deal.'

'No! A boy's life against *my* life!' King shouted.

'Doug, Doug, don't insult my intelligence! This wouldn't be the end for you. Don't say your "life" as if—'

'My life, my life!' King insisted. 'Just that! Everything I've worked for since as long as I can remember. This business is a part of me, Diane, don't you realize that?'

'The hell with the business,' she snapped. 'I don't care if you never own Granger Shoe! I simply don't care. If you owned Granger, if you owned United States Steel and got them by letting a boy die . . .'

'It's my life, my *life*!'

'And it's his death! Your life against his death!'

'Don't throw semantics at me,' King said angrily. He put his glass down on the coffee table and rose suddenly, beginning to pace the room. 'It's my death, too. What happens to me if I pay that ransom? I'll tell you what happens. Benjamin and his goddamn vultures will team up with the Old Man and kick me into the street. You were worried about what I did to Robinson, about his ever getting a job again. Okay, do you know what they'll do to *me*? My name'll be mud in the industry. A power grab that failed! Do you think any other firm would trust me after that? Do you think I'd ever get this far again? I'd be finished, Diane. Finished!'

'You could start again. You could—'

'Where? Where do I start? And how far do I go? Goddammit, even the office boys would watch me to make sure I never got too big again. I'd be chained to a desk. Is that what you want for me? Is that living?'

'Yes, it's living. There are hundreds of men chained to—'

'Not me! Never.' He paused. 'And what about yourself, Diane? Think of yourself. All this would go.' He gestured wildly with his hands. 'The house, the cars, the way we live, even the goddamn food we eat!'

'I'd choke!' Diane said. 'If you let Jeff die, I'd choke with every bite I took.'

'Then who's supposed to die? Me? Am I supposed to die for him? What is he to me?'

'He's a human being, that's all. Another human being. You used to care about . . .'

'All right, and I'm a human being, too. What the hell do I owe humanity, this great faceless mass named by the gentle spirits of our time? What has humanity, anonymous *humanity*, ever handed me? Nothing! I've clawed an existence for myself, clawed it out of solid rock until my hands are bleeding. How could you know, Diane, how could you possibly know? You were attending a private school while I was working my ass off in Granger's stockroom. I've worked for this business all my life, don't you see, all my life! And only because I could see into the future, the time when—'

'I don't want to hear it. If you mention the business

again, I'll . . . I'll punch you. I swear to God, I'll punch you!'

'All right, forget the business. Just tell me why *I* should pay. How many people out there have more money than I'll ever have. I'm poor, for God's sake. By comparison, I'm poor. It's taken me years to reach the point where I can afford this deal. There are people who make deals like this every day of the week, pick up a phone, close it by saying yes or no. Why haven't we had munificent offers from some of them? Why don't *they* pay the goddamn ransom?'

'That couple in Calm's Point offered you a thousand dollars, Doug. And they're probably poorer than you ever were.'

'Sure, a thousand dollars. What percentage of their life's savings is that? How much have they got in the bank *besides* that? Have they got five thousand? Okay, let's send them a return wire and ask for the entire sum, the entire five, not just the portion of it represented by the thousand they offered. Let's tell them they have to give us their life savings or a boy will die. What plans have they made for that money, Diane? A down payment on a house in the country? A new car? A trip to Europe? What? Ask *them* to give up their plans and their dreams for a kid who means nothing to them. Go ahead, ask them. Ask anybody in the world! Ask all of your sweet loving humanity! Ask humanity to commit suicide for a brother!'

'*You* were asked,' Diane said. 'You can't pass the buck.'

'I know I was asked, and I'm saying it's unfair. It's idiotic! I'm saying *nobody* should be asked.'

Diane sat at his feet suddenly. She took his hands in

her own and looked up into his face. 'Look,' she said gently, 'if . . . if Jeff were drowning and . . . and you were standing there on the shore . . . why, you'd automatically jump in after him, wouldn't you? You'd save him. That's all I'm asking of you now. Save him, Doug. Save him, please, please, pl—'

'But why me?' King said plaintively. 'Because I took the trouble to learn how to swim? Why didn't Reynolds learn to swim? Why should he come to me now and say, "Save my son! I never bothered to learn how to swim!"?'

'Are you blaming Reynolds for what happened?'

'Don't be silly, how could I?'

'For what then? For being a chauffeur? For not having five hundred thousand dollars?'

'Okay, I *have* got five hundred thousand, and I didn't get it by sitting around and watching the world go by. So where's the justice? I've worked hard for everything I've ever—'

'Reynolds has worked hard, too!'

'Not hard enough, then! Not half as hard! If he had, I wouldn't have to ransom his goddamn son! He's a sitter, Diane. And the sitters all want something for nothing. The big jackpot! The big country of quiz programmes that pay thousands of dollars for worthless information! Want a million dollars? Sure, go out and win it! Bull! Go out and work for it! Work like a bastard, until your fingers are—'

'Stop it, stop it,' she said.

'What is Reynolds saying to me? He's saying, "Help me, I'm helpless." Well, I don't want to help. I don't want to help anybody but myself.'

'You don't mean that,' Diane said, dropping his hands. 'You can't mean that.'

'I do mean it. Don't you think I'm tired too, Diane? Don't you think I'd like to *sit*?'

'I don't know what to think. I don't know anything about you any more.'

'You don't have to know anything about me. I'm a man fighting for his life. That's all you have to know.'

'And Jeff's life?' she asked, suddenly rising. 'Do you want them to kill him?'

'Of course I don't!' he shouted.

'Don't yell at me, Doug! They will kill him. You know they will!'

'I don't know they will! And it's not my problem. He's not mine. He's not my son!'

'He's there *because* of your son!' Diane shouted.

'I'm sorry about that, but it wasn't my—'

'You're *not* sorry! You don't care what they do to him. Oh, my God, you don't give a damn what happens to that—'

'That's not true, Diane. You know I . . .'

'What's happened to you, anyway?' she said. 'What's become of you? Where's Douglas King?'

'I don't know what you . . .'

'Maybe I shouldn't have stood by watching all these years, never raising a finger. Yes, you clawed, oh God, *how* you clawed your way, but I told myself this was an admirable trait, a desirable trait. This was a *man*, I told myself, the man I love. Even when I realized what you were doing to people, I excused it, I said it was simply your way. I convinced myself that you weren't cruel and ruthless and—'

'How does this make me ruthless? Isn't self-preservation more important than—'

'Shut up and listen to me!' Diane said. 'All those

years, God, all those years and this was what you were becoming! *This!* I watched when you crushed Di Angelo to get the cutting-room-foreman job, and I watched while you smashed half a dozen men in that factory to get to the top, and I watched while you ruined Robinson, and I was ready to watch on this Boston thing, knowing you'd throw the Old Man, *and* Benjamin, *and* how many others into the street! With resignations, Doug? Would you have allowed them to resign? Oh, God!' She covered her face with her hands, unwilling to sob, unwilling to show any sign of weakness.

'This is a different thing entirely,' King said.

'No, this is the same damn thing! The same pattern! Over and over and over again. People just don't mean anything to you any more, do they? You just don't care about anything but yourself!'

'That isn't true, Diane, and you know it. Haven't I always given you whatever you wanted? Haven't I been a good father to Bobby? A good husband to—'

'What have you ever given to me or Bobby? A roof? Food? Trinkets? What have you ever given of *yourself*, Doug? When have I ever meant more to you than your business? What am I now but a good bed companion?'

'Diane . . .'

'Admit it to yourself! You said the business was your life, and you meant it! Nothing else matters a damn to you! And now you're ready to murder a boy! After all these years, you've arrived! You're finally ready to murder an innocent little boy!'

'Murder, murder, you throw the word around as if—'

'It's murder! Pure and simple! You can call it what you want, but it's murder! You are about to commit a murder and, goddammit, this time I won't watch you do it!'

'What do you mean? What are you talking about?'

'I mean *this*, Doug. I mean you'll pay those kidnappers.'

'No. I won't, Diane. I can't.'

'You can, Doug, and you will. Because you're going to have to choose between your business and something besides Jeff's life.'

'What?'

'If you don't pay them, Doug, I'm leaving.'

'Leav—'

'I'm taking Bobby and I'm getting out of this house.'

'Now, come on, Diane, you don't know what you're saying. You're . . .'

'I know exactly what I'm saying, Doug. Pay those men, because I don't want to be anywhere near you if you don't! I don't want to be anywhere near something that's turned rotten and filthy.'

'Diane . . .'

'Rotten and filthy,' she repeated. 'Like one of the machines in your factory. A filth-clogged—'

'Honey, honey,' he said, and he reached out for her. 'Can't you—'

'Get away from me!' she shrieked, and she pulled away from his grasp. 'Not this time, Doug! This time you don't drag me into bed and make everything all right that way! I don't want your hands on me, Doug. This time you're doing murder, and I've had it – right up to here!'

'I can't pay,' he said. 'You can't ask me to.'

'I'm not asking, Doug,' she said coldly. 'I'm telling. When those men call tomorrow morning, you'd better have the money for them. It had better be ready and waiting for their instructions, Doug. It had better be.'

'I can't give it to them,' he said. 'Diane, I can't pay. You can't ask me to.'

But she had already walked out of the room.

# 10.

**MORNING.**

The city slumbers. The piercing cold is designed for late sleeping. It couples with the blackness outside to make the bed a sanctuary. There are cold floors in this city, and no one is anxious to touch them with bare feet.

The alarm clocks begin to ring when it is still dark. There is no sign of the sun as yet. The stars are beginning to flee the vault of night, but there is no spark of warmth on the horizon to the east. The morning is filled with blackness, and the alarm clocks penetrate the gloom with their staccato rings and persistent hums, their automatically tuned music, Good morning, America, it's time to rise and shine.

Go to hell, and the hands reach out to silence the never sleeping voices of time, go to hell, and a shoulder is turned into a warm blanket, flesh touches flesh, George, it's time to get up.

Mrmmbbb.

George, honey, it's time to get up.

The Georges of the city slip from beneath the blankets, leaving the warm womb of the connubial bed, their toes touching icy floors. The Georges of the city shiver and dress quickly, and the water in the tap (hot or cold, it makes no difference) all feels as if it is rushing from an icy mountain stream. It is a chore to shave. The light in the bathroom casts a cold eerie glow.

The wife and the kids are still asleep, and there is something unnatural about being the only person awake in the apartment, one of a million Georges who are awake throughout the city, performing their early-morning toilets. It is still cold in the apartment, but the radiators are beginning to bang now, and soon there will be the hiss of heat, the penetrating smell of heat. The coffee pot in the kitchen is beginning to perk, and the rich aroma of the brew will invade the apartment soon. Even the water from the tap feels a little warmer now. But best of all, the sun is coming up.

It rises without a problem. Boldly, it peers over the edge of the night, wearing a halo that turns the bowl of the sky upon itself, sends it rushing away, spikes of yellow intimidating the deep blue, fiery oranges boldly pushing at the night, rising, rising, like a giant suddenly standing, the sun touches the east, lines the edges of the building with sudden yellow, washes the River Harb in gold, covers the streets with warmth, no problems has the sun, no complexities, it is simply a matter of rising, it is simply a matter of shining. Good morning, America, it's time to rise and shine.

The neon lamps blink in sudden weakness against the overwhelming power of the sun. In the empty canyons of the city, the traffic signals click monotonously. There is no traffic; the reds and greens are meaningless. There are no pedestrians to heed the Walks and Don't Walks. Reds and greens flash, and the sun's single hot eye reflects on the countless glass eyes of the traffic signals, lights the windows of the tall buildings so that they gleam eastward with a hundred torrid glares.

A blind man taps his way along the pavement.

On the river, the traffic comes to life. The Georges of

the river wake to the smell of brine and cooking bacon. The whistles begin to hoot up and down the curving waterfront. On a Navy vessel, reveille is piped over the loudspeaker system.

The street lamps go out.

There is only the sun now.

A patrolman makes his silent rounds, trying the knobs of stores, leaning close to the plate-glass doors, peering into shops. He glances at his watch. Five-forty-five. In a few hours he will be relieved on post.

It has been a long, cold night.

But now it is morning.

She packed in the silence of the sun-washed bedroom. Dust motes climbed the shaft of sunshine, limning her figure as she methodically filled the bag. Liz Bellew watched her, sipping at a cup of coffee, curled up on the chaise longue alongside the bed.

'I haven't been up this early since the morning Alpha Beta Tau staged a panty raid,' Liz said.

'I remember,' Diane answered.

'Flaming youth, where have you gone? Alpha Beta Tau raided panties, and all Harold raids is the icebox.'

'We all have to grow up sometime, Liz,' Diane said. She opened one of the dresser drawers, removed a pile of slips from it and brought them to the bed.

'Do we?' Liz asked. 'And when do you grow up, honey? This seems like a pretty childish thing to me.'

'Does it?'

'Yes, it does. Unless you happen to have a suicidal urge.' Liz pulled a face and sipped at her coffee. 'But I always had you pegged as a pretty levelheaded girl. So now you're asking Doug to ruin himself and you besides. That doesn't make sense.'

'Doesn't it?'

'No.' Liz frowned. 'I wish you'd stop picking up the tail ends of my sentences and turning them into questions. It sounds a bit like imitation Hemingway.'

'I'm sorry.' Diane smoothed out a slip, folded it and put it into the bag. 'Suppose it were one of your children out there, Liz?'

'I'd cut off my arm to save him,' Liz answered unhesitatingly.

'And suppose it were my boy – Bobby – and they asked *you* for the money?'

Liz took a long pull at the coffee. It was still early morning, and she wore no make-up, but she was beautiful even without it, and her eyes were clear. 'Darling,' she said, 'I love you like a sister. Always have, and this isn't just a college-days-remembrance bit. But I'm not sure I'd part with five hundred thousand bucks to save your son. I'm just not sure, Diane. And if that makes me a bitch, so be it.'

'I'm surprised,' Diane said.

'Why? Because I'm a mother? I'm only a mother to the three little monsters who cavort through the house on the hill. I'm not a mother to all humanity, thank God.' Liz paused. 'Three pregnancies were enough.'

They were silent for a while. Liz finished her coffee and put down the empty cup. Diane continued packing.

'It was good of you to offer me a place, Liz,' she said.

'The least,' Liz said breezily. 'But if Doug asks me what I think about all this, I'll tell him quite frankly that you are nuts.'

'You needn't bother. He thinks so already.'

'Are you sure this kidnapping business is behind your leave-taking?' Liz asked. 'There's not something else? This is Aunt Lizzie, darling, so don't be afraid to—' She stopped suddenly. 'He's still good in bed, isn't he?'

'Yes, he's fine.'

'Then what the hell's wrong with you? Unpack that bag and go down and kiss him, for God's sake.'

'Liz,' Diane said calmly, 'he's *out* of bed sixteen hours a day.'

'Darling, we mustn't be greedy,' Liz said, lifting one eyebrow.

'Don't joke, Liz, please. This isn't fun for me.'

'I'm sorry.'

'He knocked on the door three times during the night,' Diane said. 'The last time, he sounded as if he was crying. Can you imagine Doug crying?' She paused. 'I wouldn't open the door for him. He's got to know I'm serious. He's got to know I'm leaving unless he pays that ransom.'

'Why don't you simply ask him to shoot himself in the head?' Liz said.

'I'm only asking him to do what any other human being would do.'

'Don't talk about human beings when you talk about tycoons,' Liz answered. 'They're a breed apart.'

'Then I want no part of the tycoon. If money and power are all that matter in life . . .'

'That's only a small part of it,' Liz said. 'Tycoonery is a disease. We laymen call it ants in the pants. Men like Doug and Harold couldn't sit still if you nailed them to the chair. They've got to be moving, they've got to be *doing* something. Render them inactive, and you're draining their life's blood.'

'And does "tycoonery" include the loss of all pity and

compassion for your fellow men?' Diane asked. 'Does it include all that, Liz?'

A knock sounded on the bedroom door.

'Who is it?' Diane asked.

'Me. Pete.'

'Would you get that, Liz?'

Liz Bellew uncurled herself from the lounge and went to the door. Opening it, she said, 'Good morning,' and Cameron looked at her in surprise.

'Liz,' he said. 'Didn't expect you here. Didn't even know you got up so early in the morning.'

'I always wake up early,' Liz answered. 'And always refreshed. How'd you sleep, Mr Cameron?'

'Fine, Mrs Bellew. Considering.'

'Then you haven't reached tycoon status yet. When you do, you'll begin scheming at night, too.'

Cameron smiled. 'I do all my scheming during the day, Liz.'

'Mmm, I'll bet you do,' she answered. 'And all your best work at night.' Their eyes locked. Diane, packing the bag, did not seem to notice. 'What brings you to the lady's boudoir?' Liz asked.

'A problem. I've got Doug's cheque in my pocket, Diane. What do I do? Go up to Boston with it? Or tear it up?'

'You'll have to ask him.'

'I ought to tear it up,' Cameron said. 'He's going to pay that ransom. I'm sure of it.'

'What makes you so sure?'

'He has to, don't you see?'

'No, I'm afraid I don't.'

'Well, look, let's say I go to Boston to close this deal, right? Douglas King then gets control of Granger Shoe.

But the newspapers'll smear him from here to China and back. Douglas King, they'll say, the man who now controls Granger Shoe, the man who refused to save a little boy's life. Hell, the publicity will ruin him. Do you think anybody would buy a pair of Granger shoes after that?'

'No, I don't suppose so. I hadn't thought of it that way.'

'Sure,' Cameron said. 'And you can bet Doug is considering that angle of it right now. That's why I'm certain he'll pay.'

'If that were his only reason for paying—' Diane started.

'What time did they say they'd call?' Liz interrupted.

'The kidnappers? They didn't say.'

Liz shook her head. 'And when they call, they ask the big question. I think the television quiz shows are more humane, don't you? At least they give you a week to decide.'

There was a cough at the door to the bedroom. They all turned. Douglas King stood there in robe and pyjamas. He was unshaven and his eyes were rimmed with red, but there was a cold deadly purposefulness to his stance. He stood in the doorframe like a spectre suddenly materialized. He issued his single cough and then said nothing, simply standing there and staring into the room.

'Good morning, Doug,' Cameron said. 'Sleep well?'

'No, I didn't sleep well.'

'God, you look awful, Doug,' Liz said.

'I'm supposed to look awful, didn't you know? My sins are all catching up with me. I'm a cruel, heartless bastard, that's me,' King paused. 'What are you doing here so early?'

'I called her last night, Doug,' Diane said. 'I'm taking Bobby there.'

'All ready for the big Sinking Ship scene, huh? Women and children first.' He turned to Cameron. 'When are you leaving, Pete?'

'What?'

'I said when are you leaving?'

'Well, I . . . I don't know.'

'What do you mean, you don't know? What plane are you on?'

'I didn't make a reservation,' Cameron said.

'Why not?'

'I thought . . .'

'It's not your job to think. I told you to get a reservation, didn't I? I gave you a cheque to deliver, didn't I?'

'Yes, but . . . I didn't know whether you still wanted me to.'

'Nothing's changed. Get downstairs and call the airport.' Cameron nodded and left the room.

Resignedly, Diane said, 'I guess I'd better finish packing, Liz.'

King stared at her for a moment and then went out of the room and downstairs. Cameron was already on the telephone.

'Eastern Airlines, please,' he said. 'Hello? I'd like to make a reservation for your first available flight to Boston. This morning.' He paused. 'Yes. This morning. Yes, I'll wait.' He cupped the mouthpiece and turned to King. 'They're checking it, Doug.'

'You should have taken care of this last night.'

'You going to let them kill that boy, Doug?' King opened his mouth, ready to answer, and Cameron turned back to the phone. 'Hello? Yes? Twelve noon? Hold on a minute, will you?' He cupped the mouth-piece again. 'Earliest flight is twelve noon. The others are filled.'

'Book it,' King said.

'All right, would you list me, please?' Cameron said into the phone. 'Mr Peter Cameron. That's C as in Charlie, a-m-e-r-o-n. Cameron. I've got a U-card, would you please – Yes, it's listed for Granger Shoe Company . . . . That's right, Granger with a G . . . . Check-in time is what? . . . All right, thank you.' He hung up and then turned to face King. 'Okay,' he said, 'we just chopped off Jeffry Reynolds's head.'

'Cut it out.'

'It's true, isn't it?'

'I said cut it out!'

'You are killing an eight-year-old boy, aren't you?'

'Yes, yes, I'm killing an eight-year-old boy – all right? I drink the blood of infants – all right? Don't you like what I'm doing? If you don't, pack your bag with the rest and get the hell out!'

'Now hold it a minute, Doug. There's no reason to—'

'I don't need any reason for anything! I'm just a ruthless, filth-clogged machine, and if you don't like my smell, you can leave with the rest of them!'

'Well, I guess that's putting it pretty plainly.'

'That's putting it pretty goddamn plainly, if you ask me. Make up your mind.'

'I still say it's murder,' Cameron said.

'Okay. If you think so, fine. I don't need men around me who—'

'Doug, listen to me. If our relationship has ever meant anything to you, for God's sake listen to me! Let the deal go! Save that kid! He's a young, defenceless child! You can't just . . .'

'When did you start loving young, defenceless children?'

'Aw, Doug, everybody loves kids! God, you can't be that—'

'And especially Pete Cameron, huh? The big child-lover. Don't you know this Boston deal will help you, too? Surely you know that, Pete. Hasn't any of my cold-hearted business acumen rubbed off on you after all these years?'

'Sure, I know it. But . . .'

'But it doesn't matter, huh? You love kids that much, do you? You love little runny-nosed Jeff Reynolds so much that Pete Cameron's career doesn't matter. Well, that's interesting. That's pretty damn interesting.'

'I'm not saying he matters more than my career, Doug. I'm saying . . .'

'Just what the hell *are* you saying?' Doug shouted, and the room went silent.

'Well . . .'

'Well?'

'I'm saying a boy's life is important.'

'But more important than this deal, right?'

'No, not more important, but . . .'

'More important or less important? Which?'

'Well, when you put it that way, I suppose . . .'

'If I pay the ransom, the deal falls flat on its face.

Now do you want the deal to collapse, or don't you? What's the matter, Pete? I've never seen you tongue-tied before. Does murder startle you?'

'No, no, it's just that . . .'

'Do you want this deal to fold, or don't you? Answer me.'

'No, I don't,' Cameron said.

'Then why are you so interested in the welfare of Jeffry Reynolds? When did you get so fatherly, Pete? I'm wondering when you got so ninety-nine per cent paternal?'

'It's for the boy,' Cameron said. 'How can we stand by and let a young defenceless—'

'If you give me that young, defenceless child crap again, I'll puke! What is it, Pete? What's the real reason?' King paused. A crafty glint touched his eyes. 'You got something of your own cooking? Is that it?'

'What? Me? Someth—Me?'

'Well, now,' King said. He moved a little closer to Cameron, a cold smile twisting his mouth. '*Well*, now. Now we're getting close, huh? Now we're . . .'

'Doug, don't be silly.'

'Why'd you call Benjamin yesterday? And never mind the Far Eastern Brocade baloney! What are you planning with him?'

'Me? Nothing. Doug, don't be ridiculous. I wouldn't plan anything with Benjamin.'

'Who *would* you plan something with?'

'Nobody.' Cameron laughed feebly. 'Nobody, Doug.'

'Did you tell Benjamin about this Boston deal?'

'Boston? Why, no. No.'

'Then why'd you call him?'

'About the Far Eastern Brocade line. I told you, Doug. The sales meeting . . .'

'Your secretary could have handled that! Why'd you make a personal call to Benjamin's house?'

'I . . . I wanted to tell him personally. I thought he'd be offended if I . . .'

'Yeah? Go ahead.'

'I . . . I just thought he'd be offended, that's all.'

King stared at Cameron silently for several moments. Then he went directly to the telephone and began dialling.

'What are you doing?' Cameron asked.

King did not answer. He stood with the phone to his ear, facing Cameron, waiting.

'The Benjamin residence,' a voice said.

'Get me Mr Benjamin,' King said.

'Who's calling, please?'

'Douglas King.'

'One moment, Mr King.'

'Why are you calling *him?*' Cameron said. 'I told you . . .'

'Hello?' a voice on the other end asked.

'George?' King said sweetly. 'This is Doug.'

'What is it, Doug?' Benjamin answered.

'How are you, George?'

'I'm fine. It's a little early in the morning, isn't it, to be exchanging—'

'George, I've been giving your proposition a lot of thought.' King continued staring at Cameron, who sat poised on the edge of his chair.

'Have you?' Benjamin said.

'Yes. It doesn't sound half bad to me.'

'Oh, doesn't it?' Benjamin said smugly. 'Well, well.'

'I'm thinking I may throw in with you, George.'

'Oh, you may, hey?'

'Yes. After all, there's more than myself to think about. There're a lot of other people who've served me loyally over the years. This would mean a lot to them, too.'

'You're such a Good Samaritan, Doug.'

'Well, I know I behaved badly yesterday, but, as I say, I've been doing a lot of thinking. Refusing your offer would simply be unfair to the people around me.'

'You should have done your thinking a little earlier, Doug,' Benjamin said triumphantly. 'You should have done your thinking before this kidnapping fouled up your deal in Boston!'

King's face changed. Studying Cameron, his mouth lengthened into a tight hard line and his eyes turned suddenly cold. 'My deal in Boston?' he repeated, and Cameron stiffened.

'Yes, yes, I know all about it, so don't get innocent with me,' Benjamin said.

'Well, that was just . . .'

That was just something that happened to fall through! Well, it's too damn bad, Mr King, but you played your cards and you played them wrong. My offer has been withdrawn. In fact, you might start looking for another job. You're going to need one as soon as we can call a meeting.'

'I see,' King said softly.

'I hope you do.'

'I guess I know when I'm over a barrel, George. But I hope this won't affect your attitude toward any of the people who've worked closely with me. Believe me, Pete knew nothing about what I was planning. I'd hate to see him pay for my errors. He's a good worker, George, and a bright—'

'Don't you worry about Pete!' Benjamin said, laughing. 'We'll take care of him.'

'You're not going to fire him, are you?'

'*Fire* him?' Benjamin's laughter grew louder. '*Fire* him? Fire your trusted, loyal assistant? Don't be ridiculous, Doug.' The laughter trailed off. 'If you don't mind, I'm late for the links now. Goodbye, Doug.' There was a click on the line. Slowly, King put down the phone.

'You son of a bitch,' he said to Cameron.

'Yes.'

'You told him about Boston.'

'Yes.'

'You gave him everything.'

'Yes.'

'Everything, you son of a bitch!'

'Yes, yes!' Cameron said, rising from his chair with nothing to lose now, exploding with a vengeance. 'Yes, I told him everything! And now you're going *out*! Out!'

'Oh, that's what you think, sweetheart!'

That's what I know, sweetheart. Benjamin's got the Old Man on his team now. You're going out, Mr King, and *I'm* going in. Me! Take a good look. Me!'

'I'm looking, you son of a bitch!'

'Look long and look hard! The next look you get is from the bottom of the heap!

'I'm looking! I'm looking, you miserable . . .'

'No more miserable than you, pal. I learned in your school. Did you expect me to bow and scrape forever? Did you expect Pete Cameron to be an assistant bottle washer for the rest of his life? Not me, pal. I learned. I learned fast!'

'Oh, you learned! I ought to strangle you, you bastard!'

'Why? What do you see, Doug? Yourself? Yourself ten years ago?'

'Myself ten—'

Take another look. I'm not you ten years ago. I'm you tomorrow! Tomorrow you're in the gutter. You're out, and I'm in. Tomorrow!'

'Not if this Boston thing goes through!'

'You haven't got the guts to kill that kid!'

'Haven't I? But you have, huh, Pete? Then why not me? We're alike, aren't we? The same school, no? Blood brothers, no? Both sons of bitches, no?'

He suddenly seized Cameron by the lapels of his suit and flung him across the room.

'Get out of my house!' he yelled.

'With pleasure, Mr—'

'Get out! Get out!'

Cameron went to the closet and quickly pulled his coat from a hanger. He reached into his trouser pocket, took out King's cheque, crumpled it into a ball, and threw it across the room.

'Get out!' King screamed. 'Get out, get out, *get out*!' The door slammed on his words, and still he shouted, '*Get out, get out, get out!*'

# 11.

**THE BOY WAS** cold.

She had given him her overcoat, but he still complained of the cold in the draughty farmhouse. He wanted cocoa, he said, something hot to drink, but there was nothing but coffee and evaporated milk in the house, and the boy sat on the edge of the bed as the sun stained the winter sky, and he shivered visibly and contained the sobs he would not release.

The two street maps had been set up alongside the radio equipment, and the men arranged them now so that they were clearly visible and easily read. The first map was a detailed map of Isola with Smoke Rise and the King estate marked with a red circle. A red line was inked onto the streets leading from the estate, following a tortuous route crosstown and over to the Black Rock Span. Once over the bridge, the red line took to the highways that crisscrossed Sands Spit, proceeding past a spot marked with a blue star, and then continuing out to the farthest tip of the peninsula. There did not seem to be much direction to the aimless meanderings of the inked red line. It moved from Smoke Rise erratically and then swooped toward the bridge with the precision of an arrow, only to assume an erratic course again once it hit the Sands Spit highways. The red line continued to reel drunkenly until it had passed the spot marked with the blue star, after which it again straightened, rushing with direct purposefulness toward the ocean. Perhaps significantly, it steered a wide course around a dot on the map which was marked simply 'Farm.'

Sitting with her arms around the shivering boy, Kathy tried to make some sense out of the maps, the radio equipment, and the snatches of conversation she overheard between Sy and her husband. The radio equipment was a necessary part of their plan, she knew, but she could not understand how they hoped to utilize it. The maps, too, were important, but again she could forge no connecting link between the radio and the maps set up near the chair in front of the equipment. The radio equipment included the oscillators and the transmitter Sy had mentioned, in addition to a microphone, and a dial which seemed far removed from any radio equipment she had ever seen.

She knew from the conversation that another phone call to King was in order, this one to ascertain that he had the money and to give him instructions about its delivery. After that, she knew, Sy was going to leave the house in the car while Eddie remained behind. More than that she did not know.

The boy trembled in her arms, and she held him close, and she wondered for perhaps the fiftieth time how the man she loved could possibly have become involved in a crime she considered heinous. The word 'heinous' did not enter her mind; it wasn't even a part of her vocabulary. But she considered kidnapping something unspeakably horrible, something almost inhuman, and she wondered what it was in Eddie, what drive, what lust for money, what search for identity, that could have led him into this final shattering act. It was her fault, of course. She knew that instantly. She knew with the intuition of a Cleopatra detaining an Antony, a Helen launching the Trojan war. The affairs of men were governed by women. This she knew, as all women know, with infallible instinct. And if Eddie had taken part in a kidnapping, was *now* taking part in the final stages of the theft of a child, then she was in part responsible for it.

She recognized in her own attitude about crime a peculiar dichotomy. She had, for example, sanctioned yesterday's excursion because she presumed Eddie and Sy were going out to rob a bank. The concept was almost amusing. In the hands of skilled players, it could indeed become a hilarious satirical sketch. 'Is this what you do to me?' the actress gun moll complains to the returning actor gangster. 'After I've given you the best years of my life? You go out to rob a bank, and you bring home a kid instead?' Very funny. Ha-ha. It was not humorous to Kathy, because it happened to be true in her case. Believing he was about to rob a bank, she had in effect given him her blessings. Confronted with a kidnapping instead, she heaped upon him her scorn.

Nor could she honestly say that she had exercised a great deal of effort over the years in pulling her husband away from crime. He had been in trouble as a youth, had been sent to reform school, where, under the skilled tutelage of tougher, more experienced youths, he had learned tricks he had never dreamed of. She hadn't met him until he was twenty-six, and by that time crime was as much a part of Eddie Folsom as his kidney. Was it this about him which had first attracted her? This attitude of nonconformity carried to its furthest extreme? This anti-social outlook which made the beatniks seem like members of a British soccer team? Perhaps, but she did not really believe so.

Eddie Folsom, in the eyes of Kathy Folsom, his wife, was not a crook. It is probably difficult to understand that because the good-guy/bad-guy concept is a part of our heredity, drummed into our minds together with the knight-on-a-white-charger ideal, and the only-bad-girls-lay taboo, and the slit-dresses-are-sexy fetish. There are good guys and bad guys, dammit, we all know that. Sure. But does the bad guy ever think of himself as a bad guy? When a gangster watches a gangster movie, does he identify with the police or with Humphrey Bogart?

Eddie Folsom, you see, was a man.

Short and simple, sweet and easily understood. Man. M-a-n. Kathy knew him as a man, and loved him as a man, and thought of him as a man who earned his living through stealing. But this did not make him a crook. True, Kathy knew the difference between right and wrong, between law and anarchy, between good and evil. But this did not make her husband a crook. A crook was the man at the butcher shop who thumbed the scale when weighing out lamb chops. A crook was the cab driver who had shortchanged Kathy in Philadelphia once. Crooks were people in charge of labour unions. Crooks were hired killers. Crooks were men who ran huge corporations.

And, unfortunately, crooks were people who planned and executed kidnappings.

And perhaps this was why the job disturbed her so much. In a single day, in the space of several hours, Eddie Folsom had stopped being a person who earned his living by stealing and had begun being a crook. And if this were the end product, if a person as sweet and as kind and as full of love as Eddie could turn into a crook, was not his wife to blame? And if she was to blame, where along the line had she compromised the ideal? Where had the good-guy/bad-guy concept ceased to have any real meaning? When had she decided that stealing was not a crime? It simply wasn't the kind of life she wanted for her man.

Wasn't this why she wanted to go to Mexico? So that Eddie could stop stealing, so that he could have his radio and do with it what he wanted, so that the demands of everyday living – simple things like wanting to eat, and wanting to be warm, and wanting a roof over one's head – could be satisfied with a maximum of security and a minimum of cold hard cash? A bank job, a last-time big splash. No more hiding, no more running. Mexico, and sun-washed streets, and skies as blue as Monday morning. Safety. Wasn't this all she really wanted for herself and her man?

Now, clutching a shivering eight-year-old boy to her bosom, Kathy Folsom felt something she had never in her life felt before. Holding a boy who was not her own, listening to the whispered plans of the men across the room, she wanted more than safety. She wanted the good to return and the bad to be over with. The trembling of the boy touched something deep inside her, a well-spring as old as Eve. She knew in that instant that the good-guy/bad-guy fiction was a legend designed not to fool but to inspire. And she knew why she was at fault in leading Eddie into his current dilemma. There was good in her man, a great deal of good. She had done a disservice to the good by casually accepting the evil. What she wanted to voice now was something spouted by every thief in every Grade-B melodrama. What she wanted to cry now were the words that poured from the mouth of the gangster as he lay bleeding in the gutter. What she wanted to sob out was the criminal's straight-man dialogue designed as a setup for Jack Webb's devastating closing punch line.

'Give me a break, will you?'

In the movies, the thief is instantly manacled and dragged bleeding to jail. On the television screen, the thief's eyes are wide with pleading. 'Give me a break, will you? Please. Give me a break.' And the taciturn spokesman for the Los Angeles Police Department answers, 'Did you give *him* one?'

There are no punch lines in real life.

Kathy Folsom wanted a break, a lousy break, another chance.

And she knew with intuitive female logic that many more lives than Jeff Reynolds's depended on the outcome of this job.

'Eddie,' she said.

He turned from the transmitter. 'What is it, hon?'

'The boy's still cold.'

'Who cares?' Sy said. 'What the hell are we running here? A nursery school?'

'He needs something hot to drink,' Kathy said. 'Would you go for something, Eddie?'

'I will never – never in my life – understand dames!' Sy said, an amazed expression on his face. 'The nearest store is maybe ten miles from here, and God alone knows how many cops are roaming the highways, and you want to send him out for a hot drink? That takes the prize, Kathy!'

'Will you, Eddie?'

'I don't know. I mean . . .'

'One of you has to go out to make the call, anyway,' Kathy said.

'Ahh, she's been listening. That's right, one of us does have to go out. But if it's me, I ain't running into any grocery store to buy something we can heat up.' He paused. 'And you're not either, Eddie. There's too much risk involved.'

'There's more risk involved if the boy gets sick,' Kathy said.

'Once we get the dough, we're never going to see this kid again, anyway,' Sy said.

'What do you mean?'

'Don't get excited! I meant we're leaving him here. You're going to Mexico, I don't know where the hell I'm going. So who cares if he gets sick?'

'It may be a while before they get to him,' Kathy said. 'If he got sick . . . if something happened to him . . .'

'She has a point, Sy,' Eddie said. 'Why make things tougher for ourselves? Look at the kid. He's shaking.'

' 'Cause he's scared.'

'I'm not scared,' Jeff said in a small voice.

'Won't you have to go to that store to make the call, anyway?' Kathy said.

'Yeah, but . . .'

'Won't it seem less conspicuous if you went in to buy something, and then just *happened* to make the call?'

Sy studied her with disgruntled admiration. 'That's not a bad idea,' he said. 'What do you think, Eddie?'

'I think so.'

'Okay. When you make the call, get the kid what he needs.'

'I'm going?' Eddie asked.

'Why not?'

'No, no reason. I'll go.'

'You know what to do? Find out if he's got the loot first. Then tell him to leave the house at' – Sy studied his watch – 'ten o'clock on the button. Tell him to go straight to his car, the Caddy with the DK-74 license plate – make sure you specify, Eddie. We don't want him using the wrong car. He's just liable to use his wife's Thunderbird.'

'All right,' Eddie said.

'So specify the Caddy. Tell him to go straight to the car and begin driving away from Smoke Rise. Tell him he'll be met by someone with further instructions. Make sure you say he'll be *met*.'

'Who's going to do the meeting?' Kathy asked. 'You?'

'Nobody,' Sy said, and he grinned. 'Tell him he'll be watched every step of the way and if he's followed by the police, we'll kill the boy. That's it. Then hurry back here. It's only eight now, and it shouldn't take you more than forty minutes or so to get to the store, make the call and come back. That gives us plenty of time.'

'Okay,' Eddie said. 'What do you want me to get, Kathy?' He went to the closet and put on his coat.

'A package of hot chocolate and some milk. Get some cookies, too, or some cupcakes. Whatever they have.'

He went to her and kissed her on the cheek. 'I'll be back soon.'

'Be careful.'

'Good luck, kid,' Sy said.

Eddie started for the door and then stopped. 'King's number.'

'Oh, yeah.' Sy opened his wallet and handed Eddie a scrap of paper. 'That the right one?' he asked.

'Yeah,' Eddie said.

'Can you read my Chinky handwriting?'

'Yeah.'

'Okay, take off.'

Eddie went to Kathy again, and again he kissed her on the cheek, and again she said, 'Be careful.'

Sy unlocked the door for him, and he went out of the house. They heard his footsteps on the gravel in the front yard, and then the sound of a car door slamming, and then the car starting. Sy waited until the car pulled out of the yard, waited until he could no longer hear the engine.

Then, locking the door again, he grinned and said, 'Well, well, alone at last.'

There were memories Steve Carella carried like heavy stones in his mind. There were things connected with police work which he would never forget, which would lurk always at the back of his skull, waiting to be called up fresh and painfully clear. He knew that the image of Charles Reynolds talking with Douglas King would become one of those memories, and even as he watched the man he wanted to leave the room, wanted to get away from the scene before it registered on his unconscious, before it joined the other lurking shapes.

He would never forget the smell of whisky in the liquor shop on the night he investigated the murder of Annie Boone, the broken trail of bottles, the girl's body pressed lifelessly to the wooden floor, her red hair afloat in alcohol.

He would never forget the moment of shocked surprise when he faced a boy with a gun, a boy he was certain would not shoot, and suddenly realized there'd been a lance of fire and an explosion, suddenly realized there was pain engulfing his chest, suddenly realized the boy had indeed pulled the trigger, the ground going out of focus, falling, falling, he would never forget that cold day in the park although he had already forgotten the name of the boy who had shot him.

He would never forget bursting into Teddy's apartment before she became his wife, confronting a killer who had literally been sent there by a reporter named Cliff Savage, firing low and firing fast before the man with the .45 could take a careful bead. He would never forget the scent, the feel of Teddy in his arms when it was all over. He would never forget these things.

And now, listening to Charles Reynolds, he wanted to plug up his ears, close his eyes, blot out what was happening, because he knew with certainty that the scene would haunt him for the rest of his life.

The man had come into the living room through the dining-room arch, standing hesitantly in the archway, waiting for Douglas King to notice him. King had been busy lighting a cigarette, his hands trembling slightly, and Carella had been sitting at the wiretap, watching King, and then suddenly aware that Reynolds was standing on the threshold to the room. There was on Reynolds's face a look of utter despair which, through contamination, infected his entire body. His shoulders were slumped, and his hands hung limply at his sides. Patiently, lifelessly, he stood in the doorway, waiting for King to turn, waiting for the owner of the house, his employer, to notice him.

King walked away from the coffee table, blew out an impatient stream of smoke, said, 'They probably won't even call—' and noticed Reynolds. He pulled up short, sucked in on the cigarette again, and said, 'You startled me, Reynolds.'

'I'm sorry, sir,' Reynolds paused. 'Sir, I . . . I would like to talk to you.' He paused again. 'Mr King, I would like to talk to you,' and Carella knew from those first words that this was going to be painful, and he wanted to get out of the room.

'Reynolds, couldn't . . .' King started, and then hesitated. 'All right, what is it? What do you want, Reynolds?'

Reynolds took a single step into the room, as if that was as far as he was prepared to go, as if even that single step was a break of the rules he had formulated for himself before making his entrance. His shoulders slumped, his hands hanging awkwardly, he said, 'I want to ask you to pay the ransom for my son, Mr King.'

'Don't ask me,' King said, and he turned away.

'I'm asking you, Mr King,' Reynolds said, and he extended his hand as if to pull the retreating King closer to him. But he did not budge from his spot just inside the entrance archway. He stood with his hand extended and pleading, until King turned to face him again from the other end of the room. And then, separated by forty feet of living-room area, separated by God alone knew how many miles, the two men faced each other like knights about to charge with lances, and Carella felt like a spectator who had no favourite.

'I have to ask you, Mr King,' Reynolds said. 'You see that, don't you?'

'No. No, I don't. Please, Reynolds, I really feel . . .'

'I have never begged in my life,' Reynolds said awkwardly, 'but I'm begging you now. Please, Mr King. Please get my son back.'

'I don't want to listen,' King said.

'You have to listen, Mr King. I'm talking to you like a man now. A father to a father. I'm pleading with you to save my son. God, God, please save my son!'

'You're coming to the wrong person, Reynolds! I can't help you. I can't help Jeff.'

'I don't believe that, Mr King.'

'It's true.'

'I . . . I have no right. I know I have no right. But where else can I go? Who else can I turn to?'

'Do you know what you're asking me to do?' King said. 'You're asking me to ruin myself. Am I supposed to do that? Goddammit, Reynolds, I wouldn't ask that of *you*!'

'I *have* to ask!' Reynolds said. 'Is there a choice for me, Mr King? Is there someplace I can go, someplace to get five hundred thousand dollars? Where? Tell me. I'll go. I'll go. But where? No place.' He shook his head. 'I'm coming to you. I'm asking you. Please, please . . .'

'No!'

'What do you want me to do, Mr King? Name it. I'll do it. Anything you say. I'll work for the rest of my life, I'll . . . '

'Don't talk nonsense. What can you possibly . . . ?'

'Do you want me to get down on my knees, Mr King? Shall I get on my knees and beg you?'

He dropped to his knees, and Carella winced and

turned away. Separated by forty feet of broadloom, the men stared at each other, Reynolds on his knees, his hands clasped, King standing with one hand in the pocket of his robe, the other hand holding a trembling cigarette.

'Get up, for God's sake,' King said.

'I'm on my hands and knees, Mr King,' Reynolds said. 'I'm begging you. Begging you. Please, please, please . . .'

'Get up, get up!' King said, and his voice was close to breaking. 'Good God, man, can't you—'

'. . . save my son.'

'Reynolds, please.' King turned away, but not before Carella saw him squeeze his eyes shut tightly. 'Please, get up. Please, man. Please. Could you . . . could you leave me alone? Could you? Could you please do that? Please?'

Reynolds got to his feet. With great dignity, he dusted off the knees of his trousers. He did not say another word. He turned and walked stiffly out of the room.

Humiliated, Douglas King stared at the door.

'Does it make you feel like a big turd, Mr King?' Carella asked.

'Shut up!'

'It should. Because that's what you are.'

'Goddammit, Carella, I don't want to listen to—'

'Oh, go to hell, Mr King,' Carella said angrily. 'Just go to hell!'

'What's the matter with you, Steve?' Byrnes asked, coming down the steps. 'Let's cut that out.'

'I'm sorry,' Carella said.

'I was just on the phone upstairs,' Byrnes said. 'I

checked our list of stolen cars and, sure enough, there she was. A grey 1949 Ford. Teletype's going out on it now. I don't suppose the licence plate'll still be the same one as on that list, do you?'

'No, sir.'

'Now just cut it out, Steve,' Byrnes said.

'Cut what out, sir?'

'The slow burn.'

'I wasn't—'

'You were, and don't lie to me, and remember that we've got a job to do here, and we're not going to get it done if everybody goes around with his ass being—' He cut himself short. Liz Bellew was coming down the steps, one hand clutching a valise, the other holding Bobby King's hand.

'Good morning,' she said. 'Any word yet?'

'No, ma'am,' Byrnes said.

'Daddy?' Bobby said.

'What is it, son?'

'Is Jeff back yet?'

'No, son. He isn't.'

'I thought you were getting him back.'

There was a long uncomfortable silence. Carella watched them and devoutly hoped he would never see the look that was on Bobby King's face at this moment on the face of his son, Mark, in years to come.

'Bobby, you should never throw questions at a tycoon so early in the morning,' Liz said breezily. 'He's coming over to my house for now, Doug.' She winked. 'It'll work out.'

'Where's Diane?'

'Upstairs putting on the finishing touches.'

'Did you . . . ?'

'I talked to her.' Liz shook her head. 'It's no go. But give her time.' She turned to Byrnes. 'Do I get a police escort, Lieutenant?'

'Darn right you do.'

'Make it the tall redheaded cop,' Liz said. 'The one with the white streak in his hair.'

'Detective Hawes?'

'Is that his name? Yes, him.'

'I'll see if I can.'

'He's just outside the door, Lieutenant, getting some air. I saw him from the upstairs window. Shall I tell him his services are required?'

'Yes, yes,' Byrnes said, a look of puzzlement on his face. 'Yes, please tell him.'

'I shall tell him. Come along, Bobby, we're going to meet a handsome policeman.' She walked him toward the front door. At the door, Bobby turned.

'*Aren't* you getting him back, Dad?' he asked, and Liz pulled him through the open doorway and shouted, 'Yoo-hoo! Detective Hawes! Yoo-hoo!'

The door closed behind them.

'I feel I should make my position clear to you gentlemen,' King said, clearing his throat. 'I know that on the surface my refusal . . .'

The telephone rang.

King stopped speaking. Byrnes looked at Carella, and Carella rushed to the wiretap equipment.

'You'd better get on the trunk line, Pete!' he said, and Byrnes ran to the other phone and picked up the receiver, ready to speak.

'Go ahead, Mr King,' Carella said, 'answer it. If it's our man, keep him on the line.'

Over the ringing of the telephone, King said, 'What . . . what shall I tell him?'

'Just keep him talking. About anything. Keep him on the line.'

'And . . . the money?'

'Tell him you've got it,' Byrnes said.

'Pete . . .'

'It's our only chance, Steve. They've got to think we're playing ball with them.'

'Answer it, answer it!'

King hesitated a moment and then lifted the receiver. 'Hello?'

'Mr King?'

The voice was not the one King had heard before. A frown crossed his forehead. 'Yes, this is Mr King,' he said. 'Who's calling, please?'

'You know who's calling,' the voice said. 'Don't play dumb.'

'I'm sorry. I didn't recognize your voice,' King said, and he nodded to Byrnes, who instantly said into the trunk line phone, 'He's on the other wire now. Get moving.'

Sitting at the wiretap equipment with the head-phones over his ears, Carella watched the spools of tape revolving as they recorded the conversation. Scarcely daring to breathe, he listened to the voice on the other end.

'Have you got the money, Mr King?'

'Well . . .'

'Yes or no? Have you got it?'

'Keep him talking,' Byrnes whispered.

'Yes, I have it. That is, I have most of it.'

'What do you mean, most of it? We told you . . .'

'Well, the rest should be here momentarily. You specified small bills, didn't you?'

'What's that got to do with it?'

'And no consecutive serial numbers. Five hundred thousand dollars is a lot of money, you know. And there wasn't much time. The remainder is being counted out at the bank now. It should be here within the half hour.'

'All right, fine. Now here's what you're to do. Do you have a wrist watch, Mr King?'

'Yes. Yes, I have one.'

'I want you to set it so that it's synchronized with mine. Take it off your wrist now.'

'All right. Just a moment.'

'Keep him talking,' Carella said. 'Keep him talking.'

'You got it, King?'

'Yes, I'm getting it.'

Into the trunk line phone, Byrnes said, 'What's happening there? For God's sake, I *told* you he was on the line!'

'How about it, King?' the voice asked impatiently.

'All right.'

'My watch says exactly eight-thirty-one. Set yours for the same time.'

'All right.'

'Did you set it?'

'Yes. I set it.'

'Fine. Now the rest I'm going to say fast and only once, so get it all the first time. You are to leave the house at ten o'clock sharp, and you are to be carrying the money in a plain carton. You will go straight to the garage, and you will get into the black Cadillac with the license tag DK-74. That is the car you will use, Mr King. Do you understand?'

'Yes, I understand,' King said.

'Hurry, hurry!' Byrnes whispered into his receiver.

'You will drive away from the house and away from Smoke Rise. You will be watched, Mr King, so don't attempt to take anyone in the car with you, and don't allow the police to follow you. If you are followed, we will kill the boy right away. Do you understand that?'

'Yes, I do. I have it.'

'Have they got it yet?' Carella whispered to Byrnes.

'The damn fools are . . .'

'You will continue driving, Mr King, until someone meets you with instructions. That's all you have to know for now. Leave the house at ten sharp, alone, *with* the money. Goodbye, Mr—'

'Wait!'

'Keep him talking,' Byrnes said. 'They've got it traced to Central on Sands Spit!'

'What is it, Mr King?'

'When do we get the boy back?'

'When we get the money, we'll call again.'

'How . . . how do we know he's still alive?'

'He's still alive.'

'Can I talk to him?'

'No. Goodbye, Mr King.'

'Wait! You . . .'

'He's gone!' Carella said, ripping off the headset.

'Son of a bitch!' Byrnes said. Into the phone, he shouted, 'He just hung up. How far have you . . . What? Oh. Oh, I see. Okay. Okay, thanks.' He hung up. 'Didn't matter a damn. He was using a dial phone. As soon as they traced it to Central, it got lost in the automatic equipment.' He turned to Carella. 'What'd he say, Steve?'

'A lot. Want me to play it back?'

'Yes, go ahead. Nice work, Mr King.'

'Thank you,' King said dully.

'His voice sounded different,' Carella said. 'Didn't you think so?'

'Yes,' King answered.

'I think we got a different customer this time,' Carella said. 'Mind if I start the playback with the previous call, Pete? Just to check the voices?'

'No, go right ahead.'

Carella looked at his watch. 'Eight-thirty-five. We've still got time,' he said, and he flipped the switch that reversed the tape.

It was eight-thirty-three when Eddie Folsom came out of the telephone booth. The ride to the grocery store had taken longer than Sy had estimated, but there was still nothing to worry about. It would be a long, long time before ten o'clock rolled around.

Casually, he walked to the counter.

'Let me have a package of hot chocolate,' he said, 'and a bottle of milk, and a box of those cookies there.'

# 12.

**KATHY HAD BEGUN** pacing at eight-thirty. Now, at eight-forty-five, she wandered the room aimlessly, the window facing the front yard serving as the focal point of her ramblings. She would walk to the window, lift the shade and look out at the front yard, draw the shade again, pace, wander, light a cigarette, and then end up back at the window again.

'Where is he?' she asked. 'Shouldn't he be back by now?'

'He'll be back,' Sy said. 'Relax.' He paused. 'He not only had to make the call, you know. He also had to do the daily marketing.'

'The boy . . .'

'The boy, the boy, the boy? I hear another word about the boy, I'm going to start a club for underprivileged kids! Man, am I sick to death of this job! I should have known better than to tie up with a jerk who runs out to buy milk!'

'He went out to make the call,' Kathy said. 'Someone had to do it.'

'He's also buying milk. And *hot chocolate*,' Sy said, using a falsetto on the words, giving them a mincing, oversweet quality.

'The boy is cold.' She glanced at Jeff where he lay huddled on the bed, Kathy's coat around him, a blanket over that. 'You're lucky he hasn't started crying.'

'You're lucky *I* haven't started crying,' Sy said. 'That money is so damn close I can taste it.'

'Sy, when Eddie comes back—'

'What time is it?'

Kathy looked at her watch. 'Eight-fifty. When he comes back, what are you going to do?'

'Nothing. Not until a little before ten.'

'And then what?'

'Stop worrying. Your milkman will return, and everything'll come off all right, and we'll be rich as hell. And you know why? Because Sy Barnard is handling this little shindig. If a small-time punk like Eddie was in charge—'

'He's not a small-time punk!'

'No? Okay, he's a big operator, okay? How'd you ever get involved with such a big operator, huh?'

'Oh, what do you care?'

Nervously, she walked to the dresser and opened her purse. Nervously, she began combing out her hair.

'I'm interested,' Sy said. 'Really.'

'We just met, that's all.'

'Where?'

'I don't remember.'

'The Safecrackers' Ball?'

'That's not funny, Sy.'

'But you knew he was in the rackets?'

'Yes, I knew. It didn't matter to me.' She paused. 'Eddie is good.'

'Yeah, he's a doll.'

'I'm not joking. Oh, why am I even talking to you!' She hurled the comb into her purse and then snapped it shut and walked to the window again.

'Didn't I say he was a doll?'

'He's in this because it's the only thing he knows,' Kathy said. 'But if he got away from it, if I helped him to get away from it, he'd be good. I know he would. I'd see to it.'

'Why'd you marry him?'

'I love him.'

'Warm for his form, huh?'

'When are you going to let me go?' Jeff said from the bed.

'Shut up, kid.'

'Aren't you ever?'

'I said shut up. I've had you up to here already!'

Kathy lifted the shade and scanned the yard again. Sighing, she turned away from the window.

'You worried about him?'

'Of course I am,' she said.

'What for? There's other fish in the ocean. Bigger fish. Smarter fish.'

'He's my husband.'

'Pull down the shade.'

'It's morning. Why can't . . . ?'

'I don't want nobody peeping in here.'

'There isn't a soul around for miles!'

'Pull it down!'

Kathy lowered the shade, walked to the dresser again, fished into her purse for a cigarette and, discovering she was out, snapped the bag shut angrily.

'Stop worrying,' Sy said. 'Husbands are for the birds. All they are is a piece of legal paper and a gold circle. Who the hell ever takes husbands seriously?'

'I do,' Kathy said. 'I love him.'

'Love is what they make up for teenagers. There ain't no such animal.'

'You're mistaken. You just don't know.'

'I know more than you think, baby, and about a lot of things. I know, for example, that your darling boy is rotten clean through. There ain't nothing you can do for him no more. It's too late now.'

'It's not too late. Once this is over . . .'

'Once this is over, there'll be another job, and another one after that, and then another and another and another! Who the hell are you kidding? Yourself? I seen bums like Eddie in prisons all over this country. He's rotten! He stinks! He's *me*, for Pete's sake! Do you think *I'm* such a prize?'

'I don't want to listen.'

'Okay, don't. The big reformer there. Gonna make a silk purse. Bullshit!'

'Don't talk like that, Sy. I don't . . .'

'Why? What are you gonna do about it?'

'I'll – Just don't talk like that.'

'You sound actually threatening, you know that? I got to watch my step, huh? Got to be careful. Not like little Blondie there, huh? He don't have to be careful.' Sy paused and then looked at the radio receiver. 'Eddie shoulda turned on the monster before he went out. We ain't heard nothing for a long while.'

'There's nothing to hear but the road blocks.'

'So? I find road blocks interesting.' He paused and studied her. 'Listen, you want a little drink?'

'So early in the morning?'

'Sure. Puts hair on your chest. Come on.'

'No.'

'What's the matter, baby? Don't you drink?'

'I drink.'

'So, come on, have one. For Pete's sake, we're sitting

on a fortune, you realize it? Are we supposed to mope around like a couple of corpses? What the hell is this, a graveyard? Come on, baby, loosen up.'

'If you want a drink, take one. Nobody's stopping you.'

'Right, baby! Nobody stops me from nothing I want!' He studied her speculatively for a moment, and then walked to the dresser. Picking up a pint bottle from its top, he held it aloft, said, 'Cheers,' and tilted it to his mouth. 'Good stuff. Change your mind?'

'I don't want any. Where's Eddie?'

'You getting nervous, huh?' He held the bottle out to Jeff. 'Want a slug, kid? Warm the cockles. No, huh?' He shrugged and wiped his mouth. 'You worry too much, Kathy. We could be having ourselves a real ball, insteada worrying. A real ball.' He smiled and nodded, staring at her. Kathy moved toward the window again, crossing her arms over the front of her sweater. 'You know what your trouble is, baby? You don't know how to live, that's what. You're all tensed up because darling hubby went to the grocery store. You got to learn to relax. Look at me. Cops covering the city like a plague. Do I worry? Hell, no.'

'How can I relax when Eddie may have run into trouble?'

'You can start by forgetting all about Eddie. Come on, have a little drink.'

'Oh, Sy, don't bother me! I don't want a drink.'

'Excuse *me*, I didn't know I was bothering you. Okay, stand around and worry if that's what you want to do. I can think of a lot better ways to kill the time, though.' He walked closer to her, his eyes on the front of her sweater. 'A dame like you should have good clothes, you know that? Where'd you get that crumby, moth-eaten sweater? Eddie should be ashamed of himself! You should be wearing fancy, lacy stuff. It ain't every dame can fill clothes like you.'

'I'm not interested.'

'What the hell's the matter now? For Pete's sake, I'm complimenting you!'

'Thanks,' she said dryly.

'Boy, there sure ain't no mutual-affection society here, is there? All the affection goes out to Blondie, don't it? Or Eddie, depending on who's around. But none to Sy, that's for sure. Well, you want to know what I think? I think you're wasting your time with a punk like Eddie, that's what I think. Best thing could happen to you is for the bulls to pick him up.'

'Shut up,' Kathy said.

'I'm shooting you the goods. Pretty little piece like you tied down to a second-rate punk. Who needs him? I can run this job alone. Honey, you're wasting your talents on him. What you need is somebody who knows the score, somebody who can—'

'Shut up, Sy!'

'Tell me the truth, ain't you hoping they pick him up? You was against this job to begin with, wasn't you? All you're worried about is little Blondie over there, will we hurt him, will we—'

'Shut up, *shut up*!'

'What is it? You got a yen for a family of your own? Is that it?' He laughed bitterly and tilted the bottle to his mouth again. Kathy walked to the window and raised the shade. Sy pulled the bottle from his mouth and shouted, 'Lower the goddamn shade!' She glared at him sullenly and then obeyed. 'Boy, this is some cheerful party, ain't it? Will I be glad when this gig is over. Man!' He held the bottle aloft in a toast. 'Here's to the object of the lady's affection, the dear little kidnap victim. Cheers, Blondie.' He drank. 'How about that, you little bastard? I just drank a toast to you.'

Jeff did not answer.

'I just toasted you,' Sy repeated. 'What's the matter, ain't you got no manners? Didn't your mother never teach you to say thanks? Or don't you know how to talk?'

'I know how to talk,' Jeff said. He was still trembling, both from the cold and from a very real fear which had begun the moment Eddie left the farmhouse.

'Then say something,' Sy said. 'The goddamn cops are chasing all over the city looking for me, and my partner is out marketing and I'm cooped up here with a frigid bitch, and on top of all that I drink a toast to your health, you little bastard. That's pretty damn white of me, I would say. How about a thank-you?'

'Thank you.'

'Or maybe you don't know the reason I'm cooped up here with Little Miss Cold Ass. Maybe you don't know *you're* the reason, huh? Or maybe you think I like this?' He paused. 'You know you're the cause of my misery?'

'I . . . Yes.'

'Oh, you know, huh?'

'Y-yes,' Jeff said, hugging the blanket to him.

'So what the hell're you gonna do about it?'

'Stop picking on the boy, Sy. And watch your language.'

'Stop picking on the boy, Sy, and watch your language,' he mimicked. 'Good to see that something gets a rise out of you, anyway. I was beginning to think maybe you had died and was already laid out.' He turned back to Jeff. 'I asked you a question, Blondie.'

'I . . . I don't know what to do about it.'

'Well, that's a hell of an attitude!' He paused. 'Isn't it?'

'Yes, I suppose . . .'

'Y-yes, sir.'

'One hell of an attitude, I would say. You're the cause of all my misery, and you don't know what to do about it. Well, how about thinking a little? A smart little bastard like you should be able to figure out something, don't you think?'

'Sy, leave him alone!'

'Yeah, and watch my language, I know. Well, you can go straight to hell, baby.'

'Why are you picking on the boy?'

'Who's picking on him? We're chatting. You want me to stop?'

'Yes.'

'Make it worth my while. Convince me.' Sy laughed and turned back to Jeff. 'Start thinking, kid. I'm waiting.'

'I don't know what you want me to say, sir.'

'I want you to come up with some ideas.'

'I haven't got any ideas, sir.'

'Well, now, ain't that a crying shame? No ideas. Tch, tch, tch. You just don't care what happens to me, is that it?'

'I . . . I don't know what to say, sir.'

'Say whatever the hell's in your head, stupid! When somebody asks you something, say what you think!'

'Y-yes, sir.'

'Okay. Would you like to see me get the electric chair?'

'I . . . I don't know.'

'*Sir!*'

'Sir,' Jeff said, beginning to get rattled. 'I don't know, sir.'

'You do know. Yes or no? Give me a yes or no answer. You want me to get the electric chair?'

'Sy, stop it!'

'Yes or no?' Sy persisted.

'Yes, sir. I . . .'

'What?'

'I would like to see you get . . .'

'What? What, you little bastard!'

'Sy, you're scaring him half to death! Can't you see?'

'You keep your ass out of this! Unless you've got some ideas!'

Jeff suddenly scrambled off the bed and rushed to where Kathy was standing, burying his head in her sweater, throwing his arms around her waist. Like a jealous suitor, Sy shouted, 'Get your hands off her!'

Kathy pulled the boy closer. 'That's enough, Sy.'

'What's enough? Who the hell are you – What the hell are you saying to me? You're telling *me*? There ain't a skirt alive who can tell *me* what to do!' He seized Jeff's arm and tore him away from her, flinging him across the room. 'There!' Sy said. 'How about that? How about that, you two-bit slut?' and Kathy slapped him with all the power of her arm, her shoulder, and her outstretched palm.

His hand flashed to his face. Slowly he lowered it. 'You want to play, huh?' He said. He reached into his pocket, and the knife came into view, the blade opening almost before it had cleared his pocket.

'You're finally ready to play, huh?' he said, and he swiped at her with the knife, forcing her to back away from him. He followed her across the room, slashing at her with the knife, not intending to cut her, simply toying with her, forcing her back until she collided with the door, and then he crouched before her with the knife swinging in front of his body in a wide arc.

'Sy, don't . . .'

'Don't what, baby? Don't cut you? Baby, would I cut you?' he said, and he lashed out with the razor-sharp blade, catching Kathy's sweater with the tip, drawing it away from her body, and then suddenly ripping upward with the knife, slashing the sweater up the front toward the neck.

'Sy!'

Again he slashed, using the knife with the precision of a duellist, ripping at the sweater, exposing her brassière. She tried to cross her arms over her breasts, but the knife flashed again, and she pulled her hands away from her body, the sweater hanging in tatters over the white brassière.

Sy grinned. 'Now the bra,' he said.

Her hands moved instantly, instinctively, to cover her breasts. He thrust out with the knife, and she pulled her hands back again, gasping uncontrollably now, waiting for the rip of steel that would sever the cotton bra.

'We're gonna let them beauties free,' Sy said, and he moved closer to her with the knife. 'Keep your hands down. I'd hate like hell to cut you! We're gonna let them big ripe . . .'

The boy seemed to materialize from nowhere. He landed on Sy's back with the ferocity of a wildcat, clawing, pummelling, punching, pulling at Sy's hair in a frenzy of unleashed anger. Sy straightened up, surprised, and then swung about and tried to shake the boy loose as Kathy ran for the door. He reached behind him for a grip, clutched at the boy's trousers and tore him loose, flinging him halfway across the room. Kathy, at the door, was fumbling with the lock. He reached her in two bounds, caught her arm, and pulled her to him, the knife tight in his right hand.

'Maybe you just better relax, baby,' he said. 'Maybe you'll like it better that—'

The three knocks sounded on the door. Leaning against the door as they were, Sy and Kathy recoiled sharply from the minor explosions against the wood.

'It's Eddie,' Kathy whispered, and she said the words like a prayer.

Sy backed away from her instantly. 'Put your coat on. Hurry up!'

She moved away from the door rapidly, took her coat from the bed, slipped into it and buttoned it to the throat.

'You mention a word of this to Eddie,' Sy said, 'and the kid is dead. You hear me? The kid is dead.'

Kathy nodded dumbly.

Sy went to the boy and sat beside him. 'Okay,' he said. 'Open it.'

Kathy stepped close to the door again. 'Eddie?' she said.

'Yeah. How about it? Open up, willya?'

She opened the door. He stepped into the room quickly, closing the door behind him and locking it.

'Jesus, what took you so—' he started, and then he saw Kathy's face and knew instantly that something was wrong.

'Welcome home, hero,' Sy said nonchalantly. 'You get the milk?'

'Yeah,' Eddie said. He carried his package to the table. Kathy began unpacking it silently. Eddie watched her. 'Hey, what's the matter here?' he said.

'Nothing,' Kathy said. 'Everything's fine, Eddie.'

'Kathy and I just had a little spat, that's all,' Sy said.

'What about?' Eddie asked. He looked at his wife again. 'What are you wearing a coat for?'

'I'm . . . It got chilly in here.'

'What'd you fight about?'

'She doesn't like the idea of the whole damn job,' Sy said. He shrugged. 'I shouldn'ta flown off the handle, I guess. I'm sorry, Eddie. You run into any trouble out there?'

'No. I didn't see a single cop the whole time I was on the road.' He looked at the pair suspiciously again. 'This is no time to be squabbling,' he said ineffectively. 'I mean, what the hell.'

'I said I was sorry,' Sy said.

'Yeah. Well.' Eddie shrugged.

'I'll make you some hot chocolate,' Kathy said to Jeff.

'Tune in the monster, Eddie. Let's see what's happening out there.'

'What time is it?'

Sy looked at his watch. 'Little after nine. I should leave by about nine-thirty, just to make sure.'

'Yeah,' Eddie said from the receiver. He threw a switch and began tuning the set. 'I still don't know what you two had to fight about. We're almost near the end now, and you . . .'

'. . . *POSSIBLE LICENSE PLATE RN 6220. THAT'S . . .*'

'Jesus, lower that, will you?' Sy shouted over the sudden roar from the radio. Eddie quickly turned down the volume.

'. . . *a 1949 Ford sedan,grey,possible license plate RN 6210.*'

'Wh—?' Sy said.

'*Once more for the West Coast,*' the police dispatcher said. '*Car used in the Jeff Reynolds kidnapping may have been a 1949 Ford sedan, grey, possible license plate RN 6210 . . .*'

'They know the car!'

'Don't get excited!' Sy snapped.

'And I was driving it! Even with the changed plates, they could have—'

'Relax! For Pete's sake, don't panic!'

'They coulda picked me up. I coulda – Hey! How we gonna . . . ? Sy, the car figures in our plan. How we gonna use it now?'

'I don't know. Take it easy now.' Sy began pacing the room.

'What are we supposed to do? We can't let all that money go!'

'No. No. we can't. We won't have to. You said the roads were clear from here to the grocery store. Okay, chances are they don't have road blocks everywhere, how could they? Okay, that radio is gonna tell us just where they *do* have the road blocks! It's just a question of listening all over again, and taking down the information this time.'

'Sy, that don't sound safe!'

'What the hell are you worried about? It's me who'll be driving the car.'

'Still . . .'

Sy looked at his watch. 'We got about a half hour. Let's hope they give a lot during that time. Because whether they do or not, that car leaves here at nine-thirty. And you better be ready to do your share come ten o'clock.'

'Sy, if they get one of us, the whole damn job'll . . .'

'Don't you worry about me, kid,' Sy said. 'Nobody's gonna get this boy. Not when five hundred thousand bucks is riding on his back.'

'. . . *corner of Agatha and two-one-oh . . .*'

'Shhh,' Sy said.

'. . . *to relieve Car 108 in road block. You got that, 112?*'

'*This is 112. Roger.*'

'Good,' Sy said, nodding his head vigorously. 'Spiel it out, boy. Keep spieling it out.'

# 13.

**AT TEN O'CLOCK** in the morning, the front door of Douglas King's house opened. Douglas King, wearing a dark overcoat, black Homburg and pearl-grey gloves, stepped out of the house. He was carrying a brown carton stuffed with newspapers. He walked to the side of the house, looking briskly about him, went directly to the garage, pulled up the overhead door, entered the black Cadillac parked there and started the engine. He let the engine idle for several moments and then pulled the car out of the garage, executed a turn, and drove up the driveway to where the twin stone pillars flanked the road. He turned onto Smoke Rise Road and glanced into the rearview mirror. There was not a car or a person in sight. If anyone was watching his departure, that person was certainly well hidden.

He began driving aimlessly, going on a straight course for several blocks, turning off Smoke Rise Road and onto the viaduct over the River Highway, and then heading crosstown. No police cars were behind him. To the observer, Douglas King was following instructions to the letter. He had left the house at 10 A.M. carrying a plain carton full of money. He had got into his car alone and begun driving, awaiting further contact.

Any observer, casual or intent, could not possibly have known that Detective Steve Carella had entered the garage at 9.30 A.M. through the door leading from the kitchen, or that he had then climbed into the Cadillac and made himself comfortable on the floor in the back.

Lying there now, he said, 'Do you see anything?'

'What do you mean?' King answered.

'A car following us? A pedestrian signalling us? A helicopter hovering?'

'No. Nothing.'

'How the hell are they going to make contact?' Carella grumbled. 'Is God going to send down a thunderbolt?'

At ten o'clock in the morning, Eddie Folsom began warming up his radio equipment. Sy had left at nine-thirty with a list of road blocks clutched in his hand and embossed on his mind. Now, as the tubes glowed with life, as the hum of the oscillators and the transmitter filled the room, Eddie could feel a nervousness starting somewhere at the pit of his stomach and spreading through his body. He consulted his meters again, made sure he was on the right frequency, and then sat down before the equipment, the microphone set up directly before his face, the street maps not two feet from where he sat, the dial three inches from his right hand. He looked at his watch. It was ten-oh-three. He would give King another seven minutes. And then at ten-ten it would start.

'Anything yet?' Carella asked.

'No.'

'What time is it?'

'Ten-five.'

'Why'd you come along, Mr King?'

'That's my business.'

'You didn't have to. A detective could have taken your place.'

'I know.'

'Besides, I doubt very much that the house is being watched. Unless this gang is enormous, they couldn't possibly have that many . . .'

'Are you married, Mr Carella?'

'Yes.'

'Do you love your wife?'

'Yes.'

'I love mine, too. She walked out on me this morning. After all these years of marriage, she walked out on me. Do you know why?'

'I think so.'

'Sure. Because I wouldn't ransom Reynolds's boy,' King nodded his head, his eyes glued to the road. 'You think that's pretty rotten of me, too, don't you?'

'You won't win the Nobel Prize for it, Mr King.'

'Maybe not. But then, I don't want the Nobel Prize. All I want is Granger Shoe.'

'Then it shouldn't bother you that your wife walked out.'

'No, I guess it shouldn't. If Granger Shoe were all I wanted, I wouldn't care very much about Diane, or Bobby, or anybody, would I?'

'I guess not.'

'Then what am I doing here?'

'I asked first, Mr King.'

'I don't know what I'm doing here, Mr Carella. I only know this. I cannot pay that boy's ransom. I cannot because it would mean destroying myself, and that's impossible. I don't believe in fairy tales, do you?'

'No, I don't.'

'I'm what I am, Mr Carella. I don't think I'll ever change. Business is a part of my life and without it I might as well be dead. That's what I am. I make no apologies for it. And maybe I've been rotten, yes, maybe I have. And maybe I've hurt men, but I've never gone out to get anybody without a damn good reason, and that's what I am, and I make no apologies. It's taken me a long time to get where I am today, Mr Carella.'

'Where are you today, Mr King?'

'In a car, waiting for instructions from a thief.' King smiled thinly. 'You know what I mean. It's taken me a long time to get the things I always felt I needed. A man doesn't change, Mr Carella. Diane doesn't know what poverty is. How would she know? She's had money all her life. Not me, Mr Carella. I was dirt-poor. I was hungry. You don't forget poverty, and you don't forget hunger. I started working for Granger when I was sixteen. In the stockroom. I worked harder than the others. I stacked more damn shoes, and I carried more damn shoes, and I took pride in what was the cruddiest part of the plant because I knew that someday I was going to own that company. That sounds crazy, doesn't it?'

'Ambition never sounds crazy.'

'Well, maybe not. I learned that factory inside out and backwards. Every position, every phase, every person. I learned shoes. I learned shoes because this was going to be my company. It was going to be the only thing I ever knew or ever wanted. By the time I met Diane . . .'

'Where'd you meet her, Mr King?'

'I picked her up. The war was still on. World War Two, I mean.'

'Was there any other war?' Carella asked.

'I was in on furlough, a sergeant, a T-five. Were you in the Army?'

'Yes.'

'Then I don't have to explain how lonely your own home town can seem when you're home on furlough. I picked up Diane at the U.S.O. She was one of those rich girls doing their bit for the enlisted man. We danced together a few times. We clicked. Just like that. The rich girl from Stewart City had met the poor boy from Kelly's Corners and – Do you know the city well, Mr Carella?'

'Fairly.'

'Then you know the part familiarly referred to as Stewart City, hugging the river on the south of Isola, very fancy, doormen, penthouses, air conditioning. And you know where Kelly's Corners is, we used to call it Smelly Corners when I was a kid. We met, Mr Carella. Never the twain, but we met. And we clicked. And she married me. I went back to Granger after I was discharged. I was earning about sixty dollars a week for the first year of our marriage. That wasn't enough. Not enough for Diane, and not enough for me. So I began doing what had to be done. I began solidifying my position in that factory, and I stamped on anyone who got in my way because nothing had changed. I was still going to own it. I was going to make Diane Kessler's father eat his words. I was going to trudge up to his Stewart City apartment with the air conditioning and the mile-high carpeting and make him apologize to me for ever referring to me as a "worthless nobody." As a matter of fact, I never tasted that particular revenge. The old man died before I really got a toehold. And he died without asking for his daughter and never having spoken to her since that day we broke the news to him. I never had my revenge.'

'Revenge isn't sweet,' Carella said. 'It's only boring.'

'Sure, but I would have liked it. I know I would have. Five years later, I was ready to spit in his eye, but he was six feet underground, and you don't go to a man's grave to dance on it. Five years later, I bought the house in Smoke Rise. I wasn't quite ready for the house yet, but I knew the house would be important to me. And it was. A house is a wonderful bargaining tool, Mr Carella. You'd be surprised how many people in this world are impressed by the accoutrements of everyday living, the houses, the silverware, the cars – the window dressing. And now . . . here I am. I've still got the house, and I own or am about to own enough stock to make me president of Granger. My son goes to a private school, and I've got a cook, and a chauffeur, and a gardener, and a housemaid, and a sports car for my wife, and a Cadillac for me, and enough money to get whatever I want, Mr Carella. Whatever I want.'

'Then why are you here?' Carella asked. 'Why are you driving your own car waiting for contacts from men who may turn out to be worse than murderers?'

'I don't know. Or, yes, I do know. I can't give those men the money they want. I can't because it would kill me. If that makes me rotten, then all right, I'm rotten. But I can't change the way I am, Mr Carella. That's for the fairy tales. The mean witch who turns into a lovely princess, the toad who turns into a prince, the rotten louse who suddenly sees the error of his ways and vows to do good for the rest of his life, fairy tales, pap for the television viewers of America. I'll never change. I know it, and Diane knows it, and she'll come back to me, Mr Carella, because she loves me. I'll never change. And if I'm rotten, I'm rotten. But I've fought all my life, and if I can't give those men the money they want, I can fight them this way, by going along, by *doing* something.'

He shook his head.

'I know none of this makes any sense. For the first six months of my married life, we lived in an apartment that had cockroaches the size of flying bats. I never want that again, Mr Carella. I want my house in Smoke Rise, and I want my servants, and I want a Cadillac with a telephone hanging from the dashboard, and I want—'

And in that instant, the telephone hanging from the dashboard rang.

It had been a simple matter to learn the frequency band within which all automobile telephones in the vicinity operated. Once this had been learned, it was equally simple to steal the necessary equipment: the 600-volt oscillator and the 1600-volt oscillator, the transmitter and the various relays and switches, and lastly the batteries. It was a little more difficult to come across the dial which Kathy had thought seemed alien to a radio set – and only because it *was alien*. The dial was a telephone dial hooked to the battery and the relay, so that it could key the telephone in King's car and cause it to ring. Once King picked up the telephone, Eddie could speak to him over the microphone attached to his transmitter. King's automobile telephone number, quite naturally, had been obtained from the telephone company.

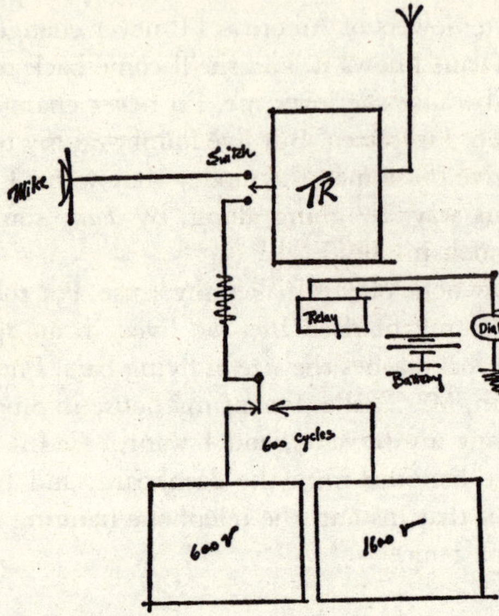


Eddie Folsom's preliminary sketches from the setup had looked like the diagram above.

The setup was now a reality before him. He had dialled King's number nervously. He waited now, one hand trembling around the microphone, the receiver tuned to pick up King's voice, the transmitter ready to relay Eddie's instructions.

Pick up the phone, he thought.

*Pick it up!*

'Wh—?' King said.

'What's—?' Carella said from the back seat.

'The telephone! The telephone's ringing.'

'Holy God, that's how – Answer it! Go ahead, answer it!' King lifted the receiver from where it hung on the dash. 'Hello?' he said.

'*All right, Mr King, this is it,*' Eddie said. '*You listen carefully, because you'll be receiving your instructions over this telephone for however long it takes you to get where we want you to go. Do you understand?*'

'Yes. Yes, I'm listening.'

'*Nobody's going to help you now, Mr King, because this conversation can't possibly be traced. I'm using a radio transmitter and not a telephone. So get that out of your mind in case you had any idea of stopping and telling anyone about this. We know exactly how long it should take you to get where you're going, so no tricks, please. Now. Where are you?*'

'I'm . . . I don't know.'

'*All right, keep that phone in your hand. You are not to hang up until this trip is over. Keep it in your hand, and as you pass the next cross street, tell me where you are.*'

'All right.'

'What is it?' Carella whispered. He was kneeling close to the back of his seat, his mouth alongside King's ear. King shook his head and pointed to the telephone.

'You think he'll hear us?' Carella whispered.

King nodded.

'I'm coming up front. I'll talk to him from now on. The reception on these damn things isn't hi-fi, that's for sure. We'll have to hope he doesn't recognize the change of voice. What does he want?'

'Cross street,' King whispered as Carella climbed over the seat and took the phone from King's hand. He looked through the windshield and then brought the receiver to his mouth.

'I'm approaching North Thirty-ninth and Culver,' he said into the phone.

Apparently, Eddie did not detect the difference in the voices. His own voice level and calm, he said, '*Turn left on North Fortieth. Continue in a southerly direction until you reach Grover Avenue, then turn left again. Go uptown until Forty-eighth, where you will see a crosstown entrance into the park. Take that entrance and continue driving. When you reach Hall Avenue, let me know. Have you got that?*'

'Left on North Fortieth,' Carella repeated. 'South until Grover, then left again. Uptown to Forty-eighth, and then into the park. Right.'

He covered the mouthpiece with his hand. 'Have you got that, King?'

'Yes,' King said.

'He's giving it to us piecemeal so we can't alert the nearest traffic cop as to just where we're heading. These are shrewd bastards, Mr King.' Carella's brow furrowed. 'I wish I knew how to stop them. I just wish I knew.'

Sitting in the parked car, Sy Barnard smoked his tenth cigarette in the past half hour. Anxiously, he looked at his watch. Then he glanced again at the road. The car was parked in the woods, completely shielded from the road by an old electric-company repair shack. The screening, in all truth, was unnecessary. Only one car had driven by in the past half hour, and on the day he and Eddie had chosen the site they had clocked only three cars in two and a half hours. The chances of being spotted by a curious motorist were negligible, almost nonexistent. Nor was there much possibility of a police car cruising by. Studying the list of road blocks, Sy knew that the nearest police barricade was at a big intersection some fifteen miles to the west. He had easily avoided it in getting here, and he knew he could easily go around it when driving back to the farmhouse.

Even if King refused to obey orders, even if, for example, a squad car were following the black Cadillac at this moment, the plan was still foolproof. And the part of it that made it so beautiful was the fact that no one but King knew where he was going, and even he was getting it in small bits and pieces so that he couldn't possibly give any meaningful information to a third party. The electric-company shack was just around a curve in the road. If a police car were following King, it would have to maintain a respectable distance or risk being detected. Detection would endanger the boy, and so Sy knew that any following police would stay pretty far behind the lead car. Communicating with King via the telephone, Eddie would know when King was about five miles away from the site. He would tell him to pull over to the side of the road and lower his right-hand window. Then he would tell King to begin driving again. At a point a half mile from the shack, Eddie would tell King that he was approaching a curve in the road. As soon as he rounded that bend, he wanted King to slow down, pull over, stop, and drop the carton of money out of the window and into the bushes on the right-hand side of the road. He was to drive away from the spot as quickly as possible then, following the instructions that came to him over the telephone.

And therein lay the beauty of the plan. A following squad car would be nowhere in sight when the drop was made. By the time they approached the electric-company shack, King would have driven off. They would continue to follow, not having witnessed the drop, not even knowing it had taken place. Eddie would continue talking to King. He would lead him out to the very tip of Sands Spit, turn him around at the end of the peninsula, and then lead him back to the city via another route. The following police car, if there was one, would continue tailing the lead car. Eddie would continue talking to King until Sy had picked up the money and driven back to the farmhouse. The moment Sy stepped through the door, Eddie would stop transmitting. King – and the police, if there were any – would then be on their own. They would be free to drive wherever the hell they wanted to. They could even drive back to the electric-company shack if they so chose; Sy would have left there long ago.

The plan, then, was beautiful.

And yet he was nervous.

He could not quell the persistent feeling that something would go wrong.

And yet he couldn't figure what.

He was not, you see, a Bible-reading man.

He did not know that the meek shall inherit the earth.

Studying the street map, Eddie Folsom said, 'All right, you're now approaching the Black Rock Span. There's a toll booth there, and the toll is a quarter, Mr King, twenty-five cents. Get the change out of your pocket now, and have it ready. Don't hand the attendant a hundred-dollar bill or anything like that to attract attention. And don't say anything to him. It won't do you any good at all to have police following you. If there are any cops when it comes time to make the drop, we'll call the whole thing off and kill the boy. Do you hear me, Mr King?'

'*Yes, I hear you*,' Carella answered.

'Good,' Eddie said. 'Go through the toll booth and onto the bridge. Let me know as you're driving off the bridge, and I'll tell you what to do next. It won't help to say anything to the cop collecting the toll because you still don't know where you're going. Any tricks, and we kill the boy.'

Listening to her husband, Kathy winced at the words.

Kill the boy.

*Kill the boy.*

My husband, she thought.

My fault.

In the automobile, Steve Carella reached into his back pocket and took out his wallet. He hastily opened it to where his shield was pinned to the leather. He unpinned the shield, took out his notebook rapidly scribbled:

*Call police headquarters. Tell them King contacted by radio transmission to car telephone. Try to get a fix. Hurry!*

*Detective Steve Carella*

He pinned his shield to the note, took a quarter from his pocket, and motioned King to pull over to the booth accepting quarters from the window opposite the driver's seat.

'*You at the booth yet, King?*' Eddie asked.

'Just approaching it.' Carella said.

'*Have you got the change?*'

'Yes, I've got a quarter.'

*'Good. No funny stuff.'*

The car slowed and pulled up alongside the toll booth. Carella handed the uniformed cop on duty a quarter, the note and his police shield. He nodded tersely at the cop as King pulled away and joined the steady stream of traffic moving across the bridge.

'You're coming off the bridge now, is that right?' Eddie asked.

*'That's right,'* Carella answered.

'Okay, bear to your left. I don't want you going out to Calm's Point. There's a big sign reading Mid-Sands Highway. That's the road I want you to take.'

Standing behind her husband, Kathy began to piece together a clear picture of what the markings on the street maps meant. The spot outlined with the red circle was obviously the Douglas King house, and the route marked in red was the route over which Eddie was leading him. The place marked 'Farm' was, of course, the farmhouse, situated on Fairlane Road, about a half a mile from Stanberry Road. And the spot marked with the blue star . . . ?

'Keep driving until you reach Exit Seventeen,' Eddie said. 'Have you got that, King?'

*'I've got it,'* Carella said.

The blue star confused Kathy because the red line went directly past it and then continued on out to the end of the peninsula, where it once again turned and headed back for the city. If the drop . . .

But of course.

The blue star indicated Sy's hiding place. They would ask King to drop the money and then keep him driving, simply to get him away from the spot or to confuse any followers. Of course. Sy Barnard, then, was lying in wait at . . .

She studied the map more closely.

. . . Tantamount Road, just around the curve in Route 127.

'Eddie,' she said.

'Not now, for God's sake!' he yelled, one hand cupped over the microphone.

'Eddie, let's get out of this. Please. Please.'

'No!' he said. 'Where are you now, King?' he asked into the microphone.

'Approaching Exit Fifteen,' Carella answered.

'*Let me know when you pass Sixteen*,' Eddie said.

'All right,' Carella covered the mouthpiece of the telephone.

'Where do you suppose he's leading us?' King asked.

'I don't know. Somewhere out on the peninsula.' He shook his head. 'If we knew that, Mr King . . .'

Sy Barnard looked at his watch again.

It shouldn't be long now. Come on, Eddie, he thought. Hurry them up. Get them over here with the gold. Let them make the drop, and let me pick it up, and let me get back to that farmhouse safely.

Come on. Please. Hurry up.

Sy didn't realize it, but he was praying.

'What do you make of this, Harry?' the uniformed cop asked.

The cop in the adjoining toll booth handed a motorist his change and said, 'What?'

'Lower that radio a minute, will you?'

'Sure.' He turned down the volume. 'What is it?'

'Guy just handed me this. What do you make of it?'

Harry studied the shield and the note. 'What do I make of it? You damn fool, this guy's a bull! Get on the phone right away!'

'How do you know he's legit?'

'Mister, you can't buy shields like that in the five and ten!'

'Headquarters, Detective Snyder.'

'Listen, this is Patrolman Umberson, shield number 63457, I'm in a toll booth on the Black Rock Span.'

'Yeah, what is it, Umberson?'

'A black Caddy just went through the toll stop. Guy handed me a badge and a note asking me to call Headquarters.'

'What kind of a badge?'

'Detective.'

'What's the number on it?'

'Just a second.' There was a pause on the line. 'Number 8712,' Umberson said.

'So what about it?'

'The note said to tell Headquarters that King was contacted by radio transmission to the car telephone. It said to try to get a fix. Does that make any sense to you?'

'King contacted by . . .' Detective Snyder shrugged. 'I just came on duty,' he said, 'It don't mean nothing to me. I'll check on that badge number, see if it's legitimate tin. What was the guy's name again?'

'King.'

'King, huh? Like the guy in that kidnapping over in

Smoke—' Snyder started and then suddenly said, 'Oh, my God!'

'Call it off, Eddie,' Kathy said. 'End it. We'll take the boy and—'

'I'm not calling anything off!' Eddie snapped. 'I have to do this, Kathy! I have to!'

'Please. If you love me, I'm asking you to . . .'

'*All right, we just passed Exit Seventeen*,' Carella said.

'Fine. Turn off at Seventeen and drive four blocks north. Then double back until you hit the parkway entrance below this one. You'll be heading in the opposite direction,' Eddie said. 'Drive down one exit to Exit Fifteen. Let me know when you—'

'The boy is in a farmhouse on Fairlane Road, a half mile from Stanberry!' Kathy suddenly shouted into the open microphone.

'What the hell—' Eddie started, and he turned to face her, but he was too late, the lid had blown, the words were spouting from her mouth.

*'Sy Barnard is waiting in a car . . .'*

*'Kathy, stop it, are you crazy?'*

*'. . . on Tantamount Road, around the curve in 127.'*

'Did you hear that?' Carella shouted.

'I heard it,' King said.

Carella slammed the receiver down onto the hook. 'Head for Tantamount Road, Route 127,' he said to King. 'Straight ahead, turn off at Exit Twenty-two. Step on it. Never mind the speed limit.' He lifted the receiver from the hook again and waited for the operator.

'Your call, please?'

'This is a police officer,' Carella said. 'Get me Headquarters immediately.'

'Yes, sir!' the operator said.

Sy Barnard was sitting in the automobile smoking his fifteenth cigarette when the black Cadillac rounded the bend in the road.

*This is it*, he thought. *This is it*.

The car slowed to a stop. The window on the right-hand side of the car was open. Sy watched, expecting to see a pair of hands appear at the window, expecting to see a carton of money drop into the bushes. Instead, the door opened and a man with a gun in his hand leaped out.

*What the* . . . ? Sy thought, and then he cursed Eddie for not having warned him somehow, and then stopped cursing because he realized it had been impossible to warn him, and then wondered what had gone wrong, and then turned the ignition key and started the car, and then ducked because that son of a bitch with the gun had opened fire. He drove straight for the man with the gun. The man kept firing. Two bullets shattered the windshield, but Sy drove past, seeing another man jump out of the Cadillac. The car had no sooner hit the macadam highway than Sy heard a fusillade of shots and felt the car give a sudden lurch, and knew at once that a tyre had been hit. The back window shattered and Sy figured he'd be better off on foot from here on in. He drove the limping car for another few yards, hopped out before it had stopped rolling, and began running into the woods.

The guy with the gun was reloading.

The other guy, a tall man with greying temples, began running after Sy.

Sy instantly drew his own pistol, turned, and fired twice, missing.

He thrashed into the woods.

'Give it up!' the man behind him yelled. 'We know where your partner is!'

'Go to hell!' Sy shouted, and he turned and fired again but the big man behind him did not slow his pace. He stamped into the woods after Sy and again Sy fired, and again, and suddenly the gun was empty. He threw away the useless pistol. He reached into his pocket, and the switch knife flashed into view, and suddenly the big man came around an outcropping of rocks, and Sy said softly, 'Hold it!'

'Hold crap!' Douglas King said, and he lunged.

The knife ripped upward, cutting a swath across King's overcoat. Again it slashed, digging deeper this time, tearing into King's jacket and running a thin line of blood across his flesh. King's hands tightened on Sy's throat.

'You son of a bitch! You lousy son of a bitch!' King muttered, his hands tightening, tightening, as he backed Sy against a tree. The knife flashed erratically now, searching for flesh. King's grip on Sy's throat would not loosen. A powerful man with hands that once had cut leather, he battered Sy's head against the tree, never relaxing his grip, silently, coldly, viciously pounding the other man until the knife dropped quietly from his lax fingers.

Exhausted, dizzy from the pounding, Sy Barnard only mumbled, 'Give . . . give me a break, will you?'

Douglas King didn't know the *Dragnet* answer. He held Sy until Carella came up with the handcuffs.

And that was that.

The patrolmen who responded to the call from Headquarters drove into the front yard of the farm and stopped the squad car. They drew their revolvers and took up positions flanking the door, listening. The house was silent. One patrolman cautiously tried the knob, and the door eased open.

An eight-year-old boy was sitting in the centre of an open sofa bed, a blanket draped over his shoulders.

'Jeff?' the patrolman asked.

'Yes.'

'You okay?'

'Yes.'

The patrolman studied the room. 'Anybody here with you?'

'No.'

'Where'd they go?' the second patrolman asked.

Jeff Reynolds hesitated a long time before answering. Then he said, 'Where'd *who* go?'

'The people who were holding you here,' the patrolman said.

'No people were holding me here,' Jeff answered.

'Huh?' the first patrolman said. He studied his black note pad. 'Look,' he said patiently, as if he were talking to a confused adult rather than a child, 'a detective named Carella called Headquarters from a car telephone. He said you were being held in a farmhouse on Fairlane, half a mile from Stanberry. Okay, so here you are. He also said a dame named Kathy had shouted the dope over a radio microphone, and that there was a guy with her. Now where are they, son? Where'd they go?'

'I don't know who you're talking about,' Jeff said. 'I've been all alone here ever since Sy left.'

The two patrolmen stared at each other.

'He must be in shock,' one of them said.

Jeff stuck to his story.

And, if life must have its little surprises, Sy Barnard corroborated the child's fable. He did not know whom the police were talking about, he said. He knew of no one named Kathy. He had engineered and executed the job singlehanded.

'You're lying and we know you're lying,' Lieutenant Byrnes said. 'Somebody had to be there to operate that transmitter.'

'Maybe it was a Martian,' Sy said.

'What the hell do you hope to gain by lying?' Carella asked. 'Who are you protecting? Don't you know the woman was the one who gave you away?'

'What woman?' Sy said.

'A woman named Kathy. The man yelled her name the minute she blew her stack.'

'I don't know any dame named Kathy,' Sy said.

'What's this, some code of yours? The law of the pack? No squealers allowed? *She told us exactly where we would find you. Barnard!'*

'I don't know who coulda told you, because I was in this alone,' Sy insisted.

'We'll get them, Barnard. With or without your help.'

'Will you?' Sy asked. 'I don't know how you're gonna get somebody that doesn't exist.'

'One thing makes me want to puke,' Parker said, 'is thieves who got honour.'

'So puke,' Sy said, and Parker hit him suddenly and viciously.

'What's the broad's last name?' Parker asked.

'I don't know who you mean!'

Parker hit him again.

'Kathy, Kathy,' Parker said. 'Kathy what?'

'I don't know who you mean,' Sy said.

'What are you selling us?' Parker said. 'You know damn well who . . .'

'I ain't selling you nothing,' Sy said.

Parker drew back his fist.

'Put away your hands, Andy,' Carella said.

I'd like to . . .'

'Put them away.' Carella turned to Sy. 'You're not doing yourself any good, Barnard, and you're not helping your pals, either. We'll get them. You're not giving them anything but time.'

'Maybe time is all they need,' Sy said, and there was a sudden sadness in his voice. 'Maybe a little time is all anybody ever needs.'

'Lock him up,' Byrnes said.

# 14.

**IN THE SQUADROOM** of the 87th Precinct, Detective Steve Carella typed up his final report on the Jeffry Reynolds kidnapping. It was a bitter-cold day at the end of November, and the steam rising from the cup of coffee on his desk gave a feeling of coziness to the otherwise drab squadroom. The feeble November sunshine sifted through the meshed grille-work covering the long windows, patched the floor in pale gold. Carella ripped the three copies of the report from the machine, separated them from the carbon copies, turned to Meyer Meyer and said, 'Finis.'

'End of story,' Meyer Meyer said. 'Steve Carella, star reporter for the *Isola Rag*, writes thirty to another dazzling assignment. Justice once more triumphs. Sy Barnard rots in jail. The police are jubilant. Another threat to the safety of John Q. Public is eliminated. Steve Carella, star reporter, lights a cigarette and meditates on crime and punishment, justice and the power of the press. Hooray for Carella, the crowd shouts. Long live Carella, the crowd roars. Carella for Presi—'

'Up yours,' Carella said.

'But what of those behind the scenes?' Meyer asked grandiosely. 'What of the mysterious woman known only as Kathy? What of the man who shouted her name into the transmitter microphone in that lonely deserted farmhouse? Where are they now? You might well ask,' Meyer said, 'because even the intrepid star reporter doesn't know.'

'Out of the country is my guess,' Carella said. 'I wish them luck.'

'What the hell for? Kidnappers?'

'Kids are like puppies,' Carella said. 'If Jeff Reynolds refused to bite somebody's hand, that hand must have been kind to him. That's the way I figure it. Who the hell knows what was behind all this, Meyer? Barnard isn't telling, and he never will. He'd rather get the chair than the mark of a squealer. His silence makes him a big man at Castleview Prison, the hoodlum the cops couldn't break. Okay, give the louse his day of glory. Maybe everybody's entitled to his day of glory.' Carella paused. 'Kathy. That's a nice name.'

'Sure. She must be a nice girl, too,' Meyer said. 'She only took part in a kidnapping.'

'We don't know the facts,' Carella said. 'Maybe she deserved what Jeff Reynolds gave her. Who knows?'

'Steve Carella's flintlike eyes softened,' Meyer said, 'for beneath the crusty exterior of this star reporter's breast there beat the heart of an old washerwoman,' Meyer sighed. 'Who do we whitewash next? Douglas King?'

'He got his lumps,' Carella said.

'He brought them on himself. You know what the bastard was most pleased about after all this was over? The fact that his damn stock deal went through and that he's going to be president of his lousy shoe company. Now how about that, Steve? Just how about that?'

'Some guys always pick up all the marbles,' Carella

said. 'His wife went back to him, you know that, don't you?'

'Sure. Why do the louses of the world always get the rewards?'

'While the good die young,' Carella finished for him.

'I ain't dead yet,' Meyer said.

'Neither is King. Maybe nobody got ransomed in this damn case, or maybe *everybody* did.'

'How's that again?' Meyer asked.

'Give the man time. He didn't have to stick his neck out against that switchblade.'

'Just because a guy has the guts to face a knife,' Meyer said, 'it doesn't necessarily mean he has the guts to face himself.'

'Pearls, pearls,' Carella said. 'Give him time. He figures he can't change. I figure he *has* to change, or he's dead. Why do you think his wife went back to him? Because he helps old ladies across the street?'

'Because she's got an investment in the louse, that's why,' Meyer said.

'Sure. But not in Granger Shoe, though. Her investment is in Douglas King. And she struck me as the kind of woman who knows when to sell a stock that's falling.'

'Careful or we'll switch you to the financial pages,' Meyer said.

'Whoo!' Andy Parker said from the gate in the slatted rail divider, slapping his arms at his sides, stamping into the room. 'If it gets much colder out there, I'm leaving for the South Pole.'

'What's the street like?'

'Cold.'

'I mean . . .'

'Who knows? You think I look for crime on days like this? I look for warm candy stores, that's what I look for.'

'Everybody changes, huh?' Meyer said. 'The day Andy Parker changes is the day I become a street cleaner.'

'You're a street cleaner already,' Parker said. 'Where'd you get that coffee, Stevie?'

'From Miscolo.'

'Hey, Miscolo!' Parker bellowed. 'Bring in the joe!'

'He'll have to pay it one day,' Carella said thoughtfully.

'Huh? Who'll have to pay what?' Parker asked.

'King,' Carella said. 'His *own* ransom.'

'I don't like riddles on cold days,' Parker said.

'Then why'd you become a cop?'

'My mother forced me.' He paused. 'Miscolo, where's the goddamn coffee?'

'Coming, coming,' Miscolo yelled back.

'I hate to file this,' Carella said, studying the report.

'Why?' Meyer asked.

'Maybe because I feel the case is still open. For a lot of people, Meyer, it's still open.'

Meyer grinned. 'You only *hope* it is,' he said, and the coffee came into the room, Miscolo staggering under the load of the cups and the huge pot, the aroma assailing the nostrils. The men poured and drank and told their dirty jokes.

Outside the squadroom, the city crouched.

# MONEY MONEY MONEY

This—as always and forever—is for my wife,
Dragica Dimitrijević-Hunter

# 1.

**THE TWO MEN ON THE NARROW DIRT STRIP WERE BOTH** wearing white cotton pants and shirts. They stood beside the Piper Warrior III in broad daylight, waiting for Cass to hand over the locked aluminum suitcase. She gave it to the larger of the two men, and watched as they walked to a dark blue Mercedes-Benz glistening in the sun alongside the cornfield. The doors on either side slammed shut into the stillness, and then there was only the sound of insects racketing in the scraggly woods nearby.

Today was Pearl Harbor Day, the seventh of December, though it didn't much feel like it here in Guenerando, Mexico. Cass stood beside the airplane, sweating in the afternoon heat. She assumed there was money in the aluminum suitcase. She further assumed they were counting it over there in the Benz. She guessed that the cargo they'd be turning over in exchange for the money would be dope—either heroin or cocaine. She didn't care much either way. She stood in the shade of a spindly eucalyptus for almost forty minutes. At last, the two men came out of the Benz and handed the aluminum suitcase back to her. The one with the mustache was grinning. He handed her a long white business envelope with a rubber band around it. The other one watched solemnly, expectantly.

"Open it, *por favor,*" the one with the mustache said.

She slipped the rubber band over her wrist, opened the

envelope. There was a whole bunch of hundred-dollar bills in it.

"Count them," the serious one said.

She counted them.

There seemed to be ten thousand dollars in that envelope.

"For me?" she asked.

*"Para ti,"* the one with the mustache said.

Damn if they weren't tipping her!

"Well thanks," she said. *"Muchas gracias."*

*"Muchas gracias,"* the one with the mustache said, grinning.

*"Muchas gracias,"* the other one said. He was grinning now, too.

She couldn't help grinning herself.

THE BABOQUIVARI MOUNTAINS STRETCHED NORTHWARD to Kitt Peak. She flew low behind them. There was an anti-drug radar blimp in the sky over Fort Huachuca, but she had talked to other pilots who'd made the identical run dozens of times and who knew there was a so-called radar deficiency within plus-or-minus four degrees of the Kitt Peak Observatory. If she flew northward through "Gringo Pass," as the security gap was called, she could avoid detection. Besides, she'd be on the ground again near Avra Valley in eighteen minutes, so even in the unlikely event that she *did* show up on radar, there wouldn't be enough time for Customs planes to take off and chase her.

She didn't even know the last name of the man who was paying her $200,000 to do this little job for him, a quarter of it already in a bank account back East, where she'd rented an apartment within ten minutes of laying her hands on all that cash. She'd first met him in Eagle Branch, Texas, after one of her whistle-stop hops. What she did was fly light machinery, chickens in crates, melons, computer parts, sandals, what have you, all over Mexico in single-engine planes that were new when Zapata was still a boy. She'd occasionally been dating a Texas Ranger named Randolph Biggs, who made frequent trips to the Rio Grande where he helped the border patrol dissuade wetbacks from entering the sacred shores Cass had gone to the Persian Gulf to preserve and protect. In a bar one night, he'd introduced her to this guy named Frank. Kind of cute, but no last name. Just Frank. Frank's enough, he'd told her. She wondered now how much Randy had got for introducing him to a good pilot willing to take risks.

Instruments on the Warrior—such a mighty name for a single-engine light aircraft—were kindergarten compared to the Chinook helicopter Cass had flown during the Gulf War. Way they played it on television back home, everything was a surgical strike and nobody but the enemy suffered any casualties, which of course was a crock. More hardware up there in the Iraqi skies than she'd care to fly through ever again in her lifetime. Little different here in Arizona. Better pay, too.

She could see the lights of some quiet little desert town down below in the near distance. What's a bad girl like you doing in a nice place like this? she wondered. Don't ask, don't tell. Man says fly four shipments for me from Texas to Mexico, I'll give you fifty grand a trip, two hundred total, you tell him Mister, you've got a deal. This was the last of the four trips. Rented the Warrior in San Antone, nice little rig that handled like a dream. She'd drop the plane off at the Phoenix airport later tonight, as pre-arranged, hop a commercial liner back East, be snug in her own apartment long before Christmas.

There.

Just below.

The signal light.

She flashed her own wing lights, dipped in lower for a better look. When you came in low over Baghdad, it was to drop a smart bomb down Saddam Hussein's chimney. Only trouble was they'd never got to him, ended the war too damn soon. Well, some you win, some you lose. She guessed.

She made a pass over the site, and then swung around for her actual approach into the wind. A car's headlights came on, illuminating the strand of sand more fully. It was long and narrow. She watched the altimeter, pulled back on the flaps, leveled the pedals, glanced at the speedometer, this would be a piece of cake, douse your lights, boys, who needs them?

The strip here was level and flat, she felt the wheels touching, hit the brakes, lowered the flaps, and rolled along the beach to a full stop some twenty yards from where she'd seen the headlights. She cut the engine. The night was still. Immediately, she took the forty-five from the flap pocket of her jump suit.

She waited inside the cockpit, in the dark.

Kept waiting.

In the Gulf, she'd packed a forty-five automatic in a holster at her waist, case she got shot down, a distinct possibility. Lots of unfriendly people down there, waiting to get their hands on an American pilot, well, who could blame them? A female pilot, no less. Cassandra Jean Ridley, Lieutenant, U.S. Army, 714-56-32, that's all she was obliged to tell them. Didn't even have to say she was with the 101st Airborne. Here, she didn't know *who'd* be waiting for her.

But she knew she had a hundred and fifty thousand coming for delivering this last suitcase. Money like that, a girl couldn't be too careful.

The rap on the window startled her.

She slid it back, right hand tight around the walnut grip of the Browning in her lap. She had to pee. First thing you did when you got back to base was rush to barracks to pee. The male pilots just unzipped and pissed right where they'd landed.

"Welcome to Arizona," someone said.

Cheerful voice, the speaker nothing more than a blur in the dark. Two other men with him. She did not loosen her grip on the automatic. She was waiting for the single word that would tell her these were the people expecting the shipment. Buried any which way in whatever sentence they chose to use. But until she heard it, she sat right where she was with the gun in her hand and her finger inside the trigger guard.

"Nice night," one of the men said.

Try again, sweetheart.

"Hasn't been much rain."

Rain.

Bingo.

"Who's got my money?" she asked.

"Where's the suitcase?"

She released the door lever, climbed out onto the wing, and dropped to the ground, the gun dangling lazily, familiarly at her side.

"You won't need that," one of the men said.

"Gee, I hope not," she answered.

The desert air was a bit chilly. She wished she had on her flight jacket. One of the men was carrying a small leather case the size of a laptop. He placed it on the rim of the door, snapped it open. Another man turned on a penlight. She was looking at a lot of U.S. currency.

"A hundred and fifty thousand," one of the men said. "Final payment. As agreed."

"Where's the suitcase?" another man said.

"Mind if I count it first?" Cass said.

"Why don't we all just sit out here in the open till Customs spots us?" the third man said.

"Count it out for me," Cass said.

"Count it out for her," the first man said.

He was the one with the cheerful voice. He sounded a trifle impatient now, but she didn't give a damn *how* he sounded. One thing she'd learned in the Army was you didn't back off. Not on the ground, not in the air. So far all the risk these guys had taken was to sit here in Shit Wallow, Arizona, waiting for her. She was the one carrying the cargo, she was the one who *still* had the cargo sitting in a plane *she'd* rented. So go right ahead, she thought, *get* impatient. That's *my* money you're treating so casually there.

The one who'd mentioned Customs slipped the thick rubber band from one of the packets and looped it over his wrist. There was a small tattoo on the back of his left hand. Some kind of bird, looked like a hawk, wings spread wide, claws gripping a fish. He spread the bills to show her there weren't any pieces of newspaper cut to size in the bundle. Then he began counting them out loud, one by one, ". . . five, six, seven," Cass holding the gun, watching, listening, "eight, nine, ten, a thousand. One, two, three, four . . ."

On and on. There were fifty bills in the packet, all of them hundred-dollar bills. When he counted out the last bill, he rubber-banded the stack again, and dropped it back into the leather case. There were thirty packets of bills in all, each of them about three-quarters of an inch thick. It took the man less than fifteen minutes to count them all out. He snapped the lid on the case shut, and handed it to the first man, who folded his arms across it and held it against his chest like a schoolgirl carrying books. She suddenly thought of Fall River, Massachusetts, where Lizzie Borden had got away with killing her father and her stepmother and where, coincidentally, Cassandra Jean Ridley had spent the first fifteen years of her life, my how the time did fly. What am I doing *here?* she wondered.

"The suitcase," he said.

Cass climbed back into the plane and pulled out the suitcase from where she'd stowed it. She carried it out again in her left hand, the gun in her right, still hanging loose. She was thinking they could shoot her dead the minute she dropped to the ground again, grab the suitcase full of dope, she was sure it was, ride off into the night with the dope *and* the money they'd so patiently counted out for her.

It didn't happen.

She revved up the engine again, the little leather case with $150,000 sitting on the seat beside her, another ten grand in the flap pocket of her jump suit. Tonight I'll be back in the big bad city, she thought. Her heart was pounding as fiercely as it had over the sands of Iraq.

HANUKKAH WOULD START AT SUNDOWN TODAY, THE twenty-first day of December. Will didn't much care. He wasn't even Jewish.

This was always the most dangerous time, going in. Well, coming *out* was no picnic, either, but then you could march right through the front door, say you'd been there to fix the toilet or the sink, nice day, ain't it? Somebody saw you going in, though, that was another story. Specially when you were going in through a window on a fire escape, now *that* was a little difficult to explain.

He'd been watching the apartment from the roof across the way for the better part of a week now, knew when the lady came and went, even had an opportunity once to see her in the altogether, though inadvertently, he wasn't no damn Peeping Tom. Redheaded as a cardinal, she was, carpet matching the drapes, a fair sight to behold and a rarity in this day and age. He always so-called cased a joint, he hated criminal jargon, for at least a week before he went in, sometimes two or three, because the one yearning he did not have was to spend any more time behind bars.

Lady was putting on a short red fox jacket now, which meant maybe there were more furs in there than he'd figured. Thing that had first attracted him to her when he was scoping *all* the apartments across the way was a sable coat came down to the floor, had to be worth fifty large at least. You could always tell a woman with a new fur coat, she pranced in front of the mirror with it all day long. He decided that going into the apartment for just the sable alone might be worth it, plus whatever other little goodies he might find in there. The building was on South Ealey Street in a section of Isola called Silvermine. It was a doorman building, which usually meant any other kind of security was lacking. The lady was heading for the front door now—

"There we go," Will said out loud.

He still spoke with a Texas twang he should've lost after thirty-seven years on this planet, especially since he'd left the state when he was eighteen and never did go back except for his mother's funeral. He was still a sophomore at UCLA when she died. He guessed maybe her death had something to do with him flunking out the very next year. Her dying so young and all. He sometimes wondered if his life might've turned out different if she hadn't died and he hadn't flunked out of college. He wondered if he'd've become a burglar, anyway. He guessed maybe he would've.

Will gave her ten minutes to get clear.

Then he jumped the airshaft to the roof of her building, and came down the fire escape to the ninth floor. He wasn't expecting any kind of burglar alarm, and there wasn't any. He jimmied the turnbolt lock on the window, and was inside the apartment in ten seconds flat. No need for a flashlight here in the living room at ten in the morning. Anyway, there was nothing to steal in this room but a TV set and a stereo and he wasn't any junkie burglar, thank you. He went into the bedroom, went to the windows first to pull down the shades so nobody would look in and see a guy six feet tall at a buck-ninety roaming a bedroom where a lady lived alone. Only when the shades were down did he go to the wall switch and snap on the overhead lights. Bed nicely made, he surely did appreciate neat people. He yanked back the cover, stripped both pillows of their pillow cases, and then went to the closet. The door was closed. He opened it and found—well, oh my stars—not only the long sable coat but a mink stole as well, the lady really *had* been on a shopping spree. Both were too bulky to fit inside the pillow cases, he tossed them on the bed for now, and went to the dresser.

Everything neatly laid out here, too, rolled nylons and pantyhose in one drawer, tank tops and cotton panties in another, T-shirts and sweaters, all precisely put away as if they were color-coded or something, he figured all at once that either the lady was a nurse or else she'd been in the military. In the top drawer, there was a jewelry box. He opened it. Nothing in it but a bunch of cheap costume jewelry and a long white business envelope with a rubber band around it. He slid the rubber band off, opened the envelope. What he was looking at was a whole big bunch of U.S. currency. He fished in his jacket pocket for his eyeglass case, slipped the glasses out of it, hung them on his nose and his ears, and looked into the envelope again.

The money in there was hundred-dollar bills.

HE DIDN'T STOP TO COUNT THEM TILL HE WAS SAFE AT home again in his apartment on South Twelfth Street, just off Stemmler Avenue. This was now close to twelve noon, and it had begun snowing outside. He sat in an easy chair under a lamp with a lamp shade that somehow had ketchup stains on it, and took the white envelope out of his jacket pocket, and then took the rubber band off the envelope again, and took out the bills and began counting them.

What it turned out to be was $8,500 in hundred-dollar bills.

Will hadn't expected such a big haul, and the very idea of sitting alone here four days before Christmas, in an apartment even he admitted was dingy, seemed illogical for a suddenly wealthy individual. He took $500 from the stack of hundreds, put on his coat, and went out whistling.

IT WAS SNOWING QUITE HEAVILY BY THE TIME CASS GOT back to the apartment at two-thirty that afternoon. She went into the living room, tossed the red fox jacket over the arm of the sofa, turned on the Christmas tree lights, and then poured herself a Courvoisier on the rocks. Sitting alone in a chair by the window, she sipped the cognac and basked in the winking glow of the Christmas tree, thinking how lucky she was to have a nice apartment like this one in this wonderful city at this very special time of the year. She wondered what she might like to buy next. Or should she wait till after Christmas, when she could get everything on sale? Today was the twenty-first. Christmas wasn't too far off.

She eased out of her pumps, $400 at Bruno Magli, stretched her legs, and suddenly realized just how tired she was. Rising, carrying the shoes in one hand and the brandy snifter in the other, she walked into the bedroom, snapped on the light switch, and almost spilled cognac all over her brand-new dress, $2,100 at Romeo Gigli. The closet door was open. She saw in a single eye swipe that the sable and the mink were gone. All the dresser drawers were open, too. Her envelope with what was left of the Mexican tip money was gone. She felt an immediate sense of violation, someone had been in here, someone had taken her things, gone through her private possessions, taken her goddamn *things!* She felt as angry as she had when some twerps in Basic pissed in her footlocker, felt like rushing to the still-open window and screaming at the top of her lungs, "You goddamn *thief!,"* a lot of good that would do. Calming herself slightly, but only slightly, she checked the closet and the dresser more closely, trying to ascertain if he'd taken anything more than the obvious. It seemed that was it. Hadn't bothered with the Angela Cummings bracelet she'd bought last week, all shiny and bright in its aqua-blue box. Hadn't been lured by the Hermès scarf, or the cashmere sweater, or the pre-Hellenic winged Eros pendant from an antiques shop on Jefferson, had satisfied himself merely—*merely!*—with the sable and the mink and what was $8,500 in cash the last time she'd counted it, the son of a bitch!

She actually pounded the dresser top in anger, pounded it again and again with her closed fist, screaming, "You mother-fucking son of a bitch bastard!," obscenities she hadn't used since the war, and then calmed down just a little bit and went to the phone and dialed 911.

WILL WAS TELLING THE BLONDE THAT HE'D BEEN BORN and raised in San Antonio, Texas, but that he hadn't been back there in quite a while.

"What's the Will for?" she asked. "William?"

"No, Wilbur," he said.

"Wilbur Struthers?"

"Wilbur Struthers is what it is, ma'am."

She almost burst out laughing. She didn't. She even managed to keep herself from smiling, which he certainly appreciated. They were sitting in a booth in a bar called Flanagan's, on Twenty-first and Culver. Will had first ordered a bottle of Veuve Cliquot, which the waiter didn't know what it was, or care to know, it was that kind of bar. So he had asked Jasmine—that was her name—what she might prefer instead, and she had ordered a Harvey Wallbanger, and he had ordered a bourbon and water for himself, and they were now on their third drink each, with their knees touching under the table, and their heads very close together above the table. He figured if he played this one correctly, she would soon be in his bed back at the apartment.

He told her how he'd booked onto a tramp steamer after he quit college, headed for the Pacific Rim, found himself in Cambodia just about when the Khmer Rouge were rampaging there, got himself taken prisoner, and spent two years waiting for them to blow his brains out before he attempted a daring escape that landed him first in Manila and next in Singapore. Jasmine figured he was full of shit, but he had the tall rugged look of a cowboy, wearing a dark blue turtleneck that complemented the lighter blue of his eyes. Gray sports jacket, darker gray slacks. His hair a sort of sunwashed brown, rather than truly blond. Good strong face, good strong hands. Southern accent—or whatever it was—that didn't hurt the Home-on-the-Range image. Too bad he's a trick, she thought, although he hadn't yet asked her how much this would cost him, or anything so crass as that, which she considered the sign of a true gent. She figured he'd get around to it sooner or later, but meanwhile she enjoyed listening to him tell her about the time a Khmer Rouge soldier put the barrel of a pistol in his mouth, which only happened to her every night of the week, more or less.

When it got time to pay for the drinks, Will handed the waiter a hundred-dollar bill, and then asked her if she'd made any other plans for the night. If she hadn't, did she think she might enjoy accompanying him back to his place? Perhaps they could find a liquor store that sold Veuve Cliquot, a truly astonishing champagne, he told her, which they could drink while watching a movie on HBO. She still figured he was full of shit, but she thought this might be a good time to mention that she got five bills for the night, Around-the-World understood, of course.

Will blinked.

"I'm a working girl," she said. "I thought you knew."

"I'm sorry, ma'am, I surely didn't."

"So what do you think?"

"I never paid for a lady's favors in my life," Will said.

"Always a first time, cowboy. Teach you things you never dreamed of."

"I dreamed most everything," he said.

"Does that mean yes or no?"

"I guess it means no," he said. "I'm sorry."

"No sorrier'n I am," Jasmine said, and picked up her handbag and said, "Have a nice Christmas," and threw her coat over her shoulders and went swiveling toward the front door, passing within a few feet of where the waiter was handing Will's hundred-dollar bill to the cashier.

The cashier, a woman named Savina Girasole, held up the bill to the light to check the otherwise invisible polyester strip. The embedded security tape revealed itself at once, the upside down *USA 100 USA 100 USA 100* repeating itself over and over again down the left-hand side of the bill. So it's genuine, Savina thought. But there was something about the feel of it—well, not exactly the *feel,* the paper certainly *felt* as reliable as any other U.S. bill. But . . .

Well . . . the *look* of it.

The funny writing in ink across Franklin's face, for one thing. The *smell* of it, too. It had a sort of sweet smell. Savina didn't normally go around sniffing money that came in, but this bill really did have an odd aroma. Not like marijuana, nothing like that. More like some kind of cheap perfume. As if it had been between the breasts of some girl who bought her brassieres off downtown pushcarts.

The guy whose bill it was sat in the booth all alone now, nursing his drink as sad as could be. He looked like an all-

American back yard barbecue champ, which didn't mean he was above passing a phony hundred-dollar bill, which if it ended up in her cash register would cause Mr. O'Brien to fire her. Ronnie O'Brien was the owner of the place and not anybody named Flanagan, no matter what it said on the sign outside. Savina didn't want to lose her job. So she picked up the phone resting alongside the credit card machine, and called the number she had Scotch-taped to the side of the cash register.

"SO AS I UNDERSTAND THIS," ONE OF THE DETECTIVES was telling Cass, "all this guy took is two expensive furs, is that it?"

"Yes, that's it," Cass said.

She hadn't mentioned the missing cash, and she didn't intend to.

"One of them a full-length sable coat . . ."

"Yes, from Revillon."

"How much would you say it's worth, Miss?"

"Forty-five thousand dollars," she said.

"And the mink stole? How much was *that* worth?"

"Six thousand."

"Insured?"

"No."

"You should insure things, Miss."

"I intended to."

"Your initials in either of them?"

"Both of them."

"And what would those initials be?"

"CJR."

"For?"

"Cassandra Jean Ridley."

"Could you please spell Ridley for us?"

"R-I-D-L-E-Y," she said. "What are the chances of getting them back?"

One of the detectives was redheaded. With a white streak in his hair. The other was short. She figured the chances were nil.

"We have a very good recovery record, don't we, Hal?" the redheaded one said.

"Well, so-so," the short one said, and smiled.

Which confirmed Cass's doubts.

"We'll let you know if we come up with anything," the redheaded one said. "Here's my card, I'll write my beeper number on the back in case you think of anything else." The card said he was Detective/Second Grade Cotton Hawes of the Eighty-seventh Detective Squad.

"Thank you," Cass said, though she couldn't imagine what else she might think of to call them about.

"We know just how you feel," the short one said.

"Oops!" the redheaded one said, and stopped dead in his tracks and bent to pick up a black eyeglass case on the floor near the dresser. "Almost stepped on them," he said.

Cass did not wear eyeglasses.

"Thank you," she said at once, and took the case.

"Have a nice Christmas," the short one said.

"You, too," Cass said.

She led them to the door, and locked it behind them. The minute they were gone, she looked at the name and address imprinted on the case in barely legible gold letters:

Eyewear Fashions, Inc.
1137 Stemmler Avenue
(corner of 22nd Street)

Cass went to the closet for her red fox jacket.

THE KNOCK ON THE DOOR CAME AT A LITTLE PAST FOUR that afternoon. Will went to the door and said, "Yes?"

"Secret Service," a voice said. "Mind opening the door for us?"

Secret *what?* Will thought.

"Say again?" he said.

"Special Agent David A. Horne," the voice said. "Few questions I'd like to ask you, sir. Routine matter."

Which to Will meant he ought to go out the window this very minute. Trouble was, there was no fire escape outside the window.

"Just a minute, let me put something on," he said, even though he was fully clothed. In the next thirty seconds, he debated whether he should go hide the stolen hundred-dollar bills in the toilet tank or the freezer compartment of the fridge, both of which places would be searched at once if this was related to the burglary he'd committed on South Ealey. He decided to play it cool.

"Just a minute," he said again, and went to the door and opened it.

The man standing there was tall and thin and blue-jowled, wearing a neon blue parka and a woolen hat with ear flaps. "Special Agent David A. Horne," he said again, "with an 'e,' " and opened a little leather case to show a gold star that looked like the ones the Texas Rangers carried back home. Will tried to think if there were any outstanding warrants on him back home. He couldn't think of a single one.

"Good evening," he said. "What can I do for you?"

"It's still afternoon," Horne corrected. "Is your name Wilbur Struthers?"

"It is."

"Ask me in," Horne said, and smiled.

"Sure, come on in," Will said.

He was somewhat frightened now, but he spoke calmly and politely because it was always best to be polite to policemen. Even back home in Texas, Will spoke politely to policemen, whose long suit was definitely not courtesy. But Horne was a Secret Service agent with considerably more sophistication, he hoped. He stepped into the room now, looking around as if there might be an accomplice or two lurking about.

"You were in Flanagan's earlier today," Horne said. It was not a question.

"That's right," Will said.

The hooker, he thought at once. Something happened to the hooker, so now the Secret Service is here to question me about her. He hoped it was nothing serious. He hoped nobody had killed her or raped her.

"You had some drinks there," Horne said.

"I did."

Had she been poisoned?

"You paid for them with a hundred-dollar bill," Horne said. *"This* bill," he said, and removed from the inside pocket of the bulky blue parka a narrow folder that looked like the kind you put money in for a Christmas gift to your mailman or your doorman, except that it had a gold star embossed on the front of it. Horne opened the folder and took a hundred-dollar bill from it. "Recognize it?" he asked, and handed it to Will.

"All hundred-dollar bills look alike to me," he said.

"Where'd you get *this* hundred-dollar bill?" Horne asked.

"I won it in a crap game," Will said.

"Won a hundred dollars in a crap game."

"Yes, I did."

"Where? What crap game?"

"Pickup game on Laramie," he said.

"Where on Laramie?"

"Don't recall the address," he said.

Two different agendas here, he was thinking. Man here wants to know all about this hundred-dollar bill, I want to make sure he don't find out I stole it.

"This all you won in the crap game?"

"Just the hundred, that's all."

"Went out to spend it, is that right?"

"That's right."

Listen, he thought, why the fuck are you asking all these questions?

But knew better than to say.

Two different agendas here.

"I talked to a girl named Jasmine before I came up here," Horne said.

"Oh?"

"Got your name from her."

"So?"

"Ran a computer check."

Will said nothing.

"Seems you ran into a little trouble here in this city, is that right, Wilbur?"

"It's Will, by the way."

"Sorry, I didn't know that, Will."

"That's okay," Will said.

He was thinking it still didn't take the curse off the oldest cop trick in the world, calling a suspected perp by his first name, which reduced him to the status of a menial. What this was here was *Will* and *Mr.* David Horne.

"Burglarized a gas station seven years ago, did time for the deed up at Castleview. That the only burglary you ever committed, Will?"

"The one and only," Will lied.

"That's commendable," Horne said. "But nonetheless, on the basis of this hundred-dollar bill here, I was able to obtain a search warrant."

"A *what?"*

"I believe you heard me," Horne said, and handed Will a court order with a judge's signature and all on the bottom of it, authorizing a search of this very apartment for monies paid as ransom . . .

*"Ransom?"* Will said.

"Ransom in a kidnapping, is what it says. *Ransom* money, Will."

"That's not my bill," Will said at once. "I told you. I won it in a crap game."

"Well, that's good, Will, because the serial numbers on this bill match the serial numbers on one of the bills paid as ransom in a kidnapping case we're investigating. Do you understand the implications of that?"

"I'm not a kidnapper," Will said.

"That's good, too, Will, because I have a search warrant to look for any *other* bills that may have been part of the ransom payment," Horne said, and took off the blue parka to reveal a dark blue suit, a white shirt, and a red tie. The suit jacket was taut over bulging pectorals and broad shoulders. The man was a fitness freak. He took off the hat with the ear flaps, revealing a head of very black, very thick hair.

"Is it the President?" Will asked.

"Is what the President?"

"Who got kidnapped?"

"I have to warn you not to say anything that might prove incriminating," Horne said.

Oh, Jesus, it's the President, Will thought. Because if it *wasn't* the President, then what was the Secret Service doing in this? It was the *FBI* who investigated kidnappings, wasn't it? All the Secret Service did was protect the President of the United States. And his family. So it had to be somebody in the White House who'd got kidnapped.

Horne was moving over to the closet now, where the bills sat in a shoe box on the shelf over the hanging sable coat and mink stole, both of which Will had also stolen. I can run right this minute, he thought, go visit my cousin Earl living in Fort Worth with a girl used to be Miss Texas in the Miss America contest, came within a curly blond crotch hair of winning it. Spend a few weeks down there till this whole kidnapping thing blew over, which he hadn't done anyway, *damn it!* All he'd done was burglarize a fucking apartment!

"Well, well, what have we here?" Horne said.

He was looking in at the sable coat and the mink stole.

"Your search warrant says you're supposed to look for money," Will said.

"These are in plain view," Horne said.

"In plain view" was an expression the police used when they appropriated something without benefit of a search warrant.

"They're my girlfriend's," Will said.

"What's her name?"

"Jasmine. Who you talked to."

"She told us you only just met," Horne said.

"Well, that's true."

"And she left her furs here?"

"She trusts me."

Horne gave him a look. But he didn't pursue the matter of the furs any further, perhaps because his mind was on the President's kidnapping, who it had to be, or else someone in his family, otherwise why the Secret Service? I ought to run for it right this minute, Will thought. Horne was reaching for a shoe box on the shelf. Run for it or not? Will thought. Horne took down the box. Which? Horne took the lid off the box and looked into it. He reached in for a white envelope with a rubber band around it. He took the rubber band off the envelope. He opened the envelope.

"Well, well," he said again.

"That's not plain view," Will said.

"Now it is," Horne said, and fanned the bills. "Where'd you get *these* little mothers?"

"Same crap game," Will said.

Horne began counting.

"This is a lot of money here," he said.

"Yeah, it was a big crap game."

"Looks like five, six thousand dollars here."

"More like eight," Will said.

"You won eight thousand dollars in a crap game?"

"I got lucky."

"Who was in this game?"

"Bunch of guys I never saw in my life."

"So let me get this straight, Will," Horne said. "You're asking me to believe that one or more of the men in this crap game of yours *could* have been the kidnappers to whom these bills were paid as ransom, is that it?"

"I guess that's it," Will said.

He knew he was already in the toilet. He knew Horne would yank out a gun and a pair of handcuffs in the next minute. He'd be spending Christmas Day in jail for a goddamn kidnapping he didn't do.

"Listen," he said, "you really do have the wrong person here."

"Maybe so," Horne said, and gave him a long, hard look.

Will's hands were shaking. He put them in his pockets so Horne wouldn't see. He hated himself for being so goddamn scared here, but he couldn't help it. A kidnapping was serious stuff.

"Tell you what," Horne said.

Will waited.

"What I think I should do is confiscate this money here," Horne said. "Give you a receipt for it, check the serial numbers downtown, get back to you later today."

Sure, Will thought.

Secret Service or not, every cop in the world was identical to every other cop, and they were all fuckin crooks. Next thing you knew, eight thousand bucks would find its way into a fund for the widows of Secret Service men who had died in the line of duty. Only thing he didn't understand was why Horne was granting a possible kidnapper the opportunity to flee. He watched as the man meticulously copied the serial numbers on all the bills, signed the sheet of paper with the numbers on it, and handed it to Will. He looked for his parka, found it where he'd draped it over one of the chairs, and put it on.

"I don't have to warn you not to leave the city," he said.

"Not while you've got all my money," Will said.

"See you later," Horne said, and put on the hat with the ear flaps, and walked out of the apartment.

It was twenty minutes to five.

So what do I do now? Will wondered.

Hell, I'm an innocent man here!

Except for the burglary.

But Horne hadn't been interested in any burglary, Horne didn't even know any burglary had *happened.* Horne had been interested only in the hundred-dollar bills that had maybe or maybe not been paid as ransom in a kidnapping case he was investigating—but how come the Secret Service? Anyway, that was the entire scope of Special Agent David A. Horne's interest. The money. Check the serial numbers. If they match, come fetch old Wilbur here.

But let's say the serial numbers do *not* match. I mean, out of all the millions of apartments in New York City, what are the odds on my breaking into the only one that happens to be the apartment of a redhead who'd done a kidnapping and stashed the ransom money there? What are the odds on that kind of thing happening? I mean, *really.* A thousand to one? A million to one? I'll take odds like that on a horse any day of the week.

So the odds have got to be in my favor, right? The serial numbers will not match, Horne will come back with my money, I'll sign off on the receipt, and he'll apologize for having taken so much of my time.

I hope, he thought.

AT FIVE MINUTES TO SIX THAT THURSDAY EVENING, CASS walked into Eyewear Fashions, Inc. on Stemmler Avenue and Twenty-second Street. The evening was clear and cold. Pinprick points of stars dotted a black sky, and the streets and sidewalks glistened with fresh snow, but Cass did not have a white Christmas on her mind. All she wanted to do was find the man who'd taken her money and her mink stole and her long sable coat, which should have been keeping her toasty warm on this frighteningly cold day. She'd been a cold puppy all her life, and the first thing she'd purchased from the money she'd earned on the Mexico job was the sable. Hell with people who went around in the nude protesting the wearing of furs. Anyone ever tried to spray paint on her furs was somebody who'd better already own a funeral plot.

Instead of the stolen sable, she was wearing the short red fox jacket over blue jeans and a green turtleneck sweater, freezing her ass off nonetheless. One of the reasons she'd left Fall River, Massachusetts, was that it had been so damn cold up there. That and her father shouting hell and damnation at her day and night. Her mother was a mathematics teacher. Cass guessed she thought it made sense to marry a Presbyterian minister and then present him with two daughters, one of whom grew up to be a holy person like Papa. The second and youngest, Cassandra Jean Ridley herself, fed up to here, ran away from home instead. Went to live on a commune in New Hampshire, which was even colder than it was here on this street corner in Isola. Left there when the group's youth advisor came into her room naked one midnight clear, determined to read to her out loud a short story from *Hustler* magazine. Cass clobbered him with a frying pan.

"Hi," she said to the man behind the counter, "my name is Harriet Daniels," which was the name of the woman who'd run the rooming house she'd lived in down in Eagle Branch, Texas. "I found an eyeglass case with your store name on it, and I was wondering if you could help me locate the owner of the glasses."

"Well, gee, I don't know," the man said.

"You are?" she asked.

"Wesley Hand," he said.

He was perhaps twenty-eight or twenty-nine, a round little man with moist blue eyes and a pleasant looking face except for the complexion. He looked sincerely concerned about the eyeglass case she now put on the counter top. He also looked bewildered. She guessed that was his natural expression.

"Is there some way you could do that for me?" she asked. "Help me locate the owner?"

"That might be difficult," he said. "Except for some very special prescriptions, most eyeglasses . . ."

"Isn't there some machine or something you can put them on?" she asked. "To see what the prescription is?"

"Well, sure, but . . ."

"Because maybe it's one of the *special* ones, you see."

"Well . . ."

"I would appreciate it," she said, and flashed what she hoped was a warm and convincing smile.

"I close at six," he said, and glanced up at the clock.

"Well, how long would it take . . . ?"

"And I have to be someplace."

"The thing is, I found them earlier today," she said. "So chances are he'll be missing them by now."

"Uh-huh."

"So could you put these on your machine and see if . . . ?"

"Not now," he said. He was already moving around the counter toward a small closet on the side of the shop. "Call me tomorrow morning," he said.

"Thank you," she said. He was putting on his coat. "I

appreciate it," she said, and smiled sweetly.

You prick, she thought.

**HORNE CAME BACK TO SEE WILL AT TEN-THIRTY THAT** night. He came unannounced, and when he pressed the buzzer downstairs to say he was there, Will was enormously surprised. He'd never expected to see those hundred-dollar bills again. Tonight, Horne was wearing a blue car coat with a faux fur collar, wide wale, dark brown corduroy trousers, and a brown fedora. By comparison to this afternoon, he looked positively dapper.

"Will, I must apologize," he said.

"Why's that?" Will asked.

"These are *not* the ransom bills."

"I didn't think they were," Will said, but he was tremendously relieved nonetheless.

"We checked the serial numbers, and except for that one bill they simply didn't match. So . . . I'm sorry for whatever inconvenience the Department may have caused you . . ."

"What department is that, by the way?"

"Why, the Treasury Department," Horne said, looking surprised. "The U.S. Secret Service is part of the Treasury Department."

"I didn't know that," Will said.

"Not many people do," Horne said. "So if you'll just let me have that receipt I gave you earlier today . . ."

"Okay," Will said, and fished in his wallet for it.

Horne carried the receipt to the kitchen table, sat, removed from his briefcase a sheaf of hundred-dollar bills, and handed them to Will.

"If you'll just count these," he said.

"I'm sure I can trust the Treasury Department," Will said.

"Even so," Horne said, "I'd feel safer if you counted them."

Will sat across from him at the kitchen table, and began counting the bills. Horne took out his pen and drew a straight line under the list of serial numbers on the receipt. Just below the line, he wrote the words ***Receipt of $8,000 acknowledged in full.*** It took maybe a minute and a half for Will to count all eighty bills. They were all there.

"If you'll just sign this," Horne said, and handed him the pen, and passed the receipt across the table to him. Will signed his name to it. Horne folded the receipt and put it into his briefcase.

"Mr. Struthers," he said, and extended his hand. "Please keep your nose clean."

"You, too, David," Will said, and opened the door for him. Horne stepped out into the hallway. Will closed and locked the door behind him. He listened at the wood until he could no longer hear Horne's footfalls in the hallway or on the steps. Then he whirled away from the door, grinning, and slapped his hand on his thigh and shouted, "Will Struthers, you are one lucky son of a bitch!"

**CASS'S PHONE RANG AT PRECISELY TWO MINUTES PAST** ten on Friday morning. Today was the first full day of Hanukkah, the twenty-second of December, three days before Christmas. The man calling was Wesley Hand.

"The optician?" he said.

"Yes, Mr. Hand?"

"I checked the glasses . . ."

"And?" she said at once.

"As I told you, most prescriptions fall into routine categories," he said, "what we call plus-one biopters, absolutely commonplace. That was the case here. But I remembered the frames. He insisted on the mocha brown frames, even though I said they wouldn't go well with his coloring."

"What *was* his coloring?" Cass asked.

"Dirty blond hair, blue eyes, the mocha brown frames were all wrong. He'd have done much better with the midnight blue."

"But he insisted on the brown."

"Yes."

"Which is how you remembered him."

"Yes."

"What was his name?" she asked at once.

"I have it right here," he said. "It's Wilbur Struthers."

"Do you have an address for him?"

"I do," Wesley said. "Are you sure it's okay for me to give this to you?"

"Oh, yes, I'm positive. May I have it, please?"

"Well . . ."

"Please?" she said.

"Well," he said again, and read off the address like a prisoner of war revealing under torture the location of an infantry division.

"I can't thank you enough," Cass said.

"YES?" A MAN'S VOICE SAID.

"Delivery," she said.

"What kind of delivery?"

"Pair of eyeglasses," she said.

"What?"

"I'm from Eyewear Fashions. Somebody found your glasses,

brought them in this morning. Did you want me to bring them up?"

"Thank you, yes, come on up. Hey, terrific. It's 2C, on the second floor."

The buzzer sounded. Cass opened the entry door at once and felt in her tote bag for the reassuring grip of the Browning automatic. No elevator, of course. She climbed the steps to the second floor and yanked the gun out of the bag as she came down the corridor. She used the muzzle to tap gently on the door to 2C.

When Will opened the door, he saw the redheaded woman whose apartment he'd ripped off. Moreover, she was holding in her fist what appeared to be a .45 automatic. He tried to slam the door shut on her, but she hit it with her shoulder at once, shoving it in against him, almost knocking him off his feet, he hadn't realized she was that strong. She was in the apartment in a wink, slamming the door behind her, and whirling on him with the automatic pointed at his head.

"Where's my money?" she asked.

"Don't get excited," he said.

"My money," she said. "My furs," she said. "You're a thief," she said. She kept using the gun for punctuation, which made Will believe she was somewhat unstable and therefore capable of hysterically pulling the trigger.

"Don't get excited," he said again. "Everything's here, all of it's here, no need to go waving the gun around like that."

She was maybe five-eight, five-nine, taller than she'd looked from the rooftop across the way, a tall good-looking redhead wearing a red fox jacket open over blue jeans and a bulky green turtleneck sweater that made her look like Christmas although it was still three days away.

"Get it," she said.

"Would you mind putting up the gun?" he said. "Makes me nervous, you standing there with a gun in your hand."

"Get my stuff," she said.

"Right away," he said.

"You fucking *crook,"* she said.

He wanted to tell her that a Khmer Rouge soldier had once pistol-whipped him with a weapon just like the one in her hand, but instead he went to the closet and took from it the long sable coat and the mink stole, and carried them to where she was standing alongside the sofa, the gun still in her hand, and dumped them onto the cushions, and then went back to the closet to take down from the shelf the shoe box containing what he'd last counted out for Horne as $8,000 dollars in hundred-dollar bills. He was hoping she knew how to handle that big gun in her fist because he sure didn't want to get hurt here.

"Take off the lid," she said, and waved the gun again.

"It's all here, I just counted it last night."

"That what you do in your spare time, you crook? Count other people's money?"

"I'll be happy to count it for you now," he said, taking the rubber-banded white envelope from the box. "Or you might want to put down the gun and do it yourself."

"You count it," she said.

He removed the rubber band, took the bills from the envelope, began counting the money for the second time in as many days, a hundred, two hundred, five hundred, six hundred, seven hundred, eight hundred, nine hundred, a thous . . .

"Stop!" she said.

"What?" he said.

"Hold it right there!"

"Why? What . . . ?"

"That isn't my money," she said.

"What do you . . . ?"

"That is *not* my money! What are you trying to pull here?"

"Ma'am, I can assure you . . ."

"That is *not* my money! My money had funny marks on it. And it smelled sweet."

"Lady, *all* money smells sweet."

"Where are the marks?"

"What marks?"

"The writing, the funny writing!" She picked up a handful of bills, spread them open like a fan. "Do you see any writing on these bills? These bills are clean! Smell them! Do you smell anything sweet?"

"No, ma'am, but . . ."

"What did you do with my money?"

"This *is* your money."

"It is *not* my money! What'd you do with my money?"

"Lady, I'm telling you for the last time, this *is* your money. In *your* envelope. They even gave me a receipt with the serial numbers on it. I had to sign it to . . ."

"What do you mean? Who?"

"To get the money back. I had to sign the receipt."

"Get it *back?* Where *was* it?"

"At the Department."

"What department? What are you *talking* about?"

"The Treasury Department. A Secret Service agent took the money to check the serial numbers."

Oh Jesus, she thought. Those Mexicans tipped me with hot money. Slowly, trying not to lose control, reminding herself that she had been in worse situations than this—she had once flown a Chinook helicopter over a desert blooming with black shrapnel, she had flown through horrific firestorms from below and had not lost it, she was not going to lose it now—slowly, carefully, she asked, "Why did they want to check the serial numbers?"

"Don't worry, they didn't match," he said.

"But why did they want to check them?"

"They thought they were ransom bills."

Calm, she thought. Stay calm. Just hear him out. Just try to get to the bottom of this.

"What ransom?" she asked calmly.

"There was a kidnapping," he said. "The ransom was paid in hundred-dollar bills. They thought these might be the bills."

"What made them think that?" she asked evenly, calmly.

"Because the serial numbers on a bill I cashed . . ."

"You cashed *my* money?"

"Just that one bill. I didn't spend any more than that. And the serial numbers on it *did* match."

Don't shoot him, she thought. Just remain extremely calm.

"Did match *what?*" she asked.

"Did match the numbers on one of the ransom bills."

"A bill the Secret Service was looking for."

"Yes."

"Why the Secret Service?"

"I don't know."

"And you say they took the *rest* of the money . . ."

"Yes. To check the serial numbers. Which did *not* match. So they brought all of it back."

"Brought back *this* money here on the table."

"Yes. Your money. In your very envelope. Right there on the table."

She stood there nodding, looking down at the money, trying to make some sense of everything he'd told her. Then she said, "This is not my money."

Will wished she would stop repeating the same words over and over again when her goddamn money was sitting right there on the kitchen table, in plain view for the entire world to see. Why wouldn't she just let him *count* it, for Christ's sake, and then get out of here with her goddamn furs and her gun?

"Ma'am," he said, "I am telling you for the last time that this is your money that the Treasury Department returned to me. I gave them a signed receipt with all the serial numbers on it, stating that the money was all here because I counted it last night and there was indeed eight thousand dollars here. Now if you'll let me count it for you now, ma'am, I'm sure it will come to eight thousand dollars all over again because nobody has touched a cent of it since Mr. David A. Horne, with an 'e,' left here."

"I'll let you count it for me," she said. "But it isn't my money."

Goddamn broken record, he thought, and began counting all over again. She kept watching the bills as he passed them from one hand to the other, counting, "twenty-one, twenty-two, twenty-three . . . ," shaking her head as if trying to dope out the great mystery of what had happened here, when it was all so simple a caterpillar could grasp it, "thirty-four, thirty-five" and on and on, money, money, money, "fifty-seven, fifty-eight, fifty-nine, sixty," if he had to count these damn bills one more time, "seventy-one, seventy-two . . ." and at last he counted the eightieth and last bill, and looked up at her and said, "Satisfied?"

She did not answer him. She rubber-banded the bills again, and dropped the wad into her tote, leaving the white envelope on the table. Then she took off the red fox, put on the sable, draped the fox and the mink over her arm . . .

"Would you like something to carry those in?" he asked.

She looked at him.

"Little bulky that way," he said. "Let me see if I've got anything."

Not trusting him for a minute, she followed him into a bedroom with an unmade bed and what looked like a week's laundry strewn all over the floor. He opened a closet door, rummaged around inside there, and came up with a duffel that looked like the one she'd carried in the Army, except her name and rank weren't stenciled in black on the side.

"Thanks," she said, and folded her furs into the bag, first the fox jacket and then the mink stole. Pulling the drawstrings tight through the grommets, she wondered if she should offer to pay for the duffel, and then asked herself if she was losing her mind, the man here was a thief who'd caused her a great deal of unnecessary trouble. She slung the duffel over her shoulder, backed toward the front door with the gun still in her hand, and without saying another word, walked out.

Will still considered himself lucky.

She'd forgotten to ask for the four hundred dollars and change he still had left over from the five he'd borrowed yesterday.

SHE STOPPED AT A BANK OSTENSIBLY TO CHANGE THREE of the hundreds into twenties, tens, and fives, but actually to test the bills. She was still wondering why a Secret Service agent had exchanged her own world-weary hundreds for these obviously used but relatively fresh ones, and she was relieved when the teller held them up to the light to check the security strip, and then changed them without raising either an eyebrow or a fuss. It was close to three when she came out of the bank but yesterday had been the shortest day of the year, and with the heavy clouds overhead, the afternoon seemed already succumbing to dusk. The day was still piercingly cold. She was grateful for the sable, luxuriating in its long silken swirl, feeling like a Russian empress all at once, $8,000 in cash in her handbag, the city all aglitter for Christmas, what more could a person wish for?

How about caviar and champagne? she thought.

**THE TWO MEN WERE SITTING IN THEIR OVERCOATS, ONE** on either side of the Christmas tree in her living room. They popped out of the dusky gloom the moment she turned on the lights. The larger of the two men had a gun in his hand and it was pointing up at Cass's head.

*"Buenas noches,"* he said and smiled. "We are here for dee money."

She thought at once that it was really shitty of Wilbur Struthers to recruit two Latino goons to reclaim the money he'd stolen from her in the first place, the son of a bitch. But here they were, both of them smiling now, somewhat apologetically it seemed to her, but perhaps she was mistaken. She put down the brown paper bag with the caviar she'd bought at Hildy's Market and the Dom Perignon she'd bought in the liquor store on Twenty-sixth Street.

"What money?" she said.

"One million seven hun'red t'ousan dollars," the one on the other side of the tree said.

"I think you're in the wrong apartment," she said.

"I don't theenk so," the first one said.

Very heavy Spanish accents on both of them, something suddenly clicked. The men on the narrow dirt strip in Guenerando, Mexico, except that earlier this month they'd been wearing baggy white cotton pants and wrinkled shirts.

"I don't know what money you're talking about," she said.

"Dee money we paid you for a hun'red kilos of pure cocaine," the one with the gun said.

"I don't want to know anything about that cargo," she said.

"You delivered the money, we gave you dee fockin cocaine . . ."

"I didn't know what the cargo was. I don't know anything about the money, either. All I did was hand it over."

"We know that."

"We know you were only dee messenger."

"We want to know who *gave* you dee money."

"I don't know his name. Look, if the money was short, I'm sorry. You should have counted it more carefully. Anyway . . ."

"We did coun' it carefully."

"It took us a fockin *hour* to coun' it."

"We counted it *very* carefully."

"Dee money *wassen* short," the one with the gun said. "Who gave it to you?"

"I told you, I don't . . ."

"His name, *por favor.*"

The gun was in her face now.

"He called himself Frank. But I'm sure that wasn't his real name."

"Frank what?"

"All he gave me was Frank."

"Where wass this?"

"I was living in Eagle Branch at the time. He was introduced to me by someone I know."

"And *his* name? The one who introduce you?"

"I don't want to get anyone in trouble. If the money was short . . ."

"Dee money *wassen* short."

The gun in her face again.

"Then why . . . ?"

"We delivered quality cocaine. We expected . . ."

"I don't want to know about it."

"Where *wass* this in Eagle Branch?"

"A bar."

"Tell us his name. The one who introduce you."

She suddenly wondered how much Randy Biggs had got for introducing her to the man who'd paid her $200,000 for making four trips to Mexico, to transport—at least on the last trip, anyway—what now turned out to be cocaine.

"Wha' wass his name?" the one with the gun said again.

"I told you . . ."

"We don' want to kill you," the other one said.

"Then tell him to put the gun away."

*"Su nombre,"* the one with the gun said.

She knew with absolute certainty that he would kill her in the next instant if she did not give up Randolph Biggs. She wondered what she owed Randy, wondered what she owed the one who'd called himself Frank and who seemed to have offended these men in some unspeakable way. She decided this was not the Persian Gulf. She was not sworn to tell them only her name, rank, and serial number.

"His name was Randolph Biggs," she said.

# 2.

**DETECTIVE STEVE CARELLA WISHED THAT ONE OF THE** lions hadn't dragged the victim's left leg into the 88th Precinct. That was what brought Fat Ollie Weeks into the case. As it was, most of the vic's body was being consumed by three lionesses, a young lion, and a big thickly maned patriarch, apparent leader of the pride, none of whom seemed at all disturbed by a fascinated audience of detectives, zoo personnel, and television reporters gathered outside the Lion Habitat at the Grover Park Zoo.

Half of the zoo was in the 87th Precinct.

The other half was in the 88th.

By Carella's rough estimate, four-fifths of the vic's body was in the Eight-Seven. The remaining fifth, the vic's leg, was over there in the Eight-Eight, where Fat Ollie—watching a young lion claw and gnaw at the leg—was beginning to get hungry himself.

This was Saturday morning, the twenty-third day of December, the true start of the big Christmas weekend that only yesterday had included the first full day of Hanukkah, now history. Carella and Meyer had caught the squeal some twenty minutes ago, at a quarter past seven, when the man in charge of the zoo's Animal Commissary called the police to report that a woman had wandered into the habitat and was at that very moment being attacked by a pride of lions who hadn't yet been fed this morning.

At seven-thirty-seven A.M., there was a heavy layer of snow on the paths that wound past the barred fence, and the moat beyond that, and then the island habitat where the lions and lionesses feasted. The television reporters were having a field day. Never before had a photo op like this one presented itself, a pride of lions tearing apart a woman wearing nothing at all on one of the coldest days of the year, the animals greedily feasting on the woman's flesh and bones. Some fifty feet away, in the 88th Precinct, a solitary lion contentedly gnawed on the victim's leg.

Detective Oliver Wendell Weeks had caught the squeal some ten minutes after Carella and Meyer had, which was when the young lion had dragged the leg over into the Eight-Eight. None of the detectives were particularly happy to have caught a case like this one—or *any* case for that matter—a half-hour or so before their shifts ended, especially on a holiday weekend, when they had shopping to do and trees to put up and gifts to wrap.

On a morning when the temperature hovered at just above freezing, Ollie was wearing only a sports jacket over dark slacks, a white shirt, a food-stained tie, white socks, black shoes, and a red woolen watch cap. He had eaten breakfast an hour ago, but all the activity out there on the island was making him wonder if the zoo's coffee shop was open yet. By contrast, Carella and Meyer were both wearing heavy overcoats, gloves, and mufflers. They were each and separately wishing Fat Ollie hadn't been dragged into the case by the victim's leg. They were each and separately wondering how they were going to get the victim off the island before there was nothing left of her but chewed-over bones.

The Emergency Services truck had arrived not five

minutes ago, and the captain in charge of the ES Squad was talking to the zoo's Assistant Director, a man named William Boyd, who had been notified at home by the Commissary Superintendent who'd told him that one of their people had just finished feeding the great apes and was approaching the Lion Habitat to deliver two hundred pounds of horse meat enriched with vitamins and minerals when he spotted a woman being attacked on the island there. Boyd was now advising the ES Captain that he should take his truck and his team and go home.

"Our own personnel are quite capable of getting onto the island and recovering whatever's left of the dead woman," he said.

The ES Captain told him it might be very risky for a "civilian" to go over there to retrieve the body while the lions were in a "feeding frenzy," as he put it, though in all truth the animals seemed to be taking their morning meal in a leisurely manner. The ES Captain's team tended to agree with him. The team had rescued people trapped in elevators, had scissored open automobiles with people squashed inside them, had plucked charred bodies from sizzling electrical cables, had even picked the locks on cell doors when hookers plugged them with bubble gum to avoid court appearances. This, however, was the first time they'd ever seen a woman being chewed to ribbons by half a dozen lions. Which did not stop them from becoming instant experts.

One of the guys on the team suggested that maybe they should go for the leg first, as a sort of training exercise. Throw the young lion over there in the Eight-Eight something *else* to eat, lure him away from the leg, lay a ladder across the moat, snatch the leg away from him while he was thus distracted. The ES Captain was of the opinion that human flesh was something of a treat for these animals and it might not be easy to tempt them away from it with ordinary fare. Ollie was getting hungrier and hungrier. Carella and Meyer were watching the pride at work. Over on the island, the ground around the kill was disturbed, the snow trampled and spattered with blood.

Ollie wandered over to where the ES Captain and his team were discussing their next move. The Captain's name was Ernie Levine. This being the Hanukkah weekend and all, Ollie figured it wouldn't hurt to remind Levine that he was a Jew.

"Hey, Ernie," he said, "what're you doing on the job, your holiday and all?"

Levine knew Ollie from previous jobs. He greeted him with something less than enthusiasm.

"Hello, Ollie," he said briefly.

"You put up your Hanukkah bush yet?" Ollie asked.

"We don't have anything like that in our house," Levine said.

"You light all ten of your candles?"

"Nine," Levine corrected.

"You think that lady out there is kosher?" Ollie asked. "Cause I hear lions don't eat pork."

"Eat *this* a while," Levine said, and briefly grasped his crotch, and then walked over to where the zoo's General Director had just arrived in a dither. The director's name was Alfred Hardy. He was in his late thirties, Carella guessed, a tall slender man you'd figure for a lawyer or an accountant rather than somebody running a small city. Which was what the Grover Park Zoo was, in effect: a small city within a much larger city. Hardy took one look at the situation and told Levine he wanted everyone out of here while his people performed what to him was a simple rescue operation. Levine explained that there was nobody to rescue anymore. The victim was already dead and in fact being consumed at this very moment. Hardy said there were five healthy *lions* to rescue. Levine said he would have to clear that with his Deputy-Inspector.

"Fine," Hardy said heatedly, "you go do that. Meanwhile, I'll be getting my lions off that island." He turned to Boyd. "Make sure nobody tries to go out there. I'll be in the holding area," he said, and marched off in a huff. Carella figured that anyone who arrived in a dither and went off in a huff couldn't be all bad. Levine went back to the truck to call his superior. Ollie shrugged and turned to where Carella and Meyer were still watching the lions. A pretty blonde from Channel Four News sidled up to Carella and said, "Fascinating, isn't it?"

"Thrilling," Ollie said.

The blonde turned to him as if surprised to learn that a hippopotamus could speak.

"Want to go for some breakfast?" Ollie asked.

"Thanks, I've already eaten," she said.

"I didn't mean you, Miss," he said, and grinned. "I was talking to my colleagues here. These superior sleuths from the Eighty-seventh Precinct."

"Better wait till the ME gets here, don't you think?" Carella said.

"But now that you mention it, I'm Detective/First Grade Oliver Wendell Weeks," Ollie said, turning back to the blonde. "Want to interview me?"

"What for?"

"The leg over there is in my jurisdiction."

"Then why don't you go take it away from that lion?"

"I might in a little while."

"Good. You go get the leg, and then I'll interview you."

"I also play piano," he said.

"A shame we don't have a piano here in the park," the blonde said, and turned back to Carella. "How do you suppose the woman got out there?" she asked.

"I've been taking lessons for almost two weeks now," Ollie said. "Right now, I'm working on 'Night and Day.' "

Boyd had been told to make sure no one went out onto the island. But he had just heard the blonde's question and he wanted to get a little closer to someone who looked so leggy and all in a short skirt and high-heeled boots and a brown leather jacket. So he came over to explain that the way personnel got onto the island was through a tunnel under the moat . . .

"The lions are brought inside every night," he explained. "To cages in the holding area."

"That's very interesting," the blonde said.

"I'm gonna learn five songs," Ollie said.

"That's very interesting, too," the blonde said, and turned back to where Carella and Meyer were still watching the lions. It was a frighteningly cold morning, but neither of the men was wearing a hat. Carella's hair was brown, dancing on his head now in a brisk wind. Meyer was totally bald; his barren pate made him look colder than he actually was. The two detectives stood like bookends flanking Fat Ollie, whose little red watch cap was tilted at a rakish angle. Actually, Ollie thought he cut a fine figure of sartorial elegance.

"My name is Honey Blair," the blonde told Carella, "I rove for the Five o'Clock News."

"Hello, Honey," Ollie said. "I rove for the Eighty-eighth Squad."

Honey was thinking the two big detectives made a nice picture standing there watching the voracious lions. They were both tall and wide-shouldered, the bald guy looking solid and serious, the other one looking sexy as hell in a way she couldn't quite understand, he wasn't that good-looking. Something about the way his eyes slanted downward maybe, giving him a sort of Chinese appearance, though he certainly wasn't Oriental. Something about the *look* in the eyes, maybe. Dark and brooding. As if it pained him to see the woman out there being torn to shreds.

"You new in the job?" she asked him.

"New? Me?" he said, and smiled, and shook his head.

The smile got to her, too.

"Want me to take your picture?" she asked.

"Sure," Ollie said.

"You and your partner," Honey said. "Looking over at the lions."

"I don't think so, thanks," Carella said.

"Why not?"

"Wouldn't be professional," he said.

"Make a nice shot, though," Honey said, and beamed a dazzling smile at him.

Meyer raised his eyebrows.

"Thanks, no," Carella said again.

"Think it over," she said, and turned away and walked back toward her camera crew, flirty little skirt fluttering about her elegant long legs. Ollie watched her go. So did Meyer. Carella walked over to where Levine was still on the phone with the DI.

"We're going to have to get on that island soon," Levine

was saying. "Before the Five o'Clock News tells everybody we let wild animals eat 'em for Christmas." He listened, and then said, "You think so?" He listened again. "I'm not sure the CEO here is gonna buy that." He listened, nodded, said, "Okay, Boss, whatever you say," and put the phone back on its bracket in the truck's cab. He turned to Carella and said, "Quote: 'If a dangerous animal is threatening human life, destroy it.' Period. Unquote."

"So what does he want?"

"A team of sharpshooters."

"Mr. Hardy won't like that."

"Just what I told the DI."

"Let me go talk to him. You call SWAT, tell them we need enough sharpshooters to take care of five healthy lions."

Meyer walked over to the truck.

"What are we doing?" he asked.

"Shooting the lions," Carella said.

"I'LL HAVE THEM OFF THAT ISLAND BEFORE YOUR sharpshooters get here," Hardy said. "What's the sense in killing them? The woman is already dead. Besides, it isn't as if they escaped confinement and went *looking* for prey. The woman found her own way onto the island somehow. These are wild animals. Carnivores. It was in their *nature* to attack her and devour her."

"Sir, I'm merely telling you what we plan to do," Carella said. He looked at his watch. "A SWAT team should be here in ten, twelve minutes. They'll dispose of the animals at that time."

"Meanwhile, I'll have them off the island. You have your plan, I have mine."

"What's *your* plan, Mr. Hardy?"

"I'll have my vets anesthetize the animals and carry them back here to the holding cages."

"Back here" was a bunker-like building connected to the island by a ramp and a tunnel that ran under the moat. By now, a considerable number of zoo people had gathered here in the holding area. In addition to zookeepers of various grade levels, there were people from the Curation Department, and two animal behaviorists, and the three veterinarians who would be handling the anesthetizing of the animals out there.

The way Hardy explained it to Carella and Meyer—and to Ollie, who had now joined them—the forthcoming operation was really a simple one. The vets would use either dart guns or blowpipes to administer the anesthetic. The holding cages inside the bunker were flanked by keeper walkways. Guillotine doors opened from squeeze cages on the walkways into the larger holding cages. A five foot high concrete wall formed the back of each cage. The front of each cage was constructed of steel wire mesh. The keeper work area ran down the center of the building. There were access doors to the cages on either side of the work area. The anesthetized animals would be carried from the island to the ramp to the walkways and into the holding cages.

Considering that Carella had told Hardy the shooters would be here in ten to twelve minutes, he took his time debating with his staff the procedures they would use in safely anesthetizing and transporting the lions from the island to the holding area. Should they use an explosive projectile dart or a blowdart? Should they use a dissociative anesthetic, a tranquilizer, a non-narcotic sedative, or a narcotic drug?

"Even smaller cats than the ones out there are dangerous to handle without anesthesia," Hardy explained. "The young lion who carried off that woman's leg must weigh at least four hundred pounds. I'd say he measures ten feet long including his tail and stands at least three feet at the shoulders. You try to put a net on a wild animal that size, you're asking for trouble."

The drug they debated using was ketamine hydrochloride, a dissociative anesthetic most commonly delivered intramuscularly in doses of 100 to 200 mg/ml. For a dose sufficient enough to provide a rapid effect, a larger dart and more powerful delivery force was required. One of the keepers argued that this heightened the possibility of injury to the animal. Another argued that ketamine HCl was a painful injection. One of the vets argued that the drug induced a tendency for the animal to convulse. With three minutes to spare, they agreed to use the drug, after all, and decided that instead of using a blowdart, which had a higher probability of successful injection, they would use an explosive projectile dart, which had a traumatic impact but which was necessary because the drug was ketamine HCl.

At seven minutes to nine, just as Carella thought he heard the approaching siren of the van bearing the SWAT team, Hardy's own team went through the steel guillotine doors, out onto the run, down the ramp, and into the tunnel that led to a second pair of guillotine doors that opened discreetly onto the jungle-like environment where the young lion was gnawing on the woman's severed leg. If the lion heard the guillotine doors opening, he gave no sign of it. He was still busy with the bone—which was what the woman's leg had now become—when the first of the darts hit him in the forehead. The vets were going for the frontal or dissociative cortex of the brain. But as often happened with explosive projectile darts, the impact was insufficient to detonate the charge. Freddie, which was the lion's name, lifted his head from the bone, spotted the three vets crouched behind one of the habitat bushes—

"Easy now, Freddie," one of vets whispered.

—crouched for just an instant, and then charged them.

They ran for the guillotine doors, the lion behind them, ran into the tunnel under the moat, and up the ramp, into the run behind the holding cages, startling Hardy, who realized too late that a lion was loose. He stabbed at the button that began closing the guillotine doors behind the three vets—but the lion was inside as well. The doors clanged shut. Everyone was suddenly in a long narrow holding cage with a lion who'd just had his first taste of human flesh.

The access door to the work area was at the far end of the cage. Between that door and the lion were four zookeepers, three veterinarians, two animal behaviorists, two curators, an assistant director, a director, three detectives, and a partridge in a pear tree.

One of the detectives was Steve Carella.

The lion went directly for him.

Maybe it was his smile.

But Carella wasn't smiling. In fact, he was terrified, his eyes bulging, his mouth falling wide open as the lion leaped into the air at him. He brought his hands up defensively. Four hundred and some odd pounds of animal force knocked him flat on his back to the concrete floor of the cage. Pinned by enormous paws, Carella looked up at a head the size of a beach ball, all tawny fur and yellow eyes and open jaws and teeth. The lion's roar resounded through every nerve in Carella's body. He twisted his head away just as the animal lunged for his face.

A shot rang out.

It took the lion clean between the eyes.

He collapsed onto Carella like a huge smelly rug in somebody's den.

Fat Ollie Weeks waddled over, grinning, a nine-millimeter Glock in his hand.

He flipped back his jacket, holstered the gun, and said, "You owe me one, Steve-a-rino."

**OVER ALFRED HARDY'S VIOLENT OBJECTIONS, THE** SWAT team disposed of the remaining four lions in short order. Honey Blair got some nice shots of the sharpshooters doing their job, aiming down their rifle barrels and all, the lions happily munching away on the lady out there, whoever she was, unaware that in minutes they would be merely trophies. Hardy refused to let Honey take any pictures of the carcasses on the island, animal or human, and ordered her off the premises. She went over to where a pair of paramedics were searching Carella for any cuts or bruises caused by what they insisted was a "mauling."

"I was *not* mauled," Carella told them over and over again. "I was almost *eaten,* but I was not mauled."

"Sounds like a good idea either way," Honey said, and smiled. "Here's my card. You ever feel like discussing police work or television reportage, give me a ring. Or even just a cappuccino, mm?" she said, and smiled again. *"Ciao, bambino."*

Carella watched her walking off.

He looked at the card.

And tossed it into the trash bin near the railing where he sat.

The paramedics thought the lion mauling him had damaged his brain.

THE THING THAT BOTHERED CARELLA MOST ABOUT THE dead woman—or what was left of her, which wasn't very much—was that she was naked.

"Woman wandering around the zoo without any clothes on, dead of winter," Carella said.

"Which does seem peculiar," Meyer agreed.

"Almost makes it seem as if she didn't *want* to be identified."

He was thinking that this was the worst time of the year for suicides. Girl loses her man, her job, her mind, her gold watch—she wasn't wearing a watch, he noticed, unless one of the lions ate it—she decides to end it all. Ashamed of the act she's about to commit, she strips herself naked, goes for a bare-assed walk in the zoo, straight into the lion's den.

Another thing that bothered him was the fact that Ollie Weeks had saved his life. Once upon a time, Bert Kling had saved a Puerto Rican courier from a near-fatal baseball-bat beating. The man's name was José Herrera, and he had informed Kling that in certain cultures—Asian or North American Indian, he wasn't sure which—if you saved a person's life, you were responsible for that person's life forever. The one thing Carella did not want was Fat Ollie Weeks being responsible for his life forever.

"You think somebody *threw* her to those lions?" he asked Meyer.

"Be a new one, all right," Meyer answered.

*

CARL BLANEY HATED EXAMINING BODIES THAT WERE IN parts. If he'd wanted to become a butcher, he would not have gone to medical school. This one was particularly disgusting. All chewed over and everything. Your cases involving severed parts were usually your blunt force injuries, where a person got run over by a truck or a subway train. The other times you got a bundle of disconnected arms and legs was when somebody was trying to dispose of a murder victim, and sawed the body up into pieces and packed them in a trunk. This particular corpse, he'd been told, had been attacked by lions, of all things, you'd think this city was the African veldt.

There was not much more than the bare bones remaining of the victim's left leg. All the tissue and muscle had been torn away, leaving the exposed femur, patella, tibia, and fibula, portions of which had been gnawed through as well. The right leg was in a similar state of obliteration, the bones cracked open, the marrow sucked out. The woman's right breast was completely gone, her left breast consumed to almost where it joined the chest. Her right arm was still connected to the body, but the hand had been consumed, bones and all, and from the wrist up to the elbow, the tissue and muscle were gone, exposing the ulna and radius.

The heart, the liver, the pancreas, the stomach—all the tasty parts—were gone. He was examining the woman's head and face, which had been partially consumed, the nose and ears gone, the lips gone, the eyes gone, when he noticed—

But how could that be?

He was looking at a tiny circular perforation in the skull, just above what was left of the woman's hairline.

To the naked eye, it looked a great deal like a small-caliber pistol wound.

**IT WAS TWO-THIRTY THAT SATURDAY AFTERNOON WHEN** the phone on Carella's desk rang. He picked up the receiver.

"Carella," he said.

"Blaney here."

"Hey, Carl."

"On this dead girl who got eaten by lions?" Blaney said, as if he still couldn't quite believe it. "I've lifted a good thumbprint and two fingerprints. I don't imagine you know much about her . . ."

"Not a thing so far."

"Reason I'm asking . . . I've come up with something interesting."

"What's that, Carl?"

"I found a tiny perforation in the left temporal region of the skull. At first, it looked like a bullet wound, but upon further . . ."

"Looked like a *what?"* Carella said.

"But it wasn't."

"What was it?"

"An ice-pick wound. Somebody stabbed her with an ice pick."

He waited while Carella absorbed this.

"The tract passed into the brain as deep as the left cerebral peduncle," he said. "Now, the reason this is interesting, such a wound will rarely cause instant death. Absent concussion of the brain, we've had victims surviving for as long as five days after an assault."

"I'm not sure I understand what you're saying, Carl."

"I'm saying there are cases on record of victims walking long distances from the scene of the trauma. Eventually, there'll be either subcortical or subdural hemorrhaging from the wound, with subsequent compression of the brain and resultant death. But *before* then . . ."

"Before then, she could've walked to the park, is that it?"

"Yes. Or someone could have transferred her there from wherever the trauma occurred. In either case, I'm merely stating as a positive fact that she was stabbed first. With an ice pick."

"When will I have those prints?" Carella asked.

"They're on the way now," Blaney said.

THE PRINTS REACHED CARELLA BY MESSENGER AT three-seventeen that afternoon. A half-hour later, AFIS—the automated fingerprint identification system—got back to him with a hit on a United States Army lieutenant named Cassandra Jean Ridley.

# 3.

THE TELEPHONE DIRECTORY GAVE THEM A LISTING FOR A C J Ridley on South Ealey Street in Silvermine. Carella and Ollie went there at once. They had phoned ahead and a pair of technicians from the Mobile Crime Unit were waiting for them downstairs. The building was a twelve-story red brick a block away from the oval. They introduced themselves to the doorman, and asked to speak to the superintendent, a man named Peter Dooley, who immediately took them up to apartment 9C and unlocked the door for them.

Carella and Ollie stayed out in the hall with Dooley while the techs got to work. The super was a tall, wide-shouldered man with a shock of black hair and piercing blue eyes. He was wearing wide-wale blue corduroy trousers and a navy-blue sweater vest over a red plaid shirt. He told them the woman lived here alone, took the apartment in November, was gone for a little while, came back again early in December. He figured she was worth a little something, the fur coats and all, don't y'know.

"When's the last time you saw her?" Carella asked.

"She was in and out a lot the past few days," Dooley said. "Doing her Christmas shopping, I guess. This the same case as the other one?"

Carella and Ollie looked at each other, puzzled.

"Had some detectives from the Eight-Seven here the other day," Dooley said.

"Oh? When was that?" Ollie asked.

"The other day. Thursday."

"What do you mean by the other case?" Carella asked.

"The break-in. We had a patrol car come by and then two detectives."

"No, this has nothing to do with that."

"I thought . . . well . . . Miss Ridley and all."

"What do you mean?"

"It was her apartment got broken into. She had me change the lock on the door the very next day."

"Let me get this straight," Carella said.

"There was a burglary here?" Ollie said.

"On Thursday, yes, sir. I changed the lock on this door only yesterday."

"Because the apartment was broken into?" Ollie said.

"Yep. I was outside with the doorman when your two detectives come by to investigate," Dooley said. "One of them a redhead, the other one this short little fellow with curly black hair. Doorman called upstairs, Miss Ridley told him to send them right up."

"Who were they, do you know?"

"Thought you might."

Carella was already on the cell phone.

"Anybody else here for the lady in recent days?" Ollie asked.

"Not that I noticed. I'm busy in the office most of the time."

"Bert?" Carella said. "This is Steve. Can you check with the Loot, see if Willis and Hawes responded to a burglary here on South Ealey this past Thursday?" He listened. "321," he said. "Apartment 9C. Sure." He turned to Ollie. "Kling. He's checking."

"Did you see anyone coming out of the building with Miss Ridley late last night, early this morning?" Ollie asked the super.

"I go home at six," Dooley said. "You're lucky you caught me."

"Which doorman was on last night, would you know?"

"Same one as now."

"Can you send him up, please?"

"Sure," Dooley said, and walked off toward the elevator.

"Yeah," Carella said into the phone. "Just what I thought. Are either of them there now? Put him on, willya?" He turned to Ollie. "Willis and Hawes were here around four Thursday," he said. "He's getting Willis now."

They waited.

The apartment seemed suddenly very still.

"Hal, hi, it's Steve," he said. "Bert tells me you investigated a burg here at 321 South Ealey this past Thursday. Can you tell me a little about it?" He listened. "No, this is a homicide. Right. The lady got stabbed with an ice pick and thrown into the lion exhibit at the zoo. No, I'm dead serious. Can you give me the back story?" He listened. "A sable worth forty-five grand, right. And a mink stole worth six. Initials in both of them, CJR. Is that it? Okay, good, thanks a lot." He hit the END button, flipped the lid shut, turned to Ollie. "You heard?" he said.

"I heard."

Dooley was back with a man wearing a blue uniform with gold trim, blue hat with a shiny black peak. He looked Hispanic to Ollie, but Dooley introduced him as Muhammad Hassid, which meant he had just arrived from the Sahara and was plotting to blow up the nearest municipal building. Ollie asked him if he'd seen Miss Ridley leaving the building with anyone anytime last night.

"No, sir, I have seen no one," Hassid said.

"What time did you leave here?" Ollie asked.

"I was relieved at eleven-forty-five," Hassid said.

"Who came on after you?"

"Manuel Escovar."

"We'll want his address and phone number," Carella told Dooley.

"I have them in the office," Dooley said. "Will you be needin either of us any further?"

"Not right now," Ollie said. "We'll stop by on our way out."

"Good luck to you, lads," Dooley said.

"Thank you, sirs," Hassid said.

IT TOOK A GOOD HOUR AND A HALF FOR THE TECHS TO vacuum the place for fibers and hair and to dust for fingerprints. The lights were on when Carella and Ollie finally went in to join them.

"Got some nice latents," one of the techs said. "How urgent is this?"

"It's a fuckin homicide," Ollie said. "What do you mean, how urgent is it?"

"Cause what I can do . . ."

"The fuckin lady got chewed to bits by lions!" Ollie said.

"I can run the prints for you, was what I was gonna suggest, save a little time," the tech said, unruffled. "Call you if I get a make."

"That'd be a help," Carella said.

"My name's Murphy, here's my card," he said. "Probably be late tonight, early tomorrow morning."

"Gee, that's a *big* fuckin help," Ollie said.

Murphy looked at him.

"Talk to you later," he said to Carella and walked out shaking his head.

The apartment was a one-bedroom with a good-sized living room and a utility kitchen. They started in the bedroom, which was where they hoped to learn the most about the woman.

Three furs were hanging in the closet there: an ankle-length sable, a mink stole, and a red fox jacket. The initials in each of the furs were CJR.

Ollie turned to Carella.

"Didn't you say . . . ?"

"That's what Willis told me."

"So what are they doing here?"

"Maybe she had two of each."

"Maybe my aunt has balls," Ollie said.

There were also two woolen cloth coats in the closet, and a fleece-lined brown-leather flight jacket. The jacket had a silver bar on each shoulder and a diamond-shaped leather name patch over the left breast: Lt. C. J. Ridley. Hanging lengthwise on trouser hangers were two pairs of blue jeans and three pairs of tailored slacks. Hanging in the rest of the closet were dresses, skirts, and several bulky sweaters.

The clothes in her dresser drawer were laid out like soldiers lined up for inspection, rolled nylons and pantyhose in one drawer, tank tops and cotton panties in another, T-shirts and sweaters in the bottom drawer, all precisely stored away.

In the top drawer of the night table on the left-hand side of the bed, they found a candy tin with a floral design on its lid. They opened the tin. Inside the box was a stack of photographs, several airmail letters, and a small black ring box that contained a slender gold wedding band. The letters were from a Captain Mark William Ridley—the return address indicated he was stationed with the U.S. Air Force in Germany—to a woman named Cassandra Jean Ridley in Eagle Branch, Texas.

"Probably her husband," Ollie said. "Got killed over there in Germany for some reason or other, and the letter's from a chaplain or somebody, telling her he was dead and returning the wedding band."

"Very romantic," Carella said.

"Let's read 'em."

"Also there's no war going on in Germany right this minute."

"Be the only place there isn't," Ollie said.

They opened one of the letters.

It was dated November 13 of this year, and it was from the dead woman's brother. He was telling her he'd just received a Dear John letter from his wife back in Montana, and he was sending their wedding band to Cassandra Jean to dispose of because he couldn't bear doing that himself, nor could he bear even looking at it ever again.

"That's romantic, too," Ollie said.

The letter went on to say that the job his sister had lined up for the early part of December sounded good to him, "so long as you won't be flying anything that might get you in trouble."

"Might've got her in a whole *lot* of trouble," Carella said. "Let's take these, read 'em all later."

Sitting on the living room desk was an appointment calendar for the current year. They immediately flipped to the week of December 3. Someone—presumably Cassandra Jean Ridley—had scrawled the word *Mexico* into the box for Sunday the third. An inked arrow ran over the boxes for the next four days, its point leading to the box for December 7, Pearl Harbor Day, where the words *End Mexico* were written in the same hand. The single word *East* was written in the box for December 8.

In the top drawer on the right hand side of the kneehole, they found a checkbook from Chase, another for Midlands, and a savings account passbook from a bank called First Peoples. For yet another bank called Banque Française, they found a safe deposit box key in a little red packet with a snap catch.

A pile of rubber-banded hundred-dollar bills was resting on edge, at the right hand side of the drawer.

There were eighty of them.

$8,000 in cash.

They wished they could take a peek at her Banque Française safe deposit box, but this was the Saturday before Christmas Day, and the bank had closed at noon. Even a court order would not get it to open again before Tuesday morning, the twenty-sixth.

They went to see Manuel Escovar instead.

THE STREETS OF LITTLE SANTO DOMINGO WERE ABLAZE with light when they got there at eight that night. Stringed white lights hung from sidewalk to sidewalk, and dancing red and green lights flashed in every window overlooking the street. Spotlighted banners wished FELIZ NAVIDAD to the world. All up and down the street, pushcarts lighted with flashlights displayed last-minute gifts ranging from Louis Vuitton handbags to Hermès scarves and Rolex watches. Christmastime was the biggest thriller of the year, and the countdown had begun in earnest.

"All of this shit fell off the back of a truck," Ollie commented.

They found Escovar in a little bar off Swift Street, where he was enjoying a few beers with his cronies before heading off to work at eleven. Nervously, he told them his shift began at midnight and ended at eight in the morning. Anything more than two beers would be dangerous, he told them, but he assured them he was all right with just two. Ollie suspected Mr. Escovar here did not have a green card. He suspected the man did not wish the slightest bit of trouble with the law. Which was why his hands were trembling as he smilingly explained that he was just a mellow little man with a sporty little mustache enjoying a few peaceful brews with his pals. My ass, Ollie thought. Instinctively, he knew Escovar had something to hide if only because he was a spic.

"There's a woman who lives at 321 South Ealey," Ollie said. "Her name's Cassandra Jean Ridley. Does that name mean anything to you?"

"Miss Ridley, yes," Escovar said, nodding at once. "Appar'menn nine C."

"That's the one," Ollie said. "Did you see her leaving the building at anytime late last night, early this morning?"

Escovar thought this one over. Because he's getting ready to lie, Ollie thought. He had never met anyone of Spanish descent who gave you a straight answer. Then again, he had never met any Jew, Chinaman, Polack, Irishman, or Wop, for that matter—present company excluded—who could look you in the eye and give you an unequivocal yes or no. Ollie was a consummate bigot. He knew that virtually everyone he met in this business was inferior to Detective/First Grade Oliver Wendell Weeks. That was simply the way it was, kiddies, take it or leave it. Otherwise, a fart on thee.

Escovar's drinking buddies had moved from the bar to one of the booths, but they were watching the action here with intense interest now. Ollie glanced in their direction, and they all turned their heads away. He figured *they* didn't have green cards, either. Escovar was still thinking.

"Take all the time you need, ah yes," Ollie said, doing his world-famous W. C. Fields imitation.

Escovar took the suggestion to heart, the dumb little spic. The detectives waited.

"This might have been very early in the morning," Carella suggested. "Four, five o'clock, around then."

"I'm trine to remember," Escovar said.

Try speaking a little English, Ollie thought.

"She might have seemed disoriented," Carella said.

She might have had an ice pick in her forehead, Ollie thought.

"I thought she wass drunk," Escovar said.

The way he finally tells it, Miss Ridley got out of the elevator at about four-thirty this morning, accompanied by two girls—he called them "gorls"—one on each side of her, each holding one of her arms to support her, it looked like to him.

"Can you describe these girls?" Carella asked.

"They wass big gorls. Very tall."

"White? Black? Hispanic?"

"White," Escovar said.

"What color hair? Black? Blond? Red?"

"It wass two blondies," Escovar said.

Blondies, Ollie thought. Jesus.

"Skinny? Fat?" he asked.

"They wass wearin overcoats."

Ollie wondered what the fuck that had to do with the question.

"You can still tell if a person's skinny or fat," he said. "Look at me. Am I skinny or fat?"

Escovar hesitated.

"Go ahead, you won't hurt my feelings, I know I'm fat."

"If you say so," Escovar said shrewdly.

"In fact, I like being fat. It means I eat good."

"Okay," Escovar said.

"So were these two broads skinny or fat?"

"They wass healthy," Escovar said.

"What does that mean, healthy? Big tits? Did they have *tetas grandes, amigo?"*

Escovar grinned.

"Big *tetas,* huh?" Ollie said, grinning with him.

"Bigger than they gorlfrenn, anyhow," Escovar said, still grinning.

"How do you know she was their girlfriend?" Ollie asked. He was no longer grinning.

Neither was Escovar.

"How do you know Miss Ridley was their girlfriend?" Ollie asked.

Escovar looked at him blankly.

"Answer the question, Pancho."

"My name iss Manuel," Escovar said.

"Answer the fuckin question!"

"Slow down, Ollie," Carella warned.

"Never mind that man behind the curtain," Ollie said, jerking his thumb at Carella. "He's just being Good Cop. I'm the *Bad* Cop, Pancho, you dig? And in a minute I'm gonna ask you for your green card."

"I hass a green card."

"Oh, I'm sure you do."

"I hass it home."

"I'm sure that's just where you have it. How'd you know they were Miss Ridley's girlfriends?"

"They tole me they wass."

"Oh? When was this? When they carried her out of the fuckin elevator? They stopped and told you they were all good girlfriends here, is that it?"

*"Sí,* that wass when."

"You're lying, Pancho."

"That wass when."

"You sure it wasn't when they came *in?"*

Escovar looked at Carella again.

"Don't look at him, he ain't gonna help you. What'd they do, slip you a few bills to let them upstairs without buzzing the apartment?"

Escovar went pale.

"That's it, ain't it, Pancho?"

"They had a bahl of champagne," Escovar said. "They tole me it wass her burr'day. They said they wass good frenns, they wann to sorprise her."

"How much did they give you?"

"Ten dollars."

"To let them in, huh?"

"They said they wass frenns."

"Some friends, they stuck a fuckin ice pick in her head. What was she wearing, Pancho?"

"I tole you. Overcoats."

"Miss *Ridley.* What was *she* wearing when they carried her out of there? She wasn't naked, was she?"

"Naked? No. A gray suit. Jacket, skirt, a suit."

"Was she wearing shoes?" Carella asked.

"Shoes?" Escovar said, looking offended. "Of course, shoes, *señor.* The two gorlfrenns walk her by where I am holdin dee door open for them, out in the street. I thought she wass drunk," he said. "I thought it wass dee champagne. I wash them . . ."

He watched them as they walked up the street to a black Lincoln Town Car parked just outside the Korean nails place. Both of the girls got in the back seat with Miss Ridley. The car drove off around five, five-fifteen.

"Chauffeur driving the car?"

"I theenk so, yes."

"You didn't happen to notice the license plate number, did you?" Carella asked.

"I'm sorry, *señor,*" Escovar said. "I did not."

It was too early for Christmas presents.

**OR MAYBE NOT.**

At nine that night, when Carella went back to the squadroom to check on any phone calls and to sign out, there was a message that a detective named John Murphy had called to say he'd run the prints he'd lifted from the vic's apartment and had got hits on an Army lieutenant named Cassandra Jean Ridley and a guy named Wilbur Colley Struthers who'd taken a burglary fall in this city seven years ago. Struthers had dropped the better part of a five-and-dime at Castleview before getting released on parole two years ago. His last known address was 1117 South Twelfth . . .

"Right up there in the Eight-Seven," Murphy said. "Now ain't *that* a stroke of luck?"

Carella figured maybe it was.

*

HE WENT THERE WITH THREE OTHER DETECTIVES AS backup; the man was a convicted felon whose fingerprints had been found all over the vic's apartment. The building on South Twelfth was a brick walkup, no doorman. The name under the doorbell was W. Struthers. Carella rang every other doorbell in the row. To the first voice that erupted on the speaker, he said, "Police, want to buzz me in, please?"

"What?" the voice said.

"Detective Carella, Eighty-seventh Squad," he said. "Please buzz me in, sir."

"What is it?"

"We need access to the roof. Buzz us in, sir."

"But what is it?"

"An air vent," Carella said.

Hawes shook his head, suppressed a smile. The buzz sounded a moment later.

"Thank you, sir," Carella said to the speaker, and the four detectives entered the building. Hawes was still shaking his head and smiling. Outside the door to 2C, Carella put his ear to the wood. Meyer was behind him, on his right. Brown was standing to the left of the door. This was ten o'clock on the Saturday night before Christmas, the building was alive with sound. Radios and television sets going, toilets flushing, people talking behind closed doors, there was a city in miniature inside the walls of this building. They had no warrant, hadn't even bothered to approach a judge for one because they'd felt certain Struthers' fingerprints alone would not constitute probable cause for arrest. They had to hope that the man inside there did not bolt for a window the minute they knocked on the door and announced themselves as policemen. Like most cops, they considered burglars—even convicted burglars—people who were not particularly dangerous. The "Burglars-Are-Gents" myth persisted, even though a surprised burglar could turn as violent as any other thief in the world.

There was music behind the closed door, coming from either a radio, an audio system, or a TV set, Carella couldn't tell which. Christmas music. He kept listening. He heard nothing but the music.

He turned to the others, shrugged.

Nobody said anything.

They all stood there with drawn weapons pointing up at the ceiling. Meyer Meyer, bald and blue-eyed and burly, looking patient and attentive and somewhat bored, to tell the truth; Cotton Hawes standing tall and square and redheaded, a white streak in the temple over his left ear, memento of an assailant whose name he'd long since forgotten, still looking amused by Carella's doorbell bullshit; Arthur Brown resembling nothing so much as a dark, scowling Sherman tank. Stalwarts of the law. Waiting for a signal either to come down the chimney or go home.

Carella shrugged again, knocked on the door.

There was silence except for the music, and then, "Yes?" A man's voice.

"Police," Carella said, what the hell.

"Shit, what is it *this* time?" the man said.

They heard footsteps approaching the door. Heard a lock turning, tumblers falling, a chain coming off. The door opened wide. The man inside backed away the instant he saw four guys standing outside there with guns in their hands. He was about six feet tall in his bare feet, Carella guessed, wearing blue jeans and a brown woolen sweater with the sleeves shoved up to his elbows. His hair was a muddy blond color and his eyes were blue, opened wide now in either fear or surprise or both. A Christmas special was on the television set behind him.

"For Christ's sake, don't shoot," he said, and threw his hands up alongside his head. The cops in the hallway suddenly felt like horses' asses.

"Okay to come in?" Carella asked, and showed the tin.

"Yes, fine, come in," the man said, his hands still up. "Just watch how you handle them pieces, okay?"

"Your name Struthers?" Brown asked.

"Yes, sir, that's my name," Struthers said.

"Wilbur Struthers?"

"But you can call me Will, sir. Is this the kidnapping again?"

"What kidnapping?" Carella asked at once.

The detectives were maneuvering so that he was the center of a loose circle, their guns still drawn, nobody even dreaming of holstering them now that they'd heard the word "kidnapping," which was a federal offense that carried with it the death penalty.

"Is it the President's been kidnapped?" Struthers asked, and Carella thought, Oh dear, we've got ourselves a nutcase here, but he still didn't put up the gun.

"Know anybody named Cassandra Jean Ridley?" he asked.

Recognition flashed in Struthers' eyes.

"Do you know her?" Carella asked.

"I have met her, yes. But I do not *know* her, sirs. I would not say I truly *know* her. Excuse me, Officers, but it's been my experience that when there are firearms on the scene, one of them is bound to go off, either because of undue excitement or some other impulse of the moment. So, if it's all right with you, I'd appreciate it . . ."

"How'd your fingerprints get in her apartment?" Carella asked.

"Her goods and her money have already been returned," Struthers said.

The detectives looked at each other.

"What goods? What money?" Carella asked.

"I gave it all back to her yesterday," Struthers said.

"What are you saying?"

"He's saying he burglarized the joint," Brown said.

"Is that it?"

"No, no. There was a misunderstanding, that's all," Struthers said.

"What kind of misunderstanding?"

"Two of her furs came into my possession, was all. And a little cash, too. But everything was returned to her yesterday. Officers, if you think I'm armed and dangerous, why not simply frisk me, so I can put my hands down?"

Hawes frisked him. He was still smiling. He was finding all of this somehow very comical. He nodded okay to the other detectives. They all holstered their guns except Brown, who had grown up in a neighborhood where people sometimes hid weapons up their asses. Struthers lowered his hands. He looked relieved.

"When yesterday?" Carella asked.

Struthers blinked at him, puzzled.

"Did you return her stuff?" Carella explained.

"Oh. She came here around ten-thirty in the morning."

"How'd she know where to find you?"

"I think through my eyeglasses," Struthers said.

Carella was still thinking the man was a bit off his

rocker. Hawes was still smiling. Brown still had his gun in his hand. Meyer was wondering what the man had meant about a kidnapping.

"What kidnapping?" he asked.

"What do you mean, through your eyeglasses?" Carella asked.

"I think she may have found my eyeglasses. She said she was delivering my eyeglasses."

"Found them where?" Carella asked.

"I don't know."

"What kidnapping?" Meyer asked again.

"The man from the Secret Service said there'd been a kidnapping."

Next comes the CIA giving him instructions, Carella thought. Through his radio or his television set.

"Said the President had been kidnapped?" he asked.

"No, that was *my* notion."

*"You* thought the President had been kidnapped."

"Well, why else the Secret Service?"

Why else indeed? Carella thought.

Hawes was still smiling. Nodding his head and smiling. This was turning out to be a very amusing evening after all. Meyer was thinking if the Secret Service had really been here, then maybe someone in the White House had really been kidnapped. Brown was beginning to think along the same lines as Carella: the man was a loonie. He kept his gun in his hand, just in case.

"When was the Secret Service here?" Meyer asked.

"Day before yesterday," Struthers said, "around four in the afternoon. And he came back again that night, around ten, ten-thirty."

"Who was this? Did he give you a name?"

"Yes, sir, he did. Special Agent David A. Horne. With an 'e.' "

"Show you any ID?"

"Showed me his badge, yes, sir."

"What'd it look like?"

"You know that gold star the Texas Rangers carry? It looked a lot like that."

"And he told you he was with the Secret Service, is that right?"

"Yes, sir. The U.S. Treasury Department."

"What'd he want here?"

"He said a hundred-dollar bill I'd spent earlier in the day had serial numbers that matched the ones paid as ransom in a kidnapping. Which is why I thought it might be the President, the Secret Service and all."

"Naturally," Carella said.

"He took the rest of the money with him," Struthers said.

"The rest of *what* money?" Hawes asked.

"The money that was part of the misunderstanding between me and the Ridley woman."

"The money you *burglarized,"* Brown said, and waved the nine for emphasis.

Struthers looked at the gun.

"I'm not admitting to any burglary here," he said. "Or anything else."

"Like what?" Carella asked.

"Like anything at all," Struthers said.

"Maybe you'd like to tell us how your prints got in her apartment," Brown said.

"I took down her drapes," Struthers said.

Carella tried to remember if there'd been any drapes in the dead woman's apartment.

"Because I was going to paint the place for her," Struthers said. "Which is why I thought she wanted the furs moved. So they wouldn't get any paint on them." He nodded to the detectives, seeking approval and encouragement. "That was the misunderstanding," he said. *"I* thought she wanted the furs moved, whereas *she* didn't want them moved."

"How about the money?" Brown asked.

"That, too," Struthers said.

"You didn't want to get paint all over the money, is that it?"

"Exactly. There was just a misunderstanding, is all. She didn't know I was planning to move it, you see."

"Maybe she thought you'd be painting the place green."

"Huh?" Struthers said.

"The color of money."

"No, no . . ."

"In which case it wouldn't've mattered if you got paint all over it."

"No, it was beige."

"Which made a difference, of course."

"Yes."

"So you moved the furs and the cash before you took down the drapes and got your fingerprints all over everything."

"Well . . . yes."

"Man, you are so full of shit," Brown said.

"It wouldn't have been eight thousand in cash, would it?" Carella asked.

"The money was returned to her," Struthers said. "And I didn't kill her."

Whoa now, Carella thought.

"Who said anything about her being *dead?"* he asked.

"Television," Struthers said.

They all looked at him.

"I saw you and some fat cop on television early this morning. At the zoo? Where some lady got tossed to the lions? That was her, wasn't it? That's what this is all about, ain't it?"

THE MAN THEY KNEW ONLY AS FRANK HOLT WAS waiting in the other room while they tasted and tested the cocaine. What he was selling them here was a hundred kilos divided into ten-kilo packets. He was getting a million-nine for the lot, so they wanted to make sure it was good stuff. If it was anything but what he'd advertised it to be, they would kill him. He knew that, he was no fool.

The apartment they were in was a second-floor walkup on Decatur and Eighth. Tigo and Wiggy the Lid were in the second bedroom, such as it was. The man who called himself Frank was waiting outside, in what passed for a living room, chatting with a third man whose name was Thomas, and who was carrying a nine-millimeter Uzi. A radio playing rap music was on in the living room. Frank was the only white man in the apartment. He and Thomas were talking about recent movies they had seen. Thomas was saying he didn't believe none of the gunplay shit in any of the so-called action-adventure movies because all that ricochet stuff and sparks flying and sound effects like zing zang zing was all full of shit. Most gun fights didn't last an hour and a half, anyway. You shot somebody, he was either dead or gonna shoot you so *you* were dead. Frank tended to agree, though he himself had never been in a gun fight. He admitted this to Thomas now.

"You never shot nobody?" Thomas said.

"Never," Frank said.

"Shit, man," Thomas said unbelievingly, and began chuckling. "Where you from, man, the planet Mars?"

"I've just never found the opportunity."

"How long you been doing this?" Thomas asked.

"Almost eight years now."

"And you never found no opportunity to shoot nobody?"

"Most people I deal with aren't interested in ripping anyone off. We're traders, pure and simple."

"I got to tell you bout Wiggy," Thomas said. "He ain't such a pure and simple trader, man."

"He seems like your average businessman."

"He ain't so average, neither. You know how many people *he* has found the opportunity to kill?"

"I'd rather not know," Frank said.

"He got the name Wiggy not ony cause his lass name's Wiggins. It's also cause he wigs *out* whenever things don't go his way. Blows his *lid,* that's the second part of the handle, he Wiggy the *Lid,* man. Reason he so tempermennul, is he doped up day and night. This is one man involved in dealing shit who don't believe shit is *shit,* you take my meanin? He believes shit is *good* for a person. I don't know how much you sellin him in there . . ."

"A hundred keys."

"Wiggy goan snort half that fore the week is out."

"I know you're exaggerating."

"I am. But the man *do* like his cocaine. And when he's stoned, why, man, that's when he wigs out, that's when he blows his lid, that is when you has to shoot him first or he goan shoot you dead, man. He shot and killed . . ."

"I don't want to know. Really."

". . . twelve niggers ony last year," Thomas said, and shrugged. "It was Nigger of the Month Club roun here."

Frank never felt safe when black men—especially black men named Thomas—began calling themselves niggers in his presence because he never knew when the inside familiarity would suddenly turn against him. And whereas he'd never shot a man, he did not particularly encourage situations where gunplay might be called for. He himself carried a Walther P-38. It made him feel like a Nazi in a war movie. They had not relieved him of the gun when he'd come up here. Perhaps because they knew he'd be crazy to attempt a shootout. Anyway, he'd have handed it over in a minute because there was no need to worry about his cocaine failing any test put to it.

The stuff Frank was selling had been grown in Bolivia and processed in Colombia for about $4,000 a kilo. That came to a growing-and-manufacturing cost of $400,000. The Mexicans he'd purchased it from in Guenerando had probably paid $800,000 for it, and had sold it to him for $1,700,000. He was now about to turn it over for $19,000 a key—$1,900,000. That's the way it worked. A pyramid with everyone making a profit from top to bottom. Eight hundred large in Colombia, a million-seven in Guenerando and now a million-nine in New York.

But Frank served a much higher cause than any of these assholes knew about.

Besides, he had a decided edge.

WIGGY HAD TASTED THE COKE, AND SO HAD TIGO, BUT tasting it meant nothing because you could get bad stuff'd fool the keenest taste buds. Ony way to make sure was the trio of tests Wiggy called the TNT, for "Tried 'N' True."

First test you got straight from the water tap.

Opened the faucet, filled the glass with a few ounces of plain water, then scooped a spoonful of shit out of the plastic bag and dropped it in. If it dissolved directly, it was pure cocaine hydrochloride. If any of it stayed solid, the dope had been cut with sugar.

Second of the TNT was Clorox.

Put a little in a glass jar, drop a spoonful of the powder in it, and watch the movie. If you got a white halo trailing the powder, it was cocaine, my dear. If you got red following the powder as it fell, the stuff was cut with some kind of synthetic, and somebody was going to get killed.

Last of the three was the best of them all, cobalt thiocyanate. What you did with the chemical was you dropped it onto the cocaine, also known as the White Leash, or the White Lady, or Lady, or sometimes just plain Girl, or any one of a thousand other cute little names to lure the kiddies in. If the powder turns blue, you've got cocaine. The brighter the blue, the better the Girl. Is what they say, man. The brighter the blue.

Frank's stuff lit up the sky like neon.

Wiggy had been taught to distrust every white man in the universe. He turned to Tigo and said in something like astonishment, "Why, the honkie's honest!"

But Wiggy also served a much higher cause.

Himself.

And he, too, had a decided edge.

# 4.

OLLIE WEEKS HAD CALLED HIS SISTER TO TELL HER HE might not be able to make it there on Christmas Day cause he'd caught a leg being chewed on by a lion, and she'd said, "You ought to find yourself another job." Typical Isabelle Weeks remark, the jackass.

Now, to make matters worse, here was a dead guy stuffed in a garbage can, with a bullet hole at the back of his head. Your classic Mafia-style murder, except that the gangs up here in the Eight-Eight were all either black or Hispanic. Ollie could remember a time when the Mob ruled this part of the city, and all the Negroes and spics were running around doing the legwork for them while the Wops pulled in all the hard cash. Now it was different. The Wops should have learned to speak Spanish or so-called black English, which meant saying, "I done gone sell some dope to school chillun."

Ollie loved using the word "Negro" because he knew it pissed off "people of color," as they sometimes chose to be called. "Blacks" was another favorite, they should make up their fuckin minds. Same thing with the spics up here, which word he didn't dare use to their faces or they would cut him up and serve him from a *cuchifrito* stand. They didn't know whether to call themselves "Hispanics," which sounded too much like "spics," or "Latinos," which sounded like a team of tango dancers. Ollie thought maybe they should concentrate instead on calling themselves "American," huh? and not flying Puerto Rican or Dominican Republic flags from their car antennas. Or marching in Columbus Day parades, the Wops. Or St. Patrick's Day parades, the Irish micks, getting drunk and puking all over the city streets, while cops got paid time and a half for overtime. Ollie hated all this high-profile nationalism for countries that weren't the U.S. of A. If they liked Santo Domingo or San Juan or Islamabad or Jerusalem or Dublin or Calcutta so fuckin much, they should go back home instead of leaving dead bodies in garbage cans. Ollie hated everyone and everything except food.

They had stuffed the corpse in the garbage can feet first, knees up, which was considerate of them. It meant that you could look the dead man right in the eyes. Looked like some kind of sculpture you could find in one of the elite, highbrow, so-called art museums downtown. Ollie could remember a time when a person could stroll along the avenue and buy an artistic landscape in real oil paints for twenty-five bucks. Nowadays, you got a dead man in a garbage can who looked like he was alive and posing for some *artiste* except that he had a bullet hole at the base of his skull.

The medical examiner had come and gone, offering his learned opinion that the guy in the garbage can was indeed dead and that the possible cause of death . . .

"Possible," he'd actually said.

. . . was a bullet wound in the head.

With the help of the Mobile Unit techs—who had arrived some ten minutes ago and were dusting the alleyway as if it would reveal anything surprising about the corpse in the garbage can—Ollie lifted him out, and spread him on the alley floor. He was aware of the fact that in about ten minutes, an ambulance would arrive to pick up the body and carry it to the morgue, where they would cut it open to make sure the guy hadn't been poisoned *before* he got shot, a distinct possibility in police work, where nothing was as it appeared to be, ah yes, m'dear. Sometimes, Ollie even *thought* like W. C. Fields.

The dead man was carrying a wallet with a lot of identification in it. There was a driver's license that gave his name as Jerome L. Hoskins (no relation to the disease, Ollie hoped) and his address as 327 Front Street in Calm's Point—shit, he'd have to make a trip all the way to a section of the city for which he had no particular fondness. There was an American Express credit card made out to Jerome L. Hoskins, and MasterCard and Visa cards made out to the same name. There was a MetTrans card for the subway and bus lines in this considerate city, and also a health plan card from an outfit called MediPlan, whose main offices were in Omaha, Nebraska, wherever that was. There was seven hundred dollars in hundred-dollar bills in the wallet, plus three twenties, a ten, and eight singles. A little card said that the person to notify in case of an emergency was Clara Hoskins at the same address in Calm's Point, who could be reached at 722-1314. Great. He just *loved* breaking the news to somebody's wife, mother, or sister.

A handful of change was in the right-hand pocket of the stiff's trousers, along with what appeared to be a house key, a mailbox key, and a car key with a big gold L for Lexus in a circle on its black plastic head. The luxury car maybe spelled dope, though the vehicle of choice these days was a Range Rover, there being not much difference between big-city dope dealers and Hollywood producers, ah, yes.

Strengthening the possibility of the stiff being drug-connected (as who wasn't up here these days?) was a carry pistol-permit tucked into one of the wallet flaps.

The carry was for a P-38 Walther, however, a somewhat ancient weapon for anyone in the drug trade, but perhaps the man was merely a diamond merchant who'd wandered uptown in search of black pussy and flirted by mistake with the girlfriend of a Negro warlord named High Five or some such. The gun itself was in a shoulder holster under the man's hand-tailored suit jacket. He was wearing no overcoat; when you're about to shoot a man at the back of his head, you don't dress him for the cold weather outdoors.

Well, Ollie guessed he had to talk to this Clara Hoskins, whoever she might turn out to be, find out if she was home, and then go all the way out to Calm's Point to give her the sad tidings, ah yes. He gave one of the techs his card, and asked him to call if he came up with any valuable fingerprints, Fat Chance Department. He also advised them to keep an eye out for a meat wagon from St. Mary Boniface, which should be along any minute now. He could tell the techs didn't like fat people. Hell with them. *He* didn't like nerds who tip-toed around alleyways treating garbage as if it was some priceless piece of evidence instead of the messy shit it actually was.

"Have a merry Christmas," he told them.

"You, too," one of the techs said cheerlessly.

A fart on thee, Ollie thought, and smiled in farewell.

This was now twenty-seven minutes past ten on Sunday morning, the twenty-fourth day of December—Christmas Eve, by Ollie's own reckoning, ah yes.

His jackass sister was probably in church.

*

CARELLA'S PHONE DIRECTORY FOR LAW ENFORCEMENT agencies gave him a number for the U.S. Treasury Department at 427 High Street, all the way downtown, close to where the old police headquarters building used to be located. A recorded message told him the offices were closed for the holiday and would not reopen until Tuesday morning, December 26.

On the offchance that Special Agent David A. Horne might be listed in one of the city's five telephone directories, Carella tried the Isola book first and came up with dozens of listings for the surname Horne, but none for a David A. Horne. He began dialing, anyway. On his twelfth try, he hit paydirt.

"David Horne, please," he said.

"Who's this?"

"Detective Steve Carella, Eighty-seventh Squad."

"This is David Horne."

"Mr. Horne, we're investigating a homicide here, woman named Cassandra Jean Ridley . . ."

"Yes?"

". . . whom we've linked to a man named Wilbur Struthers . . ."

"Yes?"

"Did three and a third at Castleview on a burglary fall . . ."

"Yes, I know the man. I questioned him about some suspect hundred-dollar bills."

"Related to a kidnapping," Carella said, nodding.

There was a silence on the line.

"Can you tell me which kidnapping that was?" Carella asked.

"No, I'm afraid that's classified information," Horne said.

"Even to a fellow law enforcement officer?"

"I'm afraid so."

"This is a homicide, you know."

"So you told me."

"Well, can you at least tell me how it worked out?"

"How what worked out?"

"The questioning."

"I confiscated eight thousand dollars in hundred-dollar bills, checked the serial numbers against our list, and came up negative. I returned the bills to Mr. Struthers that very same day. End of story."

"Which list would that be? That you checked the bills against?"

"I'm afraid that's classified, too."

"Who was kidnapped, Mr. Horne? Can you tell me that?"

"Classified."

"If I showed you the bills we recovered in the victim's apartment, could you tell me if they're the same ones you checked against this mysterious list of yours?"

"Do I detect a note of sarcasm in your voice, Detective Coppola?"

"It's Carella."

"Oh, forgive me. But this is Christmas Eve, you know . . ."

"Yes, I know that."

"And I'm home here with my family. If you can . . ."

"Gee, *I'm* still here at the office," Carella said.

"That's admirable, I'm sure. Call me on Tuesday, okay? Perhaps we can talk then."

"Mr. Horne, the victim won't *ever* be talking again."

"That's unfortunate. But I'm certain our separate cases aren't at all linked."

"Then why were the serial numbers on her money being

checked against bills paid in ransom, isn't that what you said?"

"I said nothing of the sort."

"Then it's what Struthers told me."

"A man with a criminal record."

Carella could almost hear the dismissive shrug.

"He seemed to be telling the truth," Carella said.

"Be that as it may."

"Mr. Horne, I'm trying to find out who . . ."

"It's Special Agent Horne, by the way."

"Oh, forgive me. But somebody tossed a woman to the lions the other day . . ."

"Is that a metaphor, Detective?"

"I wish. We're trying to find out who. Any help you can give us . . ."

"I have no help to offer. Our case is, as I said, classified. Besides, the bills we checked have nothing to do with that woman's death."

"How do you know that?"

"I feel certain they're unrelated."

"Then why were you checking them?"

"Detective . . ."

"Please don't sound so annoyed," Carella said.

He wanted to say, Don't sound so fucking annoyed, okay, Mr. Special Agent Horne?

"I can subpoena those serial numbers," he said.

"You'd never get a court order."

"Why not?"

"Detective," Horne said, and paused. "Let it go, okay? Leave it alone."

"Sure," Carella said, and hung up.

He had no intention of leaving it alone.

CLARA HOSKINS, AS IT TURNED OUT, WAS JEROME Hoskins' wife. On the phone, Ollie told her he was investigating something or other . . .

Actually, he mumbled the words "identification process" so that they were unintelligible, a bullshit ploy that did nothing to quell Mrs. Hoskins' curiosity.

"You're investigating *what?"* she asked.

"Routine matter," he said. "Better to discuss it in person. Okay to come out there, Mrs. Hoskins?"

"Well, all right, I guess," she said. "But you'd better have identification."

The drive to Calm's Point took him half an hour from the North Side of the city to the bridge and over it into a community only recently reclaimed from urban decay. Hillside Commons consisted of low-rise tenements which had been inhabited by runaway hippies during the Sixties and Seventies, immigrant Hispanics in the early Eighties, Koreans in the Nineties, and now—here in the bright new millennium—upwardly mobile Yuppies yearning for a glimpse of the distant towers across the River Dix. The way Ollie looked at it, all those former immigrant residents could move right next door to Hillside Heights, where there were still street gangs and dope pushers and prostitutes and all the other amenities they were used to. Not that he liked the fuckin preppie Yuppies, either, but if an individual couldn't speak the fucking language, he had no right living in a nice neighborhood.

Clara Hoskins spoke the language just fine.

She would not open the door until Ollie had flashed both his ID card and his gold detective's shield, and then she unlocked two locks and took off a security chain before letting him in. She was a blonde in her early forties, Ollie guessed, dressed in tailored gray slacks and a tight red sweater with a little Santa Claus pin over the left breast. Five-seven, five-eight, he supposed, good-looking woman except for the suspicious blue eyes and the frown. She led him into the living room, where a Christmas tree was ablaze with light in one corner of the room. There was the scent of greenery all over the apartment, in fact. All the place needed was a log burning on the hearth, but this was the city, and only cannel coal was allowed, and not even that was in evidence.

"Mrs. Hoskins," he said, figuring he'd get straight to the point, "I'm afraid I have bad news for you."

"Oh Jesus," she said.

"Your husband is dead, ma'am, I'm sorry to have to tell you this way."

"Oh Jesus," she said again.

They all reacted in different ways. Some of them burst into tears, some of them staggered around the room like drunks, some of them looked as if they'd been hit by a locomotive, some of them couldn't speak for ten, fifteen minutes, some of them denied it, told you you'd made a mistake, or this was all a horrible joke, anything to get away from the fact that the Grim Reaper had come to the door and knocked on it and found somebody home. Clara Hoskins just stood there staring at him.

"Tell me what happened," she said.

"He was murdered," Ollie said.

"Are you a homicide detective?" she asked.

"No, ma'am, that's not the way we work it here. The precinct detective who catches the squeal . . ."

He caught himself.

"The responding detective follows the case through to its conclusion, ma'am, is the way we work it here in this city."

"Where was this?" she asked.

"In a section of the city called Diamondback, ma'am."

"That's black, isn't it?" she said.

"Largely, ma'am. And Hispanic."

"What was Jerry doing up there?"

"I thought maybe you could help me with that."

"Diamondback," she said, and shook her head.

"Do I smell something baking, ma'am?" Ollie asked.

"Oh my God," she said, "thank you," and turned away from him and rushed into the kitchen. He watched as she yanked open the oven door and took from it a steaming cake. "Caught it just in time," she said, and put it down on the counter top. "I bake one every Christmas," she said.

"What is it, ma'am?"

"An apple upside down cake."

"I'll bet it's delicious," Ollie said.

But she didn't offer him any.

Instead, she suddenly burst into tears. Sometimes apple upside down cakes did that to people. Or maybe she had just realized her husband was dead. Either way, if she wasn't going to offer him anything to eat, he had no sympathy at all for the woman.

"Ma'am," he said, "weren't you concerned when your husband didn't come home last night?"

"He's often gone a lot," Clara said.

"Were you expecting him home?"

"Not necessarily."

"Well, did he call to say he *wouldn't* be home?"

"No, he didn't. But that's usual. I don't worry about him. He comes and goes."

"What does he do for a living, ma'am?"

"He sells books."

"He works in a bookstore?"

"No, he's a book *salesman.* For Wadsworth and Dodds. The publishing house. His territory is the entire northeast corridor. He goes all the way up to Maine and down to Washington, D.C. He's gone a lot."

Ollie tried to think if there were any bookstores in Diamondback. He couldn't recall a single one.

"Does he make stops in Diamondback?" he asked.

"I don't know where he makes stops," Clara said, and yanked a Kleenex from a box on the counter. "Can't you see I'm crying here?" she said. "Don't you have any sensitivity at all?"

"I'm sorry, ma'am, but I'm trying to learn who might have killed him. Your husband wasn't doing drugs, was he?"

"What!"

"I said . . ."

"I heard what you said. How *dare* you?"

"Mrs. Hoskins, I was simply asking a question. Your husband was found in a garbage can in Diamon . . ."

"A garbage can!"

"Yes, ma'am, with a bullet hole in the back of . . ."

"A bullet hole!"

"Yes, ma'am, which all sounds very strange for a man who sells books for a living, wouldn't you say? Did you know that he carried a gun?"

"A gun!"

"Yes, ma'am, a P-38 Walther was the make. In a holster on his right side. Was he left-handed, ma'am?"

"Yes. I have to tell you, Detective Weeks, I find all of this extremely upsetting." She pulled another tissue from the box, and blew her nose. Ollie hoped she wouldn't get snot all over the cake. She still hadn't offered him a piece. "I can't imagine *what* my husband was doing up there in Diamondback, or why he was carrying a gun, or why anyone would want to kill him. This is all simply beyond belief," she said, and blew her nose again.

"Yes, well, I'm terribly sorry it happened, too, ma'am, or even that I had to report it to you."

He was thinking he would like a piece of her apple upside down cake.

He was also thinking he would like to grab her ass.

"Your husband had a permit for the gun," he said.

"A permit!"

She had a very bad habit of repeating the key words in everything he said and shouting them back at him, very loudly, as if he were deaf. Each time she did that, he winced. The kitchen was redolent with baking smells. He felt like grabbing that cake in both his hands and gobbling it down.

"You sure he wasn't doing drugs?" he asked.

"No, I'm *not* sure, how would I *know* if he was doing drugs or not? He was on the road two, three weeks at a time, for all I know he was robbing banks with his goddamn P-thirty-six . . ."

"Eight, ma'am."

"Whatever, and shooting heroin in his veins, how the hell would *I* know what he was doing when he wasn't here? He ends up in a garbage can, how the hell do *I* know what he was or even *who* he was?"

"That's just my point, ma'am."

"I fail to see your point."

"Just that it seems so strange."

"It does," she agreed, and burst into tears again.

He wanted to take her in his arms and comfort her. He

wanted to reach up under that tight red sweater.

"I wish I could play piano for you sometime," he said.

She looked at him.

She had very blue sad wet eyes.

"To ease your pain," he said.

"Thank you," she said, "that's very kind of you."

"I play piano," he said.

"I wouldn't have suspected it," she said.

"I'm sorry for your trouble," he said. "Here's my card. Call me if you think of anything."

"What would I think of?" she asked.

"Anything that might help us find your husband's murderer."

She burst into tears again.

"Where do I go to . . . to claim . . . to . . . to . . . where is he now? His body?"

"At the St. Mary Boniface morgue," Ollie said. "You can identify the remains . . ."

"Remains!" she said.

"Yes, ma'am, his body, ma'am. You don't think he had a black girlfriend up there, do you?"

"A what!"

"I guess not," he said. "Call me, okay? I know 'Night and Day,' if you happen to like that song."

She was sitting by the Christmas tree in the living room, weeping, when he left the apartment. He could smell the goddamn apple upside down cake all the way down to the street.

*

THE HALLS OF JUSTICE WERE SOMEWHAT LESS THAN thronged with judges eager to hand down rulings at three o'clock on this Christmas Eve, which also happened to be a

Sunday. Most pickpockets, shoplifters, and daytime burglars had called it a day yesterday, packing it in at six o'clock, when all the stores closed. Most of the judges had done the two-step at around the same time, the Christian judges eager to get back to their homes and hearths so they could start the Yuletide festivities, the judges of other faiths heading to vacation spots where they could escape a holiday that excluded them so completely. Only skeleton crews manned the courtrooms. The entire Criminal Courts building resembled nothing so much as a marble mausoleum.

Abe Feinstein was the judge who read Carella's petition for a search warrant. He was sixty-three years old, and he'd been a criminal court judge for twenty-three years now, having been appointed at the age of forty, which was relatively young for such a judgeship. He read the signed affidavit and then peered over the rims of his eyeglasses and the top of his bench, and said in a rather astonished voice, "You want a warrant to search the offices of the U.S. *Treasury* Department?"

"Yes, Your Honor."

"Because—if I'm reading this correctly—you wish to examine a list of *serial* numbers . . ."

"Yes, sir."

". . . for hundred-dollar bills that you believe may have been used as *ransom* money in a kidnapping?"

He still sounded astonished.

"Yes, Your Honor," Carella said.

"Which kidnapping would that have been, Detective?"

"I don't know, sir. That's what I'm trying to find out."

"I must be missing something," Feinstein said, and shook his head.

"Your Honor, a special agent named David A. Horne confiscated eight thousand dollars in hundred-dollar . . ."

"Hold it, hold it, where's that on the affidavit?"

"Paragraph number three, Your Honor."

" 'Upon personal knowledge and belief,' " Feinstein quoted, " 'and facts supplied to me by . . .' "

"Yes, Your Honor, by an ex-con named Wilbur Struthers, who burglarized the suspect money from the apartment of a woman now deceased, the victim of a homicide. That's all in paragraph three, Your Honor."

"Eaten by *lions,* does this say?"

"Yes, sir. At the Grover Park Zoo yesterday. But that wasn't the cause of death. The woman was first stabbed with an ice pick."

"I see that, yes."

"In the head, Your Honor."

"Yes. And you think her murder may be related to this kidnapping you mention?"

"Yes, Your Honor, I do."

"But you don't know anything about this kidnapping?"

"Only what Struthers reported to me."

"Does he seem reliable?"

"As reliable as any thief can be, Your Honor."

"Have you contacted the Secret Service?"

"I spoke personally to Special Agent Horne, yes, Your Honor."

"And what did he have to say?"

"He advised me to leave it alone."

"Any idea why he would have made such a suggestion?"

"He told me the case was classified, sir."

"I see. And you're asking for a search warrant that would invade this confidentiality, is that it?"

"A woman was murdered, Your Honor. An ice pick . . ."

"I have no idea what this kidnapping case is about—and neither do you, I might add. Which means you don't have probable cause, Detective. If the Secret Service has deemed its case classified, I'm not going to allow you to poke around confidential documents. Take Horne's advice, Detective. Leave it alone. Petition denied."

"Thank you, Your Honor," Carella said.

"Merry Christmas," Feinstein said.

OLLIE WEEKS CALLED THE OFFICES OF WADSWORTH AND Dodds at four that afternoon. He got a message telling him the firm was closed for the holidays and would not reopen until Tuesday morning, December 26.

He figured he was the only person working in this fucking city, so he went home.

# 5.

**SO THIS IS WHAT THE FAMILY HAS TURNED OUT TO BE,** Carella thought.

This is what this family has become on this Christmas Day in the new millennium.

There's still me and Teddy, thank God, and the twins, thank God again, although he didn't appreciate the fact that they were slowly inching their way toward puberty. Before he knew it, Mark would be reading *Penthouse* and April would be dating seniors, and he and Teddy would be in wheelchairs in a nursing home. Forty years old, he thought. Jesus. Where did it all go so soon?

There was his sister Angela, too, of course, with her own twins—they ran in the family—and their older sister. Tess was eight, the twins four, all three far distant from puberty. Angela had named the twins Cynthia and Melinda, and then had begun calling them Cindy and Mindy, as if they were a tap-dancing team in Vegas, shame on you, Sis, even though their father had insisted they be called Cynthia and Melinda as originally planned, a noble thought.

Tommy wasn't here this Christmas, the little girls' father was God-knew-where on this bright cold afternoon as everyone was called to dinner, or lunch, or whatever it was at two in the afternoon. Tommy Giordano wasn't here today because he and Angela were divorced now—but not because he'd insisted on calling his daughters by their true and proper names. Tommy Giordano had been caught having a love affair, was still having a love affair, but the lady in question wasn't a lady at all, although she was often called that. Tommy Giordano was having a love affair with cocaine. He had tried psychiatric help, had tried rehabilitation, had tried every damn thing he and the family could think of, but he was hooked through the bag and back again, and nothing had worked. The marriage had fallen apart when Angela just couldn't take it any longer. Tommy was still snorting the Devil's Dandruff, *wherever* he was—the last time they'd heard it was Santa Fe, New Mexico.

In Tommy's place today was an assistant district attorney named Henry Lowell, who had received his undergraduate degree from Duke, his law degree from Harvard, and a smattering of lesser education from Oxford University, or so the precinct locker-room jive maintained. Lowell had been with the D.A.'s Office for almost five years now. In that time, he had racked up thirty-eight convictions, an impressive record, four of them on murder cases. The only murder case he'd ever lost, in fact, was the one he'd prosecuted against the man who'd killed Carella's father.

Maybe this was why Carella didn't like him too much.

Gee.

What Carella couldn't understand was why his *sister* was sleeping with the son of a bitch, and bringing him around to his mother's house on every goddamn holiday that came along. That was what Carella couldn't understand, but maybe he was just old-fashioned. Maybe he thought real life here in the big bad city wasn't the same thing as Greek tragedy where you slept with your father's murderer or ate your own children. Given that the murderer had finally been gunned down by Carella himself or maybe Brown, who'd been standing by his side and firing at the same time . . .

Or maybe both of them . . .

Given that bygones should be bygones . . .

Justice had been served . . .

An eye for an eye and all that . . .

*Given* all that . . .

Should Angela *really* be considering marriage to the man?

But even worse than *her* defection . . .

How could his *mother* have forgotten so soon?

THE SECOND INTERLOPER AT THE TABLE TODAY WAS A man named Luigi Fontero from Milan, Italy. Henry Lowell was sitting on Angela's right, and Luigi Fontero was sitting on Louise Carella's right—Carella's *mother's* right, right! Nor was this the "Luigi" of ancient television fame, a fruit peddler or whatever the hell he'd been, a man who spoke broken English the way the immigrants at the turn of the century had, although the show took place in the Fifties, Carella guessed, he'd only seen a single rerun on the *Nick at Nite* channel or one of the other hundred and ninety-nine channels proliferating like fleas on a dog.

*This* Luigi was a furniture manufacturer. *This* Luigi made furniture fashioned by some of Europe's most important designers. *This* Luigi spoke fluent English with merely the faintest trace of an accent. *This* Luigi wore suits hand-tailored in Rome, and shoes hand-cobbled in Florence. *This* Luigi was holding his mother's hand. If this were Greek tragedy, Carella would have cut off *this* Luigi's hand at the wrist.

"How was the weather when you left Milan?" Lowell asked pleasantly.

"Milan is always the same this time of year," Fontero replied pleasantly. "Drizzly and cold. Very much like Paris."

Two old buddies chatting about the weather.

Carella wanted to kill them both.

"Could *we* go to Paris sometime?" April asked her mother, simultaneously signing.

Teddy signed back, *Yes, next weekend, darling.*

"Really?" April said, her eyes opening wide.

Image of her mother, black hair and brown eyes. Talked up a storm, a constant chatterer—well, exactly like her mother in that respect as well, except that Teddy could only talk with her hands and her eyes. Born deaf, she had never heard a human voice, never heard any sound at all. Almost everyone at this table knew how to sign, some perfectly, some to a lesser degree. Except the interlopers, of course. They looked at Teddy's hands as if she were scribbling Sanskrit on the air.

April was wearing lipstick. Not yet thirteen, and wearing lipstick. Teddy assured Carella it was all right. Carella didn't want to think his daughter was growing up. He didn't want to think his sister would be marrying the man who'd let their father's killer go free. He didn't want to think his mother was starting up with some Italian gigolo so soon after his father's death. On Christmas Day a year ago, she'd burst into tears whenever his father's name was mentioned. Now she was openly holding hands with a man who looked too fucking much like a young Marcello Mastroianni.

Maybe I've had too much wine, Carella thought.

"I love Italian furniture," Angela said.

Right, Sis, Carella thought. Aiding and abetting.

"Yes, it is quite beautiful," Fontero said.

In all modesty, Carella thought.

"Lamps, too," Angela said.

Compounding the felony, Carella thought.

"What's the name of your company?" Lowell asked.

"Mobili Fontero."

"Could I have more lasagna, please?" Mark asked.

The conversation ebbed and flowed, washing the table in familiar sound, except for the voices of the inept district attorney and the sartorially resplendent furniture man from Milan. Carella's mother had been on a diet for the past two months. Now he knew why. She was styling her hair differently. Now he knew why. He wondered how long they'd known each other. Wondered how they'd met. Wondered . . .

"How'd you two guys meet, anyway?" Lowell asked.

You two guys. As if they were teenagers. His mother was sixty-three years old. Fontero was sixty-seven if he was a day. You two guys.

"You tell him, Luigi," his mother said, and patted his hand.

Looking like a schoolgirl. The funeral meats not yet cold upon the table. He suddenly remembered his brief stay in college, remembered playing a bearded Claudius to Sarah Gelb's Gertrude, a girl he'd later taken to bed—if you could call it that—in the back seat of his father's car.

He missed his father so very much.

Luigi was telling them about Louise's best friend—

That was Carella's mother he was talking about. Louise. Louise Carella. Luigi and Louise. And, of course, Luigi was Louis in Italian, Carella's middle name, Louis and Louise, oh how *cute!*

—Louise's best friend Kate, who lived next door, and

who was related somehow to Luigi's brother in Florence (Firenze, Luigi said) who had suggested that Luigi stop by to say hello while he was on his business trip to America, which he had done, taking a taxi the first time . . .

"That was a mistake," Louise Carella said, his mother said, rolling her eyes. "Luigi didn't know how much it would cost, all the way up here to Riverhead."

"You should have asked for a flat rate," Angela suggested.

"Well, at home they warn us all the time about the taxi drivers in this city, but I must tell you I have never once been cheated on any of my visits here."

"How often do you come here?" Lowell asked.

"Three, four times a year. To sell my line to American dealers. But also because I love this city." He smiled. Beautiful white teeth. Marcello Mastroianni teeth. "Now I have reason to come more often," he said, and squeezed Louise's hand, squeezed Carella's mother's hand.

"To make a long story short," his mother said, Louise said, "I was there having coffee with Katie when this taxi pulled up and Luigi stepped out . . ."

"This was in October," Luigi said.

"He was wearing a gray coat with a black fur collar . . ."

Like a Russian diplomat, Carella thought.

"No hat," Louise said.

Carella noticed that he had thick black hair, Luigi did.

"He came up the walk, and rang the doorbell," Louise said. "Katie was expecting him, of course, but not until much later. He introduced himself . . ."

"I soon forgot I was there to say hello to my brother's friend," Luigi said, and squeezed her hand again, Carella's mother's hand, Louise's.

"We went out to dinner, the three of us," Louise said.

"I asked Katie to join us for the sake of courtesy," Luigi said.

A beard, Carella thought.

"And that's how we met," Louise said.

"I came back the very next month."

"Before Thanksgiving."

"We talk every day on the phone."

"We've known each other since October fifteenth," Louise said.

Birthdate of great men, Carella thought, but did not say.

"Seventy-one days today," Luigi said.

But who's counting? Carella thought.

His sister's eyes met his.

There was something like a warning in them.

*Et tu, brute?* he thought.

He'd played Caesar, too. And had gone to bed with Portia after the opening-night party. A year and seven months in college, and he'd been able to score with only two girls, big Lothario. How did he suddenly get to be forty? It occurred to him that he had never been to bed with another woman since the day he met Teddy. Nor did he ever plan to. Nor had he ever felt the slightest desire for any other woman. He wondered how many women *Signore* Marcello over there had been to bed with, *Signore* Casanova, wondered if he'd already been to bed with Carella's mother, Louise, with her stylish new clothes and her svelte new figure and her elegant new coiffure, wondered if his mother had already forgotten that once upon a time there'd been a gentle, loving man named Anthony Carella who'd been shot to death during a holdup in his bakery shop, wondered if sooner or later everyone who dies is forgotten, and thought, curiously, Shakespeare isn't forgotten, I was Claudius, I was Caesar.

He poured himself another glass of wine.

This time, it was his wife's eyes that shot a warning across the table.

He smiled at her and raised his glass in a silent toast.

She sighed and turned away.

SHE DID NOT SAY ANYTHING TO HIM UNTIL SHE WAS certain the children were asleep. Carella was already in bed when she came to him. She sat on the edge of the bed, and in the light of the lamp burning on the night table, her fingers and her eyes told him what was on her mind.

*You're drinking too much,* she said.

"Come on," he said, "a few glasses of wine, what's wrong with you?"

*It started in November, when Danny Gimp got killed . . .*

"Danny was a stool pigeon," he said.

*He was your friend.*

"I never considered him a friend."

*He came to the hospital.*

"That was a long time ago."

*He came when you were hurt. And now he's dead. And you never cried for him.*

"He meant nothing to me," Carella said.

*Did your father mean something to you?*

Carella looked at her.

*You didn't cry for him, either.*

"I cried," Carella said.

*No!* her hands shouted. Her eyes were flashing. He realized all at once that she was containing enormous anger.

"I cried inside," he said.

*Why are you still so angry with Henry?*

"Oh for Christ's sake, is he *Henry* already?" Carella said.

*Your sister's going to* marry *him!* Teddy said. *You have no right to make her feel guilty about it! She* loves *him!*

"Love!" Carella said.

*Is that all at once a dirty word?*

"He lost the case!"

*Do you think he wanted to?*

"He let the man who killed my father . . ."

*Steve,* she said, and put her hand on his arm. *Sonny Cole is dead. You killed him, Steve. He's dead. Let it go, honey. Leave it alone.*

"Seems everyone's asking me to do that these days," he said, and shook his head.

*What does that mean?*

"Nothing," he said. "Forget it."

*You never used to say Nothing, forget it.*

Her hands stopped, the room went suddenly still. She looked at him for what seemed a very long time.

*Steve?* she said at last. *Do you still love me?*

"I adore you," he said.

*Then what is it? Is it the job?*

He shook his head.

*Is it?*

"No. No, I love the job."

She took a deep breath.

And in the stillness of the night, she asked him why he'd drunk so much at his mother's house today, and at first he told her he hadn't drunk that much at all, a glass or two of wine, and then he admitted he'd had at least a full bottle, but this was Christmas Day, so what the hell, she didn't have to start talking to him as if he was some kind of *drunkard,* this wasn't Tommy Giordano here sniffing his life up his nose in Santa Fe or wherever. Then he admitted that he was annoyed that his sister would even *consider* marriage to the man who'd let Sonny Cole walk out of that courtroom . . .

"Never mind that it ended with me shooting him, do you think that's something I *enjoy* doing?" he asked. "Gunning down a man? Do you think I became a cop so I could shoot people dead in the street, twenty yards from the house where my wife and my children are sleeping, do you think I *enjoy* doing that?"

I think the job is getting to you, she said, and he told her Don't be ridiculous, and she said I think the job is beginning to get to you, honey, you're not the same since your father got killed, you just aren't the same man I married, and she began sobbing into his shoulder. He told her Come on, nothing's changed, I *love* the job. And I *did* cry for my father, you don't know how much I cried. I cried for Danny, too, he *was* a friend, I know he was, he practically died in my arms! Jesus, Teddy, don't you think I *care* for people, don't you think I have any feelings?

And suddenly he was crying again—or perhaps for the first time.

She moved out of his arms.

She sat up.

*Listen to me,* she said.

He nodded. His nose was running. Tears were rolling down his cheeks.

*If it's the job,* she said, *I want you to leave it.*

He shook his head. No. Kept shaking it. No.

*I don't want to lose my husband to the job.*

Tears kept streaming from his eyes.

*I don't want you eating your gun one day.*

He kept sobbing.

At last, she turned out the light and went to bed with him cradled in her arms.

He fell asleep thinking that only two days ago, he'd seen a woman chewed to pieces like raw meat.

**VISIONS OF SUGAR PLUM FAIRIES DANCED IN OLLIE'S** head, even though Christmas Day had come and almost gone. Visions of roast beef slices, too. And candied yams. And buttered beans. And thick apple pie with vanilla ice cream sitting on its flaky crust. And red Delicious apples, and Bartlett pears, and Baci chocolates with a sort of fortune-cookie message that read *A woman's soul is like an angel's kiss.* Lying alone in bed, he thought of all the delicious things his sister had served for Christmas dinner today, and he forgot all about the two separate—or so he thought—cases he was currently investigating. Suddenly famished, he got out of bed and went to the refrigerator.

He fixed himself a thick Genoa salami sandwich on rye bread smothered with butter and mustard, and poured himself a glass of whole milk, and carried these to the upright piano he'd rented.

It was almost midnight.

He sat down and started playing "Night and Day."

Somebody in the building yelled, "Shaddup, you jackass!"

A fart on thee, Ollie thought, and continued playing.

He had to admit he wasn't yet a jazz giant, but tomorrow was another day.

**WALTER WIGGINS, BETTER KNOWN AS WIGGY THE LID,** liked to frequent a bar on St. Sebastian's and Boyle because there were very often white hookers in here. Wiggy was in the mood for a white hooker tonight. Not any of your Puerto Rican hookers who *looked* white because they were of Spanish and not African descent. What he wanted was a genuine white hooker.

As a black kid growing up in America, Wiggy had played basketball in the schoolyard, had joined a street gang when he was thirteen, had convinced a twelve-year-old deb member of the gang that slobbering the Johnson wasn't the same thing as having sex, had killed two other black kids from opposing gangs when he was sixteen, had decided when he was eighteen that gang-busting was for the fools of this world, had become fond of cocaine while serving as a mule for a Colombian dope dealer whose business he'd later acquired after he'd shot the man with a Desert Eagle semi-automatic he purchased from a black gun dealer.

As a grown man living in America—Wiggy had just turned twenty-three—he earned more each year than the head of General Motors did, but he still lived in Diamondback, the almost exclusively black section of the city, and he still dated black women, and went to a black barber who knew how to cut his hair, and wore expensive clothes he bought from a shop on Concord Av because the black owner knew what looked best on a black man. He liked eating steak and potatoes, but he also liked collard greens, and fried chicken, and grits. He enjoyed television shows and movies with all-black casts. He didn't read much, but when he did it was mostly novels about crime—none of them by white writers, who he felt didn't know shit about black thieves, and shouldn't even try. In fact, Wiggy distrusted *all* white people because the men believed he was a criminal—which he happened to be, by the way—and the women believed he was a rapist, which he *didn't* happen to be, and had *never* been, by the way. He especially distrusted cops because he'd suffered too many beatings from them when he was coming along, and he was now paying off too many of them to look the other way when it came to this small matter of dealing controlled substances. Having a few dozen cops in your pocket did not engender faith in the criminal justice system.

Wiggy generally steered away from white neighborhoods altogether because he felt reviled there, observed, suspected, never treated with the respect he earned on his home turf. As a result, his universe was largely defined by the *absence* of white people in it. This was why he liked to go to bed with white hookers. Same way lots of white dudes came uptown looking for black hookers, because these girls were something outside of they purlieu, so to speak. The Starlight Bar often had white hookers in it, which is why he was not surprised when along around twelve-fifteen or so on Christmas night, this leggy blonde walked in all alone and took the stool to his right at the bar, and crossed her legs to show enough gartered stocking to qualify her for porn stardom. This little girl seemed most definitely for sale. If she was Puerto Rican, however, he didn't want her. Because to his mind, that meant she wasn't white, she was just a spic.

America was a peculiar place.

"Merry Christmas," he said.

"Merry Christmas," she said and turned to him, and smiled.

"Merry Christmas, Miss," the black bartender said. "Something to drink?"

"I'll have a Tanqueray martini," she said. "On the rocks. A twist."

"Another scotch, Mr. Wiggins?" the bartender asked.

"No, John, I think I'll try what the lady's drinking," Wiggy said, and swung his stool around to face her. "What'd you just order there, Miss?"

"A Tanqueray martini."

"Sounds good to me," Wiggy said.

"It is," she said, and smiled.

He had never drunk a martini in his life. He did not know what Tanqueray was, either. He had, however, seen a lot of James Bond movies.

"Stirred or shaken?" he asked.

He did not like Bond making it with black girls. The girl here looked very white indeed. But if so, what was she doing in a black bar at midnight on Christmas Day?

"Shaken is better," she said, and smiled.

"Shakin it, huh?" he said. "Is better, you think?"

"Oh yes," she said. "Much."

"Then, John," he said, "you best shake it for me, too."

"Two martinis comin right up, Mr. Wiggins," the bartender said.

"So," Wiggy said to the blonde, "how was your Christmas?"

"Very nice, thank you," she said. "And yours?"

"Spent it with my mama," he said, which was the truth. His mama didn't know he was dealing drugs. She thought he got lucky as a day trader. Only person in his family knew he was thus involved was his cousin Ashley, who was one of his runners. Kid made more money than Wiggy's father did, who was a mailman. "How about you?"

"Uh-huh," she said, but he noticed she hadn't mentioned who with, or exactly how she'd spent the day.

"Santa treat you nice?" he asked.

"Oh yes," she said.

"Two martinis on the rocks, a twist," John said.

"Thank you, m'man," Wiggy said, and raised his glass to the blonde. "Cheers," he said, "Merry Christmas."

"Merry Christmas," she said again, and clinked her glass against his.

Wiggy tasted the drink.

"Mm," he said. "Good."

"Told you, didn't I?"

"So you did."

Not a trace of Spanish accent, but lots of these third-generation spics spoke English good as he did. Last thing he needed was a roll with a girl had six diseases she'd picked up in San Juan.

"Walter Wiggins," he said, and put his glass down, and extended his right hand. She took it in her own hand; it was cold from holding the drink.

"I'm Sheryl," she said.

"Nice to meet you, Sheryl."

Didn't sound like any Spanish name he knew, maybe she was white, after all. Or Jewish maybe, which was even better. You got some of these Jewgirls in bed, they screamed down the whole fuckin hood.

"You live up here in Diamondback?" he asked.

Smattering of spics lived up here, maybe she was one of them, after all. He was tempted to take John aside, ask him who the blonde with the long legs and the big tits was. A Spanish working girl or an import?

"No, I spent the day here with a girlfriend," she said.

"She live up here?"

"Her mother does."

"She a black girl?"

"No."

"Spanish?"

He looked her dead in the eye.

"White," she said. "Same as me."

"Where do *you* live?" he asked.

"Same place my girlfriend does. We're roommates."

"And where's that?"

"Downtown. Hastings and Palm. Near the Triangle."

"Nice neighborhood," he said. "So what are you doing up here?"

"I told you. My girlfriend's mother invited us for Christmas."

"White woman living up here?" he asked.

"On the *park,"* she said. "What is it with you?"

"I thought you might be Puerto Rican."

"I'm not. But what difference would it make?"

"None at all."

"So what's the bullshit?" she asked. "I mean, what is it, are *you* so fucking white?"

All at once, he liked her.

"Have another drink," he said.

"Oh, am I suddenly white enough for you?"

"You're white enough, honey," he said, and put his hand on her thigh. She looked into his eyes.

"Another Tanqueray," she told the bartender.

"How about you, Mr. Wiggins?"

"I'll join the lady, sure," Wiggy said, and squeezed her thigh. She kept looking into his eyes. She was jiggling her foot now. She had terrific tits in a very low cut black dress.

"So what are you doing here at the Starlight?" he asked.

"What are *you* doing here at the Starlight?"

"Hoping to meet a gorgeous blonde from downtown on

Hastings and Palm," he said. "Near the Triangle."

"So you met her," Sheryl said, and covered his hand on her thigh with her own. Her hand was no longer cold.

"Seems I have," Wiggy said.

Sheryl looked at her watch. "My girlfriend's picking me up in five minutes," she said. "We've got a car and a driver. You want to come downtown with us, honey?"

"Let's have our drinks first," Wiggy said.

THE LIMO WAS A BLACK LINCOLN TOWN CAR DRIVEN BY A black chauffeur. There was another blonde on the back seat, wearing a black dress like Sheryl's, high-heeled black shoes like her, a black cloth coat identical to hers, little black fur collar at the neck. The car felt warm and smelled of expensive perfume. "Hi," the other blonde said, extending her hand. "I'm Toni." Wiggy slid onto the seat beside her, took her hand. "Hi, honey," she said, and leaned across him to kiss Sheryl on the cheek. He felt her breasts against his arm. Her dress was high on her thighs. The door on Sheryl's side slammed shut. She moved closer to him. The brother came into the car, made himself comfortable behind the wheel.

"We're going home," Toni told him, and the tinted glass separating front from back slid up at once.

"Excuse me, ladies," Wiggy said, "but how much is this going to cost me?"

"One million, nine hundred thousand dollars," Toni said.

He turned to look at her.

She was holding an AK-47 in her lap.

# 6.

THE OFFICES OF WADSWORTH AND DODDS WERE IN A side street off Headley Square, close to the Municipal Theater and the Briley School of Art. As Ollie crossed the small park outside the school, and then the square itself, a fierce wind almost blew his hat from his head. He clutched at it with both hands, cursed at the wind, and at God—who was also on his list of people, places, things, and supernatural beings he hated—and then proceeded across the square to the building in which the publishing firm was housed. The wind moaned beneath the eaves of the old landmark building as he mounted the low flat entrance steps and walked into the lobby, stomping slush from his shoes. He checked the lobby directory—Wadsworth and Dodds was on the fourth floor of the six-story building—and walked toward the waiting elevator, its fancy grillwork door looking like it had come out of a spy movie set in Vienna.

"Whoosh!" he said to the elevator operator, and took off his hat when he noticed there was a lady in the car. The gesture did not go unnoticed. The woman, a good-looking broad in her late fifties, Ollie guessed, with still splendid legs and *poitrines,* ah yes, smiled almost imperceptibly. He figured she worked out a lot. One of these days, he'd have to go to a gym, lose a few pounds, though not anytime soon. Maybe after he learned his five songs. His next lesson was tomorrow night, he could hardly wait.

Wadsworth and Dodds occupied the entire fourth floor of the building. Ollie took one look at the receptionist behind the desk and figured she could have profited from the same aerobics classes the broad in the elevator most likely attended. Ollie hated fat people. He considered them unsightly and weak-willed whereas he thought of his own girth as perfectly suited to his height and his large bone structure. When Fat Ollie Weeks looked into a mirror he saw an impressive figure of a man, whose very presence struck fear into the hearts of underworld types.

"May I help you, sir?" the fat lady behind the desk asked.

Ollie flashed the tin.

"Detective Weeks," he said, cutting to the chase. "I'd like to talk to whoever runs the place here."

"You'd want Mr. Halloway, our publisher."

"Okay," Ollie said, and snapped the leather case shut. "Could you let him know I'm here, please?"

The fat lady picked up her phone, pressed a button on her desk panel, listened, said, "A Detective Weeks to see you, sir," listened again, said, "Yes, sir," looked up at Ollie, and asked, "May I ask what this is in reference to, sir?"

"No," Ollie said.

The fat lady looked startled. "Uh," she said into the phone, "he won't tell me. Yes, sir," she said. "Yes, sir." She hung up, smiled at Ollie, and said, "He'll be with you in a moment, sir. Won't you please have a seat?"

"Thanks," Ollie said, and began roaming the waiting room.

Framed posters of Wadsworth and Dodds books lined the walls. The firm's logo was a distinctive open hand with a silver globe sitting on the palm and radiating rays of light, the fingers tentatively closed around it. Ollie didn't recognize any of the titles.

Behind him, he heard a buzz from the phone on the fat lady's desk.

"Mr. Weeks?" she said. "He'll see you now. It's the end of the corridor, the door on the right."

Ollie nodded.

The corridor leading to Halloway's office was similarly lined with framed posters of books Ollie never heard of. The closed walnut door on the right, at the end of corridor, had no markings on it. He knocked, heard a man's voice call, "Come in, please," twisted the brass doorknob, and entered. He was in a corner office with floor-to-ceiling bookcases on two walls. The other two walls were windowed, enclosing a walnut desk that matched the entrance door. A white-haired man in his early fifties, Ollie guessed, sat behind the desk. He rose the moment Ollie entered the room. Extending his hand, he said, "Richard Halloway, how do you do?"

Ollie took the hand.

"Detective Oliver Weeks," he said, "Eighty-eighth Squad."

"Sit down," Halloway said. "Please," and gestured to a brown leather wingback chair studded with brass buttons. Ollie sank into the chair.

"How can I help you?" Halloway asked.

"One of your salesmen was murdered on Christmas Eve," Ollie said. "His name . . ."

"What?" Halloway said.

"Yes, sir. His name's Jerome Hoskins. From what his wife . . ."

"Oh my God!" Halloway said.

"From what his wife tells me, he sold books in your northeast corridor."

"Yes. Yes, he did. Forgive me, I'm . . . forgive me."

He was shaking his head now, demonstrating how overwhelmed he was. Little white-haired guy in a gray flannel suit and a bow tie with red polka dots on a black field, shaking his head and looking appalled and overcome with sudden grief, all of which seemed somewhat phony to Ollie. Then again, he'd never met a book publisher before.

"Did his territory include Diamondback?" he asked.

"Yes, it did."

"Lots of bookstores up there, I guess."

"Not many. But enough. We're a small firm, last of the family publishing houses in this city, in fact. We're constantly trying to expand our market."

"You sell your books for cash, Mr. Halloway?"

"I'm sorry, I don't understand the question."

"Hoskins had seven hundred dollars and change in his wallet. Seemed like a lot of cash to be carrying around."

"I have no idea why he would have . . ."

"Any idea why he might have been carrying a gun?"

"Diamondback is a dangerous section of the . . ."

"Tell me about it."

"Perhaps he felt he needed protection."

"Do all of your salesmen carry guns?"

"Not to my knowledge. In fact, I didn't know *Jerry* carried one until this very moment."

"How many salesmen are there?"

"Including Jerry, only five. As I told you, we're a small firm."

"Is Mr. Wadsworth still alive? Or Mr. Dodds?"

"Both dead. Christine Dodds is the sole stockholder now.

Henry Dodds's granddaughter."

"How about you? Are you a member of the family?"

"Me? No. No, what gave you that idea?"

"Well, you being the *publisher* and all . . ."

"Oh, that's just a title," Halloway said airily. "Like President or Vice President or Senior Editor."

"Pretty important title, though, huh?"

"Well . . . yes."

"Who are these other four salesmen? I'll need to talk to them."

"Jerry was the only one based here, you know. In this city."

"Where are the other ones?"

"Illinois, Minnesota, Texas, and California."

"Can you give me a list of names and phone numbers?"

"Yes, of course."

"And the names, addresses, and phone numbers of the bookstores Mr. Hoskins visited in Diamondback."

"I'll ask Charmaine to get those ready for you," he said.

Charmaine, Ollie thought. A slender wraith who weighs a ton and a half bone dry. He watched as Halloway picked up the receiver, pressed a button, and told his receptionist what he needed. There was something crisp and efficient about his motions and the way he rapped out instructions. When at last he replaced the receiver on the cradle, he seemed to suddenly realize that Ollie had been observing his every move. He smiled pleasantly. "She'll have those for you when you leave," he said.

"Thanks," Ollie said. "Tell me what you know about Jerry Hoskins, okay?"

"Tell me what you're looking for."

"Well," Ollie said, "I guess I want to know what a book

salesman was doing with types who'll shoot a man at the back of his head and drop him in a garbage can."

"Good Lord!" Halloway said.

Ollie didn't know there was anyone still left on the planet who said, "Good Lord!" He had the feeling all over again that Richard Halloway was faking surprise and sorrow.

"Most of the gangs in Diamondback are dealing drugs," he said, and watched Halloway's eyes. Nothing flickered there. "Hoskins wasn't doing dope, was he?"

"Not to my knowledge."

"Who *would* know?" Ollie asked.

"Pardon?"

"If he was doing drugs. Or dealing drugs. Or involved in any way with controlled substances."

"I can't possibly imagine Jerry . . ."

"Who *could* possibly imagine it, Mr. Halloway?"

"I suppose our sales manager would have known him better than anyone else in the firm."

"What's his name?"

"She's a woman."

"Okay," Ollie said.

"I'll ask her to come in."

CARELLA AND MEYER WENT TO THE BANQUE FRANÇAISE at ten that morning of the twenty-sixth with a court order to open Cassandra Jean Ridley's safe deposit box. The manager of the bank was a Frenchman from Lyon. His name was Pascal Prouteau. In a charming accent, he said he had read about Mademoiselle "Reed-ley's" death in the newspapers and was very sorry. "She was a lovely person," he said. "It is a shame what 'appen."

"When did she first open the box, can you tell us?" Meyer asked.

*"Oui, messieurs,* I 'ave her records here," Prouteau said. "It was on the sixteenth of November."

"How many times has she been in that box since?"

Prouteau consulted the signature card.

"She was 'ere a great deal," he said, looking surprised, and handed the card to Carella. He and Meyer looked at it together. "We'll need a copy of this, please," Meyer said.

*"Mais, oui, certainement,"* Prouteau said.

"Let's take a look in the box," Carella said.

What they found in the box was $96,000 in hundred-dollar bills.

There was also a sheet of paper with a lot of figures on it.

They asked Prouteau for a copy of that as well.

THEY KNEW THE LADY HAD BEEN SMURFING EVEN BEFORE they checked the figures against her two checkbooks and her passbook.

The handwritten notes in her safe deposit box looked like this:

*Deposit: November 16*
*$50,000*

| | |
|---|---|
| *Current Balance:* | *$50,000* |
| *Withdrawals:* | |
| *November 20:* | *$6,500* |
| *November 21:* | *$9,000* |
| *November 22:* | *$7,000* |
| *November 24:* | *$5,430* |

"Missed a day," Meyer said.

"Thanksgiving," Carella said.

| | |
|---|---|
| November 25: | $6,070 |
| November 27: | $8,000 |
| November 28: | $4,000 |
| Current Balance: | $4,000 |

The next deposit was made almost two weeks later.

"According to her calendar, she came East on the eighth of December," Carella said.

Deposit: December 11

$150,000

| | |
|---|---|
| Current Balance: | $154,000 |
| Withdrawals: | |
| December 12: | $4,000 |
| December 13: | $9,000 |
| December 14: | $7,500 |
| December 15: | $7,500 |
| December 18: | $8,300 |
| December 19: | $9,400 |
| December 20: | $8,600 |
| December 21: | $3,700 |
| Current Balance: | $96,000 |

On the identical dates she had listed for withdrawals from the safe deposit box, there were corresponding deposits in either of her two checking accounts or her savings account. Each deposit was for a sum of money less than $10,000, the maximum cash deposit allowed under a federal law that had gone into effect almost three decades ago. Anything more than that sum had to be reported to the Internal Revenue Service on a so-called CTR, the acronym for Currency Transaction Report. Cassandra Jean Ridley, it would appear, had been engaged in money laundering, albeit on a relatively minor scale. Smurfing, as it was called in the trade.

In order to be charged with laundering, a person had to disguise the origin or ownership of illegally gained funds to make them appear legitimate. Hiding legitimately acquired money to avoid taxation also qualified as money laundering. The U.S. Treasury Department cautiously accepted a State Department Fact Sheet estimating that as much as four hundred billion dollars was laundered worldwide annually. Of this, fifty to a hundred billion was said to have come from drug profits in the United States alone.

If Cassandra Jean Ridley's transfers of cash were indeed necessitated because the money came from drugs, she was small potatoes indeed. According to the evidence they now possessed, she had introduced a mere $200,000 into the banking system, and had then separated it from its possible criminal origins by passing it through several financial transactions. In police jargon, this was called "placement" and "layering." But street sales of drugs were usually transacted in five- or ten-dollar bills, and the $96,000 they found in her safe deposit box was in hundreds. It seemed certain she hadn't been running around the street selling dime bags of coke to teenagers.

Her checkbooks showed somewhat substantial amounts written to department stores all over the city in the weeks before her murder. The lady had been moving money around and spending it profligately. The only sum they could not account for was the $8,000 in $100 bills they'd found nestling in the top right-hand drawer of her desk—presumably currency suspected in a kidnapping that had drawn the attention of the Secret Service.

They knew several other things about Cassandra Jean Ridley.

She had been a pilot in the U.S. Army.

She had lived in Eagle Branch, Texas.

This last bit of information might not later have proved significant if Ollie Weeks wasn't at that very moment speaking to Jerome Hoskins' sales manager in the publishing offices of Wadsworth and Dodds.

KAREN ANDERSEN WAS A TALL BRUNETTE WEARING A charcoal black business suit with wide lapels and white pin stripes. Her handshake was firm and her smile was welcoming. Ollie wondered at once if she was wearing black thong panties and a garter belt under the tailored slacks. Halloway filled her in on the reason for Ollie's visit—

She seemed equally appalled by the news of Hoskins' murder.

—and then left them alone in his office while he attended a meeting in the firm's conference room. Karen asked Ollie if he'd care for a cup of coffee. It was close to twelve noon; he was beginning to get hungry. He wondered if the offer included a croissant, a donut, or at least a slice of toast. He accepted it nonetheless, watching Karen's ass as she walked to a folding door that opened to reveal a small kitchen unit. A coffee maker was already prepared for brewing. She hit a button. A red light went on. Karen walked to a chair facing him. She crossed her long legs. He wished she was wearing a skirt. She tented her hands. Long narrow fingers, the nails painted a red to match her lipstick. The savory aroma of perking coffee set Ollie's salivary glands flowing.

"So," she said, "what is it you want to know?"

"What was he doing in Diamondback?" Ollie asked.

"Selling books, I'd expect."

"At one A.M. on Christmas Eve?"

Karen looked at him.

"That's the ME's estimated post mortem interval. The time of his death. The time someone fired a nine-millimeter pistol into the base of his neck."

"I can't even *imagine* what he was doing up there at that hour."

"How many bookstores was he selling to?" Ollie asked. "In Diamondback?"

"Four. We're trying to expand our market there."

"What sort of books do you sell?"

"Mostly non-fiction. We have a small fiction list, but nothing significant."

"Books that would appeal to a Negro audience?"

"To a what?"

"A Negro audience."

"You said Negro."

"Yes."

"Some of them."

"Like what?"

"Oh, any number of our titles."

"Was Hoskins having any kind of trouble with his accounts?"

"Trouble?"

"Deadbeats. Slow payers. Whatever. Personality differences?"

"No problems that I know of. We're an easy firm to deal with. As I said, we're trying to expand our markets. Not only in Diamondback, but all over the United States. Coffee's ready," she said, and uncrossed her legs. She rose, walked to the kitchenette, poured coffee for both of them. "Sugar?" she asked. "Cream?"

"Both," he said.

He was hoping she'd offer him something to eat. His eyes whipped the counter top, saw nothing but an open box of granulated sugar. She knelt to open a mini-fridge under the counter, took from it a container of skim milk. She spooned sugar into his cup . . .

"Two, please," he said.

. . . added milk, carried it to where he sat. She smelled of expensive perfume. He wondered what the hell she was doing selling books for a rinky-dink firm like Wadsworth and Dodds.

"Five salesmen," Ollie said. "Was what Mr. Halloway told me. Charmaine's supposed to be getting me their names and phone numbers."

"Why?" Karen said.

"I want to talk to them. See what they can tell me about him."

"I doubt if any of them knew him that well. Aside from sales conferences, their paths wouldn't have crossed all that often."

"Worth a few phone calls," Ollie said, and shrugged.

"I'll see how she's doing," Karen said.

She lifted the phone on Halloway's desk, stabbed at a button on the face of the cradle. "Hi," she said, "it's Karen. Have you got that information for Detective Weeks?" She listened, hung up, nodded, said, "She's bringing it in," and then folded her arms across her chest, and looked across the room at Ollie.

"Would you guys be interested in a book by a bona fide police officer?" he asked.

Karen looked surprised.

"Would you?" he asked.

"What kind of a book?"

"You know, make-believe."

"Fiction?"

"Sure, fiction. But by somebody who really *knows* police work, never mind these faggots who make it all up."

"Who'd you have in mind?" Karen asked.

"Me," Ollie said.

"I didn't know you were a writer."

"You probably didn't know I play piano, either."

"I confess I didn't."

"Do you like 'Night and Day'? I can play that for you sometime."

"It was never one of my favorites."

"I can even play it with a Latin beat, if you like."

"I don't think so, thanks. Why? Do I look Latin?"

"Well, the dark hair and eyes."

"Actually, my parents were Swedish."

"So would you be interested?"

"In what?"

"A fictious book about police work? I've had lots of experience."

"Would it have a Latin beat?" Karen asked, and smiled.

"I had more of an American cop in mind."

"We sell lots of books in the Southwest."

"What's that got to do with the price of fish?"

"Large Latino audience," Karen said, and shrugged.

"I could throw in a few wetbacks, I suppose," Ollie said dubiously. "But it might ruin the subtle mix."

"Oh, you already have a mix in mind, is that it?"

"No, but I thought if I could talk to somebody up here, one of your editors . . ."

"I see."

". . . he could maybe fill me in on your needs, and I could prepare an outline or something. I have to explain something to you, Miss Andersen . . ."

"Yes, what's that?"

"If a person is creative in one way, he's usually creative in another. That's been my experience, anyway. Take Picasso, you ever heard of Pancho Picasso?"

"Does he write police novels?"

"Come on, he was a famous painter, you heard of him. The point is, he also made pots."

"I see."

"What I'm saying is, if you're creative in one way, you're creative in another. My piano teacher says there's no limits to where I can go."

"Maybe you'll even play at Clarendon Hall one day."

"Who knows? So have you got an editor up here I can talk to? Give your company an exclusive look at the book?"

"I'm not sure any of our editors are free just now," Karen said. "But we may have something you can look at."

"What do you mean *look* at?"

"Something one of our editors may have prepared. Defining our needs. As I said, we don't publish much fiction . . ."

"Always room for a bestseller, though, am I right?"

"Always room."

"You had more bestsellers, maybe your salesmen wouldn't

end up in garbage cans with bullet holes in their heads."

"Maybe not."

"Was he doing drugs?" Ollie asked.

"Not to my knowledge."

"Did he have a black girlfriend up there?"

"He was married."

"Did he have a black girlfriend up there?" Ollie asked again.

"He was *happily* married."

Dainty Charmaine came in with the names and addresses of Hoskins' customers in Diamondback, and the names and addresses of his fellow sales reps in the United States.

One of them lived in Eagle Branch, Texas.

WALTER WIGGINS HAD GROWN UP TO BELIEVE THAT beating the system was the only way to cope with the system. The way he looked at it, the system was stacked against the black man, and any man of color would be foolish to try living within the rules white men had established to control and punish the black man.

Wiggy committed his first theft—a two-dollar water pistol from a variety store on Hayley Avenue, the wide thoroughfare that skewered Diamondback north to south—when he was six years old. His mother forced him to take the toy pistol back to the owner, which Wiggy did after much wailing and protesting. Two days later, he went back to the store again—without his mother this time—and stole the water pistol all over again.

The owner of the store was white, but Wiggy didn't feel he was striking a blow for black power—which words were all the rage then—or anything else. He merely felt he was getting a water pistol for free, fuck his mother. He kept committing petty thefts until the time he was thirteen and joined a street gang named Orion, after which his life became a merry round of rumbling, doing drugs, dealing drugs, and eventually master-minding (he thought of it as such) the ring (he called it a posse, in the Colombian style) that now supported him in the lifestyle to which he had become accustomed. It would never have occurred to Wiggy that living within the system was a possible alternative to the life he'd chosen. Wiggy the Lid was a big man in this part of the city. He even fancied himself to be famous outside of the six square-blocks he controlled in Diamondback.

It annoyed him enormously that he'd had to pay for cocaine being peddled by a man he thought of as an amateur. It annoyed him even further that he'd had to hand over the money to a pair of white chicks holding guns bigger than they were. This guy Frank Holt—if that was his name, which Wiggy doubted—had come recommended by a cousin of Wiggy's in Mobile, Alabama, who said he'd met him with a man named Randolph Biggs in Dallas, Texas, when the three of them were setting up a run from Mexico. This was four years ago. Apparently this Frank Holt person—who'd later found himself stuffed feet first in a garbage can with a bullet hole at the back of his head, courtesy of Wiggy the Lid himself—had recently purchased some very good shit in Guenerando, Mexico, and through various levels of subterfuge had smuggled it into the metropolitan area where he was peddling a hundred keys for a million-nine. One look at the guy, you knew he was new at the trade, however long ago Wiggy's cousin had worked with him. Patted him down, found him carrying an ancient piece out of *Casablanca,* trusted Tigo and him alone to test the shit while he sat outside with a brother named Thomas who could've broke him in half with his bare hands. Beating the system was what this was all about. Why pay a white man a mill-nine when you could shoot him in the head and take the booty home free? Like the water pistol.

Not that there wasn't profit enough in the trade even if Wiggy had played it by the book. Pay Frank Holt—or whatever his name was—the money he wanted for his hundred keys of truly very good shit, and then take it from there. In the long run, because Wiggy'd been careless or stupid or both, he'd had to fork over $19,000 a key to the two blondes in the Lincoln Town Car, who'd driven him back to his so-called office on Decatur and watched while he'd opened the safe, the one named Toni—which he was sure wasn't *her* goddamn name, either—sitting there with the AK-47 leveled at his head while he twirled the combination dial, a smile on her face, her splendid white-cunt legs crossed.

Wiggy had failed to beat the system.

Oh yes, he knew he'd be selling off his newly acquired ten-key lots for twenty-three grand a key, a twenty-one percent profit on each key, for a virtual overnight gain of $400,000 on his $1,900,000 investment. Yes, he knew that, and that wasn't bad for a kid who'd stolen his first water pistol at the age of six. He knew, too, that there'd be profits for everyone down the line, but he didn't give a shit about anyone but himself. His one-kilo buyers would step on the drug by a third, diluting it to produce 1,333 grams or some 47 ounces of cocaine. This would be sold for about $800 an ounce, the profit margin rising the closer the drug came to the street. What had started in Mexico for

$1,700,000 would end up on the streets of Diamondback at a retail price of close to $9,000,000. From door to door, all anybody made was money, money, money, but Wiggy was in this for Numero Uno alone. It did not disturb him to know that some of the kids buying highly diluted shit from sad-assed street dealers were scarcely older than he himself had been when he swiped that water gun.

What bothered him was that he'd allowed two titty blondes to cold-cock him and deprive him of an even greater profit. He would have to get that money back somehow.

What he didn't know was that his $1,900,000 had already been wire-transferred to Iran—where it would buy even more money at a huge discount.

**THE REDHEADED PILOT HAD TOLD THEM THE MAN'S NAME** was Randolph Biggs and had said he lived in Eagle Branch, Texas. She'd given them a fairly good description, too: a tall, broad-shouldered man with thick black hair and a black mustache. She had told them he was a Texas Ranger, but they couldn't go ask about *that,* eh, *amigo?* And besides they felt she was either lying or had been lied to. How could a Texas Ranger be involved in a scheme flying dope out of Guenerando, Mexico?

Eagle Branch was just across the Rio Grande from Piedras Rosas, Mexico—where, legend held, a former U.S. Marine had broken an American drug-prisoner out of jail there, oh, twenty, thirty years ago. Legends die hard. The people in Eagle Branch still talked about the daring escape. To them, it had become almost mythic. They insisted that the escaped prisoner's girlfriend had lived and taught school right there in Eagle Branch. Who knew? It could be true. The people in Piedras Rosas were indifferent to the story. They wouldn't have cared if a whole Marine *battalion* had freed the entire prison population. They were of a mind to believe that the corrupt guards at the local jail, if paid enough *mordida,* would let everybody go free, anyway. Most of the people in Piedras Rosas were more intent on crossing the river and making their way north, where Wiggy the Lid was selling cocaine to dealers lower down the chain of command who would eventually step on the drug and sell it to Mexican immigrants without green cards living in shitty neighborhoods where they pined for the good old days in Piedras Rosas.

Both Francisco Octavio Ortiz and Cesar Villada possessed green cards and were therefore free to come and go as they pleased, taking trips hither and yon in pursuit of their chosen occupation, which was earning—if that was the word—millions of dollars smuggling drugs up from Colombia and selling them to assorted gringos from across the border. On the seventh day of December this year, they had turned over to a pretty redheaded pilot one hundred keys of very high quality cocaine they'd purchased from the Cali cartel, a notorious association of traffickers operating out of Colombia's third-largest city. She had given them in return $1,700,000 in hundred-dollar bills, which they'd counted to ascertain the proper value and then—generously, they felt—had skimmed ten thousand dollars off the top, to give to her as a gratuity.

They had smiled all around.

*Gracias, gracias, muchas gracias.*

Now, in this little border town of what they estimated to be fifteen, twenty thousand people, they were looking for a man named Randolph Biggs, who had given the lady the money she'd subsequently passed on to them.

They didn't mind losing the ten thousand, which, after all, had been offered of their own free will, in gratitude, as an act of South of the Border generosity.

What annoyed them was that *all* the money was counterfeit.

# 7.

**THE RESTAURANT SPECIALIZED IN MIDDLE EASTERN** and Mediterranean cuisine. Here, in the virtual shadow of the mosque near the ramp approach to the River Dix Drive, one could feast upon delicious dishes from Turkey, Israel, Lebanon, Morocco, Tunisia, Syria, Iran, Iraq, the United Arab Republic. The restaurant was smoke-filled even at lunch time, when it was packed with men and women—but mostly men—on breaks and longing for the taste and the aroma of the food and drink they had enjoyed in Damascus or Baghdad, Beirut or Teheran. The entertainment, even during the lunch hour, helped to remind them of their homelands, but it was the fare that drew them here, exquisite to the taste and to memories too long submerged in an accursed foreign land.

Mahmoud Gharib looked the most benign of the three men sitting at the little round table near the small stage where a Raqs Sharqui belly dancer gyrated to a recorded mix of electronic instruments and violins. Resembling a chubby cheerful standup comic from the good old days before comedians turned lean, mean, and obscene, he sported a tiny mustache somewhat uptilted at the tips, giving him the appearance of a man who was perpetually smiling. His complexion was the color of bread lightly toasted, his eyes the color of the very dark brown Turkish coffee they brewed here. His comrades knew him as Mahmoud. The dispatcher at the cab company for which he worked called him Moe, which Mahmoud knew was a Jewish name, and therefore a hundredfold more offensive. He looked plump and jolly and content. He was the most dangerous of the three men.

The men were talking about the proper way to prepare a fish dish that was enormously popular throughout the Middle East. Jassim, the smallest of the men, was saying that the secret was in refrigerating the fish for an hour before it was cooked. Akbar, who worked for a sporting goods store on the South Side, told him that refrigeration had nothing to do with it, he had eaten the fish in poor little villages where no one had even *heard* of ice. Jassim insisted it was the refrigeration. You had to keep the fish on ice for an hour before placing it in the skillet, skin side down, and cooking it. It was the refrigeration, he said, that caused the skin to crisp so swiftly and effectively. Mahmoud said that was nonsense.

"The fish is inconsequential to the dish," he said, waving his hand in a manner that defined leadership and dismissed argumentation. The gesture seemed exceptionally grandiose in light of the comic little mustache under his nose. "You can use any kind of white-fleshed fish," he said. "So long as you wash it clean and season it with salt, pepper, and lemon juice, you can let it stand outside while you make the sauce. I'm not saying forever. It is dangerous to let any fish stand forever. But it's the sauce and the nuts that give the dish its succulent flavor."

"The onions," Akbar agreed.

"The caramelized onions, yes," Jassim said, nodding.

"But especially the pine nuts," Mahmoud said, again superseding all discussion. "Swiftly fried in oil, browned to a pale golden perfection, and then *showered* on the fish."

"On a bed of rice," Akbar said.

"On a bed of rice," Mahmoud said, and kissed his fingertips.

It was odd that the men were discussing fish because at the moment they were eating pancakes stuffed with cheese. In Morocco, where they were cooked on one side only and served with only a warm honey-butter sauce, these little semolina-yeast crepes were traditionally served on the feast of *aid el seghir,* toward the end of the Islamic month of fasting called Ramadan. Here in this restaurant, the pancakes were prepared in the Lebanese manner, stuffed with ricotta and shreds of mozzarella, broiled on both sides to a succulent crispness, and then drizzled with a syrup made of sugar, lemon juice, orange blossom honey, and orange flower water. The men ate ravenously. Jassim licked his lips. Mahmoud found this disgusting, but he made no comment.

A dark-eyed, dark-haired waitress brought them thick black coffee. The belly dancer was wearing a beaded bra and matching belt, a sequined skirt over a body stocking. Her veil work was hardly Egyptian. To Mahmoud, it looked more like the modified striptease one would find in the so-called American Nightclub style. The girl was wearing finger cymbals, although they had for the most part gone out of style in Egypt. She was more adept at twirling her veil and snapping her hips than she was at playing the cymbals.

"When does the Big Jew arrive?" Akbar asked.

Given the origins and political dispositions of the trio, this could have been a derogatory remark, but it was not meant to be. Svi Cohen was in fact an Israeli Jew, and he was in fact a very big man, standing some six feet, three inches tall and weighing close to two hundred and forty pounds.

"Tomorrow," Mahmoud said.

"And his performance at Clarendon?" Jassim asked. He was still licking traces of syrup from his lips. His fingernails were grimy with traces of his trade; he worked as an automobile mechanic in a garage at the foot of the Calm's Point Bridge. Mahmoud found the filthy fingernails disgusting, too.

"On the thirtieth," he said. "This Saturday night."

"So where's the money?" Akbar asked.

It was a good question.

**THE SQUADROOM WAS RELATIVELY CALM ON THAT WEDNESDAY** morning two days after Christmas. Today was only the twenty-seventh and the week was lurching steadily forward into another big weekend that would culminate on Sunday with the tolling of the bells and the falling of the ball in the square. But the squadroom was enjoying a comparative period of calm, a respite from the usual hubbub and hullabaloo that accompanied its normal pace.

Carella and Meyer sat poring over the letters Mark Ridley had written to his sister in the months and weeks preceding her death. From references he made to her own letters, it became clear almost at once that she was terribly excited about a job she'd be flying early in December, which would change her circumstances considerably, enabling her to move East, where she'd always wanted to live, be there long before Christmas, in fact. In the letter they'd already read—the one dated November 13—her brother wrote to say that the job sounded good to him, "so long as you won't be flying anything that might get you in trouble."

The words still rang meaningfully in the stillness of the squadroom.

On November 16, Cassandra Jean Ridley opened a safe deposit box at Banque Française here in this city and placed in it $50,000 in cash. Apparently, her circumstances had in *fact* changed considerably by then. They were to change even more dramatically. Her calendar for December 7 was marked with the words "End Mexico." On December 8, she presumably flew East again. Three days later, she placed another $150,000 in the safe deposit box. Twelve days after that, she was dead.

Their computer told them there'd been seventy-four reported incidents of kidnapping in the United States during the first three weeks of December. Most of these were abductions of children from parents in divorced or separated circumstances. Some of these cases might have attracted the attention of the FBI, in that state lines had been crossed. None of them would have warranted the attention of the Secret Service.

Yet the Treasury Department had braced a small-time burglar named Wilbur Struthers, confiscating bills he'd stolen from Cassandra Jean Ridley's apartment, checking out the serial numbers against ransom notes used in an alleged kidnapping, and then—remarkably—giving him a clean bill of health and returning the bills to him that very same day.

Something stank in the state of Denmark.

They figured it was time they paid a personal visit to Special Agent David A. Horne.

*

**A WHOLE LOT OF HUNDRED-DOLLAR BILLS WERE FANNED** out on Horne's desk.

"A hundred and four thousand dollars," Carella said.

"Some of it recovered in the dead woman's apartment," Meyer said.

"The rest from her safe deposit box."

"All receipted and accounted for," Meyer said.

"So?" Horne said.

He looked like a used car salesman who'd eaten and drunk too much over the weekend, jowly though not paunchy in a dark blue suit, brown shoes, a white button-down shirt, and a blue tie. The circular seal of the Department of the Treasury hung on the wall behind his desk, its gold shield decorated with a pair of scales representing justice, a key symbolizing official authority, and a blue chevron with thirteen stars for the original thirteen states. A little black plastic placard, with Horne's name on it in white lettering, sat near his telephone.

"We think the eight thousand we found in her apartment is the money you appropriated from Wilbur Struthers," Carella said flat out.

"What makes you believe that?"

"Struthers does. Apparently, Miss Ridley located him and went to get her money back. At gun point, incidentally."

"I'm assuming Struthers told you this as well."

"Yes."

"A petty thief," Horne said, dismissing him.

"Big enough to have captured your attention, though," Meyer reminded him.

Horne looked at him. "I don't like unannounced visits," he said belatedly.

"We'd like to see that list of ransom-note serial numbers," Carella said.

"As I told you on the phone . . ."

"We'd like to know just which kidnapping you were investigating," Meyer said.

"I have no authority to release that information to you. And you have no authority to request it."

"We're investigating a murder," Carella said.

"Top of the food chain," Meyer reminded Horne.

"I'm sorry," Horne said, and shook his head.

"We won't go away, you know," Carella said.

"Detective," Horne said, and paused to give the word weight. "Go home, okay? Go arrest some pushers around the schoolyard. Keep your nose out of affairs that don't concern you."

"Gee," Carella said, "all at once I'm *really* interested."

"Me, too," Meyer said.

Horne looked at them both. He sighed heavily.

"I'm not free to discuss any case currently under investigation," he said. "I can, however, show you the list of suspect serial numbers for you to make a comparison check. You'll have to do it here in this office, under my supervision. If that's satisfactory to you . . ."

"It's a start," Carella said.

THE SERIAL NUMBERS WERE A RANDOM LOT.

There were numbers in the A series . . .

A63842516A, A5315898964A, A06152860A . . .

. . . and numbers in the B series . . .

B35817751D, B40565942E . . .

. . . and numbers in the C and F and H and G and E and L and K and D series . . .

But none of these numbers matched those on the separate caches of hundred-dollar bills they'd seized by court order from Cassandra Jean Ridley's desk and her safe deposit box.

They thanked Horne for his time and courtesy . . .

"Always a pleasure," he said.

. . . and went back to the squadroom.

It was not yet twelve noon.

DAVID HORNE WAS TRYING TO CONVINCE HIS BOSS THAT the two Keystone Kops had no idea the bills had been switched.

"This is like the old shell game," he said. "You have to guess which shell the pea is under. But the pea is really in the palm of our hand."

"I'm not familiar with the shell game," Parsons said.

His full name was Winslow Parsons III, and he had been recruited into the Secret Service when he was twenty-two and a senior at Harvard. He'd been present in Dallas, walking alongside the presidential limo when Kennedy was assassinated, but he hadn't been the one to protect the President with his own body—well, no one had, for that matter. Similarly, when John Hinckley, Jr. shot Ronald Reagan in 1981, Parsons had missed his big chance at immortality by not hurling himself in the path of the bullet. At the age of sixty-four, he was still tall and lean and he had all his hair, albeit turning gray, and he thought he looked like Charlton Heston, whom he greatly admired, but he bore no resemblance to him at all. In any case, he didn't know what a shell game was. In Cambridge, they did not have such things as shell games.

"You palm the pea," Horne explained. Or tried to explain. "Same way we palmed the bills."

He was thinking this is four days before New Year's Eve, and we're having a big party, and I should be checking my booze, see how much I have to order. Setups, too.

"How did they come across the bills in the first place?" Parsons asked.

"A case they're investigating."

"What kind of case?"

"A woman was murdered."

Parsons looked at him.

"It gets complicated," Horne said.

"Life gets complicated," Parsons replied.

"Yes, sir, it does."

"Life *is* complicated."

"Yes, sir, it most certainly is."

"How'd *we* get involved in this, is what I'd like to know," Parsons said. "If you please."

"A flagged super showed up on our list, sir. Man who passed it had eight thousand total in similar bills. We yanked them out of circulation. Should have been the end of the story." Horne shrugged. "Instead, the woman got killed and suddenly it's Mickey Mouse time."

"What's the woman got to do with it?"

"He stole the bills from her."

"The eight thousand?"

"Yes, sir."

"He admitted that?"

"No, sir. He told me he won them in a crap game."

"Is that likely?"

"Hardly."

"And you say you recovered eight thousand supers?"

"Yes, sir, and replaced them with clears. The old shell game, sir," he said, and smiled.

Parsons did not smile back.

"Why the hell did you do that?" he asked.

"Do what, sir?"

"Give the man good money for bad?"

"In retrospect, I'm glad I did, sir. All this sudden police interest."

Parsons looked at him skeptically.

"Never mind in retrospect," he said. "Why did you do it in the *first* place?"

"I thought he might make a fuss, sir, if we simply grabbed eight thousand dollars of his."

"Has this man got a record?" Parsons asked.

"Yes, sir. Took a burglary fall seven years ago, did three and a third at Castleview."

"Ex-cons don't usually make fusses."

"But he might have, sir."

"Any chance we can pop him back in?"

"Not unless he commits a crime, sir."

"How'd this woman get the eight thousand?"

"I have no idea. But, sir . . ."

"Yes?"

"There's more."

"Let me hear it."

"The locals found close to a hundred thousand in her safe deposit box."

"Supers?"

"I didn't check them, sir."

"Why not?"

"Well, they had them in their possession, sir. They were here to look at the list of serial numbers used in a kidnapping . . ."

"What kidnapping?" Parsons asked at once. "Has there been a kidnapping?"

"No, sir, that was just confetti."

"But you say they were here with a hundred thousand dollars . . ."

"Ninety-six, actually, sir."

". . . that they found in her safe deposit box?"

"Yes, sir."

"And you didn't check the *bills?*"

His eyes were wide open now.

"I had no opportunity to do so, sir. Without arousing suspicion."

"Suspicion is *already* aroused," Parsons said. "Why the hell do you think they came here? They're *already* suspicious!"

"I don't think so, sir. They're a simple pair of flatfoots investigating a murder. Nothing more."

"Nothing more," Parsons said sourly. "Nothing more than a murder."

"That's all, sir."

"Ninety-six thousand dollars in cash and you don't think they're going to smell something fishy?"

"Sir, my job was to yank those supers out of circulation. That's what I did, sir."

"Splendid," Parsons said.

Horne never knew when he meant it.

"But how long do you think it'll be before these nitwits realize there are *more* phony hundreds out there?" Parsons asked. "How long will it be before they come back to us?"

The room went silent.

"Why was the woman killed, do you know?" Parsons asked.

"I would suspect to keep her quiet," Horne said.

"Do you think this may be Witches and Dragons again?"

"It could be, sir."

Parsons nodded.

"Find out," he said. "Give Mother a call."

THE SIGN OVER THE CASH REGISTER READ:

WE WILL NOT CASH BILLS LARGER THAN
$50. SORRY FOR ANY INCONVENIENCE.
THANK YOU.

Wilbur Struthers took umbrage at this.

Perhaps this was because the only money he had in his wallet was a pair of singles and $400 in hundred-dollar bills. A glance at the cash register total informed him that he had spent $95.95 for two bottles of Simi Chardonnay, two bottles of Gordon's gin, and a bottle of Veuve Cliquot champagne.

"I'm afraid I only have hundred-dollar bills," he told the cashier.

"We accept American Express, MasterCard, and Visa," the cashier said.

"I only have cash."

"Take a personal check, too, if you have proper ID," the cashier said. "Driver's license, or even a MetTrans card with a photo on it."

"I only have cash."

"We can't accept a hundred-dollar bill, I'm sorry," the cashier said.

"Why's that?"

"Been burned too often. Lots of phonies in circulation."

"These aren't phonies," Struthers said.

"Hard to tell 'em apart nowadays," the cashier said.

So much easier to stick up the fuckin joint, Struthers was thinking.

"Tell you what I'm gonna do," he said. "I'm gonna lay a hundred-dollar bill right on the counter here and forget all about the four dollars and change I got coming. You can either pick up the bill and put it in your cash register and tell me 'Thanks for your business, sir,' or you can shove it up your ass. Either way, I'm walkin out of here with my purchases. Good day to you, sir."

The Eighty-seventh Precinct car patrolling Adam Sector picked him up before he'd walked three blocks from the store.

FIRST THING DETECTIVE ANDY PARKER LEARNED ABOUT the perp the blues brought in was that he'd walked out of a liquor store with purchases totaling close to a hundred bucks without paying for them—or at least paying for them with a bill the cashier had refused to accept because it might have been counterfeit. Nobody—least of all Parker—as yet knew whether the bill was queer or not. That wasn't the point. You could not simply walk out of a store without paying for your purchases even if you kept insisting afterward that you *had* paid for them—which Struthers was insisting now, over and over again, bending Parker's ear and breaking his balls.

This was not a court of law here. This was a police station. Parker was a detective and not a judge. He was not being paid to administer justice here, any more than cops in a park during a riot were expected to determine whether a crowd of unruly assholes were *actually* sticking their hands up under girls' skirts. Those cops were being paid to sit on park benches and watch the parade go by. Parker was being paid to sit here and write up a DD form that would follow this man through the criminal justice system—where, by the way, the dude had been before, Parker was just noticing on his computer. This did not bode too well for Mr. Wilbur Struthers here, who seemed to have taken a burglary fall not too long ago and done some fine time upstate. This was enough to put Mr. Struthers in serious trouble here, though certainly Parker did not wish to seem judgmental.

"What you did, it looks like," he said, "was walk out of a store with close to a hundred bucks in merchandise, without paying for it. Is what you seem to have done, Willie."

"I paid for the merchandise," Struthers said.

"Man said you placed a possibly phony . . ."

"Man had no reason to believe the bill was phony."

"Says you forced it on him even though he told you it was store policy not to accept . . ."

"No one forced anything on him. I merely placed the bill politely on the counter top . . ."

"And told him to shove it up his ass."

"He could've also just put it in the cash register and shut his fuckin mouth."

"Language, Willie, language."

"Well, he could've avoided a lot of unnecessary trouble here."

"Which he chose not to do because his boss has been stung with queer C-notes before."

"This one was not queer."

"How do you know?"

"The Secret Service told me," Struthers said.

This was not exactly true.

The Secret Service had told him that $8,000 of the

$8,500 he'd stolen from Cassandra Jean Ridley's apartment was not part of a ransom paid in some mysterious goddamn White House kidnapping, but they had not said the bills weren't counterfeit. In any case, the lady had reclaimed the eight large and had been eaten by lions for her boldness. The $100 bill Struthers had subsequently passed across the counter of S&L Liquors on Stemmler Avenue was one of the bills first Special Agent David A. Horne and later the red-headed lady herself had overlooked in their zeal to make everything right again. Struthers had no idea whether it was phony or not.

Besides, intent was ninety percent of the law, a jailhouse attorney had once informed him, true or not. He'd had no intention of passing counterfeit money. His only intention was to stock up on alcoholic beverages for New Year's Eve, which he hoped to perhaps spend with that girl Jasmine he'd tried to introduce to good champagne, if ever he could find her again. He now had $300 left of the money he'd stolen from the Lion Lady, as he thought of her, and if Jasmine would accept that in trade, he would be willing to pay for a woman for the first time in his life. What the hell, a new year was coming. After which, he figured he might have to run out and do another little burglary, provided this asshole detective here in the rumpled suit and the razor cuts all over his face let him go. Struthers didn't see that anybody had a case here. He'd paid for the goddamn booze!

"Here's the way I look at it," Parker said. "If the bill you gave that guy was genuine, then you in fact paid for the merchandise, and we've got no beef. If, however, the bill is phony, then not only were you passing bad money, you were also committing Petit Larceny, a class-A misdemeanor as defined in Section 155.30 of the Penal Law, punishable by a term not to exceed a year in the slammer. I'm not paid to be judgmental," Parker said judgmentally, "but why waste the city's time and money if in fact the bill is genuine?"

Struthers held his breath.

"Let's take a walk over to the bank," Parker said.

"Let's," Struthers said confidently.

"Well, well, look who's here," Meyer called from the corridor. He swung open the gate in the slatted wooden railing, walked into the squadroom, tossed his hat at the hat rack, and missed. Kneeling to retrieve it, he asked, "What's it this time, Will?"

"Walkaway," Parker said.

"Oh dear," Meyer said.

"Hello, Will," Carella said, just behind him.

Struthers didn't like all this fucking cordiality. He wanted to go to the bank, show the bill to whoever understood counterfeits there, and get on with his preparations for New Year's Eve.

"Also he insisted on passing a C-note may be phony," Parker said.

"I was paying for my merchandise. Incidentally," he said, "there's no law against innocently passing a counterfeit bill if there is no intent to deceive."

The detectives looked at him.

Parker sighed.

"We were just on our way to the bank," he said.

"Where'd you get that bill?" Carella asked.

Struthers didn't answer.

"Will? Where'd you get that C-note?"

Still no answer.

"Was it part of the money you stole from Cass Ridley?"

Struthers didn't know what he might be getting into here. He figured maybe he just ought to keep still.

"Was it?"

No answer.

"Cause I'll tell you what," Carella said. "We've got a whole pile of *other* hundred-dollar bills here. Why don't we all walk over to the bank?"

**IT WAS TEN MINUTES TO THREE WHEN STRUTHERS AND** the detectives walked through the revolving doors of the First Federal Bank on Van Buren Circle. Not too long ago—well, perhaps longer ago than Carella chose to admit—a criminal alternately known to the squad as "Taubman" or "L. Sordo" or most commonly "The Deaf Man"—had tried to rob this bank, *twice.* Carella still felt a faint shiver of apprehension at the memory. They had not heard from The Deaf Man in a long, long time—well, perhaps not as long a time as Carella might have wished—and he had no desire to hear from him again anytime soon.

The manager back then had been named Somebody Alton, Carella no longer remembered the first name, if ever he'd known it. The new manager was a woman named Antonia Belandres, a stately plump brunette in her forties, wearing no makeup and a dark gray suit. She looked up at the clock the moment they approached her desk.

"Little late for business, gentlemen," she said.

Carella showed his shield.

"Detective Carella," he said. "Eighty-seventh Squad."

"This is the Eighty-*sixth* Precinct," she said.

Carella didn't know what that had to do with anything. The bank was on the Circle, directly across Tenth, the wide avenue that slivered the two precincts roughly in half, north to south. First Federal was most convenient to the station house, and besides it was a federal bank. If anybody should know anything about counterfeit money, it was the Feds.

"We're just across the avenue," Parker explained helpfully.

"We're investigating a homicide," Carella said.

She looked at the clock again.

"We need some suspect bills checked," Meyer said.

"We're kind of in a hurry here," Struthers added.

Antonia turned to look at him. Something flashed in her dark eyes. Perhaps she was wondering if he was in charge of this little band of Homicide detectives. He certainly looked intelligent enough. Perhaps she liked the long rugged cowboy look of him. Whatever it was, she addressed her next question to him. With a smile.

"May I see the bills, please?" she said.

They spread the bills on her desk.

$96,000 in hundreds from Cass Ridley's safe deposit box . . .

$8,000 in hundreds from the desk drawer in her apartment . . .

And next the solitary hundred-dollar bill Struthers had placed on the counter at S&L Liquors in payment for his various alcohol purchases.

"You have to understand," Antonia said, as she delicately leafed through the money, "that for every man, woman, and child in the United States, there are six or seven hundred-dollar bills in circulation. That means for every person in the work force, there are more than a *dozen* hundred-dollar bills out there. That comes to something like a billion and a half dollars."

It had begun snowing again. The snow was fierce. Tiny little needle-like crystals blown by a bitter wind. The snow and the wind lashed the long windows of the bank where they sat around Antonia's desk covered with hundred-dollar bills.

"Now who do you think is in possession of *most* of those bills?" she asked, and smiled at Struthers.

"Who?" he asked.

"Vicious criminals, drug dealers, and tax cheats," Antonia said.

"I'm not any one of those," Struthers explained to the detectives.

They did not appear impressed.

"The Secret Service gave me a clean bill of health," he explained to Antonia. She seemed more impressed than the detectives. She raised her eyebrows appreciatively, gave him an approving little nod.

"You may not know," she said, "that the United States Secret Service is part of the Treasury Department."

"Yes, I *did* know that, in fact," Struthers said. "It was explained to me."

"They don't merely protect the life of the President of the United States. Actually, the *major* part of their job is the detection and prevention of currency counterfeiting. Not many people know that," she said.

"*That* I didn't know till this very minute," Struthers said—kissing ass, Parker thought.

"I'm happy you came to me today," Antonia said. "I've had occasion to work with the Secret Service before, you see, on cases regarding counterfeit United States currency." She was carefully turning over the stack of hundreds on her desk, bill by bill, checking for whatever. "Though at first glance, I must say these bills do not strike me as being super-bills. Or super-dollars, whichever terminology you gentlemen prefer. Or even super-notes. Which *do* you prefer, Lieutenant?"

Struthers realized she was addressing him.

"I never heard any of those terms in my life," he said.

"The Arabic writing on the face of some of these bills is suspect, of course," Antonia said, "but not all bills passing through the Middle East are fake. In fact, sixty percent of *all* United States currency is in circulation abroad. You probably didn't know that, either."

"I certainly didn't," Struthers said.

"In fact, the hundred-dollar bill is the most widely held paper currency in the world. Which is what makes it such an attractive target for counterfeiters," Antonia said. "What I'm trying to tell you, however, is that the signature of a money-changer—on this bill, for example, the handwriting means 'Son of Ahmad'—in itself does not indicate a fake bill. As a matter of pride, a money-changer will sign or put some other personal mark on a stack of bills. It's like an author signing his book at Barnes & Noble."

Struthers thought a money-changer was some guy who cashed checks on Lambert Av, up in Diamondback. And he didn't know any authors who signed books.

"In the Arab world," Antonia said, "money-changers are financial middlemen. They've been around since well before Jesus. You need to buy commodities in the West? Simple. You just take your cash to a second-story office in the old quarter of Damascus. The money-changer will arrange for the transfer. I've seen these money-changers' signatures many times before," she said, exhibiting another of the bills. "They don't necessarily indicate a bill is counterfeit. We see entire *families* of counterfeit bills . . ."

Families, Struthers thought.

". . . with the same serial numbers on them," Antonia said. "But none of this larger stack of bills belongs to any of those families."

"Then they're genuine," Carella said.

"They're not counterfeit, that's right," Antonia said, and shoved the stack of bills to one side of her desk, summarily dismissing $104,000 as beneath further scrutiny. "But let's look more closely at this lone hundred-dollar bill here," she said, and picked up the bill Struthers had used in the liquor store. "Henry Loo," she said, staring at the face of the bill.

The man on the bill looked like Benjamin Franklin to Struthers, but he didn't say anything.

"The manager of Ban Hin Lee," she said. "The bank I worked for in Singapore, many years ago. On Robinson Road."

"I know Robinson Road," Struthers said.

"You do?"

"I was in Singapore many years ago, too," Struthers said.

"What's Henry Loo got to do with this bill?" Carella asked.

"He was the first person who showed me a super-bill," Antonia said. "Or a super-dollar, if you prefer. Or a super-note."

Struthers was trying to figure what the rap might be for passing a phony hundred-dollar bill he hadn't known was phony to begin with.

"I studied economics in Manila," she told Struthers, trying to impress him, Parker figured. "After graduation, I got a job at Ban Hin Lee . . ."

"I spent some time in Manila, too," Struthers told her—still kissing ass, Parker thought. "After I escaped from the Khmer Rouge. But that's another story," he said, and Antonia noticed for the first time the almost imperceptible tic and small white scar near the corner of his left eye.

"And later in Singapore," he said. "That's how I happen to know Robinson Road."

"It's a small world," Antonia said.

"I'm amazed we didn't meet there," he said. "In Singapore. We probably passed each other all the time on Robinson Road."

"Yes," she said. "We probably did."

Staring at each other across the desk where the genuine bills were stacked to one side, and Struthers' lone C-note was sitting in front of her.

"I started as a bank messenger," Antonia said. "Worked my way up to teller and then assistant manager, which was when Henry Loo showed me a hundred-dollar bill so *real*-looking I thought old Ben Franklin would any minute go fly a kite off it!"

Antonia laughed at her own witticism.

"But it was as queer as monkey soup," she said, on a comic roll. "A lot of these C-series hundreds were coming through at the time, all of them printed in Teheran on high-tech intaglio presses."

"*What* kind of presses?" Carella asked.

"Intaglio," she said.

"What's intaglio?" Meyer asked.

"An embossing technique that uses a very thick gummy ink."

"Is that what intaglio means?" Parker asked Carella. "Thick and gummy?"

"How should I know what intaglio means?" Carella said.

"Maybe it means embossing technique," Meyer suggested.

"I thought you were supposed to be Italian," Parker said, and shrugged.

"Intaglio produces a three-dimensional effect you can't get with any other printing technique," Antonia said. "Whatever the engraver designs, intaglio gives you *exactly.*"

"And you say these presses exist in *Teheran?*" Parker asked. He was thinking *Teheran?* Where they wear baggy pants and turbans?

"Yes," Antonia said. "Identical to the ones used by the Bureau of Engraving and Printing."

"Bureau of Engraving presses in *Teheran?*" Meyer said. He was thinking *Teheran?* Where they shoot guns in the air and burn American flags?

"Oh yes," Antonia said.

"Let me get this straight," Carella said. "You're saying . . ."

"I'm saying that the late Shah of Iran bought two high-tech intaglio presses from the United States to print his own currency. When the mullahs took over, they put the presses to their own use."

"Printing counterfeit hundreds, you're saying," Parker said.

"Printing super-bills, yes. On plates and paper purchased from the East Germans, yes. Is what I'm saying."

"Printing high-quality . . ."

"Printing *super*-bills," Antonia repeated, stressing the word this time. "Notes so close to the original, they're virtually impossible to tell apart. In fact, I suspect *this* may be a super-bill," she said, and gingerly tapped Struthers' hundred-dollar note.

Uh-oh, he thought.

"How can you tell?" Carella asked.

"Experience," she said.

He looked at her.

"How?" he asked. "If they're so close to the original . . ."

"There are detection machines at the Federal Reserve," she said.

"Do you have one of those machines here?"

"No. I'm judging by eye."

"I thought you said it was virtually impossible . . ."

"Yes, well, I have a trained eye."

He looked at her again. It suddenly occurred to him that she didn't *know* for sure whether or not that hundred-dollar bill was a phony.

"But if it's so *easy,*" he said.

"No one said it's easy."

"Well, you took one look at that bill . . ."

"I've been looking at it all along."

"Without a machine, without even a magnifying glass . . ."

"There are machines at the Federal Reserve. I told you . . ."

"But not here."

"That's right. We send any suspect bills to the Fed."

"How many suspect bills do you get on any given day?"

"We get them every now and then."

"How often?"

"Not very often. Now that the Big Bens are in circulation . . ."

"The what?"

"The new hundreds with the big picture of Franklin on them. Little by little, they're replacing all the old hundreds. That means all the super-bills will eventually be pulled out of circulation, too."

"When?"

"That's difficult to say. It might take years."

"How many years?"

"Five? Ten? Why are you being so hostile?" Antonia asked.

Struthers was wondering the same thing.

"Maybe because a woman was killed," Carella said. "And you're telling me a bill stolen from her apartment may be one of these *super*-bills that are so good nobody can tell them from the real thing."

"The Federal Reserve can detect them. They have machines."

"But how about mere mortals? Can *we* detect them?"

"I just told you this bill looks suspicious, didn't I?"

"Which means you'll be sending it to the Federal Reserve to check on one of its secret machines, right?"

"They're not *secret* machines. Everyone knows they exist."

"How many of these super-bills find their way to those machines?"

"I'm sorry?"

"How many of the bills end up in the Federal Reserve's vaults?"

"The Fed doesn't release those figures."

"Well, how many of them are still in *circulation?* I'm not talking about the ones you see here at your bank, I'm talking about . . ."

"I don't understand your question."

"I'm asking how *many* of these super-bills are still floating around out there."

"I've heard an estimate."

"And what's the estimate?"

"Twenty billion dollars," Antonia said.

# 8.

**IN THIS BUSINESS, YOU DO NOT EXPECT FAKE MONEY.** Fake names, yes, but not fake money.

Fake money can get you killed, whereas a fake name can save your life. Even the two Mexicans, whose real names *were* Francisco Octavio Ortiz and Cesar Villada, used fake names when they were doing business with types trading in controlled substances. No one buying or selling a hundred keys of dope gives you his real name, unless he is *loco*—which, by the way, was a distinct possibility with the people who'd paid a million-seven in fake hundreds to two dangerous *hombres* like themselves. They suspected that the man the redheaded pilot had fingered as Randolph Biggs wasn't a Randolph Biggs at all, nor was he even the Texas State Ranger he'd pretended to be. The problem was in finding him first in a good-sized town like Eagle Branch, and next in Piedras Rosas, the teeming border town just across the river.

If you are dealing in controlled substances, you do not buy radio commercials or newspaper ads announcing that you are in town looking for a man who paid you with bad money. You play it cool, which is difficult to do when you are eager to tie a man to a chair and pull out his fingernails. Villada and Ortiz merely kept flashing money everywhere they went. They were either rich tourists from Barcelona—

in a shitty border town like Piedras Rosas?—or else they were looking to make a drug deal. There were drugs and drug dealers in Eagle Branch, and there were drugs and drug dealers in Piedras Rosas, too. You could not go anywhere in the world today and not find drugs or drug dealers, even in those nations where the penalty for possession was death. This was a very sad fact of life to Ortiz and Villada, but what could one do in a world obsessed with money?

The color of their money blinked like green neon. Money, money, money. The scent of human greed on their hundred-dollar bills floated on the hot Mexican air. Prostitutes blatantly tendered their sloppy favors. Men proffered high-stakes card games, cock fights, dog fights. Lower-level street pushers looking like *bandidos* out of old black-and-white movies offered rolled sticks of marijuana, dime bags of diluted cocaine. Urchins asked if the gentlemen would care to fuck their sisters. Ortiz and Villada were even afraid to drink the water.

Randolph Biggs—or someone who could have been Randolph Biggs—surfaced that afternoon.

THEY WERE SITTING AT A TABLE IN AN OUTDOOR BAR, flashing the green as always, trolling. The white man who took a table adjacent to theirs was tall and broad-shouldered, with a broad neatly trimmed mustache under a nose that sniffed the air disdainfully as he sat and signaled to a harried waiter. He was wearing a neatly pressed tan tropical suit. White linen shirt open at the throat. Tan loafers. No socks. A huge man, the redhead had told them. Randolph Biggs?

Looking bored, he ordered tequila, lime, salt. His dark

brown eyes grazed their table. He looked at his watch. Sniffed again, as if he'd just smelled an open toilet, which in all likelihood he had. Looked around as if expecting cockroaches or rats in a place like this, another likelihood. The waiter brought his drink and the props. He thanked him in fluent Spanish, told him to keep the tab running. Villada and Ortiz were impressed.

He squirted lime juice on the back of his hand, sprinkled salt onto it, licked at the solution, drank some tequila. They were further impressed. He signaled to a man selling cigarettes from a tray hanging around his neck. Loose or by the pack? the man asked in Spanish. He bought an unopened package of Marlboros, paid with Mexican *pesos* he peeled from a grubby roll of bills.

The three men, at separate adjacent tables, sat drinking in the gaudy heat of the Mexican afternoon. There were guitars somewhere. There was the liquid laughter of women from alleyways and upstairs rooms. Everything smelled sweaty and smoky. Buses rolled past. Taxicabs honked their horns. This was a busy bustling little city the size of some neighborhood ghettos in North America. Walk into any one of those ghettos, you'd see the same faces you saw here, you'd hear the same language. The man sitting here in his fancy tropical suit and his neatly groomed mustache looked as out of place as Meg Ryan might have.

*"Perdoname,"* he said. *"¿Tiene usted un cerillo?"*

He was holding one of the Marlboros between the forefinger and middle fingers of his right hand, close to his lips, leaning over toward them now. Ortiz triggered a gold Cartier cigarette lighter into flame. The man inhaled, let out a cloud of smoke, grinned in satisfaction. In Spanish, he said, "I've been trying to quit."

"A bad habit," Ortiz agreed in Spanish, and snapped the lid of the lighter shut.

Randolph Biggs?

"What brings you to this lovely city?" the man asked, and raised his eyebrows to emphasize the sarcasm.

"Passing through," Villada said.

"On your way to?"

"Mexico City."

They were still speaking Spanish. His Spanish was very good.

"And you?" Ortiz asked.

"I live in Eagle Branch," the man said.

They waited for his name. Nothing came.

"Manuel Arrellano," Ortiz said, reaching his hand across the tables, giving the name he frequently used during drug transactions, though he did not yet know whether or not this man was at all involved in the trade. "My partner Luis Larios," he said, giving Villada's *nom de guerre.*

"Randolph Biggs," the man said.

Ortiz's eyes narrowed just the tiniest bit.

The men shook hands all around.

"What business are you in?" Biggs asked. "You said you were partners."

"We export pottery," Villada said in Spanish.

"And you?" Ortiz asked in English. Shift to the man's own tongue, make him feel a little more comfortable about asking if the gentlemen here were in reality selling high-octane shit and not some crockery worth a buck and a half.

"I'm a law enforcement officer," Biggs said. "Texas Rangers." He raised the flap of his jacket, reached into his side pocket, took out a thick leather billfold, opened it to show a gold star pinned to the flap. Ortiz and Villada were impressed all over again. But the redheaded pilot had told them all this. A Texas Ranger named Randolph Biggs was the man who'd introduced her to Frank Holt, another bullshit name, who'd arranged for her to fly to Guenerando to pick up the dope. And pay for it with focking fonny money.

"Do you know a woman named Cassandra Jean Ridley?" Villada asked in English.

Stick to English now, he was thinking.

Make this all perfectly clear to Mr. Randolph Biggs here.

The name registered.

Biggs looked across the table to where Ortiz was sitting with a pistol in his lap, pointing at his belly.

"We have a car," Villada said.

OLLIE'S PIANO TEACHER WAS A WOMAN NAMED HELEN Hobson. She was in her late fifties somewhere, he guessed, he'd never asked, a rail of a woman who always wore a green cardigan sweater over a brown woolen skirt, he wondered if she had any other clothes in her closet. He thought it ironic, the way fate worked. In November, he'd caught a little dead colored girl in an apartment downstairs, turned out Helen had been the one who discovered the body. Now he was taking piano lessons from her and well on the way to becoming an accomplished musician. It was all so strange and wonderful.

It seemed odd to find a grand piano in what was basically a slum apartment, but Helen had crowded one into a corner of her small living room, and it was here that Ollie shared a piano bench with her while he pored over the sheet music for "Night and Day." Helen sat perched to his right on one scant corner of the bench, Ollie's wide buttocks overwhelming the remainder of it. He kept pecking away at the keys.

"I'm having trouble with the notes in the first few bars," he said.

He loved musical terms.

Until now, a bar was just a place where you went to have a beer.

Helen looked at him.

"The notes in the first few *bars?"* she asked.

"Yeah. They're giving me trouble," he said.

"There is only *one* note in the first few bars," she said. "It is the same note repeated three times. G. The note is G. Three times. Bom, bom, bom. Night. And. Day. That is the same note, Mr. Weeks. How can it be giving you trouble?"

"I don't know, it's just giving me trouble."

"Mr. Weeks, we've been working on the first six measures of this song for the past little while now . . ."

"Yeah, I know."

"Without, I must confess, noticeable progress. Are you *sure* you want to take piano lessons?"

"I am very sure. Yes, Miss Hobson. My ambition is to play five songs on the piano."

"Because . . . and this is a possibility you may wish to consider, Mr. Weeks . . . perhaps you have no talent."

"Oh, I have talent, all right."

"Perhaps not."

"I have talent to spare. I think I'm just in some kind of slump, is all. Not bein able to get past those first three notes."

"But those first three notes are one and the *same* note! Bom, bom, bom," she said, demonstrating, striking the note three times in succession. "Night. And. *Day!*" she said, striking the same note again and again and again. "It is impossible for you to be having trouble with the identical note struck three times. It is physically impossible, Mr. Weeks. Bom, bom, bom," she said, hitting the note again. "It's so simple a *rodent* could tap it out with his nose."

"It isn't that I haven't been practicing," he said.

"Bom, bom, bom," she said.

"It's just I caught these two murder cases . . ."

"Please," she said, and lowered her eyes.

"I'm sorry, I know you don't like to hear about . . ."

"I truly don't."

"I'm just trying to explain I've been very busy. And also, I've begun writing a book."

Helen turned to look at him.

"Yeah," he said, and grinned. "A novel."

She kept staring at him.

"A novel," she said. "My."

"Yeah," he said. "I know."

He went on to explain that he'd been a cop for almost twenty years now, and a detective for fifteen of those years, so he knew a little bit more about police work than your average run-of-the-mill aspiring writer, didn't he?

"I'm sure you do," Helen said.

So he'd picked up what he guessed was some sort of form letter this editor at Wadsworth and Dodds . . .

"Which is where I'm investigating the second murder . . ."

. . . writes to people who make inquiries and it had really been very helpful, and had probably started him on yet another worthwhile career, though not one so satisfying as yet as playing the piano . . .

"If I can just get past those first three notes," he said.

"The *same* note, Mr. Weeks. It is the *identical* note. Bom, bom, *bom,"* she said, pounding the G key.

"His name is Henry Daggert," Ollie said.

"Whose name?"

"This editor at Wadsworth and Dodds. He's a senior editor and vice president. I practically memorized everything he wrote."

"But you can't memorize the first note of this song," Helen said, tapping the sheet music. "Such a *simple* note, too. Just think of the three notes as the *same* note, can you do that? Place your index finger over the G key, and strike it once, bom. Let it resonate, and then strike it again, bom. Can you do that?"

"Oh sure," Ollie said.

Helen looked at the keyboard somewhat despairingly. "We have a few more minutes," she said. "Do you think we can try it one more time?"

AT FIRST, HE INSISTED HE KNEW NO ONE NAMED Cassandra Jean Ridley. Knew no one named Frank, either. Of *any* last name whatever. No Franks at all in his busy life as a Texas Ranger.

But this was sunny Mexico.

So they used a cattle prod on his testicles.

He all at once remembered the good-looking redhead and this man named Frank Whoever, but all he'd done was introduce the pair, *"Verdad,"* he said in Spanish, he scarcely knew them at all, really. Cassie—the guys in the bar used to call her Cassie—was an attractive redhead, and Frank was just someone he'd seen around, nice-enough fellow, he thought they might hit it off together, didn't even know his last name, *verdad, amigos.*

"I'm a Texas Ranger," he told them. "What I do mostly is border patrol, trying to keep the wetbacks out, you know . . ."

He actually used the word "wetbacks" in the presence of two Mexicans who were holding a cattle prod an inch away from his quivering balls . . .

"No offense meant," he said immediately. "The point is . . ."

The point was he knew nothing about any money that was flown south of the border by Lieutenant Ridley or anyone else, knew nothing about any deals made between these two obviously fine gentlemen here and anyone in the entire universe, did not know anything about Frank Whatever-His-Last-Name-Was, whom he'd only met in a bar, did not know how much a key of cocaine was worth, did not even know what cocaine *was,* ask him any other question, he was very good at geography.

They gave him a longer jolt this time.

His balls shriveled right up into his throat.

Okay, he told them, the man's name is Frank Holt, I knew him only as an independent contractor who was normally very reliable. I had no idea what kind of deal was going down in Mexico, I merely put together a man and a pilot. The man needed a delivery and pickup, and the pilot had to be willing to take risks—which, by the way, Lieutenant Ridley had taken plenty of during the Gulf War, from what he'd heard about her. He believed she'd been decorated for valor, in fact. An honorable woman who'd served her nation well in times of dire stress, he felt sure she would not have had any part of a scheme designed to bilk anyone out of fair payment in exchange for his goods, whatever those goods might have been, though he'd had no idea the lady would be picking up cocaine across the border. He told them he'd certainly hadn't the faintest *notion* that counterfeit money was being flown to Mexico in exchange for what was undoubtedly very high-grade coke indeed, the two gentlemen here seeming trustworthy and entirely professional. In short, he'd been a mere instrument of convenience, an enabler, a facilitator, so to speak, an all-around nice guy who'd tried to be helpful, was all. If the gentlemen here had got stung, Randolph L. Biggs hadn't had anything to do with it. They would have to look elsewhere for satisfaction.

"So, gentlemen . . ."

Villada nodded to Ortiz.

Ten seconds later, Biggs was telling them that Frank Holt's real name was Jerome Hoskins and that he worked for a company called Wadsworth and Dodds, back East in the big bad city.

CARELLA FINALLY REACHED CAPTAIN MARK WILLIAM Ridley at a little past six that evening. He was cognizant of the fact that it was already midnight in Binsfeld, Germany, but when he'd tried earlier that day, he was informed that the captain had still not returned to base.

Now—at six-oh-six exactly on the face of the squadroom clock—Carella listened to the captain's voice coming over the line from somewhere outside Frankfurt, explaining at great length that Spangdahlem's commanding officer, the brigadier general in charge of the 52nd Fighter Wing, had decided to divide more or less evenly among the base's five thousand U.S. active-duty military members and their seven thousand dependents, the holiday season's twelve-day sequence that had begun on December 21, the start of

Hanukkah, and would end on New Year's Day.

"That is because our wing mission is to be constantly ready at all times to promote stability and thwart naked aggression," he said.

"I see," Carella said.

"In order to achieve U.S. and NATO objectives," Ridley added, "yessir."

Carella wished the man didn't sound as if he'd been drinking.

"I drew December 21 to December 27," Ridley said. "I just got back from Italy fifteen minutes ago. Did I understand you to say you are a detective, sir?"

"Yes, I am," Carella said.

"Why are you calling me here in the Rhineland, may I ask, sir?"

Carella was calling to tell him his sister was dead.

He took a deep breath.

He guessed he'd performed this drill a hundred times before, perhaps a thousand times before, telling a wife or a mother or a father or a son or a brother or an aunt that someone near and dear was suddenly, inexplicably dead, and then listening to the silence or the tears or sometimes the hysterical laughter that greeted this unexpected, unwanted news from a total stranger, he guessed he had spoken these same damn more or less identical words a million times before it sometimes seemed.

Ridley was silent for several moments.

Then he said, "It comes in bunches, don't it, sir?" He sounded suddenly quite sober. "First my wife leaves me . . ."

He fell silent again.

Carella waited.

"I'm sorry," Ridley said.

Carella suspected he was crying, but he could hear no tears over the crackling line. He waited.

"Captain," he said at last, "I wonder if I could ask you some questions. I know this is a bad time . . ."

He let the sentence trail.

Ridley said nothing.

"Captain?" Carella said.

"Yes. Yes, sure," Ridley said. "Go ahead. Sure. I'm sorry. Go ahead."

"We read some letters you sent to your sister . . ."

"Yes, we corresponded a lot."

"In one of them, you made reference to one of *her* letters . . ."

"Yes."

". . . where she told you she'd be flying a job early in December . . ."

"Yes."

". . . which apparently she felt would change her circumstances considerably, was how she put it in the letter to you, which you were quoting."

"Yes."

"What was that job, Captain Ridley? Would you know?"

The captain was silent.

"Sir? Apparently she wrote to say she'd be moving East sometime after this job . . ."

"Yes."

". . . be there long before Christmas, in fact, was apparently what she wrote to you, if your letter was quoting her exactly."

Again, the captain was silent.

"You see, sir, she was killed just before Christmas, and

we were wondering if this job she flew had anything to do with her murder."

"How was she killed?" Ridley asked.

"Someone stuck an ice pick in her," Carella said.

And waited.

"She was flying dope," Ridley said.

"To Mexico, is that right?"

"Yes. Four runs."

"On December seventh, she flew to Mexico for the last time, is that right?"

"Yes. How do you know that?"

"There was an entry in her calendar."

"She called me right afterward."

"Called you there in Germany?"

"Yes."

"To say what, Captain?"

"That she'd flown the four runs, and they turned out to be a piece of cake."

"How do you know they were drug runs?"

"She told me."

"On an open phone?"

"No, in one of her letters. After I warned her not to do anything that might get her in trouble. She assured me these would be short flights, simple pickups and deliveries. Just like chickens or sandals, she said. Just like that."

"Where was she flying? From where to where?"

"Texas to Mexico to Arizona."

"What kind of pickups and deliveries?"

"Money for drugs."

"How much money?"

"They didn't tell her. It was in locked suitcases."

"What drug? Heroin? Cocaine?"

"I don't know. I don't think she knew, either."

"Who was she working for?"

"A man named Frank Holt. He was the one who gave her the suitcases with the money in them. He was the one buying the stuff."

"Who is he, do you know?"

"Some guy she got introduced to in a bar in Eagle Branch. This is why I thought it all sounded so risky. I mean who the hell *were* these people? She said they were okay. Ordinary guys, she told me. Guys trying to make a buck. One of them was a Texas Ranger she'd dated once or twice. The guy who introduced her to Holt."

"What was *his* name? The Ranger?"

"Riggs? Briggs? Something like that."

"How much were they paying her?"

"A *lot* of money."

"How much?"

"Two hundred thousand dollars."

"That's a lot," Carella agreed. He was thinking they had to be big buys. You didn't pay fifty grand a pop for a two-bit pickup and delivery.

"How'd they pay her, did she say? Was it in hundred-dollar bills?"

"I don't know. She got fifty on a handshake, the rest after the last run." Ridley paused. "Plus what they tipped her."

"What do you mean? Tipped her?"

"Yeah, they tipped her."

"Who did?"

"The Mexicans in Guenerando. They gave her a ten-thousand-dollar tip. She told me she was going to buy a couple of fur coats."

The line went silent.

"Did she ever buy the coats?" Ridley asked. "Would you know?"

"She bought the coats," Carella said.

FAT OLLIE WEEKS STOPPED BY AFTER HIS PIANO LESSON to see if anybody up the Eight-Seven wanted to go for pizza or anything. They went to a place on Culver and U. Ollie ordered a large pie for himself. Meyer and Carella shared a nine-incher. The men were off-duty, they ordered beers all around.

"You look tired," Ollie told Carella.

"Must be all this accounting work," Carella said.

Ollie bit into a wedge of pizza. Cheese and sauce spilled onto the lapel of his sports jacket. He dipped up a dollop of mozzarella with the tip of his forefinger, and daintily brought it to his mouth. Licking it off, he asked, "What accounting?"

"On the Ridley case."

"What accounting?" Ollie asked again.

"I've been trying to chase down all her money. I spoke to her brother in Germany half an hour ago . . ."

"The one whose wife dumped him," Ollie said, nodding. He was already on his second slice of pizza. "The one who sent the wedding band."

"That's the one. He told me she got paid two hundred grand for picking up some dope in Mexico."

"We're in the wrong racket," Ollie said.

*"Plus* a ten-grand tip."

"Dope dealers are tipping people nowadays, huh?"

"The way I figure it, she kept the ten grand aside for petty cash. Struthers stole whatever was left of it."

"Eight thousand bucks," Meyer said.

He was wondering how many calories were in the slice of pizza he now picked off the tray. Ollie seemed to have no such problems.

"Popped two hundred grand into her safe deposit box," Carella said, "and then slowly transferred it into two separate checking accounts and a savings account."

"Placement and layering," Meyer said.

"Smurfing," Ollie agreed, and picked up a third slice of pizza.

"All accounted for," Carella said. "And, incidentally, all good money. What's left of it."

"Who says?"

"A lady at the bank."

"Reliable?"

"Maybe."

Ollie raised a skeptical eyebrow.

"But for the moment, let's say the two hundred grand is *not* counterfeit, okay?" Carella said.

"Okay. Two hundred large in nice clean money."

"That leaves only the *ten* grand she got as a tip."

*"Only?"* Ollie said. "That's bigger than the weekly collection from Riverhead."

Cops were always joking about payoffs from Riverhead or Calm's Point being short or being late or withheld for one reason or another. Some of the cops weren't joking. Meyer figured Ollie for an honest cop, though. Only a cop with a clear conscience could eat the way Ollie did.

He watched him as he washed down the third slice of pizza with a huge swallow of beer, thought What the hell, and bit ferociously into his own pizza wedge. With his right hand, Ollie signaled to the waitress for another pie. With his left hand, he was reaching for a fourth slice. Meyer wondered what he would look like if he had three hands.

"A ten-grand tip from the boys in Mexico," Carella said. "Which Cass keeps around the house to use for incidentals while she's distributing the *big* money in her various accounts. Okay. Struthers breaks in, finds eight thousand—or maybe more—sitting in a shoe box or wherever, and swipes it. He tries to spend one of the hundreds, but gets nailed by the Secret Service, who tell him they're investigating a kidnapping . . ."

"Bullshit," Ollie said.

"I agree. In any case, they return the bills and send him on his way."

"Why?"

"Good question. Now here's what's troubling me . . ."

Ollie bit into the fourth slice of pizza. Chewing, he looked across the table at Carella. Meyer was looking at him, too.

"Struthers tried to cash another bill earlier today. Which makes me think he originally swiped more than the eight G's. But never mind. We take the bill to the bank, lady there thinks it's a phony—something called a super-bill the Iranians are running off on presses they . . ."

"Bullshit," Ollie said again.

"I'm not so sure. But forget the Iranians for a minute, okay? Maybe that *is* bullshit, who knows? Let's just say, for now, that the bill *is* phony. Let's say every *one* of those hundred-dollar bills Cass Ridley got as a tip were phony. Ten thousand bucks in fake hundreds. Can we say that for a moment?"

Meyer was frowning.

"What?" Carella asked.

"If that ten grand was fake . . ."

"Right."

"And Struthers stole it . . ."

"Or what was left of it."

"And the Secret Service checked it out . . ."

"Yes."

"How come they didn't recognize it as fake?"

"That's just what's troubling me," Carella said, and nodded, and bit into his cold slice of pizza.

"I must be missing something," Ollie said.

"If the Secret Service had its hands on eight thousand bucks in bad money," Carella said, "why didn't they just confiscate it? Why'd they return it to Struthers?"

"I'll bite," Ollie said, and bit into another slice of pizza. The waitress was arriving with the fresh one. He ordered another round of beers from her. Now, two-fisted and ham-handed, he began lifting slices of pizza from both trays, some hot, some cold, all disappearing with remarkable rapidity into his briskly energetic mouth. "Why *did* they return the money to him?"

"All I can figure is they didn't," Carella said.

"You just said . . ."

"They returned eight thousand dollars to him, yes, but it wasn't the eight thousand they'd taken from him earlier. They returned *good* money to him. Even the lady at the bank said it was good."

"Why would they do that?"

"Because they didn't want anybody making waves down the line. Take his money from him, he might start trouble later on, who knows? Might even come squawking to *us,* who knows?"

"An ex-con?" Ollie said.

"Who knows? But give him back eight grand in *real* bills . . ."

"They probably got a slush fund," Meyer said. "Same as us."

"I'll bet. They pull eight large from it, send Struthers on his way, nice to know you, kid, don't bother us anymore."

Ollie looked at him.

"Too fucking deep for me," he said.

"Don't you see?" Carella said. "Why would two blond hitters carrying a bottle of champagne go up to a lone woman's apartment on a bullshit birthday story, stick an ice pick in her head, waltz her over to the park, strip her naked, and toss her into the lion's den where she gets eaten beyond all recognition? Why did they want her to disappear?"

"Why?" Ollie asked.

"Because she stumbled into something down there in Eagle Branch, Texas."

"Eagle Branch?" Ollie said, and stopped chewing.

"What is it?" Carella said at once.

"My publisher has a sales rep lives down there."

"Your publisher?"

"Yeah, I'm writing a book, didn't I tell you?"

Carella glanced at Meyer.

"I happened by chance on a publisher looking for a good thriller," Ollie said. "So when I'm not practicing piano, I work on the book. The countdown has *begun!"* he announced dramatically, and popped another slice of pizza into his mouth.

"You happened upon a publisher by chance," Carella said. "With a sales rep who lives . . ."

"I caught a guy stuffed in a garbage can on Christmas Eve," Ollie explained. "Bullet at the back of his head. Looked like a drug hit to me, but turned out he's an honest-to-God sales rep. Wadsworth and Dodds. That's the name of the publishing house he worked for."

"Ollie," Carella said. "Eagle Branch is where Cass Ridley hooked up with the two guys who sent her to Mexico."

"Well, I *know* that, Steve-a-rino."

"Eagle Branch is where this all *started.*"

"Well, why do you think I mentioned it?"

"Are you saying you've got a linked homicide?"

"I'm not saying that at all. I'm saying I caught a stiff who worked for a publishing house that has a sales rep who lives in Eagle Branch, Texas. Is what I'm saying."

"What's his name, this guy in Texas?"

"Randolph Biggs."

"The Texas Ranger," Carella said to Meyer.

"No, he's a sales rep," Ollie said.

"Your stiff didn't happen to be carrying any phony hundred-dollar bills, did he?" Meyer asked.

"Well, I don't know if they're phony or not," Ollie said, "but you're welcome to look at them. I already turned them over to the Property Clerk's Office."

**THEY SIGNED FOR AND CHECKED OUT THE SEVEN $100** bills Detective Oliver Wendell Weeks had recovered from Jerome Hoskins' wallet and deposited for security with the Property Clerk's Office. At ten minutes to ten that night, when the last FBI pouch left for Washington, D.C., the money was on the plane, together with an urgent note to the Federal Reserve, asking for an immediate authenticity pop.

The bills and the response from the Fed were waiting on Carella's desk when he got to work early the next morning, the twenty-eighth day of December.

The money was real.

# 9.

**IT REALLY UPSET NIKMADDU ZARZOUR TO BE TREATED** like a terrorist. Even if he looked like one. Even if he *was* one. Which, in fact, he happened to be.

The problems started the moment he transferred from Air France's flight 613 from Damascus to Paris, onto their connecting flight 006 to the United States. He was wearing a black linen suit, a white shirt without a tie, and a little red fez of the sort favored by Turkish gentlemen though he was neither Turkish nor a gentleman. On the Syrian leg of the flight, he was merely another Arab, his complexion the color of desert sand, his black mustache neatly trimmed, a single gold tooth occasionally glinting in the upper left-hand corner of his mouth. But the moment he transferred planes in Paris he became someone whose shabby-looking suitcase and clothes called him to the attention of the security guard who was boarding the 3:15 P.M. flight to the States. It never occurred to the guard that if Nikmaddu were truly a terrorist—which, in fact, he was—he would have been carrying a Louis Vuitton suitcase or something less likely to call attention to his appearance. The guard riffled through his meager belongings, and then questioned—and confiscated—the little box of fresh figs Nikmaddu said he was taking to the U.S. for his maiden aunt. The guard did not suspect that the battered and scarred brown leather suitcase contained a false bottom. He could not have imagined that close to two million dollars in U.S. currency was neatly layered along the bottom of the suitcase; X-ray machines do not pick up paper.

And, of course, there was the same hassle coming through Customs and Immigration here on the eastern shores of the munificent United States of America, even though his passport was in order, even though he showed them a visa, little did it matter to them. He looked like a terrorist, ergo he *was* a terrorist. Which, in fact, he was. But it rankled.

Now . . .

At last.

*"Uhlan wa-Sahian."* Welcome.

*"Ahlan Bikum,"* Nikmaddu said.

The proper reply, in plural because he was talking to three of them. He had never met any of them before. The men introduced themselves now. One of them, the obvious leader, sported a tiny uptilted mustache that made him look as if he were smiling. He had been trained in Afghanistan, was said to have links with the Egyptian Islamic Jihad.

*"Ismi Mahmoud Gharib,"* he said. My name is Mahmoud Gharib.

The second man had the harsh, leathery look of a desert camel driver, deep creases on his brown face, thick veins standing out on the backs of his strong hands. He told Nikmaddu his name was Akbar. He had the unsettling grin of a shark, all teeth and no sincerity. He was their demolitions expert.

The man who introduced himself as Jassim had the look of a pit viper, small and dark and pock-marked. His handshake was remarkably strong, his fingernails encrusted with a deep dark residue, perhaps the traces of explosive powders or oils. He was the one who would go in with the bomb.

One who smiles only with his mustache, Nikmaddu thought, another who smiles with false teeth, and a third —with dirty fingernails—who does not smile at all.

"So you're here at last," the third one said. Jassim.

*"Il-Hamdu-Allah,"* Nikmaddu answered. Thanks be to God.

"Was it a pleasant flight?" Akbar asked. All false glittering smile and bright dark eyes.

Nikmaddu shrugged.

"Did you bring the money?" Mahmoud asked. Mustache smiling. A direct question. Without the money, there would be no explosives. Without the money, there would be no preparations. Without the money, there would be no escape routes afterward, no safe passages home. Without the money, there would be nothing.

"I brought the money," Nikmaddu said.

And now they could discuss the business at hand.

THE APARTMENT THEY WERE MEETING IN WAS RENTED by Mahmoud himself. He was already three months in arrears, another reason for him having asked so soon about the money, his bloodsucking Jew landlord threatening eviction on an almost daily basis. The apartment was in a four-story walkup in a section of the city called Majesta after Her Majesty, the late lamented virgin queen of England, when these United States were still colonies. Once upon a time, Majesta was inhabited by Irish immigrants. Then it became Italian. Then it became Puerto Rican. Now it was populated largely by immigrants—many of them illegal—from third-world nations in the Middle East. The men sat sipping strong Turkish coffee as they looked out past the swirling snow to the towers of the Majesta Bridge in the misty distance. Jassim would have loved to wire that bridge with explosives, but Mahmoud was of a more conservative bent.

It was Mahmoud's opinion that all successful terrorist acts were premised on what had happened in Algiers almost half a century ago. It was there that the Arab struggle for independence from France began in 1954, culminating in July of 1962, when the Democratic and Popular Government of Algeria was formed. It was during those eight years that terrorism discovered its claws and its fangs. It was then that women wearing long dresses as prescribed in the Koran—*O prophet, tell your wives, your daughters, and the wives of the believers that they shall lengthen their garments. Thus, they will be recognized and avoid being insulted*—wearing as well the *hijab* that covered all of the face except the eyes, and the *khimar* that covered their bosoms, strolled unrecognized into grocery stores or onto buses, carrying shopping bags full of high explosives which they conveniently left behind while they went home to their families.

The world of terrorism—Mahmoud now told Nikmaddu—had expanded too greatly. The leaders were thinking too big. Their plans were too grandiose. Why bomb a World Trade Center in New York or a Federal Building in Oklahoma City or a U.S. Embassy in Nairobi or Dar es Salaam? Why bring down an airplane over Lockerbie or LaGuardia? Events such as these only created intense scrutiny and enormous animosity. Why not settle instead for leaving a small bomb in a cinema? Or a railroad station? Why not compromise instead for leaving a satchel with explosives under a sixth row orchestra seat at Clarendon Hall on the night Svi Cohen would be playing Beethoven's "Spring" sonata in F Major, or his "Kreutzer" in A Minor, or whichever other tune the Big Jew chose to perform on his accursed Zionist fiddle?

"Why not commit *tiny* acts of terrorism that will allow them to realize we can strike anywhere, anytime we choose?" Mahmoud asked.

"Clarendon Hall is not so tiny," Akbar said, grinning.

"You understand my point," Mahmoud said reasonably to Nikmaddu.

"I understand your point," Nikmaddu answered reasonably.

He was enjoying the coffee. He was not so sure he was enjoying the terrorist beliefs of a half-lira philosopher like the man with the comic mustache here. Nikmaddu himself had worked with Osama bin Laden on the Dhahran bombing attack in which nineteen U.S. servicemen were killed. It was his own belief that only *major* attacks of terrorism would leave any impression at all on the forces of evil polluting the Arab world. Only desperation measures would provoke wholesale departures. The withdrawal of all U.S. and western forces from Moslem countries in general and from the Arabian Peninsula in particular was the stated goal of *al Quaida.* Killing all Americans, including civilians, everywhere in the world was merely a means toward this end. But Nikmaddu was nothing if not a faithful servant of God. Someone higher up had ordered the Clarendon Hall bombing. He was here merely to serve.

They sat sipping coffee.

"Tell me the plan," Nikmaddu said.

*

THE OWNER OF DIAMONDBACK BOOKS WAS NAMED Jotham Davis. He was in his early forties, Ollie guessed, a black man with an entirely bald and very shiny head. He was wearing black jeans, black loafers, and a black turtleneck sweater. A gold chain hung around his neck, dangling to somewhere in the middle of his narrow chest. He told them that in the Bible, Jotham was the youngest of Gideon's seventy sons. He told them things were quiet after Christmas. He told them fifty percent of a bookstore's sales were in the three months before Christmas. He told them if a bookstore didn't make it at Christmastime, it might as well fold. Ollie thought he was full of shit. That was because Ollie figured a Negro couldn't possibly know anything about selling books.

It was now almost twelve noon on the twenty-eighth day of December, three days before New Year's Eve, six minutes or so before lunch time. Ollie was always aware of the clock, but only because it announced mealtimes. He and Carella had been in the shop for almost ten minutes now, listening to this bald jackass telling them about the book business when all they wanted was information about Jerome Hoskins who'd been shot at the back of the head and stuffed in a garbage can four days ago.

"You sell many books from Wadsworth and Dodds?" Ollie asked. "In the three months before Christmas?" He was thinking these people would probably be his publishers once he finished his book, so he wanted to know how well their books sold.

"Not too many," Jotham said. "They publish mostly technical stuff, you know."

"What do you mean, technical?" Carella asked.

"Engineering stuff, architectural. Like that."

"How about thrillers?" Ollie asked.

"Haven't seen any thrillers from them," Jotham said.

"They told me they do some thrillers."

"Maybe so. I just haven't seen any."

"Did their salesman mention any thrillers to you?"

"No, I don't recall him mentioning any thrillers."

"Man named Jerome Hoskins? He never mentioned any thrillers to you?"

"No, I don't think so."

"When's the last time he came by?" Carella asked.

"Must've been in September? Maybe October. Sometime around then. That's when most of the reps come around. Right after they have their sales conferences."

"Was he in here last week?" Ollie asked.

"Nossir."

"Two days before Christmas, to be exact."

"Nossir, he definitely was not in here two days before Christmas."

"You read newspapers?" Ollie asked.

"I do."

"You watch television?"

"I do."

"Read or see anything about Hoskins in the past few days?"

"No, I didn't. What happened to him?"

"How do you know anything happened to him?" Carella asked.

Jotham gave him a look that said Man, when you were born and raised in this neighborhood and two cops come calling on you one fine morning, and start asking questions about the last time a sales rep was in here, you know damn well they ain't here to buy no book about electrical engineering.

"Thanks for your time," Carella said.

Not three blocks away from the bookstore, Wiggy the Lid was talking to the bartender at the Starlight Bar, where he'd met one of the blondes who'd cold-cocked him on Christmas night.

"I NEVER SEED HER BEFORE THAT NIGHT," THE bartender said.

"Just walked in out of the blue, is that it, John?"

"That's what it was, Mr. Wiggins."

"She ever been in here before?"

"Don't recollect seeing her."

"Or another blonde looked just like her?"

"I'd've remembered somebody looked like that," John said.

"Neither one of them come in here, ast did a man named Wiggy Wiggins frequent this place?"

"No, neither one of 'em, Mr. Wiggins."

"Man named Wiggy the Lid? Did either one of 'em come in here, ax for me by that name?"

"Nobody come in here axin for you by no name at all."

"Cause I think she come in lookin for me, John."

"I wouldn't know about that."

"I think she knew I'd be here, come in here lookin for me specific."

John the bartender clucked his tongue in sympathy.

"Found out somehow that I drop in here every now and then, come in here to *get* me, John."

John the bartender clucked his tongue again.

"You didn't happen to see me get in that limo with her, did you?"

"Well, yes, I was watchin thu the winder."

Wiggy opened his eyes wide.

"You didn't happen to see the license plate, did you?"

John the bartender grinned from ear to ear.

**IN THE NEXT THREE BOOKSHOPS ON THE LIST OLLIE HAD** obtained from Wadsworth and Dodds, the two detectives learned a few things about the publishing business in general and his prospective publisher in particular.

"A sales rep'll make fifty to seventy K a year," the first of the booksellers told them. His name was Oscar Haynes. He asked them to call him Oz. Ollie figured him for a fag because he was wearing a purple shirt.

"To cover the U.S., you've got to hire, what, twenty to thirty reps?" Oz said. "That comes to big bucks. Frankly, I don't see how a small firm like W&D can afford that kind of coverage."

"They've only got five reps," Ollie said.

"Even so, that comes to two hundred and fifty K minimum," Oz said. "That's a lot of bread."

In the second bookstore, they learned from a bookseller whose last name was African and unpronounceable—he asked them to call him Ali—that most publishers have a two-season list, and it was therefore not unusual for Jerome Hoskins to make calls here only twice a year. "Unless a house has a big bestseller, where there'll be reorders, a rep has no reason to come by again. W&D has never had a bestseller in its history, take it from me."

*"Never?"* Ollie said, dismayed.

"Not that I know of. You want my opinion, W&D publishes books nobody wants to read."

In the third and last of the bookshops, they learned that a firm the size of Wadsworth and Dodds usually employs a distribution company to peddle its books. "A distributor will handle sales for a hundred or so small companies," the bookseller told them. His name was David. He was black, too, and he was wearing a pink shirt. Ollie figured him for another fag. Ollie was beginning to think the entire industry was populated with faggot Negro booksellers. "I'm surprised W&D has its own reps, really," David said.

"Did Jerome Hoskins stop by here on the twenty-third?" Carella asked.

"If he did, it had to be after five o'clock. That's when I closed."

"When's the last time you saw him?" Ollie asked.

"September sometime. October. Around then."

"Ever see him with any other W&D reps?"

"Nope."

"Man named Randolph Biggs? Ever meet him? From Texas?"

"Nope."

It was time for lunch and all they'd learned about Hoskins was that he hadn't visited any of his bookshop customers on the twenty-third. Which meant he'd been up here for some other reason. Some other reason that had got him shot in the head and dumped in a garbage can.

"Total fucking loss," Ollie said.

"Not entirely," Carella said. "We now know Wadsworth and Dodds is a two-bit publisher that never had a bestseller in its history."

"Who gives a shit?" Ollie said. Actually, he was heartbroken; he'd been hoping his first novel would sell millions of copies.

"But they hired five sales reps, anyway," Carella said. "At

fifty to seventy grand a pop. To peddle a list of books nobody wants to read."

"Let's go eat," Ollie said.

SINCE THE ABILITY TO FIX TICKETS FOR TRAFFIC violations was essential to Wiggy the Lid's business, one of the people on his payroll was a sergeant in the Motor Vehicles Bureau. He called the man—whose name was Evan Grimes—at one o'clock that afternoon, and asked if he could trace a car for him, and then gave him the license plate number John the bartender had seen through the window of the Starlight on Christmas night. Grimes got back to him ten minutes later. He told him that the car was registered to a company called West Side Limousine, and he gave Wiggy an address and a telephone number he could call. He also advised Wiggy not to call him at work again and hung up abruptly, which was tantamount to a gladiator thumbing his nose at the emperor. Wiggy called him back, at work, an instant later.

"Let me splain the rules of the game, shithead," he said.

Grimes listened.

Carefully.

Then he personally called the city's Taxi and Limousine Commission and asked if a trip sheet had been filed by West Side Limo for a pickup at the Starlight Bar on St. Sebastian and Boyle around one A.M. on December twenty-sixth. "License plate would've been WU 3200," Grimes said, "I don't have the car number." The guy at T&L asked him to wait while he checked, and then came back on the line some five minutes later.

"I think I got what you want," he told Grimes. "But I don't have it as the Starlight Bar. I've got it as 1271 St. Sebastian."

"What time would that have been?"

"Ten past one."

"That'd be it. Who ordered the car?"

"Company named Wadsworth and Dodds. You need an address?"

"Please," Grimes said.

Which is how, within minutes of each other that Thursday afternoon, three people converged on the old landmark building off Headley Square.

One of them was Wiggy Wiggins himself.

The other two were Detectives Steve Carella and Ollie Weeks.

ACTUALLY, THEY RODE UP IN THE ELEVATOR TOGETHER.

Wiggy knew these two dudes were cops the minute they stepped into the car. He could smell cops from a hundred miles away. Even if he hadn't seen the butt of a nine-millimeter pistol showing under the fat one's jacket, he'd have spotted him for plainclothes. The other one, tall and slender, had Chinese eyes that didn't hide the look of awareness about him, as if he was expecting a crime to erupt around him any minute and was getting ready for it to happen. The fat one was saying that was the worse pastrami sandwich he'd ever had in his life. Half of it was on his jacket, from the looks of it, mustard stains on one of the lapels, ketchup stains on the other. Wiggy looked up at the ceiling.

The elevator operator was a pimply-faced white kid wearing a brown uniform with gold braid. "Fourth floor," he said, as the elevator ground to a halt. He slid open the door and looked over his shoulder at all three of them. The two cops—Wiggy was sure they were—stepped out into a large waiting room with framed posters of books lining the walls. Wiggy hesitated.

"Sir?" the elevator operator said. "This is the fourth floor."

In the next ten seconds, Wiggy did some quick calculations. Two blondes had forced him to give up the money he'd taken from Frank Holt before he'd shot him dead and stuffed him in a garbage can. Now two cops were here at the place that had hired the limo for the two blondes. Was it possible the cops were also looking for the blondes? If so, how long would it be before they linked Wiggy himself to the murder of Frank Holt?

"I think I made a mistake here," he said to the elevator operator.

"Hi, Charmaine," the fat cop said to the fat broad behind the reception desk.

"Take me back to the lobby," Wiggy said.

The elevator operator shrugged and started to pull the door shut.

The tall, slender cop turned and took a look at Wiggy just as the closing door blocked him from view.

**THE MAN WHO INTRODUCED HIMSELF AS THE PUBLISHER** here at Wadsworth and Dodds was wearing a brown suit, darker brown shoes, a corn-colored shirt, and a green bow tie sprinkled with gold polka dots. He had snow white hair, and he told Carella his name was Richard Halloway. He remembered Ollie as Detective *Watts,* a misapprehension Ollie quickly corrected.

"It's *Weeks,* sir," he said. "Detective Oliver *Weeks.*"

"Yes, of course, how stupid of me," Halloway said. "Sit down, gentlemen, please. Some coffee?"

"I could use a cup," Ollie said.

"Detective Carella?"

"Yes, please."

Halloway lifted the receiver on his phone, pressed a button on the base, and asked someone to bring in some coffee. He put down the receiver, turned to the detectives, smiled, and said, "So. What brings you back here, Detective Weeks?"

"We're still trying to figure out what Jerry Hoskins was doing up in Diamondback on December twenty-third," Ollie said. "According to his customers, he wasn't there to see any of them."

"It is peculiar, isn't it?" Halloway said.

"A couple of the booksellers seemed surprised you had sales reps at all," Carella said.

"Oh? Did they?"

"Seemed to think a firm this size might do better with a distributor."

"We've considered that, of course. But then we wouldn't get the personal service we now enjoy."

"Five sales reps altogether," Carella said.

"Yes."

"One of them in Texas, is that right?"

Before Halloway could answer, a knock sounded on the door, and the receptionist came in with a tray on which there was a pot of coffee, three cups and saucers, a pitcher of milk, and a bowl containing an assortment of white, pink, and blue packets.

"Ah, thank you, Charmaine," Halloway said.

Charmaine put the tray down on the coffee table in front of the sofa.

"You wouldn't have any cookies or anything, would you, Charmaine?" Ollie asked.

"Well . . . uh . . ."

"See if we have any cookies," Halloway said.

"Yes, sir," she said, and went out.

Ollie was already pouring.

"How do you take this?" he asked.

"Black for me," Halloway said.

"A little milk, one sugar," Carella said.

He was watching Halloway. A good three or four minutes had passed since he'd asked about the sales rep in Texas, more than enough time for Halloway to frame an answer. Halloway seemed to be engrossed in Ollie's short order technique. Ollie was opening a packet of sugar now, pouring it into Carella's cup. He handed it to him, and then carried Halloway's black coffee to the desk. Charmaine came in with a platter of Fig Newtons, just as Ollie sat on the couch beside Carella again.

"Thank you, Charmaine," he said.

Charmaine smiled at him and went out.

"Your rep in Texas," Carella said.

"Yes."

"He lives in Eagle Branch, is that right?"

"Yes, Eagle Branch."

"You listed his name as Randolph Biggs . . ."

"Yes, that's his name."

"Would this be a side job for him?"

"A side job?"

"A second job. He wouldn't have another job, would he?"

"Not that I know of. Another job? No. Why would he have another job? Working for us keeps him busy enough, I'm sure."

"He wouldn't be a Texas Ranger, would he?"

Halloway burst out laughing.

"Forgive me," he said, "a Texas *Ranger?* I hardly think so."

"Have you ever met him?"

"Of course I've met him."

"Did Jerry Hoskins know him?" Ollie asked.

"Yes, I'm sure they knew each other. I'm sure they were at sales conferences together."

"Twice a year, is that right?" Carella asked.

"Yes. In the spring and the fall."

"Would they have seen each other this year?"

"I feel certain."

"This spring? This fall?"

"Yes, I'm sure."

"Where, Mr. Halloway?"

"Why, here. We had both conferences at the Century Hotel."

"You didn't have your conferences in Texas, did you?"

"No."

"Eagle Branch, Texas?"

"No."

"So they couldn't have met down there, could they?"

"Hardly."

"When's the last time you yourself saw Mr. Biggs?"

"When he was up here in September. For our last sales conference."

"Do you talk to him often?"

"Every now and then."

"Will you be talking to him anytime soon?"

"I would imagine."

"Tell him we were asking for him, will you?"

"I'll be sure to."

There seemed nothing further to say.

Carella was wondering if they had enough on Biggs to justify an arrest warrant and extradition from Texas. Ollie was thinking he would like to ask this little white-haired son of a bitch if he knew that Biggs had introduced Cassandra Ridley to his friend Frank Holt, who'd paid her two hundred thousand dollars to fly dope up from Mexico. He wanted to ask him if maybe Biggs had a *third* job besides sales rep and Texas Ranger, and could that third job possibly be smuggling drugs? He wanted to suggest that if one of Halloway's sales reps was fucking with drugs down in Mexico then maybe *another* of his reps was doing the same thing up in Diamondback, which was maybe what had got him killed. Ollie wanted to scare the shit out of Halloway, was what he wanted. Sometimes, if you scared them hard enough, they jumped the wrong way.

The silence lengthened.

"Well," Carella said, "thanks for your time. We appreciate it."

"*And* the delightful repast," Ollie said, and stuffed some Fig Newtons into his jacket pocket.

They were walking out of the Headley Building, toward the square across the street with its statue of William George Douglas Rae, the gentleman scholar who had captivated the heart of the city with his grace, his charm, and his sparkling wit, when Ollie said, "What do you think? Is the flyboy's word enough for an arrest warrant?"

"What flyboy?"

"Cass Ridley's brother in Germany."

"Depends on what judge we get."

"You think Halloway's in on this?"

"In on what?"

"On whatever the fuck it *is.*"

"If he is, we've got him thinking."

"We shoulda scared him more."

"I think we scared him enough," Carella said.

But Halloway's bad day was just beginning.

THE DETECTIVES DIDN'T NOTICE WALTER WIGGINS CROSS the street and head toward the Headley Building the moment he spotted them coming out onto the sidewalk. Nor did they notice the two Hispanic-looking men who crossed the little park in the square and walked toward the building, reaching it at just about the same time Wiggy did. The two men were Francisco Octavio Ortiz and Cesar Villada, and they had just arrived from Mexico this morning.

They got into the elevator with Wiggy, and all three men told the operator they wanted the fourth floor. The two Mexicans gave Wiggy a glance and then turned away. To Wiggy, they looked like spic hit men. He was beginning to regret having come here altogether. First two bulls in the elevator and now two big hitters. "Fourth floor," the elevator operator said, and yanked open the door. Wiggy was looking out at the same reception room he'd seen half an hour ago, same fat white chick behind the desk. The two Latinos stepped out of the elevator ahead of him, no fuckin manners. They walked to the desk, Wiggy right behind them.

"We're looking for a man who works here named Jerome Hoskins," one of them said.

It came out, "We lookin for a man worrs here name Jerr-o Hosk."

"Frank Holt," the other one said.

The last name came out "Hote."

Which was clear enough to Wiggy, who all at once began

to think these two Spanish-American gentlemen were not two hitters but were instead two detectives from the Eight-Eight, investigating the murder of Frank Holt. He almost bolted for the elevator.

"I can't understand what you're saying," the receptionist said, squinting.

"What's *your* name?" the first man asked.

He made it sound like a threat, even though it came out with a Spanish accent as thick as guacamole.

"Charmaine," she said.

"You know a man name Randoff Beegs?" he said. "In Texas?"

"Eagle Branch," the other one said.

Wiggy was trying to remember if Frank Holt had told him he'd come up from Eagle Branch, Texas. All he could recall was him saying the hundred keys of cocaine had come up from Guenerando, Mexico. He wondered now if Guenerando was anywhere near Eagle Branch. He tried to appear as if he was not listening to the conversation between these two possible dicks and the fat chick behind the desk, but he was standing only three feet behind them, and it was impossible to appear small and insignificant when he weighed two hundred and ten pounds and stood an even six feet tall. He wondered if he should go sit on the bench against the wall, but then he'd miss this fascinating conversation about the man he'd shot in the head. So he stood where he was and pretended not to be eavesdropping. He would have whistled to show how nonchalant he was, but he thought that might only attract attention to him.

"What was that name again?" Charmaine asked. "In Texas?"

"Randolph Biggs," the first man said.

It still came out "Randoff Beegs."

"Oh. Yes," she said, decoding the accent at last. "Let me see if our sales manager is free." She lifted the receiver on her phone, pressed a button in its base, asked, "Whom shall I say is here?" and raised her eyes expectantly.

"Francisco Ortiz," one of the men said.

"Cesar Villada," the other one said.

Wiggy noticed that they did not flash gold badges or identify themselves as detectives. Maybe they were associated with Mr. Holt in some other way. Maybe they were from Eagle Branch, Texas. Maybe they were good old buddies of Frank Holt's, here to inquire how come he was now dead. In which case, Wiggy *still* felt he ought to get out of here fast.

"Miss Andersen," Charmaine said, "there are two gentlemen here inquiring about Mr. Biggs." She listened, nodded, looked up at the two men again. "May I say what firm you're with?" she asked.

"Villada and Ortiz," Ortiz said.

"Villada and Ortiz," Charmaine said. She listened again. "Is that a bookstore?" she asked.

"Yes, it's a bookstore," Villada said.

"In Eagle Branch," Ortiz said. "Texas," he said. "Villada and Ortiz, Booksellers."

Charmaine relayed the information, listened again, put the phone receiver back on its cradle, rose, and said, "I'll show you in." She turned to Wiggy as she came around the desk, said, "I'll be with you in a moment, sir, won't you have a seat?" and walked off with the two men Wiggy now knew owned a bookstore in Eagle Branch, Texas, which sounded like total bullshit to him.

He went over to the wall on the left of the elevator doors,

and sat on the bench there. He looked around the room at the posters hanging on the walls. He'd never heard of any of the books. In a minute or so, Charmaine came back. Instead of going to her desk, though, she walked over to where he was waiting, and sat beside him on the bench.

"So," she said, and smiled. "How can I help you, sir?"

"On Christmas night," Wiggy said, "somebody up here phoned for a limo. I want to talk to whoever that might've been."

"That's very fanciful," Charmaine said, and smiled coquettishly. "Are you a writer?"

"No, I'm a drug dealer," Wiggy said, and grinned like a shark.

"I'll bet," Charmaine said.

"I run a posse up in Diamondback," he said.

"Oh, sure," she said.

"Who do I talk to about this limo was called for?"

"If *anyone* called for a limo, it would've been Douglas Good, our publicity director. But no one was here on Christmas night. We closed on Christmas Eve at three in the afternoon, and didn't open again till the following Tuesday. But I'll see if Mr. Good will talk to you."

"Just tell him Mr. *Bad* is here," Wiggy said, and grinned again.

KAREN ANDERSEN WAS TELLING THE TWO MEXICANS THAT Randolph Biggs did indeed work for them, and so had Jerry Hoskins. But she hadn't seen Randy since their sales conference in September, and Jerry had been the victim of a fatal shooting on Christmas Eve. Was there anything *she* could do for the gentlemen?

The gentlemen explained to her—in halting English

which she nonetheless understood—that Jerry Hoskins, who until recently they had known only as Frank Holt, had purchased from them a hundred keys of excellent cocaine . . .

"I beg your pardon," Karen said, looking astonished.

. . . for which they had been paid in hundred-dollar bills . . .

"Gentlemen, I'm sorry," she said, "but . . ."

"Yes, we're sorry, too," Villada said.

"Because the money was bad," Ortiz said.

DOUGLAS GOOD WAS A BLACK MAN WHO DID NOT appreciate brothers who looked or sounded like Walter Wiggins.

"Two girls named Sheryl and Toni," Wiggins was telling him.

"Yes?" Douglas said.

"West Side Limo," Wiggins said. "The Starlight Bar."

"Mr. Wiggins . . ."

"Somebody here called a limo from West Side to take two girls named Sheryl and Toni uptown to a bar named the Starlight on St. Sab's and Boyle on Christmas night," Wiggins said. "St. Sebastian's," he explained.

"Somebody from Wadsworth and *Dodds* called a limo . . ."

"Is the information I have."

". . . for two girls named Sheryl and Toni?"

"That's they names. The ladies owe me some money, bro."

Douglas didn't like black men who looked or sounded like Walter Wiggins to call him "bro."

"Mr. Wiggins," he said, "we don't have any women named Sheryl and Toni working for us."

"Two very tall blond ladies," Wiggins said.

"I'm sorry."

"This was a limo from West Side," Wiggins explained again, patiently. "Black Lincoln Town Car with a chauffeur same color as the car. The blonde named Toni was sittin in it, and she picked up me and the blonde named Sheryl outside the Starlight and drove me to my office on Decatur Av, where they relieved me of a certain amount of money, at gun point, on Christmas night."

"No one was here on Christmas night," Douglas said.

"The Taxi and Limousine Commission seems to believe otherwise, bro."

"The Taxi and Limousine Commission made a mistake," Douglas said.

"I don't think so," Wiggins said.

"Let me ask Mr. Halloway to come in," Douglas said.

"Who's Mr. Halloway?"

"Our publisher."

He went to the desk phone, picked up the receiver, and hit Halloway's extension button.

"Halloway."

"Richard, it's Douglas."

"Yes, Douglas."

"I have a man with me who thinks we sent a limo up to Diamondback on Christmas night. His name is Walter Wiggins."

"He should've left well enough alone," Halloway said.

"I thought you might like to meet him."

"I'll be right in," Halloway said.

Douglas put the receiver back on the cradle, smiled at Wiggins, and said, "He's on his way."

*

**KAREN ANDERSEN WAS STILL TRYING TO BLUFF HER WAY** out of this.

"Bad money?" she said.

"Counterfeit," Ortiz said. "We wass paid with queer money."

"One million seven hun'red t'ousan dollars of it," Villada said.

Karen smiled.

"We don't think it's so funny, Miss," Ortiz said.

"In any case," Karen said, "Jerry Hoskins is dead."

"In any case," Ortiz said, "so is Randolph Biggs."

Karen looked at them.

"He met with an electrical accident in Piedras Rosas, Mexico," Villada said, and nodded.

"We want our money," Ortiz said.

"Gentlemen, I have absolutely *no* idea what you're talking about," Karen said.

"We are talking about one million seven hun'red t'ousan dollars two people who worr for you company focked us out of in Mehico," Villada said.

Or something like that.

Which Karen Andersen all at once understood clearly because Ortiz suddenly seemed to be holding a gun in his hand.

**DOUGLAS GOOD DIDN'T WANT TO SAY ANYTHING FURTHER** to Mr. Wiggins here until Halloway joined them. Wiggins had obviously done a little research, first locating West Side's name and next tracing them back to the offices here. Douglas figured the man was here to get his money back, which wasn't his money at all since he should have paid it to Jerry Hoskins after the cocaine had been turned over. Wiggins's oversight had resulted in a visit from "The Weird Sisters," as Sheryl and Toni were affectionately called even though they were not related. W&D's oversight—or rather Halloway's—had been in not dispatching the man the moment the money was in their hands. Halloway had ruled out such an action, partially because he had no real evidence that Wiggins had been responsible for the murder of one of their best people, secondly because black-white relationships were touchy enough in Diamondback without giving the drug people up there a reason to distrust future commerce with Whitey. In any case, Wiggins should have left well enough alone. Instead, here he was, the fool.

"You know why I'm here, don't you?" Wiggins asked, and smiled wisely.

"I have no idea," Douglas said.

"No, huh? Then why'd you ax your boss to come in?"

Douglas had called Halloway because he was the only person sanctioned to order Wiggins's death—as he should have done on Christmas night. If Wiggins had anything incriminating to say, he wanted Halloway to hear it first hand. So that maybe he'd give the goddamn correct orders this time around.

"I'm here for my money," Wiggins said.

Big surprise, Douglas thought, and Halloway walked in without knocking. "Hello, Mr. Wiggins," he said, extending his hand. "Nice to meet you." The men shook hands. Their eyes met. Douglas figured Wiggins should have known in that single meeting of eyes that he was a dead man. But maybe he was stupid.

"Are you authorized to make a payout?" he asked Halloway. "Cause what I need fum you is one million nine hundred thousand dollars in cash."

IN ALL HER YEARS WITH W&D, KAREN ANDERSEN HAD never before looked down the barrel of a gun or into the eyes of a person who would have no qualms about pulling the trigger of that gun. She wondered briefly what Halloway would do in similar circumstances. She had seen him perform admirably in comparably challenging situations, but those had been when they were in bed together, and always during the window of opportunity Viagra presented. She was surprised now to discover that she was not at all frightened. Calmly, coolly, she said, "Please don't force me to call the police."

Villada laughed.

Karen reached for the phone on her desk, intending not to call the police but to summon Halloway for help. Ortiz slammed the butt of his revolver down on her hand. She pulled it back, winced, held the throbbing fingers to her breasts. Her lip was quivering, but she did not scream.

"We'll be back," Ortiz said. There was blood on the butt of the pistol. He yanked a tissue from the box on Karen's desk, wiped the butt clean, and tossed the stained tissue into an ashtray. "Get the fockin money," he said. *"Real* money this time, *comprende?"*

"Or we'll kill every fockin one of you who works here," Villada said.

Not if we kill you first, Karen thought.

"I HAVE NO IDEA WHAT MONEY YOU MEAN," HALLOWAY said.

"The money your two blond ladies took from me," Wiggins said.

"I don't know which ladies you mean."

"Sheryl and Toni. With the long legs and the AK-47."

"We have no such employees. Mr. Wiggins," Halloway said, slowly and distinctly, "you are making a terrible mistake here."

Their eyes met again.

This time Wiggins read the meaning in them.

Which was perhaps why he drew a pistol from a holster under his jacket. He pointed the gun first at Halloway, and then swung it around toward Douglas, as if to emphasize that his enmity was large enough to include both of them. The gun looked like a snub-nosed .38. Douglas didn't think the man was foolish enough to kill them here in their own offices, especially since he was here to negotiate the return of money he felt was his. But who knew with these street thugs?

Halloway had been in hairier situations than this one. Not for nothing was he in charge here. He looked at the gun in Wiggins' hand, and then raised his eyes to meet Wiggins' again. His eyes seemed to say *This is only about money, friend. Do you really want to die for it?* But would Wiggins have pulled a gun on them if he didn't realize he was already a dead man?

"You don't want to do this," Halloway said.

"I've done it before," Wiggins said.

"Not with the consequences this would bring."

Douglas knew this was bullshit. If Wiggins had in fact killed Jerry Hoskins, there had been no consequences at all. Wiggins must have realized this, too. He had blown one of them away, and the only thing that had happened was The Weird Sisters coming to call. Douglas wondered if, in retrospect, Halloway was thinking he should have given the termination order back then on Christmas night. A bit late now, though.

"Tell you what," Wiggins said. "I realize you don't have that kind of money juss layin aroun in cash. But go get it, okay? I'll come see you sometime soon," he said, and backed away toward the door.

Sometime soon, you'll be dead, Douglas thought. Bro.

Wiggins stepped out into the hallway.

THE THREE MEN REACHED THE ELEVATOR AT ABOUT THE same time. One of the two Mexicans pressed the bell button set in the wall.

"How'd it go?" Wiggy asked them.

"Fockin people still owe us money," Ortiz said.

Which was how a rather strange triumvirate was founded.

IT WAS STILL THURSDAY ON WHAT WAS SHAPING UP TO be the longest day of the year, never mind what the almanac said. Sitting at his desk at a quarter to five that evening, the squadroom almost deserted, Carella tried to make some sense of this bewildering case that seemed to focus entirely on money, real or largely imagined. The *imagined* cash appeared to originate in Iran, where billions of dollars in so-called super-bills were being printed on intaglio presses with plates provided by the good old U.S. of A., talk about payback time.

Carella knew some things for certain. The rest he could only guess at. He knew that Cass Ridley had made four trips to Mexico with a certain amount of money she'd exchanged for some kind of controlled substance, and had been paid $200,000 in cash for her efforts. This money was real, if the lady at First Federal could be trusted, whatever her name was. But Cass Ridley had also been given a ten-grand tip by the pair of Mexicans involved in the transaction, whoever *they* were, and *that* money was fake. Poor Will Struthers, trying to spend the cash he'd pilfered, had twice been nailed passing phony hundreds. According to the lady at First Federal, Antonia Lugosi or something, twenty billion dollars in counterfeit hundreds were floating around out there, enough bogus bills to concern the Treasury Department, who had relieved Struthers of the phonies he'd stolen and given him real cash in exchange—but that was only a guess. Belandres! Antonia *Belandres!* Hence the Lugosi association, for *Bela* Lugosi, the best Dracula there ever was, the mind worked in curious ways its wonders to reveal.

Carella wished with all his heart that this case would reveal itself as clearly to him as Lucy's throat had been revealed to the count all those years back when Carella first saw the black-and-white film on television, the count's head descending, his lips drawing back, the fangs bared, Carella had almost wet his pants.

The money in Jerry Hoskins' wallet was real, too. No question about that, the Federal Reserve had run it through their machines, the hundred-dollar bills were genuine. But Jerry Hoskins had worked for Wadsworth and Dodds, and the man who'd set up the flying arrangement with Cass Ridley also worked for W&D, though there seemed to be some confusion about whether or not Randolph Biggs was *also* a Texas Ranger, which Carella sincerely doubted—but that, too, was a guess.

Lots of guesswork here, no hard facts.

He wondered what time it was in Texas.

He looked up at the wall clock, opened the bottom drawer of his desk, took out his massive directory of law enforcement agencies, found a listing for the Texas Department of Public Safety headquarters in Austin, figured somebody would be there no matter *what* time it was, and dialed the number. He told the woman who answered the phone what he was looking for, was connected to a sergeant named Dewayne Ralston, repeated everything again, and was asked to "Hang on, Detective." He hung on. Some five minutes later, Ralston came back onto the line.

"Nobody in the Ranger Division named Randolph Biggs," he said. "You landed yourself an imposter, Detective."

"While I've got you on the line," Carella said, "could you check for a criminal record?"

"Don't go away," Ralston said.

Carella didn't go away. Across the room, he could see Kling at his desk, hunched over a computer. Cotton Hawes was just coming through the railing that divided the squadroom from the corridor outside. Telephones were ringing. In one corner of the room, the squad's meager Christmas tree blinked holiday cheer to the street outside. From the Clerical Office down the hall, he could smell the aroma of coffee brewing. This was a very familiar place to him. He felt suddenly sad and could not have explained why.

"You still there?" Ralston asked.

"Still here."

"No record on a Randolph Biggs, B-I-G-G-S. But if this is the same dude, he turned up dead in Piedras Rosas two days ago. Found him floating in a tub of water with a plugged-in cattle prod. Death by electrocution. Apparent suicide."

"That makes two," Carella said.

"Pardon?"

"One of his colleagues was murdered up here on Christmas Eve."

"Looks like you got your hands full," Ralston said.

"Looks that way," Carella said.

THE PHONE ON OLLIE WEEKS' DESK RANG SOME FIVE minutes later.

"Weeks," he said.

"You handlin that murder happened last week?" a man's voice asked.

"Which murder would that be?" Ollie asked.

Up here in the Eight-Eight, there were 10,247 murders every day of the year.

"The newspaper said he was Jerry Hoskins," the man said. "To me, he was Frank Holt."

"Who's this?" Ollie asked at once.

"Nev' mine who's this," the man said. "I know who killed him."

Ollie pulled a pad into place.

"Tell me your name," he said.

"Is they a reward?"

"Maybe. I can't deal with you unless you tell me your name."

"Tito Gomez," the man said.

"Can you come up here in half an hour?"

"I rather meet you someplace else."

"Sure. Where?"

"The Eight' Street footpath into Grover. Fourth bench in."

Ollie looked up at the wall clock.

"Make it a quarter to six," he said.

"See you," Tito said, and hung up.

Ollie hit the files.

**IT DID NOT TAKE WIGGY AND THE TWO MEXICANS** long to discover that what they had in common was a hundred keys of cocaine. It also appeared they had each been stiffed by a company that purported to publish books, but which instead seemed to be involved in the transport and sale of controlled substances. They did not yet know they were fucking with something much bigger here. For the time being their shared grievances were enough to provide motivation for what they planned to do sometime tomorrow.

They were discussing all this over beers in a bar on Grover Avenue, not too distant from Grover Park, where Ollie and Gomez would be meeting twenty minutes from now. In many ways, the big bad city was just a small town.

"I can't get over these people payin you queer money for your goods," Wiggy was saying. "Which by the way was very high quality shit, I have to tell you."

*"Gracias, señor,"* Ortiz said, pride of product glowing in his eyes.

"Which is a shame," Wiggy said, "them stiffing you that way. But I have to tell you the money *I* paid *them* was hundred-percent genuine American currency, and I want it back cause they sent two blondes to take it away from me."

This was not entirely true. Wiggy had never paid a single penny to Hoskins or Holt or whoever he was. He had shot him in the head instead.

"They stole *your* money, too?" Ortiz asked incredulously.

"For damn sure."

Neither was this entirely true. They had, in fact, taken the money from his safe, but this was not stealing from him. This was collecting money rightfully owed them for the hundred keys of cocaine they'd delivered as promised.

"So they are stealing from *all* of us," Villada said.

"Basic thieves is what they are," Wiggy said.

"Like us," Ortiz said, and all three men burst out laughing.

"So what we're gonna do tomorrow . . ." Wiggy said.

**AT FIRST, IT LOOKED AS IF THERE WAS NOTHING ON HIM** but a marijuana violation two years ago. But at the time of the bust, Tito Gomez—whose street name was Tigo—had worked for a place named King Auto Body, and this rang a bell with Ollie. So he cross-checked the files and lo and behold, there it was. A massive conspiracy arrest some six months back. Ollie went to his desk and phoned Carella.

"Steve," he said, "I got a call from somebody says he knows who killed Hoskins. I'm meeting him in Grover Park ten minutes from now. You want to join us?"

"Where in Grover?" Carella asked.

**"WE GO UP THERE TOGETHER," WIGGY SAID. "WE TELL** them give us the fuckin money you owe us or you all dead men. Your million-seven. My million-nine."

Nobody owed Wiggy anything. But he already believed himself the true owner of the million-nine the blondes had taken in rightful payment for the drugs he'd purchased.

"Fockin crooks," Villada said, shaking his head.

Ortiz was shaking his head, too. But only because he didn't like the plan. His reasoning was simple. Threats and warnings were one thing. Reality was another. In his broken English, he explained that between yesterday and today, nobody up at Wadsworth and Dodds could have gathered together the million-seven his partner had demanded, much less the million-nine their new associate was seeking. That came to a total of three-million-six . . .

"Which ees a ho lot of money," Ortiz explained.

Wiggy was thinking there was once a time in his life when two dollars for a water pistol seemed like a whole lot of money.

TITO GOMEZ WAS SITTING ON THE FOURTH BENCH INTO the park when Carella got there at ten minutes to six that Thursday night. The two seemed to be hitting it off extremely well. Gomez was smoking a cigarette and listening to Ollie intently as he concluded what was apparently a joke because Gomez burst out laughing just as Carella approached.

"Hey, Steve!" Ollie called. "You know the one about the guy who puts a condom on his piano?"

"Yes," Carella said.

He sat on the bench beside Gomez, the two detectives flanking him like mismatched bookends. "This the man you were telling me about?" he asked Ollie.

"This is him," Ollie said. "Tito Gomez. Otherwise known as Tigo. Meet Detective Carella, Tigo."

Tigo nodded.

"So I understand you want to talk to us about something," Carella said.

"Yeah, but I ain't got all day here. You got any more detectives you need to call?" he asked Ollie.

"No, this is all of us," Ollie said affably. "He says he

knows who killed Jerry Hoskins, ain't that interesting? He wants to know if there's a reward."

"We can maybe come up with a little something," Carella said.

"What do you mean *maybe?"*

"We can talk to the commissioner, see what this case means to him."

He was thinking with counterfeit super-bills somehow involved, the commissioner might be able to come up with a little something.

"What I have in mind is fifty thousand dollars," Tigo said.

"That's a lot of money, Tigo."

"But that's what makes the world go round, no?" Tigo said, and grinned. "Money, money, money."

"Well, that all depends on the value of the information you have for us, eh, *amigo?"* Ollie said, still affably.

Tigo didn't like to be called *"amigo."* His father was from Puerto Rico, true enough, but his mother was black, and he was proud of his heritage on her side of the family. As pleasantly as he could—these were, after all, cops he was dealing with—he said, "I don't speak Spanish, *amigo,"* which was a lie, but which seemed to make his point.

"Oh, sorry," Ollie said, "I didn't realize. So tell us why you wanted to see us."

"There was this buy on Decatur Av?" Tigo said, making it sound like a question. "Guy runs a posse from a crib on the whole second floor there, knocked out the walls of three apartments? He brings up dope from Mexico, Colombia, Peru, sells it in ten-kilo lots for forty, fifty a pop, whatever the traffic will bear. I've been workin for him almost two years now, you'd think he'd start talkin bout makin me a partner, but no. He's still got me on salary . . ."

So that's why he's ratting him out, Carella thought.

". . . treats me like a fuckin courier, don't get me started. I used to make more money driving the truck. I used to drive a tow truck for this auto body shop on Mason."

"What's this guy's name?" Carella said.

"First tell me how much the commissioner's gonna okay on this," Tigo said.

"Well, we haven't talked to him yet," Ollie said affably. "We have to *go* to him with something, you see. We tell him there's this guy *maybe* has information, he'll say go take a walk, fellas."

"Can you at least tell us when this buy went down?" Carella asked.

"Sure," Tigo said. "Four, five days ago."

"When exactly?"

"What's today?"

"The twenty-eighth."

"So it must've been . . . let me see." He began counting back on his fingers. "Last Saturday night? When was that? Christmas Eve?"

"No, the twenty-third," Ollie said.

"So that's when it was. Like I said. Four, five days ago."

"Where?" Carella asked.

"I told you, this crib on Decatur. It's these three apartments, this person we're talking about knocked out the . . ."

"What's the address?"

"1280 Decatur."

"Were you there when the buy went down?"

"Yeah. This dude was waitin in the front room while we tested the shit. He was supposed to get a mill-nine for the hundred keys."

"What was his name?"

"Frank Holt. But his picture in the paper said he was Jerry Hoskins. The same guy, right?"

"The same guy," Carella said. "Tell us what happened."

"This is where the bus stops," Tigo said. "Go talk to the commissioner."

"Suppose we go to 1280 Decatur instead, talk to whoever's got the second floor there, tell him his trusted employee just ratted him out?" Carella said.

"Now, now, Steve," Ollie said affably. "The man hasn't ratted out anyone yet, have you, Tigo?"

"Not till I see the green."

"You just told us you participated in a drug deal, do you realize that?" Carella said. He was thinking this was an odd reversal of roles, him playing Bad Cop to Ollie's Good.

"Gee, did I?" Tigo said. "Are you wired, Detective? If not, who's your witness? Another cop? A bullshit bust, and you know it."

"I can tell you right now, nobody's giving you fifty thousand dollars so we can nail a two-bit drug dealer in Diamondback."

"Even if it's murder?"

"Even if he raped the Mayor's mother."

"How much *are* you prepared to give me?"

Sounding like a fucking lawyer all at once.

"You tell us you witnessed a murder, you give us all the details, you agree to testify at trial, we can maybe scrape up two or three . . ."

"Goodbye, gentlemen," Tigo said, and got off the bench.

"Sit down, punk," Ollie said.

Tigo looked surprised.

"I *said* sit the fuck *down.*"

Tigo sat.

"Let me tell you what you're gonna do for us," Ollie said.

"OKAY, I GOT A BETTER IDEA," WIGGY WAS TELLING THE two Mexicans. "We go in heavy, all three of us. Semi-automatics under our overcoats. We hold the mother-fuckers hostage."

Villada looked at Ortiz.

"We go in early tomorrow morning. They got the whole fourth floor, ain't nobody but us gonna know we're in there holdin guns on them. We stay there till they come up with the cash."

"The banks will be closed till Tuesday," Ortiz said.

"It's the long weekend," Villada said, nodding agreement.

"Man, they stole a mill-nine from me, you think they put that in a *bank?* These people are thieves, man. They got that money *stashed* someplace, is what. All we got to do is ask that white-haired fuck to take us to wherever it is."

"What about *our* money?" Ortiz asked.

"We'll get that, too, don't worry," Wiggy said. "One thing I know for sure, you stick a piece in some dude's face, he's gonna give you every fuckin nickel he has."

Actually, Wiggy didn't give a rat's ass about their money. Far as he was concerned, they could eat tacos and beans the rest of they fuckin lives. All he needed them for was the extra muscle they brought to the gig. He was already figuring they would be the ones who stayed behind to watch the others while him and Halloway went to retrieve the money that was rightfully his.

Ortiz was ahead of him.

"Who goes for the money?" he asked.

"Halloway. Their boss."

"Who goes *with* him?"

"Any one of us," Wiggy said.

"I think it should be either me or Cesar," Ortiz said.

"Sure, whoever," Wiggy said, and grinned.

TIGO SAID NO, HE WOULD NOT GO IN WITH NO WIRE on him.

Ollie said either he wore the wire or they would bust his ass for the Fire Lane Scam.

"What the fuck is the Fire Lane Scam?" Tigo asked.

"You drove the tow truck, remember?" Ollie said affably. In fact, he was actually smiling.

"What's the Fire Lane Scam?" Carella asked.

"What I done when Tigo called me," Ollie said, "was see what we had on him in the files. Aside from a bullshit marijuana violation two years ago . . ."

"I was acquitted."

"I told you. Bullshit. In fact, I was just about to tell Detective Carella here that there didn't seem to be anything else on you. So I figured you were clean."

"I am."

"Except for participating in a drug deal last Saturday night," Carella said.

"You got only my word for that," Tigo said, making a joke. In fact, he grinned at them as if expecting them to laugh.

Ollie didn't laugh, but he grinned back.

"Your record said you were employed by King Auto Body when you were busted for the weed," Ollie said. "So I cross-checked and found out why that name sounded familiar. I found a big, big arrest six months ago, Tigo. The

Fire Lane Scam. For which Joey King—no relation to Larry—is doing a five-and-dime at Castleview. You know what I'm talking about now, Tigo?"

"No, I don't."

"You were driving a tow truck for him, right?"

"That's right. I went out on calls for dead batteries, flat tires, lockouts, like that."

"You also went out on calls for Berry Appliances, who were in on the scam with Joey."

"I never heard of anything called Berry Appliances."

"George and Michael Berry," Ollie said. "They used to sell washing machines, refrigerators, stoves, all that shit. A shop on Twelfth and Moore, you remember it?"

"No."

"Had a little alley running alongside the shop, remember the alley?"

"No."

"What it was," Ollie explained to Carella, "George Berry went to the Fire Department and greased a few palms—they all went down together, by the way. Joey King, George and his brother, and the two Fire Department assholes who signed papers declaring the alley a so-called fire lane. They're all exercising in the yard upstate."

"Ho-hum," Tigo said.

"Yeah, ho-hum," Ollie said, and turned back to Carella again. "What it was, George and his brother posted these signs on the walls of the alley saying it was a fire lane, and you couldn't park there, or your car would be towed if you did. Guy comes back, finds his car towed, he reads the small print on the bottom of the sign, it tells him he can recover the car at King's Auto Body Shop on Mason Avenue. What Tigo here did was make a sweep of the alley every few hours, tow any car parked there. There were always five, six cars in the alley, nobody paid any attention to the signs. Tigo picked up the cars, towed them over to King's. When the owner came to collect his car, Joey told him it would cost a hundred bucks to release it. You towed maybe twenty cars a night, didn't you, Tigo? People in this city have no fuckin respect for the law. 'No Parking' signs all over the alley, 'Fire Lane,' they just ignored them. A hundred bucks a car, that's two thousand bucks these guys were splitting every night of the week. That's like fourteen grand a week, how much do we make, Steve?"

"Not that much," Carella said.

"Not even in a good week," Ollie said. "I keep tellin you, we're in the wrong business."

"Where'd you get all this shit?" Tigo said, shaking his head as if in disbelief.

"It's all in the record. You were driving the tow truck. But you told the D.A. you were just a salaried employee who didn't know anything wrong was going on, and they believed you. You were just a kid, they had bigger fish to fry. But guess what Joey King told me?"

"You talked to *Joey?*"

"Yeah, gee, I did. I figured I might need insurance if you got all pissy on me. So I called Castleview just before I left the squadroom, had a nice little chat with him. He told me they were paying you twenty bucks for every car you brought in. Three, four hundred bucks a night. Something like two grand a week. You were in on the deal, Tigo."

"I was a salaried employee. Go look at my social security records."

"Salary *plus,* Tigo. You were part of a conspiracy. You should be up there at Castleview with them."

"But I ain't," Tigo said.

"Ah, but you could be. Joey seems to think early parole sounds very nice indeed."

Tigo looked at him.

"He's ready to rat you out, friend, ah yes."

"You're full of shit," Tigo said.

"Well, maybe so," Ollie said affably.

"Tigo," Carella said, "I think he's got us."

# 10.

CHARMAINE LOOKED UP WHEN THE THREE OF THEM CAME out of the elevator. The moment the doors closed behind them, guns came out from under their coats. She was reaching for a button on her desk when Wiggy said, "Don't, Fatso." This hurt. A moment later he slapped her across the face to let her know he was serious. This hurt even more. One of the Mexicans was already rushing down the long corridor flanked with posters of books nobody ever heard of. Wiggy went directly into Halloway's office.

He was hunched over his computer keyboard, his jacket draped over the back of his chair, his bow tie hanging unknotted and loose around his neck, the top button of his shirt unbuttoned, his sleeves rolled up. He jerked his head around the moment Wiggy burst into the room, and then immediately stabbed at one of the keys on the computer. Four key strokes would have allowed him to escape the program and the machine: the Windows key to the right of the space bar, the Up arrow, the Enter key, and the Enter key again. Once the computer was shut down, no one would be able to boot it again without the proper password. Halloway managed to hit the Windows key, and was about to tap the Up arrow when Wiggy said, "Don't, Whitey." Halloway hesitated. For a moment, it seemed he might complete the action, anyway. Just tap the remaining three keys, and shut down the computer, effectively locking it.

But the gun in Wiggy's hand was very big and rather ugly.

THERE WERE EIGHT EMPLOYEES ALTOGETHER, ALL of them seated around the long conference table now. Richard Halloway sat at the head of the table, as befitted his status as publisher. David Good from Publicity sat on his left, Karen Andersen from Sales on his right. There was an editor named Michael Garrity, and another editor named Henry Daggert. There was Charmaine, the fat receptionist, and someone named George Young from the stock room, and someone else named Betty Alweiss from the Art Department. Eight of them in all. They all looked frightened.

Wiggy and the two Mexicans leaned against three of the walls, weapons in their hands. Wiggy was holding a Cobray M11-9 he had purchased last night for five hundred dollars from a man named Little Nicholas in Diamondback. Villada and Ortiz were each carrying Mark XIX Desert Eagle pistols. The clock on the conference room wall read twenty minutes to ten. They had caught everyone by surprise, and now they were about to lay their demands on the table.

The Mexicans had decided to let Wiggy do all the talking. Ortiz had objected to this at first, on the grounds that his English was impeccable. Villada had convinced him at last. The men leaned against the walls nonchalantly. Their weapons—dangling casually in their hands—looked almost nonthreatening. The three of them figured they had nothing to worry about here with these bookish types. Little did they know.

"Now, this here's the story," Wiggy said. "Our grievance

is a mill-seven for my frens here, and a mill-nine for me. We don't know where you keep your stash, but one of you's gonna go with one of us to get the cash an' bring it back here. Then we'll all be on our way, and you alls can go home to enjoy the ress of the holiday. Do I make myself clear?"

"We don't have that kind of money," Halloway said.

"We're bettin you do," Wiggy said. "We're bettin you'll go get it before . . ."

He looked up at the clock.

"Before six o'clock tonight. That's eight hours from now, more or less. Cause for every hour we sit here without goin for the money, we're gonna hafta shoot one of you. Eight hours, eight people. By six o'clock, you all be dead less'n we has our money. Do I make myself clear now?"

The room was silent.

"I'll have to make some calls," Halloway said.

"We'll be listening," Wiggy said.

The Mexicans were smiling.

Wiggy figured he had made himself clear.

THE MEN OF THE 87TH DETECTIVE SQUAD COULDN'T seem to keep their minds on business at their weekly Friday-morning, think-tank meeting. Carella was trying to tell them what he and Ollie had learned from Tito "Tigo" Gomez. He was trying to tell them that if Tigo could be trusted, a dope dealer named Walter "Wiggy" Wiggins was responsible for the murder of Jerome "Jerry" Hoskins, alias Frank Holt . . .

"Was that in this precinct?" Lieutenant Byrnes asked.

"No, but the murdered woman was."

"What murdered woman?" Andy Parker asked.

He was dressed for undercover work today, which meant he hadn't shaved, and he was wearing jeans and a black turtleneck sweater and a brown leather jacket and motorcycle boots. He thought he looked like an upscale drug dealer. Actually, he looked like a slob.

"The woman who got eaten by lions," Meyer said.

"Ha-ha, very funny," Parker said.

"This happened a week ago, where have you been?" Brown said.

"She got stabbed with an ice pick first," Carella explained.

"What's Hoskins got to do with her?" Byrnes asked impatiently. He was thinking if any of this had happened in some other precinct, he'd be glad to get it off his plate.

"He paid her to pick up some dope in Mexico," Meyer said.

"Which he later sold to this Wiggy character," Carella said.

"Who paid *him* with a bullet in the head."

"Here in the Eight-Seven?"

"No, the Eight-Eight. Fat Ollie caught it."

"So let him keep it."

"He also caught one-fifth of the Ridley case."

"Who's Ridley?" Parker asked.

"The lady who got eaten by lions," Kling said.

"Ha-ha, very funny," Parker said.

"How can you catch one-fifth of a case?" Willis asked.

"Her leg," Meyer said.

"Am I supposed to be following this?" Parker asked.

"Nobody else is," Byrnes said. "Why should you be an exception?"

"The point is," Carella said, somewhat edgily, "we're sending Gomez in with a wire."

"Why?" Brown asked.

"Cause we've maybe got a line on the perp in a homicide."

"This Wiggy character?"

"Right. Who maybe killed Jerry Hoskins, who for sure hired Cass Ridley to go to Mexico for him."

"And *we* caught the Ridley case, is what you're saying."

"Four-fifths of her."

"Why's this so important, anyway?" Parker asked, and looked around the room, and shrugged, and said, "Don't anybody want a bagel?" and went to help himself from the tray on Byrnes' desk.

"There's funny money involved," Carella said.

"So let the Secret Service worry," Byrnes said.

"They *are* worrying," Carella said. "They grabbed eight grand in queer bills from a two-bit burglar and gave him real currency in return."

"The lunatics have taken over the asylum," Hawes said.

"I don't like complicated cases," Parker said.

"Neither do I," Byrnes said.

"Well, that's truly unfortunate," Carella said, "but I didn't ask to *catch* this one, either."

"What the hell's wrong with *you* this morning?" Parker asked.

"I'm trying to make some sense of this goddamn case, that's all, and you guys are . . ."

"Relax, okay? Have a bagel."

"There's dope involved here," Carella said, gathering steam, "and counterfeit money, and the Secret Service, and Christ knows what . . ."

"So let our new President handle it," Parker said.

"Sure."

"Our beloved flounder," Willis said.

"Let *him* ask the Secret Service what's going on here," Brown said.

"Sure."

"Next motorcade he's in," Hawes said, "he can wave out of his limo and ask them what they know about a lady got eaten by lions."

"Go on, Steve, have a bagel," Parker said.

"I don't want a bagel," Carella said.

"You know who woulda made a better President than the one we got now?" Hawes said.

"Who?" Kling asked.

"Martin Sheen."

"The guy on *The West Wing,* you're right!"

"He'd call the Secret Service on the carpet, tell them to quit handing out good money for bad."

"No, you know who'd do that? If he was President?" Willis said.

"Who?" Kling asked.

"Harrison Ford."

*"Air Force One!"*

"President James Marshall!"

"Oh, yeah!" Brown said. "He was maybe the *best* President we ever had. Remember what he said? 'Peace ain't merely the absence of conflict, but the presence of justice.' Man, that's fancy talking."

"Remember what the *bad* guy said?" Willis asked.

"Who cares what bad guys say?" Parker said, and took another bagel from the tray.

"He said, 'You murdered a hundred thousand Iraqis to save a nickel a gallon on gas. Don't lecture me on the rules of war.' *That's* fancy talking, man."

"That was Bush he was talking about," Kling said.

"No, that was President James Marshall," Willis said.

"Yeah, but that was *Bush* who started the Gulf War."

"You want to know who was an even *better* President than Harrison Ford?" Hawes said.

"Who?"

"Michael Douglas."

"Oh, *yeah.*"

"He was maybe the best President we ever had. You see that movie, Steve?"

"No," Carella said curtly.

"Have a bagel, sourpuss," Parker said.

*"The American President.* That was the movie. Michael Douglas was President Andrew Shepherd."

"You remember who his aide was?" Kling asked.

"No, who?"

"Martin Sheen! Who is now *President!"*

"President Josiah Bartlet!"

"President *Jed* Bartlet."

"What goes around, comes around."

"What's *his* aide's name?"

"Who cares?" Parker asked.

"He might be President one day."

"Fredric March was a good President, too," Byrnes suggested.

"Who's Fredric March?" Kling asked.

*"Seven Days in May."*

"Never heard of it."

"Or Henry Fonda," Byrnes said. "In *Fail-Safe."*

"That was the same movie, wasn't it?" Brown asked.

"It only *seemed* like the same movie," Hawes said.

"Who's Henry Fonda?" Kling asked.

"How about Kevin Kline?" Willis asked.

"Yes, he was a very good President," Meyer said solemnly.

"He was also this guy who *looked* like the President."

"Dave."

"That was the name of the movie. *Dave.*"

"It was also the name of the lookalike. Dave Kovic."

"Because the *real* President had a stroke while fucking his secretary. I saw that movie," Parker said. "This sexy broad."

"Yeah," Willis said, remembering.

"Yeah," Brown said, nodding.

They all had another bagel.

"But you know who was the *best* actor?" Meyer asked. "Who ever played the President?"

"Who?" Kling said.

"Ronald Reagan."

"Oh yes," Kling said.

"Yes," Hawes agreed.

"Unquestionably," Byrnes said.

What's the use? Carella thought, and took a bagel from the tray.

THE CALL FROM CARELLA'S SISTER CAME AT A LITTLE before ten that Friday morning. The surveillance equipment from the Tech Unit had already arrived. Across the room, Meyer Meyer was helping Fat Ollie Weeks tape the battery-powered recorder to Tito Gomez's chest.

"Who's gonna be on the other end of this?" Tigo asked.

"Nobody," Ollie said. "It ain't a transmitter, it's a recorder."

"Then who's gonna come save my ass if Wiggy tips?"

"Don't worry about it," Meyer said.

"I worry," Tigo said.

On the telephone, Angela was asking Carella if he could come to Mama's house tonight after work.

"Why?" Carella said.

"We want to talk to you."

"We're talking right now," Carella said.

"You're at work and so am I."

"What do you want to talk about?"

"We'll tell you when you get here."

"I'm working a homicide, I may not get out of here till late," he said.

"That's okay, we'll wait."

"What is it, Angela?"

"A surprise," she said.

"I'm a cop," he said. "I hate surprises."

"I'm leaving early today. Can you get to Riverhead by five?"

"Only if I'm out of here by four."

"Whenever," she said. "I'll see you later."

He put the receiver back on its base and walked across the room to where Tigo was complaining that the tapes were too tight.

"You don't want the gadget rattling around, do you?" Ollie asked.

"I don't want the gadget, period," Tigo said.

"It'll save you a lot of time upstate," Meyer said.

*"If* he says anything."

"That's your job," Carella said. "To get him talking."

"He's not so fuckin dumb, you know. I start talkin about that night, he's gonna wonder why."

"Make it sound casual," Meyer suggested.

"Sure. Hey, Wiggy, remember the night you shot that dude in the back of his head and dropped him in a garbage can? Boy, that was fun, wasn't it?"

"Do it over a few drinks," Carella suggested.

"Sure. Have another beer, Wiggy. Remember the night you shot that dude in the back of . . ."

"Just play it cool," Meyer said. "Don't even think about the wire. Make believe you're two guys shootin the breeze."

"Sure."

"The mike's right here," Ollie said. "It looks like a button on your shirt."

"Suppose he *spots* the fuckin thing?"

"He won't."

"But *if* he does."

"Don't worry, he won't be thinking about a wire."

"What if he *starts* thinking about a wire? This man can become very violent. He is not called Wiggy the Lid for no reason."

"Just tell him you work for a record company," Meyer said.

"Tell him you're a talent scout for Motown," Ollie said. "Tuck your shirt in your pants."

Tigo tucked in his shirt.

He turned to face the cops.

"How do I look?" he asked.

He looked extremely worried.

"You look great," Meyer said.

Kling came over from across the room.

"You're wearing a wire, right?" he said.

"Yeah," Tigo said. "Why?"

"I never would've guessed," Kling said.

*

HALLOWAY TOLD THEM HE WOULD HAVE TO CALL THEIR treasurer. Wiggy asked what his name was.

"Her," Halloway said. "Her name is Susan."

Susan was a code word. The moment whoever answered the phone heard the name "Susan," he or she would know there was trouble.

"Make sure you talk to her and her alone," Wiggy said. "Give me the number. I'll dial it."

The clock on the wall read ten minutes past ten.

Halloway wrote the number on a slip of paper. Wiggy looked at it as he dialed. The instant he heard it ringing on the other end, he handed the receiver to Halloway and picked up an extension phone. The phone rang once, twice . . .

"Hello?"

A woman's voice.

"Susan?" Halloway said.

"Yes?"

"This is Dick Halloway. Happy New Year."

"Thank you, Dick," she said. "Same to you."

His use of the familiar diminutive told her he was not alone. If Karen Andersen had announced herself as Karey, or David Good as Davey, it would have meant the same thing. By repeating the diminutive, the woman on the other end of the line was telling Halloway she understood he had company.

"Did you try to reach me yesterday?" she asked.

"Yes, I called around three," he said.

He was telling her there were three people there with him.

"Sorry I missed you. How can I help?"

"We need some cash," he said.

"How much?" she asked.

To Wiggy, listening on the extension, this all sounded legitimate so far.

"Are you sitting down?" Halloway asked, and smiled.

Wiggy smiled, too.

So did the Mexicans.

Everyone was smiling at Halloway's witticism.

"That much, huh?" Susan said.

Her name wasn't Susan, but that's who Wiggy thought she was. He also thought this was going along splendidly so far. He didn't have the slightest notion that he and his two pals were being set up.

"Three-million-six," Halloway said.

"Oh dear," Susan said.

"Indeed," Halloway said, and rolled his eyes heavenward.

Wiggy nodded encouragement. You're doing fine so far, his nod said.

"Where do you want it?" Susan asked.

Wiggy motioned for Halloway to cover the mouthpiece with his hand.

"Tell her you'll come there for it," he whispered.

"I'll come there for it, Sue."

Warning her again that he had company, three in number, remember? Trouble, Sue. Or Suzie. Big trouble here. Come help us, Suze.

"How soon can you get it together?" he asked.

"How soon will you need it?"

"As soon as possible, Sue."

"How does one o'clock sound?"

Halloway looked at Wiggy. Wiggy nodded.

"One o'clock sounds fine," Halloway said.

"Allow yourself a half-hour to get here," Susan said.

This meant he could expect help at twelve-thirty.

"I'll have to make three or four calls, Dick."

She was telling him she'd be sending three or four people.

"And, Dick . . . ?"

"Yes, Sue?"

"They're doing some work out front, lots of heavy machinery all over the place. Come in the back way, will you?"

"See you in a bit," he said.

She had told him they'd be heavily armed. She had told him they'd come up the emergency staircase at the rear of the Headley Building. She had so much as told him that Walter Wiggins and his Mexican associates were already as good as dead.

The hands on the wall clock now read a quarter past ten.

"Charmaine?" Wiggy said. "Why don't you make us all some coffee?"

WILL STRUTHERS DIDN'T CALL THE BANK UNTIL TEN-twenty that morning. As a former bank employee himself, he knew there was always an early-morning rush of customers, and he suspected Antonia Belandres would have been particularly busy until now, it being the start of the big New Year's Eve weekend and all.

"Miss Belandres," she said.

The "Miss" pleased Will. It meant a) she was single, and b) she wasn't one of these damn feminists who called themselves "Ms." and aspired to pee in men's rooms.

"Hello, Miss Belandres," he said, "this is Will Struthers."

"Lieutenant Struthers!" she said, sounding enormously surprised. "How *are* you?"

"Fine, thank you," Will said, not bothering to correct her. "And you?"

"Busy, busy, busy," she said. "We close at noon today, and it's been bedlam."

"I know just how it is," Will said.

"I know you do," she said. "So tell me, are you looking forward to the new year?"

"Actually, I never have liked New Year's Eve," he said. "It always seems like a big disappointment to me. I don't know why."

"I feel exactly the same way."

"You do?"

"Yes. I've been to small parties and big ones, I've stayed home and I've gone to nightclubs, and it's always the same thing. A big buildup to an even bigger letdown."

"Gee," he said.

"Yes," she said.

There was a short silence.

"Miss Belandres . . ." he said.

"Antonia," she said.

"Antonia," he said. "I know this is short notice . . ."

Silence again. He could hear her breathing on the other end of the line.

"But I was . . . ah . . . wondering . . ."

"Yes, Lieutenant?"

"If you don't . . . ah . . . have any other plans . . ."

"Yes?"

"Do you think you might care to have dinner with me tonight?"

"Why, I think that would be lovely," she said.

"Good," he said at once. "Good. Does seven o'clock sound convenient to you?"

"Seven o'clock sounds lovely."

"Do you like Italian food?"

"I love Italian food."

"Seven o'clock then, good," he said. "Good. Where shall I pick you up?"

"It's 347 South Shelby, apartment 12C."

"I'll be there at seven on the dorothy," he said.

"I'll be waiting," she said.

He was thinking, Antonia, you and me are going to be millionaires.

"THIS IS CLARENDON HALL," MAHMOUD SAID.

Nikmaddu wished the man's little mustache didn't make him look as if he were constantly smiling. This was a serious matter here.

"Jassim will be sitting here, in row F in the center section."

Jassim of the dirty fingernails and no smile nodded. He was familiar with the seating plan, knew exactly what he was to do tomorrow night.

"Seat number 101 on the aisle," Mahmoud said.

Nikmaddu looked at the plan more closely.

"If we're lucky," Mahmoud said, "the explosion will carry to the stage. If not, we will have made our point, anyway."

"Killing the Jew is not the point, you understand," Akbar said. The desert camel driver, deep creases on his brown face, thick veins on the backs of his strong hands. Their demolitions expert. "We are teaching them that we can strike anywhere, anytime. We are telling them that they are completely vulnerable. Unless they wish to strip-search every American entering a theater, a movie house, a concert hall, a restaurant, a coffee shop, a supermarket, anywhere. They are at our mercy, is what we will be proving to them tomorrow night."

"Still, getting the Jew would be a bonus," Jassim said.

"But not a *priority,*" Akbar insisted. "If we get the Jew, fine. If not, many others will die. Our point will be made."

"To die for Allah would be an honor," Jassim said. He was the one going in with the bomb. By rights, he should have the last word. But Akbar had fashioned the bomb and the timing device.

"Akbar is right," Nikmaddu said. "It will be better if no sacrifice were involved this time." He was referring to the suicide bombing of the United States destroyer in Yemen. "We must let them know we are professionals, not fanatics."

Jassim took this as a personal affront. He gave Nikmaddu what he hoped was a disdainful look, and then lighted a cigarette.

"When will this happen?" Nikmaddu asked.

"After the intermission," Akbar said.

"*Precisely* when?" Nikmaddu asked.

"The Jew is the guest artist in the second half of the evening. We now know he will be playing Mendelssohn's violin concerto in E Minor. The bomb will be set to go off sometime during the first movement."

"When, precisely, during the first movement?"

"It is difficult to time the music precisely," Akbar said. "The first movement is about twelve and a half minutes long, depending."

"Depending on what?"

"The performer, the conductor—artistic license. But it will rarely run much longer than that. In any event, the bomb will be set to go off at nine-thirty."

"At *precisely* nine-thirty?"

"Precisely, yes. It will explode toward the end of the first movement, trust me."

Nikmaddu was beginning to realize that although this man looked as if he belonged in a tent on the desert, he was perhaps more intelligent than any of the others.

"What do you mean by movement?" Jassim asked. The stupidest of the lot. And the one with the most responsibility. The one who would go in with the bomb. "What does movement mean?"

"The Mendelssohn concerto has three movements," Akbar explained.

"But what is a movement?"

"It's not important that you know," Akbar said. "You will place the bomb and leave the hall. The rest is up to Allah."

"Will Jassim have enough time to get back to his seat, leave the bomb, and make his departure?" Nikmaddu asked.

"A good point," Mahmoud said. "Have you timed all this?"

"I have been to six concerts this season," Akbar said. "And hated them all. I know exactly how long it takes to get from the street to the lobby, and from there back to the seat in row F. Without rushing, Jassim should be out of there before the bomb explodes."

"At nine-thirty precisely," Nikmaddu said, seeking confirmation yet another time.

"Yes, at nine-thirty precisely," Akbar said. "A fitting climax to the first movement."

The men laughed. All but Jassim, who found nothing humorous in any of this.

"What kind of bomb are you using?" Nikmaddu asked.

"A simple pipe bomb. Two of them actually. Taped together and packed with black powder, nails, and screws. Similar to the one in Atlanta four years ago."

"And the timer?"

"A battery-powered clock."

"How will he carry it in?" Nikmaddu asked.

"In a handbag," Akbar said.

"I'll be carrying a *handbag?"* Jassim said.

"A *man's* handbag. Europeans carry them all the time. Besides, I've taken one into the hall on six different occasions now. There is no security check. Women go in with handbags, even shopping bags, men carry briefcases. They are very sure of themselves, these Americans."

"That will all change tomorrow night," Nikmaddu said.

"Yes, it will," Akbar said.

*"Inshallah,"* Mahmoud said.

*"Inshallah,"* the others said in unison.

MAN SEEMED TO HAVE DISAPPEARED FROM THE FACE of the earth.

First place Tigo tried was the crib on Decatur. Thomas—who on the night of the murder had been chatting with Mr. Jerry Hoskins, alias Frank Holt, while Tigo and Wiggy tested the dope in the other room—was watching television when Tigo waltzed in.

"Hey, man," he said.

"Whut'choo watchin?" Tigo asked.

This was ten to eleven in the morning, man was sittin here watching television.

"I don't even know," Thomas said. "Suppin with Sylvester Stallone."

Tigo watched the screen for a moment.

Sylvester Stallone was dangling from a rope.

"Where's Wiggy?" he asked.

"You got me, man."

"You seed him today?"

"Nope."

"When'd you get here?"

"Bout an hour ago."

"He wasn't here?"

"Nope."

"He come back, you tell him I'm lookin for him, okay?"

"Peace, brother," Thomas said.

My ass, Tigo thought.

Next place he tried was Wiggy's barber. This was a man named Roland, who cut mighty fine hair and also took in numbers on the side. Or vice versa. Tigo figured Wiggy might be here gettin a trim, New Year's Eve comin up and all. He could use a trim hisself, matter of fact. Roland said he hadn't seen hide nor hair—

"You get it?" he asked.

—of Wiggy since a week ago today when he last cut the man's hair.

"Try L&G," he suggested.

L&G was short for Lewis and Gregory, who were two brothers owned a haberdashery on Chase Street. Both brothers were there when Tigo arrived at eleven that Friday. The shop was packed with people returning ties, and shirts and shit they'd got for Christmas and had no use for. Greg told him he hadn't seen Wiggy since before Thanksgiving, was the man all right? He usually came in here and splurged two, three times a year. Tigo told him Wiggy was fine, just'd been busy was all. Greg said, "Tell him I said happy new year, hear?"

"I'll tell him," Tigo said.

He was wondering had Wiggy vanished from sight?

This business, vanishing from sight was always a distinct possibility.

He tried a bar called the Starlight, which was already doing very good business at a quarter past eleven, two days before New Year's Eve. Tigo could just imagine what the place would be like on the big night itself. But John the bartender told him he'd seen Mr. Wiggins on Christmas night, when he was sittin here at the bar hittin on a blonde who'd come in out the cold, and again just yesterday aroun this time.

"Is that so?" Tigo asked. "A blonde?"

It was too bad the tape recorder wasn't turned on because first it missed a hair joke from Wiggy's barber, and now it just missed a thickening of the plot with Wiggy working a blonde on Christmas night. He told John if Mr. Wiggins came in again to tell him he was lookin for him, okay, and then—so it shouldn't be a total loss—he tossed off a shot of Dewar's before he went out into the cold again.

It was beginning to snow.

No snow for Christmas, but now it was coming down to beat all hell.

Tigo looked at his watch. It was twenty minutes past eleven. He didn't know where to go next.

He tried the pool hall on Culver and Third, but nobody there had seen Wiggy, and then he tried The Corset Lady on South Fifth, which was run by a foxy chick named Aleda who made very fine ladies' underwears and who used to go with Wiggy, but not for six months or so now, but she hadn't seen him and didn't *care* to see him, thanks. Then he tried the First Bap on St. Sab's because believe it or not

Walter Wiggins was a religious man who went to church every Sunday, but the Reverend Gabriel Foster hadn't seen him since, in fact, last Sunday, had anything happened to him? Foster was always looking for something that had happened to anybody in the black community, some cause he could champion on his radio show, some put-upon black he could go march to City Hall about. Tigo was beginning to think maybe something *had* happened to Wiggy. This business, things happened.

He finally tried a man named Little Nicholas, who did business out the back of a laundromat he owned and operated on Lyons and South Thirty-fifth. Little Nicholas was about five-feet, eight-inches tall and Tigo guessed he weighed something like three, four hundred pounds. What Little Nicholas did was sell guns. He told Tigo that Wiggy had been in there late last night, and had purchased a beautiful submachine gun called the Cobray M11-9, would Tigo be interested in seeing some very fine banned weapons and silencers that had come in from all over the nation only yesterday? Tigo asked had he seed Wiggy anytime *today?* Little Nicholas said No, he hadn't had the pleasure.

It was a quarter to twelve.

The snow was coming down pretty hard now.

Tigo wondered where the fuck Wiggy could be.

**WIGGY WAS SITTING AT HALLOWAY'S COMPUTER UP AT** W&D. One of the Mexicans—he guessed it was Ortiz—came out of the conference room where they were holding the staff, and asked him shouldn't he be going for the money soon? They had already decided, after some sound reasoning from Wiggy, that he should be the one who went for the cash, in case there was any language problem, not that he meant to be disparaging. He looked up at the wall clock now. It was only twelve noon, and Halloway's accountant had advised them to allow a half-hour to get there for their one o'clock appointment, which meant there was still plenty of time before him and Halloway had to go out into what looked like a full-fledged blizzard.

"I got time yet," he told Ortiz, or Villada, or whoever the hell he was. *Whoever* he was, Wiggy planned never to see him or his partner ever again the minute he got his hands on that money. *Adios, amigos,* it was very nice knowing you.

Meanwhile, there was some very interesting information on the W&D computer.

CARELLA AND MEYER WERE HAVING LUNCH IN A DINER on Culver and Eighth, not far from the station house. Meyer was eating a salad and drinking iced tea. Carella was eating a hamburger and fries. Meyer told him that just two days ago, his wife had told him they should go buy him some clothes for the new year.

"She said we'd have to go to a shop for *large* men, was what she called it. I said, 'Why do we have to go to a large men's shop?' She said, 'Because we won't find anything to fit you in a regular men's store.' I said, 'Hey, come on, Sarah, I can buy clothes off the rack at any store in town! Large men's shops are for men who are *obese.'* So she looks me dead in the eye and says, 'Well?' "

"Sarah said that, huh?"

"Sarah."

"Said you were fat, in effect."

"Obese."

"In effect."

"Do you think I'm obese?"

"No. Ollie Weeks is obese," Carella said, and popped a fry into his mouth. "You're what I'd call chubby."

"Chubby! That's *worse* than obese!"

"Well . . . plump maybe."

"Keep going. How's your damn hamburger?"

"Terrific."

"The fries?"

"Splendid."

"You forgot stout."

"Stout's a good one, too."

"You ever have a weight problem?"

"Never. I've always been svelte."

"I've always been borderline."

"Borderline what?"

"Obese!" Meyer said, and both men burst out laughing.

The laughter trailed.

"I've got other problems, though," Carella said.

"Yeah?"

"Yeah."

Meyer looked at him. Carella's face, his eyes were suddenly very serious.

"Tell me," Meyer said.

"You think I've changed?" Carella asked.

"How do you mean?"

"I don't know. Am I different?"

"You seem the same to me."

"Teddy says I've changed since my father got killed. She says I never cried for him. She says I never cried for Danny, either, Danny Gimp. I don't even remember if I did. She says I've been drinking too much, she says . . ."

"Ah, shit, Steve, you haven't, have you?"

"No. I don't think so. I hope not. It's just . . ."

"What?"

"Ah, Jesus."

"What, Steve? Tell me."

"I think I'm scared."

"Come on. You're not scared."

"I think I am. Teddy's afraid I might eat my own gun one day. I'll tell you the truth . . ."

"Don't even say it."

Both men fell silent.

Carella was looking down at his hands.

"I think I'm scared," he said again. "Really, Meyer."

"Come on, scared. Of what?"

"Dying," Carella said. "I'm afraid I'll get killed."

"We're all afraid we'll get killed."

"I came so close, Meyer."

"We've all come close, one time or another. O'Brien comes close every day of his life."

"O'Brien's a hard luck cop. And he never had a lion sitting on his chest."

"So what are you scared of? Another lion sitting on your chest? Come on, Steve."

"He almost had my head in his mouth, I could feel his breath on my face, I could smell his breath. Another minute, he'd have closed his jaws on me. I never came that close to dying before."

"And you'll never come that close again. What do you think this is, the African plains? Come on. This is a *city,* Steve. You don't run into lions on the streets here."

"I dream about that lion every night, Meyer. Every fucking night, I see that lion in my dreams. I wake up sweating, Meyer, shaking. I'm scared it'll happen again. And next time . . ."

"It's okay to be scared," Meyer said.

"Not if you're a cop."

"We're all scared."

"Cops shouldn't . . ."

"Not only cops. Everybody. We're all scared, Steve. If you meet another lion, just look him in the eye. Stare him down."

Carella's hands were trembling.

"Come on," Meyer said. He slid out of the booth, came around the table, sat beside his friend, and put his arm around his shoulder. "Come on, Steve."

Tito Gomez walked in just then.

"How tender," he said.

"Go fuck yourself," Meyer explained.

"Nice talk. I can't find Wiggy. I don't know where he is. What now?"

WIGGY WAS STILL AT HALLOWAY'S COMPUTER.

There was a folder named MOTHER, which he couldn't open because whenever he double-clicked on it, he was told to enter a password. But when he double-clicked on a folder called WITCHES AND DRAGONS—which he thought at first might be some kind of a game—it opened to his touch, and he found a whole list of files with names like ADA and NETTIE and DIANA and EM and TESSIE and RONI and BELA and GINA. Was W&D in the business of tracking hurricanes, or had he lucked into Halloway's personal little black book of cuties, oh you sly old dog, you! Or were these the names of writers the company published? But then why use first names? And even some nicknames?

Intrigued now, Wiggy double-clicked on the file labeled

TESSIE because that was the name of the first girl he'd ever talked into licking Frick and Frack, a thirteen-year-old high yaller beauty fresh up from the South with her grandma. There wasn't nothing in that file about girls, mellow or otherwise. What was in there was information about the West Side Limousine Corporation, which it would appear was a subsidiary of Wadsworth and Dodds here, and which made all kinds of trips to and from the city's two airports and the one across the river in the next state, not to mention a trip to Diamondback on Christmas night.

He began wondering why a file about a limousine company would be called TESSIE, and then he realized that there were two S's in the words WEST SIDE, and also a T, and—lo and behold—an I and an E! So what you had here was little old TESSIE all curled up in the back seat of a WEST SIDE limo!

He double-clicked on the file labeled EM.

What was in there was an itemized list of drug deals that made Wiggy's little operation in Diamondback look like somebody selling lemonade by the side of the road. Dates, places, number of kilos purchased, dollars paid for them. He wasn't surprised that the list existed; everybody kept records *someplace,* man. In fact, his own transactions uptown were recorded on a computer disc called HAPPY DAYS that could only be opened with the password WW2, which stood not for World War II, but instead for his initials and the month of his—it suddenly occurred to him that WITCHES AND DRAGONS stood for Wadsworth and Dodds.

What he was looking at here was a record of drug buys the book publishers had made in Mexico over the past two years. And suddenly he realized that the name EM was buried in the word MEXICO, same as TESSIE was buried in WEST SIDE, was in fact the first two letters of that word, reversed, and he began wondering how many of the *other* girls' names in the WITCHES AND DRAGONS folder were buried in larger words, hiding there, so to speak, lurking there in the dark for somebody smart like Wiggy to find.

He kept opening file after file.

When finally he double-clicked on the file named DIANA, his eyes opened wide.

He was reading all about Diamondback, which was where he conducted business, the uptown ghetto where Jerry Hoskins alias Frank Holt had come calling with a hundred keys of prime cocaine purchased in Mexico.

DIAMONDBACK.

Little ole white girl DIANA hiding up there in the blackest of black holes.

The magnitude of his discovery made him suddenly want to pee.

Grabbing the Cobray from where it was resting on the floor at his feet, he went down the hall to the men's room at the rear of the office complex.

At that very moment, The Weird Sisters and two very tall, very broad black men were entering the Headley Building through the back door in an alley that was posted with NO PARKING—FIRE LANE signs. This time around, Sheryl and Toni—whose real names were Anna and Mary Jo—were *each* carrying guns with silencers affixed to the muzzles.

So were the black men.

*

WIGGY DIDN'T HEAR ANY SHOOTING BECAUSE THE weapons were wearing silencers.

All he heard was screaming.

The screaming wasn't coming from the two Mexicans, who were dead within minutes after the assassins entered the conference room. Instead, they were coming from Charmaine the receptionist, and Betty Alweiss from the Art Department. Karen Andersen wasn't screaming. She was learning how to be as cold-bloodedly unemotional as her boss and sometime lover.

"There's a third one," Halloway said.

By that time, Wiggy was down the fire stairs and out of the building.

THE WEIRD SISTERS UNASHAMEDLY STRIPPED THE Mexicans naked and wrapped them in tarpaulin. Their two black associates carried the bodies down the fire stairs, hoisted them into the back of a white ML320 Mercedes-Benz, and transported them to a garbage dump on Sands Spit, not far from the airport. It was Halloway's surmise that the Mexicans would never be identified and therefore would never be missed.

At about four-thirty that afternoon—just as Carella was leaving the squadroom—Anna and Mary Jo went up to Diamondback to look for Walter Wiggins. This time, their orders were to kill him.

CARELLA GOT TO HIS MOTHER'S HOUSE IN RIVERHEAD at a little past six that evening. He recognized his sister's car in the driveway outside the house, and parked just behind it. His mother's Christmas tree glowed behind the windows fronting the house. At least a foot of snow covered the walk to the front door, and it was still coming down. He climbed the low flat steps, pressed the button set in the door jamb, and heard familiar chimes sounding inside the house. He waited. Falling flakes covered his hair and the shoulders of his overcoat. He was about to ring again when the door opened.

"Hey," his mother said, and hugged him. "You should wear a hat."

"I know," he said. "You told me."

"From when you were six," she said.

"Three," he corrected.

"Come in. Angela's already here."

"I saw her car."

"Come in."

He followed his mother into the house. This was where he'd grown up. This was what he'd called home during his childhood, his adolescence, and his early manhood. Home. It seemed strange to him now, smaller, somehow cheerless. He wondered if that was because his father no longer lived here. Angela was sitting at the big dining-room table, drinking a glass of red wine. Another glass of wine was on the table, just opposite her. He remembered when they were kids and used to hide together under this very table. He remembered Sunday afternoons here in his parents' house, the penny-ante poker games, he and Angela hiding under the dining-room table. He remembered his sister once breaking his head with the clasp on a pocketbook she'd swung at him in anger. He couldn't remember now what had so enraged her. Something he'd said jokingly. He'd loved her to death when they were kids. He still did. She kissed him on the cheek in greeting.

"How's the traffic?" she asked.

"Pretty bad. The roads are getting slick."

"Steve, some wine?" his mother asked. "Something stronger?"

"A little wine, yes," he said. "Thanks."

He sat alongside Angela. Outside the window, the snow was coming down heavily. He didn't live very far from here, but the roads were already bad. He was beginning to regret not having gone straight home from the office. His mother brought him his glass of wine, and went to sit opposite him and Angela at the table. They all lifted their glasses.

*"Salute,"* his mother said in Italian.

"Cheers," Carella said.

"Health," Angela said.

They drank.

"So," Angela said.

"So," his mother said.

They were both smiling.

Carella looked across the table at his mother. He turned to look at his sister.

"What?" he said.

"We're getting married together," Angela said.

"A double wedding," his mother said.

"Me and Henry, Mama and . . ."

"I don't want to hear this," Carella said.

He was already standing, surprised to find himself on his feet, wondering when he'd got up. Was it when they'd both started smiling? Was it then that the feeling of impending dread had lurched from his heart into his throat?

"Sit down," his mother said.

"No, Mom. I'm sorry, but . . ."

"Sit down, Steve."

"No. I don't want to hear about you getting married so soon after . . ."

"Your father's been dead almost . . ."

"I don't want to *hear* it!" Carella shouted, and whirled on his sister. "And I don't want to hear about you marrying the man who . . ."

"What the hell is wrong with you?" Angela asked.

"Oh no," he said. "Oh no, you don't."

"Have you lost your . . . ?"

"Never mind what's wrong with *me!* What's wrong with you? Have you both forgotten Papa already? How can you sit here in *his* house . . ."

"Papa is dead, Steve."

"Oh, is he? Gee, no kidding. What do you think this is about here? What are we talking about here? What are you both planning to do if not spit on Papa's . . ."

"Don't you *dare!"* his mother said.

"Oh, for Christ's sake, Mom, stop behaving like a schoolgirl. And you stop encouraging her!" he shouted, whirling on Angela. "You want to marry that jackass, at least have the decency to leave her out of it."

Angela was shaking her head.

"Sure, shake your head," he said. "I'm wrong, right? She meets a Wop fresh off the boat . . ."

"Not in my house," his mother said. "Never use that word in my house."

"Oh, forgive me, what is he? A Yankee Doodle Dandy?"

"I think that lion scrambled your brains," Angela said.

"And never mind the fucking *lion!"* he shouted.

"Not in my *house!"* his mother said, and slapped him.

He looked at her.

"I'm sorry," she said.

"Sure."

Angela suddenly began crying.

"All we wanted was your blessing," she said.

"Well, you didn't get it," he said. "If you can both forget Papa so easily, I can't. Goodnight, Mom. Thanks for the wine."

He turned and was starting for the door when his mother said, "I'm not a schoolgirl, Steve."

He continued going for the door.

"I love him and I'm going to marry him," she said.

His hand was on the doorknob.

"Whether you like it or not," she said.

"Goodnight," he said again, and opened the door, and walked out into the fiercely falling snow.

THE TAPE RECORDER WAS GOING.

Tigo couldn't believe what he was hearing. Nor did he *want* to be hearing what he was hearing. He wanted to get this conversation back to the reason he was wearing a wire to begin with. He wanted Wiggy to start talking about December twenty-third.

He wondered suddenly if this was all bullshit Wiggy was giving him here. Did Wiggy maybe *know* he was wired? Was he maybe making up a good story so the fuzz would get off the scent? It sure was a peculiar story he was telling here. Almost made Tigo forget why he was here. Almost made Tigo sorry he had finally found the man.

"You really think all this is true, huh?" he asked. "Cause to me . . ."

"Man, I was lookin straight into they computer! I seed all this stuff with my own eyes!"

"It just sounds, you know, like science-fiction, you

know?" Tigo said. "This file named Mothah you can't open cause you need a password, an all this money floatin aroun, and these dope deals here an there, and these people causin trouble all over the world, an tryin'a fuck us right here in Diamon'back, I mean, man, it sounds like suppin you'd see in a *movie,* you know what I'm sayin, man?"

"It'd make a *good* movie, that's for damn sure," Wiggy said, "but it's *true,* man! I got it from they *computer!"*

"That don't mean it couldn't of been garbage in there," Tigo said, and shrugged.

"The point is, whut we gonna do about it, Tigo? I mean, these guys are messin with our *people!"*

Tigo had never particularly felt that any of these people they sold dope to were necessarily *related* to him in any way. Maybe *Wiggy* thought of they customers as his "people" but Tigo didn't share the sentiment. To tell the truth, if they was money to be made recycling dope here in the hood, Tigo didn't care *who* sold them the dope to begin with or where the proceeds of the sale were going. In fact, the only thing he wanted to do right this minute was talk about what he'd come here to talk about so he could go back to the police and collect his reward. He planned to retire from the dope business—

He didn't yet realize how close his retirement was.

—soon as he got his hands on however much money the commissioner gave him for this valuable stuff he was about to tape. So he didn't need to know about any *conspiracy* Wiggy had tapped into through somebody's computer. Nor did he want to *do* anything about any such conspiracy, even if it did exist, which he strongly doubted because Wiggy's story sounded like so much jive to him. So—subtly and not wishing to appear too aggressive or inquisitive—he asked, "How'd it feel killing that dude on Christmas Eve?"

"I think we should go to the police," Wiggy said, "tell *them* the story."

And suddenly, he shoved himself out of his chair and went marching straight for the telephone.

**CARELLA WAS ON HIS WAY HOME WHEN THE CELL PHONE** in his car rang. Ollie Weeks was on the other end.

"Guess what?" he said.

"Surprise me," Carella said.

"I just got a call from Walter Wiggins."

"What?"

"Ah yes."

"The man Gomez is supposed to be taping?"

"The very same."

"The man who maybe shot and killed Jerry Hoskins?"

"That's the one."

"Is he confessing?"

"I don't think so. But he wants to talk to us."

"What about?"

"Some kind of big conspiracy."

"Uh-huh," Carella said.

"I'm on my way to 1280 Decatur. You want to meet me?"

Carella looked at the dashboard clock.

"Give me half an hour," he said.

**ANTONIA BELANDRES WAS VERY IMPRESSED THAT** Will had managed to find his way here in all this snow. He jokingly told her he used to drive a dog sled team in Alaska, which somehow she took to be the truth, and was even more impressed. He now had two lies to account for. He hoped he did not lose her when he told her he was not a police lieutenant, and had never been to Alaska in his life.

There wasn't a single cab in sight when they came downstairs from her apartment. He had deliberately picked an Italian restaurant not too distant from where she lived on South Shelby, but it was really coming down and he apologized for asking her to walk the six blocks, but he was afraid they might lose their reservation.

"Don't be silly, Lieutenant," she said. "I *love* walking."

Lieutenant, he thought. Boy.

As it was, he needn't have worried about the reservation. The restaurant was almost empty. In fact, the owner fawned over them as if they were the Mayor and his wife who'd braved the storm to come here. He offered them a bottle of wine on the house, and then reeled off the specials for the night, all of which sounded delicious. Antonia ordered the *osso buco.* Will ordered the veal Milanese, which turned out to be breaded veal cutlets, oh well.

"By the way," he said, when they had each drunk a glass of wine and Will was pouring again, "I'm not a police lieutenant. In fact, I'm not even a cop."

"Oh?" she said.

"That's right," he said. "Here's to golden days and purple nights," and clinked his glass against hers.

"Where'd you learn that toast?" she asked. "Golden days and purple nights."

"Singapore."

"Me, too."

"So here's *to* them," he said.

"Here's *to* them," she said. "Golden days and purple nights."

They drank.

"Then what were you doing with all those detectives?" she asked. "If you're not a cop."

"I was sort of with them," Will said.

"If you're not a cop, what are you?"

"Actually, a burglar," he said.

"Really?"

"Yeah," he said, and shrugged.

"Did they arrest you for burglary? Was that it?"

"Not exactly."

"Then what?"

"They thought I passed a phony hundred-dollar bill."

"Was that the super-bill they asked me to examine?"

"I guess so. It sure looked real to me. I think that's why they let me go."

"What do you mean?"

"Well, I think it fooled *them,* too. I mean, if *they* couldn't tell it was fake, how was I supposed to know?"

"Well, you did work in a bank once."

"Yeah, but I never saw a super-bill in my life. They told me they could've charged me with a class-A mis, but this was Christmas, what the hell. They let me go."

"So as I understand this . . ."

"That's right . . ."

". . . you're a common thief."

"Well, I'm a burglar. That's not so common."

Antonia laughed. Will figured this was a good sign.

"Also, I have some plans that ain't so common neither," he said.

"Oh? What plans?"

"I'll tell you later," he said.

Antonia was thinking the plans he was talking about had

to do with sex. He was referring to possibly taking her to bed later on tonight. After dinner. While the storm raged outside. Which wasn't a bad idea at all. Except that he was a common thief. Well, a burglar.

"What makes a burglar so special?" she asked.

"Well, first of all, we're like doctors."

"I see. Doctors."

"Yes. Our motto is 'Do no harm.' In fact, we go out of our way to keep from harming people. We see a light burning in an apartment, we think there's somebody in there, we'll avoid it like the plague."

"Why is that?"

"I just told you. We don't want some old lady screaming so we'll have to hurt her. Do no harm. Also, the rap is bigger. If you hurt somebody while you're inside a dwelling, or even if you're just carrying a gun. It goes up from Burg Two to Burg One. That's a difference of ten years, when it comes to sentencing."

"You sound very familiar with all this," Antonia said.

"Oh sure," he said. "Well, I've been doing it for a long time now."

She was wondering why she was still sitting here. The man had just told her he was a burglar, a *thief.*

"I thought you said you worked in a bank," she said.

"Long time ago," he said. "I was just a kid when I went out on the Rim."

"But you never saw a super-bill," she said.

"Never."

"I'm surprised. Plenty of them in Southeast Asia."

"Plenty of them *everywhere,* from what you said."

"Where'd you get the one you tried to cash?"

"I stole it."

"Why am I not surprised?" she said, and rolled her eyes.

"That's okay. Not many people get to dine with burglars."

"Lucky me," she said, and rolled her eyes again.

"That might turn out to be the case," he said.

She still thought he was talking about taking her to bed later on. Which she still thought might not be such a bad idea.

"You know that woman who got eaten by lions in Grover Park?" he said. "The zoo there? Did you see that on television?"

"No," she said. "But I read about it in the newspaper."

"That was who I stole the money from."

"Oh my, you're famous," she said.

"Well, *she* was, I guess. It's not everybody gets eaten by lions."

"What do you suppose she was doing in the lion's cage?"

"I have no idea. I only talked to the lady once in my entire life."

"*You* didn't have anything to do with . . ."

"No, hey, *no,*" he said, "I'm a burglar!"

"Yes," she said. "So I'm beginning to understand."

Their food arrived. She was thoughtfully silent for a while. Then she said, "So, if you were me, what would you do here?"

"What do you mean?"

"Would *you* go to bed with you, knowing you're a burglar? Or would you eat your dinner and go home like a nice little girl?"

"You could do both," Will suggested.

**TIGO GOMEZ WAS GETTING VERY NERVOUS.**

Wiggy had just told him that the man who was on his

way here was the very same person who'd strapped this tape recorder to his chest—"That's just great," Tigo said—none other than Detective Oliver Wendell Weeks of the Eighty-eighth Detective Squad.

"You maybe seed him aroun the streets," Wiggy said. "Fat Ollie Weeks. He's this big fat guy."

No kidding, Tigo thought.

The problem was that Wiggy thought he'd be doing a favor for the police, when all *they* wanted to do was send him up for Murder One. The further problem was that Tigo couldn't warn the man how dangerous this fat hump was because then he'd have to reveal that he himself had visited the police to ask for a favor of his own by way of a cash reward, and they'd wired him tight as Dick's hatband, which is why he was sitting here this very minute, still attempting to get information he could use as a bargaining tool when the Law arrived and the shit hit the fan.

"You goan tell him you a drug dealer?" he asked.

"No, I don't have to tell him that."

"Then how come you *know* these people are sellin dope up here?"

"I coulda heard."

"*How* you coulda heard, Wigg? You goan tell the fuzz this man Hoskins come up here Christmastime, sold you a hundred keys of coke to distribute to li'l kiddies in the streets?"

"No. But I could . . ."

"You goan tell 'em you shot this man Hoskins back of the head an dropped him in a garbage can? You goan do that, Wigg?"

"I'm sayin it don't seem right, what these mothahs are doin to our people."

"They's evil folk in this world," Tigo said, "it *is* a shame."

He was thinking Jerry Hoskins may have brought that shit up from Mexico and sold it to Wiggy, but Wiggy was the one passin it down the line till it got to his "people" in the streets. And he *still* hadn't said one damn word about the Christmas Eve murder. Tigo was about to prod him again, get this show on the road here, nem mine feelin sorry for all the drug addicts in this sorry world of ours, when Wiggy said, "You know what the name Nettie stans for?"

"Nettie, you say?"

"N-E-T-T-I-E," Wiggy said, spelling it out for him. "You know what word that name is hidin' in?"

"No, I has to admit I do not," Tigo said.

"Counterfeit. That's the word. You search that word, you find Nettie lurkin in there. You double-click on her name, you transported straight to Nettieland. You want to hear this, man, or you want to stay ignorant the ress of your life?"

Tigo did not want to hear anything but how Wiggy had killed Hoskins—but neither did he wish to remain ignorant the rest of his life. He nodded wearily, and listened as Wiggy began telling him all about his adventures in Nettieland. Gradually, he began to lean closer. Gradually, his eyes opened wide. He was listening intently, his attention completely captured, when all at once he heard footsteps pounding in the hallway outside. He turned toward the front door. An instant later, he heard the sound of rapid gunfire, and all at once the door flew off its hinges.

At that very moment, Steve Carella was turning his car into Decatur Avenue, never once realizing he was about to meet another lion.

*

TIGO WAS RUNNING FOR THE WINDOW EVEN BEFORE THE two blond ladies burst into the room. Somewhere behind him Wiggy screamed in pain. Tigo dove through the glass head first, came through onto the fire escape in a cascade of shattering shards, heard more firing from inside the apartment.

"The window!" one of the women yelled, but he was already on his feet and charging down the ladder. The iron rungs were crusted with snow, slippery underfoot. He almost lost his balance, almost went over the rail, but continued running, sliding, slipping, almost flying down those steps while above him the blondes were on automatic, bullets kicking up snow everywhere around him, clanging against the iron of the fire escape. He jumped the dozen feet or so to the ground, began broken-field running across the back yard, the blondes still firing, and was climbing the fence between this yard and the next one over, when they finally found the range. He heard wood splintering everywhere around him, and then felt slugs ripping across his back as he came over the top of the fence. Another slug ripped through his right hand. He dropped to the ground, zig-zagged toward the alleyway alongside the building, tucking his bloody hand in against his body, cradling it, blood leaking onto the white snow from his hand and his chest as he ran.

The storm had kept most people off the street.

He stumbled out of the alleyway, fell, got to his feet again.

He turned to look behind him, fell again, and began crawling toward the streetlamp on the corner. He was lying there under the lamp for perhaps two or three minutes when a tall hatless man came running around the corner.

Tigo did not know whether the shots had attracted him or whether there'd been some other disturbance in the hood. He only knew he was glad to see him. The man knelt beside him. Tigo recognized him at once.

"You know who did this to you?" Carella asked.

Tigo nodded.

"Who, Tigo? Can you tell me?"

Carella's lion had just followed Tigo's trail of blood up the alleyway.

"Mother," Tigo said.

"Your *mother* shot . . . ?"

"Nettie," Tigo said.

"Is that your mother's name?"

Carella's lion was just running out of the alleyway behind them.

"Diana," Tigo said.

"I don't under . . ."

But Tito Gomez was already dead.

And Carella's lion was almost upon him.

He turned just in time to see someone dressed entirely in black, carrying what was unmistakably an AK-47.

*If you meet another lion, just look him in the eye. Stare him down.*

This lion wasn't a male.

There was merely a surprised instant that robbed Carella's eye of steely intent and lessened the speed of his gun hand, but that was all it took to give the blonde the advantage she needed. He registered three things in the tick of a heart beat. A car pulling into the street. The blonde angling the weapon toward his head. A man getting out of the car.

The blonde was about to squeeze the trigger when Fat

Ollie Weeks shot her in the back, dropping her in her tracks.

"That's two, Steve," he told Carella, and grinned into the flying snow.

# 11.

**WILL GUESSED** this was why he'd never been to bed with a hooker.

You went to bed with somebody who you had to pay, she put on her clothes directly afterward, said, "Thanks, I had a nice time," and went home. He guessed. But with a woman like Antonia Belandres, you sat here on a Saturday morning, drinking orange juice and coffee, and eating the chocolate croissants he'd gone down to the bakery to get, and it was . . . well . . . intimate. You could have sex with a hooker, but he didn't guess you could get intimate with one.

Antonia was wearing nothing but a little silky peignoir she'd taken from her bedroom closet. Will was wearing the slacks and shirt he'd put on when he went downstairs for the croissants. It was a little past ten-thirty. The snow had stopped and the sun was shining. In the street outside, everything looked clean and white and sparkling. He told Antonia that maybe they should go for a walk later on, if she thought she might like that. She told him she might like that a lot. He smiled and nodded. She smiled and nodded back.

He didn't tell her his plan until they were in her bed together again, and then only after they'd made love yet another time. She was cuddled in his arms, the blanket pulled up over their shoulders, frost still limning the window across the room, sunlight striking the glass.

"I know how we can both become millionaires," he said.

"Yes, how?" she said.

Black hair fanned out on the pillow. Brown eyes opened wide. Wearing no makeup. Her face looking as expectant as a child's on Christmas Day.

"We use the bills."

"What bills?" she asked.

"The super-bills."

"Use them?" she asked. "How do you mean?"

"You said you send any suspect bills to the Federal Reserve."

"Yes?"

"That's what you told the detectives."

"That's right. That's what we do."

"Somebody brings in a bill that looks phony . . ."

"Right, we send it to the Fed."

"You confiscate the bill, is that right?"

"That's right."

"Do you give the person a genuine bill in exchange?"

Which was just what the Treasury Department had done with the eight grand they'd taken from him. But he didn't know that.

"Of course not," she said. "That would be the same as condoning counterfeiting."

"Do you give the person a receipt for the bill?"

"Not if we know for certain it's counterfeit," she said. "In that case, we simply take the bill out of circulation."

"Even if the person didn't know it was counterfeit?"

"Too bad for him."

"How about if you're not *sure* it's counterfeit? If it's one of those terrific bills you have to send to the Fed?"

"Then we give the customer a receipt for it, yes."

"And if the Fed decides it's phony?"

"It never comes back to us. They take it out of circulation, and notify us. We in turn notify the customer, and that's that."

"What if they say it's real?"

"They return it to us, we notify the customer, and he comes to pick it up. No harm done all around."

"Okay, what if you *don't* send a suspect bill to the Fed? What if you just take it from the customer, give him a receipt for it . . . and keep it."

"Keep it?"

"Yes. And then two weeks later . . . or however long it usually takes the Fed to get back to you . . ."

"It varies."

"Two weeks, three weeks, whatever, you call the customer and tell him Sorry, your bill was phony and the Fed has confiscated it. Goodbye, sir, and good luck."

Antonia looked at him.

"That would be stealing," she said.

"Yes," he said. "But it wouldn't be stealing *real* money."

Antonia was still looking at him.

"It would be stealing *counterfeit* money," he said.

"What's the difference?" she said. "I fail to see the difference."

"That's exactly my point. If nobody can *tell* the difference, we can use tons of fake money just as if it's real money. We can use fake money to pay for anything we buy."

Which was just what Jerry Hoskins had tried to do with the Mexicans. But Will didn't know this, either.

"It still seems like stealing to me," Antonia said.

"Ain't nothing wrong with stealing," Will said, and kissed her again.

"Do you like violin music?" she asked.

FAT OLLIE WAS EATING.

He was also listening.

For him, he was eating lightly. That is to say, he was eating a baloney sandwich on rye with butter and mustard, and a sour pickle, and a potato knish, and a banana, and he was drinking coffee while he and Carella listened to the tape they'd retrieved from the recorder Tigo Gomez was wearing when the unidentified blonde—now in the hospital, and *still* unidentified—shot and killed him. Carella was eating a tuna and tomato sandwich on white, and drinking a glass of milk. The two detectives were in the interrogation room at the Eight-Seven, where Ollie seemed to be spending a lot of time lately, now that he was responsible for Carella's life two times over. Carella devoutly wished he would not save his life a third time, otherwise he might become a permanent fixture up here.

Ollie much preferred eating to listening to tapes.

The trouble with police tapes was that they were very rarely interesting. If you went to see a movie or watched a television show, or even if you were desperate and decided to read a book, there was usually a story you could follow. Listening to a tape was the same as hearing people talking, except that when you were in a room with people and they were babbling away, you didn't always recognize how boring it was. Listening to a tape, you were always aware of the fact that you were hoping these people would *say* something you could use against them. Usually, there was one person wearing the wire and the other person or persons present were totally unaware that they were being recorded. So they rambled on about anything under the sun, while you sat there with your thumb up your ass waiting for some kind of plot development. Even though Ollie did not much enjoy reading books, he knew all about plot development now that he'd started writing his thriller, which to tell the truth he'd found much easier than learning the first three bars of "Night and Day." In fact, he couldn't understand why the guys who wrote such shit got paid so much money for it.

The interesting thing about the tape Gomez had recorded was that Wiggins hadn't shot him at once. Because anyone listening to it—as Ollie and Carella were listening to it now—had to recognize from minute one that Tigo was on a fishing expedition and that what he was fishing for was an admission of murder. But Wiggins had something else on his mind, and as the detectives listened and ate—Ollie's banana was particularly tasty with a baloney sandwich smothered in mustard—they began to become more and more interested in what Wiggins was saying than in Gomez's inept attempts to wring a confession from him.

Since Gomez's voice was the only one they'd heard before now, they cleverly detected which of the two speakers was the one wearing the wire and doing the fishing, which easily enabled them to assign the other voice to Wiggins. And since both detectives were used to *reading* transcripts of tapes, they automatically began *listening* that way, labeling each voice as it came from the recorder. They were frankly getting bored stiff with Tigo's clumsy interrogation, expecting Wiggy to yell "The fuck you *doin,* man?" and shoot the silly jackass dead, when all at once Wiggy began talking about the computers he'd tapped into up at Wadsworth and Dodds. Ollie wondered what the man had been doing up there at his future publishing house, but Wiggy wasn't about to explain that. Instead, he began talking about what he'd found on the computers. Ollie looked at Carella. Carella shrugged.

WIGGY: All these files labeled with girls' names.
TIGO: Whut you mean names?
WIGGY: Rina and Bela and Ada and Gina and Tessie, and here's the one really got me . . . Diana.
TIGO: Like Princess Di?
WIGGY: Yeah, but it's Diamondback. It's code for Diamondback.
TIGO: How you know that, Wigg?
WIGGY: It was on the PC. Man left it wide open for me when I showed him the ugly. D-I-A-N-A. Right there in the name Diamondback, juss mixed up and turned all aroun, is all.
TIGO: If the man put a code in there, why he want to go *splain* it to you?
WIGGY: Nobody splained it to me, man. I doped it out all by myself. Same as how B-E-L-A is for Lebanon. And G-I-N-A is for Nicaragua.
TIGO: Why they want to do that for, Wigg?
WIGGY: To hide what they *doin* in those places. Man, don't get me wrong. I don't give a shit bout the mischief they into anyplace else. But when they buyin dope in Mexico and sellin it up here in Diamondback . . .
TIGO: We selling dope here, too, Wigg.
WIGGY: It ain't the same thing, man. They sellin dope

up here for altogether different reasons. Man, they shittin on us black folk is what they doin.

TIGO: I just don't know, Wigg. I mean . . .

WIGGY: What is it you don't know? I just *tole* you what's happening, what is it you don't unnerstan?

There was a long silence on the tape. Ollie peeled another banana. He looked at Carella again. Carella shrugged again.

TIGO: You really think all this is true, huh? Cause to me . . .

WIGGY: Man, I was lookin straight in they computer! I seed all this stuff with my own eyes!

TIGO: It just sounds, you know, like science-fiction, you know? This file named Mothah you can't open cause you need a password, an all this money floatin aroun, and these people causin trouble all over the world, an tryin'a fuck us right here in Diamon'back, I mean, man, it sounds like suppin you'd see in a *movie,* you know what I'm sayin, man?

WIGGY: It'd make a *good* movie, that's for damn sure, but it's *true,* man! I got it from they *computer!*

TIGO: That don't mean it couldn't of been garbage in there.

WIGGY: The point is, whut we gonna *do* about it, Tigo? I mean, these guys are messin with our *people!*

There was another long silence.

"What the hell's he talkin about?" Ollie asked.

"Shhh," Carella said.

WIGGY: I think we should go to the police, tell *them* the story.

"Good idea," Ollie said to the tape.

There was the sound of a phone being dialed.

"He's calling me," Ollie said.

"I figured."

They listened to Wiggy's end of the conversation. Ollie opened a bag of potato chips. Carella finished his glass of milk. There was the sound of the phone receiver clicking onto the cradle. Ollie dipped into the bag of chips.

WIGGY: Weeks is on the way.

TIGO: That's just great.

WIGGY: You maybe seed him aroun the streets. Fat Ollie Weeks. He's this big fat guy.

"Hey, watch it," Ollie said.

TIGO: You goan tell him you a drug dealer?

WIGGY: No, I don't have to tell him that.

TIGO: Then how come you *know* these people are sellin dope up here?

WIGGY: I coulda heard.

TIGO: *How* you coulda heard, Wigg? You goan tell the fuzz this man Hoskins come up here Christmastime, sold you a hundred keys of coke to distribute to li'l kiddies in the streets?

"Here we go," Ollie said.

"Shhh," Carella said again.

| | |
|---|---|
| WIGGY: | No. But I could . . . |
| TIGO: | You goan tell him you shot this man Hoskins back of the head an dropped him in a garbage can? You goan do that, Wigg? |

"Go for it, man," Ollie said.

| | |
|---|---|
| WIGGY: | I'm sayin' it don't seem right, what these mothahs are doin to our people. |
| TIGO: | They's evil folk in this world, it *is* a shame. |
| WIGGY: | You know what the name Nettie stans for? |
| TIGO: | Nettie, you say? |
| WIGGY: | N-E-T-T-I-E. You know what word that name is hidin' in? |
| TIGO: | No, I has to admit I do not. |
| WIGGY: | Counterfeit. That's the word. You search that word, you find Nettie lurkin in there. You double-click on her name, you transported straight to Nettieland. You want to hear this, man, or you want to stay ignorant the ress of your life? |

"This is all bullshit," Ollie said.

"Let's hear what the man . . ."

"He's hallucinatin," Ollie said.

"For Christ's *sake!*" Carella said, and snapped off the recorder, and shot Ollie a look. Ollie dug into the bag of chips again. Carella hit the rewind button. Ollie looked offended.

WIGGY: . . . hear this, man, or you want to stay ignorant the ress of your life? What these mothahs doin, they buyin fake money in I-ran. Hunnerd-dollar bills. So good you want to lick 'em right off the page. They buy 'em at a fifty-percent discount. That means they pays half a century for a C-note, they ahead of the game by fifty already, you dig, man?

TIGO: I'm listening.

WIGGY: They takes this fake money to Mexico, where they buy high quality shit with it. You member what that white dude was sellin us aroun Christmastime?

TIGO: The one you shot and thowed in the garbage can?

WIGGY: The hunnerd keys we tested, you member it?

TIGO: I member you shootin him. Why'd you kill that man, Wigg?

WIGGY: Point I'm makin is them hunnerd keys was purchased with funny money, man. They gettin *twice* the dope they should be gettin cause they payin for it with bills coss 'em ony *half* what they face value is. You see the scam they got goin here, man?

TIGO: Wish we'da thought of it, Wigg.

WIGGY: But *we* ain't gettin no fifty-percent payback here in Diamondback, man! We payin the full an honorable price for the shit. And they takin the big profit they make up here an usin it for financin all they activities all over the world, you know what I'm sayin? Man, we payin 'em good money, an they usin it to start some revolution in *Africa* someplace!

TIGO: Who you mean by *they,* man? Who's *they?*

WIGGY: I don't *know* who they is. But I'll bet you any amount of money it's right there in that folder marked *Mothah.* You fine the password to that folder, man, you on the way to trackin down *zackly* who these people are.

TIGO: Why you so keen on knowin that, man?

WIGGY: What's the matter with you, Teeg, you some kind of fool? They fuckin us six ways from the middle! You close Nettie and you double-click on Diana, you know what you fine in that Diamondback file? You fine what the plan is for *us,* man. You see what they *really* doin up here, you see how this thing comes full circle.

TIGO: What is it they doin, Wigg? I'm sorry, but I don't see what . . .

WIGGY: They buildin a community of *dope* fiends, man. They keepin the nigger in his place so he can't work, he can't vote, he can't do a fuckin thing but shoot H in his arm or sniff coke up his nose! They turnin us into fuckin slaves all over again.

TIGO: Man, Wiggy.

WIGGY: Yeah, man, is right. That's why I called that fat hump cop. They got to know what's goin on here, Teeg. Somebody got to put a stop to it.

TIGO: One thing I don't get, Wigg.

WIGGY: What's that?

TIGO: These dudes in I-ran? The ones gettin paid *real* money for the fake stuff?

WIGGY: Who gives a shit about them, man? You unnerstan what I'm *sayin* here?

TIGO: I was juss wonderin what they *do* with that money, that's all.

The shots exploding from the recorder startled both detectives. Ollie actually dropped the bag of potato chips. Screams erupted over the ugly stutter of automatic gunfire. A woman's voice shouted, "The window!" There was the sound of glass breaking. Heavy breathing. More shots. Footsteps clanging on metal. The breathing harsher now. Yet more shots. More footsteps pounding. And then Carella's own voice came from the machine.

CARELLA: You know who did this to you? Who, Tigo? Can you tell me?
TIGO: Mother.
CARELLA: Your *mother* shot . . . ?
TIGO: Nettie.
CARELLA: Is that your mother's name?
TIGO: Diana.
CARELLA: I don't under . . .

There was more shooting.
Heavy breathing.

OLLIE: That's two, Steve.

"Who the fuck is Mother?" Ollie asked.

FROM WHERE SVI COHEN STOOD CENTER STAGE, HE could see the vast enclosing arms of Clarendon Hall, from the orchestra level soaring upward to the first and second tiers, and the dress circle, and the front and rear balconies. A giant of a man himself, he felt dwarfed by the golden sweep of the most prestigious concert hall in the United States. It was here that Jascha Heifetz, a seventeen-year-old Russian violinist, made his explosive American debut in 1917. It was here—not a decade later—that a ten-year-old prodigy named Yehudi Menuhin stunned the world of classical music with a violin style that combined the elegance of Kreisler, the sonority of Elman, and the technique of Heifetz himself. Here, too, on this very stage, the great Russian pianist Svetlana Dyalovich had made her American debut. Svi stood staring out at the red-carpeted space, overwhelmed.

"So how does it look to you?" Arthur Rankin asked, beaming.

Rankin was the Philharmonic's conductor, a man in his sixties, a man who'd been playing violin since he was four years old and conducting since he was thirty, but in the presence of this thirty-seven-year-old genius from Tel Aviv, he was virtually awe-stricken.

"Wait till you hear the sound," he said.

"I can imagine," Svi said.

The orchestra was beginning to tune up.

Tonight's program would start with "La Gazza Ladra"—the "Thieving Magpie" overture from Rossini's *The Barber of Seville.* They would then play Mozart's no. 40 in G Minor to conclude the first half of the evening. There would be a twelve-minute intermission, and then Svi Cohen would take the stage. The orchestra had been rehearsing all of the pieces for the past week now, but this was the first time they would be playing the Mendelssohn E Minor with the Israeli violinist.

Rankin tapped his baton for silence.

"Gentlemen?" he said. "May I introduce our honored guest?"

THE PLAN WAS A SIMPLE ONE.

They had been trained to believe that all good plans were simple ones.

Part of the seed money had been spent for false identity papers created for them by a master forger who'd been trained in Bucharest and who now lived in a small town upstate, where he sold antiques as a sideline. Passports, green cards, driver's licenses, social security cards, credit cards—all that anyone might need to move freely around the United States, or indeed around the world. From the stock of a Cadillac dealership in the state across the river, Nikmaddu—using the assumed name on his new driver's license—had purchased outright a black DeVille sedan. The car would be used in the attack tonight, and then driven to Florida, where it would be disposed of before all four men parted company. Akbar, Mahmoud, and Jassim would board separate flights to Zurich, Paris, and Frankfurt, and would then disperse to the far corners of the Arab world. Nikmaddu would leave first for Chicago, and then San Francisco, and finally Los Angeles. The attack here in this city would have put only a small dent in the cash he'd carried from home. Activities elsewhere in the United States required money, too. Money was what made the world of terrorism—or, as he preferred to call it, liberation—go round. Money was both the engine and the fuel.

At seven-forty-five tonight Akbar, wearing a chauffeur's uniform, would drive the Cadillac—

They called this luxurious car a Caddy, the Americans.

They also used this word to describe the menial who carried a golfer's clubs. A strange country.

He would drive the Caddy, then, to the front door of Clarendon Hall. Jassim, barbered and bathed and manicured and groomed, well-tailored in a black business suit, carrying a man's handbag purchased at Gucci on Hall Avenue, would present his ticket and enter the hall. If he was asked to open the bag, which was highly unlikely, they would find in it only a package of cigarettes, a gold and enamel cigarette lighter also purchased at Gucci, a Coach leather wallet, and a paperback copy of *Catcher in the Rye.* It was not until later that Jassim would re-enter the hall carrying the armed bomb.

"Where will you be during the first part of the concert?" Nikmaddu asked.

Akbar, who had assembled the bomb, and who would be responsible for arming it before Jassim went back in, said, "I'll be parked just across the street."

"Wouldn't it be better to park directly outside?"

"It is forbidden to park in front of the hall. Or, in fact, anywhere on that side of the street. Most of the limo drivers park across the way or around the corner. Jassim knows where I'll be. We've run this through many times already."

Mahmoud looked at him skeptically.

"Half the taxicab and limousine drivers in this city are from the Middle East," Akbar said. "I will not arouse any suspicion. I will sit behind the wheel quietly, minding my own business, smoking a cigarette and waiting for my fat Jew employer to come out of the hall. Jassim and I will find each other, don't worry."

"You've got only twelve minutes to find each other," Mahmoud reminded them.

"I'll be watching for him to come out," Akbar said. "We'll have more than enough time, believe me."

"What time does the concert start?" Nikmaddu asked.

"It's supposed to begin at eight. Experience has taught me that it always starts some five or ten minutes later."

"And the intermission is when?"

"The Rossini overture can take anywhere between nine and eleven minutes and the Mozart symphony between twenty-five and thirty-five. On average, I would expect the first half of the concert to run some forty minutes. The intermission should start at around nine or a little bit after."

"Can you not be more precise?" Nikmaddu asked.

"I'm sorry," Akbar said. "Western music is not always precise. In any case, I'll arm the bomb when Jassim returns to the limousine. I'll place it in his bag, and he'll go back into the hall. You'd be surprised how long a time twelve minutes is."

"I hope so. I wouldn't want the bomb to explode while he's still outside on the sidewalk."

"No, that can't possibly happen. The intermission will end, let's say, at nine-fifteen. They will allow at most five minutes for everyone to get settled again. Let's say the Jew comes on stage at nine-twenty. The bomb will be set to explode at nine-thirty. Jassim will be long gone by then."

*"Inshallah,"* Mahmoud said.

*"Inshallah,"* the others repeated.

The men fell silent.

"The weather is supposed to be clear and cold tonight," Nikmaddu said at last.

"Good," Mahmoud said. "Then our drive to Florida should be trouble free."

"Someday, I would love to spend some time in Florida," Akbar said, almost wistfully.

THE BLONDE OLLIE HAD SHOT IN THE BACK WAS IN A room on the sixth floor of Hoch Memorial. A male police officer was stationed outside the door to the room. The clock on the wall behind him read twelve-forty P.M. The blonde had plastic tubes trailing out of her nose. The blonde had lines running into her arm. Neither Carella nor Ollie felt the slightest bit of pity or compassion for her on this cold December afternoon at the end of the year.

"Want to tell us who you are?" Carella asked.

"I don't have to tell you anything," she said. "You're making a grave mistake here."

"You're the one who made the grave mistake," Ollie said.

*"Three* of them," Carella said.

The blonde smiled.

"What's your name?" he asked.

"I don't have to tell you that."

"You killed two civilians and tried to kill a police officer. Do you know what kind of trouble you're in here?"

"I'm not in any trouble at all."

"Two counts of Murder Two . . ."

"Another count of Attempted . . ."

"On our block, that's pretty serious," Ollie said.

"On my block, it's routine," she said.

"And where's that, Miss?"

"What's your name, Miss?"

"Where do you live?"

"How come you weren't carrying any identification?"

The blonde smiled again.

"You think this is pretty funny, don't you?" Ollie said.

"Trying to kill a police officer."

"How about a police officer shooting me in the back?" she said. "Do you think *that's* funny?"

"Not as funny as it might have been if I'd killed you," Ollie said. "That really would've been comical."

"You think so, huh? Just wait, Mister."

"For what?" Ollie said.

"Just wait."

"What it is, you see, we don't like cops getting shot in this city."

"Then cops in this city should keep their noses out of other people's business."

"Which people are you talking about?"

"People with more important matters on their minds than two piss-ant dope dealers."

"Oh?" Carella said.

"Oh?" Ollie said.

"You knew they were dealing, huh?"

The blonde smiled.

"What else did you know about them?"

She shook her head.

"Did you know one of them killed a man named Jerry Hoskins?"

She kept smiling, shaking her head.

"Ever hear that name?"

"Jerry Hoskins?"

"Got himself shot on Christmas Eve by one of the guys *you* shot last night? Think there might be a connection?"

"Stop blowing smoke up my skirt," she said.

"Jerry Hoskins? Frank Holt?" Ollie said.

"One and the same person," Carella said.

"Sold Wiggins a hundred keys of coke on Christmas Eve . . ."

"Got paid for it with a bullet at the back of his head. Ever hear of him?"

"Jerry Hoskins?"

"Frank Holt?"

The blonde said nothing.

"Ever hear of a woman named Cass Ridley?" Ollie said.

"Cassandra Ridley?" Carella said.

"Flew a hundred keys of shit out of Mexico for Jerry Hoskins. Ever hear of *her?*"

"I'm not saying anything until my people contact you."

"Oh? Your people? Who are these people?"

"You'll find out."

"You got friends in high places?" Ollie asked.

"The Mayor's office?"

"The Governor's mansion?"

"The White House?"

"Go ahead, laugh," she said.

"Nobody's laughing," Ollie said. "What it looks like is you knew Walter Wiggins was dealing drugs, and maybe you also knew Hoskins was in the same business . . ."

"Keep blowing smoke," she said.

"Did you also know Cass Ridley, who flew the shit up from Mexico?"

"Did you happen to take a bottle of champagne to her apartment?"

"Did you and another fine lady walk her over to the zoo?"

"You and another blond lady?"

"Both of you wearing black?"

"We got a doorman just *itching* to identify you."

"Keep blowing, I'm beginning to enjoy it."

"I wonder how you'll enjoy your date with the D.A."

*"You've* got a date with my people," she said. "But you don't seem to . . ."

"We're dying to meet them," Carella said.

"Tell us who they are, we'll go pay them a visit."

"Maybe they can explain how come you killed Wiggins who killed Hoskins who hired Ridley to fly dope for him."

"Maybe they can explain how Ridley ended up in that lion's cage," Ollie said.

"No ID on her," Carella said.

"Maybe your people can explain all that."

"Maybe my people can have you both walking beats tomorrow morning."

"Oooo," Carella said. "A threat, Ollie."

"Oooo," Ollie said.

There was nothing he liked better than a perp trying to pull rank. Especially when the perp had tried to gun down a cop.

"You think these important people you know'll come riding to the rescue, is that it?" he said.

"You don't know what you're messing with here."

"Gee, I thought we were messing with an Attempted Murder One and a pair of Murder Twos."

"You'd never make it to trial. They'll step on you like a bug."

"Who? Your important people in high places?"

The blonde smiled.

Ollie just loved it when they smiled.

"If your friends take you out of here, they'll be harboring a fugitive," he said. "That's called Hindering Prosecution in the first degree, Section 205.65 of the Penal Law. Want to hear it?"

"Shove it up your ass," the blonde said.

"Nice talk on the lady," Ollie said. "Hindering prosecution is rendering criminal assistance to a person who's committed a class-A felony. Murder Two is a class-A felony. So's Attempted Murder One. If your friends whisk you out of here, they'll be staring at a seven-year max in the slammer. Maybe that's why they're not here yet, huh?"

"All in good time," the blonde said.

"Oh sure, I hear them thundering down the hallway right this minute."

The blonde actually cocked her head toward the door.

"But maybe not," Ollie said. "Ballistics is checking the slugs that killed the two dealers. If they match the ones we test-fire from that cannon you were carrying . . ."

"Save it. I'm not interested."

"Well, let me tell you what else we've got," Carella said. "It might change your mind."

"I got shot last night. I'm tired. Goodbye, Mr. Detective."

"We've got one of the guys you killed wearing a wire. We've got the other guy you killed *talking* on that wire. Saying a lot of interesting things about a company called Wadsworth and Dodds, ever hear of them?"

"No."

"W&D?"

"No."

"Witches and Dragons?" Carella said. "Is that a glimmer I see in your eye? How about Mother? Do you know who Mother is?"

The blonde said nothing.

"Ever see that name on a W&D computer?"

The blonde was still silent.

"Ever hear that name anyplace?"

"Why don't you go home, Mr. Detective?"

"People keep telling me to go home," Carella said to Ollie.

"Maybe you should," Ollie said.

"Yeah, but gee, I'd like to finish this, you know?"

"So finish it."

"Here's where we're coming from, Miss," Carella said, turning back to the bed. "A person is guilty of Murder in the First Degree when the intended victim is a police officer who at the time of the killing is engaged in the course of performing his official duties, quote, unquote, Section 125.27 of the state's Penal Law. You tried to kill a police officer last night, honey. *Me. Would* have killed me, in fact, if another police officer—Detective Oliver Wendell Weeks here—hadn't expediently intervened. That makes the crime *Attempt* to Commit Murder, which in this case is an A-1 felony. Add to that the *actual* murders of both Tito Alberico Gomez and Walter Kennedy Wiggins, and you're looking at twenty-five years to life, three times over. That comes to seventy-five years in the slammer. You'll be a hundred years old when you get out."

"A hundred and five," the blonde said.

"That's if we don't get a positive ID from the doorman."

"What doorman?"

"The one who let you in Cass Ridley's apartment building. Where you stuck an ice pick in her forehead. You can add another twenty-five for that one."

"You think so? *I* think I'll be out of here before you jerks leave the building."

"You got shot when?" Ollie said. "Seven, seven-thirty last night? You know what time it is now? Almost one o'clock the next day. Has anyone been here to see you? Has anyone even called you? Where's the cavalry, sweetheart? They're riding into the sunset, that's where they are, and leaving you to take the fall. But, hey, be loyal. Seventy-five years behind bars may seem better to you than anything we've got to offer."

The blonde was looking at him.

Ollie figured he had her attention.

"Want to hear it?"

"No. I want to go to sleep."

"Okay, go to sleep. I guess we'll have to charge her on all three counts, Steve."

"Maybe four if we get lucky with the doorman," Carella said. "Too bad she can't help us get our search warrant, huh?"

"A crying shame," Ollie said.

"Well, what are you gonna do?" Carella said, and shrugged. "Let's go home."

"So long, Miss," Ollie said, and both detectives started out of the room.

"What do you mean?" thc blonde asked.

They turned back to the bed.

"About a search warrant?" she said.

"Let me be honest with you, okay?" Ollie said, which was the last thing he wished to be with her. "We know you won't admit you're a hitter for W&D because that would make this Murder for Hire, and that means the Valium cocktail if you're convicted."

"The death penalty," Carella explained. "Lethal injection."

"I hear it's actually pleasant," Ollie said, and smiled. "But we know you won't admit that somebody *paid* you for offing the redhead and the two Negroes, so all we've really got for sure are the pair of Twos and the One-Ten. Which is enough to put you away for seventy-five, I might remind you, ah yes, if that's the route you choose to take."

"Or," Carella said.

"Or," Ollie agreed, and nodded.

"Or *what?* Let me hear it."

"To the point, I like that in a woman," Ollie said. "Do you know what's on any of the W&D computers?"

"Let's say I *can* know what's on them if I *need* to know what's on them."

"Let's say you *need* to know what's on them if you want to deal here," Ollie said.

"But of course we can't speak for the D.A.," Carella said.

"Of course not. But *if* the lady wants to deal, she would have to tell us she knows what's on those computers."

"You're both so full of shit," she said. "Tell me what you want me to say."

"We want you to say that evidence of a crime exists on W&D's computers."

"What crime?"

"From what we understand, the Criminal Sale of Controlled Substances."

"In the first degree," Carella said.

"Section 220.43."

"An A-1 felony."

"Twenty-five to life upstate."

"Heavy," Carella said.

"That's the crime," Ollie said. "From what we understand."

"And how do you happen to understand this?"

"A good question," Ollie said. "We've got a tape, remember?"

"We want you to listen to that tape," Carella said.

"Tell us it's accurate . . ."

". . . so we can get a search warrant on probable cause."

"Reliable information from a cooperative witness and all that," Ollie said.

*"If* I cooperate," the blonde said.

"Well, that's entirely up to you, m'little chickadee, ah yes."

"What do I get in return?"

"We'll drop the One-Ten," Ollie said. "That okay with you, Steve? I mean, you're the one she tried to kill."

"That's fine with me, if it's okay with the D.A."

"Yeah, well, it's not fine with me," the blonde said.

"Then you tell us."

"Drop everything."

"We can't do that."

"Oh, yes you can. I walk, you get the big boys."

"Well, maybe we can reduce the murder counts to manslaughter."

"Well, maybe I don't think that's good enough, either, okay?"

"Two counts of Manslaughter One? That's *very* good," Ollie said. "And we'll drop the Attempted, don't forget."

"Sorry, boys."

"Somewhere between five and twenty-five on each?" Carella said. "That's a good deal. Don't you think that's a good deal, Ollie?"

"I do indeed. What do you say, Miss?"

"I say I want five, not twenty-five."

Carella pretended to be thinking this over. He looked at Ollie. Ollie sighed.

"Okay, five," Carella said.

"And you run the sentences concurrently," the blonde said.

"No, we can't do that," Carella said. "That'd come to only two and a half on each hit."

"Come on, honey, be realistic," Ollie said.

"The guys who got whacked were a pair of shits," the blonde said. "I did society a favor."

"Still, just five *concurrently?"* Carella said.

"For a *double hit?"* Ollie said.

"That's all they're worth," the blonde said.

"Let me call the D.A.," Carella said. "Play the tape for her, Ollie."

# 12.

**THEY INTERROGATED RICHARD HALLOWAY AT TEN** minutes to five that Saturday afternoon. He was wearing gray flannel slacks, a blue blazer, a blue button-down shirt, and a green bow tie printed with little red prancing deer. He had waived his right to an attorney, and so there were only four people in the interrogation room—Halloway himself, Detectives Carella and Weeks, and Detective-Lieutenant Byrnes—all of them sitting around the long cigarette-scarred table, drinking coffee. Halloway seemed completely relaxed and supremely self-assured.

"Mr. Halloway," Carella said, "when we entered the offices of Wadsworth and Dodds this afternoon at three-thirty, were you packing to move?"

"Is it a crime to move one's offices?" Halloway asked.

"Only if you're moving to conceal evidence of a crime."

"I see. And what crime was I supposed to have been concealing?"

"We have a warrant to open your computers, Mr. Halloway."

"So open them," Halloway said, and smiled, and added, "If you can."

"Oh, we will."

"Good luck."

"We think we might find some interesting stuff on your database."

"If you find sales figures interesting."

"Tell me about that database, okay?"

"Sure. Which book?"

"A folder called Witches and Dragons."

"I'm not familiar with that title. How about *Diagnostic and Statistical Manual of . . . ?*"

"How about a file named Diana?"

"Don't know that title, either."

"Or Em. Interesting file, Em. Seems to list all the drug deals your firm has made in Mexico over the past two years. Dates, locations, number of kilos, purchase prices, etcetera, etcetera, the whole megillah."

"I'm more familiar with *Practical Classroom Chemistry* by Guthrie Frane. I know we have a file on that."

"Do you have a file called Nettie?"

"Not to my knowledge."

"The Feds might be interested in that one. We think Nettie stands for 'counterfeiting.' We think you've been buying counterfeit money in Iran and using it to finance your various drug transactions."

"My, my, all this crime in such a small publishing house."

"We think your database will provide evidence of those crimes. And other interesting activities."

"Assuming, of course, that you can get into our computers."

"I think we can."

"Well, you can certainly try."

"Our nerds are very determined."

"I'm sure they are," Halloway said, and finished his coffee, and stood up, and smiled. "Well, I have things to do," he said, "as I'm sure you do, too. So let's not waste any more time here, hmm? I know you believe . . ."

"You're under arrest here, Mr. Halloway," Byrnes said. "Please don't forget that."

"Perhaps *you* should forget exactly that," Halloway said. "Believe me, you're not going to pick up any marbles this time. Not this time, boys. So, if there's nothing further . . ."

"Sit down," Byrnes said.

Halloway smiled. But he sat.

"We're charging you with the criminal sale of controlled substances in the first degree," Byrnes said. "That's Section 220.43 of the Penal Law, an A-1 felony punishable by a term of twenty-five years to life. We've got twenty-four hours to arraign you before McNabb-Mallory kicks in. That means you'll be before a criminal court judge early tomorrow morning. We'll ask for sky-high bail, you're an international drug dealer. If he goes along with that, we'll have six days to crack your goddamn computers and present our case to a grand jury. Any questions?"

Halloway was still smiling.

"Let me give you some advice," he said. "You should have listened to the Secret Service when they told you to back off, but you didn't. So here we are, at an awkward juncture that could have been avoided. I certainly shouldn't be here, but neither should you. Which is why I'm suggesting you listen to me now." He looked at his watch. "When I walk out of here in five minutes, you will forget you ever saw me, you will forget a woman named Cass Ridley met a horrible fate in the zoo's Lion Habitat, you will forget . . ."

"What are you, a hypnotist?" Ollie said.

"Allow me to finish, Detective Weeks. I am advising you to put all of this behind you. Forget Jerry Hoskins was murdered, forget that two black drug dealers in Diamondback were subsequently killed, forget everything that's happened since December twenty-third, forget you ever woke *up* that morning. There are bad people in this world, boys. Pursuing this any further . . ."

"People like you," Carella said, nodding.

"No, you've got it backwards. I'm one of the *good* guys. I'm talking about people who are *terrorists.* People who consider us the Great Satan. People who wish us nothing but harm. These people all believe in the same cause. And that cause is to drive Americans out of the Arab world."

His tone had changed all at once, his voice sounding suddenly portentous and, to tell the truth, somewhat frightening.

"There's a vast network of individual terrorist cells out there," he said, "take my word for it. Three or four dedicated individuals in each cell, that's all it takes to do considerable mischief. Anonymous little *gangs,* if you will, who get their orders and their financing from the top, and then use their own judgment in executing those orders. Makes it enormously difficult to zero in on them, no less stop them. Why do you think those two men who bombed the *Cole* still can't be traced back to bin Laden? Why do you think . . . ?"

"What's any of this got to do with you buying and selling dope?" Ollie said.

"No one has yet produced any evidence to that effect," Halloway said. "Once I walk through that door . . ."

"You're not walking through any door," Byrnes said. "You're going straight to a detention cell downstairs."

"That would be inadvisable."

"Who the fuck do you think you are?" Ollie asked. "The CIA?"

Halloway smiled.

"Cause you want my opinion, there *ain't* no CIA. Any outfit so fuckin stupid has got to be a cover for our *real* intelligence agency."

"I'll have to remember that one," Halloway said, and actually laughed. "No CIA, that's very funny. On the other hand, *you* might wish to consider the possibility that the CIA, *if* it exists, has adopted the same techniques as the people they're fighting. If there *is* a CIA—and perhaps you're right, perhaps there isn't—but on the slight off-chance that there *might* be, then perhaps they've splintered into hundreds of little *counter*-terrorist cells all over the globe. Little self-reliant units that take orders from the top and carry them out autonomously. Authorized roving bands of brothers, you might say—sisters, too, if you wish to be politically correct. Legitimate loose cannons. And if this is actually so, then perhaps you stepped . . ."

"Authorized by *who?*" Ollie said.

"Well, if there *is* a CIA, then the authorization comes directly from the President or the National Security Council, doesn't it?" He smiled again. Looked at his watch again. "Let's say you stepped in the way of a rolling cannon on a tilting deck, boys. You stumbled into something far more vital to the interests of the United States than a bunch of dumb flatfoots, believe me. You should have known enough to step aside, boys. Instead, you stepped in shit. Wipe off your shoes and go home."

"Somebody else telling us to go home," Carella said.

"I'm telling you it's possible to get chewed to shreds by lions," Halloway said.

"He's saying don't go in the lion's cage tonight," Ollie said.

"For the lions are ferocious and they bite," Carella said.

"Well, Mr. Halloway," Byrnes said, and stabbed at a button on his intercom, "I appreciate your advice, truly. But you see we might feel derelict in our duty if we just let you walk out of here. So with the permission of the President and the National . . ."

"Sir?" a voice said.

"I'll need an officer to take a prisoner down," Byrnes said.

"I'll send someone forthwith, sir."

"Thanks," Byrnes said, and clicked off.

"I want to warn you again not to do this," Halloway said. "Don't open a can of peas that might explode in your face. Don't threaten our very existence, our sacred undertaking, our . . ."

"Gee, sacred," Ollie said.

"Because if you do, if you destroy everything we've been trying to accomplish, if you open our files to public scrut . . ."

"I thought your computers were sacred, too," Ollie said.

The door to Byrnes's office opened.

"Sir?" a uniformed officer said.

"Maggie, find a cell downstairs for this gentleman, will you?" He turned to Halloway. "Do we have to cuff you?" he asked.

"Only lions bite," Halloway said, and smiled thinly. "You'll never even get me arraigned, I promise you. You've got to be kidding here. The Commissioner will come down on you so hard you'll wish you lived on Mars. You think we'll let a Mickey Mouse detective squad in the asshole of the universe jeopardize everything we've been working for? Who'd stop those bastards *then,* can you tell me? Who'd stop them from poisoning our reservoirs or blowing up our trains? Who'd stop them from planting bombs in day care centers or baseball parks? Who'd stop them from destroying this land of ours? This *world* of ours? This *free* world of ours? You? Are you the ones who'll save us? Don't make me laugh! You should get on your hands and knees and praise God we exist! Because if it weren't for us, there'd be nobody! Nobody at all! They'd make it impossible to walk the streets! They'd blow up your babies in their cribs! Without us, who the hell on earth would even *try* to stop them? I'm asking you. *Who?*"

**WILL STRUTHERS HELPED ANTONIA OUT OF THE TAXI** in front of Clarendon Hall and looked up at the falling snow. The snow added a somewhat festive air to the evening. In a city of strangers, people were actually smiling at each other as they entered the old limestone building. Will looked up at the television monitors spaced high on the walls everywhere around the lobby, all of them showing the stage inside. "For the benefit of latecomers," Antonia explained, which Will didn't quite understand, but he followed her as she handed their tickets to a man standing at one of the entrance doors to the hall itself. Together, they stepped into the vast space, all red and gold and magnificent, glittering like an outsized Christmas present left by Santa himself. Will had never seen anything so splendiferous in his life. Not even in Texas.

**THE SHORT, SLIGHT MAN WHO STEPPED OUT OF THE BLACK** Cadillac DeVille was wearing a black overcoat with a mink collar. The trousers of a black suit showed below the bottom edge of the coat. He was wearing a black homburg and highly polished black shoes. Hanging from a strap over his left shoulder was a man's black leather handbag. The hat, the coat's collar, the coat's shoulders became immediately dusted with falling snow. The tinted glass window of the limo slid down silently. The man leaned into it and gave the driver some instructions in English. The driver answered in English and then the window slid up again, and the limo pulled away from the curb.

Standing in the falling snow on the sidewalk outside Clarendon Hall, Jassim Saiyed reached into the handbag, removed from it a package of Marlboro cigarettes, shook one free, and lighted it. He glanced at his wristwatch. It was fifteen minutes to eight. Puffing calmly on his cigarette, Jassim watched the crowd of smiling Americans entering the building.

THEY TOOK THEIR SEATS IN ROW G, SEVEN ROWS BACK from the stage, numbers 2 and 4 on the aisle.

"Good, huh?" Antonia said, grinning. "One of my best customers plays oboe with the orchestra. This was his Christmas present to me."

Will was thinking that when he and Antonia became millionaires, they would come to places like this all the time, never mind free handouts from anybody. There was a sense of excitement and anticipation in this opulent place, resounding now with the repeated sounds of strings and horns tuning up. Leafing through the program, he noticed that one of the pieces they'd be playing tonight was something called "La Gazza Ladra," which he saw was translated as "The Thieving Magpie."

He showed this to Antonia, and then whispered, "I hope this isn't anything personal."

Antonia laughed.

A hush fell over the audience.

The concert was about to begin.

JASSIM LOOKED AT HIS WRISTWATCH.

If Akbar's calculations were correct, the intermission would begin at approximately nine o'clock. Jassim would go up the aisle, and out into the lobby, and hence into the street, where Akbar would be waiting in the Cadillac. He would arm the bomb's timing device, and Jassim would come back into the hall, and take his seat again. Several moments later, after the Jew had started playing, Jassim would rise again from his seat, apparently on his way to the men's room, leaving behind him his hat, his coat, and the bag containing the bomb. At precisely nine-thirty, the bomb would explode.

Jassim wondered why he felt so calm.

WILL WAS BORED TO DEATH.

The kind of music he liked best was what he heard back home in Texas. Songs about cowboys. Songs about women with broken hearts. Songs about true-blue hound dogs. The orchestra up on the stage there sounded like it was practicing.

He could hardly wait for the intermission.

TERROR WAS THE ONLY THOUGHT ON JASSIM'S MIND.

Strike terror into their hearts.

Deliver fatal blows all over the world.

He rose the moment the lights came up, placed his coat and his hat on the seat, and began walking swiftly toward the back of the hall. His watch read exactly three minutes past nine. He wanted to be back in his seat again by nine-fifteen, when the intermission would end. The aisle was thronged with concert-goers making their way to the rest rooms or the street outside. Patiently, Jassim milled along with them, but his heart was pounding inside his chest. He tried not to look at his watch again until he reached the lobby outside.

Nine-oh-six.

He raced through the lobby and out onto the sidewalk.

He looked across the street.

The Cadillac was parked exactly where Akbar said it would be.

But a policeman in a black rain slicker was standing outside the door on the driver's side.

THERE WAS IN THE LOBBY A PALPABLE AIR OF ANTICIPATION. The first part of the concert had been agreeable enough, but this glittery crowd was not here for the Rossini or the Mozart. In fact, they were not even here for the Mendelssohn. They were here for the man who would be *playing* the Mendelssohn. The chatter was about Christmas gifts received and exchanged, and plans for tomorrow night's celebration, and the weather and the market and the latest war abroad, but the people here in the lobby or smoking in the falling snow on the sidewalk outside were merely trying to conceal their excitement over the imminent appearance of the Israeli violinist. Like children careful not to wish for sunshine for fear it might rain upon their circus, they dared not even breathe his name lest he vanish somehow in a puff of smoke, disappointing their expectations.

THE POLICEMAN STOOD LEANING INTO THE OPEN window on the driver's side of the Cadillac, a massive man in a slippery black coat, the snow falling everywhere around him. Akbar was handing documents to him. The policeman was examining the documents. Akbar was smiling at him politely. The snow kept falling.

Jassim looked at his watch.

**THE TELEVISION MONITORS SPACED AROUND THE LOBBY** showed only an empty stage now, its lights dimmed. Will kept hoping they'd show a football game or something.

"Are you enjoying it so far?" Antonia asked.

"Oh yes indeed," he said.

So far, it was putting him to sleep.

"So far, I love it," he said.

"Just wait," she said. "The real fireworks won't begin till the Israeli starts playing."

**THE POLICEMAN DID NOT WALK AWAY FROM THE CADILLAC** until fourteen minutes past nine. Dodging heavy traffic on the street, Jassim ran across to it, and yanked open the rear door on the curb side. Slamming into the car, he whispered, "What happened? What did he want?"

"Profiling!" Akbar shouted.

"What?"

"Profiling, *profiling,* never mind, give me the fucking *bag!"*

Jassim handed him the bag. He looked at his watch and then glanced immediately over his shoulder through the rear window. The intermission would end in less than a minute; the sidewalk outside Clarendon Hall was rapidly clearing. In the front seat, Akbar was working on the timing device. Jassim could hear his heavy breathing, could see perspiration beading on his forehead, could hear as well the ticking of the clock to which Akbar was wiring the detonator. He waited. His palms were sweating. He looked back over his shoulder again. The sidewalk was clear now. He caught his breath. Waited. Kept waiting. The windows of the car were beginning to fog with their exhaled breaths. It seemed to Jassim that he could hear the beating of his own heart in the steamy darkness of the vehicle. At last, he heard a faint click. The bomb was armed, the timer and detonator wires securely fastened to the two taped pipes. Akbar eased the device into the bag. He closed the flap, snapped the bag shut.

Jassim looked at his watch.

The time was twenty minutes past nine.

The intermission had ended five minutes ago.

But he still had ten minutes to get back to his seat, plant the bomb, and get out of the hall before it went off. He stepped out onto the sidewalk and ran across the street to the lobby entrance doors. The lobby was empty. The huge ornate brass clock over the center entrance doors read nine-twenty-one. There was violin music coming from within the hall. The second part of the concert had already begun. On all the television monitors circling the lobby, a miniature Svi Cohen was standing before the orchestra, violin under his chin, head bent as if in prayer, deeply engrossed in his playing. Jassim noticed that the Jew held the fiddle in his unclean hand. He was reaching for the brass handle on the door nearest him when a man wearing a gray uniform said, "I'm sorry, sir."

Jassim turned to him, puzzled.

"I can't let you in until the first movement is over."

Jassim blinked.

"It started three minutes ago, sir. I'm sorry, those are my orders."

The time was nine-twenty-two.

The Mendelssohn concerto had started at nine-nineteen, and the bomb was set to detonate at nine-thirty.

WILL WAS WONDERING HOW LONG HE'D HAVE TO SIT here. He was thinking that maybe him and Antonia could go for a bite to eat after this fiddle player did his thing, there seemed to be a nice Italian restaurant right across the avenue.

He was also wondering if anybody had ever tried to steal instruments from this place. Was there a room where they stored tubas and trombones and such? Or did all those musicians up there have their own instruments? He guessed maybe they did. Besides, he had to stop thinking like a thief. If Antonia went along with his scheme, he would never in his lifetime have to commit another burglary.

But, man, was *this* boring!

JASSIM LOOKED AT HIS WATCH AGAIN.

It was now nine-twenty-four.

The first movement of Mendelssohn's accursed violin concerto was about twelve and a half minutes long. The Jew had started playing it at nineteen minutes past nine, which meant he would end the first movement at a bit past nine-thirty-one, perhaps later, nine-thirty-three, even nine-thirty-four, depending on how much artistic license he took with the piece. Jassim could not wait until any of those times because the bomb was set to go off at nine-thirty, which meant that unless he went into the hall, it would explode right here in the lobby in six minutes.

He took a deep breath.

"Hey!" the guard shouted, but he was too late.

Jassim had thrown open one of the doors and was already running down the aisle on the right-hand side of the hall.

WILL TURNED TO LOOK UP THE AISLE WHEN HE HEARD somebody screaming. The person screaming was a short dark man carrying a handbag, holding it by the straps and beginning to twirl it over his head as he ran toward the stage, screaming. Will didn't know what the man was screaming because it was in a foreign language, but whatever it was, there was enormous rage in the words. As the man rapidly approached the stage where the Israeli was playing, he almost looked like an undersized David twirling a slingshot to hurl a stone at a giant Goliath.

Will got to his feet the moment he realized this was close to what the little man intended.

"Hey! What the hell you doing?" he shouted, and threw himself at the man, intending to tackle him, but missing by a hair. He stumbled forward, off balance, as the man stopped some three feet from the stage and shouted something else in the same foreign language.

Will didn't know quite why he hurled himself at the man again. Perhaps he was simply trying to impress Antonia, who sat in the seventh row, watching him with her mouth agape and her eyes wide. Perhaps he was remembering that the Khmer Rouge who'd tortured him had also spoken a language he couldn't understand. Whatever the reason, he threw himself into the air again just as the man released his grip on the handbag's straps. The Israeli tried to deflect the missile coming at him, raising the violin by its slender neck, simultaneously stepping aside to his right.

In that instant, Will landed on the man's back.

In the next instant, the bag exploded.

# 13.

**NEW YEAR'S EVE DAWNED BRIGHT AND CLEAR AND** piercingly cold. Something had gone wrong with Hoch Memorial's heating system during the night, and while technicians fiddled with thermostats and nozzles and valves, nurses ran around wearing sweaters or even coats over their starched white uniforms.

A multitude of people had drifted into Will's room at all hours of the night, there to take his temperature or his blood pressure, to change the dressings on his face and his hands, to offer him medication and the sort of tender loving care a wounded individual deserved. When he heard voices outside the door to his room, he thought it might be more nurses coming in to change the sheets or the dressings or the bags hanging by the bed, but instead it was just someone asking a nurse if it was okay for him to go in and talk to the patient.

The man who entered his room looked a lot like Detective Stephen Louis Carella.

"Hey, hi," Will said. "What're *you* doing here?"

Carella had just supervised the orderly discharge and transfer of one Anna DiPalumbo—which turned out to be the blond shooter's true and honorable name—from Hoch Memorial to the hospital wing at the Women's House of Detention downtown, but he didn't offer this information to Will because discussing an informant with a person who was a known felon was simply stupid and might come back to haunt him later on. If Halloway's threats were at all realistic, the arraignment later this morning might be sent south even without any further help, but it didn't hurt to err on the side of caution, as the sage once remarked.

"I had some business here," Carella said, which was true enough. "How are you doing?"

"Well, okay, I guess," Will said. "A lot better than some of the others, that's for sure."

The newspapers this morning had reported that the Israeli violinist, Svi Cohen, had been killed in what was cautiously being called "a supposed terrorist bombing" at Clarendon Hall. Six musicians in the string section had also been killed. Plus eight concert-goers sitting in the first two rows. Plus the unidentified bomber himself. Carella didn't think Halloway's case would be helped by the fact that the person who'd tried to stop the bomber was a professional burglar and not one of W&D's own elite band of brothers, as he'd called them, or sisters if you included Anna DiPalumbo, who was now on her way downtown in an ambulance, and whom Carella never cared to meet again on any snow-covered street anywhere in the world, thank you. But where were you when we needed you, Mr. Halloway? When push came to shove last night, where were all your knights in shining armor? The only hero last night had been little ole Wilbur Struthers here, sitting up in bed now and grinning like a kid on Christmas Day.

"Your picture's on the front page of two newspapers, did you know that?" Carella said.

"Yeah, I saw them. I was on TV, too, early this morning. They came here to my hospital room, can you believe it? I guess it was because of the book deal."

"What book deal?" Carella asked.

"Man from a publisher here in the city came to see me, offered me a whole bunch of money for my life story. Not as much as they gave Hillary, but a goodly sum of money anyhow. I figured I ought to take it."

"Are you free to say how *much* money?" Carella asked.

"A million-five," Will said.

"That's a goodly sum of money, all right," Carella said.

"I guess there's more than one way to make a killing, after all, huh?"

"I guess so," Carella said.

**HE STOPPED AT HIS MOTHER'S HOUSE ON THE WAY HOME.** The front walk had been shoveled clean, he wondered who had shoveled it for her. He rang the doorbell, and heard chimes sounding inside, and then her voice calling, "Just a minute." He waited.

When she opened the door, he almost burst into tears.

He had seen her only two days ago, but she seemed so suddenly old all at once.

He took her in his arms.

They hugged.

"Are you okay, son?" his mother asked.

"I'm fine, Mom."

"I love you, Steve," she said.

"I love you, too, Mom."

They sat at the kitchen table the way they used to when he was a boy eating breakfast before heading off to school, sat there now drinking coffee, and he told her he'd just come from an arraignment on what was going to shape up as a very difficult case, but at least they'd got past the first two hurdles. It was a miracle they'd managed to get the guy arraigned at all, and whereas they were hoping at best for bail in the millions, the judge had denied bail altogether, which was very good for their side. He told her all this sitting at the kitchen table, the way he used to sit there after school when he was a kid, drinking his milk and telling her everything that had happened that day.

She asked him what he and Teddy would be doing tonight, and he told her they'd be staying home with the kids, before you knew it Mark and April would be old enough to go to New Year's Eve parties on their own, might as well enjoy the few years they still had left with them. His mother asked him if Teddy would be making lentils for the new year, it was good luck to serve cold lentils when the clock struck twelve, and he told her he remembered how she used to do that when he was a boy . . .

"Well, I still do it," his mother said.

"I know, Mom. I'll tell Teddy."

"Tell her," his mother said. "It's good luck, really."

They both fell suddenly silent.

He could hear the clock ticking in the living room.

He remembered his father winding that clock every Sunday night.

"Well," he said, and there was nothing left to say except that he was sorry.

"I love you, Mom," he said. "If you want to get married, I'll lead you down the aisle. Angela, too, I love you both, I'm sorry I behaved like a shit. I think maybe it was the lion, I think Ange was right, I think that lion scrambled my brains. But there are no more lions now, I'm okay now, I promise you. I'm cool with it, really. I love you both, I'm sorry, life's too damn short, I love you."

They hugged again.

At the front door, she reminded him that the lentils had to be served at midnight, not before.

"For luck in the new year," she said.

"I'll remember," he said.

"Good luck with your case," she said.

"Thanks, Mom."

He was starting for the car when he turned to her and said, "Mom?"

She was just about to close the door.

"Mom?" he said again.

"Yes, son?"

"Say hello to . . . uh . . . Luigi for me, okay?"

"Yes, son," she said. "I'll say hello."

"Don't forget now, okay?"

"I won't forget."

"Happy New Year, Mom."

"Happy New Year, Steve."

He waved, and nodded, and then turned and walked swiftly to where he'd parked the car.

BAD MONEY

a novel by

Oliver Wendell Weeks

It was a dark and stormy night.

Detective/First Grade Oswald Wesley Watts wasn't overly fond of this section of the city because a lot of Negroes lived here, and they could infrequently be dangerous. On the other hand, "Big Ozzie Watts" as he was affectionately known to the residents of Rubytown, was here on an errand of mercy.

An evil individual was using government funds to enslave these oppressed folk, just the way the British had done in Japan, turning the entire populace into a nation of junkies before the Opium War put an end to <u>that</u> little gambit. Someone in this building was involved in the purchase and recycling of narcotics like cocaine. In police work, this illicit drug was called a "controlled substance." It was sold in what was known as "keys," which was an underworld expression for "kilograms." A kilogram was 2.2 pounds. "Big Ozzie" knew all this valuable information because he had been a highly decorated (for bravery) law enforcement officer for a good many years now.

Tall and handsome, broad of shoulder and wide of chest, slender of waist and fleet of foot, Detective "Big Ozzie" Watts, pistol in hand (a nine-millimeter semi-automatic Glock, by the way), boldly climbed the steps to the fourth floor of the reeking tenement and knocked on the door to apartment 4C. The sound of music came from somewhere inside the apartment. Its noisome beat filled the hallway tremblingly. He heard the stammering click of high-heeled shoes approaching the door.

The woman who opened the door was a very gorgeous twenty-seven-year-old blonde, thirty-six, twenty-two, thirty-four, wearing a long green gown slit up the side to show her extremely curvaceous thigh. Leaning against the door jamb, the gown's quite low neckline exposed fulsome white creamy breasts. She smiled dazzlingly out into the hall.

"Hello, Detective Watts," she exclaimed.

"So, Mother," he retorted. "We meet again."

## A WORD FROM THE AUTHOR

I began outlining *Money Money Money* in April 2000, and started the actual writing at the beginning of May. By the end of July, when I left for a month-long vacation in the south of France, I had finished 226 pages of the book. After Labor Day—this was a year before the World Trade Center attacks—I picked up where I'd left off, rewriting the first 226 pages and bringing the book to page 337 by the end of the month. (If you're wondering, I keep meticulous work calendars; it's the only way I know I'll ever actually finish a book.) By the end of November, I had brought the book to a rough finish at 420 manuscript pages, and on 20 December 2000, I FedExed the final draft to my agent.

The book's official publication date was 6 September 2001. On that day I started a book tour in New York City, and then drove to Bryn Mawr, Pennsylvania on the 8th. The 9th of September was my fourth wedding anniversary. I spent it at home in Connecticut with my wife, Dragica, to whom the book is dedicated. We enjoyed a quiet dinner in a lovely French restaurant—I magnaminously ordered champagne for everyone in the house, not such a big deal since there were only a dozen other diners.

On 10 September, I flew to Dayton, Ohio, and on 11 September I flew early to Chicago. The escort picked me up at the airport early in the morning; Chicago is an hour behind New York City. In the car, on the way to the hotel, his cell phone rang. Someone was calling to tell him what had just happened at the World Trade Center. We turned on the radio. The second plane had just hit. I thought, God, it's happening. I was shocked but not surprised; the research I had done into terrorism seemed to indicate that America itself was a prime target for bin Laden.

The book tour was cancelled that very day. I rented a car with the journalist Rick Bragg—whose book tour was similarly cancelled that day—and together we drove back to a New York City gone sudenly silent.

Following the attacks, I learnt more about terrorism than I could ever have imagined while I was writing the book. But the words "Follow the money" resonated every time I opened a newspaper or watched television, and even now, as Afghanistan harvests its largest opium crop in decades, I am reminded of the vast Money—Dope—Terrorist conspiracy in these pages. And I pray that smaller terrorist attacks like the one depicted here will never come to these shores.

Ed McBain
Weston, Connecticut

*available from*

THE ORION PUBLISHING GROUP

---

☐ **Candyland** £5.99
EVAN HUNTER/ED MCBAIN
0 75284 410 5

☐ **Money Money Money** £5.99
ED MCBAIN
0 75284 839 9

☐ **Cop Hater** £5.99
ED MCBAIN
0 75285 791 6

☐ **The Mugger** £6.99
ED MCBAIN
0 75285 792 4

☐ **The Pusher** £6.99
ED MCBAIN
0 75285 793 2

☐ **The Con Man** £5.99
ED MCBAIN
0 75285 794 0

☐ **'Til Death** £5.99
ED MCBAIN
0 75285 795 9

☐ **King's Ransom** £5.99
ED MCBAIN
0 75285 796 7

☐ **Fat Ollie's Book** £5.99
ED MCBAIN
0 75284 276 5

☐ **The Moment She Was Gone** £6.99
EVAN HUNTER
0 75285 904 8

☐ **The Heckler** £6.99
ED MCBAIN
0 75286 378 9

☐ **See Them Die** £6.99
ED MCBAIN
0 75286 379 7

☐ **Give the Boys a Great Big Hand** £6.99
ED MCBAIN
0 75285 979 X

☐ **The Frumious Bandersnatch** £6.99
ED MCBAIN
0 75285 916 1

☐ **The Empty Hours** £6.99
ED MCBAIN
0 75286 411 4

☐ **Lady, Lady, I Did It!** £6.99
ED MCBAIN
0 75286 410 6

☐ **Hark!** £6.99
ED MCBAIN
0 75286 564 1

☐ **Like Love** £6.99
ED MCBAIN
0 75286 546 3

☐ **Alice in Jeopardy** £6.99
ED MCBAIN
0 75286 503 X